Secrets and Blood

Secrets and Blood

Dewey Hensley

Hydra
Publications

ISBN: 978-1-958414-97-2

Hydra Publications

Goshen, Kentucky 40026

Hydrapublications.com

Acknowledgments

This book would not be possible without the patience and encouragement of my wonderful wife, Kathy, and my son, Daxon. My brother James provided effective feedback, insights, a sympathetic ear, and numerous cover designs. My other brothers, Dave, Mike, and Jerry, also inspired me.

I must thank Tony Acree and his family at Hydra Publications for their confidence and expertise.

"There is no greater agony than bearing an untold story inside you."
    Maya Angelou

Chapter 1
She Ain't No Lady

Evangeline slipped between the lawless trees on the hillside and the wild weeds near the yard. A blackberry bush speared her pants and shirt sleeve. She sighed and pulled free from the tiny daggers. That's Eastern Kentucky for you. At first, the hills give you a soft hug, but then the embrace tightens, trapping you in a chokehold.

She drew her gun and pointed it toward the ground. She watched the target—a two-story white house with a wraparound porch between the three hills surrounding the land.

The late afternoon sun half-dipped behind the mountains to the west, causing the pine tree shadows to stretch across the yard. Those elongated forms reminded Evangeline of how her father would drop his hat on her head and lift her onto his shoulders. He had galloped around the yard, the singular silhouette bouncing on the grass beside them. "You will be ten feet tall someday," he had told her. Except now, in the mid-October wind of Hammond Creek, she no longer rode his broad shoulders. Instead, she felt like an unsteady leaf anxious to detach from a Pin Oak. The single fiber holding her in place on the branch was her kin.

1

She hurried toward the backyard, staying low and navigating around a blackened metal coal bucket and several Ironweed plants, their purple blossoms pushing back against the change of season. The blooms sprouted near the ground, so someone pruned the plants in June.

A fat-bellied washing machine with a mounted black and white clothes wringer concealed one back porch window while a yellow curtain covered the other. A clothesline stretched between two crosses in the yard. White bedding, small and dotted with dragons and boats, saddled the line, causing it to sag. The emerging night sky and the soft wind made the sheets sway and shimmy like the old ladies testifying at a Freewill Baptist Church service.

Evangeline remained low, and her head swiveled as she assessed the exterior. She pushed the earpiece into her ear and clicked the radio with three consecutive bursts, signaling her team to proceed.

Nobody in 2002 uses a wringer washing machine. She shook her head and muttered, "Focus, Evangeline, focus." She knew better than to be distracted when doing God's work, but she needed to sweep away the dust in her mind. She was on the verge of finding the Highlander if the informant were honest. Then she could soar away from this place.

However, she felt poised to fall, not fly.

*****

Deputy Art Butcher emerged from the other side of the house, and Evangeline signaled for him to meet her on the front porch. He arrived first, and the plank floor moaned with each of his cautious footsteps. When she walked onto the porch, her boots did not register.

The sheriff had permitted Luke Porter to be the lead at the

back door. He would knock and announce the warrant while she and Butcher covered the front porch. It was a psychological trick her father taught her to keep the drug dealers off balance. Evangeline heard Thud. Thud. Thud. Three knocks on the back door.

Luke said, "This is the Madden County Sheriff's Department. We have the warrant to search your premises on suspicion of drug possession and firearms. We will use forced-entry procedures if you do not allow us to come in."

Evangeline pictured Luke all puffed up at the door. Forced entry procedures would be Luke's preferred method to check out library books if he could get away with it.

The radio growled, and Luke said, "No response, Sheriff."

Evangeline turned to Art and pointed toward the entrance. Butcher leaned back, raising his boot to kick the front door off its hinges. She waved and flashed a closed-fist signal. The deputy froze, a heavily muscled flamingo yard decoration, his thick leg waist high and the other planted on the floorboards.

Art was a hammer, even when you needed needle-nosed pliers. Albeit, he was the best hammer in the toolbox. His large frame blocked the naked bulb swinging above the door. She mimed turning the doorknob, and Butcher nodded, stepped closer, and turned the bronze handle. The latch clicked, and the door opened to reveal darkness. The deputy smiled at the sheriff and shrugged his massive shoulders. She rolled her eyes, feigning dismay. *Better safe than bloody,* her father would say. Evangeline clicked her mic button, "Enter with caution. There may be innocents inside."

*****

Evangeline slipped across the threshold. A television played, its glow as dim as the porch light and the volume muted. First, she heard whispering inside the house, then silence. The covered windows darkened the room, so she felt for a light switch on the wall with her left hand while raising the gun in her right.

When the light rose, the room came alive. A teenager, thin as a cattail, bounced up from his chair at a card table and darted toward the back door.

"Everyone, this is the Sheriff's Department, and we have the warrant to search this house. Stay where you are and show your hands, and this will go just fine." Her voice and her grip on the gun were steady.

The runner continued, but the man at the table sat and raised his hands. The woman wrapped her arms around the bundle she held in her lap.

Art clicked his radio and said, "Luke and Junebug—a runner is coming your way. Appears unarmed."

Luke Porter met the cattail at the back door. The officer pointed his gun at the runner's face, leading the kid to freeze. Luke grabbed him by the arm and towed him toward the backyard.

Sheriff Grace eyed the seated suspects until she heard a moan behind her. She swung her body a quarter turn to monitor the couch with her peripheral vision while holding the gun high. Evangeline backpedaled toward the sofa where a young woman in a "Just Do It" tee shirt curled into a ball, her unwashed brown hair covering her face. The crying girl wrapped her skinny arms across her chest.

The sheriff paused. The damn girl appeared to be eighteen or nineteen. The age Evangeline was when she left for college at Eastern Kentucky University. Another kid wasted. *This county mangles lives before they even begin. I will never figure—focus, focus, focus.* The sheriff shifted her feet so she could view the kitchen table, the sofa, and the hallway to her left.

The man remained as wooden as the chairs at the kitchen table while the silent woman clutched the bundle, a tiny baby, to her chest and caressed the child's back with her slim fingers. She was out of place, causing Evangeline to picture the Ironweed plants in the yard. Her long, gray hair, high cheekbones, and delicate skin presented an aura of royalty. For a moment, the sheriff expected her to sing a sweet lullaby.

However, the large man was a bowling ball. He was broad-shouldered, his cheeks covered with wiry red tufts of hair, and an odd orange glow emanated from his balding head. His bulging eyes and tight lips suggested he might explode at any moment.

Big Orange said, "What do you want? We ain't doin' nothin' or hurtin' nobody. Why you all comin' at us like this?"

Before the sheriff replied, a crash on the second floor drew everyone's attention.

Sheriff Grace aimed her gun at the table as Art hustled from the living room toward the stairs. The older woman said, "Don't hurt him, please."

The younger woman moaned and stood. Her yellow sweat-pants and shirt said Madden County Miners, with the same emblem of a dragon breathing flames in the shape of a Nike symbol.

"No one will be hurt as long as you remain calm. Ma'am, please keep the baby safe in your arms," Evangeline said. The woman acknowledged her words with a single nod and held the baby closer to her chest.

Evangeline stared at Big Orange. "You ain't doing nothing, huh? What is that in front of you, then?"

"They ain't no drugs here," he replied, touching his chin with his fingertips, "I mean, besides the ones in these bags." He pointed toward a plastic bag half filled with marijuana and a sandwich bag with several tablets and pills.

Before Evangeline could ask him again, Luke entered from the kitchen into the living room. He towed the now handcuffed runner by the shirt. In the light, Evangeline could see the runner was just a kid, even younger than the sofa girl. She could see the boy's eye was red and swollen, and blood ran from a cut above his eyebrow onto his battered right cheek. He could not be much older than her brother.

"What the hell, Luke? Are you kidding me?" Evangeline glared at Porter.

Junebug entered the room behind Luke and the kid. The sheriff turned to her youngest deputy. "Junebug, what happened?"

Junebug Spears avoided eye contact with his boss.

Luke interrupted. "This kid made an aggressive move toward me and Junebug, Sheriff. I responded." Luke did not look at Evangeline. He turned to the other officer. "That's right, isn't it, Bug?" Luke glared at Junebug.

Evangeline examined the boy's bruised face, then turned to Junebug again. The officer did not look much older than the handcuffed runner. His black hair peeked under his cap, a little longer than her father would have permitted, and his face appeared conflicted. Still, he refused to look at her. "Deputy?"

"What Luke said is right, Sheriff," Junebug said. He glanced at Luke and averted his eyes.

"Bullshit," Big Orange said from the table. "Cyrus wouldn't tip a soul. He ain't even a drinker, let alone a druggie like me." The big man was agitated—governed by anger and pride instead of common sense and self-control. Enough stupid coursed through his blood to cause a wrong decision. She braced as he flung the card table aside and stomped toward the sheriff, his hands extended to bowl over her.

The sheriff holstered her gun and sidestepped to the right in one motion. She kicked downward at the man's leg, her heel striking him above the left knee. He stopped and reached for his wounded leg. His body turned, allowing her to grab his right wrist. With a torquing motion, she spun him upright and, using his wrist as a lever, wrangled him to the floor and onto his back. Big Orange yelled in pain as she planted her foot against his shoulder while retaining control of his arm. The sheriff snarled at the man's cardinal-red face.

Junebug and Luke froze, although they had seen the sheriff in action before. The teenager, his face swelling, stood next to Junebug, and the girl on the sofa shrieked, causing the baby to cry. The woman cradled the child and walked toward Junebug. Bug's eyes widened as the woman passed the bundle into his arms and walked to the couch. She sat and held the young woman as she cried. As she rocked the teenager, the older woman's despair caused Evangeline's lower lip to tremble.

Luke stepped over and retrieved his handcuffs from his belt. "Looks like the lady just kicked your ass," he said as he grasped the man's other hand.

"She ain't no lady," Big Orange said.

Luke laughed as he eyed Sheriff Grace. "Both of us saw action today, Sheriff."

"We will return to this issue later, Deputy," the sheriff said as she released the man's arm. "Just cuff him, Luke, and be quiet."

Junebug waltzed with the baby, moving back and forth as he secured her in his arms. "Officer Spears," the sheriff said, "hold the baby while I search this area."

Before Evangeline moved, a deep, menacing growl drifted from the first-floor hallway. Evangeline lifted her gun toward the sound.

"Don't hurt my dog." The linoleum floor muffled Big Orange's words. "Sam Bowie, stay in there, buddy. Don't come out. Please don't shoot him, Sheriff."

Evangeline placed her gun at eye level in response to the man's words, and Junebug retreated with the baby. In her thirteen years in law enforcement, Evangeline had dealt with Pitbulls, pinchers, and other dangerous dogs. It was common for drug dealers to train big dogs to attack law enforcement or anyone who posed a threat.

Without shifting her aim, the sheriff put her hand in her pocket and searched.

"Stay, Sam Bowie, stay," Big Orange said, his cheek pressed against the floor.

Sam's deep growl reverberated as he moved closer to the living room until a large white and blue speckled hound meandered out of the darkness.

Evangeline held out her hand. The Blue Tick hound stopped, stared at Evangeline, turned toward Big Orange, and bore his teeth. He shuffled toward the sheriff, sniffed her shoes, and lifted his big head toward her hand.

She fed him the dog treat from her palm, placed her gun in her holster, kneeled to his level, and scratched Sam Bowie behind the ears. The big dog leaned into her rubs and then yawned, his mouth gaping wide. The hound dropped his treat onto the floor, stretched his crooked front legs forward, yawned again, and gazed up at the sheriff as he devoured the snack. Evangeline fed him another cookie.

*****

Butcher's voice boomed upstairs, "Stop kickin', old man."

As Luke monitored the others and Junebug cared for the baby, the sheriff sprinted up the stairs toward the commotion.

She followed Deputy Butcher's voice to an open bathroom doorway. Art was holstering his gun, so she straddled the threshold, allowing her to monitor the bathroom and hallway. Two naked legs dangled from the open bathroom window. The wedged man kicked like a drowning swimmer, but the window frame made escape impossible despite his thin frame. The deputy extracted him with little effort and sat him on the floor.

"You okay, Art?" Evangeline said. Butcher's width blocked her view of the man.

Art responded, "Oh no...."

"What is it?" Evangeline charged into the room. She said again, "Art, what is it?"

Art said, "I'm sorry, Evangeline." He lifted the ragged man to his feet and turned him.

The sheriff viewed the older man's bare legs, his sagging underwear bunched at his knees. His testicles hung like fruit on the vine. Her gaze traveled up the man's pale, half-naked body to his red "Madden County Apple Festival" tee shirt. However, when the sheriff's eyes settled on the man's face, she recognized the hollowed cheeks and sunken eyes possessing the same hazel hue as her own.

Evangeline lowered the gun and said, "Oh, Uncle Willie...."

Chapter 2
A Cracker Barrel on the Moon

"I ought to kick your big ass for suggesting it." The sheriff stared at the computer monitor on the table.

"You know it would be easy. For instance, what if I didn't read Willie his rights? No one saw me do it. I'm sure Junebug would go along if I told him—"

"Is that what you think of me, Art? You believe I'd give up my integrity and the shield to boot based on a lie? That's not how I work." She turned toward him, relaxed her face, and smiled. "Still, I appreciate it."

They returned to the monitor and watched Willie Grace, her father's brother, fiddle with his hands in the interrogation room. "Shoot, we only recovered a handful of pain pills, some marijuana, and a crying baby," Butcher said. "With the drug avalanche in Madden County, that's not worth seizing." Art sipped coffee from an oversized University of Kentucky mug. "Willie's not the Highlander you want to lock up, now, is he?"

"Thank you, defense attorney Butcher," she said. "We will catch the Highlander by following the little fish into the big fish's mouth."

"The problem is," Art said, "this fish is family, and, knowing Willie, he won't be anxious to share it even if he has the Highlander's home address."

Evangeline checked her watch. The days moved fast at the station; she should have remembered that before talking to Sheldon.

"Do you have somewhere to be, Sheriff? A date, maybe, or a hair appointment?" Art tried hiding his grin behind another swig of coffee, but Evangeline knew him too well.

"Do you want an appointment at the unemployment office? I can put it on your calendar," Evangeline replied.

Both officers smiled.

Art turned to the black and white screen. "So we are right back where we started. What's the plan, Sheriff?"

They watched the seventy-four-year-old man on the screen. He slumped, causing his back to bow even more than it did when he stood. His shoulders were narrow, and his thin face was as rough as a gravel road. Willie's orange jumpsuit and his chin's gray stubble reminded Evangeline of an overripe peach.

She glanced at her watch again and stared up at Art. Evangeline was two inches taller than most women, yet she resembled an elementary school student standing beside him. Most people looked up at him or tried to see around him. His crossed arms were so thick they pressed against the fabric of his uniform like overfilled sacks of flour. Butcher had played tackle at the University of Kentucky and was an All-Southeastern Conference powerlifter. Although forty-two years old, he competed in national strongman competitions and made as much money lifting as working for the Sheriff's Office. Yes, Art was a smart-ass, but the strongman could also read her better than anyone else, and Evangeline trusted him to be honest and loyal.

Butcher raised his palm, inviting her to answer his question. "If you don't have plans, tell me why you're watching the clock like it's New Year's Eve."

"You know, in Madden County, it is never too late to make a big mistake," Evangeline said. "I was afraid he would hear about it at school, so I told Sheldon we arrested Uncle Willie last night."

Art's nose wrinkled like he smelled rotten cabbage. "Shit fire. Sheldon loves that old man. Damn, you would finish second in the Big Sister of the Year contest at your own house."

The sheriff shook her head. "I'm running a distant third behind the Playstation 2 thing and the microwave."

Art continued, "So you have arrested the boy's favorite person, and you intend to pull him from the high school and his friends to relocate him to Louisville. Why don't you neuter him and throw away his television? Are you sure you don't want to leave him here to live with Maria and me?"

"When you say it, I almost sound insensitive," she said. "And no, for the hundredth time, my brother can't stay with you. I promised Dad I would never separate from Sheldon until he grew up. For Daddy, grown meant thirty years old."

"And your motive for leaving town? To get on the fast track to being a police chief, right? I am sure Sheldon noticed you are already head honcho here in Madden County, your hometown. You know, this place where people love the hell out of your family. If I were Sheldon, you would have to transport me in the trunk, and it would involve rope and a bag over my head."

"How you got Maria to marry you is your business." She glanced at her watch again. "Yep, I am destroying my brother's life. My evil plan...." She observed Willie on the monitor. He was laughing. Then he fell silent again. His eyes were still red, and his face was like a map, lined with forking roads and blue rivers.

Evangeline continued, "Changing the subject, I want you to lead the Hammond Creek interrogation. It avoids any hint of corruption. Get Willie's interview over with as soon as you can."

"I don't believe Willie would sell drugs or hurt anyone—he is a consumer, not a producer." Art paused, retrieved a green notebook from his back pocket, and opened it to check his notes. "The big house belongs to Faith Cornett. She was the older woman at the table. She and Willie are close friends. Kimmy Meade is her niece and the cute baby girl's mommy. The big boy you almost broke into pieces is her nephew, Tucker. She took them in after her sister died of lung cancer in 1995. The kids haven't handled losing their mom very well. But the runner, Cyrus, is Ms. Cornett's baby boy and a senior at Madden High School."

"Ms. Cornett is a little young for Willie, don't you think?"

"I don't know. Maria is ten years younger than me, which worked out well."

"For you, maybe. Maria is a saint." The sheriff suppressed her grin. She had been the best man at Art and Maria's wedding eight years before. Now the couple had two beautiful children, with one more on the way.

"I'm waiting for her to wise up," Art responded. "But you know what I wish?" He paused but did not hide his giant smile.

"No, Art. Come on. We've been through this—"

"What if you didn't sign the contract? What if the deadline slipped by, and you stayed in Madden County? You would win the upcoming election on your last name alone. You could stay, and my kids would have their godmother nearby. The baby hasn't seen a ray of sunshine and is already asking for you."

The sheriff looked to the ceiling. Art had promised he'd ask her to stay in Madden County at least once a day until she was gone, and he had kept his word. Often, they laughed at his clever transitions into the subject. However, this time she felt guilt blended with shame. She pushed aside her short auburn hair and half turned her toned back to Butcher.

He continued, despite her body language, "Are you sure Louisville is what you want? I mean, the grass isn't always greener—"

"Jesus, Art," Evangeline said. "The grass isn't greener on the other side argument?" She shook her head. "Madden County is a war zone. The people can't, or won't, function here. Heroin and meth, pills, and the mines are dying. Any day now, I might be the Sheriff who allowed the Madden Massacre to happen in 2002." Her volume rose. "You know, even if I stayed, the people are more apt to vote for Luke Porter than they are me. Then what? Let's face it. This place has about as much hope as a Cracker Barrel on the moon."

"Okay, but I have to point out Louisville may have coffee shops and fancy restaurants, but it isn't a paradise. A Louisville officer told me about one patrol where he picked up a naked baby crawling out on the street. As bad as it was, at least the little one last night was in a crib and the house with her mommy."

Evangeline envisioned a Venn Diagram she had made in middle school. The teacher assigned the class to compare two different places, so she made the obvious choices of Madden County and New York City. She had described Madden as "black and white" and New York as "colorful." Small-time and Big-time. Rich and Poor. The only commonalities she had listed were that both places supported a police department and heroes like her father. Even then, with poster board and markers spread across her bed, she had felt the pull of faraway places.

"It was my plan, Art. I headed to college and the police academy. Madden will always be home, but I aimed to be somewhere else. I thought about it, dreamed about it, and took steps toward it, but I never did it. Now, with Daddy gone, I can follow my plan and leave the mountains."

"I understand," Art said, "but—"

"I have worked hard for twelve years to make Madden County better despite the feuds, drugs, and way of thinking about people like me. I want to lock away the Highlander thug and make my plan real. It has been one year and one month since the planes took down the towers in New York. Don't you remember how we watched the first responders running into the smoke and debris to help people? We wanted to be there, making the whole world safer." She took a long breath.

"All due respect, Evangeline, but you see the weaknesses here, and that's all. I don't. We tend to see what we want in people. If we want to find good or bad, we find it. You want to believe the job here is impossible, but you've increased the number of raids on drug dens, and you certainly aren't just riding out your last days. The spotlight may not be as bright here as in Louisville, but in Madden County, you are the law and make good things happen."

"I'm not my father, Art. I can advance in the Louisville police. I want to be where I can show...." Her voice trailed off. "Besides, when Dad persuaded me to come home after the Academy, I said it would be temporary. People say he passed because he lost Mom, but I'm convinced he died to keep me chained to the family business."

"That's bull, Boss." The deputy shifted his feet and lowered his volume. Evangeline liked when he wrinkled his nose and became earnest. "You can even see what you want to see in yourself. We all are saints and sinners, that's for sure. You are not your Daddy, and I don't think he would want you to be. But he cared about the people here and took care of you. You took care of him. Mountain people are about family. He knew you would make a difference here."

A chill ran up her spine, and an image of her father in a hospital bed, lines and cables stretching like tentacles to monitors and machines, flashed across her memory—his tortured smile was so out of place on his thinning face.

Evangeline turned to the monitor, hoping to signal the conversation was over. She leaned closer to the screen when Willie mumbled and rose from his chair. Another shiver rippled across her skin. What would her father think now? Madden County was a mess, and she had just arrested his only surviving brother, who had always treated her well.

Willie opened his eyes, sat up as if someone had hurled an insult, and pointed his fingers to lecture the speaker.

Evangeline massaged her neck. Seeing him made her ache. Uncle Willie had always helped Sheldon and her, especially when her father was sick and after he died. But now was the time for her to quit standing on the diving board and jump into the water. As soon as she could get beyond this family catastrophe, she would speed toward Louisville and a new life, leaving Madden in her rearview mirror.

Chapter 3

The Crystal, the Needle, and the Silver Spoon

An invisible knife lacerated Willie Grace's brain, and he welcomed it. The cell shrank as if his niece had turned the crank of a torture device, drawing the walls toward him. When he was younger, he had handled detox better—because there hadn't been a mix of alcohol, weed, pills, and heroin floating in his system. Now, Willie felt his body withdrawing, his heart like hummingbird wings while his stomach and head churned.

"Sometimes, I wonder what's worse. Is it the weaning or the curse?" Despite the pain, he laughed at the rhyme. "A whole poem is hiding in that line."

Willie reflected on his evolution as a curse victim. For his first fifteen years, he grew up with numerous school friends and had expected a successful life. Glorious ignorance protected him during the following twenty years by convincing him a typical life was possible. When his hope crashed, he spent the next twenty-four years shielded from reality by Jim Beam and the weed he could grow on Mole Branch. However, the summons had grown louder and bolder in the last twelve years. The older he became, the more it grew from a whisper, then a word, and now a sharp blade of dread. The voice was so intense only the pills, the crystal, the needle, and the silver spoon kept the evil at bay.

Willie called the voice a summons because it reminded him of the job his younger brother, Earl, helped him get, serving subpoenas and court documents. As a server, he felt sorry for the people avoiding him. One man had donned a wig and women's clothes to evade the summons, and another had hidden in his car's trunk whenever he and his wife had exited their garage. The trunk guy had almost died when his wife had abandoned him in the car for over ten hours.

That's why Willie felt sorry for himself. This court server was more persistent and devious than Willie had ever been. The Agent did not give up, seldom shut up, and did everything possible to shatter Willie's sanity and resolve.

Willie chuckled and whispered under his breath. "I would not be an attractive woman, that's for sure." Then the old man spoke aloud to the empty room. "Don't you agree, Barlow? If only I had the good sense to be like the souls who accepted the summons and told me to screw off. Balls the size of cantaloupes."

Willie giggled again after he received no response. "Mine are little hazelnuts, isn't that right, you sonuvabitch?"

*****

Willie hoped to survive long enough for this binge to pass, so his mind was intact during these last days. He had lived beyond his expiration date. Although Willie feared that Little Dep—his pet name for his niece—would not believe his story, it was time.

Evangeline's direct bloodline included Willie's father, Sheldon, and Willie's younger brother, the famous Sheriffs of Madden County. She walked, talked, and even held her chin up like Earl had whenever challenged in an argument. Willie remembered playing Cops and Robbers with Lil' Dep in the yard—her badge pinned to her shirt and packing her cowboy pistol like her daddy carried his. Willie was the criminal then, and she had arrested him.

How far they had come.

Although the interrogation room was warm, a chill traveled down his bare arms. The orange jumpsuit they had provided to cover his butt did not fit well. Willie regretted Little Dep seeing his boys swinging free at Faith's house, but it was no surprise. Willie had lived bare-naked since his older brother Robert had gift-wrapped the summons for him back in 1958. He had become a peasant with no clothes to hide the one thing he could not reveal —the secret.

Do you think you should tell her about me, Wee Willie? I have a better idea. You could die with the secret. The whisper was faint. The Agent was like a candle flame, diminished but casting a shimmering shadow. *You don't tell her, and I will let you be. Let. You. Be.*

Willie rattled his head to shake away the familiar lyrics. "I knew you lurked close, Agent," Willie said, staring at the unnatural darkness in the corner.

Let. You. Be. The Agent paused after each word, increasing the volume from a murmur to a penetrating growl.

"As if you will ever leave me alone," Willie said. "You don't let anything be, you serpent. I will not permit you to kill everybody in this county, especially how you like to kill. Don't blame me for holding you back. You're the one who told Robert the rules. He had sense enough to pass them on to me."

The laughter bounced inside Willie's brain.

It's mountain shit like you I shall miss when I wipe you off my shoe, Willie Grace. You may be a turd, but you are the shiniest one in the outhouse. Or, as you and yours refer to it, home.

Willie feigned disinterest, but over the years, he had learned to listen to the disembodied voice, even when the Agent reverted to playground-level insults.

You know, Willie, I may be two scores older than you, but you remind me of my dearly departed dad up in Boston. He always called me "Dull Daniel" because he thought I was stupid. I used to tell him how sharp he was. I would say, "After all, you own a knife company." The trouble was he didn't enjoy jokes, so he would take a razor strap and beat me till I bled. That's why I went to the war. I figured Germans couldn't be as bad as him.

The Agent's voice adopted a sing-song tone again. *Now, look at me. With another old man preaching about what he won't let happen. Even in this wasteland, you give me a home in your thick skull, Willie.*

You live in my head, alright, Willie whispered to himself or aloud. He wasn't sure which, and it did not matter. This filthy monster had become his rider long ago. "Agent, I am your jackass, your dying camel, your Derby favorite. Your sharp heels have dug into my sore ribs for nearly sixty years."

You have learned so much from me, Willie Grace.

Willie paused, then smiled. "But soon, I can buck your evil ass and head into the hills. I've earned the reward, oh Lord, I have earned it."

The bars fragmented the light coming into the room. But in the corner, Willie could see the tall man's shape and the outline of his old suit, visible only in silhouette. The shadow of the Agent's fedora stretched across the cell wall, a dull knife blade cutting the light until it bled.

Chapter 4
The King, Judge, and Jury

"This is the most entertaining one-man show ever. What's your uncle doing?" Art asked, pointing toward the monitor. Willie's finger dotted the air and his face twisted in anger, but all Evangeline could hear was her uncle mumbling. He resembled a sidewalk prophet in an argument with the world.

"Look at him, Art. Willie's my flesh and blood. But we can't be too surprised. His troubles have always led him to take risks." She pointed to her uncle's face. It was as if Willie heard her through the monitor. He raised his shoulders, and his head swayed, turning back and forth as if something might bite his ear—damn pills and heroin.

Butcher cleared his throat. "I remember when your Dad did a traffic stop on him," he said. "Willie was so drunk he parked at the Super Mart air machine and tried to use the air hose to fill his gas tank."

"Yes, but the mighty Sheriff Grace let him go, didn't he?" Evangeline's brow furrowed, and she turned toward her deputy. She could picture her father, his head held high, preaching to his older brother about being a bootlegger and a drunk. "Earl Grace was the king, judge, and jury. I don't have the influence here, not like he had. His legacy smothers me because my decisions put me in everyone's crosshairs. All they know is my daddy's rules."

Art said, "His footprint is large here in Madden. Hell, this county loved your daddy, and everybody knew he wasn't the straightest arrow in the quill. People knew he did what was right, so they left him alone. Earl took many a man to his family instead of the Courthouse. And a few ladies, too."

"I know better than anyone, Art. He's why I became a police officer." Evangeline's father had wanted her to come home, so she had. He had wanted her to be a deputy, so she was. He had wanted her to live in his house and help him take care of Sheldon, so she had sacrificed, and when he got sick, he appointed her the interim sheriff and told her she could not say no, so she hadn't.

Evangeline pictured her father standing on the courthouse lawn, cameras flashing. She still loved and admired him more than anyone else, but he was enormous because Madden County was not. She wanted to prove he was substantial, but she was, too.

"Willie has always been different, Art. I once asked my father about his risky behavior with drugs and alcohol." She watched Willie push his wild thick gray hair back with his fingers. "He said, 'Willie shoulders a heavy burden. It was a sack plumb full of the past, and Willie had no place to sling it.' I said addictions are something you don't want, but you can't let it go."

"I heard Willie was a great writer. Old codgers call him a crazy genius. There was talk he had a full scholarship to Marshall University to study writing. That's pretty impressive," Art said. "Which reminds me, he asked for a legal pad, a pen, and an envelope earlier. I told him not until I was sure he could handle it, but I sent them to his cell. He will have it after he leaves the interrogation room today."

"Are you sure sharp objects are a good idea right now?" Evangeline asked.

Art did not respond.

Evangeline adjusted the monitor's volume. "...and it doesn't matter, does it?" Willie was saying. He was alone, but his words had purpose and audience. "You will find me no matter where I hide, won't you, Detective?"

Evangeline and Art watched as Willie rested his head on the table.

"What the hell is he saying? I hope he doesn't mean you and me." Butcher glanced at the sheriff. "Last night, he was high when we got him, but not as bad as Kimmy, the young woman on the couch. She was out of her mind. Ms. Cornet and Cyrus tested negative, while the others had pills, weed, and alcohol in their blood.

Evangeline nodded. She felt guilty for listening to an unreliable informant. Maybe this problem would not be in her lap if she had been more critical and strategic. What would Dad call it? Jackassery. He had always expected her to be sharper than the rest, including State Police detectives. It was flattering, but it tethered her to his approval.

But now, one big mistake could deny her the position she coveted in Louisville. Even worse, the perception of her giving unjust preference to her Uncle Willie could make headlines and brand her as corrupt. Not even her friend Sylvia at the Louisville Metro Police could help her then.

"Art, it's best if you and Luke question Willie today about the Highlander. I want you to lead the investigation. I can't even allow the scent of my giving unfair treatment or leniency to Willie. Gene Begley will contact the Louisville Police Department if I misstep."

Butcher nodded. He turned away, but Evangeline registered his disappointment. She almost expected another go at changing her mind about the job offer across the state.

Evangeline wanted to tell Art the truth, but it sank inside her like a rock in a pond.

"Junebug and I will respond to calls and bring Luke into work with you." She stared at the monitor. Willie's lips moved as if he were in a fierce conversation. "Who knows? He may reveal who he's talking to in there."

As Art nodded, Evangeline wanted to tell him more. Instead, she swallowed even more guilt and walked to her office without telling her best friend the truth.

She had signed the LPD contract moments before departing for Hammond Creek.

Chapter 5
I Don't Disappear If You Go

Sheldon Grace knew he was lucky, which only amplified his anger. Despite his efforts to contain his angst, he poured it on Sarah Wainscott the most. They had stopped for a milkshake at Spence's Diner while walking to the police station. As first-year students at Madden County High School, they were too young to drive but old enough to walk thirty minutes to the courthouse.

When they had turned fourteen, both had experienced a growth spurt. Sheldon had filled out, losing his baby fat and replacing it with muscle and acne. Sarah was still a half-foot shorter than Sheldon and thin, but years of volleyball had toned her body, and even seniors noticed her thick black hair and blue eyes.

Sheldon noticed, too. In middle school, they had been friends. Now, they were something different. He slipped his hand into hers as they crossed Eden Street, heading toward the police station and the jail.

"She's the only one who matters," Sheldon said. "It is always her way or no way. I don't have any voice."

"I understand, Sheldon. But to Evangeline, the job in Louisville is a big deal. Plus, she has always been out of place here." Sarah squeezed his hand to hold him back as an old pickup truck rolled through the intersection, gears grinding. "In Louisville, she will be a big shot. There is nothing big about Madden County."

"That's not true, Sarah." They stepped on the cracked sidewalk and walked over broken chunks of cement. "I have friends here. I don't want to go to Louisville. Besides, you're here. That's enough for me."

She squeezed his hand again. "I won't disappear if you go to Louisville, Sheldon."

"Yes, but I will." He released her hand on the other side of the street.

"Have you talked to Vangie about this? Does she know how much you hate the idea?" Sarah leaned against him, her shoulder resting on the sleeve of his thin school jacket.

"I can't," he said. "I promised our dad I would stay close and help her. I can't break my promise to him. Besides, I want her to stay in Madden because she wants to, not for me. I've been a burden since I was born. I could not live with myself...."

They passed the local newspaper office where Sarah worked for Gene Begley. A women's clothing store with a large sign reading "Debbie's Place" was next door, and the Shear Magic barber shop followed before Adele's Bookstore. Across the street, the old gas station and convenience store displayed ancient signs advertising Texaco, the "Doctors Recommend Chesterfields," and Red Man Chewing Tobacco, contrasted with the modern gas pumps and neon signage. Madden was a small town where Sheldon felt safe.

Several blocks later, Sheldon and Sarah paused at an iron placard near the courthouse and police station. The monument's raised metal lettering read, "Honoring Sheriff Sheldon Grace, 1894-1979."

The historical society had secured the placard to a substantial chunk of granite. Sheldon and Sarah had seen the monument so often they usually gave it little notice. However, today Sheldon stopped so they could examine the metal plate. The artist had cast a representation of Sheldon's grandfather in the center. Beneath the raised imprint were the words, "Legendary Lawman, Sheriff Grace, through courage and negotiation, kept the peace in Madden County during the Kentucky Coal Wars in the late 1920s. He was a hero and a man of peace."

Hero, Sheldon thought. *Right Here. Our home. But that's not good enough for her.*

Sheldon's anger percolated again. Without context, he said, "And look what she's done to Uncle Willie. All the druggies and alcoholics around Madden County, yet my sister manages to arrest our uncle. And she is thirty-six years old. My God, she is too old to do anything else pretty soon. She's as ancient as this sign." He knew it was time to stop when Sarah did not respond. He retook her hand, and this time, he squeezed it to apologize.

*****

Sheldon opened the police station door for Sarah and then stepped forward to greet Paulene at the reception desk.

"Hi, Sweet Pauline," he said. He placed his elbows on the counter and leaned toward the receptionist. The older woman smiled. Her blonde hair and red lipstick lightened her face. He estimated she was in her mid to late '40s and had worked at the police station for as long as he could remember. When his father had brought him to the office, Paulene always fussed and teased him about girls.

"Howdy, handsome." She glanced over Sheldon's shoulder toward Sarah. "You got you a fine catch here, little Missy. Don't you forget it."

Sarah was silent, but Sheldon imagined her trademark eye-roll and smirk.

"My sister is expecting me," he said, his cheeks burning.

"I will let her know you're here," Pauline said. She smiled as she picked up the phone but was formal when Evangeline answered. *Funny,* Sheldon thought, *maybe my sister treats people like I get treated at home. They can only tell her what she wants to hear.*

As soon as Paulene ended the call, the phone rang again. She waved bye to Sheldon and Sarah and clicked the lock release. Sheldon mouthed, *thank you,* as they headed to the Sheriff's Office.

When Sarah and Sheldon stepped through the door, they saw the sheriff and Junebug bolting toward them. The officers wore their usual shit-colored uniforms and black jackets. Evangeline had her trusty sidearm on her hip, and Bug pushed back his hair as he put on his turdy Madden County Law Enforcement hat. Sheldon understood Evangeline needed to be somewhere he wasn't. *Big surprise.*

"I'm so sorry, Sheldon," his sister said as they passed. "I waited, but now I have to go on a call at Spence's Diner."

"Really? Is it half-priced donut day again, and you must get there before Officer Butcher?" Sheldon glanced at Sarah, hoping to see her smiling. She wasn't.

"My brother, the comedian," Evangeline said as she continued toward the exit. "Sarah, try to teach him a thing or two."

"We are visiting Uncle Willie, right?" Sheldon tried not to whine, but he recognized the mewl in his voice. "You promised I would get to see him today."

Evangeline spoke as she moved further away, her words cascading behind her like nickels dropping from her pocket. "You will, Sheldon. It's just I have to run out first. I'll be right back—"

"I've heard that one before," Sheldon said. His sister's athletic build stood out despite the drab brown uniform and the fact she was in her mid-thirties.

"I'm doing my best here." The sheriff turned and backpedaled through the door as she spoke. "I will get back as soon as I can. This call shouldn't take long."

Sheldon stared at his sister and then turned to Sarah. He struggled to contain his disappointment and anger. He loved Evangeline as his sister but could not say the same about her as his guardian. It wasn't as if she didn't try to be both a good sister and a responsible parent figure. She did. However, the attempt made her ineffective in both roles. Uncle Willie's arrest kindled his anger, but her plan to drag him from the only place he had ever known had been the latest spark.

"We will visit without you if you aren't back by 5:30 PM," Sheldon said. *Strength. That's all she knows.* "Whether you like it or not."

Evangeline exited the side door to the police vehicle lot. Junebug Spears nodded and turned to follow Evangeline as she jogged toward the car.

Chapter 6
No Greater Fury

After she started the cruiser, Evangeline inhaled the vinyl and sweat of the car and stretched her neck from side to side.

"Junebug," she said, "there is no greater fury than a teenager scorned."

The deputy smiled, removed his hat, and rested it on his right knee. "Sheldon is a good kid," he said. "All of us go through stuff at his age. My parents threatened to lock me out of the house unless I stopped moping and making a mess trying to build a computer."

"I wonder if Steve Jobs's parents told him to quit making a mess?" Evangeline said. "He just became a billionaire."

Rarely did Junebug fully commit to a smile, but he did now. She watched it evaporate as he cleared his throat. "You put me in some big-name company, Sheriff. I'm not in his league, that's for sure."

It was common for Junebug to downplay his skillset and contribution to the team. Her dad had hired him back in 1997, fresh out of Morehead State University, to upgrade the technology at the station. Junebug had revamped the system using a state law enforcement grant to improve the network.

"Someday, all police department technology systems will be called Junebug," she said.

"Everybody has called me Junebug my whole life. My dad is also named Bentley Spears. They began calling me Junior, but it became Junebug for some reason."

"Sweet," she replied. However, an adult with a name like Junebug was a marked man outside Madden County.

"Not really," he replied without elaboration. "Your father never called me Junebug in the short time I worked with him. He always called me Ben, Spears, or Kid."

"I see," the sheriff responded. She stared ahead as the streets changed into roads. There wasn't time to explore the deputy's words because Spence's Diner had already appeared in the distance. Still, she recalled the controversy when her father's illness had required Junebug to simultaneously serve as an enforcement officer and provide the station's technical support. Junebug had never protested, though he had dreaded the training and now the extra work, especially considering he received no additional pay. Luke Porter had complained the most, arguing "the geek" could not hold his own in the field.

"Daddy read people well and believed in your ability to contribute to the team. You would not be here if I disagreed," the sheriff said as she steered toward the diner.

The deputy gazed toward the hat on his knee. "I'm sorry, Sheriff," he said. "I should have done better at the Hammond Creek raid. I should have—"

"You should have told me the truth about Porter and the kid in the yard, Junebug," she said as she accelerated toward the parking lot.

Chapter 7
Boys, Madden County is Poison

"Where's the sheriff?" Willie asked.

Art could tell Willie was more coherent than earlier, but he still acted like a squirrel perched on an unstable branch.

"I want to talk to her and only her."

"Sorry, Mr. Grace," Luke said before Art could respond. "You will work with us today. It would be a conflict of interest for the Sheriff to—"

"No," Willie said. "I need to see Evangeline now." Art noted that the old man ignored Luke, preferring to speak to him. "And I don't need Samson and Delilah in the room." He motioned like a carnival caller toward the two officers. Willie's arms were long and thin, with highways of veins traveling along his skin. His dirty gray hair appeared prepared to spring forward at any moment.

Art smiled, but knew his partner would not like the Delilah reference. Luke spent many hours at the gym lifting, which showed, but his workouts had done little to ease his insecurity.

Luke's spine stiffened, as did his tone. "What are you talkin' about, old man? You don't get to choose who questions you, even if your last name is Grace. You refuse a lawyer but want to tell us who interrogates you?" He lowered his voice. "Damn meth head."

Art noted how Luke now wore suits to work each day. It was another signal he was confident about his campaign for County Sheriff in November, considering his grandfather was the Judge Executive. Art watched his colleague's red tie unfurl from the wooden tabletop as he leaned away from Willie. Luke shifted in his seat to appear taller than his 5'8" frame. For show, he rested his elbows on the table and flexed his biceps.

"So I take it she's not out there watching," Willie said, nodding toward the door. "You are too pussy to act all tough in front of her. Your balls didn't drop until my niece mentioned leaving Madden."

Luke lifted his butt off the chair as if to lunge at Willie but stopped short.

"What's wrong, Porter?" Willie said. "You just realize I'm not a boy you can use as a punching bag?"

Art put his hand on Luke's shoulder. "Settle down, Porter. Willie, with all due respect, you might want to rethink your decision about a lawyer. Especially talking to us like this." He observed Willie's reaction. "It's not like you killed anybody," Art said.

Wille's expression tightened. His sober, intense eyes were inconsistent with his shaky hands and restless body.

"I haven't killed a soul, Butch, but this is about life and death. People will die if I can't see the sheriff before it's too late."

Luke chuckled. "That's damn dramatic and convenient, Willie. You and your niece negotiating your future as she gets ready to leave town? That's the bull I aim to end here in Madden County." Luke's voice escalated as he spoke, then trailed off when Art stared at him.

"This isn't a stump speech, Luke. Get off the stage," Art said. "Willie, what are you talkin' about? We want to help you, but you're not making it easy. You face a ten-year minimum sentence if you are involved in pill and heroin distribution. You may end up dying in prison."

"There's a good chance I don't leave your jail, Butch. That's why I need to see Evangeline. I have to tell her something."

"Well, just tell us," Art said. "We will let her know what—"

Willie shook his head. "I can't do it, Art. It has to be her." He paused, managed a deep breath, and a smile lifted his cheeks. "I am a joke. That's what everyone thinks—even you, Butcher. I have known you since you were born. And Porter, everybody knows your family runs the courthouse. It would not surprise me to find out every proper person in Madden believes I'm an addict and future looney bin inmate. I understand why you boys might laugh as I plead to speak to the Sheriff. But I am telling you, if I don't tell her what I know, there will be dire consequences for this county."

Both officers stared at Willie, making no effort to speak. Art shook his head as Willie's smile receded.

Willie slammed his hand down on the table with such force Art and Luke jumped. "I need her *now*."

"She isn't here, Willie," Art said. "It's not in her professional interest to be with you alone."

"I agree," Willie said, "but I've put it off as long as I can—"

"You have only been in here a minute," Luke said.

"You idiot. I have postponed it for pert near fifty years. She is the only one it makes sense for me to tell."

Art tapped his fingers on the table and wondered how to help Willie without exposing Evangeline to conflict of interest accusations. Willie's urgency made him uneasy. *If he is this passionate about seeing her, it should happen.* "I imagine she hopes to meet with you today outside her role as sheriff—in the visitor's room. Others will be present."

"That's more like it," Willie said. "I don't know anything about meth, heroin, or pills. If I did, I'd try to get me some." Willie laughed, but his face hardened again. Art watched as Willie leaned back, massaged his chest, and said, "Boys, Madden County is poison. It has been for a long time."

Chapter 8
War Makes Men of Substance

"Thank you, Otis," Willie said as the officer closed the cell door. "How are Loretta and the girls doing? Imagine your oldest one's about to get married."

"She sure is, Willie," Otis responded. He reached into his uniform pocket and retrieved his wallet. "Here's a picture of her and her man at the engagement party in Ashland. That's where his people live. Hell, you know his daddy. She's marrying Denny Maynard's son. He's in school to be an eye doctor."

"She's a pretty one, Otis," Willie said. "Guess she takes after Loretta." They laughed as the officer nodded and walked down the hallway.

"I'll see you later, Willie," Otis said. "I hope this is over soon."

"Don't worry, my friend. Everything ends at the appropriate time."

When Otis exited, Willie spoke aloud. "What're you waiting for, Agent? You're hanging in the corner like a vulture circling roadkill."

I sometimes wonder why they let you hillbillies breed, Willie.

The Agent's voice echoed inside Willie's brain. *Look at that fat ass with his pictures.*

Willie stared at the figure in the corner. When he first became afflicted, Willie struggled to identify the Agent's shadow. However, now it was easy to discern the shape no matter where it formed. "If I remember, your Daddy was a prince, Barlow. That's how you turned out to be such a sweetheart."

The Agent's familiar laugh engulfed Willie's brain. The Agent first entered Willie's mind moments after Robert Grace had told Willie he existed. Willie had fought for decades to keep the secret like a rabid dog locked in a cage, for the Agent remained an evil shadow, unable to wreak havoc on anyone else's life as long as Willie stayed alive and told no one about him. Willie excelled at keeping the secret. However, he could not deny death.

Oh yes, my father was royalty indeed, the Agent said. *I told you he owned a knife company. He made big money selling knives and bayonets to both sides of World War I. Our boys and German boys were trying to run each other through with blades shaped right in my old dad's factory. My father was a piker when it came to spending money on me. However, he used to take me downtown in Boston to see the hoofers and go to the swankiest whorehouses around.*

"See, that's a classy thing to do in the sophisticated Northeast. Made your mama proud, I bet."

Willie detected a pause in the Agent's banter.

My mother left long before we attended the burlesque shows. When I was your sissy-boy nephew's age, my father introduced me to a gypsy girl working at the show. She was a fortune teller and the most beautiful woman I had ever seen.

"Vadoma, again? How many times will you tell me this story, Agent? I have heard it so many times I hallucinate it happened to me."

The Agent's dark shadow rolled like smoke in the corner of the room. For half a century, Willie had listened as the Agent shared bits and pieces of his life—the war, how he had become a Baldwin agent, even bragging about the men he had killed. Willie had heard him babble on and on about his wealthy, underhanded father.

Vadoma was six years older than me. Her eyes were as black as rich soil, and her black hair and jewels hung around her neck. It would appear like a dye job and a costume for most women, but on her, the jewelry shined real, and her face—

"So you got laid when you were a boy. Big deal, Barlow. I know this story."

The voice amplified in Willie's mind.

You don't have any sense, do you, hillbilly? It's another reason I cannot wait to tear the soul out of this place.

Willie laughed. "I always hit a nerve there, don't I, Agent? I feared your scary tales and threats for decades. But they have helped me see you are a sensitive, fragile fellow. How about you finish up your little whore story."

I will finish this tale as a sign, Willie Grace, to acknowledge we will complete our business very soon. I will hurt you even if it delays my plans to return Madden County to the wilderness it used to be. I first came to Madden County to distribute justice, and I will no matter how long it takes.

The Agent would do it. Still, Willie wanted to keep him talking and stoke his anger. It would prime him to end Willie's life soon. Ultimately, Willie's death could save others' lives because of Evangeline. If anyone could carry the secret and outlast this demon, it was her.

"Then please, get back to Vadoma, the love of your life."

My father left us alone at her table. I asked if she could see the future. She held my hand and opened the palm. I thought this was all a big show, of course, but when she caressed my palm, I knew it was real. Her fingertips touched my life as if she were turning the pages to peek ahead at chapters in a book.

Willie noted the legal pad and ballpoint pen on his pillow but pushed them from his mind.

Her dark opals shined as she leaned away from me. Vadoma said, "You will come home from a great war, your body whole, but your soul will splinter when you walk through these doors." Her Roma accent was thick, but she wasn't like the low class you have climbing these mountains like goats. I could understand her."

Willie listened and said, "Do you expect me to feel something based on this anecdote? Barlow, are you setting me up for some cruel punchline to a long joke? Perhaps that's all you are, an old-time Vaudeville comedian."

The Agent ignored him. *Over the next two years, I visited her whenever possible. She taught me things your weak brain will not comprehend. She roamed from Louisiana to Boston with her friends. When they left, she stayed in Boston, dancing at the theater, serving hooch, and reading fortunes. They called her Gypsy Viv.*

The Agent's voice scattered in Willie's mind, a hurt dog dodging a boot. He was unsure if he imagined it, but the shadow in the corner shrank.

Sometimes patrons laughed and mocked Vadoma, but she was wiser than people like my father, who gawked at her. Because I respected her, she became my revealer. She taught me revenge and the black art of curses. Of course, I loved her. But when I expressed my love and begged to be with her, Vadoma would not answer or offer an ounce of encouragement. She did not want me as I was. She wanted someone who had substance.

Willie shook his head as if someone had shouted an incorrect answer at school or tripped over their own feet. "Thanks for reminding me. My entire life has been a curse. My brother's death was some magical curse so you could get revenge." Willie laughed. His thin chest rose and fell with each breath. "You want the people who never did a damn thing to you to pay, so you curse me to ensure people die if I mention you exist. That sounds about right. So, tell me what happened to you and your Gypsy witch."

The war happened, Agent Barlow said. *Uncle Sam drafted me to kill Germans. Vadoma had envisioned it years before—me on a battlefield, blood dripping from my hands. Not my precious blood, of course. I left her, but I knew I could return as the man she wanted. War makes men of substance.*

"Was she right about the other part?" Willie said. "Your soul splintering?"

The moment I walked into my father's house, I could feel his glee. I did not know why until she descended the stairs. She was a porcelain doll. I had thought about her every day for three years of war. My heart was a cannonball.

"What did you say to her?"

I wanted to tell her about how I had changed during the war. Let her see I wasn't a boy now. I was a man ready to take care of her. Unlike you and your kind, I was a well-bred Bostonian. The world prepared me to cut a path through it so clear she could follow right along. That's what I wanted to say.

Willie calculated possible outcomes for any response he might give. After a moment, he replied, "Is that what you said to her? Did you tell her you had a crush on her and wanted to come a-courting?"

No, I did not speak to her because my father spoke first.

"I bet he said, *I bought you a present, Danny boy.*"

Barlow's harsh voice reverberated as if from inside a drum. Willie wondered if any sound could be darker, more grating, and more evil.

He said, "Say hello to your new mom, son."

"My favorite part of the story, Agent," Willie said, "Your Daddy stole your fortune teller right from under your army boots. I could hear that scene a million more times, but I'm getting the feeling I won't."

You know your time is short. You have hindered me for too long. I want you to know me well because I will end you, Willie. To be honest, I hate you. Even if it takes longer to get this place's stink off my skin, I will kill you.

Chapter 9
There is Always a Battleground Somewhere

Sheriff Grace bounced to a stop in the gravel parking lot of Spence's Diner. Junebug raised his hand to the dashboard to steady himself. "When will these guys quit?" he asked.

The sheriff grabbed the radio to call dispatch. Evangeline felt the aftershocks of her conversation with Sheldon. She was always backpedaling and apologizing to him. Why couldn't her brother understand the reasons behind her decisions? She would help Willie, but not at the cost of a better future for them.

"Otis, we're here at the diner. It's the usual crowd jawing out front. It looks intense, so be on alert if we need backup." She released the mic button and looked at her deputy. "They will quit when they can't reach each other across the graveyard. But then, their sons and daughters will carry on the hate. Can't you see why I must get leave this crazy county?"

As usual, Junebug remained stoic, staring straight ahead. Evangeline thought her departure would affect Junebug the most —because Luke disrespected him—yet Junebug never attempted to persuade her to stay. She turned toward him. He resembled a kid pretending to be a cop. She wondered if he wanted to leave Madden, too. Perhaps they both wore costumes.

"Copy," Otis responded.

Evangeline and Junebug watched as two rival groups stood toe to toe like in a scene from *West Side Story*. Anger molded each person's face into a mask of hate. The two men in the middle pecked at each other, roosters in a cockfight.

The only barrier restraining them was Clyde Perry. Clyde stood between the men, his muscular brown arms stretched like a traffic cop signaling both sides to stop. Many assumed Clyde backed the miner's union because he drove a coal truck. Indeed, his economic security hinged on the coal industry, Evangeline thought, but as he had said to her back in the summer, "I believe violence won't work either way or for either side. That's why I own my truck outright, so I can go across the Tug River into West Virginia if I need to find work."

As the sheriff and deputy approached the ring, Clyde lowered his arms and stepped away, drifting toward his coal truck parked in the background.

George Spence, the diner's owner, had reported the trouble. He peered through the glass plate window, so she waved at him.

Evangeline could not decipher what they were saying, but she guessed it was the same contentious quarrel Baron Mills and Carl Ramey had had for a century. The exact words, the same battle, and the same result—except now it wasn't about a broken fence like the feud their grandparents had ignited. Today their fights were about carbon-based emissions and economic feasibility. *Now that's progress.*

Memories are like coal trains—the farther away they are, the smaller they become. But the tracks always remain. It was easy for the Wainscotts, Mills, and Ramey feuds to pick up steam and commence again at the sound of the whistle. The rails were in place.

"There is always a battleground somewhere," Evangeline told Junebug as she motioned for him to secure the onlookers.

The officer moved to the outer ring while the sheriff entered the center. She stepped between Mills and Ramey and said, "That's enough."

Baron said, "It sure as hell is, Sheriff. How long will you twiddle your handcuffs while these men rape the land and destroy what little dignity we have left in Madden County?" He was a tall man with a ponytail collected in a rubber band behind his narrow face and head. His finger pointed toward Evangeline like a crooked stick.

Before she could respond, Carl interrupted, "Please, Sheriff, put this man out of my misery. Dignity, my ass. If he had his way, this whole county would be on food stamps and welfare, and the mines would shut down." He turned his attention back toward Baron. "There ain't no dignity when you can't feed your family, dumbass."

"Christ on a cracker, Carl. What in the hell has Madden Mining done for you? Wainscott and his boys get rich while we stay poor, and the mountains die. Do you want the rich to grow richer?" Baron's face tightened more. His finger retreated into a fist. Evangeline had known Baron Mills for most of her life, and his daughter, Sandy, was her teammate on the Madden County High School basketball team.

"Madden will become a ghost town when the mines close, Baron. Can't you see it? If we don't have jobs, we got nothing. Will you stay here when there ain't a store to shop in or enough kids to have a school system?" Carl snarled, his thick hands gesturing to line up his argument on the runway. He was broad-shouldered with short-cropped hair. Carl Ramey was a pallbearer at her mom and dad's funerals. He was the union steward for the local United Mine Workers at Madden Coal. "I have taken on Wainscott more than anyone in the county. There is no love lost between me and him. But it's not about him. It's about us and this place."

Junebug raised his voice in the background to silence the spectators. "You better close your mouth, kid." Evangeline stared at the most animated roosters—two high school boys acting grown. She hoped they would comply with his commands.

"Yes, sir, Barney Fife," one teenager said. The other laughed and nudged his friend with his elbow.

"Don't shoot us with your one bullet," the second teen added, shaking his hands in mock fear.

Baron and Carl moved closer, causing the two groups of onlookers to flow toward each other like two water drops preparing to become one.

Carl's fists clenched tighter, his forehead and scalp turning crimson. "Baron, your friends up north and in Louisville sure didn't complain when coal built the factories and big cities they used to get rich, did they? They didn't mind taking poor, desperate people's mineral rights for nothing and laughing about it. Hell, they're the ones who benefited the most from tearing down the hills. It's easy to find God and stop swindling people when you got all you want and need."

"Who do you think sold 'em the mineral rights, Carl?" Baron's ponytail swung behind him. "The old-timers like the Mayo family and the Wainscotts used mountain people's hunger to get them to sell their rights. Your beef ought to be with them. But no, you kiss their boots and thank them for letting you."

The two men leaned closer, causing Evangeline to picture two burning logs standing upright in a campfire.

She placed her hands on the men's shoulders and pried them apart. She stepped into the fire.

"That's it. You're too good to stand outside the diner, acting like fools. You all have had two run-ins in town this month. It isn't right, and I am to the point where if I have to, I will haul you to the courthouse to end this nonsense." Evangeline glanced at the diner's large glass window. Two small kids pressed their noses against the glass. "Carl, look over there. Do you see the two babies in the window?"

She pointed to the teens near Junebug. "Baron, they are two idiots who should be at Madden High School instead of here. Is this what you want to do—scare the children, rile up the teenagers, and accomplish nothing except getting your rear ends tossed in jail for disturbing the peace?"

The men lowered their gazes and paused for several moments. Each man exhaled. Their anger subsided, and their fists unclenched.

Carl spoke first. "I'm sorry, Evangeline. You know I respect the law. But if these tree huggers make it harder to work, there won't be any county to protect. Madden County is hard-working people, not a bunch of hills." Frustration framed his voice. "We want to live here—not starve to death here. When Baron wins the battle to save the mountains, the coal companies will cross the river to West Virginia or hightail it to Western Kentucky. Wainscott is management, but he still gives much more than he takes. I don't work for him. I work for my family and our kid's futures."

Baron adopted the same tone. "I apologize, too, Sheriff. I don't mean harm, but the coal tycoons have trapped feeble-minded people like Carl in the mindset the companies want. Wainscott wants us to think we can't make it without him and the other coal companies. We give them a license to destroy the land for profit. Unless the coal companies hightail it out of here, there won't be water fit to drink or clean air to breathe."

Evangeline knew these arguments well and realized easy answers were rare. She placed a hand on each man's arm. She sat beside her father when he had dealt with the United Mine Workers lawyers from out of state, the prominent city environmentalists who came to town, and the stakeholders in the mining companies in Madden. None represented these men, and her father had told them so to their faces.

Her voice was so low Junebug could not hear her ten feet away. "Enough with the speeches. I can't make you get along, gentlemen, but I can arrest you. The next drama gets you an all-expenses paid trip to my jail."

"This age-old war won't end until the coal runs out or these puppets come to their senses," Baron said, pointing at Carl.

"Or you destroy our home. Maybe people will come to their senses then," Carl replied. "I will see you again, Baron."

"You can count on it, Carl."

The men sneered at each other. Their hatred radiated like heat from a coal stove. She didn't have time to douse the flames if she wanted to return to the station in time to watch Luke and Art interrogate Willie and visit Uncle Willie with Sheldon. If anything halted her attempts to support Madden County before she left town, it would be how the people held her head under the creek water, refusing to allow her to do the work.

"Go home, and don't let this happen again. You are God-fearin' men...." Her voice trailed off. She knew prayer would not lead to resolution, only a seismic change of hearts and minds.

She glanced at her watch and realized she would be late. Before she could exhale, the dispatcher's voice sounded on the radio.

"Sheriff Grace, there is an issue at the middle school. Someone is in distress in the football field bleachers. EMTs are also on the way, but the coach requested police assistance, too."

Chapter 10
Life is Short, but the Days are too Damn Long

Willie knew the secret held Agent Barlow back. There was no reasoning, no kindness, no moment untainted by the Agent's dirty hands. Nope. Only the secret shielded all these people—a secret secured like a box of dirty magazines labeled "Old Shoes" and stashed under the bed. Except Willie was the shoe box, bursting at the joints. Willie could bear it. He had given up on creating value in his life long ago. The old man had cut it close with his reckless use of drugs, but now he would collapse and bask in the freedom death offered.

"Life is short," he mumbled, "but the days are too damn long."

When Willie stepped into the visitation area, he stopped. His heart raced as he scanned the entire room.

Sheldon and Sarah sat at a small table. Alone.

As they stood to greet him, Willie realized they had registered his disappointment.

"Where's your sister?" Willie regretted selecting those as his first words.

"It's good to see you, too, Uncle Willie. Are you alright?" Sheldon stood, his arms extended to embrace him.

Willie said, "I need words with your sister."

"Good luck on that," Sheldon replied. "Our great sheriff is fighting crime, arresting jaywalkers or little old ladies who tore the labels from mattresses. She said she would be here, but as you can see...."

Willie hugged his nephew and sat down. "Sarah, you are a beautiful young lady." Before she uttered her thanks, Willie turned his full attention to Sheldon. "Listen, son. I must see Lil Dep. I have to talk to her."

"Certainly, Uncle Willie. I hope she has enough sense to get you out of this trouble. You don't deserve it."

"I am guilty as hell, son. That's not my point." Willie placed his damp palm on Sheldon's forearm. "I must see her for another reason—to give her something. It's not about my little mess of trouble because prison doesn't matter an ounce of coal dust."

"Well, this is a big deal to me," Sheldon said. "She will help you tomorrow if she doesn't make it today."

"Jesus Christ, boy. That may be too late. I am old and rubbed to a nub. It's hard to tell how much my abused ticker can handle." Willie tapped his finger against the orange jumpsuit over his heart.

"Whoa, Willie," Sheldon said. "You're talkin' crazy."

"Sheldon, I am crazy as an opossum with rabies. How long has it taken you to realize it?"

Willie sat as Sheldon sank into his chair. Sarah placed her hand on Sheldon's arm.

Willie stared beyond the two kids, his eyes narrowing. In the corner, the Agent's gray outline shaded the beige wall. The shadow's fedora and the sharp angles of his tailored suit floated up and down.

The voice echoed in Willie's brain. *Yes, yes, yes, Willie, yes, yes. Tell him about me. Then I can finally shut your mouth forever.*

"Fuck you," Willie blurted. He could see Sheldon and Sarah

cower. "Not you," he said to them while waving his hands. "I didn't mean you."

Willie lifted his shoulders toward his ears as he inhaled, stopping to stare at the backs of his hands before exhaling. The dark spots and scars that spread across his pale wrists to his knuckles reminded him of a constellation of dim, dying stars. "I'm sorry, Shel. I am losing it locked up in here, I guess."

It wasn't enough. Sheldon resembled a wounded pup, and the girl leaned away as though she feared Willie might strike her at any moment.

"Sarah." Willie composed himself as he spoke. "Would you mind giving us some time alone?"

She looked at Sheldon. Willie liked her, even though she was a Wainscott, but the fewer people present, the better.

This will be good. Barlow's deep voice jabbed his mind.

"I will be near if you need me, Sheldon," Sarah said as she stood. Walking away, she glanced back at them. Willie waved and smiled to signal Sheldon would be fine.

Willie commenced the moment she was gone. "I don't have much time, Sheldon, so I need you to listen. You don't understand everything playing out here. It is a force older and eviler than you can imagine." Willie glanced into the corner and watched the shadow grow like a stain.

"What do you mean, Uncle Willie? You're scaring me."

"You better be scared, Sheldon. It is better to be afraid than not believe in the world's wickedness, and Madden County is no exception."

Again, Willie studied the corner.

"What are you seeing, Willie? Are you hallucinating? You have to quit the drugs."

"Yes, that's it. I see things. Had a rough few months." Willie reached into his orange jumpsuit. "I have something I need you to do, Sheldon. It is vital." He shifted his body to hide his actions. He retrieved a thick, white envelope from his orange jumpsuit and slid it across the table to Sheldon. Face up, the words "Evangeline Grace" were printed across the front.

"I need you to deliver this to your sister, son." He stared into Sheldon's eyes, direct, unwavering. "It has to go to her and only her. I don't want anyone else reading it, and you cannot lose it. Tell her not to open it until tomorrow morning. You will give me time..."

Willie recognized the questions forming on Sheldon's lips. "I can't tell you what it is, so don't ask. Please do this, Sheldon. I would not put this in your hand if I had another way. Tell Evangeline not to share it with anyone." He glanced at the shadow again. "The only thing I can tell you is I won't be around anymore after she reads this letter."

"Okay, Willie." Sheldon clutched the envelope. "I will give it to her tonight. Is it your will or something?"

"I told you I can't say anything. Except, I love you and your sister more than anyone on Earth. Someday she will question it, and I don't blame her. I know I rue the day I got..." The Agent drifted closer, as if hoping Willie would reveal something. "Sheldon, I won't last long after she reads this letter. I wish I hadn't done everything I did, but tell your sis I am proud of her, love her, and I'm sorry." Although he felt tears pushing against his eyes, Willie smiled. "Your daddy, your sister, and you... Well, you are my family."

"What do you mean, Uncle Willie? What are you saying?" Sheldon's voice cracked, and Willie read the confusion and fear on his face. Sheldon reminded Willie of his late sister-in-law. He had teased his brother Earl when he had married Millie by suggesting her only imperfection was her eyesight.

Sheldon also reminded him of Robert, his brother. Intelligent, tall, kind—until the moment he had passed Willie the secret and lifted off as though he was flying away, free as the softest Kentucky winds.

"Hey, asshole," Willie said. This time he made it clear he was not talking to the boy by rising from the chair and yelling toward the corner. "I won't break the rules. I haven't for sixty years, so don't expect it to happen by accident now."

The door opened, and Otis entered the room. "Sit down, Willie," he said.

"I don't blame you for being afraid, you cocksucker." Willie continued his rant. He stood taller now, and his face revealed anger and hate. "You will meet your match with her. She will end this, and I pray to God you suffer the searing flames of hell."

Otis rushed over to Willie, grabbed him by the arm, and led him away from the table. Willie stared past Sheldon.

I wager I will see you tonight, Willie. It's time to wipe you off my shoe. I will enjoy it, too, old man. Your little Dumb Dora will not be able to deny me the pleasure. The Agent's laughter followed Willie as the officer forced the fragile man toward the door.

Willie turned to his nephew. "You be a good man, Sheldon. Your dad named you after someone who wasn't always so good. Remember, do what I told you to do and take care of Lil Dep. She will need you. I wish I could find another way."

As the jailer pulled him through the door, Sheldon stood alone at the table, pushing the thick envelope into his jacket pocket.

Chapter 11
The Deepest Scars

E vangeline gazed at her watch and the couple lying on the grass beside the bleachers.

"Wow, I am only two hours late for our visit with Willie," the sheriff said to herself.

Ambulance lights flashed in a circular pattern, the red beams dying against the early evening sky before being reborn. The spectators stood on the bleachers as if they were posing for a Shelby Lee Adams photograph—even the trees and the wind stopped to watch the Emergency Medical Technicians' urgent work.

An older man approached Evangeline and stood beside her. He whispered, "Hello, Sheriff. I was the first to respond when the couple fell to the ground."

Evangeline's blood pressure rose. Whenever there was an event, someone in Madden was anxious to give the scoop and add their personal touch. They inserted themselves into the tragedy and told everyone at the hardware store, grocery, hair salon, or courthouse wall about the incident as if it were their story. This elderly gentleman, dressed in a Madden Middle Football jacket, leaped at his chance. It was yet another thing she would not miss when she left.

The sheriff motioned for Junebug to come over. "Please provide your statement to Officer Spears, sir." Before the man could respond, Evangeline spoke to the deputy, "Officer, please take this man's statement." She turned her attention toward the bleachers and the spectators observing the EMS workers and the two people sprawled on the grass.

Junebug removed his notebook from his pocket. Evangeline listened and kept the officer and the old man in her peripheral vision. Junebug's professionalism and kindness made her smile.

"Sir, can I have your name, please?"

"Warren Davis, Deputy. I live out on Route 40 near Wells Grocery store."

"Thank you, Mr. Davis," Junebug said. "Please tell me what you witnessed today."

"Everybody was watching the boys play ball," the man said. His embroidered jacket suggested it wasn't his first game. "My grandson plays on the team..." Junebug did not write anything, but he listened to every word. Bug was always attentive to others. When her father had interviewed deputy candidates five years ago, she had advocated for Spears. Not only did he have the technology chops the department needed, but she also recognized a quiet determination suggesting he could do much more than service technology.

Evangeline would miss him when she departed for Louisville.

When Mr. Davis paused, she assumed he wanted to provide Junebug time to write. However, tears rolled down the old man's cheeks, and he struggled to compose himself.

"Just take your time," Junebug said.

The sheriff felt a pang of guilt. She had assumed the man was an attention seeker. *I'm jumping to conclusions about people without evidence. Way to go, Evangeline.* Since she had returned to

Madden County to help her father and brother, she had experienced so much violence and tragedy she expected the worst on these calls. It made her feel like an intuitive, well-trained officer when she was right. When she was wrong, it made her an ignorant cop.

After he cleared his throat, the man continued, "Chris and Trina huddled up and weren't watching the game. I thought it was a shame because their boy Brett is about as good a running back as I've seen at the middle school level. He had just picked up a first down on a twelve-yard run. He is a good kid, too."

Junebug raised his notebook with his pen poised to write. It was a subtle signal to get to the point.

"Trina stood up. She stumbled and swayed back and forth. Within seconds she tumbled onto the grass by the bleachers. Chris said her name, and I headed over there. But a few seconds later, Chris fell right next to her."

Junebug's pen scribbled on the page.

"All I knew to do was yell for someone to call an ambulance. I rolled both over when I got there to make breathing easier. Trina struggled the most, so I tilted her head, cleared her air passage, and started CPR. I worked in the mines for forty years, so I have some first aid training, but it has been a while. Wanda, Hank, and some others came over to help Chris."

Evangeline leaned into the man's words. Her guilty heart pounded because she had pre-judged him, so now she needed to listen—not an easy task. The two EMTs leaned over the couple and worked with urgency. A small, empty plastic baggie was on the ground near the man's leg, and she made brief eye contact with the female technician. The young woman, her black hair pulled into a woven strand away from her face, appeared to be at least part Native American. Her intense focus on helping the unconscious man and woman caused Evangeline to refocus on the grandfather giving his testimony. *Get your head in the game, Evangeline.*

"It took just a few minutes before the ambulance arrived, and they told us all to step away. But Deputy, before I did, I could see Trina had a pill bottle and a syringe next to her. I already told the EMTs." The man paused again to get his composure. "Sheriff, these dang fools are killin' themselves for nothing, and if that ain't bad enough, they are destroying..." Again, he paused and strained to gain composure. When he achieved it, he said, "It feels like this place is falling apart."

"It's alright, sir," Junebug said, putting his hand on the man's shoulder.

"No, it's not," he stated, his voice breaking again. Then, unable to explain, he pointed toward the field.

Evangeline noticed the football players grouped by the fence. All the players surrounded one kid sitting on his helmet, his arms above his head. His face was hardened like concrete, and his eyes were vacant as the exposed pea-gravel. Some players touched his shoulder pads or sat beside him on the field.

"Can you imagine what that poor boy feels right now?" The grandfather shook his head. "All of us carry scars people give us. But the deepest ones come from our own family."

Chapter 12
I'm a Trained Detective, You Know

When Evangeline arrived home, she stood in the yard for a moment. Her childhood and most of her adult life had transpired in this modest two-story home. The white and green exterior, with a red front door and the thicket of hedges in the front, brought her both comfort and concern.

Indeed, she was fortunate. So many others who lived in the matchbox-sized trailers or prefab homes dotting the hillsides would love to have her house. But she longed to live somewhere different and new. She could envision a condo or a shotgun home downtown in Louisville, just steps from neighbors, coffee shops, restaurants, and bookstores. Sylvia, her friend since the academy in Richmond, was already scouting places closer to the Crescent Hill police station and downtown. She had encouraged Evangeline to bring Sheldon and stay at her house in the Clifton neighborhood until they found the place she wanted.

Maybe she would paint the front door red.

The lights glowed in Sheldon's upstairs room. He was pissed, no doubt, because she had missed their visit with Willie. She would address her brother with care—like one approaches an angry bear. Paulene had said Shel and Sarah had waited a long time. She had reported the visit had not ended well, so perhaps it was best Evangeline missed it.

As sheriff, she wanted to keep her distance from Willie. All she needed was a significant controversy triggered by Gene Begley or the County Judge claiming she was conspiring to hide evidence against her uncle. She pictured the front page of next week's newspaper: "Sheriff Grace Serves and Protects Family First." It would go a long way toward ending her time in Louisville before her first day.

When the sheriff entered the house, she placed her keys and radio in a wicker basket near the door and locked her Glock in the gun safe. She surveyed the living room to her left and the dining room to her right. Sheldon had draped a small gray blanket across the sofa, and the dining room table was empty except for a biology textbook and a notebook. She walked into the kitchen, but Sheldon was not there, so she ascended the stairs.

Evangeline took a deep breath. Sheldon's room was quiet, but light escaped beneath the door, so she tapped her knuckles against the frame.

"You awake, Shel?" Silence. She knocked again. "I am a trained detective, you know. I can see the light under your door." She smiled as if to signal she was kidding.

Stillness.

"I'm sorry I didn't make it back to visit Uncle Willie, Sheldon. I wanted to but had a difficult call and ended up at the hospital with a family."

"You are big on family, aren't you, sis?"

Evangeline winced.

"That's not fair, Shel," she said. "You know it isn't."

"I don't know anything, Evangeline."

"What do you mean?" She leaned closer to the door and placed her hand near the knob.

"Sarah and I met with Willie today. He was talking about crazy things." Sheldon's voice grew louder. "The only thing he said, which didn't sound like insane rambling, was he wanted to see his Lil Dep. But that's too much to ask, I guess."

"So now you get it. Willie is troubled, Sheldon. He always has been. I can't let him distract our chance to—"

"Willie is in trouble, Vangie. There's a difference. He is talking crazy but needs you to be there for him. Like he was for us when Dad died. You're too busy lusting for Louisville to see what's happening under your nose. You might be a detective, but you don't know where to look for clues, that's for sure."

Evangeline's face grew hot as she clenched her jaw. She was too tired to take a lecture. She walked away toward the master bedroom. When her father died, she had moved into her parent's room and given her old space to Sheldon. Of course, Sheldon had refused at first but later accepted the larger room.

Evangeline was twenty-two years older than him, but he was never reluctant to judge her. She sensed he hated the idea of relocating to Louisville, but she could not break her promise to her father. Her dad had said he expected her to keep Sheldon at her side until he was an adult. It was the next to last thing her father had asked her to do before he had passed. The last thing was to replace him as sheriff. She was leaving enough undone business as the chief law enforcer. She did not need to mess up with Sheldon, too.

Nonetheless, her brother frustrated her because he was never grateful. Dad had just turned forty-two, and mom had been thirty-nine when Sheldon was born. His birth had changed the lives of everyone involved in dramatic ways. It had changed her future.

"Sheldon, I'm exhausted and heading to bed. I'm sorry," Evangeline said as she walked away. She heard a noise from his bedroom, so she stopped and turned around. The light under the door had disappeared.

Chapter 13
River of Earth

S heldon waited to turn on the desk lamp. Red numbers glowed on his alarm clock—9:15 PM. Instead of reading or doing homework, he sat down, placed his elbows on the flat surface, and rested his chin on his fist. When he heard Evangeline's shower start, Sheldon took a deep breath and examined the books braced between the brown bookends on the desk.

"Am I too tough on her?" He shook his head and added, "Why is everything so hard?"

Sheldon had spent his first ten years trying to connect with his sister and his father. His father had shared time with him. However, their dad viewed his hours with Evangeline as an investment in the future. Sheldon realized his sister had held a special place in his father's heart. While his dad loved, played with, and disciplined him, it had never been with the high expectations he held for Evangeline. She was his legacy. Sheldon was his accident.

Whenever they had been home at the same time, his dad and sister had relived the dramatic arrests of the day, or Dad would explain why he had made certain decisions regarding a case. They would laugh, argue, and sometimes stand up and act out their theories as if rehearsing a scene for a play. Often they had asked Sheldon for his opinion as though he had been some arbitrator or judge. They had laughed when he had shared his thoughts, even when he had tried his best to be helpful. However, when they had not asked, Sheldon had drifted away, back to his room and his *Star Wars* action figures, books about dinosaurs, and CDs.

Since his father's illness and death four years earlier, Sheldon had wanted his sister to see him as a person instead of a chain around her ankle holding her in Madden County. Despite his efforts, he hadn't been successful. Rather than prove himself, Sheldon had continued to irritate her. Now he could either keep silent and do what she wanted or continue to weigh her down. Talk about no good answers to a problem.

An old, tattered copy of *River of Earth*, his dad's favorite novel, leaned against the other books on his desk. It was the only one Sheldon never removed or replaced. He had read it numerous times because his father had read it to him during elementary school. Sure, his dad's fondness for James Still's masterpiece made it special, but he continued to love the novel as he matured because it was so good. His father and mother were avid readers and passed the love of books on to him. Sheldon picked up the novel and flipped through the pages. He stopped at a passage:

"Their hearts are black as Satan," Mother said. "I'd rather live in this smokehouse than stay down there with them. A big house draws kinfolks like a horse draws nit-flies."

In the novel, the mother burned down the family's home and moved into the smokehouse to get the relatives to leave. Maybe that was the best strategy for Evangeline—burn the house so he would have to go with her.

When he was nine years old, Sheldon had ventured into Vangie's bedroom to share what he had read about animals with his fourth-grade teacher, Mrs. Elliott. Whenever possible, Sheldon had shaped conversations with Evangeline so they could joke about their dad. He had realized she worked with their father all day and then lived with him, too, so when they could get a laugh at Daddy's expense, they bonded.

Sheldon had intended to inform her that a cow poops sixteen times a day—or almost as much as Dad on a regular day after beans and cornbread. However, when he had reached her door, he had heard his sister talking on the phone.

"You're telling me!" she had said into the receiver. "I don't have a chance around here, Sylvia."

Sheldon stood outside the half-open door watching his sister stretch her athletic frame across the bed, facing the wall.

"It's crazy. My dad and brother have me trapped here. I'm taking care of Sheldon like he's mine, and I have to watch out for Dad at work because he has been so distracted since Mom passed. I'm afraid he will get himself shot."

After a pause, Evangeline had said, "Yes, that's right. I wouldn't be here if it weren't for him. My whole life changed when my mom died giving birth to Sheldon. It is like I am on a stakeout, watching my life unravel. I work hard, but nothing happens. My plan...our plans are on hold."

Ice had encased Sheldon's heart. For the first time, he had realized his mother's death had not occurred when he was born—it had happened *because* he was born. Kids had often asked why his sister picked him up at school or why his mom never came to his games. He had always said his mom had died at the hospital. But that night, listening to Evangeline, he had realized his version was not the entire story. Not only had he killed his mom, but he had also hung an anchor around his sister's neck.

Sheldon had not been able to listen further, so he had run to his room, where he had climbed into bed and covered his head with a blanket.

Sheldon still suffered for what he had done to his mother every day. He could never melt the ice surrounding his heart nor shake the guilt of denying his sister's happiness. "You don't have to burn down the house, Evangeline," he said aloud.

He lifted the white envelope and held it beneath the lampshade. The yellow paper and red lines sealed inside were visible in the bright light, and he could sense Willie's words scribbled across the pages, and after a moment's thought, he opened the letter.

My Dear Little Dep,

It made me happy to tell you nighttime stories when you were little. Although I hoped to teach you a thing or two about the world, my fables were twisted tales created right there in your room.

Perhaps those stories embodied my dreams of someday writing an important story, a literary work about goodness overcoming the evil invading our mountains. I guess I do get the chance to write something significant. However, this horrible truth will ring as convoluted and fictitious as the bedtime stories. Although you will think this letter is the mad raving of your eccentric uncle, you must believe what I tell you and act on it.

The real hero of this story is your other uncle, Robert Grace.

Minutes later, after reading the entire letter, Sheldon reread the four pages several times. Then he folded it, returned it to the envelope, and checked the clock on the wall. It was 9:25 PM. He staggered when he stood from the desk as if his uncle's words had made him dizzy. He was on a tightrope and needed to collect his bearings. Chilled by the room, he wished he was under the blanket instead of standing there, Willie's words ringing in his head.

Sheldon was worried, but not because he had read the letter instead of delivering it to Evangeline. His uncle's rantings made it clear Willie had lost his sanity.

In truth, despite his anger, Sheldon was worried for his sister. It would cause her pain to read Willie's tirade and implausible description of Robert's death and the so-called secret he had protected all these years. It would confirm her view of Madden County as a wasteland engulfing her family. Yet another puzzle piece would fall off the table, leaving the picture even more incomplete.

Perhaps Evangeline was right. Although he loved Sarah and his school friends, Louisville might be the only hope for her happiness. Maybe she did not need to read this story at all. Perhaps he could protect his sister from losing another person. He owed her that much for what he had stolen years ago.

"Or am I just trying to save my ass?"

Sheldon drifted to his bed and eased beneath the green blanket. Still dizzy, he rested his head on his pillow and stared at the ceiling plaster. The room spun one way, stopped, and changed direction. Sheldon closed his eyes and hoped the space would quit spinning. After a few minutes, he stared at the ceiling again, clutching his blanket with one hand and the letter with the other.

When Sheldon was ten, Uncle Willie carted him to a flea market in Salyersburg, where Willie had bought him a wooden box made by a local Native American artist. Now, Sheldon rolled from his bed and walked over to his dresser. He picked up the decorative container. Its carvings were intricate, intertwining branches and leaves across the sides. "It is a place to keep important things," Willie had said. Shel would keep the note there until his sister got home, then tell her he understood and would be happy to go to Louisville with her.

Chapter 14
What Do You Do With Good Ol' Boys Like Me?

Willie's cell felt bigger since he had sent the letter. He figured Lil Dep would crack open the envelope in the morning and laugh about it but then would change her mind after the Agent killed him.

To be free, by God, to be free. Willie knew Barlow would not let him live much longer since two people carried the secret. Besides, Willie had goaded and poked the Agent for decades. If Barlow had any weakness, it was his ego, so most likely the Grim Reaper had an appointment with ole Willie tomorrow.

"Who knows," he said aloud, "Perhaps it's true—the condemned man gets the best night of sleep." He peered through the bars to check the clock attached to the wall outside the cells. Its black hands indicated 9:19 PM.

Willie did not remember the last time he had felt so free. He stretched out on the cot and sang the chorus of a Don Williams song. "...those Williams boys still mean a lot to me/ Hank and Tennessee/ but what do you do with good ole boys like me?"

Again, he pictured the day Robert told him the secret. They had hiked to the top of Two Mile Hill. Most called this spot the

Pinnacle because the rocks jutted from the mountainside, over-looking miles of hills and hollers. When the trees turned, vibrant reds, browns, and greens dotted the landscape. Below the cliffs, boulders formed the base hundreds of feet below.

Robert had brought Hershey bars, Moon Pies, and Nehi Orange pop in a lunchbox. The brothers had talked for an hour before Robert had broached the secret. When he had started, it had been like a black-and-white middle school instructional movie about hygiene or how boys should treat girls. At any moment, Willie had expected him to produce a chart with a bell curve or a picture of human anatomy to point out the secret's location.

That moment had initiated the pain and suffering Willie had endured for his lifetime. It had put him into a crucible and crushed him until only this broken, drug-addicted husk remained.

But now.

Willie closed his eyes. He heard Faith Cornett's soft voice singing on the porch at Hammond Creek. "What will I leave behind, Lord? What will I leave behind."

The whisperer came. His shadow formed in the corner.

The Agent's deep voice drowned Faith's gentle tone with a harsh echo inside a dark cave. *So you will be free, Turdwhacker? That's what you think? Everything is jake in your tiny little white-trash brain. Our conflict will just work out because you told a secret? Shit, you're smarter with a snout full of whiskey.*

Willie smiled and stared into the shadow, finding the Agent's shape as he had many times. "I appreciate you visiting, Barlow. Some prisoners don't get visitors."

And here you are getting three visitors in one day, the Agent said. *You are as lucky as a Rockefeller.*

Willie was surprised but not afraid. It was good news the Agent remained a shadow. Throughout the years, Willie's ability to locate the Agent lurking in the corners of rooms or the geometrical shapes between tree branches and bushes had become a survival skill. He had developed the ability to withstand the Agent's banter inside his head with enough resolve to argue rather than comply. Over five decades, stubbornness and self-medicating can build calluses on your soul.

Thankfully, the Agent stopped talking. Willie hoped the silence would carry him to sleep.

*****

Willie was uncertain how much time had passed before the Agent spoke again.

"Sometimes, Willie, my genius surprises me." Barlow was always arrogant, but something did not feel right to Willie. It was the sound of Barlow's voice—it emanated from outside Willie's head as if the Agent spoke to his ears instead of his mind.

Willie rubbed his ear and peered into the corner. The Agent, a perverse combination of light and dark, had transformed. The figure was tangible, a concrete yet unfinished human form resembling a man rather than a shadow on the sidewalk or fog clinging to wet morning grass.

Evangeline must have read the letter earlier than expected. Just like her daddy—always searching for clues.

"Oh, well," Willie said. He had wished for death so many times that to cry about it now would be hypocritical. He had passed the secret and fulfilled his responsibility. Tonight. Tomorrow. It made no difference to his tired body and broken soul.

"You aren't smart, Agent, just evil. You thought you had me, didn't you? You wanted me to die and allow you to go wild, but it didn't work out." Willie squinted to make sense of the Agent's new form. "Now, you will deal with an enemy smarter than us."

"Damn, Willie. Give yourself some credit," the Agent said as he stepped away from the wall. Barlow was an obscene caricature formed from ash, clay, and blood. His face, hands, and skin resem-

bled paper mache. Willie's heart thundered. This Barlow had appeared once before—on the Pinnacle, with cliffs high above the rocks, trees, and gorge. *"Willie boy, you sure are stupid, but even loaded to the muzzle with coffin varnish, you are as smart as a fifteen-year-old."*

Willie's jaw dropped.

Sheldon had read the letter.

He tensed as the monster advanced across the concrete floor and bent to his face, their noses almost touching. Up close, the Agent's skin was a grotesque shaded pencil sketch. Scars pocked his cheeks. It reminded Willie of a target at a shooting range, marked with spots and flaps of tissue peeled away but attached by a small skin tag.

"Oh, it pleases me to see you all balled up, Hillbilly," the Agent said.

Barlow's chilled breath fanned Willie's face. It was how Willie imagined an exhumed, open casket might smell. He gagged.

"You thought the little pip would deliver your letter like the Pony Express. Shit, you are a goof, old man."

"What do you mean?" Willie felt his hope crumble like dried chunks of slate outside a mine. How could he warn Sheldon and Evangeline about the danger? But there was no pathway, only an empty, darkened hallway leading to the other cells on the second floor. The officers had provided him with a cell away from other inmates as an act of kindness. However, it isolated him, and since the cameras only monitored the interrogation rooms, he was alone.

Stop, Willie Grace. Now is the moment you have long hoped for, so why dread it?

Willie stopped searching for exits, answers, and resolve. He thought, right or wrong, his days would end soon, along with the pain and burden of the secret. *I get to accept the summons from the server's hand.*

"I wish I had the hair of the dog for you, Willie." The Agent

clicked his tongue as he paced beside the cot. His slow stride and the skin hanging from his face did not hide his stature. His broad shoulders and thick arms bulged beneath the 1920s suit molded to his body. *"Damn drugs, I thought they would kill you a long time ago, but I guess when you add shit to shit, all you get is fresher shit."*

Willie speculated Sheldon had opened the letter despite his request because that's what kids do. *He is close to my age when I inherited the curse. Sheldon understands the letter and knows his sister will be upset with him for reading something meant for her. He will do what I would've done. Sheldon won't tell her, and he will not share the letter. Dear God, please don't let him share the message with his girlfriend.*

"You see, your little man didn't respect you, Willie. Surprise, surprise." The Agent glided closer. Willie felt the Agent hovering over him like a boxer taunting a fallen opponent. *"Little Sheldon read the letter as if I wrote it for you and him to perform at the Shubert in downtown Boston. It would be a comedy of errors."*

The old man stared ahead as the Agent laughed. Willie slid his hand beneath the pillow beside him. "Speaking of the dog that bit me—I hope you don't mind if I take one of my joy pills." He swiped an object from under the pillowcase and popped it into his mouth. He swallowed hard, forcing it down his throat before the Agent could react.

"You pitiful drug addicts," the Agent said. *"Willie, no pills or liquor will relieve your pain when I finish with you. Only death."*

Willie's eyes filled with tears, but he glared at Barlow. "You and I will talk again in hell when Madden County gets rid of you. A letter or no letter, someone will cast your evil carcass into eternal—" Willie choked as he struggled to breathe and swallow.

"Oh, that's swell, Willie." The Agent's tone shifted. *"All this time, and you didn't realize this place is hell. Damn, it's why I'm here. I am eternal, stuck in hell with the world's worst fornicators. I am the retribution for what you people have done to the world."* His

eyes burned like embers popping from the flames. The Agent stood and stretched—his bones crackled as he rose to his full height, well over six feet tall.

"*Still,*" the Agent said, "*I want to give you a present, Willie. Maybe I should regale you with Vadoma's final chapter. Yes, that'll do.*"

Willie cleared his throat and rasped, "Really? Why don't I tell you the Vadoma story, and we title it *The End?*"

The Agent laughed. "*You are not the only one hiding secrets. Since you have spilled your guts, you can hear the saga's end.*"

Willie watched as the Agent drew a knife from inside his suit jacket. Barlow's image was vivid when he stood in the light. His tailored suit and his melting skin disgusted Willie. The Agent's coat and pants were faded, dirty blue, covering a blue vest and a shirt as white as milk. A bright red handkerchief poked from the jacket pocket, and his dress pants creased like a fancy, yet wine-stained, tablecloth. The Agent's brown shoes, etched with intricate designs in the leather, reflected light like mirrored glass. The gray and blue fedora melded with his massive head.

"*Vadoma married my father out of necessity. Our fates were tied, she said, so she needed to stay in Boston. The speakeasy decided they didn't need her anymore, so she cozied up to dear old dad.*"

It was odd to hear the Agent's voice instead of an echo blaring inside his head.

The Agent continued, "*So when I returned from the war, as Vadoma predicted, we became even closer. I stayed at home, receiving the small check the government gave soldiers to hold us over. Vadoma, my stepmother, and I were inseparable, right there in my old man's place.*"

Barlow had talked about Vadoma for fifty years, praising her beauty, wisdom, and magic. But he had never ventured this far. The stories had always stopped when he arrived at his home in

Boston after World War I. Willie understood this was the Agent's goodbye gift.

"Vadoma taught me more than all my schooling and time in the service. Months later, she told me I needed a job doing something I did well. I became a detective for the Baldwin Agency, kicking asses and cracking heads. I worked security at night, so when my father left for the knife factory, I would slip in to continue my lessons—"

"I am sure you did," Willie said.

"She taught me how the darkest magic surrounds us and, when called upon, gives the knowledgeable caller great power. She showed me how to tap into the arts for three more years—not the love potions and soft spells, but the curses she said I would need in the future. Revenge. Control. Mastering Death itself. She ensured I was well-read on every subject."

Willie's throat hurt from swallowing, but he still managed a husky laugh. "Barlow the Friendly Ghost," he said. "Go ahead. Kill me. It can't hurt as much as listening to you whine about your lost love."

The Agent examined the blade. Without redirecting his focus, he said, *"But the story isn't over yet, so you better pipe down."* Barlow moved closer again.

Willie could not avoid the foul breath. He had nowhere else to go.

"One day, my father came home early from the factory. I have never forgotten Vadoma's calm reaction. We were in the bed she shared with him, but she showed no shame or fear. She did not try to cover up her naked body and stared as though she had expected him. I jumped up and attempted to explain. He walked to me and said with an unfamiliar kind tone, 'Don't worry, son. It's not your fault. It is this evil witch.' That is when he struck me with his fist right in the head."

Willie watched Barlow's paper mache face wrinkle even more.

"When I awoke, there was Vadoma next to me on the bed like

when we were together. Except now, her brains covered the white pillows, the nightstand, and the headboard. My father had placed the gun in her right hand and positioned her arm and the pistol, so it appeared she had killed herself."

Willie sat up straighter with his back flat against the cinder block wall.

"I know what you are thinking, you piker. Your weak mind predicts I took the gun or this knife," the Agent said as he ran his finger along the blade's edge, "and chased my father to avenge Vadoma's murder."

Willie continued to swallow as hard as he could, advancing the bulge deeper into his throat. The storm brewed, and the lightning would strike soon. He nodded, signaling yes in response to the Agent's claim, not because he cared about the story but to buy himself a moment.

"But I did not. The war showed I was not opposed to killing people on my side, but this was my father. Instead, I touched Vadoma's shoulder and thanked her for all she had taught me. I vowed to study and use the darkness to hurt anyone who crossed me. I loaded her books, cards, and crystal into my knapsack and left my father's house to find my way. I have never been back to that house."

As the Agent's mottled face and blood-red eyes remained frozen in thought, Willie covered his face with his fingers and swallowed hard a final time. He knew the Agent could only see the constellation of age marks on the back of his hands. "Robert," Willie said, "I did my best."

"I know you, Willie Grace," the Agent said, flipping the knife into the air and catching it by its handle. "You would end your life because you have given away the secret. Why not? You have no reason to live. I am content—no, I am pleased—to end you and your shitty, meaningless life myself." The blade reflected the light from the hallway. In the silver, Willie's face flowed as if liquified by light and steel.

"Besides, your little nephew will be around a long time, and he will tell someone. Maybe his little girlfriend. His weakness will give me the strength to end this town."

Willie's breathing came in abbreviated bursts, sounding like hiccups as he leaned back, his thin shoulders touching the wall. "Since I will die, why don't you tell me something, Agent? Tell me who or what you are. Why do you hate us enough to curse our lives?" Willie's voice squeaked and cracked like a broken whistle. His head felt light, and the pain in his throat spread.

"You know, Sheldon gave me one good idea. He opened your letter. I will open you like a letter. Look at this letter opener, Willie. Look at it."

Willie peered at the 8-inch blade as Barlow turned it around in his hand again. Willie remembered when he and Earl had played mumbly peg in the yard on summer days. He would drop the knife with such precision it had stood straight up near his brother's bare feet. Back then Willie had been the protector.

Death was giving him one last chance to smile and accept the summons from the Agent's coal-black hands. Accept it and say goodbye.

The old man stared through the Agent, ignoring Barlow's incessant words and the blade he used to open the envelope holding Willie's heart.

Chapter 15
Beyond Those Pines and Poplars

E vangeline slipped beneath the sheets. Instead of sleep, images invaded her thoughts—a haunting hybrid of the present and the past. She stood at the football field, only now, no one else was there except for the grandfather, Mr. Davis. He sat in the bleachers with his back to her. The embroidery on his jacket glowed. She tried to ask why he was still there, but she could not speak. When he turned, it wasn't the grandfather at all. Instead, it was her father. His lips moved, but his words were aborted, replaced by the buzz of her phone.

Snapping awake, Evangeline fumbled with the phone, then said, "Yes?"

Art's voice filled her ear. "Evangeline, you'd better come to the station. Something has happened to Willie."

Within minutes Sheriff Grace's car roared toward town. The crescent moon escorted her down the winding roads. Her dream abandoned her, replaced by Uncle Willie's face and her memory of her father in the hospital bed, both unsettling visions.

She shifted her groggy thoughts to the football field again.

Helpless and hopeless were the only words to describe Brett's expression. She remembered how he had sat across the fence and watched EMTs save his parents' lives, but the kid's pain would not end there. Helpless and hopeless.

Her father and mother had protected her, so such despair did not visit her as a child. Perhaps that was why the boy's expression haunted her so much. Even with Uncle Willie, Sheldon, Sylvia, the contract, and her doubts about her future, she drowned in the sadness on Brett's face.

Brett's parents would survive, for now, thanks to the grandfather and first responders. Evangeline thought about what the boy had endured and how Madden County had just erased his childhood like the night sky pushing aside the sun.

Her headlights cut through the dark. Evangeline imagined how isolated events could shape a child's worldview. She recalled an event much less traumatic than Brett had experienced but remained with her twenty-five years later.

Evangeline rode in the backseat of her father's cruiser, daydreaming. She had insisted on riding with him rather than with her mother an hour later. Her mind rehearsed what would happen during the rally. Her father, a heroic lawman, would stand alongside the Governor of Kentucky. Her Social Studies teacher, Mr. Conley, proclaimed the governor a great man. This great man would praise her father's work before all her friends and classmates. Even Mr. Goble, her principal, would be there, and she valued his opinion. She imagined standing in the hallway, chatting with Mr. Goble about her father's greatness.

More than all the other times she had ridden in his police car, that ride held a special place in Evangeline's memory. She noticed the green trees, the houses and trailers perched on hillsides, and the blue sky as background like she never had before then. On the way, she hoped her dad would give a speech about his approach to stopping crime.

"Tell them about the time you caught the dangerous robbers from Tennessee, Daddy," Evangeline said from the backseat.

"What did you say, Vangie?" her father said.

Evangeline had already retreated into her brain where the governor admired her father and cameras flashed. Reporters scribbled as fast as possible to catch each gold nugget before it fell to the courthouse yard.

"When you take a picture with the governor, can I be in it, Dad?"

This time he heard her. "We will see, Vangie. I expect it to be a hectic day."

She looked out the car window and smiled because she knew he had said yes.

When they arrived at the courthouse, the wooden platform on the lawn was smaller than she had anticipated. It held a few folding chairs, a podium with a microphone, and a single electric speaker aimed toward the yard and Main Street. The County Judge Executive stood nearby as several workers scurried about stringing caution tape to reserve a section for journalists.

A mannequin with perfect blonde hair and glowing white teeth talked with the judge. He appeared to have leapt off the cover of her mom's *People* magazine to take charge of this event. He directed the workers to set up more folding chairs inside the taped section and smiled as if he planned to sell everyone a used car.

Daddy's deputies must sit in that section, Evangeline thought. *Maybe I can sit with them.* But it didn't feel right. She needed to be closer—as close as possible to her father. Being near him was more important than seeing the stage up close. She wanted to feel the flashing lights, the rumble of applause, and the warm adoration. Evangeline wanted to be him.

She scouted the scene and recognized an opportunity. The workers left gaps between the planks supporting the platform's foundation. Evangeline checked for witnesses and snaked between the boards to find a safe place beneath the stage.

The stakeout commenced. Sunlight cut through the slats and drew lines on the grass around Evangeline's legs. Vangie viewed the chairs where the dignitaries, like her father, would sit and slid her butt across the grass to see the podium at the platform's edge.

Footsteps vibrated the boards above her. Two men laughed as they approached the chairs. Mr. *People* magazine led as the other man—her teacher's hero, Governor Bradley—followed. Their well-groomed hair and fancy suits made the men's heads appear too massive for their thin necks.

Governor Bradley spoke to the Cover Boy while they waved at people entering the courthouse yard. The governor's smile stretched across his giant head like a carved mouth on a pumpkin. "That's why you must get me out of this godforsaken dump," Bradley said. "Did you see the sheet someone used to welcome us into town? I'm sure it had piss stains." Both men snickered while they pointed, waved, and offered thumbs-up gestures to the crowd.

"That's rich, Boss," the assistant said. His plastic smile reminded Evangeline of the giant billboard near US 23 on the way to the shooting range. Accompanying the Wizard of Oz-sized head plastered across the sign were the words, "Aaron Cohen, Lawyer. Why settle for the rest when you can have the best?"

"Oh Gawd, is he the shit-kicker sheriff we dealt with last year in Frankfort? Don't tell me he'll be on the platform," the governor said to his sidekick. Evangeline's heart paused, then somersaulted, before beating again. *What did he say?*

"I'm afraid that's him. He's the worst." Cover Boy leaned closer to the governor but did not bother to whisper. "I can run cover for you if you want. I'll boot him without much effort. However, it would be tough to exclude him from the photo op at the end."

The space under the porch shrank. Evangeline wanted to leap

through the floor onto the stage like a killer whale breaking the ocean's surface.

"He thinks he is a big deal because he has power in this one-stoplight town. Assholes like him grab my ear and hang on as if I care what they have to say. They believe they are big shots when they don't matter. Holy shit, he questioned everything I said at the law enforcement conference last year."

People magazine said, "He sure as hell hurt us in Eastern Kentucky during the last election. Here he comes now. I will take care of it, don't you worry. I dealt with his kind in Virginia."

As the assistant headed toward the makeshift stairs, Evangeline tried to reach her father first. Her breath was shallow as she held back tears. However, extracting herself from her perch beneath the floor was difficult. The slats felt tighter, and Evangeline was more awkward than when she had squirreled her way under the stage.

When Evangeline exited, it was too late. Cover Boy was speaking to her father and pointing toward a designated area outside the taped area. Her father nodded, shrugged his broad shoulders, and walked away. Her heart pounded.

Evangeline stood outside the chairs with all the others relegated to the outer edges. Older people, kids, and a small group of miners were outside the tape. Listening was difficult because she felt wounded, like when she missed a free throw at the end of a basketball game, and everyone on the other team laughed and cheered. Confusion and embarrassment swirled inside her.

There was her father standing outside the tape. Quiet.

In his speech, the governor addressed poverty in Eastern Kentucky and how he guaranteed a better future for people in the mountains. But Evangeline only heard the insults he had said earlier. "Godforsaken dump." "Shit-kicker sheriff." "Doesn't matter." His billboard head spewed meaningless words through his opossum grin. He acknowledged the County Judge, the Bank President, and even the High School Football coach, but he did not mention her father. His words were like candy—sweet and what the people wanted—however, they still gave Evangeline a belly-ache decades later.

The memory stuck in other ways, too. Evangeline's father had been a great man in a small place. If Earl Grace had lived in Louis-ville or Lexington, he would be State Police Commissioner or Governor by now. He was a goldfish in a small bowl, his growth stunted.

In her memory, the applause settled like smoke after the fire-works as people lined up for pictures with Governor Bradley. Evangeline's father stood like everyone else. As she watched the sheriff chat with Richard Duty and his wife, he looked different, even though he was in his uniform. The people around him appeared changed, too, their faces less vibrant.

"Vangie, get on over here. It's picture time," her father said. She was slower than usual but made her way to his side, where the governor's lackey rushed people through the line. Evangeline stood beside her father as he pinned a campaign button on his shirt. She wrapped her arms around herself but could not wipe away the resentment and confusion she felt. She knew her father was a great man in her bones, but he would never be more than the Sheriff of Madden County, a small place, helpless and hopeless.

Evangeline swore she would travel to where she did not settle for less. It would be far, far away from Madden County.

When it was time to go home, Evangeline told her dad she would ride with her mom. His brow wrinkled, but he said, "Sure."

She rested her cheek against the chilly car window. The rows of trees made each hillside a fortress wall, keeping the world out and the people of Madden County locked inside. She swore she would never be a prisoner. Nothing, nor anyone, could hold her there except her father and mother. The conflicting feelings stretched her. She admired her dad and wanted to protect him.

However, she needed to be significant someday. She needed to be an essential person respected as a leader and a hero. Such respect could only happen beyond those pines and poplars.

*****

As Evangeline drove through the pines and poplars, she wondered if kids like Brett would escape these dark hills. Or would he always be helpless and hopeless? Had she exchanged her opportunity to be more than a raggedy sheriff in a ragged town for her father's approval?

She scolded herself for her self-pity, considering the pain and shame the boy must feel. But he had an excuse for still living in Madden County. She was no longer her daddy's Lil Dep. Brett could have a more meaningful future, just as she still hoped to find more meaning for herself and Sheldon. Evangeline needed significance then just as now, even as she dreaded what awaited her at the station. Art had not provided details, but something was wrong. In Madden County, there always was.

She envisioned dropping the signed contract on her desk into the Outgoing Mail bin well before the October 25th deadline.

Chapter 16
The Summons

The images invading Sheldon's sleep made him nauseous. Red and black liquid spattered a white canvas, each gush accompanied by shortened breathing and gurgling. A knife descended, slashing the fragile scarecrow of a man, drawing more blood with each arc. Dark splotches covered the decaying skin of the artist's hands.

Sheldon opened his eyes. His mind hurt as if the same rotting fingers probed his brain like a surgeon gauging his responses. Someone or something lurked inside his room, maybe even inside his head. He could feel them.

Sheldon searched for an intruder and froze when he recognized a shape in the corner. It was a shadow but more than a shadow—more than the absence of light. It formed and reformed, all the while remaining the recognizable shape of a man. It was like playing name-the-cloud with Sarah at Dewey Lake.

He blinked to confirm his perception. The seven-foot shadow covered the bedroom wall and resembled a suit, sharp shoes, and a fedora like the gangsters in old black and white movies. Sheldon swung his legs over the side of his bed and sat there staring. The figure shimmered like a candle flame.

So sad, Sheldon heard inside his brain. *Your poor Uncle Willie. Was he holy? No, but he is holey now.* The voice and laughter shocked Sheldon. Rather than evaporating like his usual nightmares, the gaping holes, the vacant face, and the blood lingered. The wounds were vivid, and he heard the metal blade cut into flesh and grate against bones. Why did he feel the blood staining his hands and soaking the Oasis tee shirt if this was a dream? He was awake, yet his heart raced as though he had witnessed a murder.

Sheldon glared at the Important Box on the dresser. Willie's written words collided with the nightmare in his head, and suddenly he was sitting at the visitation room table with Uncle Willie as he had hours before. The old man leaned in to whisper, and it felt real.

However, now Willie's bloodless face stared from the nightmare's distant edges. His uncle was pleading, "Take this to Evangeline, Sheldon. Take it to your sister." Sheldon could hear wet thuds coming from behind Willie. How was this real?

Willie's right, Shel, old boy. It isn't too late to share your newfound burden with your selfish sister. The arrogant voice fogged Sheldon's mind. *She is a bird, alright, but you don't need to carry me around alone. My dad was all wet, too, but he and I got along fine. He had plenty of jack to take care of me because he owned a knife factory. Now, your big Sis isn't one to help you, but maybe if you told her everything about me—it doesn't matter a teardrop whether she believes you or not. Here, let me show you a picture...*

Willie's dead eyes were still open. The Agent stood behind Willie, a formless face, hand, and blade spotted with blood, grinning as the knife pierced the old man's body in a steady, wet, sticky rhythm.

It isn't a pretty family picture, is it?

Sheldon snatched his jeans from the bedroom floor and pulled them over his legs. His shoulders and leg muscles were tight and trembling. The images remained, imprinted on his vision like the screen at a drive-in movie. Blood. Uncle Willie's blank and lifeless face. The box on his desk. Willie tried to warn him, but he did not listen.

The voice blared, a reverberation, deep and saccharine. *You will learn, boy.*

Sheldon stumbled down the hallway and turned the knob on his sister's door. He hoped to see his sister sleeping with her legs stretched diagonally across the entire bed like she had when he was a kid. It was not the case. Evangeline's unmade bed indicated she had left in a hurry.

Within minutes, Sheldon pumped his bike pedals, heading toward the Sheriff's Station. The dark early morning Kentucky hills circled him as he pushed himself. The wind against his face burned his nostrils and lungs. He repeated, "Get to the station...get to the station...a bad dream...a bad dream..." The mantra substituted the Agent's words, but not his childhood. That was gone like the days when his father, sister, and uncle had led him to believe the world was safe.

Chapter 17
Snitches Get Stitches, Right?

"Screw you, Luke. You watched us like a hawk to make sure I didn't talk to him, but you couldn't protect him from...this?"

Evangeline gestured toward the open jail cell. The lighting and the blood painted the room burgundy and copper. Willie reclined on the cot, his shoulders and upper back propped against the wall. His chest gaped open as if prepped for surgery. Blood spatter stained the sheet and the wall above the cot. Willie's outstretched arms gave the impression he was trying to fly, and the ripped orange and scarlet jumpsuit made him an exotic bird.

Luke said, "Don't blame me. It happened a couple of hours ago, by my estimation. I had just started my shift." His biceps and chest tensed, and his face blazed.

"What does this?" Art changed the subject. "I mean, who does this?"

Luke said, "It's the drug runners. Willie must have been pretty high up in—"

Evangeline charged toward Luke. She raised her fists—her face a blend of anger, hate, and loss. Art stepped between them and wrapped his arms around the sheriff, preventing her from reaching Luke. As Art held her to his broad chest, she tensed every muscle in her body. She struggled but could not escape his embrace. For a moment, she recalled a blackberry bush with long tentacles and sharp thorns wrapped around her on a Hammond Creek hillside.

"No, Evangeline." Art said as he held her. She felt the loss rise above the anger and hate. She went limp, and the small sobs bubbled to the surface. Over her shoulder, Art said, "Now isn't the time, Luke. Keep your theories to yourself until we have some evidence."

Although Art attempted to hide the carnage in the cell, Evangeline stubbornly turned her head toward the scene. Agony flowed through her, but she assessed the crime scene. *Someone will pay for this.* She forced herself to take a mental snapshot of the carnage.

Evangeline tapped Art on the side and stood straight to tell him she had regained her composure. He eased his hold, and she slipped away. The sheriff nodded a thank you and then faced the cell.

It's not Willie anymore. It is a victim.

"Let's inspect and photograph every inch," she said. She wiped her eyes. Junebug, who had just arrived at the station, retrieved a camera while Art and Luke pulled on latex gloves and opened a tackle box investigation kit.

Willie's chest, split from the trachea to solar plexus, caved inward like a shattered windshield. Evangeline closed her eyes when she realized the killer had removed Willie's heart and placed it on her uncle's lap. She blinked, raising her hand to cover her mouth and nose. When the sheriff could bear to look again, Willie appeared as if he expected to watch television or read a book. No evidence of defensive wounds on his arms and hands. No handprints on the wall or floor.

But the contrast between Willie's wound and his face affected her. From outside the cell, his face was serene, as if this brutal violence was no surprise. She hoped his death was instantaneous. *Is it what I see or what I want to see?* She knew her uncle well, and although his face was thinner than before, she recognized the gentle patience around his dead eyes.

The sheriff faded from Art and walked toward the cell door. Each stride was punctuated with an ever-so-slight pause as if she were creeping up to surprise Willie as she had as a little girl. Before she entered the cell, Evangeline stopped at the bars to analyze the big picture. Blood spatter created continents on the wall, the blackening splotches stretching toward the ceiling like a world map in a geography book.

Snitches get stitches, right? Was Luke on target? Did the drug dealers kill Willie because they feared he would talk? People—criminals, in particular—witnessed too much violence in Madden County to risk identifying the Highlander.

Since her father's death, the Highlander had run pills and heroin into Madden. His people sent a clear message to potential competitors: we use whatever means necessary to protect our turf. Someone had killed two Madden County teens because they had driven to Lexington, bought pills, then sold the product here. A man searching for aluminum cans had found the boys floating face down in the Tug Valley River, their bodies beaten beyond recognition. Another time the Highlander's men had shot Glenn Setser because his ex-wife had spread the rumor he was a police informant. He was not.

Did the Highlander kill Willie to stop him from speaking to me? It was the only sensible explanation.

Luke stepped toward the cell. Art shook his head to warn him. Evangeline ignored Porter's presence and bent over the bed, her hands shaking as she peered into the center of her uncle's chest, then looked into his wrinkled, pallid face and soft, patient eyes so similar to her father's.

Chapter 18
Waiting to Catch His Boy if He Fell

Sheldon erupted into the squad room, his brown hair matted to his head and his breathing rapid. Despite the chilly autumn wind, his sweaty tee shirt and jeans clung to his skin. He gripped his red bike helmet like a weapon.

"Sheldon, it is two o'clock in the morning. What are you doing here?" Evangeline said. She did not want her brother to see their uncle this way. Sheldon's face reflected a desperation Evangeline had never seen before.

"I need to know. Is Uncle Willie dead?" Sheldon labored to speak and catch his breath.

Evangeline scanned the room, checking each deputy's face to ascertain who had informed her brother. Each man signaled their innocence with a head shake.

Art stepped forward and said, "Hey, Sheldon. We're taking a break for a few minutes. Come and sit down, and I will get you an Ale 8, then give you a ride home."

The teen shook his head and stared at his sister's face. His expression demanded the answer, and it needed to come from her.

Evangeline blinked and swallowed. "Yes, I am afraid he is, Sheldon." She balanced her sentence against the urge to cry again.

Sheldon stared at the scuffed hardwood flooring. He stumbled toward the chair Art had offered earlier.

"How did you know, Sheldon? No one is aware this happened except us." Evangeline walked toward him, her hands gloved.

Sheldon raised his head, his brow wrinkled and eyes narrow. The expression reminded her of when he had been six, attempting to figure out how their father's so-called magic tricks worked. But Evangeline rejected the idea. Sheldon was not a little boy anymore. A lock of his sweaty hair formed a half-crescent moon on his pale forehead. Part of her wanted to embrace Sheldon just as Art had her two hours earlier. However, as a law enforcement officer, she needed to understand how her brother knew about Willie's murder.

She knelt and placed her hand on his. Her raw sense of loss gripped her neck muscles, causing her head to ache. "We need to talk." She stood, helped him rise, and towed him to her office.

*****

Evangeline closed the door and embraced her brother.

"We will get to the bottom of this, Sheldon. It will be alright."

"It will never be alright again, Evangeline." Sheldon pulled away, leaving emptiness in his wake.

"I loved him, too, you know." Her voice faltered as he walked toward her desk. She hoped he did not notice the "Human Resources, Louisville Police Department" envelope resting on the surface. Her desk looked like a board game; the game pieces were a pen, letter opener, stapler, thumb drive, and a single picture of Sheldon and her father. The photo faced away from Evangeline, as Sheldon did now. However, she knew the image by heart. At seven years old, Sheldon sat on the back of a horse at the Madden

County Fair while her father stood nearby, waiting to catch his boy if he fell.

She did not see that little boy when Sheldon turned around. He was taller than her, and his face resembled their mother's. Although he was still slim, his shoulders had broadened. His face, contorted into a grimace, caused him to look older, angrier, and more troubled than she had seen him since their father's death. Right before he died, her father had made her promise she would take care of her brother. But she knew it was not only the promise preventing her from leaving Sheldon to live in Madden County with friends. She loved him and felt responsible. Sheldon was her only family now.

"These are terrible circumstances, Sheldon. I know you blame me, but I had to—"

"I don't blame you, sis." He stepped farther away from her. "I know not everything is your fault. You aren't that powerful, you know." Tears streamed down his cheeks—his face twisted and stark. "But you blame me, don't you?"

Evangeline winced. "You aren't to blame for any of this, Sheldon. Why would you say something so wrong?"

"Never mind, Vangie. I don't expect anything from you. With Willie's murder and the crazy thoughts I have in my head, I can't worry about you anymore. I need to grow up and be the kind of men Willie and Robert were. I have to be more like Dad."

Evangeline did not respond. *How can he say something so out of character and inaccurate?* While her heart broke for Willie, her uncle had endangered himself more than she ever could. Evangeline had loved her uncle, but whenever her father had advised him to stop drinking, taking pills, and using drugs, he had always responded with vague excuses and solemn assurances. And her brother had never even met Uncle Robert.

Sheldon wiped his tears with his sleeve and sniffed. He said,

"Uncle Willie was a hero in ways we don't even know. He was good to me." He raised his chin as if he had said what he needed.

"Yes, he was...." She wanted to ease her brother's pain, so she did not argue about Willie's hero status. Why would Sheldon say he needed to be like Willie and their father? "I will miss Uncle Willie, too. But we will leave this place as soon as I solve this. We both need space away from Madden County and a new start. I will make things better for us, Shel. I know I can."

"I wish it were true, sis, but we can't leave. Or, at least, I can't."

Cold fingertips trailed down her back.

"What are you talking about, Shel? We can't be apart from each other. It must be us like Dad wanted."

She had never met the Sheldon staring back at her. His tone became more deliberate, and his tears dried. "I have to stay," he said.

"After what's happened here? It makes more sense to start fresh somewhere else." Evangeline choked up again. An image of Willie in the jail cell flooded her thoughts. "You aren't thinking straight, Sheldon. Losing Willie this way has affected me too, but...." She watched as Sheldon turned away again. His arms hung by his sides, and he stared into the dark corner of her office.

"We aren't going anywhere," he mumbled. The tone was so distant and cold that Evangeline wondered if he was even talking to her.

Chapter 19
Dreams, Restless Dreams

Evangeline felt like a washcloth, twisted and drained.

Otis drove Sheldon home while she remained for the crime scene processing. She supervised as Art and Luke combed the cell for evidence, and Junebug photographed the scene in meticulous detail. Willie's body, torn and broken, paralyzed her. Her breathing came in bursts, as did her anger, despair, and disbelief.

Evangeline knew death. Her mother and father, of course, but she had also investigated many violent crime scenes and car accidents with bloody fatalities. None compared to this. Yes, it was her uncle, which made it personal. But the brutality and the impossible circumstances shocked her. Willie had suffered long before she had hauled him into her station, but to see him end in this vile way, without explanation, broke her.

Art volunteered to drive her home, but she refused.

The drive home was short, and sometimes she wished it were longer. The crooked road smoothed her longest days, allowing her to focus on the road rather than the conflicts. Today, a thousand miles of winding road could not ease her mind. Her headlights and the rising sun illuminated the spotted tree branches lining the asphalt ribbon. Each pothole bounced the lights higher onto the hillside, reminding her of when her father and Willie would drive her home after a basketball game. Back then, she would sit in the back seat, exhausted, hypnotized by the same moon and trees. But tonight, she was startled by the cracked asphalt, split and broken like Willie's body.

The sun would rise soon. Perhaps it would help her see what to do next.

*****

Evangeline climbed beneath the bedsheets. Her thoughts were a pick and shovel mining for dark memories. She almost asked herself, *How will I explain this to Dad?* Then she remembered he was not there, her mother was not there, Willie was gone, and in some inexplicable twist of reality, Sheldon already knew. "I can't call Sylvia because she would want to discuss the contract. There is no one to tell." Evangeline rolled over to stare at the wall. Soon, she fell into a fitful sleep, filled with scenes that were half memory and half dream.

"You are a badasssss," Sylvia said. "These dudes had no idea when they gave you a spot here." It made Evangeline smile as they left the gym and walked side by side toward Clooney Residence Hall at the Police Academy. "They thought we'd be easy targets in the combat training. Where did you learn to fight? Don't tell me. Your dad."

"That's all little ole' me," Evangeline said, flinging her hair back and placing her palm against her chest like a damsel in distress. "You didn't do so bad, yourself. While other girls shopped at the Huntington Mall, I practiced triangle chokes and arm bars. My father insisted. One of dad's Vietnam War buddies ran a dojo in Prestonsburg, and he trained me for years."

"We might not win the combat prize against some of these brutes," Sylvia said, "but we wiped the 'yes, ma'am' right off those hunks' faces. It impressed everyone when you took down the guy from Newport who was scoping you out instead of trying to knock you out. You are better than them in the classroom and on the shooting range, and you surprised the hell out of them in combat. Your dad trained you right."

"Earl Grace might only be a small county sheriff, but he is pretty special to me."

"I'm glad we will be in Louisville together, protecting and serving. We'd be great partners," Sylvia said. "What did your pops say when you told him you would be LMPD?"

"I'm easing into it. Dad will be fine, but he doesn't know I'm leaving Madden County. He loves the place, so I need to put some honey on it. What about you? Where did you—"

Sylvia pointed ahead. The dorm's Head Resident, Mr. Madison, approached them. "I was on my way to get you, Evangeline. You have an emergency call. The caller said it's urgent." Mr. Madison's voice shook with concern.

"Thank you, sir," Evangeline said. She smiled and patted Sylvia's arm. "I hope my boy has finally arrived. I've been waiting for nine months to see this little guy."

"I am happy for you. Hopefully, Baby Boy will kick ass just like his sister." Sylvia said. "Don't stand here. Let's run."

When they arrived at the residence hall, Evangeline and Sylvia double-timed the front steps and the stairs to their floor.

Evangeline picked up the phone in the hallway and called her father's number. As it rang in the receiver, she looked at Sylvia and smiled.

"Hey, Daddy... What's the word?"

"Hello, Lil Dep." Her dad's voice sounded distorted, as if he were hiding a pill under his tongue.

"Are you at the hospital? How does our Sheldon Lawrence Grace like the world?"

"He is good, sweetie." She had only heard her father cry two times. Once, a drunk driver killed a little boy riding his bike near the Fairgrounds. The other was when she had led the Madden County Lady Miners to the State Tournament. But she recognized the catch in his voice as he struggled to tell her something he did not want to say.

"It's Mom, isn't it?" Evangeline kept her words short to hold back the dam crumbling inside her chest. "Tell me, Dad, just tell me." Guilt. Guilt flooded her. *I should be there. I knew I should go home to make sure everything was right. Dad can't—*

"She didn't make it, Vangie. Your mom didn't make it. Hemorrhage. Doctors couldn't control it." His voice was a decrepit bridge. With each word, another beam surrendered. Soon, all she heard was his sobs.

"Of course, they couldn't control it," Evangeline said. "I hate that place. What can they manage?"

Sylvia inferred what had happened and stepped closer. Other cadets entered the hallway. They chattered but quieted after seeing Evangeline on the phone and Sylvia beside her. The hallway offered no chairs, only the pale beige walls and the black phone attached to the wall.

"I will be there as soon as possible," Evangeline said.

"I love you, Vangie." Her father's words were soft but clear.

"I love you, too," she said.

Fifteen years later, Evangeline recalled the receiver dropping from her hand, the hard surface against her back, and how she had slid down the wall to the floor before Sylvia could catch her.

Chapter 20
Dreams, Restless Dreams

"That's just what I need," Evangeline said as she arrived at the station. She leaned into the steering wheel and rested her forehead on her hands. When she left Madden County, there would be many people she missed. Gene Begley was not one.

Evangeline had dodged him since Willie's murder forty-eight hours ago. She had named Art the point of contact on Willie's case and told Paulene to concoct reasons the sheriff could not return Gene's calls. It wasn't a lie because she was drowning in meetings with local and state officials, all wanting answers.

But anyone would tell you Gene had two consistent traits—persistence and annoyance. He had parked his red Toyota pick-up truck in the parking spot labeled "Sheriff."

During Gene's thirty-five-year tenure running the *Madden Mercury* weekly newspaper, he had made a living skewering the Sheriff's Department, the school board, and the county government.

Begley had been Evangeline's chief critic since her father had appointed her Sheriff in 1998. She would never forget the headline, "Grace Gifts his Daughter with Sheriff's Badge." Venom circulated throughout the article. His editorial questioned the sheriff's judgment and implied residents might not accept a woman as the chief law enforcement officer. Gene had leveled accusations of nepotism, managing to praise Evangeline's role as a deputy while deriding her promotion. All while her father's health had worsened.

Indeed, it was uncommon for a woman to be an officer in the mountains, let alone lead the whole department, and the nepotism argument was difficult to counter.

The sheriff sat in her car a moment longer, mustering the energy to enter the station and face Gene's sharp pen.

Evangeline rattled her head back and forth to erase the images. It reminded her of an Etch A Sketch she had bought for Sheldon when he was five. Although the picture of Willie and the crime scene disappeared, it remained visible between the dark dots and lines.

*****

"Sheriff, the citizens deserve to know. You can't give me this, 'It's an open investigation,' jibber-jabber. You've acted like a deadbeat daddy, avoiding me at every turn. I appreciate Art releasing some information, but the final word must come from you. Your father kept me in the loop without complaint."

Evangeline peered back without speaking. Another thing she understood about Gene—he enjoyed his own voice.

"Media from Lexington and Louisville will arrive soon to follow up on their initial coverage. A man died in your custody. You have not apprehended the chief suspect, this Highlander criminal. I hear that someone killed your uncle in a locked cell at your station, and you have no explanation." Gene's wrinkled face registered disgust. "It better be an open investigation. But hell, if we have a killer who can walk through walls, you better let the people know."

Begley paused, scribbled on his notepad, and continued, "The best way to inform them is to provide a statement before I go to print on Monday. That's best for you and the county."

Gene always tried to push her buttons by being dramatic and mentioning Louisville and Lexington. She picked up her coffee cup on her desk and placed it in front of her without breaking eye contact. Steady. Level. Gene met her eyes without blinking.

She figured Gene Begley was nearing sixty-five years old and had served as the *Mercury* editor since she was born. She remembered articles he had written about her exploits in high school basketball and his penchant for challenging every institution, including mining regulators and companies. No entity was safe from his black-and-white pages. Gene's maroon and gray flannel shirts showed cigarette ash, spilled coffee, and yellow mustard from his trips to Spence's Diner. On second thought, it may have always been the same shirt.

Evangeline concealed her frustration and repeated her Single Overriding Communication Objective, as they had taught her at a Police Academy workshop on Media Relations.

"Gene, I can't speak about the details yet. It does no good if I provide more than the general facts. Besides, what do you want from me? No one needs the truth more than I do. I am the Sheriff, and the victim is my family. I have a double incentive to find the bastard." Evangeline paused as Gene lifted the notebook and ballpoint pen. She cleared her throat and added, "Treat all my previous statements as off-the-record, Gene."

The news editor tossed his notepad onto her desk and leaned toward her. "Sheriff, to be honest, you will have to answer questions soon enough. For months you've pissed off the courthouse by focusing on low-level pill pushers while refusing to address murder right in your front yard."

She did not take the bait. Gene wanted to rattle her and gauge her response. Evangeline smiled. They stared at each other like competing chess champions, unwilling to relinquish superiority before the next move.

"Gene, what do you want me to say?"

"Truth would be a place to start, Evangeline." He poked the bear some more. "I worked with your father for years. While we didn't always see eye to eye, I could count on him to share the plan—"

"Interesting. Now you want me to be a replica of my father, Gene. You know, that's intriguing considering your stance on nepotism and all."

"That's what this is? Your panties are still wadded up about my stories when your daddy handed you his crown?"

Evangeline refused to look away. She watched as Gene retrieved his notebook and wriggled in the chair. His wild thicket of graying ginger hair caused his green eyes to stand out, and his shoulders sloped forward. The flannel shirt resembled a sawmill worker's uniform.

"My panties are fine, Gene. You are the troubled one. Constipated, again?"

Her response caused a smile to form on Gene's self-righteous face. The sheriff awaited a sharp-toothed reply but did not receive one.

"Okay," he said after a deep breath. "I get it. We're talking about your uncle here. That's plenty painful. I've known Willie Grace my whole life, and I cannot find evidence suggesting he left this county a single time since he was in middle school. Well, at least until now. Despite being eccentric and partial to alcohol and drugs, people thought the world of him. We shared many Mason jars of fine homemade mountain products. My point is everyone knew Willie, so I have to give them something."

"Tell them he died in custody. We are investigating the circumstances and will share the details when we can. It is a tragic loss for me, my family, and his friends."

"There's a helluva lot more to it than your summary, Sheriff." Gene's crooked head and tobacco-stained teeth did not comfort the Sheriff or make him more endearing. "You arrested Willie for drug possession at the Cornett place on Hammond Creek. Within forty-eight hours, he was dead. According to the scuttlebutt, he was not just murdered but torn apart. Two days later, you remain silent on the tragedy. Do you want my summary as the front-page article, Sheriff?"

"That's one way of framing it. I can't confirm or deny because, as you know, it's an—"

"Riiight...an open investigation. Turd-buckets, Evangeline. People will demand answers within the next few days." He stood and placed his notes in his back pocket. "Have you contacted the state police yet and requested assistance? Can you at least give me something?"

Sleep loss and the tightness in her shoulders tested her ability to conceal the frustration. "Talk to Officer Butcher, Gene."

Begley sniffed and grumbled. Somehow, he even groaned with self-righteous indignation. She held her steady stare as Gene shook his head and walked away. When he reached the door, he turned.

"There is history here, Evangeline. Willie was my friend. When so many residents viewed your uncle as a crazy character, I always sensed there was more to him than he could tell me. God knows I tried to discover what made him so different from his kin."

Evangeline wrinkled her brow but did not respond. Was Begley attempting to use Willie's friendship to get a story? As she observed his slumping shoulders and intense eyes, she thought he deserved an Academy Award if he pretended to care.

Gene said, "A select few families created our history. I have lived it and researched for a long time. I am not sure what it is, but somehow the Grace, the Wainscotts, Rameys, and the Mills clans have made Madden County what it is. I have seen the good side, but bad luck runs straight through our past. Being quiet about incidents like this one won't solve Madden's problems. Transparency might be your friend if you let it be, Sheriff, because sunlight feeds the Goldenrods." He straightened his posture as if he had just been profound.

Now Evangeline's brow wrinkled, and her lips pursed. She wanted to ask questions, but Gene exited before she could interrogate him for a change. Kentucky may call the Goldenrod its state flower, but it is a weed. A yellow weed.

Chapter 21
The Sheriff Down the Hall

The *Lexington Daily Journal* littered the small kitchen table at Sheldon's house. Sarah watched Shel's eyes jerk back and forth as he scanned page three, his finger sliding along the lines.

Since Willie's murder, Sarah had witnessed Sheldon's manic evolution. Half the time, he behaved as if he was responsible for Willie's death, tormenting himself with the burden of finding the killer. He uttered cryptic phrases like, "I won't give up until we get you," or "There must be a way to end this." He spoke as if the apocalypse loomed on the horizon, prepared to end them all.

"Shel," Sarah said, "let's take a break and get out of here. I missed seeing you in the cafeteria today. We should get a chocolate shake."

Sheldon did not raise his eyes from the newsprint. "Give me a few minutes, Sarah. I am reading what Butcher told the paper to see if I can get any information about the case. My dad said you gotta read between the lines when cops speak."

She inhaled and released the breath a little at a time. "The print will not fade away before we get back, Sheldon. Not even George is that slow behind the counter."

Sheldon lifted his head and made eye contact. She noted how sleepless nights had affected his eyes and face. His skin appeared bleached, and the redness around his pupils contrasted with his pale cheeks.

He must have recognized her concern.

"You're right, Sarah," he said as he closed the paper. "I am not getting any new information anyway. The *Mercury* should give me something next week. You know that's my favorite paper because the girl working there is so hot."

She smiled but did not mention her boss's recent tirades. When the Sheriff's Office had given its statement, Gene had yelled into the telephone receiver like it was a megaphone. "Art, you and the sheriff have to give me more than this garbage. Hell, I can read this in the Lexington paper. It's a damn shame when the big city rags can get more information than I can while sitting on my ass a rock's throw away from the station. Come on..."

"Gene is doing his best to get the stories out," Sarah said. "But why do you need the press when you have the sheriff down the hall?"

His face told her it was not the best question. She needed to refine her interview skills if she planned to take Tom Brokaw's anchor position someday.

"Because my big sis believes I am a five-year-old, and she can't trust me enough to update me about my uncle's murder investigation," Sheldon said. His voice rose in volume and pitch. When he stood, his chair scraped the tile floor like nails on a chalkboard.

Sarah remained seated. She understood Sheldon's need to hear the news from Evangeline. Her father was so distant they seldom spoke. He spent his time afraid he might have to shutter the coal company. She would trade her big house any day to have her dad present and engaged at least sometimes. It occurred to her that

Sheldon had drifted away, too, absent even when standing in front of her. She did not like the revelation.

"Sheldon, don't treat me like Evangeline treats you, please. What is going on in your head? I sympathize with your pain, but it is like you are different, and it started before losing Willie." Her voice remained calm, but an urge to cry lurked beneath her calmness. "I care about you. I am worried you know something about Willie's death and don't trust your sister to do what's right."

He remained standing. The table between them might as well have been Two Mile Hill.

"Maybe I can help you return to normal," Sarah said, her voice soft and hopeful. She recognized her words affected Sheldon. He lowered his eyes.

"My dad did not talk about my mom," Sheldon said. "Once, a few years before he died, he picked me up at school, and I showed him my report card. He tried to tell me how proud my mom would be if she were here, but he choked up and turned away before getting it all out. I saw his reflection in his window. If he continued to talk about her, he would crumble."

Sarah tried to see Sheldon's face, but in this case there was no window reflection. He kept his eyes down and his face turned away. She touched his arm to comfort him.

Sheldon said, "Before he died, Dad told me he wished he had shared more stories about Mom. He described how she helped a young mom at Save-A-Lot one day because she did not have enough money to pay for groceries. But, just as before, he could not tell me the whole story."

"That's sad, Shel," Sarah said. "But I don't see how it causes you to be so distant from me. It should mean the opposite."

"If I try to tell you, it will break me. And not just me. The events happening here could end Madden County."

Frost settled on the kitchen. Sarah rose, straightening her posture. Her muscles tensed like cords, and her heartbeat drummed. Sheldon had every reason to be upset about Willie. But he did not have the right to talk nonsense.

"I have to leave," Sarah said as she lifted her backpack and opened it. "I will talk to you after I do some thinking."

"Sarah, don't go..."

She snatched her books off the table. The red and black MCHS Volleyball sticker on the side folded as she shoved the text-books into the backpack. "I will see you tomorrow, Sheldon. I hope you can get this under control. If you don't want to tell me what's going on in your head, I get it, but I am here when you need to talk." She turned and exited through the back door. The screen door clapped shut behind her.

Sheldon placed their water glasses into the sink and watched the trees wave outside the kitchen window. The back porch led to the concrete driveway where his dad had built a basketball court. He had never defeated his dad in a single game. Not one-on-one, Around the World, or HORSE. His dad had been unbeatable at HORSE. He hit hook shots from behind the basket and left-handed bank shots across the driveway. Now, his father was gone, Willie was gone, and soon his sister would be gone. Even Sarah had left him at the kitchen counter.

But was he alone?

Would Sarah believe him if he revealed the secret? When he had read Willie's letter, hadn't he thought his uncle was irrational and drug-addicted? How could Sheldon expect Sarah, or Evange-line for that matter, to understand without even reading the letter?

But since Willie's murder and his encounter with the voice, Sheldon could not convince himself it was a delusion. It was real. Barlow was a ghost, or Sheldon was as crazy as his uncle. Since Willie's death, Sheldon often found the shadow nearby as if watching him in silence.

Perhaps it was a self-hypnosis event brought on by reading the letter. Maybe it was a coincidence or a one-time ESP event like they showed on television. Sheldon remembered one episode of *Real or Fiction?* A girl had felt her parents were in danger, so she begged them not to go boating. She had been persistent, so they had stayed home. Their friend's boat sunk in the river in Madison, Indiana. *Inexplicable events happen all the time. Don't they?*

Before leaving the sink, Shel felt the summons' first ripples cascading into his brain.

If I were seventy-five years younger, I would cash that little doll, if you know what I mean, Shelly Bean.

Sheldon covered his ears, although it occurred to him he only bottled the voice inside. He searched each corner for the shadow.

Awwww, did I hurt your little feelings by sneaking up on you and listening to your fine flapper put you in your place? The voice continued and allowed no space for an answer. *She charged out of here like a dame in a men's bathroom. I hate to tell you, Shelly, but she's not buying it. Maybe you should share the secret, and everything will be jake for the two of you.*

"I don't know half of what you're saying, but I'm not telling anyone. I've figured out how long Willie kept the secret. I can do it, too, so you better get used to you and me, buddy." Sheldon wanted to sound strong, but his voice strained.

The Agent's laughter ricocheted inside Sheldon's head. After a few moments, it stopped as if someone had pushed an "Off " button. *"I have known people like you, Shelly. You act big, but when you let your sissy tell you what to do, and your girlfriend runs the roost, don't be surprised if you get razzed."*

"Why are you doing this?" Sheldon asked. He glanced at the backdoor to ensure Sarah did not come back. He did not want her to see him talking in an empty room. *Wait. Willie was not talking to us in the jailhouse visiting room.* The troubling incident had latched onto Sheldon and hurt him until this realization. Willie had been talking to the Agent.

I do this as a public service to justice, half-wit. It is a hoot that backward hillbillies have not changed. Your people cursed you, not me. Now you are paying the price.

Sheldon backpedaled but stopped before colliding with the countertop. The overhead kitchen lights dispersed the darkness everywhere except above the stove, where the shadow formed a dense, inky shape. It was visible—easy to see or not see—the outline of a person seated on the stove.

The voice dug into Sheldon's brain like gravel embedded in a bloody knee.

That's the way of the world, kid. You see, Sheldon, you cannot defeat me. You can only suffer and suffer and suffer until you die. Your dear old Uncle Willie failed to tell you that part, didn't he?

Although the voice in Sheldon's head was loud, the shifting shape drifted away as if shadows had places to go and people to see.

Chapter 22
Input Overload, Input Overload

Gene was gone, so Evangeline picked up the coffee mug she had shifted on her desk to conceal the phone message. Paulene had scribbled on the message pad, "Dr. Bell called—coming over as requested to give the prelim report." She had added a red heart beside his name, as she always did.

Daryl Bell was a local physician who served as the county's medical examiner. According to Paulene's Gospel of Gossip, the good doctor had a crush on a particular female sheriff. The receptionist and lifelong Maddenite loved to tease her, "He's a gorgeous doctor, who drives a Mercedes, flies his plane, and owns two big houses, one here and one on a Florida beach, so it's easy to see why you don't like him."

At first, the sheriff had reminded Paulene she liked Dr. Bell very much but was not attracted to him. However, it had become best to ignore the receptionist's matchmaking efforts.

The sheriff walked across the hallway and said, "Paulene, get everyone in the conference room for a briefing right now, please."

Binders and files covered the conference room table. Photos of

Willie, his eyes red and face rough as tree bark, and crime scene pictures dotted the whiteboard at the front. The dented mahogany conference table and the tattered black office chairs were so large they filled the space. Her father had bought the table when he had first become sheriff. The ragged, oversized chairs made Evangeline feel like a little girl pretending to be all grown up, and each year she asked to replace them, but the budget could not bear such a luxury as appropriate seating.

Art and Junebug entered. Junebug's oversized uniform made him look like Evangeline when she sat in the damn chairs. Bug claimed the first chair at the corner, farthest from the sheriff, and opened his laptop computer. It appeared Art might not fit inside the room. His right knee struck a chair as he sidestepped along the wall to sit at Evangeline's right. For Butcher, the chairs met the Goldilocks standard—they were just right.

Minutes later, Luke entered. His new uniform was a blue shirt with rolled sleeves and a red tie. The deputy was an American Flag lapel pin away from his family-ordained destiny of becoming the stereotypical politician—righteous even when he wasn't right.

"I appreciate you guys. It has been a tough few days, filled with emotion," Evangeline said. "I know you are working overtime to make this right. Our duty and mission remain the same. We must find whoever violated our house. We have to own it." Her voice cracked like radio static, but she cleared her throat and continued, "Willie wasn't perfect, but he did not deserve what happened." She motioned toward the crime scene photos.

The sheriff allowed the statement to hang in silence. Her heartbeat increased, but she controlled her expression and tone as she had with Gene. Evangeline's father had often said, "Keep a sense of urgency but don't panic or show pain."

Art spoke first. "Sheriff, I have not slept much since it happened. How, in God's name, did someone brutally murder a man in one of our cells? Willie... I mean, the victim was alone.

Our cameras did not show anyone leaving the hallway or heading upstairs." The deputy leaned forward, planted his elbows on the table, and intertwined his fingers as if to pray. "We examined every inch of the cell. We found mouse turds, enough hair to make Otis a wig, and some stains I would rather stay unidentified, but we didn't uncover anything you'd call evidence."

Luke added, "The other inmates were in their cells a good distance away. One man says he may have heard talking but no screams or calls for help. Our cameras can't see inside the cells, but there wasn't anyone around except Otis when he performed the scheduled walkthroughs."

Paulene appeared in the doorway. Over the receptionist's shoulder, Evangeline could see Dr. Bell, so she motioned for Paulene to bring him inside.

Whenever Dr. Bell came to the station, he was pristine. His white button-down dress shirt and brown slacks were starched and pressed. His blonde hair made him appear young, and his blue eyes were piercing and kind. Bell was only two inches taller than Evangeline, but his straight posture made him tower. Although Art often called him Madden County's resident nerd, Dr. Bell's physique appeared sculpted.

In her attempts at matchmaking, Paulene often said Daryl was a champion swimmer in Chicago, where he had grown up. He had arrived in Madden three months before Evangeline's father had appointed her sheriff. Dr. Melton, the most prominent physician in the county, had sold Dr. Bell his entire practice and headed to Flagstaff, Arizona. The purchase had provided Bell with a ready-made clinic, pharmacy, and a long list of clients.

His patients, and the entire county, fawned over Dr. Bell. It was difficult to attract physicians committed to a poor county like Madden. Unlike others, Dr. Bell never complained about isolation, the lack of recreational opportunities, or people's inability to pay their bills. He appeared to have all he needed and donated to local children's groups and schools.

"Hello, Sheriff," Bell said. "I remained at work last night to complete the examination. I figured you could not wait another day." His voice sounded steady and purposeful, as if each word needed to be the perfect one. "I apologize in advance. I have to depart in twenty minutes."

Everyone smiled when Bell talked. Junebug's imitation of the good doctor made the station howl. He would stand straight as a post and say, "Hello, Law Enforcers," as if he were a robot. Then, upon seeing the sheriff, "Input Overload, Input Overload. Why hello, darlin'." Despite the dire circumstances, Evangeline could not help but think about the impersonation and Conway Twitty.

"Thank you, Dr. Bell. I appreciate your work. What do you have for us?"

"This," Bell replied. He reached into his pocket, pulled out a small, clear evidence bag, and handed it to Evangeline.

The sheriff examined its contents. Inside was a paper-thin metal coin with faded red paint and black lettering. Upon closer examination, she could see the emblem on the front—an "M" with words etched below: "Madden Coal".

"It traces to the first two decades of the 1900s, Sheriff," Bell said as he moved closer. "Coal companies, in place of paying dollars to miners, would provide them with this currency, commonly called 'scrip'."

Both Evangeline and Art nodded. Anyone who knew the history of coal mining in Eastern Kentucky and West Virginia recognized scrip. Miners endured many indignities at the hands of coal barons, including getting paid in company money. Families were required to purchase their supplies with these tokens at the company-owned store.

"Dr. Bell, where did you find this relic?" Evangeline said as she slid the plastic bag across the table to Junebug. The deputy examined the coin for a moment and tapped on his keyboard.

"I found it wedged deep inside the victim's throat," Dr. Bell said.

The clicking keyboard stopped. Everyone stared at Dr. Bell like the conversation had hit a stone wall.

Evangeline said, "Do you mean the murderer forced Willie to...swallow it?" She watched the doctor's reaction. His square jaw flexed, and his expression was grim.

"Sheriff, the metal entered through the mouth and traveled to the esophagus," the doctor replied, "so yes."

"Are you kidding me, Doc?" Art said.

"No, Deputy Butcher. The results are odd, to be honest. Blood spatter indicated Mr. Grace's heart functioned during the attack. The murder weapon was an extremely sharp 6-inch to 8-inch blade. However, the piece of metal led to asphyxiation, so the victim possibly lost consciousness before his heart was, well, you know. Mr. Grace died due to one or the other. I could flip a coin."

Evangeline stared at Bell for a moment, but the irony of the coin reference eluded him.

Chapter 23
It's Not You, Buddy-O

The darkness behaved without kindness. Sheldon watched it narrow, swell, and fall against the light in his bedroom. He could not open his eyes enough to see the entire shape like before in the kitchen, but the presence became more apparent with every reshaping. It was something unkind.

"What is wrong with me?" Sheldon rolled over on his bed, planting his face into the pillow. Evangeline had left earlier in the morning, telling him to stay home and rest. He rolled over again but clutched the pillow as he did, pressing it over his eyes.

This room contained all of his days. When their father died, Evangeline had taken the master bedroom and persuaded him to move to her room. He was reluctant, but when he moved, the room became a safe place as he struggled through his father's death. At least until now.

Sheldon said into the pillow, "Leave me alone."

The voice occupied his head like a migraine or a song he could not shake. Images and words crowded out his perception and common sense by darting through his brain.

It's not you, buddy-o.

Secrets and Blood

A tremor rippled from his scalp down his back and into his legs. The last time he had experienced such a visceral reaction, a snake had crawled down his skin. It turned out to be a fishing lure escaping through a hole in his pocket, down his pant leg, and into his boot. But lightning had bolted through his body. He felt the same overwhelming sensation now.

Lord, what's a young man to do when he has a sister like yours? I would carry a torch for her, but she would piss on the flame.

The darkness had taken shape in the corner but remained intangible. Sheldon recognized the broad shoulders, the square jaw, the old-fashioned hat, and long legs made of fog. The sight reminded him of sitting with Sarah at Inez Lake. They would identify shapes in the clouds. This shape was evil.

"What are you?" Sheldon said.

Oh, we will get to know each other now that Willie is in the trash bin. The shadow moved closer to Sheldon like a living silhouette. *You and I will become best friends if you help me and let me help you.*

"I asked what you are, not who."

Then, let's just say I am the secret. The words covered the walls of Sheldon's brain. *Think of me as your savior, here to set things right in good ole' Madden.*

"I wish my dad were here. He would kick your ass," Sheldon said. "He would not tolerate your evil tricks."

Sorry boy, your God is the only one tricking you. He birthed you in this hellhole—you might recall how it turned out for your poor saint of a momma.

Sheldon's hatred grew inside him like a hillside wildfire.

Madden County put me in this room with you. Madden County made this bed when the coal companies sent me to straighten this crooked place. Now you are stuck sleeping in it.

The darkness crept closer and closer. "This can't be real," Sheldon told himself. He rubbed his eyes with his knuckles. The dark figure was at his side—his suit, from dark shadows, the pocket watch, his face—all obscured by darkness and the brim of his hat. Sheldon retreated, but there was nowhere to go. His back was against the headboard, and the whisperer was so close he could feel its cold.

It became quiet again, and the shape was no longer present. Sheldon scanned the entire room, searching for the character in the clouds.

Maybe you should tell your big sis on me, Sheldon. She would beat me up for you. Tell her. Tell her.

Sheldon startled.

Here's the lowdown, little man. Willie Grace passed you the buck, and then he passed on. I am the lead horse in the front of the wagon, and you are staring at my ass. Where you go is where I already am.

"Leave me alone—"

You will never be alone unless you pass the secret, kid. The shadow hovered against the cream-colored wall. The Agent managed to be genuine and unreal, like a negative of one of the old photographs Sheldon viewed at the newspaper office when he visited Sarah.

"Why are you doing this to me?"

Now the Agent laughed, loud and deep. *It figures Willie would pass the secret to someone as stupid as he was. I am Barlow. I am here now not for company money but to fill the creeks with all the tainted hillbilly blood.*

Sheldon sat up taller. The shadowy silhouette caused his hands to shake and his heart to pound. This thing killed Willie by almost cutting him in half. Was it his turn?

Real. Sheldon clung to the chance his dream was all hypnotic state or mental illness, not connected to Willie's death. But now, even he could see the shadow was tangible. Real. Sheldon heard the words and witnessed the Agent just as Willie had described.

Sheldon looked at the box on his desk. His uncle had trusted him to deliver the letter, but he had betrayed his trust. He considered his options for a few moments.

Willie had secured the secret for decades. The drugs had not been the cause of Willie's suffering—they had shielded him from pain and despair. Willie had not fought to banish the ghost from his head. His uncle had struggled to keep him there so others did not bear the fear and burden Sheldon felt now.

Sheldon wished he had not read Willie's letter.

But he had read it.

The secret. The Summons. Willie had borne this evil voice since he had been a boy. He had not revealed it to anyone, at least not until the letter. If Sheldon followed Willie's instructions, it would be his sister's evil to battle. Now, he would suffer in silence. He deserved it.

"You killed Willie," he said into the air.

It was inevitable, like the end of this place, like these turd whackers will destroy each other. Like your pretty little girlfriend of yours is a lost cause. Like you will eventually spill it out to your sister so I can rain hell on everyone's pointy little heads.

Sheldon closed his eyes, hoping the figure would go away. He understood it would not, but he needed a moment to think. Connecting the lines between his uncle, his sister, and himself only took seconds. He now guarded the secret. He remembered Willie in the visiting room, angry and defiant, not afraid.

"I'm not telling her shit, you horse's ass." Shel's voice shook, but the message was clear.

Chapter 24
Three Long Days

Evangeline surveyed her team around the table after Dr. Bell left. Luke remained quiet. Junebug stared at his screen, using his computer as a shield. Art tapped his thick fingers on the wooden tabletop.

"For almost three long days, we've scrutinized Willie's actions during his time here, and the most dangerous thing to get close to him was a ballpoint pen I provided Willie, myself," Art said. Evangeline watched as Art pinched the bridge between his eyes. "There is no easy answer to this one."

"Yes, there is," Evangeline said. She leaned forward in her big girl chair. She sounded like her father. After around-the-clock searching, they had no logical explanation for what had happened. "There is an answer to this, Art. We just haven't figured it out yet. I need all of you with your heads in the game."

Luke said, "The state police reviewed Dr. Bell's findings and agreed." Luke paused, then said, "Sheriff, they are talkin' about sending in a team of investigators from Lexington if we can't make an arrest soon."

"They are free to do that, Luke," the sheriff replied, "but I'm telling you, if they do, internal affairs will target us, not people outside the jail. For example, didn't you and Willie have some harsh words earlier?"

Luke prepared to speak but caught himself. Instead, he shot an accusatory glance at Art and then at Junebug without reason.

"Bug, any ideas?" Evangeline asked.

"It's crazy," he said. "My thinking, I mean." As usual, Junebug doubted himself. Evangeline wished he was more assertive. Her father had believed in him despite his youth and his shy nature. What if her father had led him for longer than a year? Junebug would be different now. But her dad was not the leader today, she was, and at this point, Junebug still lacked confidence.

"What isn't crazy about this, Junebug? Just spit it out," Evangeline said. "In a place like Madden County, crazy is the explanation for every problem."

Junebug nodded. "What if the killer did not force Mr. Grace to swallow the scrip? What if Willie did it on his own?"

Evangeline heard Luke snort as if Junebug's idea was inconceivable. Junebug's attention fled to his computer screen again, searching for shelter.

The sheriff glanced at Junebug and then stared at Luke, lingering on his face, before turning to Junebug again.

She asked, "Why would Willie willingly swallow a scrip? That is not a good self-defense strategy, is it?"

Junebug cleared his throat. "A killer wouldn't make someone swallow something if they planned to murder him seconds later. However, it's not as if Willie would do such a thing for no reason."

"Get to the point, Junebug," Evangeline said. She gestured with her hand as if drawing the deputy to her.

"Willie knew law enforcement because he was always around lawmen—and law women—his whole life. He knew we would find the scrip and have this conversation." Junebug gestured over his laptop, speaking directly to Evangeline.

Her two other deputies remained quiet. Luke sat back in his chair, and Art nodded.

Evangeline folded forward. "You think he wanted us to find it? You believe he was sending a message to us about who killed him?"

"It makes more sense than the killer forcing him to swallow it." Junebug held his head up a little higher as Evangeline considered his opinion.

Art said, "It makes sense, Sheriff. Why would someone who can get past us, go into a locked cell, and kill a man without dropping a single fingerprint, hair, or footprint leave anything behind?"

Evangeline sat back in her chair and pictured Willie sitting on a porch swing with her when she was a little girl. He would tell her funny stories as they waited for her dad and mom to get home.

"Willie loved his metaphors and symbols," Evangeline said. "Great job, Junebug. You are right. Willie sent us a message. But it doesn't matter unless we figure out what it means."

Everyone was silent, even Junebug. Luke lowered his eyes and straightened his tie while Junebug rubbed the peach fuzz on his cheek and stared at the keyboard. Art looked tired as he ran his large hand through his short brown hair.

"Let's consider what we know about Willie Grace." The sheriff stood and circled the table. "We have two leads. First, we have his drug dealings. We need to find out about his associates. Maybe they were scared he would give us names." She stepped up to the whiteboard and drew a line dividing the space. She wrote "Madden County Drug Pipeline" on the chart's left line.

"We also have Madden Coal scrip dating back to the 1920s." She printed "SCRIP" on the right side in large block letters. "We aim to track down how these clues are relevant toWillie's death. Perhaps where they cross is where we find the killer."

Everyone nodded.

The sheriff said, "When we talk drugs in Madden, we must consider the Highlander. He is brutal and powerful enough to hire the best. Let's pore over our recent arrests and see if we have anyone in custody who might provide insights for a deal. Also, let's return to our future raids list to see if there are any we should prioritize because of Willie's death. Junebug, you research where this scrip might fit. Maybe we can solve Willie's riddle."

Before Evangeline could check for understanding, her mobile phone rattled like buzzing cicadas.

Chapter 25
Blame and Sorrow

"Hey, Sheldon." She kept her tone soft.

"So what are we doing, Vangie?" Sheldon's raw, tired voice reeled her back into the moment. It was as if every word he uttered required restraint or vetting before he could let it go. "I need to know."

"*We* aren't doing anything. My team is investigating what happened. You are completing your algebra homework and finishing your essay. Then eating solid food and pulling yourself together for a return to school."

"When will you know more?"

He ignored her response and probed. Fear gnawed at her, but she could not identify why.

"I know the hurt is fresh, Sheldon, but you aren't usually like this. You are not accepting the realities of this situation."

She heard him mumble, "Realities? There aren't realities anymore, only stories."

"What do you mean?" She realized what had sparked her fear. Uncle Willie had often said similar things. "You don't know the truth," and, "There are more ghosts than angels in this world."

Sheldon toed the same verbal tightrope. He was unstable. His words were slow to come but darts when released. Sheldon sounded and acted like Willie. She shivered.

He threw a dart. "Jesus, can't you keep me updated about the investigation? I need to know. Do I ask you for anything, Vangie?"

"Whoa, Sheldon. Calm down. I know this is tough. Uncle Willie meant—"

"You don't know as much about Uncle Willie as you think," Sheldon said. "Don't keep me in the dark. I need help with this."

"Okay," she replied. "I will keep you in the loop. I get it." She did not get it. Of course, he loved Uncle Willie, and she did, too. Willie's murder was traumatic and inexplicable, but Sheldon's behaviors crossed the line between reason and obsession.

Sheldon's voice sounded raw. His behavior had been erratic since he had burst into the station asking about Willie. She imagined Sheldon pointing his finger and talking to himself like her uncle in the interrogation room.

Evangeline examined the photograph of Sheldon and her dad on her desk. Guilt rose inside her. Despite witnessing his change, she had not spent enough time with him since Willie's death. Sheldon was the most important person in her life, but she was too busy to address his pain. She had graduated from the police academy in Richmond, seeing her father holding Sheldon in the audience.

Willie deserved better from her. Had she been there for Willie and Sheldon instead of avoiding controversy for selfish reasons? *Who knows.* She had allowed the contract and her ambition to distract her.

Now, not only was Sheldon mourning the loss, but he sounded and acted like Willie. She did not want those thoughts, but they squeezed her like Sheldon clasping her hand when she had taught him to ride a bike.

There is no way Sheldon is using drugs. It can't be. No way.

Then she remembered Allen Jude's face. When Quinton Jude, a straight-A student at Madden High, was arrested for drug possession, Evangeline's father had ordered her to inform the parents. All the way there, she had prepared herself for the parents' reaction. She had anticipated anger because parents often defend their children no matter the evidence.

When Evangeline had met with Allen's dad, she had used the "your child is safe" approach and then had shared the bad news. "Quinton was arrested today with illegal drugs." Mr. Jude's face had flattened. His wet eyes had stayed glued to her as if he had expected her to reveal the joke or give him cause to say, "No, you have the wrong house and a different Quinton."

The time for blame and sorrow was later—after the Highlander was behind bars.

"My petty problems shouldn't distract you, so go back to getting the bad guys," Sheldon said. Evangeline stared at her phone as though it had just appeared near her ear.

"It's not that—"

"I will see you tonight unless you are too busy. If so, we will go to the visitation tomorrow."

Thank God. He planned to attend Willie's visitation at the funeral home. She had been worried Sheldon would be unable to show, and she needed him there for his sake and hers.

"Love you, bro," she said. But the abrupt end to the call left her words hanging in the air—a fluttering moth with nowhere to land.

Evangeline walked into the conference room and turned to Junebug. "I need you to do me a favor."

Chapter 26
Genetic Benevolence

Mountain people know how to honor the dead. The Phipps Family Funeral Home resembled the Madden County Fair's opening day. The powerful and the paupers circled the fairway. People spilled into other rooms, finding family, friends, and familiar stories. Except it wasn't a ride or an exhibit they waited in line to see, but Willie Grace.

Evangeline had spent her last four days trying to untangle Willie's death, which Art and Junebug had started calling a locked-room mystery. An assailant had entered a locked cell undetected—then escaped unseen. However, she found no literary novelty or complexity in the situation. Someone had slaughtered Willie while he had been under her care, so she had failed him. It was that simple.

Although she was gracious to the visitors, Evangeline continued to imagine the crime scene, and the vision caused her hands to tremble.

She recalled her father leaning back in his office chair, with a giant smile and arms crossed, saying, "Are you a time watcher or a clockmaker, Evangeline? Don't just stand there observing—investigate, make a case, and incarcerate. Be the clockmaker, not the one who announces the time."

Today Evangeline felt like a time watcher, waiting for the sand to sink to the bottom of the hourglass. It was October 16th. She had nine days to postmark the contract on her desk to meet the deadline. Before riding toward the west, she needed to find Willie's killer and protect her family's legacy. But why should she even worry about it? If she failed, the drama called Madden County would continue to play out on the stage. But what if her father watched the play from the balcony? What if the final scene before the curtain descended presented Uncle Willie sprawled across a cot like a puppet with broken strings?

Evangeline leaned into her brother as they stood beside Uncle Willie's open casket. Sheldon's face expressed an odd sense of pride. Evangeline cried. She pictured Willie swinging her around and around in their front yard, his rough cheek against her face as he whispered, "My Little Dep." She breathed the rose petal fragrance saturating the funeral home and placed her hand on the coffin's edge.

Willie had treated her with kindness even while life was not kind to him. However, Sheldon was correct. She had not known him well enough. He had been her eccentric, addicted uncle who had told her stories. Even her father, who had loved Willie, had often admitted he did not understand him. He would say, "When Robert jumped off the cliff into the rocks, he hauled Willie's future over the ledge with him."

The Phipps brothers had made Willie as presentable as they could. He resembled her father in the blue suit she had chosen, which caused her ache to radiate. Her uncle's wild hair, spotted with gray and black, was pulled back with an order he had never found in his life. The morticians had closed his eyes, making them appear more sunken into the sharp bones of his face.

People Evangeline had known her whole life circled the

parlor. Her high school basketball coach, Coach Harley, recounted the 1988 regional semi-final when Willie and another man had rolled onto the floor during the game, their fists flying. The man had called Evangeline a, "Ball hog," and it had not sat well with Willie. Everyone had cheered when Earl had grabbed both men and muscled them off the floor so the game could commence.

To her right, friends of her father stood near the coffin, chatting as if Willie's dead body, recently split from neck to pubic bone, wasn't in the room. The men, dressed in their Sunday-Go-To-Meeting clothes, ranged from sixty-five to eighty-five. Coal miners, former Sheriff's Department employees, and a couple of farmers were there in Willie's name to honor her father.

When she turned left, others mingled around the parlor. Many wore unpressed church clothes and faces filled with grief. Some were as old as the men near the coffin, but some younger than Evangeline expected. Several women sat in a semicircle on a large red sofa with matching chairs. They spoke in quiet voices and nodded, probably signaling agreement that Willie's soul was doomed.

"Excuse me, Sheriff."

Evangeline turned to see a young man she did not recognize.

"I am sorry for your loss. Willie was good..." His words trailed off as though he had forgotten a rehearsed line.

"I am sorry, young man, but I don't think I know you," she said before noticing the bruises around his eye and cheek. His black hair was shorter in the front than the back, and his dark eyes blended with the storm clouds on his face. "Yes, I do. You are Cyrus Cornett."

He looked toward his feet as if he wished she had forgotten him.

"I did not realize you and Willie were so close." Evangeline knew the teen had tested negative for drugs. Nothing connected him to a crime other than the attempt to leave the scene and Luke's handiwork. Even Willie and Big Orange vouched for him, saying he was, "A good boy."

Cyrus cleared his throat. "I wanted to watch out for Kimmy's baby. She's my little cousin," he said.

Although Evangeline had reprimanded Luke, the sheriff was skeptical of Cyrus's intentions. He had run from the police. People in Madden offered more excuses than the hills had rocks and trees.

"Cyrus, I guess you knew Uncle Willie better than I thought?"

"Yes, Willie was my friend. He tried to help me."

"You mean help you find drugs or sell drugs? Or maybe both?" As soon as she said it, Evangeline regretted it. She slipped into law enforcement mode too often nowadays—a trait she had not inherited from her father.

The kid stared straight into Evangeline's face. His shame morphed into resolve. "Willie is the reason I never tried drugs. He is Mom's friend. He connected me with Berea College and paid for my ACT testing. He encouraged me to get a college degree."

Cyrus was only a few years older than Sheldon, but he carried the countenance of hard times. Someone other than Luke had etched a moon-shaped scar into his cheek, and another one above his left eye split the eyebrow.

"So, you think Berea will like that symbol on your arm, Cyrus?"

He looked confused at first. Then he held his arm up, revealing the two tattoos adorning his forearms. One was a peace symbol, but Vangie pointed to the ink on his other arm. It was a confederate flag.

"My papaw put these on me when I was twelve, right before he got killed out on the strip mine. They did it at Darvon's garage over on Route 40. He didn't even tell me what the tats would be, but he was drunk, so I didn't say anything. It would not have turned out good for me if I had refused in front of his buddies."

"That's a poison pen if I ever heard of it," Evangeline said. "I would keep your flag covered up or never leave the county, kid. I bet your mom wasn't happy."

"Mom was mad as a hen, but she didn't buck up to Papaw since he was her daddy," he replied. "I never knew my father, so... well, Willie helped me in many ways."

Evangeline watched his eyes drop, and a curl of shame crossed his brow.

"Alright," he said with uncomfortable finality. "I'm sorry we lost Willie. He wasn't what everybody thought." The teenager nodded and drifted toward the door.

Evangeline considered calling him back to apologize, but what would she say? "Hey, sorry I'm a condescending bitch."

Then Paul Wainscott entered the room. It was rare to see him in the flesh. Wainscott spent his time jetting around the country drumming up business for the Madden Coal Company. Even though Sheldon was dating his daughter, Evangeline knew little about the man. He was handsome, in his early forties, she guessed, and only a few inches shorter than Art. She presumed Sarah's flawless, raven hair owed a debt to her father's genetic benevolence.

Wainscott picked up an obituary program from the table but did not sign the guest registry on the podium. He scanned the crowd, searching for someone, and stopped as soon as he locked eyes with her. When Wainscott walked in her direction, people stepped aside.

"Sheriff Grace," he said. Despite Paul's age, his actions reminded her of a teenager picking up his date for the prom. He shifted his weight from foot to foot, and Evangeline felt the sweat on his palm when he shook her hand.

Although they attended the same Chamber of Commerce meetings, school events, and even basketball games at MCHS, they never interacted. While social interactions were not her strength, Wainscott appeared miles out of his element.

She nodded. "I'm surprised to see you here, Mr. Wainscott."

"I am not sure why, Sheriff. Willie was a well-known character in these parts." He towered over her, but she could see the line of sweat above his lip. "I want to pay my respects."

Evangeline waited, unsure how to perceive the well-known character portrayal of her uncle. She allowed him to simmer for a moment.

Wainscott did not like the silence. He said, "I am sorry for your loss. Willie was different, but he was a good man, like your father."

"I wasn't sure you knew Willie or my dad very well," she said.

"My father always talked about Sheriff Grace and the bond between our families," Paul said.

Evangeline's skepticism rose again. "Bond?" she said. "What does that mean?"

Wainscott smiled and glanced at his feet. "I have always wondered about it, as well. I hope we can go to lunch sometime to discuss it." He raised his head, and his eyes narrowed. "Once, I asked my father why he donated to your dad's campaigns even though it was clear the sheriff didn't lean our way."

"So, what did he say?"

"It was what he didn't say that confused me," Wainscott said. "I assumed your dad either did him favors or knew something my father didn't want others to know. Aren't favors the fuel for politics?"

"Not my expertise, Mr. Wainscott," she responded. "Sarah is with my brother somewhere if you need her."

He smiled. "Speaking of no expertise. My parenting skills are lacking."

For a moment, you almost sounded human, Wainscott.

She said, "I'm only Sheldon's sister, so he has no qualms putting me in my place. Teenagers rule the world. They just lease the rest of us some space."

Wainscott's face relaxed a little, and for a second she thought he smiled. *Alert Gene at the local newspaper. The wealthiest man in Madden County smiles for the first time, and of course, it is at a funeral.*

"But I'm not searching for Sarah." His hand gestured toward her, his sweaty palm up. "I did come to extend my sympathies." He offered his hand for another handshake.

Evangeline reciprocated. As they shook, he asked, "Don't you want to know what my father said about your grandfather and father?"

She wondered if it was in her best interest to hear what old man Wainscott thought of her family.

Before she could respond, Wainscott said, "My father told me, 'I respect people who know the value of secrets and blood.'"

Evangeline remained motionless. Secrets? Blood? Willie's bloody body flashed before her eyes yet again. The room sounded louder, and she sensed others shuffling by them. Somber voices, blended with soft bouts of laughter, brought her back from the image. She took a deep breath and forced a smile.

"Thank you for coming by, Mr. Wainscott. It is appreciated." She released his hand, smiled, and turned away.

*****

Evangeline searched the funeral home for Sheldon. She could not see him, but Sarah leaned against a coat closet door in the hallway. Her silky white blouse and black skirt accentuated her tanned face and athletic legs. Her arms were crossed her chest as if she guarded the entrance.

"Sarah, your father stopped by to pay his respects. That was thoughtful of him."

"Evangeline, he is about as thoughtful as the lumps of coal he digs."

Evangeline did not bite. She wondered what her brother said

about her whenever someone mentioned her name. "What's going on? Where's Sheldon?"

Sarah shook her head and pointed over her shoulder toward the door.

"In there?" Evangeline moved toward the door and listened. She could hear Shel talking to someone. She could not decipher his words, but the murmuring made her cringe. "For how long?"

"Since we got here," Sarah said. "He's talking up a storm, telling someone to leave him alone. He is cussing, too. I am worried about...." She trailed off as if to avoid revealing something said in confidence.

Evangeline tapped on the door. "It's me, Shel. Come out here and talk." Quiet. "Uncle Willie meant a lot to you. It is okay to feel sad, but don't lock yourself away like this."

"You don't understand, Evangeline. And I can't tell you." Sheldon sounded like he was inside a well. "I will be okay in a little while."

"Is there something I don't know about, Sheldon? You can tell me anything, no matter how bad it is." She waited close to the door beside Sarah. "You can tell me anything. You know I love you."

"Please come out, Sheldon," Sarah said with gentle urgency. "You are scaring me."

The doorknob turned, and the door creaked. As soon as it was open wide enough, Evangeline pulled on it. Sheldon faced the coat room corner, his back to Sarah and his sister. Evangeline stepped inside and wrapped her arms around him.

"Come down here and let's talk," Evangeline said as she guided him toward a sitting room. Sheldon shuffled his feet, moving like a condemned man. Concern settled on Sarah's face. Evangeline glanced at her and said, "All three of us."

As they entered the sitting room, loud, angry shouts came from the funeral home's front porch.

Clyde Perry rushed through the parlor door. Evangeline had

never seen Clyde wear anything other than jeans and blue work shirts with the white Perry Coal Truck Services emblem on the pocket. Today he wore a black jacket, matching slacks, a white shirt, and a silver necktie. She started to speak, but his expression led her to remain silent. Usually, Clyde revealed little of what he thought whenever they conversed. He was amicable, thoughtful, and funny but challenging to read.

"Sheriff, I hope I'm not interrupting, but there is a problem you may want to address now rather than later." He motioned for her to follow him as he reversed his path.

"Stay with Sheldon," Evangeline said to Sarah and hurried toward the commotion.

*****

"What kind of idiots are you?" Evangeline said as she stepped onto the funeral home's front porch. "You come to my uncle's visitation and act like you have a right to fight here?"

Baron Mills, Carl Ramey, and Paul Wainscott stood in a triangle staring at each other, their faces red. Men and women stood on the porch and the grass, spectating.

"Evangeline, these fools—"

"I did not ask for an explanation, Baron. I can see what is happening." She glared, daring either man to speak. "Your hatred is so great you can't even set it aside long enough to pay respects to my uncle. Hell, you are paying disrespect."

"And look at you, fine folks." The sheriff gestured to the spectators, her anger overflowing. "Typical of our county. You would rather see a fight than stand up for law and order. That's why this place is a hellhole. It is why I can't wait..." Evangeline paused, inhaled, and refocused on the men.

Everyone remained quiet. A short man with an even smaller

woman clutching his arm stood in the grass and shook his head as if the sheriff's words were a personal insult.

"I get it, Carl. You want to earn a living. Baron, you want to save the earth and hate coal companies. Wainscott, you want your business to keep making you richer." Evangeline paused again, evaluating the three men. Disdain colored her face. "The trouble is the three of you can't live with each other, and you can't live without each other. Where does that leave the rest of us in Madden County?"

"I don't want a fight, Sheriff. I want these men to be reasonable." Wainscott's words brought sarcastic laughter from the men gathered behind Carl. Several young men walked up behind Baron.

"Reasonable? What's unreasonable about earning a living wage, Wainscott?" Carl said. Several miners stood near him, nodding in agreement.

"Between Baron's call to end mining and Carl's union draining every dollar we have to keep the company alive, don't be surprised when Madden Coal is not here to blame anymore," Wainscott said.

An angry murmur rippled through the protesters.

"Let's move this argument inside," the sheriff said. "I want to talk with all three of you."

"Bullshit," a young man standing behind Baron said. "You want to protect coal. Isn't that what Wainscott pays you for, Sheriff?" Laughter rose from the crowd. He beamed, proud of his witty remark. Then his expression changed as his sweater tightened around his neck, and his arms flailed as he levitated two feet off the grass.

"You heard the sheriff," Art said. He stood behind the man, lifting him by the back of his collar. The deputy held him as the young man waved his arms.

The crowd dispersed.

Evangeline wasn't sure who had called Art and Junebug, but

she was glad they had. Junebug herded Baron, Carl, and Wainscott through the front door while Art stood on the porch.

Before she entered, Evangeline searched for Clyde in the crowd. He stood off to the side, and she nodded. He glanced at her but did not acknowledge the appreciation. She realized the snub had bruised her as she turned toward the door.

She envisioned the contract on her desk. The postmark deadline was October 25th, and thinking about dropping it off at the post office became easier in moments like this one.

*****

"The last time we talked, Carl and Baron, I warned I would put you in jail, didn't I?" Evangeline observed their body language. Baron sniffed and straightened his ponytail. Carl crossed his thick arms and avoided eye contact. "Mr. Wainscott, we spoke moments ago. You didn't act prepared to go to war today."

Wainscott said, "Because I was not... I mean, I am not prepared to go to war."

"Then explain it to me. Including the part where the three of you deem it appropriate to fight at my uncle's visitation."

"Sheriff, I recognize how this appears," Wainscott said. "However, these men and their union members and environmental cult want more when we have less and less. They want me to close down mines and at the same time ensure the miners' jobs are protected."

"Victimhood does not wear well on the richest man in the county, Mr. Wainscott. Pardon me if I am frank, but your family has made a good living here," Evangeline said. She recognized how the remark revealed her bias. Her father had told her never to ride the fence on issues. "Riding fences leave splinters in your butt."

"You got it, Sheriff," Baron said. "His kind gets rich while we watch trees fall, our mountaintops get raped, and our quality of life worsens." Baron inflated his chest, proud of his rhetorical flurry.

The sheriff raised her hand. "His kind? Baron, the mines brought people to Madden County and provided employment. It's why you and I don't dig coal for a living. Right?"

"Hell yeah, that's right," Carl said. He uncrossed his arms and motioned toward Baron and Paul. "You have to understand my men need to make a living, or *you* don't stay rich. It is unfair if we have to work harder without pay increases, it is not fair. What else can young people do here without coal? You better wake up—"

Evangeline shook her head. "All due respect, Carl, but the world is changing. We can't stay back in the 1980s when mining jobs were so attractive that kids quit school before graduation. The mines paid dropouts more than their teachers earned. The union supported politicians on both sides in Frankfort, who sided with big coal. Those same legislators are your worst enemies since it's popular to be against the coal industry."

"You're not fair," Carl said. He continued to argue, but she tuned him out. Sheldon and Sarah sat on a red sofa in the visiting room. However, it was their third wheel that drew her attention. She would recognize the bald spot and sloping shoulders anywhere.

"Listen, gentlemen," the sheriff said as she glared at the bald spot. "Carl and Baron, I will not take you to jail as promised for one reason. I did not give Mr. Wainscott the same warning. So, I can't take him along. If I take you two, people will claim I was not fair, and the problem will only worsen."

She glared at the three men. "Don't get me wrong, I want to take you to the station, but it is not good timing right now. You know, with the funeral of my beloved uncle happening as you sit here in the principal's office."

Carl rubbed the back of his neck while Wainscott stared at the floor and Baron loosened the collar of his dress shirt.

"We have to fix this. Crazy ideas are out there—battles in the street, blasting coal mines, spiked chains in the road to wreck trucks. You are significant leaders in Madden County. What you say and do matters to all of us." She glanced back at Gene, Sheldon, and Sarah. "Just go home. Don't feel obligated to attend the burial service tomorrow unless you think you can control yourselves. She walked away as they attempted to speak to her.

Chapter 27
I Hope It Ain't Your Drinking Hand

Sheldon, Sarah, and Gene erupted in laughter as Evangeline approached. It dissolved when she arrived.

"Don't stop on my account," she said. "It is good to hear you laughing again, Sheldon." The only vacant seat was the chair beside Gene. She shuffled between the three and claimed it.

After an awkward silence, Sheldon said, "Gene was telling stories about Uncle Willie. One night Gene fell off the porch after drinking moonshine. Willie tried to catch him but fell on top of him instead. Gene told Willie his wrist felt broken. As they were lying there on the grass, Willie replied, 'I hope it ain't your drinking hand.'"

Evangeline smiled. "That sounds like something Willie would say. So, Gene, what else have you asked Sheldon and Sarah about?"

Gene rolled his eyes. "I'm just here to say goodbye to a drinking buddy, Sheriff—nothing more. I gave up moonshine some time ago, but I never forgot Willie Grace. He was a brilliant man who should have been a novelist and poet."

"Gene hasn't asked any questions, Evangeline, except how we

are doing. That's all," Sheldon said. He shifted in his seat as if in pain.

"Then what's in the folders, Gene? X-rays of your fractured wrist?" She pointed to the overfilled folders on the side table. She recognized articles and photos trapped between the folds and secured by blue rubber bands.

"It's a timeline, Sheriff," he said. "I am studying prominent families' roles in Madden County history."

"But why bring it here, Gene? Visitation is about saying goodbye—it's neither the time nor place to catch up on ancient history."

"Correct, Sheriff. However, if I decide to write a history of Madden County, I may show the past through Willie's eyes. His life is a symbol of Madden County. Smart, gifted as a writer, and equally talented as his younger brother, Earl. Yet, somehow, he fell off the track." Gene moved the folder to his lap. "I was thinking about Willie before leaving work to come here. I picked up this folder and walked to the funeral home. That's the only reason I brought it."

"What? It is your mission to find the—what did you call it in my office?—the underpinnings of Madden County's streak of bad luck," Evangeline said. "Do you plan to place Madden's problems at our feet? Is that it?" She leaned closer to better stare into his eyes and face. Her breathing accelerated, and she clenched her teeth.

If Gene Begley had a tell, he did not reveal it on his face. He accepted her words as though they might be true. His calmness deescalated her anger, so she leaned back and unclenched her jaw. *This damn arrogant little man.*

"I wish it could be so easy, Sheriff," Gene said. "All of us share Madden County's failures, me included. Failure is one thing, but the events here defy common sense. When you examine the news from years ago, there appears to be more to this place than we know."

"So where do the Grace and the Wainscott families fit into this mystery?" Evangeline adjusted her tone, but the question displayed her skepticism about Gene's intent.

"You and a few others are there at every turn. The feuds, the power exchanges, and even life and death decisions shaped modern Madden County."

Without warning, Sheldon rose from his chair. He swayed like a punch-drunk boxer, leading Sarah to stand and hold his arm. His pained face caused Evangeline to flinch and her chest to tighten.

"I need to go home now," Sheldon said. He directed the words to Sarah, then turned toward Evangeline. "Sis, I will see you at the service tomorrow if I'm not awake when you get home."

The fear tightened Evangeline's throat once again. "Of course, Sheldon," she said, stumbling on the words, "It is a difficult day, so I understand. Do you want me to drive you?"

She awaited his response, but it was as if he did not register her question. Instead, his wet, red eyes darted around the room as if he were searching for an alternative exit. When his search stopped, his eyes narrowed, and his face transformed into a snarl as he glared at the wall across the large room.

"Art Butcher said he would give us a lift home," Sarah said as she followed Sheldon toward the door.

"Mr. Begley, I will see you Monday after school," Sarah said. She caught Sheldon, propping him up as they plodded forward.

The sheriff said, "Can you see how this place affects the kids, Gene? Let me do my job. I will catch the Highlander and put his ass in jail. I can't have the people of Madden County making my job more difficult, especially when you stir them up."

"Stirred up by me?" he said. "I did not agitate the fight in the front yard, Sheriff. I am the one who called for Butch and Junebug to get over here when I saw the conflict brewing. You see, you might need the people of Madden more than you think."

*****

"Just give me one minute, Sarah," Sheldon said as they stepped into the hallway. He recognized Sarah's confusion but turned without explanation and walked in the opposite direction from the front exit. She may have said something to him, but the blood rushing to his head drowned her words.

Sheldon marched into an empty visitation room. He flipped the light switch inside the doorway and watched as the darkness evaporated, leaving only the shade in the back corners.

Sheldon identified the Agent. He recognized the human form, the fedora's shape, the creased suit, and even how the darkness shifted like a subtle rolling cloud.

You-whooo, Shelly Belly. The untethered voice sounded musical in his head. Sheldon recalled a bully who had lived near their house years ago. The older kid would hide in the bushes and taunt Sheldon, calling him names and throwing rocks at him. Like the Agent, the bigger kid had refused to beat him up and move on to another victim. Instead, he had derived pleasure from the intimidation more than meting out black eyes and butt kickings. Sheldon preferred the bruises to the drawn-out threats and mockery then and now.

Sheldon stormed toward the corner. He did not know what to do when he got there, but his anger took charge.

That's right, come this direction and let me have it, boy. I feel your hate.

The voice caused Sheldon to grit his teeth and accelerate. On the way, he swerved to the side window where a floor lamp illuminated the room. He paused long enough to reach up, rip the shade from the bulb and lift the entire fixture from the floor. The long electrical cord sagged like a jump rope.

No, don't do it, the Agent pleaded, exaggerating the first word. *Stop!*

Sheldon thrust the light into the shadow, swinging it back and forth as if he were cleaning spider webs from the corner with a flaming broom.

No, the Agent yelled inside Sheldon's head. The shadowy arms flailed like an actor performing in a Madden County drama production. *See what you have done! In a minute, I shall melt awaaaayyyyyy.*

Sheldon paused. Now he held the lamp like a flag at the end of a battle.

The Agent's laughter roared inside Sheldon's brain, and the shadow rocked in sync with each howl.

Sheldon returned the lamp to its original spot on the blue carpet without a word.

I used to call Willie Grace the best example of hillbilly sap Madden County offered, but the more I poke around in your branches, the more you win the prize, the Agent said. *At least Willie read the* Wizard of Oz *and could quote the Wicked Witch frontward and backward.*

Sheldon's body was rigid. His hands trembled, and he held his breath. He pushed against the Agent's words with images of his father walking in the yard, his arms extended. His dad would say not to let others control your actions and who you are. But how do you stop them when their words turn you inside out?

You ever wonder, Shello, what happens to you through all this? Do you think you will be the boss here in Madden when your sister leaves? Wander back and stare down into Willie's coffin if you want the answer. He is your mirror.

"Are you okay in there, Sheldon? What is happening?" Sarah had entered the room, and he could detect the confusion in her tone. "You are scaring me again, Sheldon," she said.

From her perspective, she faced the corner as though he was not alone.

"I am fine, Sarah," he said without turning around. "Hey, how about a milkshake at the diner on the way home?"

"Do we have time?" Sarah responded.

"Believe me. I have a lifetime," Sheldon said, emphasizing the final words.

Chapter 28
O Death, Where Is Your Sting?

As a little girl, Evangeline had believed burials only happened on rainy days. As she stood at Willie's gravesite, the rain pounded the Grace and Wilson family cemetery so hard that each pallbearer's steps left muddy, misshapen tracks, much like the footprints of Willie's life. The October wind blew cold, causing the reverend's breath to ascend like morning fog.

The Phipps brothers had constructed a canvas cover to protect the casket, Reverend Granville, and the family from the downpour. The pebbles of rain on the canopy reminded Evangeline of how storms drummed the tin roof of her house. Her dad had said it was God's fingers tapping the house, telling them He was watching and was there to provide comfort if they asked.

Evangeline was not good at asking for comfort or anything else. She was a lone accountable pallbearer, carrying Willie's violent death to a grave as yet undug. Evangeline clasped her left elbow as she always did when confused or uncomfortable.

Sheldon stood close enough for her to lean against him. Her

black jacket and white blouse wrinkled at the crook of her elbow, so she straightened her arm in an awkward motion.

Evangeline stared at the casket and the pastor, but in her mind, she pictured her father and Willie together as kids, hunting squirrels and wrestling on a hillside. She remembered Uncle Willie pretending to run away from her in the front yard, her small steps trailing behind his escape.

Sheldon had pulled himself together. Still, he appeared unsteady, as if a simple nudge would topple him. His blue suit fit him well, but his posture caused it to be yet another costume she had forced him to wear.

Like at the wake, the turnout surprised her with so many attendees. The gray casket was closed now, but the image of her uncle's face framed by a white pillow remained in her mind. Although most people grieved the loss of a loved one because they would never see them again, Evangeline's sadness sprang from another place. Evangeline mourned for the life Willie had not lived.

Evangeline winced, imagining Willie watching Robert take flight like the reverend's breath. She tensed as, in her mind, Sheldon's figure replaced Robert's, falling toward jagged rocks hundreds of feet below.

"Goodbye, Willie. I wish you had lived a happier life," she whispered.

Evangeline looked across the gravesite. Cyrus Cornett stood without an umbrella. Faith Cornett was half under the canvas, holding a small red umbrella above her head as tears, not rain, streaked her face. One man's eyes were closed, and his lips moved in prayer while others stood somber and silent.

Pastor Granville, a long-time friend of her dad, held an open Bible in his hand like a bird, its wings spread, a string of gold making a small, feathered tail marking the page. The pastor's black suit and thick black-rimmed glasses resembled Elvis Costello. He thanked everyone for coming to honor Willie. He managed some platitudes about Willie's "kind, but bruised soul," and his, "love of family and community so strong he did not cross the county line for over a half a century."

He said, "Today, I share a verse from 1 Corinthians 15:51-57. The scripture reminds us that while death may seem like loss, it is indeed a victory."

"Then, when our dying bodies transform into spirits that will never die, this Scripture will be fulfilled. 'Death is swallowed up in victory. O death, where is your victory? O death, where is your sting? For sin is the sting that results in death, and the law gives sin its power. But thank God! He gives us victory over sin and death through our Lord.'"

Vangie felt her brother's presence when she looked down to pray. He was not praying. Instead, he stared beyond the casket, the flowers, and the pastor onto the cover of the trees nearby. Hatred filled his eyes instead of tears.

*****

The Agent shimmered at the tree line like coal smoke. Sheldon recognized Barlow was celebrating his handiwork.

Will he be dancing by my grave someday? Will he torment me for years and then cut me open?

Sheldon shifted his eyes to Evangeline. Days before, he had thought she was evil for wanting to leave Madden County. Now Sheldon would not know evil if it was riding on his shoulders.

Sarah stood on his other side. Her dark dress and burgundy jacket highlighted her body and her black hair. She was always there for him, but for how long? Would she tolerate him if he could never tell her the reason for his anger and unpredictable behavior?

The coal smoke drifted closer. *You dress for a funeral every day, don't you, Agent?*

Think about this, Shelly Shel, the Agent's words filled his ears. *Your uncle will finally do something of value with his life. He will fertilize these horrendous hills. He is the manure he was born to be.*

Sheldon breathed slow and long. His father had always told him to focus and keep his head no matter what a bully might say or do.

Old Willie sure as hell knew how to pick 'em, didn't he? Look around at this gathering of mountain trash. Shit, even the preacher looks like he just finished off a quart jar of moonshine. He's apt to dance a jig in a minute.

Sheldon inhaled the damp air again.

And look at the old whore, Barlow said. Sheldon knew the Agent referred to Faith Cornett, her umbrella as red as a cardinal, shielding her from the downpour. *She treated your uncle better than his blood relatives, I guess.*

Sheldon covered his ears with his hands. Sarah and his sister guided his arms back to his sides.

When Shel glanced at his sister, she looked back. She wanted to say something, but her wet eyes returned to the pastor. After all, what could she tell him when mountains held them apart?

Chapter 29
Evangeline Decides on a Plan

After dropping Sarah off at her house, Evangeline and her brother rode without speaking. The Sheriff studied Sheldon as she drove. His expression was stern, and he appeared to have aged in the five days since Willie's murder. She also glanced at the rearview mirror to assess her face and noted she shouldn't judge Sheldon's appearance until she erased the dark circles surrounding her eyes.

Evangeline considered asking her brother to share his pain and what he planned to do. She aborted the idea. Her mind was too splintered to go nosing into Sheldon's psyche, so she probed her own thoughts.

Time grew short on the contract. The October 25th deadline was nine days away. Sylvia called her daily until Willie's death, so Evangeline could only imagine how stressed her friend must be now. When Evangeline refused Sylvia's offer to come to Madden and help her, Sylvia's response was kind yet suspicious.

"I will leave you alone. I know you are strong, Evangeline, but if you need me, please call, and I will be there," Sylvia had said. "Heck, I could hand deliver the contract for you to save time."

Evangeline had tried to muster laughter, but it had come out as a rough-edged sigh. Sylvia had dropped the issue.

Willie's death made the contract less like a dream and more like paper and ink. She needed to find the Highlander and force him to pay. Then she could go.

Her father had told his staff, "We speak for people who no longer have a voice. We protect and serve everyone, but when people are harmed or killed, we stand for them, so they are not forgotten or forsaken."

Back then, she had worried he expressed antiquated ideas of justice and revenge. But now, with Willie's bloody body invading her dreams, she needed justice against the drug lords who had ended her uncle's life—she needed to be Willie's voice and avenger. Only then could she set things right with Sheldon, Madden, and even her father's ghost.

However, her leadership had amounted to a lump of coal so far. Her words, unlike her father's, were hollow.

It was time to shift tactics. Instead of an inside-out strategy, Evangeline would lead the investigation. They would expand outside the station and into the hills, searching for anyone who might have wanted to hurt Willie. They would determine who had had the most to lose if Willie had talked to her. Once they established motive and opportunity, the team would follow the bloody footprints back to Willie's cell.

She glanced at Sheldon and then refocused on the wet and broken road. She would marshal her resources and trace the connections between Willie, his friends, and his enemies until she stood at the Highlander's front door. If they wanted to silence Willie, she would speak and act on his behalf and finish in time to meet the contract delivery deadline.

*****

Sheldon considered starting a conversation. However, Evangeline's white knuckles gripping the steering wheel and her distant stare told him she had other things on her mind.

Besides, any conversation would lead to Willie. He could not risk losing control and revealing everything. Willie's letter clarified Sheldon's job—to preserve the secret, so the Agent remained in check. Except that was not what it said, was it? It was Evangeline's job, not his, to save the day. He had intercepted the message and, in doing so, took responsibility.

Willie suffered, and now I will suffer in silence as he did.

Seeing the Agent's dark form and hearing his evil voice had been difficult at Willie's gravesite. Barlow took pleasure in causing pain. If he became more than a shadow, as the letter suggested could happen, the hurt would be endless. However, the Agent was quiet now, and Sheldon could think for himself. No ominous shadows rose in the backseat. He almost smiled when he pictured the Agent's silhouette strapped into a police car's back seat belt. Then fear rose again. *How do you chain a ghost? What cell can hold a shadow?*

In the letter, Willie had said to Evangeline, "If anyone could confront and end the Agent, it would be you." *My uncle believed she could make Barlow go away. Instead, could I make the evil stop?* He peered out the passenger side window again. Ditches, trees, and rocks bracketed the hillside near the road. The rain struck the glass like tiny birds hurling themselves repeatedly against the clear panes.

"I need answers," Sheldon whispered, his breath fogging the window. *What created the Agent? Why did both my uncles carry the burden?* Maybe if he found the answers, he would uncover how to defeat Barlow.

Sheldon considered recruiting Sarah and Gene to help him research what had happened in the past. Gene's access to Madden

County's history could be the key. *Even if Gene doesn't want to help a Grace, he will help Sarah.*

Sheldon leaned his forehead against the window and stared upward. Dark storm clouds rolled and shifted in the sky like a living Rorschach test where every shape was an evil man wielding a sharp blade.

Chapter 30
Can I Keep a Secret?

The road to the Cornett place on Hammond Creek turned like a corkscrew. Broken asphalt and potholes rattled the sheriff's cruiser, but Evangeline kept her foot on the gas, only braking when the hairpin curves and uneven pavement gave her no choice.

"Looks like the county judge doesn't have any family or donors living in these parts, Sheriff," Art said as he bounced with each pothole. "You know, driving here guarantees more votes in the election if you stay around."

"I don't know, but having you bouncing in the passenger's seat ensures more road damage," the Sheriff said.

"I'll try not to break our axle," Art said. "I hope Luke doesn't appear out of nowhere and pull you over for speeding, reckless driving, and getting distracted by your image in the mirror. Or in legal terms, for driving like a woman. He told me you reprimanded him for roughing up Cyrus."

Evangeline glared at Art. Both knew she was the better driver.

"So tell me, what do you think about the planning session?" The sheriff had outlined the team's strategy for finding Willie's killer. Except for Dr. Bell's discovery of the scrip lodged in Willie's throat, the investigation had provided few insights. The interviews and cameras had failed to provide a solid clue, and her speculation always led back to the Highlander. So, Evangeline created a plan. She and Art would question Willie's known acquaintances to gather information. They would hunt the people who had wanted to silence Willie the most. Junebug would research the scrip and help with a special duty. Luke would cover calls with Otis. Instead of searching for the Highlander to find Willie's killer, she would do the opposite.

"I just hope we can get people to talk." Art said as he fidgeted with his seatbelt.

"You are right on target there. Our neighbors are not known for cooperating with law enforcement," Evangeline said. "They would as soon let some killer off the hook than to say—"

Art's snicker interrupted her thought. "You must be joking, Evangeline. Even though I have known you most of your doggone life, I wonder if you grew up here." He shook his head as he smiled. "Killers in Madden don't get off the hook. Generally, a victim's family member hangs them from a hook by their feet. Your daddy understood it. When there was a killing, he knew who to go to first to tell them he was on it. If not, there would be more blood."

Art's words were accurate.

Feuds in the mountains led to bloodshed. Evangeline's father had told her the stories of famous Madden County feuds dating back to when he was a child. A disputed call in a summer picnic baseball game had led to years of violence and several deaths between the Grants and the Carsons. Her father had said it wasn't the game that mattered but the perceived disrespect. It traced back to Irish and Scottish roots, where weakness could lead to losing your livelihood to thieves. Mountain people were quick to fight and seek revenge whenever someone threatened their reputation and property.

"Judging by how people act, the old Wainscott, Mills, and Ramey feud is ready to ignite again," the sheriff said.

"Did it ever stop?" Art replied. "They've fought over coal, paychecks, timber, scabs, the environment—you name it. They'd fight over soup beans if they could conjure a controversy."

"Somehow, it feels different," Evangeline said. "At the funeral home, it felt like evil settled in, stirring things up and making Madden County even more hopeless. I sensed it at the diner, too."

"Now, who's sounding superstitious?" Art said. "When I was a boy, Benny Stumbaugh came down the road one day, carrying a 12-gauge shotgun in one hand and a bottle of Early Times whiskey in the other. Even though it was still morning, he was half-lit," Art said, his voice steady and his eyes focused ahead. "Not being the enlightened intellectual I am now—"

It was the sheriff's turn to snicker.

"...I approached him and asked what he was doing. He said, 'I'm gonna kill Frankie Money.'"

"Did he do it?"

"Nah. The old drunk stumbled into the creek. His gun and bottle went flying. I helped him up the creek bank, but I grabbed the gun, left the bottle where it fell, and walked him home."

Evangeline laughed. "Even then, you were a good peacekeeper."

"Not so good. I took Benny to his oldest son and handed him his father and the gun. I told him how Benny fell down the bank into the water on his way to kill Frankie. Two weeks later, the son killed Frankie Money in Mudtown for throwing his daddy in the creek."

"I would say you're making it up, Art, but I know you aren't," the sheriff said. "People here are a strange lot. They are hot about trivial things and cold about what matters."

"Trivial is in the eyes of the beholder, I guess," Art said. "Hey, have you talked to Sheldon about why he departed the funeral home all *Night of the Living Dead*-style? I must admit he worried me when I took him home."

"I know what you mean," Evangeline responded. "Shel is harder to understand every day. He believes he is to blame for Willie's death. He won't tell me the reason."

"There's enough blame to pass around, but it should all be handed to the Highlander, assuming he was the one who pulled this off."

"Maybe the boy is going through a rough time," Art replied. He glanced at her and shifted. "When all this is behind us, Shel will be alright. He is a good kid who can put things in their proper perspective."

"I hope I can see things the right way," the sheriff said as she turned toward the Cornett house. Brown, yellow, and orange splotches stained the leaves, and a few thrushes and sparrows darted between the branches.

The house was more prominent in full daylight. The shutters showed age and storm damage, but the Ironweed and Verbena bloomed in the front yard. Rhododendron bushes bordered one side of the yard, and a well-worn path led into the hills. Yes, she had missed too many details during the raid.

Big Orange opened the screen door and stepped onto the porch as the cruiser rolled to a stop in the gravel driveway. The blue University of Kentucky sweatshirt, jeans, and dark yellow work boots suggested he was ready to work. His broad shoulders and thick neck caused his orange head to appear too small for his body.

"He doesn't look hospitable, does he?" Art said. "I wonder who he dislikes at the police station? Oh yeah..." Art chuckled, and Evangeline shot him another of her disgruntled stares.

"Tucker is lucky I didn't press charges for attempted assault on a law officer. It's not too late, you know."

"How about not mentioning it until after questioning him?" Art said.

"Then you better do the talking on this one."

Both officers exited the car and stepped toward the porch. Evangeline rested her right hand on her belt near her Glock.

"Hello, Mr. Meade," Art said. "We want to ask you and Ms. Cornett some questions. I am sure you remember Sheriff Grace." He motioned toward Evangeline. The sheriff fixed her eyes on Tucker.

In the daylight, Big Orange's hair and the sprouts of beard on his chin and face were redder than she recalled.

"I remember her well. Sheriff, are you here to chat or to kill something? I got an opossum who comes around here and gets in the garbage sometimes if you plan to pull your piece on an animal. Or maybe you would like to beat up my baby niece inside the house?"

Evangeline fought the urge to remind him she had not hurt Sam Bowie. *Who names their dog after a UK basketball player?*

Sam lumbered across the porch as if on cue to make an appearance in the yard. His droopy eyes and blueberry-tinted skin made Evangeline smile despite her stern demeanor.

"No killin' today," Art said. "We just want to talk about Willie Grace."

"Yep, I thought you would come to see me, but I didn't figure you'd show before my court date. Sheriff, you managed to pull a gun on my dog and get the best man I ever knowed killed in a few days. Ain't that a hoot?"

"We only want to discuss who might have wanted to kill Willie," Evangeline said. "We won't take much of your time."

"I reckon I'll never forgive you for almost killing Sammy B, but I'm all in for you findin' and hangin' whatever hurt Willie."

"That's just what we aim to do," Evangeline replied. *Whatever hurt Willie?*

Big Orange invited them onto the front porch. He gestured toward two old rocking chairs and a yellow metal glider.

"You better take the heavy metal seat," the sheriff said to Art.

"Oh, that's not professional," Art replied.

Big Orange cracked open the screen door and yelled inside. "Aunt Faith, the law's here to talk to us about Willie." He waited for her by the door, refusing to engage with the officers. His belly protruded from his sweatshirt, and his denim jeans were about two sizes too large for his considerable frame.

When Faith Cornett arrived, Tucker opened the door and guided her to the gliding bench. Faith held the baby, much like during the raid. The little girl looked down at Art, and her eyes remained transfixed on his face as Faith sat beside him on the glider. Evangeline noted the older woman's straight posture and how her long fingers cradled the baby's head.

Evangeline said, "Thank you for seeing us, Ms. Cornett. Are Kimmy and Cyrus around, too? We want to talk to them, as well."

"Cyrus is at school, of course, and Kimmy, well, she's not here." Faith turned her eyes toward the road as if hoping to see her niece arrive in a cloud of dust. "I would have done anything for Willie Grace, Sheriff. He was a good friend and always treated people with respect and kindness."

Faith appeared different than she had during the raid. She pushed her graying hair away from her eyes, revealing her natural dark complexion, unblemished skin, and the sculpted contours of her face. The yellow sundress displayed her soft shoulders, although Evangeline feared she would freeze.

Big Orange stepped closer but continued standing. "I don't want you all harassing Aunt Faith, so let's get on with it, and you hit the road."

The sheriff glared up at him from her rocking chair. "Judge Endicott may have given you bail, Mr. Meade, but it doesn't mean you are off the hook. You are fortunate with how the night ended

155

when I was here last time. The drugs on the kitchen table didn't quite add up to distribution, so you are free...for now."

"Call me Tucker, Sheriff. I don't have much use for you treatin' me all respectful when you don't think highly of me. Ask what you come here to ask."

Evangeline gazed at him. She did not like how he loomed over his aunt.

Art said, "Tucker, did you have any indication someone wanted to hurt Willie before his death?"

"The only people hurtin' Willie, as far as I could tell, wore police uniforms," Tucker said. Art ignored the statement, but Evangeline knew the officer would not play Tucker's game much longer.

Faith Cornett's voice was level and soft. "Tucker, just tell them what you know." She shifted next to look at Evangeline. "Willie was one of our people. He didn't have many enemies, as Tucker said."

Big Orange's shoulders lowered, and his hands relaxed at his side. "My point is people liked Willie. He was slightly off in the head but didn't hurt anybody. He was good right back at you if you were good to him. Sometimes he was nice even if you didn't return the favor."

"What about all the drugs, Tucker?" Art said. "You know that's dirty business here in Madden County. Did he owe anybody money or drugs?"

"You all sound like you want a bad guy to pin this on," Tucker said. "The only problem is Willie wasn't in the game. He always paid for what he needed. He wasn't selling anything, and he never started trouble. I would be dead now if Aunt Faith hadn't taken me in. She did the same thing for your uncle. Faith was our family when we didn't have anyone. You ain't got no right to treat her or Willie like they ain't good people."

Faith intervened. "I tried to get Willie to stop with all the drugs. I had them at the house because I feared they would get killed in the hills dealing with drug runners from down south." She paused. "Sometimes people use drugs to forget. Willie told me the pills drowned out the ghosts haunting his head."

Faith rocked back and forth with the baby lying on her lap. The baby laughed at Art when the deputy stretched his giant finger toward her. She grasped his finger and giggled even more.

Damn metaphors, Evangeline thought. Whenever she had talked to Willie, he had challenged her to figure out what he meant, not what he said. She recalled the stories he had told her when she was a little girl.

He would always talk about two down-on-their-luck characters named Coffee Can and Sadie Tater, who would get in trouble while cleaning the barn and hog pen or some such nonsense. Her favorite was when Coffee Can kept a secret from Sadie when they rode on a coal train. The mystery was a surprise birthday party Coffee had planned for her with their equally down-on-their-luck friends. There was always a moral like, "Sometimes people keep secrets because they don't want to hurt the people they love."

Big Orange added, "He never sold a single rock or pill, so far as I could tell, although I'll admit he had his hand in the moonshine trade years ago. He was always careful not to use too much dope, just enough to help him forget. Once, I asked what he was tryin' to get out of his head. I will always remember him saying, 'The nightmare I live every day.'"

Evangeline imagined a young Willie—before life had abused and scarred his face—losing his brother to suicide. Talk about trauma. Her heart jumped in her chest. Could such a nightmare ever be erased?

"Ms. Cornett, how did you know Willie so well?" the sheriff asked.

"At first, I felt sorry for Willie. We met on Grassy Knob years ago when Pouty Combs bootlegged whiskey and beer. Pouty's wife, Sandra, was a friend of mine. Sandra always invited me over, and I would talk to her and buy beer for my daddy. One day she led me into the house, where Willie Grace and Pouty were talking up a storm. Willie asked me how I was doing and was very polite. I didn't say much. I bought two cases of Blue Ribbon, talked to Sandra for a while, and said my goodbyes.

But my car wouldn't start when I got to the gravel road. Willie tried to fix it but didn't have any luck. He offered me a ride home. Cyrus, my baby boy, was about the age of this little one, and I had just bought this house. My sister Cammy was babysitting Cyrus, and I hurried to get back home with the beer, so I accepted Willie's offer. Willie was quiet all the way there, only glancing at me a few times while driving. Willie was older than me, and it appeared he had lived a hard life, so I asked him what he did for a living. He said, 'I ain't doing much living, so I don't need much to get by.'"

"Do you know what he meant?" Evangeline asked. Art played with the baby as Tucker continued to stand near the glider. The sheriff realized Big Orange was shielding his aunt from the big orange sun.

"No idea," Faith replied. "Somehow, Willie's words made little sense, but you understood him anyway. Anyone could tell he carried more than a single burden, but he accepted it on his shoulders and still managed to keep down the anger and hate other people around Madden County showed off all the time."

"What happened then?" Evangeline said.

"We became family. We sat on the porch, drank too much, and talked about the world."

"Have you seen this before?" The sheriff retrieved a clear plastic bag from her pocket. She showed it to Faith and then Tucker.

"Willie carried the darn thing in his pocket. It is a Madden Coal Company scrip from October 1927. He said he didn't understand it himself, but it was the seed from which everything else grew," Faith said. "It was another of those things he'd say, and we all nodded as if we understood, but none of us knew what it meant. He claimed he had no details, but this scrip was a bad luck charm."

"I will never forget when he showed it to me the first time," Tucker said. We were on a strip mine getting...." Tucker paused. "I mean hanging out. I asked him why he held it since it was bad luck. He said he carried it, so no one else needed to do it."

The glider's rhythm and the baby's soft purr filled the morning air. The little girl stretched her pale, tiny arm and small fingers toward Art's face. He leaned closer and allowed her hand to grasp the tip of his nose.

"Jessica," Faith said as she smiled at Art. "Her name is Jessica."

Evangeline asked, "So did Willie do anything right or wrong to cause someone to hurt him, Ms. Cornett?"

"Right and wrong? Willie was not perfect, Sheriff, but everybody has right and wrong inside them. Anybody who can't stand imperfection shouldn't look in the mirror," Faith said as she shifted the baby from her lap into Art's massive hands. "Willie said he had an enemy he hated but wouldn't tell us who it was. We argued because he wouldn't share even though I told him everything. After a while, I figured Willie's enemy was in his head like he was at war with himself."

"If you ask me," Tucker said, "even the bad guys thought the world of Willie. Hell, they were there for him, Sheriff." Evangeline caught the implication but allowed him to continue. "I'll say this, if anyone was as close to Willie as Aunt Faith, it would be my cousin, Cyrus. They spent a lot of time together."

"Thank you, Tucker. I believe he will be our next stop," Evangeline said. "Ms. Cornett, where was Cyrus's daddy? If you don't mind me asking."

"That's one of the things Willie and I talked about the first night. You know, I promised I would never tell anyone, including

Cyrus. But I told Willie Grace. After a few hours of drinking beer, I trusted him to know something I still haven't shared with anyone, and he never betrayed me. I'm sorry, Sheriff. Cyrus is a good boy with a future, so I don't regret anything."

"I see," Evangeline said. She watched Faith rock the glider back and forth. Art half-listened and continued to play with baby Jessica, who resembled a doll in his hands.

"I know some people thought me and Willie shacked up, and some busy-bodies around here even claimed Willie was Cyrus's daddy. None of it was true. Willie Grace was my best friend. Even though he knew gossip that some people would give a kidney to know and use, he never told anyone except me." Tears traveled down the delicate features of her face, although she laughed as she cried.

"What is it?" Evangeline tilted her head to the side.

"It's just a funny thing that happened the night we met," Faith replied. "After a few hours of drinking, I got paranoid about telling so much about myself. I asked him if he could keep a secret. He chuckled, then commenced the big laugh he belted out when he found something funny. It made me laugh, too. Eventually, he said, 'Can I keep a secret? Oh yes, I can keep a secret, and I will. The only thing that'd make me reveal my secret is dying.'"

Chapter 31
Don't Rise Above Your Raising

"What are you doin' here, Junebug?"

"I'm dropping by the newspaper office, Sheldon. Hello, Sarah." Junebug nodded at Sarah. "Are you heading in to work?"

Sarah smiled and said, "It is good to see you, Deputy Spears," but she did not answer his question. They stood outside the glass door leading to the *Mercury* office, their reflections the color of asphalt.

Sheldon wrinkled his nose. It was too much of a coincidence for Junebug to drop by the newspaper. No doubt, Evangeline had ordered the officer to follow him and report back. However, Shel realized it was too late to pretend he was going somewhere else, so he said, "We need to talk with Gene for a bit."

"That's my reason for being here, too." Junebug stepped between them and opened the thick glass door, motioning for Sarah to lead the way.

Sheldon trailed behind as they entered the *Madden Mercury* office. Pictures lined the hallway, displaying washed-out faces suited to the faded wood paneling. Plaques with dull brass plates honored the paper and its accomplishments, from journalism to sponsoring Little League baseball teams.

"Gene, are you here?" Sarah had asked this question many times before. "Sheldon is with me like I said he'd be, and Deputy Spears needs to see you, too."

"Layout room." Gene's voice sounded scorched by alcohol and cigarettes.

They entered the back room, where Gene perched on a stool at a large angled drafting board. Pictures and documents littered the slanted surface, like the whiteboard in Evangeline's conference room. It was as if both Gene and his sister needed the visual layout to see the big picture.

Sheldon recognized the folder resting on the second stool. Cardboard boxes and shards of paper covered the carpeted floor around the workstations. However, Sheldon's eyes stopped when he noticed the massive model train. Sarah had described it when she had first accepted the job at the office, but it still surprised him. At least thirty feet of train track traveled around the room, looping across several long tables. Various small black train cars were linked together at the model train station. All along the way, miniature models of businesses, houses, and people stood ready to greet the engine and train cars speeding along the route. Paper mache mountains with trees, bushes, and coal mines dotted the hills framing the railroad. It was a detailed model of the county seat, Madden.

"Are you here to arrest me, Officer Junebug?" Gene smiled at the deputy. "There is a new thing called Freedom of the Press. Ask Sheriff Grace to look it up."

Junebug grinned. "Yes, sir, I will, but I won't be taking anyone to the station today. I'm here to see if you need me to help update your publishing software."

The editor creased his brow and said, "I appreciate that, Junebug. The work you did last month fixed everything."

Junebug smiled and nodded. But he didn't say any goodbyes.

Gene turned to Sarah and Sheldon. "It is about time you kids learn some history," Gene said. His stubby fingers pointed at the drafting table. "This is real history, not the sterilized storybooks they use in schools. Nowadays, they act like Abe Lincoln was gay, coal miners did more damage to the Earth than the meteorite that killed the dinosaurs, and perception and emotions are truer than reality."

Sarah moved closer to her boss and said, "Thanks for letting me bring Shel in with me, Gene."

"Shit, you are the only one keeping this place going, Sarah. I don't have much spark left in my pen anymore. Things are changing in one direction while I am backpedaling in the other."

"Mr. Begley," Sheldon said, "I am interested in what you discussed at the funeral home. About how something's been wrong in Madden County for a long time."

"Interested? You have a strange way of demonstrating your keen curiosity. You walked out on me. The sheriff isn't interested in the past, and, considering her plans, maybe not the present." Gene leaned back and rubbed his stubbled chin. "So, are you doing a research paper or something? If so, I am sure Sarah can write it for you." He turned around and organized the papers beside him. He removed an old photograph and placed it on the drafting board.

Shel recognized an insult when he heard one.

Sarah glanced at Sheldon and nodded toward the exit.

Sheldon shook his head. "Why do you hate my family so much, Mr. Begley? You hated my father and now, my sister. What did we ever do to you?"

Begley pivoted on the stool, stretching upward as he turned. The Editor's eyes narrowed beneath his errant eyebrows and turquoise glasses. "You do need a history lesson, young man."

Shel's face was hot. "You have no idea, old man. That's why I am here. I want to know the history, but I'm wondering if you know anything about—"

"Sheldon, stop it." Sarah placed her hand on his arm. "I'm sorry, Gene," she said. "He has been very stressed with Willie and Evangeline planning to leave Madden County."

Gene shifted his attention to Sarah.

"A perfect example, Sarah. Sheriff Grace put her name on the ballot but plans to skip town after the election. That's a Grace for you. Wants power up until the last possible minute."

Gene laughed and turned to face Sheldon again. "I figured Evangeline would appoint you as her replacement."

Sheldon turned toward the hallway to avoid responding in a way he might regret. He glimpsed Junebug in his peripheral. The deputy motioned palms down, urging the teen to compose himself.

Sarah was standing in quicksand, unable to step in either direction without sinking.

"I don't hate your family, Sheldon Grace," Gene said, his voice lower and calmer now.

Sheldon turned to face Gene. Sarah regained her balance. The change in Gene's tone was so immediate Sheldon wondered if Begley's insults had been a test to see if his intentions were genuine.

"You see this train right over here?" Gene slid off the stool and lumbered toward the tables. He pointed to the train set as if selling it at an auction. "For over half a century, trains like this ran top-heavy with black gold. The trains traveled toward New England, the factories in Ohio and Detroit, and the bigger cities in Kentucky, like Louisville and Lexington. The coal fed the fires in homes, industries, and government buildings, making it possible for the country to flourish. But America's fine people thought cheap energy magically appeared in their houses as if from the ether."

Gene straightened a tiny shack near the track.

"But they did not only purchase bituminous minerals," Gene said. "They bought the lives of hardworking mountain people. Those good souls were tools for the privileged. I have seen miles of coal trains speeding by company houses not big enough to hold anything but a bed and stove. The trains benefited factories and mansions, while the people in the shacks scraped together just enough to feed their children. Fathers died in mines, mother's died in childbirth, and childhood died the moment a kid became old enough to carry a pick to the mines or an ax to the mills."

Sheldon noted the red plaid shirt and how its wrinkles and pattern mirrored the scarlet on Gene's cheeks.

Gene continued, "I have always disliked how Madden County works because the division of power falls in distinct categories. First, some have power and want to keep it. Second, others don't have it and want to take it. Finally, many don't have it and recognize they never will."

Sheldon returned to Sarah's side, and Gene paused before speaking again. His voice was much softer now.

"There are kids in our county with talent and a willingness to work hard. But they hear their own kinfolks preaching at them, 'Don't rise above your raising.' To be accepted in Madden, they must know their place, as their parents and grandparents before them knew their station in life.

"You are great kids. But even if you weren't, your place is decided. I have lived here for forty years and witnessed how natural law hands some people things they did not earn. All I want is for your sister to earn her badge by protecting everybody in the county and trusting enough to be transparent."

Sheldon echoed Gene's apologetic tone. "But Evangeline is the best. She was at the top of her class in school and the State Police Academy. She could go anywhere and be amazing. There's no mystery to her. She does her best, and she earns her place."

Sheldon looked at Sarah. As he expected, there was a knowing smile. Kind words about his sister? Not an ordinary moment.

Junebug nodded in agreement. "I have worked with Sheriff Grace for a long time. She is about justice and safety for everybody."

"She's not perfect, Mr. Begley, but my sister makes Madden a better place," Sheldon said. "I want to know more so I can make the county better. Seeing Uncle Willie die the way he did and knowing this county is where I will stay no matter what Evangeline decides, I have to discover what brought us to now."

Gene considered Sheldon and Sarah. His face softened even more than his voice.

"Alright," Gene said. "Come back in tomorrow after school. Who knows? Two bright kids may provide a fresh viewpoint. Assuming you can believe what you hear. People who claim to be open minded are often the first to slam the door on anything not fitting their narrow notions."

"I don't think it will be a problem for me, Mr. Begley. Believe me when I tell you, not everything in Madden County makes sense, and my mind is a wide-open door," Shel said.

Chapter 32
We Make Our Little Corner of the World

"I see your wheels turning, Arthur. You better solve this case before we reach Madden County High," Evangeline said to her partner. It was well past time for him to crack a joke as she navigated the winding road. Afternoon shade and sunshine spun across their faces like a silent roulette wheel.

He smiled. "Don't worry, boss, I've got you covered. It's the dude from the *Invisible Man* Illustrated Comic book I read as a kid. I didn't realize it was nonfiction. This case is an Easy-Bake Oven."

"Don't worry, partner. It's common for our interviews to lead to more questions than answers. You know how Madden County works. They would rather fight a bear than give the police information. Now they will talk up a storm with their neighbors, just not us. That's why I want to keep the information loop tight." She smiled at Art and said, "What's on your mind?"

Art shifted. "I've got two kids and one on the way. Maria is a great mom, and I do my best as their dad, but I worry it's not enough."

"So baby Jessica got to you, huh?" the sheriff said.

"I see baby Jessica and wonder about her future. She lives with her aunt, who I admire now that I know her, while Kimmy gets high. Her father skipped town, just like Cyrus's daddy, I guess. Kids growing up without fathers isn't right. It's as if God says, 'You know, it's not enough for you to be poor and in a place with dwindling opportunities. Nope, I will make your teenage mom a drug addict and have your dad hit the road.'"

"How many times do I have to remind you Madden County is godforsaken?" The remark tasted bitter on Evangeline's tongue. She realized Art found it even less tasteful when the deputy shifted in his seat.

"You have told me too many times, Evangeline." His voice was kind, but his big head turned toward her. "God has not left the mountains. He put people like you and me here to change things for the better. He hasn't failed Eastern Kentucky. We have."

The sheriff did not respond. She continued along Route 40, passing dilapidated houses and tiny mobile homes wedged into hillsides. Some majestic brick houses were nestled well off the roadway. The columns and large bay windows looked down on the dilapidation and the trailers. She wondered how this winding road could lead people to the same holler but in different conditions. Her dad used to say, "All things being equal, we can conclude things are never equal.'"

Sometimes God abandons places. Other times, he was never there at all, Evangeline feared.

"It's clear people like the Highlander are tearing this place apart," she said. "If we can lock up as many of his people as possible, we can make our little corner of the world, no matter what we think of it, a better place for kids like that little girl."

"On that we agree, Sheriff," he responded as he pointed through the windshield. "I hope it's not too late for the kids over there."

Secrets and Blood

Madden County High School's large gym roof loomed in the distance. "You can show off your football awards all you want when we get there," Evangeline said. "But don't you dare mention my pictures in the trophy case, you hear me?"

He smiled again. "You must want me to talk about it."

Chapter 33
It Would Not be Good for Their Health

The high school halls were not as vast as they had been when Cyrus was a freshman. During his first year, beads of sweat had dampened his collar, and he had doubted he belonged. Despite his mother's assurances, he had recognized his life was not like many other kids' experiences. The rich and middle class always had a safety net. He did not have such a luxury. The wealthy students feared nothing other than their new Ford Mustang or Chevy Silverado getting dinged in the parking lot.

Cyrus carried fear like a hidden third eye through which he often measured the world. His mother had done so much for him, but the rest of his kin were not always so helpful. His grandfather, Aubrey Cornett, ridiculed Cyrus for counting on school as a way to find happiness. "Look, your mama graduated from high school, and where did it get her? She's worked at Save-A-Lot since she graduated and got knocked up with you. Don't go thinking you will be better than your people."

But it wasn't true, was it? Cyrus did have family beyond his mother's people. For years, he had had Willie Grace. Willie had told him fear comes and goes as it pleases, but we can steer our lives to better shores if we work hard and refuse the low expectations of others—even people who love us. Although Willie had appeared tortured by his own life, he had expected Cyrus to do better and be better. Not perfect, just better.

Cyrus had discovered a place for himself at school. Whenever anyone needed help with an advanced math problem or a science project, they cried, "Where's Cyrus Cornett?" His skills and the idea the high school needed him had carved away his preexisting doubt, sculpting someone, as the counselor told him, who needed to go to college. Some teachers measured his potential by his family tree and the brand of his clothes. But others held high expectations and gave him the support to meet them—just like Willie had.

Now he was not sure what came next.

The patrol car was visible through the tall glass doors when he entered the school lobby. "Great," he said aloud. "The police are at school, and I get called to the office." It would confirm Mrs. Dinguss's belief that he was a criminal biding his time, just like his grandpa and cousin Tucker. *Thanks, Sheriff Grace. You might as well turn on the siren while you're at it.* If it were her boy, Sheldon, and the other rich kids in school, she would be careful not to let anyone know she was there to see them. "I guess I don't matter so much."

The sheriff and Deputy Butcher were talking to Ms. King, the school principal, inside the school office. At least Sheriff Grace hadn't brought the idiot who had punched him in the face.

Mrs. King motioned for Cyrus to enter the reception area.

Evangeline spoke first. "Hello, Cyrus. We were just at your house, and Faith said we should talk to you. You aren't in any trouble—"

"I know," he responded, eyeing the principal to ensure she heard him. "You are here to talk about Willie, I guess."

Evangeline nodded and said, "Yes, we are. We hope you can shed light on his final days."

The sheriff stood close to Cyrus's height. Without her hat, the short, reddish-brown hair flattened on top and poofed out on the side. The drab police uniform did not flatter her much, but he could see she was fit and strong. Even her angular jaws appeared sculpted and muscular. Butcher was a mountain. Kids claimed he could lift a car off the ground, and once at the Apple Festival, he had bent a steel bar into a horseshoe. He reminded Cyrus of the professional wrestling matches he attended with his grandpa and Tucker.

Ms. King said, "Feel free to talk here for privacy, Sheriff." She motioned toward her office. A desk crowded with papers and two computer monitors faced the window. Framed prints adorned the wall. One depicted students wearing goggles working on some science project. A motivational poster showed a house beneath a star-dotted sky, captioned, "Shoot for the Moon. Even if You Miss, You Will Land Among the Stars." Cyrus cringed. *That's not how the moon and stars work, Mrs. King. Some things are farther away than you think.*

A glass top conference table with four chairs centered the room. The sheriff sat down first, followed by the deputy. Cyrus rolled a chair around to sit across from them like a job interview.

"Cyrus, we appreciate you talking with us. Faith and Tucker told us you and Willie were close. When we chatted at the funeral home, you said he was helping you get into college." The sheriff opened a blue spiral notebook as she spoke. Cyrus knew she expected elaboration, and he wanted to be respectful to adults. Still, she should work for it, so he peered into her eyes without speaking.

"Okay," she said. "Can you tell me how you knew Willie so well and how you got along?" Cyrus enjoyed seeing frustration cross her face, but he realized she might be the only hope for finding Willie's killer.

"Willie was kind to me. He became friends with my mom when I was a baby, and we latched onto each other. He sometimes needed someone sober enough to drive him home and stop him from going too far with the drugs. I was there for him." Cyrus's throat tightened, and tears pushed against his eyes. "When my granddaddy would give me a beating or make me do something stupid like getting a tattoo," he said, staring at the sheriff for a moment, "Willie would talk me through it. He encouraged me to go to school and not let anyone take my education away." Cyrus changed his voice to imitate Willie's speech. "'A piece of paper does not mean you are better than anyone. But getting a college degree opens doors.'"

For a moment, the sheriff looked grateful for his characterization of Willie. The look passed soon.

"But he took you along when purchasing drugs and alcohol, right?" The sheriff did not mess around. Her tone shamed Cyrus, as if he and Willie had conspired to end the world.

"Sheriff, Willie preached at me to avoid drugs and alcohol. He challenged me to go to college and not lose the chance he did. He convinced me a better life is possible and persuaded my mom to believe it, too."

"I understand, Cyrus, but you didn't answer my question. Did you go with Willie when he bought drugs? If so, he put you in danger. You could have been arrested and sent to a juvenile facility at the house the other night."

"I was trying to watch out for my baby cousin, Jessica. I arrived after Willie went upstairs to shower, so he didn't know I was there. Besides, whenever I went with Willie, he demanded I stay away to avoid trouble. I could only watch from a distance. My job was to rescue him if he got hurt, but only if I could do it safely."

"So he wanted you to be there for selfish reasons, Cyrus. That doesn't sound like a friend—"

"No, it isn't what it looks like," Cyrus snapped. "Willie said he would have died long ago, but he couldn't because it would hurt people he cared about. He told me to stay next to him if he might die and listen to him."

The principal knocked on the office door and asked, "Is everything alright?"

Deputy Butcher opened the door and said, "Everything is fine, Mrs. King." He closed the door and walked back to his chair.

Cyrus watched the sheriff for her reaction. Her expression softened as though his defense of Willie's intentions was admirable.

"Thank you, Cyrus. Did Willie have a conflict with anybody? Did he mention anyone who wanted to harm him?"

Cyrus glanced at the deputy, who, for some reason, grinned at him. The tall woman and the brute made a good team—good cop and good cop.

"We need your help," Art said. "What you said was true. Many people suffer the loss of Willie Grace. Two are in this room with me."

Cyrus glanced back and forth between the officers. The deputy was correct. Both he and the sheriff were suffering. He could see her anguish, especially when she tried to smile but failed.

"Everybody liked Willie," Cyrus said. "People would ask him for advice, and Willie even talked several young people asking Comprehensive Care for help to get clean." Cyrus paused for a moment. "The only time he got into a scrape was with some men on Two Mile Mountain."

The officers leaned closer to the table. The sheriff's eyes widened, and her lips parted, but she allowed him to continue.

"Willie was supposed to pick up some pills on the strip mine.

Believe it or not, he said they came in a lower dosage than usual, which would help him not overdo it."

The sheriff interlaced her fingers. Cyrus understood his claim sounded suspect. What addict tries to find weaker drugs? Nonetheless, he knew it was true.

"I swear, Sheriff Grace," he said. "I can't explain, but Willie needed the dope but only wanted enough to keep himself going."

"So what happened, Cyrus?" Art said.

"We got there too early, I guess. We left the car on the back-road and walked the path. Willie told me to stay hidden. About four men were standing around some vehicles in front of a camper. I remember one was a black Ford truck. When Willie was close enough, he yelled at them. You would have thought he was a zombie. They yelled at him and they pulled their guns. They stopped when they recognized it was Willie, but they didn't let him stay."

Cyrus read the confusion on the two law officers' faces.

"They said he couldn't be there when the Big Boss showed up. I asked him, of course, who the Highlander was. He said it was someone with connections but didn't know his name."

"Did you see this Highlander, Cyrus?" The sheriff's urgent tone surprised him.

"No, I didn't. We rushed to the car and left. Willie said he would get what he needed later at the Big Barn House. Willie said the Highlander was the pipeline, buried deep, but there was a faucet on Sand Gap Road back in the trees."

The sheriff peered at Art. "You thinking we should find the house on Sand Gap Road?"

"I am," he responded. "But many homesteads are hidden back in the hills on Sand Gap—some off the grid. You know it isn't the safest place in the county."

"You could take us there, right, Cyrus?" The sheriff was not requesting. Willie had described her as tough as a tank. He had also repeated many times that if anyone could change things in Madden, it would be her.

"I can show you, Sheriff. But it ain't a trip to the mall," Cyrus said. "If they figure out I'm the one who brought you to their doorstep, it won't be good for my long term health."

"If they killed my Uncle Willie, it wouldn't be good for their health either," Evangeline said.

Chapter 34
History and Mystery

"How many times, Sarah, have I told you a newspaper is like a garden?" Gene said. "Our job as writers is to put to paper what sprouts. However, too many journalists plant the seeds they want to grow and only fertilize the most personally profitable crop. Nothing is as clean and clear as it appears, even when we profess journalistic objectivity."

Sarah smiled and agreed.

Gene's quotes reminded Sheldon of his father's wise sayings and repeated jokes. Sarah sat beside Gene at the drafting board. Shel stood next to Sarah's chair while Junebug had decided Gene's invitation applied to him. He stood on the other side, near Gene.

"I have always tried to be truthful, but now I'm older and see how my so-called truths blinded me to objective stories. That's hard for an ancient newspaperman to admit."

"Mr. Begley, I'm sorry, but what does this have to do with Uncle Willie?" Sheldon leaned against a stool and glanced at Sarah and Junebug to see if they shared his confusion. Gene faced the articles and photographs covering the slanted drafting table.

"The table holds a lot of history, Mr. Begley." Sarah's interruption caused Sheldon to wince. She was kissing butt when she did not need the job.

"I decided a chronology would be too general, Sarah. Instead, I analyzed our indices and database for each time the editors mentioned the Mills, Ramey, Grace, and Wainscott families in the same articles. I added the McCoy family because they owned the sawmill."

"Why would you center on us?" Sheldon asked. "You make it sound like everything bad in the county is our fault."

Gene chuckled. "You heard what you wanted to hear, son. All these families have done good things in Madden County. Even the Mills and Ramey families contributed to the county during their feud years. Sarah knows I credit her family for creating jobs and keeping my newspaper alive with advertising. The Grace family has been the law in our county for generations, and your daddy was one of the finest men I ever knew, even though we had our hard knocks."

Sheldon pointed to the articles on the board. "Then, what is this?"

"It's me trying to understand how a county has such bad luck? You have to go back to 1925, when we were the top timber and coal producers in Kentucky, to see Madden successful. In the 1980s, coal rebounded, but overall, it's like we broke a thousand mirrors and got seven years of bad luck for each one."

Gene twisted and pointed at the board. "What or who pushed Madden County to adopt this continuous failure plan?" Gene's nicotine-stained finger tapped the white table. "Madden's history is filled with deaths in the mines, feuds, corruption, and destruction. How does this small part of the world have more deaths from drug overdoses per capita than any other place in America? How do people like Willie Grace and his older brother die in unusual, tragic ways? No one takes their kid brother to their suicide, as Robert did with Willie. No one dies in a police cell, alone, torn apart like a buck getting field dressed."

Silence followed Gene's words. Everyone stared at the board and the pictures.

"Are you trying to corrupt my students, Dad?"

Sheldon turned toward the dramatic voice. Ms. Begley, the English and drama teacher from Madden County High, still had her identification badge secured to a lanyard around her neck. Her vibrant red and white dress contrasted the office's drabness and dirty green carpet. "I'll report you to the principal if you teach without a certificate."

Her wry smile and the comical placement of her hands on her hips made it appear she was performing on the stage. Ms. Begley drew the boys' attention at school. Her red hair grazed her shoulders, and she always smiled.

Lilly's personality made it easy to forget she was Gene's daughter. Lilly was eccentric, her hand gestures theatrical and pronounced, and her clothes displayed splashes of reds, greens, and blues. She was a watercolor portrait, while her father was a pencil sketch, black and white like the print on his newspaper. Gene's manners repelled people, while students surrounded Ms. Begley because kids wanted to take her classes. She was exceptional compared to her colleagues, although she was still a young teacher.

Gene said, "Oh, don't worry, Lilly, the public school system is much better at corrupting minds than I could ever be."

Ms. Begley threw her arms around his neck from behind and kissed him on his bald spot. She said, "Sarah, don't let this geezer work you like an indentured servant. Just because Dad spends every waking hour at this place doesn't mean you have to be here all the time."

"Sheldon, has he hired you, too? Get ready for some child labor law violations," Lilly said. Her smile dimmed. "I was very sorry to hear about your uncle's passing. My condolences to you and your family."

Then she looked at Junebug and smiled. "I have seen you around, Deputy. Let's see, it's Junebug, right?"

Sheldon was sure the deputy blushed.

"Yes, ma'am, that's me. I am Bentley Spears. Ben Spears, Junior."

Shel could never recall hearing Junebug's real name, nor had he heard Junebug respond that way to anyone.

"Not sure I am journalist material, Ms. Begley." Sheldon looked back at Gene. "Right now, I would appreciate finding out what he thinks about...things."

"It's ghosts," she replied. "My dad can't accept the obvious."

Shel's heart skipped a beat. *Be quiet, lady. Don't say it out loud. You will bring the Agent here— if he isn't already sitting in the corner, watching and waiting for me to crack.* Sheldon did not know if the Agent was a ghost, a voice from hell, or a vampire, but he knew they needed to avoid unleashing Barlow on the world.

"My lovely Lilly accepts the least likely explanation first. She thinks everything is a product of a supernatural demon, fairy, or killer unicorn." Gene shook his head in dismay. "*The X-Files* is a documentary as far as she is concerned."

Ms. Begley laughed, the sound rich and full. "My dad said killer unicorns. Did you hear?' Everyone smiled, including Gene. "My father doesn't adhere to Hamlet's immortal words, 'There are more things in heaven and earth, Horatio, than is dreamt of in your philosophy.'"

The quote rang true to Sheldon. He had never dreamed his life could change so much just because he read a letter meant for his sister. Before now, he would have laughed at anyone who suggested evil spirits lurked in dark corners and minds.

"And a turd by any other name would smell just as disagreeable," Gene answered.

Sheldon listened to the banter, controlled his heartbeat, and forced a smile. However, his patience eroded. He searched the office corners. No shadows. No summons ringing in his head. No Agent. But Ms. Begley's statement reminded him of the stakes and rekindled his urgency to end this nightmare.

"If I didn't love her so much, I would opt for adoption." Gene laughed, turned around, and hugged her. "Lilly, did you come to see me, or are you heading to Adele's? She said you keep her bookstore open."

"Adele's store is the best, Dad," Lilly said as she turned to Junebug but spoke to Gene. "You should see if she has some books on the history of railways."

"That's where my little girl gets so many wild notions. Adele and her—"

"So, Mr. Begley," Sheldon said. The further the conversation veered into irrelevant things, the more anxious he felt. "What's going on here?"

"It's not so easy, Sheldon," Gene replied, not as annoyed as Sheldon expected. "If you look at your family's interactions with the other families, it traces back for generations—the late 1800s has plenty of references to families fighting over land, perceived disrespect, you name it. However, one story piqued my interest because it describes them working together. It was an incident in October of 1927 shortly after the coal company investors demanded Baldwin Agency detectives be sent into the county to protect their investment."

Sheldon shivered and leaned into Gene's words. *What if Mr. Begley figures it all out? What happens to the curse, the Agent, and the county? Does the Agent kill a moment later? Dear God, I pray we don't make things worse.*

Junebug shifted and said, "Did you say October 1927?" That date means something to him, Sheldon thought.

"The digital archive copy says..." Gene selected an article from the drafting board. "It says there was a missing boy, Leon McCoy, who brought the whole community together. Your grandfather organized search parties to find the boy, and the Baldwin hired gun, or 'agent' as they called them back then."

Sheldon's palms were sweating. He wanted to hear more, but he feared Gene would say too much or just the right thing to give the Agent what he wanted—a pathway into the world.

"While the article only names some search party participants, it doesn't beat around the bush. The sheriff, the Wainscotts, the Mills, and the McCoys were more likely to fight than collaborate. But somehow, Sheriff Grace had the wisdom or the ignorance to unite them toward the same goal of finding the child. I wish I had all the old *Mercury* editions available electronically, but I don't."

Sarah said, "That's not the Leon McCoy who used to own the sawmills. The one who lives in the little shack on Cold Springs?"

"That's him, Sarah. Older than Methuselah but still kicking," Gene said. "Madden residents claimed it was a Baldwin detective who kidnapped him when he was a boy."

"Does the Agent have him? I mean, did an agent have the kid somewhere?" Sheldon realized he sounded off-balance, as if he might stumble into Gene's story.

"That's the funny part, Sheldon. I need to search the archives for more information, but the elite search party did not find the little guy. There is mention of a company detective as the primary suspect."

"Did the agent hurt the boy in any way?" Junebug asked. "What did the agent say when they questioned him?"

"The detective hightailed it out of Madden before they could even question him. They couldn't find him, and the other thugs had no idea where he was, or so they claimed."

"He ran away, or aliens abducted him. It's all too common, you know." Lilly grinned, poking her dad on the shoulder with her knuckle. Sheldon noticed a golden sun-shaped ring on her index finger.

Gene rolled his eyes. "The lede was this—a search party found the McCoy kid alive and well. He could not say much about how he got there, and the doctors said they found no injuries or any other kind of abuse if you understand me."

"So, where was he?" Sarah asked.

"Who? The detective?" Gene said.

"No, little boy McCoy. He was missing, right? Wasn't he somewhere?" Sarah asked. She looked at Sheldon, searching for confirmation.

"Another party discovered his clothes and then found him. The boy claimed he had fallen asleep in a holler three miles from his house. He did not remember going there and had no idea why he would sleep for thirty-six hours straight," Gene replied. "Most people didn't believe Leon's wild story, but he stuck with it. People speculated the agent did something nasty to him or Leon faked the entire incident, but the kid never wavered from his story. For years people called him Rip Van Tinkle."

"Dad, I am serious now," Lilly spoke up. "For centuries, there have been stories of sleep spells and curses. Where do you think the Snow White fairy tales originated? Washington Irving based *Rip Van Winkle* on tales handed down through time. Sleeping and returning to the world have been a classical trope since storytellers first spoke around the tribal fire."

"I'm not accepting that dwarfs abducted Leon McCoy and used poisoned apples to lull him asleep, Lilly," her father said. "Maybe Leon turned into a pumpkin at midnight."

"First," she replied, "you're confusing the dwarfs with the witch, and you butchered *Cinderella* and *Snow White*. There are many cases where long periods of sleep followed conflicts with black magic practitioners like a shaman, a witch, or an occult conjurer."

Shel appeared calm, but inside, his brain and heart were helium-filled balloons in a windstorm. *What if this counted as revealing the secret? Was the Agent here right now, watching and hearing everything? Was Evangeline safe if this opened the doorway for the Agent?*

Sarah stared at him. Often it was as if she got into his head like the Agent. *Don't tell. Stay quiet.* He sensed his silence concerned her more than his questions. He tried to think of something to say. "Mr. Begley, I will help you search for answers if you want me to."

"Sheldon," Sarah said, "this is a lot to consider. Gene, how does all of this relate to Willie's death?"

"Exactly," Gene replied. "That's what I cannot figure. It may have no connection. But who knows? If you help with research, you might see something I've missed. For all I know, Lilly's magical sleep spells and unicorn turds are the cause of all Madden County's woes."

"You want the world to make sense, Dad," Lilly said. She shook her head. "Often, reality derives from perceptions or myths. No matter how strange it is, what we ignore is a product of the real world. Mystery and history rhyme for a reason."

"Please tell me you don't use such a terrible line with your students," Gene said.

Chapter 35
The Progress of Production

The basement's fluorescent lights buzzed like flies and created the shadows Sheldon despised. Oversized leather-bound archive books resembling the vertical paneling outlined the walls.

All day, Sheldon had struggled to pay attention at school because Gene had promised to take him to see the archived *Madden Mercury* editions. Sheldon dreaded finding Barlow in the archives and the basement's dark corners. He envisioned Barlow's shadow hanging like a dark drape on a window, rustling each time they unearthed clues leading to what he was.

Now Sheldon's attention sharpened, and when Gene spoke, he took notice. At least Junebug and Ms. Begley were not tagging along this time. Although, he wondered if it might have been better to have Junebug in the room because even if the deputy's task was to spy on him and report to Evangeline, somehow, Sheldon trusted the young officer.

"One good thing about getting old, kids, is seeing the progress of production. Of course, now we don't bind hard copies. Instead, we drag them into a digital folder," Gene said. He ran his fingers across several years of shelved compendiums.

"These are all past newspapers?" Sheldon said. The collection was more extensive than he had expected.

"Correct," Gene said. He carried the same worn folder with bent corners and a coffee mug stain imprinted on the outside. "It is every edition except for the fall 1956 collection and the first two months of 1957. The printers stopped working due to a fire in their Madisonville plant. Wasn't much anyone could do about the situation. Today we have many options to get the paper out if our printing company closes. Also, new editions appear on the internet."

Sarah said, "There are so many editions in the archives, Gene. What do we hope to find?"

Gene walked to a table near the room's center. He pushed back an old clock radio, some paper clips, and two pairs of scissors to make room for his folders. He sat at the table and motioned for Sarah and Sheldon to join him.

The editor removed his black-rimmed glasses from his shirt pocket. Shel noted the tobacco dip and coffee stains near the collar.

"Over time, I have developed a subjective theory. Madden County has an underlying sense of shame, kids." Gene paused, then continued. "I know it's crazy. How can a *place* have shame for anything? How can it make itself sick with guilt? I have stories about my family's deeds that'd make Judas blush. I even imagine the Wainscotts and the Grace clan don't want their dirty laundry hanging in plain sight. But a place? How can a place feel shame?"

"Do you mean we are ashamed of where we come from?" Sarah spoke with authority. The old guy had built confidence and trust with Sarah. "I don't think so, Gene. We are a proud people in Eastern Kentucky."

"I understand, Sarah. There is much good about mountain folk and their pride in family and place. History shows Appalachian people have contributed much to America," Gene said, "but sometimes, our pride is too intense."

Sarah listened, but Sheldon wished Gene would get back to the articles.

"There's evidence we brought the clan mentality from Scotland and Ireland, where perceived weaknesses put you at risk. If you want a fight, insult a mountain boy or girl. Rather than our beautiful art and contributions to America, we are famous for feuds. Appalachia provided more than its fair share of soldiers to die in wars. The media told of great industries rising in cities all around us without ever mentioning who supplied the energy for the growth. Instead of celebrating, the world portrayed us as unwashed, uneducated, and violent."

"So, where does this shame come from, Gene?" Sheldon feared they had veered off subject. He needed to find anything to help against the Agent. Since Willie and Robert had carried the secret before him, maybe there was a clue about how he could reverse it. His neck muscles tightened, and his dread swelled. He did not have time for history lessons about Daniel Boone.

Gene frowned at Shel. "A difficult question to answer, son. I am speaking in metaphor—at least, I hope I am. Can all this dysfunction and bad luck be traced back to the past? Does it even make sense to speculate on such abstract concepts as shame and luck?"

He opened the folders, flipped through sheets of paper, photographs, and newspaper clippings, removed a creased black and white photo, and placed it on the table. It displayed a celebration or party happening in a school gymnasium.

Sheldon thought the photo appeared ancient, yet the person in the center resembled a younger version of his father. "That's my grandfather in the middle, isn't it?"

"That's him," Gene said. Sarah leaned in closer. "On his right is

George Wainscott, your ancestor, Sarah. He owned Madden Coal. Beside him is Calvin Mills, the miners' union leader. On Sheriff Field's left are Lloyd Ramey and Foster McCoy. Ramey was a scab organizer, meaning he helped non-union men get jobs in the mine during the strike. McCoy owned the biggest sawmill in Madden County. He was outside the conflict between the three others, but Leon was his boy."

"Who is the man with the sniffles?" Sarah pointed to a man standing to the left of Mr. McCoy. The camera had caught the man wiping his nose with a handkerchief. He was heavier than the other men and wore a suit jacket and a white shirt. He reminded Sheldon of his American History textbook and Theodore Roosevelt. Of course, it wasn't the president, but his shape and the way he stood gave him a presidential quality.

"Best I can tell, Pastor Zendell Adams from the Southside Madden Baptist Church," Gene said. "The sheriff insisted the preacher join his search party to find the kid and the Agent Barlow feller."

"Pastor Adams doesn't appear happy," Sarah said. "They don't want their picture in the paper."

Sheldon scrutinized the photograph. His grandfather wore a suit rather than a uniform, although the badge pinned to his lapel established who he was. Wainscott was taller than the others, and his short dark hair parted to the right. The other two men wore light-colored pants and white shirts. Mills had a vest, while Ramey's hat tilted low on his brow. The four faces appeared weary. The preacher stood apart from the others, leaving a gap between him and Mr. McCoy.

Of course, Shel had seen pictures of his namesake before and had examined old photos when Vangie and their dad would coerce him into shopping at antique shops. However, the people in this picture didn't pose like the ones in the stores. Instead, the four men appeared reluctant, side-by-side in a broken semicircle, their bodies slanted forward with heads lowered to conceal their faces from the camera.

"This picture bothers me," Gene said, poking the photo with his stubby finger. "For my life, I can't identify what it is. You have four men with conflict-filled pasts. They all took to the hills to find the McCoy boy and the company thug who kidnapped him. Even though they did not find the boy or the agent, the incident ended as well as possible. Why would they socialize at a little kids' celebration if they all hated each other?"

Sarah said, "Maybe my grandpa felt terrible that someone hired by his company kidnapped a boy?"

"Yes," Gene replied, "but that's the reason to stand tall and get his picture in the paper. He should want the citizens of Madden to know he helped the sheriff search."

Sarah turned to the picture. Sheldon was unsure if her silence indicated thoughtful examination or discomfort because of her grandfather's role.

Sheldon leaned toward the photo. He stopped breathing when he examined the gap between the pastor and Mr. McCoy. His chest tightened, and blood rushed to his head. Sheldon recognized what was happening in the background but could not comment without consequences.

"Where is the story with this picture, Gene?" Sheldon said, his calm concealing the storm inside him. He knew his words jeopardized everyone in Madden if he revealed too much.

"That's where your fresh eyes help," Gene said. "Although the editors before me did a good job saving the old editions, they did not catalog the articles, pictures, and exact dates. I was not a good steward of past editions either, so I am not sure where to go first."

"Seventy-six years ago. Start there," Sheldon said. Sarah's head tilted to the right like it always did when he said something surprising. A tentative smile appeared on Gene's face.

"A particular suggestion, Sheldon. What led you to an exact number?"

Shel recalled the Agent's words, *If I were about seventy-five years younger, I would carry a torch for that little mountain filly...*

"No reason," Shel replied.

Gene said, "That's as good a year as any." He pivoted and limped toward the shelves. He pulled out a large brown binder and carried it to the dusty table. It thudded like a slammed door when he dropped it on the surface. He brought a second book, placing it gently on the table this time.

"These books are from 1927 and 1928," Gene said. "There should be 110 issues total inside. I can't guarantee this picture and story appeared in *The Mercury*, let alone promise you it is a front page."

Chapter 36
One Innocent Question

Evangeline was seldom afraid. Her father had often told her she had inherited her grandfather's brain, her daddy's heart, and her mother's courage. As an officer, Evangeline could approach any situation, even the most dangerous, with resolve and a steady hand. Nonetheless, she felt safer because Art was riding shotgun.

"This place scares the shit out of me," Art said. "There are too many ways they can get you."

So much for confidence. "Put on your big girl panties, will you, Art?"

His laughter boomed through the vehicle.

Sand Gap was a fortress of trees, rocks, and winding roads. The journey required driving in a creek bed, then trudging through water, mud, and fallen branches. The sheriff knew Cyrus had guided them to the right place when she spotted a muscular man smoking a cigarette beside a small wooden shack. His black hair touched the shoulders of his Baltimore Orioles baseball jacket. He glared at Butcher, and Art returned the stare without blinking as the cruiser passed the Oriole.

Evangeline watched the man in the side mirror. The lookout took a final drag, discarded the cigarette, and rushed into the shack, cutting through the smoke like the cruiser's wheels in the creek water. "So much for the element of surprise," she said.

The sheriff heard Cyrus move in the backseat, just like Sheldon always had when her dad had taken them on long drives. Cyrus hunkered down, his body covered by a brown blanket.

Cyrus said, "We are almost there, Sheriff. Please be careful."

*****

Evangeline and Art studied the white house concealed by the trees. Weatherproofing plastic covered the front windows, and a box fan propped open the screen door.

A two-story barn with double-wide doors stood twenty yards away from the house. Ductwork connected a sizable central air unit to the barn, just as Cyrus had described.

A shirtless man worked on a Chevy pickup truck inside the barn. The man leaned under the hood—his legs dangled as if he was half-devoured by a shark.

The sheriff stopped the car before entering the yard to hide Cyrus. She and Butcher exited and approached the barn.

"Hello," Evangeline said. "We're not here to do anything other than have a conversation."

The man did not stop tinkering under the hood, but after a few moments, he responded, "Now, why would a law-abiding citizen think you were here for any other reason, Sheriff?"

The sheriff remained steady. "Perhaps because the men in the trees and the loft are aiming rifles at us."

Art glanced at her before rotating his head like a water sprinkler until he detected the snipers. Evangeline heard his hand touch his holster.

"They're just huntin' squirrels, Sheriff. Ain't nothin' wrong with good food, now is there?" The man slid from the shark's mouth and grabbed a towel. He wiped his hands as he exited the barn and met them face to face.

Oil and dirt marked his sculpted chest. Thick biceps flexed as he rolled the cloth between his hands. Not even the grease on his face and red hair could hide his youth. His white smile was as wide as the barn door as he addressed the officers.

"I'm Lonnie Boone, and I already know both of you. Sheriff, you were the best girls' basketball player I ever saw. We got free tickets to the high school games in elementary school. I attended every home game when I was a fourth and fifth grader. You never let me down."

The sheriff smiled. This guy was a smooth talker, which increased his potential danger. "Thank you, Mr. Boone. I hope you don't let us down today. We want to ask you some questions, but your men must take Deputy Butcher and me out of their sights. If they don't, when my other deputies and the state police show up with a warrant, they may have to use those guns. You know, on squirrels."

Boone laughed and scratched his head for several long seconds.

Evangeline watched the gun barrel slide back into a hole in the barn loft. The other rifles—one on the hillside and another mounted from a deer stand in an oak tree—disappeared. Art rested his palm on his firearm's grip as he stared straight ahead at Boone. When Evangeline nodded, the deputy removed his hand from the holster.

"Thank you again, Mr. Boone."

"For what, Sheriff?" His white smile returned, so she did not bother to respond.

*****

"Sheriff, if you think me or mine hurt Willie Grace, you best get in your car and head down the road." Boone took a moment to spit on the ground. "The way I heard it, he died in your jail. If you were dumb enough to put him in the general population, that's on you."

Evangeline felt the steam rising from Art. She hoped her partner would not break Boone in half. Her father had always said the more mouthy the criminal, the less likely they will try to kill you, but Boone was a dangerous talker and a candidate to be the Highlander. The men at this site worked for him and were willing to draw guns on police officers.

"Here's the thing," the sheriff said. "Your information is a bit unreliable. Willie was never in the general population, nor did he share a cell. It would have taken someone with a real grudge to risk sneaking into a jail, kill Willie, and escape unnoticed."

Boone was quiet for a moment. His hand rubbed his red hair, causing Evangeline to survey the background. The guns remained invisible, but that did not mean they were out of commission. She smelled the firewood burning in the house's fireplace nearby.

"Let's say me and my boys happen to know a little about the world." His voice was low, and he selected each word. "Just speculating, of course, but someone who could do what you're describing would have lots of balls, and by balls, I mean influence, deep pockets, and inside knowledge."

He motioned behind him. "We do good enough to earn a living, but we ain't far up the ladder. We ain't the ones you got to worry about."

Art spoke up. "What can you tell us about the Highlander?"

Boone's eyes grew wide, and he stepped closer. "That's not a polite conversation in mixed company, officer. Sometimes in Madden County, people get a taste of power and do whatever it takes to keep it. Willie might have been old, addicted, and even good to some of us, but he was not harmless. I cannot discuss people in these parts, especially the Highlander—assuming he exists, of course."

"Why not?"

"Because if there's anyone around here high enough on that ladder to wipe out Willie and people like me, it is that dude. Not much around Madden County scares me. Not even the two of you. But strong hands pull the strings around here, usually bringing people in from the outside to do the dirty work. Me and mine don't kill kids or old men who never hurt anybody unless there was a good reason."

It was Art's turn to whisper. "Just give us a name, and we are out of your business, at least for now."

Boone rubbed his chin, so Evangeline knew he was faking consideration. He didn't know the name, or he wouldn't have said anything.

Before he could offer bullshit, Evangeline interrupted, "If you don't want to share the name, that's fine. Just answer two questions. Did the Highlander and Willie know each other?"

"Everyone knew Willie Grace, Sheriff," Boone said. "He was an odd bird, but Willie was careful around people. The only time he ever got into it with anybody was when them two high school boys got killed. You remember when it happened?"

The sheriff pictured their bloated bodies snagged in fallen branches on the Big Sandy River. She recalled the parents on television saying their boys had not deserved to be tortured and killed. The media, including Gene, had put up their Little League baseball pictures from when they were eight years old. But even their friends admitted the teens had grabbed a beast they could not tame when they became drug kingpins.

Evangeline's breath caught in her chest. "Are you saying Willie had something to do with the murder?"

"Hellfire, Sheriff," Boone said. "I don't think you could tell

Willie Grace from Willie Nelson. Do you always think the worst of people?"

Boone's words stung.

"You explain it to us," Art said, moving closer to her.

Boone shook his head. "Old Willie told the Highlander's hired muscle to relay a message to the main man. Willie told him he was wrong if he had those kids killed. Willie even said doing something stupid like killin' boys would bring trouble their boss doesn't need. One man said it sounded a threat, Willie stood his ground, and he did not take it back."

"So they returned the threat?" Art said. He still hovered near Evangeline.

"Nope. Things went haywire for Willie. He went over the edge fighting the wind and yelling at the trees. Those guys told him to stop acting crazy, and the Highlander wouldn't like his opinion of what was happening. Another said Willie was getting so cuckoo that someone might have to put him down. I heard it from a reliable source who was there."

"Did anything come of it? Did they ever come to find Willie?" Evangeline said.

"I don't know nothing. But I will say I had suspicions about the Highlander when I heard someone murdered Willie. I wouldn't be talking now if I didn't think it was what you wanted to know." Boone whispered, and his head was down. "I've been standing here speaking way too long. Anyone sees this, and I will have something in common with those murdered boys, and it won't be our love of swimming. If I didn't like Willie..." Lonnie's voice trailed.

Evangeline nodded.

Boone saluted and walked backward toward the barn, still focused on the officers. Evangeline wondered if he had turned and sprinted, would she and Art have been the ducks at a shooting gallery?

"Wait," the sheriff said. "One innocent question." Boone

nodded but did not stop his slow retreat. "Why do they call him the Highlander?"

The shirtless man paused and again chose his words with care. "Why do they call you the Madden County Sheriff? Because it's where you do your business."

Chapter 37
A Broken Spine, Gnarled and Misshapen

It was Sheldon's first time traveling this dirt road. He knew he would remember the willow tree near Leon McCoy's homestead if he had been this way before now. The road was so mottled with potholes Junebug plodded along as if driving through a minefield, yet Sheldon focused on the crooked tree. The knotted trunk rose from tangled roots near a creek bank and covered the road like an umbrella. It was a disfigured spine, gnarled and misshapen—its leaves hung like hair strands half-covering a face.

Sheldon did not look away until Junebug said, "There's the house ahead under those trees."

The faded green exterior camouflaged the house behind the web of branches. Even the rusty tin roof blended into the rust-colored leaves. The only signs of life were the lights shining through the windows and the chimney smoke escaping into the cloudless sky. An army of dying horse weed stalks blocked the pathway to the porch.

"I guess that's a fixer-upper," Sarah said. She sat next to Shel in the backseat. He could feel her hand resting on his. "Junebug, are you sure he still lives there?"

"Calvin at the post office told me Mr. McCoy's Social Security check is delivered here every month," Junebug said. Sheldon saw the officer's eyes in the rearview mirror, the thin metal lattice making him appear as if he were in a cage. "He described it to a T, even telling me to be careful because the path is overgrown and as rough as the road leading here."

Sheldon placed his elbows on his knees. *He has to live here. If Gene believes this man knows something, maybe he can help me decide what to do.*

Sarah moved her hand to Sheldon's shoulder. *She must think I am crazy, but she is still beside me.* He turned his head to look at her face. Whenever their eyes met, he found hope.

"Well, lovebirds, don't just sit back there. Let's get moving," Lilly said as Junebug opened the backdoor.

Sheldon was not surprised Ms. Begley wanted to come along for an adventure like this. So what? She was much more likable than her father.

Junebug told everyone to be careful as he took the lead. He helped Lilly, so Sheldon offered the same assistance to Sarah as they traversed the incline toward the house. Everyone stopped when the teacher stumbled over something in the yard. A bell rang, and what sounded like pop cans and bottles rattled.

"There's a thin wire stretched across the path," Lilly said.

The moment she completed the sentence, the house's front door swung open. A middle-aged man stepped onto the porch, a double-barrel shotgun against his shoulder. "You all better hightail it back the way you come if you know what's good for you." He punctuated the statement by cocking back the hammer and panning the gun from person to person.

Sheldon, like everyone except for Junebug, froze. The deputy stepped forward, his hands raised. "Sir, I am with the Madden County Sheriff's Office. We are here on official business."

The man lowered the barrel several inches but kept the butt pinned to his upper arm. "You are up agin it if you ain't tellin' me the truth, Mister. It's only me and my daddy here, and we don't cotton to people showing up uninvited."

"I understand," Junebug replied. "I have some questions. Is your daddy Mr. Leon McCoy? He can help us solve an important case."

"Leon McCoy is my daddy. He hasn't been doing too good nowadays." Sheldon could hear the sadness in the man's voice. He lowered the shotgun a few inches more. "I can't let you talk to him unless he says it is alright." The gun barrel sprang upward again without warning. "If you kids are tricking us, I swear on my mamma's grave that I will fill you full of buckshot."

"Yes, sir," Junebug said. "Tell him we want to ask him about something long ago."

"Morgan," the man said as he walked backward on the porch. "That's my name. Morgan McCoy." When the man lowered the shotgun, Sheldon breathed again. Morgan's camouflage pants and dark brown work boots clashed with his blue, short-sleeved polo shirt. He was slight and appeared much shorter than when the gun was cocked and ready. His camouflage cap was brand new. "Y'all thirsty or hungry?" Morgan said as he opened the door.

Chapter 38
Gene Sheds Light

Gene stared at the overfilled folder on his desk and said, "I'm acting like a homeless prophet roaming the wilderness, shouting about the world ending. Lilly's superstitious mumbo jumbo might be onto something. This county is a haunted house."

He walked to the window. The sky was the color of a Black Birch tree, and the stars marked the textured bark.

As a beginning journalist, Gene wanted to write about how individual actions affected history. Too often, he thought, people pin significant events on some abstraction, like systems or culture. He sought the catalyst—the person or group whose actions set the timeline in motion.

He wrote stories about Broad Form Deeds when out-of-staters like Charles Beaumont came to the mountains and purchased the mineral rights to poor people's property. The buyers would pay a paltry sum, destroy the land, and extract the coal, profiting on the backs of the poor. It left many mountain people destined for poverty. Gene shed light on corruption in both political parties and the need for educational reform in Kentucky, finding the root causes and the critical players. He received accolades and death threats but never stopped tracing the river back to the spring.

Once two opposing candidates threatened to kick his ass when they saw him. In his following editorial, he wrote about how he brought the two parties together around a worthwhile common cause.

For forty years, Gene had studied what made the county tick but soon realized he didn't understand the county any more than he could figure out Lilly. Her mother was reasonable, but Lilly had a different perspective on the world even before college. The counties around Madden had weathered the storms, grown, and advanced, but Madden failed to do so. Instead, Madden fell victim to every scandal possible. The county's moral cables appeared more frayed with each challenge.

One thing was sure; it didn't add up any better now than it did back then. Long before the Willie Grace murder, Gene had struggled to find the root causes of the decay. The connections between the Mills, Grace, Wainscott, and McCoy families confused him. He witnessed deaths, suicides, ruined mountaintops, and destructive behaviors that clung to him like moss on a rock. The battles between the miners, the coal companies, and the environmentalists threatened to destroy the county and leave it empty, yet the feuding parties could not or would not find a compromise.

"Who knows?" Gene whispered. "Maybe the kids are the answer. They did a good job searching the archives." Then he remembered Sheldon's reaction to the photograph. It was as if he had recognized something personal in a picture from 1927.

*****

Gene grasped a folder on his desk and removed the elastic

band. He had scribbled a timeline across the landscape of two pages. *Maybe this time?* He lifted his red editing pencil and reviewed the articles, pictures, and timeline again, prepared to mark anything worthy of note.

He focused on the B Section stories rather than the front pages. These secondary articles were superficial—small stories about churches, school events, reunions, and celebrations. However, he realized no matter history's significant moments, the truth often hid in the tiniest corners.

He lifted the front page about the missing boy, and behind it was a story related to the celebration of McCoy's discovery. The heading read, "Madden Celebrates the Return of McCoy." The article thanked everyone who searched for the missing child. There was a picture of Leon sitting at a table in the Church of Christ Recreation room. He looked like he would prefer a bear trap over this party. His parents sat beside him, coaxing him to eat, Gene speculated and at least pretended he was happy.

However, a puzzling image in the background attracted Gene's eyes. He recognized Sheriff Sheldon Grace talking to Wainscott and Mills as the church pastor stood nearby. Robert Grace, the sheriff's oldest son, hovered close, too. Robert's face was stern. Right behind him, a shadow stretched across the wall. It was not the boy's shadow. Gene grabbed the magnifying glass he used to read small advertising text and examined the photo. It was impossible to find the shadow's source—because the shade from a porch overhang indicated the sun shined in the opposite direction. Gene was sure this shadow was a human figure, somehow captured in the darkness, its long fingers reaching toward the boy's frightened face.

After circling the figure in the photograph, Gene shuffled through the other pictures later in the timeline. He stopped at the photo of a studious kid with unruly brown hair and an insincere smile holding a certificate in the school library. The teen gripped the certificate's corners with his fingertips. His eyes turned to one side as if he was straining to see what was beside him. Again, the silhouette of a shadowy figure stood beside a boy, invisible unless the reader searched for it. The headline read, "Willie Grace Awarded Scholarship to Marshall University."

Chapter 39
Wwbcd

Sheldon squinted as his eyes adjusted. "Have I stumbled on stage at a Metallica concert?" He said, hoping Sarah could hear him. She covered her face with her arm while Junebug and Lilly turned away from the lights.

"Sorry if it's too bright in here, y'all," Morgan said. "My dad likes to keep the room lit up. Come in and have a seat." He motioned toward a well-worn vinyl sofa bookended by floor lamps without shades to dim their glow, causing them to gleam like two burning suns. A beige loveseat and a brown recliner faced the pea-colored sofa, and a spotless red rug pulled the room together. Someone had placed a straw chair in the room's center. Sheldon would forgive anyone for believing the straw chair was a star exhibit at a furniture museum.

Four bare 100-watt bulbs hung from a fixture on the ceiling. The glowing orbs remained imprinted on Sheldon's sight when he looked away. As the images faded, other lamps were visible on every surface around the room. Flickering candles rested on the mantel above the fireplace.

Two television sets near the couch competed for attention.

The larger one was broadcasting Kentucky Educational Television's *Comment on Kentucky*. The panel, arranged in a half-circle, stared into the camera as the host spoke. Sheldon's father had been a dedicated viewer. Evangeline had always joked there were three inevitable things in life—death, taxes, and Earl Grace watching *Comment on Kentucky* each week. Sheldon realized his sister had never pointed out that the first's inevitability negated the other two.

The second television featured a rerun of *Bonanza*. Adam, Hoss, and Little Joe rode their horses full throttle along a trail toward the camera. They fired their pistols at a target unseen until a fast edit showed several other men on horseback. Going back and forth between the dueling televisions made it easy to imagine that the Cartwright boys were firing at the panel of journalists on KET.

Sheldon and his dad had watched *Bonanza* reruns whenever they could. He wondered if Adam, Hoss, and Joe had ever fought a ghost—and what would Ben Cartwright do?

"What's up with the clocks?" Sarah said, her lips close to Sheldon's ear. The televisions made it challenging to hear her, but Shel shook his head back and forth in response. Instead of pondering her question, he spent the next minute or two inspecting each living room corner, searching for errant and ominous shadows.

Once Sheldon was confident the corners were empty, he examined the walls, tables, and shelves. Different clocks covered every surface not already hosting a lamp or candle, including the front wall where a seven-foot-tall grandfather clock stood. The clockmaker had carved branches and leaves into the hood and the stand, reminding Sheldon of the wild trees surrounding the house. In every direction, clocks glowed like collectible figurines. Maybe it was a clock museum rather than a furniture exhibit. Each timepiece, old fashioned to digital, indicated 6:34 PM.

Junebug scooted the straw chair across the rug to join the others near the couch.

"No," Morgan said. He rushed toward the officer and yanked the chair away, dragging it to the original spot. "This is Daddy's chair. Always."

Junebug showed his palms and walked to the recliner.

Morgan appeared embarrassed by his outburst. He nodded toward a hallway leading further into the house. "Let me see if Dad's interested in talking with y'all."

Sheldon, Sarah, Lilly, and Junebug were silent as Morgan exited. They watched him stop, knock, and enter a room in the hallway. When Morgan opened the door, sounds from yet another television wafted into the living room. Sheldon matched the voices to the *Comment on Kentucky* panelists on the set near him.

Junebug stood when Morgan reentered. Sheldon, Sarah, and Lilly followed his lead and rose. Morgan supported an older man in a white button-down shirt and a pair of brown pants. His long white beard and pale face merged with his shirt as if God had carved him from a single piece of pearl-colored stone. Even the wrinkles and lines on his face were strands of blanched threads. Morgan propped the man up with his shoulder and arm as they walked across the rug to the straw-bottomed chair.

Junebug stepped forward to assist, but Morgan shook his head and helped his father ease into the chair.

"Daddy, this gentleman is a deputy from Madden County. Him and his friends want to talk about something from the past." The gray man's eyes widened, revealing dark blue pupils in crimson and white. "You alright to talk to 'em for a little bit?"

Leon McCoy's lips parted. "Daggone it, Morgan put us some coffee on the stove." His voice was so sharp and clear Sarah jumped.

Leon surveyed Lilly, Shel, and Sarah before making eye contact with Junebug. "Boy, if you are here to discuss Agent Barlow and the past, I reckon you're about seventy-five years too late if you ask me."

Chapter 40
There's Nothing to Secure

Evangeline parked where the shortcut ended on Two Mile Mountain. Art helped Cyrus remove branches concealing the walking trail to the strip mine a half mile up the hill. Cyrus said the faster route was the gravel road on the other side. However, he and Willie always used the dirt road on the mountain's south side and then hiked to the massive flat at the top.

Cyrus led the sheriff and deputy along the steep pathway. The teenager swerved between the branches with phenomenal grace. Each step secured a foothold, and he pushed errant tree limbs away, ensuring they did not spring back to hit the officers.

Art's heavy steps, as well as his occasional growl, trailed behind Evangeline. Although Art was born in Madden County, he spent more time in the weight room than in the hills and wasn't crazy about off-road adventures.

"You okay back there, partner?" Evangeline said over her shoulder.

"Oh, I am living the dream," Art said. "I wanted to take a leisurely climb up a steep hill toward a nonexistent mountaintop since the thermometer passed eighty degrees this morning. I was enthusiastic when I heard the first clap of thunder predicting a hard rain on the horizon. I am happy there are still some stubborn gnats and skeeters around to provide atmosphere."

Evangeline laughed while Cyrus chuckled but focused on the trail ahead. "We are almost there, Deputy Butcher."

"Cyrus," Evangeline said, "don't worry about Deputy Butcher. He is a fragile flower, but he knows I will carry him if he needs me."

"I'll keep my mouth shut," Cyrus responded, "but to be honest, I don't believe you, me, and my granddaddy's old mule working together could pack him off this mountain."

Evangeline laughed.

"Alright, you two. If any gangsters heard us, they'd know to run before our jokes killed them," Art said as he returned to grumbling.

After hiking for ten more minutes, Cyrus stopped. Thick brush, trees, and a colossal moss-covered boulder obscured the pathway's end.

"Willie told me to stay hidden behind this rock and clump of trees while he met these guys on the other side of the flat," Cyrus said. "He told me, 'if I come running, you sprint to the car.'" Cyrus motioned toward two tall Poplars surrounded by bushes and Mayapple plants at least 300 yards across the field. "The men gathered around their trucks by the camper. Willie would shoot the bull with them for a few minutes, get what he needed, and return."

The land where the mountain once peaked was wide, long, and barren. The contrast between the dead mountaintop and the dappled hills was so stark the strip mine resembled the bomb site training video the feds had shown at an Indianapolis explosives seminar. The yellow dirt and the dried clay were devoid of life, but the bruise-colored clouds rolled, and gold, red, and green trees surrounding the flat leaned away from the upcoming storm.

"So, how did the dealers bring drugs up here?" The sheriff

removed binoculars from her belt and panned across the field. A rusted-out Ford truck and a pile of black garbage bags were beside the trailer 250 yards away. The space expanded further than her map had indicated, and a strip of bare, hardened ground stretched down the center.

"Sheriff, Willie claimed the guys watching over the site would shoot anyone who came up the road or this path before the pre-agreed time," Cyrus said. "I never witnessed anything but Willie slow-stepping to the camper and back here. I stayed hidden, or they might have put me in their sights. Willie said they were packing plenty of weapons, and he was the only person they allowed to come up an old logging road. He convinced them he walked the whole way."

"Speaking of weapons," Vangie said as she passed the binoculars to Art. "A guy just exited the trailer. He wants us to say hello to his little friend."

Art raised the glasses.

"Do you recognize him, Art?" Evangeline asked.

"He's Luke's first cousin, Jesse Porter. Luke said he got a job working security for a West Virginia coal company, so why is Jesse out here?"

"Good question. We should find out," Evangeline said. She circled the rock and bushes and walked onto the barren field.

"Hell," Art said. "Wait up, Sheriff."

The man in the distance carried a shotgun, so he needed to be closer to hit them. Besides, she recognized him now. He was Luke's older cousin. She remembered seeing him with Luke on Apple Day a few years prior. The clay crunched under her boots as she glanced at the sky to gauge the storm.

Art matched her stride for stride. "It is crazy for Jesse to be out here doing security. There's nothing to secure."

The sheriff nodded. "But he looks at home on this strip mine.

Those trash bags suggest Mr. Porter has camped on this ridge for a while."

"He realizes he has visitors now," Art said.

"He sure does," Evangeline said. "Let's see if he wants company." Evangeline dropped her hand, unsnapping her holster strap in the same movement. "Let's split apart, Art. We can't let him get both of us with one blast."

As they continued their approach, Art kneeled and pretended to tie his shoe. He drifted further to the left when he rose, creating distance from the sheriff.

Porter's brown coveralls and a blue baseball cap with "Purdue" embroidered above the bill did little to conceal him against the autumn trees, yellow soil, and gray clouds. He was Evangeline's height and thin, with an unkempt brown and white goatee framing his mouth. Porter cradled the shotgun in his arms, the barrel pointing toward the ground. Evangeline's father taught her to keep the sun over her shoulder whenever possible. However, the dark clouds made it irrelevant. Nonetheless, Porter's hand shielded his eyes as he tried to identify the visitors.

He straightened when he recognized them and stood still for a moment before backpedaling to a lawn chair near the trailer entrance.

She heard Art's holster strap click. Without checking, she knew Art rested his hand on his Glock, just as she did.

As the Sheriff and Art approached, Porter placed the shotgun on his knee, retrieved a pouch from his pocket, and stuffed something into his mouth.

Evangeline raised her hand and waived, releasing her light grip on her firearm.

"Hello, Mr. Porter," she said. "It's Sheriff Grace and Deputy Butcher." She was unsure he heard her until he waved. The shotgun pointed toward the dirt, but it would not take long to ready it.

Art said, "He's still clutching the shotgun like it is his baby. If two cops approached, wouldn't you put your gun on the ground?"

"Stay alert. If Porter shoots one of us, the other has to take him out." The sheriff drifted away from Art, creating even more distance. Jesse shuffled his feet but did not raise the gun from his lap or stand.

Art drew Porter's attention by yelling, "Hello, Jesse, it's Art Butcher. I haven't seen you since the car show in Pikeville."

As they neared, the man spat a giant brown meteor onto the ground near his feet.

"Howdy, Art," he said, a wide grin crossing his face. The chewing tobacco stretched his jaw as if he held a golf ball in his cheek. When he viewed Evangeline, the smile receded. "Hello, Sheriff. I heard you have been rounding up low lives. I didn't know a hard-working man like me was in your sights."

"Jessie," she said. "What reason would I have to hassle you? Unless you're doing what you shouldn't, right?"

"My job is to guard this property." He reshuffled his feet, turned to his right, and spit another brown gob of ambeer four feet across the ground. The spit lightened as it soaked into the earth.

"This property?" Evangeline said. "What's worth protecting out here?"

Porter's eyes surveyed the tree line across the flat. "I get the feeling you two ain't alone. Who did you leave behind the rock? Is your brother riding along with his sister?"

The sheriff turned but could not see Cyrus in the distance. "I don't know what you're babbling about, Jesse. Maybe you have been out here alone too long."

"I'm concerned," Porter said. "Luke mentioned you and that boy are close. I'd hate to see anything happen to him, you know, out on one of your fishing trips."

Porter smiled and reshifted his feet, but Art's humongous hand grabbed him by the arm and lifted him from the chair before he could conjure another spit.

"If I were in your predicament, I wouldn't make threats," Art said. "I would hate to see something happen to you out here by yourself." Porter's light blue cap shifted to one side of his head, causing his face to appear cockeyed. He yanked his arm, but Art's grip only tightened.

"Deputy Butcher, please unhand Mr. Porter. That's no way to treat an outstanding citizen. Besides, he received your message," Evangeline said. It was her turn to smile. "You get what the officer is saying, don't you, Jesse?"

Art released his hold and shoved Porter. Evangeline could tell by his tears Jesse had swallowed a healthy helping of his chewing tobacco. Nonetheless, Porter straightened his shoulders and frowned at Art. He clutched the gun closer to his chest. Evangeline figured the man realized he had no chance of getting into firing position before one or both officers planted a bullet between his eyes. Still, better to be safe than bloody.

"Mr. Porter," the sheriff said. Her tone softened. "This doesn't have to be so difficult. Tell me who employs you, and we can ask them why you are up here."

"Sorry, Sheriff. I have rules to follow, just like you do."

"We will haul your ugly ass into the station," Art said. "How about it?"

Jesse stared at the sheriff, ignoring Art's threat. "What'll be the charge, Butch? Sitting around, drinking coffee, and watching the opossums climb trees? You get a warrant and come back. Then you can search my fancy trailer." He motioned to the dilapidated camper. "It don't matter none to me. But don't bother bringing my cousin. He couldn't find wind during a tornado."

"We best get going, Deputy. This man's got opossums to protect."

Butcher wrinkled his brow for a second, then nodded to her.

"Mr. Porter, thank you for your time. There's a storm brewing. About how far do you think this flat stretches?" She motioned to the west.

"Well, I guess about 650 to 750 yards."

"Just what I thought," Evangeline replied. "Please put your gun on the ground and sit in your comfy chair. I would hate to mistake a trip to the trailer to get coffee for you retrieving a rifle. Hear me?"

Porter nodded, placed the shotgun on the ground, and sidled toward the lawn chair.

Evangeline and Art edged toward the path where Cyrus waited.

"Take care, Mr. Porter," the sheriff said. "We'll catch you later."

The officers glanced over their shoulders to ensure Porter followed instructions. Leaning forward, he reminded Evangeline of a lizard lounging on a rock.

The sheriff said, "Art, do you see those tire tracks running toward us from the north?"

He did not stop but glanced downward. "Yes, I see them. Are you thinking of three-wheel ATVs? Those are big around here."

Evangeline did not respond. "Let me show you this cool trick I learned from a much older colleague." She dropped to one knee to tie her shoes, then placed her palms on the embedded tracks. Two hands wide, she thought. She extended her hand for Art to help her stand.

"Art, we might be able to solve this yet."

Chapter 41
The McCoy Story

Although Sheldon seldom drank coffee so late in the day, he sipped from his cup and listened to Leon McCoy. Everyone did.

"When I was a boy, mountain people wanted to be left alone. My daddy and the coal companies and miners worked hard, sold their labor and goods, and made a living from God's gifts to us—above and below the ground. We kids didn't have any sense. Hell, we thought Madden was the whole world." McCoy gulped his coffee and held out the cup for Morgan to fill. The son responded as if it were a daily ritual.

"If somebody went to Huntington, they'd gone to the big city. My daddy's people came from Ireland. They cut timber by hand and grew 'baccer on any flat land they could find. They had my brother, my three sisters, and me. I was the youngest, and they spoilt me like year-old milk."

Sheldon shifted on the sofa. His fear that McCoy's ramblings might trigger Barlow's rage made him anxious. *Get to it, old man.*

McCoy turned toward him as if he felt Sheldon's impatience. "You young'uns want the answers before you know the questions. I see it on the TV. Some day people will blame the Baby Boomers for creating this mess."

"Please, Mr. McCoy, continue," Junebug said.

"The devil is in the air, the water, and people's hearts, Deputy. Been there since 1927. Listening to an old shit like me for a few minutes don't add up to a weasel's pecker of time."

Sheldon straightened and stilled his racing mind. He stared at the man's weary face but did not apologize. Instead, he nodded and curbed his impatience.

"I was one of those kids who thought nothing could hurt me, so I didn't fear Baldwin Detectives or Pinkertons no matter how tough they acted." He sipped from the cup. "They come into Madden to put fear in the hearts of men. But see, I was no man. I was just a boy. What scares boys ain't real. They are afraid of ghosts and boogiemen under the bed, so they can't tell danger in life when it walks up on them like a rabid dog."

Sheldon felt a dread stir in his stomach. Although the lamps and candles illuminated the room beyond comfort, he searched the walls for well-dressed shadows.

"After the rain let up, me, your uncle, Robert Grace, and two other kids played pickle in the courthouse yard. Old men squatted on the courthouse wall, watching us. Me and Robert threw the baseball, and we had one runner trapped between the bases. The kid ran right toward Robert, and I hauled back to make the throw."

McCoy halted, drank coffee, and asked Morgan to refill. Leon's hand was less steady than before, causing the cup to tremble. Morgan held his father's hand level as he poured.

Junebug must have noticed, too. "Go ahead, Mr. McCoy. You are talking about the very time we want to discuss."

Leon McCoy's red eyes were moist. "You've done it, Deputy. Sometimes, boys make rash decisions for the wrong reasons. When I saw him walking the wet sidewalk behind Robert, I decided in a half second to do something that would last a lifetime."

"Who did you see?" Lilly asked after McCoy paused. She glanced at Junebug, then settled back in her seat.

"Everyone hated him. He walked with other detectives, wearing his fancy pressed suit and the damn hat like he was in the Sears catalog. All the agents enjoyed strutting like roosters near the courthouse yard, but he was the cock of the walk."

Again, McCoy stopped and swigged the hot coffee. Sheldon peered at Morgan, expecting him to refill the cup, but the son focused on his father's story.

"You know, God blessed me with a good arm. Other boys used to say I could knock a fly off a turd without getting a smudge on the ball. Ain't that funny?"

No one responded. Sheldon's breathing stopped, and he scanned the room for the Agent again. This innocent story scared him more than Evangeline's ghost stories about graveyards and dead men's fingers.

"It was the worst Baldwin agent. He was mean and ornery, always bullying every man and woman in Madden. He called Mary Beth a little whore because she was out of shoe polish at the store. He used to pull an ivory-handled knife to show it off. He said it was his "gutter" for anyone who'd cross him. He threatened to cut men if they didn't tell him about union meetings and plans to strike or vandalize the company. He was vile. Everyone, including the other detectives, called him the Agent."

Hearing the name spoken caused Sheldon to fold his hands and close his eyes as if in prayer.

"So I did what any fearless boy with a good arm would do. I chucked the ball over Robert's head right at the sucker's legs. It hit short and landed in a mud hole. Mud and water splashed up on his pants, suit jacket, and shiny shoes."

The room was silent until Junebug asked, "What did the detective do?"

"He turned and stared like he was painting my portrait. By this time, people had commenced laughing, and the boys with me—including Robert—snickered like the teacher had split his pants at the chalkboard. I was too brave or stupid to run. I stood there amidst the laughter, letting it all soak into me.

"What's the matter, Agent?" I said, standing my ground as only a little shit can. "Mr. Grayson says you've been buying chickens at his farm. People claim you are doing bad things to them hens. Good lord, buddy, can't you find yourself a girlfriend?"

"Everybody howled. Even the other detectives could not contain it. My friend Jacob folded his arms into wings and strutted around, flapping as he sang, 'Bok-bok-bok!'

"I jumped back into the spotlight, waved to my audience, and bowed like Mrs. Gesner had taught us during the Christmas play. People clapped and whistled.

"The Agent stared at me like he was examining a lightning bug in a jar—deciding if he'd let me go or squash me between his fingers. Everyone stopped laughing as he marched toward me while shoving his hand into his snazzy jacket. I recall every moment. I thought he planned to shoot me, and his face caused me to piss in my pants. One agent followed behind him and said, 'Agent, he's just a kid.'"

"However, the Agent did not retrieve a gun. Nope. He removed a small bottle and poured dark liquid on his palms. He rubbed his hands together like he wanted to spark a fire. But picture this—his eyes never blinked or wavered from my face.

Then he threw his head back and laughed. It broke the tension. I exhaled when he stopped in front of me. He grinned, and he did not pose any threat. Or at least I believed he meant no harm.

"He playfully patted me on my cheeks with his long, stained fingers."

Sheldon observed McCoy's face. It morphed from animated to distant as if he was reliving a confounding memory. The story-teller raised his hand to his sagging cheek. His fingers indented the skin and slid toward his chin as though wiping away an invisible scar.

The alarms split the silence with total disregard. The clocks on the walls, the floor, the mantle, and the tables blared, bleated, chimed, vibrated, and reverberated. Sarah jumped as if electricity coursed through her. Lilly, startled, grabbed Junebug's arm and fell toward him. Sheldon's hot coffee splashed onto his lap. Shock registered on Junebug's usually stoic face.

Only Leon and Morgan did not react to the clocks. They remained seated as the alarms halted their assault, reverting to quiet ornaments bathed in bright lights.

"I should have warned y'all 'bout the clocks," Morgan said. "We're used to it, but I guess it can put the fear of God in you if you never expected it. Years ago, my daddy used to get sleepy, so we set the alarms."

Sheldon, Sarah, Junebug, and Lilly wiggled in their seats.

The old man chuckled. "Looks like y'all about pissed your pants as I did back in '27 at the courthouse."

Sheldon swallowed, then spoke. "What happened next, Mr. McCoy?"

"I stood still as a wet bale of hay. Light brown fingerprints marked my face," McCoy said. "The Agent pivoted like a soldier and marched toward his buddies. They walked away as if nothing had happened. I figured I had dodged an ass-whooping or worse. But I would've been better off with a broken nose."

"What do you mean, Mr. McCoy?" Junebug asked. Lilly's hand remained on the deputy's arm.

"That night, I dreamed my parents called to me. They kept pleading for me to find them in the woods. 'We need you, son,' they begged over and over again. I searched, but branches and briar patches clung to my clothes, ripping the fabric and drawing blood. I worried my mom would get mad, so I pulled off my shirt, pants, and shoes. Even though the limbs and briars were leaving gashes on my naked legs and shoulders, I searched behind every tree and rock. Soon, the nightmare became heavy—it felt like I was carrying logs at the sawmill. It burdened me more with each step until I rested amongst the stones and thorns.

"I was butt-naked, frozen, covered in ants, curled up in a ball when they found me. My mouth felt like a bird's nest, and welts covered my legs. They reached into the dreamy fog and delivered me out of it. A man shook me, and I yelled for my mommy and daddy like a two-year-old. Finally, I settled down until they told me I had been missing for two days. I called them liars and busted out crying again."

Sheldon glanced at his friends. They were leaning in, just as he was. However, Leon McCoy did not speak next.

Morgan said, "My grandpa would not let Dad out of his sight. Of course, he went to school, but not much else. When Daddy met my mom, Granddad used the sawmill to build this little house." Morgan walked to the mantle and picked up a faded picture in a simple silver frame. He passed it to Junebug so everyone could see. Leon, at about thirty years old, stood beside an attractive redhead. Her arm stretched across his shoulder as if she was protecting him.

"She's my Dora," Leon said. "She passed back in 1995, so it's been seven years. Such a fine woman deserved so much more than me. After she died, I sold my stake in the sawmill, set aside all of it, and made it so Morgan could stay with me now but have a good life even after I joined Dora."

"He ain't left the house since Momma passed on," Morgan said. "My job is to watch out for him."

"You never leave the house?" Sarah asked Leon.

"That's right," Leon said. "Two things I don't do is sleep more than I have to and go out into the world."

Sheldon planned to ask what he thought the Agent had done to him, but Leon spoke first.

"The evil man did something to me. The sheriff said he didn't expect the Agent to return to Madden County, and I've never laid eyes on that scoundrel again. But call it what you want—hypnotizing, casting a spell, or even voodoo—the Agent got in my head and my dreams, and I have never gotten over it."

Sheldon understood McCoy but could not express it while Junebug, Sarah, and Lilly waited for him to say more.

"But the northerner taught me a lesson," Leon said. "We believe we'll wake up to the same world we left when we lay our heads on the pillow. He showed me clear as a raindrop. Some evil people can haunt your life long after they leave. They can make sure nothing is ever the same."

Shel's heartbeat increased, and his hands shook. He could imagine Barlow's shadow, Uncle Willie's mutilated body, the letter, and a life where nothing would ever be the same.

Chapter 42
Earl Will Be Proud

"You are joshing me, Evangeline?" Art said. He placed his elbows on her desk and whispered, "You better be certain because if we screw this one up, there will be a price to pay."

"It is more than a hunch. I spent the last twenty-four hours researching my theory," the sheriff said. She leaned back in her chair. "Things add up. We will ratchet up the pressure and find out. This search warrant is the first step of dethroning the Highlander."

"After all this time taking down small-time drug distributors to find the big daddy, Cyrus takes us to the clues we needed all along," Art said. "Amazing. We do this right, and Earl Grace will be proud of the whole department, especially you."

Evangeline smiled and nodded. "We got lucky, Art. It hinges on this warrant. To be the Highlander, you must have the infrastructure to make it happen, including inside information. I don't know the details, but someone will turn and talk."

Over the past two weeks, Evangeline's Louisville dream had intensified. It was the fourth quarter, and her opponents held a six-point lead with time expiring. But now, with this impending bust, she stood on the foul line with a chance to win the game. Although she could not connect the Highlander directly to Willie's murder, they would leverage the drug bust to untangle Willie's death. She could leave Madden behind as she had always planned. No guilt or shame. Her father would be proud, indeed.

Paulene stepped into the sheriff's office. "A State Policeman delivered the search warrant, Sheriff. He said to tell you well done, and the judge agreed to every term." She passed the document across the desk and patted Art on the shoulder.

Evangeline stood, grabbed her keys, and said, "Art, you ride with Luke. I want to talk to Junebug."

*****

Evangeline sensed Junebug's reluctance, but she needed to know. "This is a short drive, Junebug," she said. "Can you shine a light on Sheldon's crazy behavior?"

Junebug shifted in the passenger seat and fiddled with his camera before speaking. "He is a good kid, Sheriff."

"Don't worry, Junebug, I don't want to lock him up. I'm just worried. He has been through a lot, but there is more to it. He isn't himself, and I need to know what's causing the change."

He lowered his eyes again. "Sheriff. I have to admit something. I'm uncomfortable talking about him. Over the past few days, I have gotten to know him a lot better—"

Evangeline stared at Junebug. Her father had taught her the power of intense eye contact by applying it to her whenever his patience ran out. Earl Grace never demanded loyalty, but his people understood.

Junebug cleared his throat. "Sheldon and Sarah talked to Gene at the newspaper. They are checking on the history of Madden County and—"

"Dammit. I knew Shel was falling for Gene's bullshit," Evangeline said as she tapped the steering wheel with the heel of her hand.

"All due respect, Sheriff, but I don't know if it's bullshit or not. Mr. Begley sent us to talk to Leon McCoy over on Wolf Creek," the deputy said. "He told us about what happened to him as a child. I don't know where it fits, but it sure shook Lilly, Sarah, Sheldon, and me."

"Of course, it's a good story, Junebug. It figures Gene would send you on a snipe hunting expedition," Evangeline said. "He is still laughing about it, I bet."

"Lilly went with us, Sheriff. So he sent his daughter snipe hunting, too. I am a rational guy, not into the crazy theories, but more is going on here than we first figured."

"Did Sheldon act peculiar in any way? You know what I mean. Did my brother do anything strange or act like he was losing his mind?"

"He's a teenager, Sheriff," Junebug said. "When I was in eleventh grade, my mom ran off, and my dad took to drinking every day. By the time I graduated high school, I was so mixed up I thought... Well, let's say I didn't have good thoughts. Sheldon acted depressed or even paranoid, but he is a good kid going through a rough patch."

Junebug's forthright response caught Evangeline off guard. He was always so quiet, even private. She knew little about how he grew up. His answer revealed passion and compassion, which pleased her.

The deputy cleared his throat. "Nothing I saw indicated he was using drugs or drinking. Was he jumpy and hyper? Yes, and he was distracted at times. But I don't think he is using pills or alcohol. Sheldon is troubled about what happened and is willing to investigate his concerns. He is a lot like you, Sheriff."

Evangeline contemplated the cruiser's windshield before responding. "I'm worried he is more like his Uncle Willie."

"I know, Sheriff," Junebug said. "I will watch out for Sheldon. But if this case gets any stranger, you may need someone to follow me around, too. I hope this raid leads to the answers."

"Thank you, Junebug," Evangeline said. Although she trusted Bug, she had never witnessed Willie using drugs, either. Families never see the addict using. They only experience the consequences.

At least, if she and the team ended the Highlander, she could mail the contract and leave Madden with a clearer conscience. She could pull Sheldon away from this place, away from the dysfunction swirling around like flies. She peered off into the distant hills where fingers of fog clung to the trees, unwilling to let go.

Chapter 43
I Have Fought the Good Fight

Sheldon stood before his uncle's tombstone. The gray and silver granite read, "Robert M. Grace, August 10, 1914, to October 21st, 1943." The engraver had etched a Bible verse beneath the dates, which read, "I have fought the good fight, and I have finished the race. I have kept the faith. 2 Timothy 4:7."

Sheldon slid his hands into his jacket pockets. The sun's angle made the gravestone's shadow lean backward away from him, and in the distance, he could hear a coal truck revving its engine as it climbed a steep hill.

"I figured you would follow me here, Agent," he said, his voice weaker than he wanted it to sound.

Shelly Bean, I will be your companion forever unless you make me free. You don't have to introduce me to everyone, just someone. How hard can it be? The Agent's words flowed inside Sheldon's head. Barlow enjoyed his superiority.

Sheldon traced the wind's movement, following its gentle wave as it brushed the treetops. The Grace-Wilson Cemetery sat on the slanted hillside, surrounded by life and death. Yet, examining his uncle's grave, the faded plastic flowers in white pots resembled painted coffee cans with handles. Sheldon wondered if the mountain existed to hold up mounds of dirt and artificial flowers in rusty tin containers.

As long as the Agent was in his life, Sheldon's existence would be artificial—acting alive but not living.

"Maybe I should tell someone and be like my Uncle Robert," Sheldon said. "You know, there is plenty of room for me here in the garden."

Funny, boy. You are a regular Buster Keaton. The shadow rose from behind the stone as if ascending toward the sky.

The distorted silhouette towered above the marker. It twisted and contorted as if the wind was creating waves on a distorted television screen.

Telling the secret would be fine. Maybe I could cut your sister before you hit bottom like your Uncle Bobby. I almost cut young Willie's throat before Robert crashed on the rocks. Then, I would have been free. You and I would not be chatting at these happy holes. No need. I would have shed this dog of a county of all its blood-sucking fleas.

Sheldon refused to buckle or react. He stood still like the angel statues planted beside several graves.

"How did Uncle Willie know you could kill anyone you wanted if he died with the secret? He knew if two people carried the secret, you would become solid. So why did you kill Willie and become a shadow again?"

Willie had it coming. That strange bird suffered rather than follow my orders. Do you see why I made him hurt so bad? I hated everything he said and did.

"He got to you, then," Sheldon said, smiling. *I will give him a chance to talk.* "But how did you learn to be a ghost?"

I inherited it from her. The Agent's voice shifted like the coal truck's gears in the distance. *My Vadoma taught me how to control the future, the people around me, and even life and death. That was* her gift to me." Her teachings and the books she provided told me how to go beyond her substantial powers.

Sheldon sensed the smirk and arrogance emanating from the dark figure and wanted the Agent to keep babbling. "So she was your mom or something?"

The rules—she taught me the rules. For a curse to settle into the bones, you have to let the cursed know, then their heart fills with terror and dread. The Agent's words continued to ring inside Sheldon's head. I told Robert too much about the curse of secrets because I wanted all of Madden County to fear me, and I was confident he would be weak.

"What did we do to you? You are the one who kidnapped a little kid. All my grandfather and the other men did was try to catch you. You were free of Madden County yet decided to come back. Why would you return if you hate it so much?"

A shriek ripped through Sheldon's mind. He covered his ears with his palms not to block the noise but to keep his head intact. As the pain made a winding path through his mind, he fell to his knees beside his uncle's grave. The Agent's piercing anger thundered inside his mind.

When the shriek stopped, Sheldon rolled onto his back. The dirt and a pile of brown leaves beneath him were a pillow, steadying his pounding head. All was silent as he stared at the azure sky for a moment.

You are so much less than even your Uncle Willie, as pathetic as he was, the Agent said. You will break, and then I will slice Madden County's throat, Sheldon Grace.

Within moments the Agent was gone. The snake shed its skin inside his brain. Sheldon did not attempt to stand. Instead, he stared at the brown, red, and green leaves and beyond into the sky. He wanted to go home, but it seemed farther away than the sun above him.

Chapter 44
We Are Never as Tall

The small waiting room was packed. An old woman, her hair gray and pulled back in a bun, sat next to a younger woman in jeans and a red collared shirt with "General Dollar" embroidered near her left shoulder. A young woman with long red hair sat with a baby on her lap, and a little dark-haired boy sat in the seat next to her. A man sat across the room, his green shirt pocket tight with a pack of cigarettes and a black comb. A young man with thinning brown hair sat in the next chair. His black Madden Coal Company jacket opened at the collar, and a Cincinnati Reds baseball cap rested on his knee. A man in a blue blazer, a white shirt, and a red tie read a magazine in the final seat.

Evangeline nodded to everyone and approached the woman sitting behind the safety glass at the front desk.

"I need to see Dr. Bell," the sheriff said.

"I am sure he will see you right now, Sheriff. He often speaks fondly of you." The woman's name tag read Karla, but Vangie knew everyone called her Kay-Kay. Kay-Kay picked up the phone and said, "Tell Dr. Bell the sheriff is here to see him."

A blonde assistant at the side door said, "Sheriff, you can come on back."

Before entering, Evangeline clicked the button on her walkie-talkie and said, "Yes, let's head back to Dr. Bell's office."

Dr. Bell was waiting in the narrow hallway. His traditional white lab coat was cleaner than it had the right to be, and a stethoscope hung loosely around his neck. Daryl's sharp blue dress shirt, black pants, and the shiniest black shoes Evangeline had ever seen perfectly matched. His white smile and gleaming blue eyes made him resemble the winning coach after the final buzzer. Evangeline guessed he thought she was the trophy.

"Finally, you're taking time for a check-up," he said. Dr. Bell put out his hand and guided Evangeline toward an examination room. He looked like an actor playing a doctor on television. "You are my top priority, so step in here."

"Dr. Bell, can we talk in your office first?"

"Sure." His smile dimmed as he guided her down the narrow hallway. They passed a framed print on the wall displaying an adult swimmer helping a child out of the pool. The caption read, "We are never so tall as when we kneel to help a child."

His office was a monument to himself. Athletic trophies adorned the shelves, and framed photographs hung along the walls. Each picture displayed a younger Bell with his arms stretched upwards in triumph. His large oak desk showed perfect rows of files, medical books, and a model airplane sitting atop a small woodblock. The wall outlined his path to becoming a physician with diplomas from the University of Illinois and the University of Kentucky Medical School, accompanied by graduation photos.

Evangeline spoke first. "This is a huge building, Dr. Bell. Especially since your waiting room is tiny, you have quite a bit of available space."

"If you hope to purchase this piece of real estate, Sheriff, I'm afraid this building is not on the market." He smiled to send the impression he was joking, but his eyes indicated otherwise. His pedicured fingers twirled a paperclip.

"Do you often make it back to Chicago, Dr. Bell?" Records cataloged his frequent trips to Illinois.

"Once or twice a year, I visit my mother and her husband," he said. After a pause, he added, "But Madden is my home. I love it here. You should visit my house. Maybe for dinner."

"You fly to Chicago, don't you, Darryl?"

"Usually," he said. "It is a short trip, and the airport is near my family... That's an odd question, Evangeline."

"You also fly your Cessna down south often on weekends, don't you?"

Bell opened his mouth to reply, but a loud knock interrupted. Kay-Kay entered and said, "Dr. Bell, I am sorry to bother you, but more officers are here. Several are from the state police."

Dr. Bell glared at Evangeline. He no longer extended kindness and hospitality, and intensity pushed aside his boyish charm. "What is going on here?"

The sheriff removed the warrant from her pocket. "Darryl Bell, this is a warrant to search your facility and inventory documents for excessive prescription drugs and illegal distribution. Also, we will search for any illegal substances or weapons."

Dr. Bell snarled as he read the document. "You don't know what you are doing, Sheriff."

Evangeline did not want to explain more without another officer present. She clicked her radio. "Officer Butcher, please come to Dr. Bell's office."

As Art entered, Junebug and State Police officers walked single file down the hall toward the backdoors, as she had instructed. Art stopped near the chair beside her but did not sit. He greeted Dr. Bell with a nod. "We are here to enact a search of your—"

Before Art finished, Dr. Bell waved his hand. "I know how this goes, Deputy Butcher. I want my lawyer to read this before you search an inch of this place."

"Then you don't know how this goes, Dr. Bell. I have served the warrant, and we proceed with the search right now," Evangeline responded.

Chapter 45
The Clockmaker

The sheriff smiled when Bell's head fell back to stare at the ceiling.

She felt like the clockmaker her father had wanted her to be. Realizing the Highlander had inside connections, Evangeline had asked the Assistant State Attorney and the State Police to apply for a search warrant from a judge in Frankfort. When she and Art had questioned Jesse Porter on the ridge, she had matched the tire treads to a Cessna 172 plane. It hadn't taken long to identify Dr. Bell as the only pilot in Madden County owning a Cessna 172.

"You know, when we questioned Jesse on the ridge, he wore a Purdue baseball cap. I realized the emblem didn't match the university's colors, so I looked it up. It was the logo for Purdue Pharmaceuticals, the drug maker." Evangeline did not mind giving Bell this information. She hoped it would divide the doctor and Porter. "Pharmaceutical companies love to hand out freebies to doctors and pharmacists, who give them to employees."

Bell looked toward the wall to conceal his anger.

Evangeline said, "I saw the consequences of Oxy at a middle

school football game recently. It almost killed a mom and dad right in front of their son." Evangeline paused, then said, "Instead of being a good physician who used opioids to help those in severe pain, you distributed drugs to increase your riches."

She glanced at Art, unsure if his smile was due to Bell's discomfort or because she had noticed the logo when he had not.

"But it wasn't enough, was it, Darryl?" she said. "You extended your operation to illegal substances like heroin."

The sheriff wanted to add to his discomfort, but she resisted. She had researched Bell's former office in Chicago. He claimed to have sold the practice, but his name remained on the lease. He received frequent shipments of prescription drugs at that location. She had verified Bell used fake names and prescriptions to distribute those drugs in Kentucky, West Virginia, Ohio, and Florida.

"We even know the distribution sites you use in the county," she said. "I thought the medical profession stopped using leeches a long time ago. I guess not, since you are leeching off people's suffering here in Madden County."

Bell's breathing was a slow, deliberate rhythm. He adjusted the stethoscope around his neck every few seconds.

"Soon, we will have your accomplices and patients. One will cut a deal and spill their guts about killing Uncle Willie and Ricky Jenks and Lee Kirkland," Evangeline said. "You brought poison into the county. It's time you get a dose of it, as well."

Dr. Bell froze, then said, "Wait a minute. Do you believe I had something to do with the Willie Grace murder? You are insane, Sheriff." Spittle gathered around his lips, and his eyes widened. "I did not. No way."

"Really, now? I guess the big bad Highlander would not kill anyone? What do you think happens when you sell enough pills to kill everybody in the county, Darryl? Four people have over-dosed and died since Labor Day. Numerous others stepped onto

Death's porch and will probably revisit him soon. You are a doctor. By the way, you did not deny killing the high school kids, did you?"

She watched the physician squeeze his hands into fists. "I did not kill those boys, but I can name names if you give me something in return." He turned his attention to Art. "Deputy Butcher, make her see I do not know anything about her uncle, so don't let her try to tag me with it. I want my attorney."

Art said, "So, you know your rights, don't—"

A series of loud pops punctured the air, rolling up the hallway like an oncoming storm.

*****

"Junebug, do you copy?" Evangeline spoke into the microphone as she cracked the office door. She retrieved a bike mirror and held it to peer down the hall. The commotion—gunshots, shoes clicking against a concrete floor, and yelling—originated in the storage area. She smelled gunpowder. The sheriff drew her firearm and stepped into the empty hallway. "Bug, talk to me. Do you copy?"

"I copy, Sheriff," Junebug replied. "Two shooters, maybe three, hiding. We caught them with the door propped open, loading a truck with contraband. One state trooper shot."

"Condition?" Evangeline said. She kept her back against the wall while sidestepping down toward the warehouse.

"Bleeding from the right shoulder. Big hole. I'm applying direct pressure," Bug said. Evangeline could hear the trooper moaning. Although the deputy's words came in short bursts like gunfire, his tone was urgent yet calm. "Be careful, Sheriff. One shooter is behind the boxes at two o'clock when you enter from the hallway. Second shooter is near the propped-open back door behind an overturned table. The trooper fired twice before taking cover

235

behind some empty boxes. Not good cover. Not sure if there's more."

The sheriff felt her blood pressure rise. Whenever Evangeline heard gunshots, it triggered her father's words about the Vietnam War. In 1965 he dropped out of Morehead University to join the Marines. In basic training, he had spent hours assembling and disassembling his rifle. His sergeant tattooed the process on his brain. "I could still do it over thirty years later," he had told the department. "After weeks, a private asked the Sarge why we practiced so much. Sarge squinted and replied, 'Because you asswipes won't be able to think when you are under fire. Your brain will shift into low gear, and you won't be able to tie your boot, let alone ready your weapon. It would be best to be so automatic you don't have to think. You just do it.'"

Her father had continued, "If you stay calm, you can use your brain's creative and organized parts to solve problems. It applies to any conflict or situation."

Evangeline clicked the radio. "Art, call for an ambulance, then get out here. Junebug, don't let the trooper die. We are on the way."

*****

Art had secured Bell to a file cabinet, called an ambulance, and drew his handgun before stepping into the hallway. Evangeline leaned against the wall near the warehouse doorway. She pointed her gun toward the floor.

Art was amazed at how the sheriff handled stressful situations. She remained calm, as if the pressure that dulled others sharpened her.

The deputy slipped into position next to the sheriff. Evangeline shoved her head against his shoulder and said, "I have a plan, but I need your help."

"I can charge in there and draw fire, and then you follow and take them out. I heard the trooper on the radio, and it sounds like there isn't much time left," Art said. Before he finished, he knew it was a no-go because the sheriff shook her head.

"See if you can get them talking," Evangeline said.

The sheriff slid past him and sprinted back toward Dr. Bell's office. Art cross-stepped closer to the warehouse doorway.

"This is the Madden County Sheriff's Office," Art said. "We have more State Police on the way here. You don't get out of this, boys."

No one responded.

Art waded into the silence. "Listen to me. You can turn yourself in right this moment, and everyone gets the best outcome they can hope to get. But if you sit on your thumbs for too long, the state trooper you shot might not make it. Then you're staring at the death penalty."

"Death penalty?" Art recognized the voice but could not place it. The yell came from behind the overturned table near the concealed back door and drifted through the warehouse. Art separated from the wall and entered the warehouse door with his gun raised above his head.

"That's right. I'm telling you, it ain't worth it. We want the Highlander, so it's crazy for you boys to go down like this. For your own sake, help us ensure that that State Trooper lives."

"I didn't shoot anybody," the voice asserted.

Another voice said, "Shut your damn mouth."

Art ventured further, his hands still raised and his pistol hanging from his finger. "Let me get him out of here, and—"

A young man in a plain white tee shirt stood from behind an overturned table. He raised a shotgun and swung his long dirty brown hair out of his eyes as though he had practiced the move. Art dived toward the floor as the blast from the gun flashed and thundered, followed by three rapid shots from a handgun.

Butcher recognized the report of a Glock 17. He raised

himself to see the sheriff, her gun extended, standing in the propped open back doorway. The shooter, a stain spreading across the middle of his chest, stumbled and fell into a stack of boxes. His lifeless body thudded against the cardboard.

"Sheriff, there's more," Art said as he gripped his gun with both hands. He searched the room for others.

Another report, this time from a much larger gun, ripped the silence. Again, Art dived for the floor. As he fell, he heard the Sheriff's muffled cry.

*****

Evangeline detected another shooter rising to her right. She spun toward the threat and raised her handgun. However, before she could fire, a shotgun blast caused the sheriff to stop and drop to her knees.

The blast slammed the shooter to her right into the wall like a screw drawn to a magnet. Evangeline heard the gunman's weapon clank and scrape against the concrete floor.

Behind the overturned table, the familiar voice pleaded, "Don't shoot, don't shoot, don't shoot. I'm not gettin' the electric chair for killing a cop."

The sheriff said, "Show me the shotgun and both your hands. Hold it over your head, then stand." She paused and added, "Don't make me take you down."

First, the shotgun appeared above the table, then the arms, followed by the man's head, shoulders, chest, and stomach. Jessie Porter stood, his thin frame rigid as if he was hanging from the gun rather than holding it over his head. "Don't shoot, Sheriff. He forced me to do it, or he would've shot you. I didn't sign on to kill police."

Evangeline ignored his words. "Place your weapon on the floor before the table and walk toward me. Art, are you okay?" She spoke into her radio, "Please tell the EMS it is safe to enter."

She met Jessie halfway and yanked his arms behind him. After snapping the cuffs closed, Evangeline whispered into Porter's ear, "Too bad, big boy. There is only one way to avoid death row and the hot seat if the officer dies."

"What do I have to do?" he asked. His voice creaked like a rusty gate.

"Cut a deal with me. Tell everything you know about Dr. Bell, his reign as the Highlander, and what happened to Willie and those two boys from Madden High School."

Jessie twisted, his hands cuffed behind his back. "I can tell you about the boys, but I don't know who killed Willie. Nobody does."

Evangeline's heart beat faster now than during the gunfight.

"I mean it, Sheriff," Jesse said. "You got to believe me. I just saved your life."

The sheriff pushed Jessie toward the door. As she did, she searched for the wounded officer. Junebug stood beside him as the EMS workers kneeled. Blood covered Junebug's uniform and hands, and red splotches marked his face and neck. Evangeline glanced at the deputy and nodded. Junebug returned the nod but did not speak.

Junebug appeared older, less like a kid, for a moment.

It was the same EMS team from the middle school football field. Again, they battled time to defy death for yet another person. The young woman with raven hair had replaced Junebug and was applying direct pressure on the officer's shoulder. The sheriff felt more hopeful seeing her on the scene.

Chapter 46
Hardy Boy, Nancy Drew, and Kolchak

P aulene outdid herself this time. The receptionist planned the entire celebration while Evangeline spent the day on the phone, granting interviews and accepting pats on the back. A sizable dome-shaped cake with thick red and blue frosting dominated the conference room. Written in white across the frosting was, "MCSD Gets its Man."

Special guests roamed around the station, including the County Judge, a pregnant Maria Butcher leaning against Art, several other local dignitaries, Junebug's guest, Lilly Begley, and Sheldon with Sarah at his side. Gene Begley stood by Pauline's punchbowl, his notebook in hand. Whenever Gene headed in her direction, Evangeline maneuvered around the pods of people to avoid his questions.

As Evangeline circled, she overheard fragments of conversation.

"Things will get better...."

"Madden's biggest problem is...."

"Will she leave now..."

"I bet Luke Porter is keeping his mouth closed...."

She even heard Paulene say, "I knew something wasn't right about Dr. Bell. You know what I mean—he looked like a mean farmer who never fed his cows enough food."

Art's voice carried farther than everyone else's. He and Maria stood with a local lawyer and a prominent judge. "Judge Willingham, she read those tracks like deer scat on a trail. I would have never realized those were plane tires. Hell, I would have been flagging down wheelbarrows and three-wheelers. Genius, if you ask me."

Evangeline's cheeks turned red, and she drifted across the room where Sheldon, Sarah, and Gene huddled. Seeing the three together made her face even warmer, but for a different reason. She could not avoid Begley all afternoon, especially if he had corralled her brother to squeeze information from him.

"What do you know, here's a Hardy Boy, Nancy Drew, and Kolchak all in one place. What a treat," Evangeline said as she approached. She pinned her stare on Gene. His hair was unruly, and he wore a flannel shirt (maybe *the* flannel shirt?) while holding a cup of Paulene's punch in his hand. Evangeline admitted Gene did have a different demeanor than usual, and his interview questions celebrated the Highlander's capture.

"Kolchak? Now that's a good one, Sheriff. Has cracking the case of the century endowed you with a sense of humor and good taste in television?"

Before she could respond, Sarah said, "Congratulations, Sheriff. Thank you for making this place safer. Everyone is shocked it was Dr. Bell but happy he's under arrest."

"I would like an interview about how you unraveled this mystery, Sheriff, if you have time tomorrow," Gene said. "Art, Junebug, and the Troopers hail you as the next Sherlock Holmes. You deserve it for capturing the Highlander. Louisville and Lexington press are asking about what happened, and I have been happy to sing your praises."

"Thank you, Sarah, Gene," she said. She forced a smile and nodded. It did feel different to receive praise and acknowledgment for something in Madden. "Junebug and Art were the real heroes on this one. They deserve the credit."

Gene retrieved the notebook and pencil from his back pocket and scribbled on a page.

Evangeline said, "Would you mind if I talked to Sheldon for just a few minutes?" She turned to see Sheldon's response. Her brother's eyes rolled in frustration.

"I'm sorry, Evangeline," he said. "I promised to walk Sarah to the newspaper office."

Sarah's head turned toward Sheldon. She was skeptical, but she remained quiet.

Evangeline placed her hand on his arm. "We need to talk, and it will happen tonight when you get home. It is important."

Chapter 47
Heaven and so Much More

"Yes, we met with Gene. I figured you sent Junebug to spy on me," Sheldon said. "Besides, why does it matter? Didn't you arrest the killer today? As you said, it will end all this nonsense. We can skip to Louisville, where you will be a star. Isn't that Sylvia's plan? Oh, I mean, your plan?"

Evangeline splayed her fingers on the kitchen table. Her scrambled eggs rested on the plate untouched. She and Sheldon had not spoken more than a few words for several days, and his behaviors—fits of anger and moments of intense sadness—continued to concern her. It was not the despair they had shared when their father died, nor did his response align with his personality. It was as if his character had cracked into jagged concrete, sharp broken segments, and dust. He was not mourning Willie—he was becoming him.

"Gene wants to milk you for information about Willie's death and spread the word around Madden County like a virus to prove he was right about me from the beginning."

"That's not how it is, sis. You can ask Sarah. She will tell you he only wants the truth about Madden County."

"Gene doesn't care about the truth, Sheldon. He's about one thing—making himself look clever in the newspaper."

"Both Gene and Ms. Begley are good people," Sheldon said. "Lilly may have some ideas worth considering if you would listen."

"Gene's hippy daughter is as crazy as he is," Evangeline said. "When has Gene written anything that doesn't paint us as corrupt or incompetent?"

"Ms. Begley thinks you and her dad are avoiding the real issue. What happened was impossible, so you have to think about the impossible. She quoted Shakespeare about heaven and so much more than people know."

Evangeline leaned back in the chair, placed her hands behind her head, and closed her eyes.

"Sheldon, what are you talking about?" She recalled when he was a little boy, he would want something, a toy or ice cream, but would pretend it was in her or their father's best interest. Her father had always gotten a kick out of it. He would say, "Boy, this ice cream saved me, Sheldon. I hope it wasn't too inconvenient for you to come along."

"I may sound crazy," Sheldon said. "But you believe you know everything when you don't."

His teen angst and attitude caused Evangeline's blood to turn to acid. Nonetheless, she resisted the urge to call him an asshole.

"Sarah's dad would agree with me," Evangeline said. "He wouldn't trust Gene to hold his hat." Dark circles colored Sheldon's eyes, and his face was thinner than a few days ago. Too many kids in Madden carried the same dull expression because they turned to drugs for comfort.

"Gene lets Sarah work at the newspaper, doesn't he?"

Evangeline exhaled. "Sheldon, you know if anything is going on, you can tell me, right?"

"Oh yeah, thanks, sis." He opened the refrigerator, looked inside, then closed it. "You remember what Dad always said whenever we complained about something?" Sheldon mimicked their father. "Don't stand up to preach if your message can't save souls."

"Then tell me, Sheldon. Just tell me what's wrong." She was leaning forward now, her elbows on the table. She stared at her brother, pleading with him to confess.

"Right now, the only way I can save souls is to shut my mouth," Sheldon said.

Evangeline shook her head and rubbed her hands together. "You aren't even sixteen years old yet, Sheldon, but you speak like an old man. I don't even know you anymore. Are you doing something you shouldn't be doing?"

"You don't understand me anymore?" he laughed. "I'm doing my best, Vangie. It's all I can do. Tonight I am staying at Sarah's until late. Her dad said it was okay, and if it got too late, he said I can stay in the guest room since, well, Uncle Willie and all."

Sheldon walked toward the stairs. He leaned forward like a miner who had just finished a twelve-hour shift. His slow, deliberate stride conjured images of Uncle Willie, alone and beaten, ascending the steps.

Chapter 48
Way to Go, Super Cop

When Evangeline picked up the receiver, she heard, "I am with the *New York Times* calling about the Highlander arrest. Is it true your friend Sylvia Carter inspired you to do such exceptional police work?"

Sylvia's voice caused her to smile and feel guilty. She had neglected the contract and Sylvia for days. Evangeline treated it like a trip to the dentist, procrastinating until the last minute before mailing the contract.

"Yes, ma'am," Evangeline replied. "She pointed me in the right direction and baked some cookies for the trip."

"Did you see the story in the Lexington paper about the arrest? There's talk here in Louisville about you right now. The Chief asked me to confirm that you are *the* Evangeline Grace joining my team. This arrest highlighted your skills as an investigator and mine as a recruiter. Way to go, Supercop."

"You will end up as Chief someday," Evangeline said.

"For someone who just dismantled an illegal prescription drug cartel, you sure don't sound elated. Don't tell me I am more excited about your success than you are, Evangeline Grace. What is going on in your beautiful mind?"

"I'm sorry, Syl. I had another argument with Sheldon. Every time we talk, it is a battle."

"Is he still behaving like before?"

"Even worse. Sheldon talks to himself and is depressed. He's been going behind my back, meeting with the newspaper editor, and saying inexplicable things like his Uncle Willie used to say."

"Is he using drugs, Evangeline?" Sylvia asked.

"I am afraid to turn over his room, Sylvia," Evangeline said. She trusted Sylvia in ways she had never counted on others. It was another reason the contract caused her guilt. The time to make this bold move was now, not later. She might give up on the entire idea if she missed the deadline.

"Shit, my mom would take apart our beds, empty our book-shelves and drawers, and even call our friends if we got the hiccups," Sylvia said. "If we complained, she would say, 'when you have your own place, you get privacy. In my house, you get protected whether you want it or not.'"

"Remember, I am his sister, not his mom. It makes a differ-ence," Sarah said.

"If he's living with you for the next three years, it doesn't," Sylvia said. "If you believe he is following his uncle's path, you are justified in taking action."

"Sylvia, I miss you so much. Let me call you a bit later after I have taken care of some things."

"Of course," Sylvia said. "Remember, your work has given us a better opportunity here than before."

Evangeline ended the call. Opportunity, she thought, was all she had ever wanted. Now a red carpet would welcome her to her dream job, yet she remained trapped in a nightmare. Evangeline had seven days to mail the contract. Then she could skip to Louis-ville like Dorothy on the yellow brick road.

She stared at the ceiling for a moment. "The closest target is the only thing that matters, Lil Dep," her father had told her when he had first taught her to shoot a rifle. His thick hands had shifted the gun against her shoulder to line up the sights. "Always consider what will happen after you pull the trigger. The bullet does not just stop at the target. It travels beyond and out into the world. Decisions have consequences, which can be the difference between success and failure—life and death."

Chapter 49
Two Wolves

Evangeline changed into jeans and a black tee shirt with "Louisville Police Department: Serve and Protect" printed across the front. Sylvia had sent it to her, saying, "Try it on for size, 'cause it won't be long until you are LMPD."

Then she journeyed down the hall.

Sheldon had locked his door, but that was easy to remedy. Evangeline straightened a paper clip, rotated it in the lock a few times, and entered. She closed the door behind her, leaving it locked. After all, it had used to be her room, so she knew every trick, hiding place, and creaky floorboard.

DeNiro, Pesci, and Liotta, their faces aligned side by side above the word *Goodfellas*, met her when she turned on the light. Sheldon's bed was unmade, something her father would not have tolerated, and the silver trash can next to it was overflowing with plastic Gatorade bottles and crumbled pieces of paper.

She knelt beside the can, removed the bottles, and sifted through the scraps. Several sheets of paper, each opening, "Dear Sarah, Have you ever had something important to say but not been able to say it?" were wadded and discarded.

"Just like Uncle Willie," Evangeline whispered.

Her mind was the rope in a tug of war. Invading her brother's privacy wasn't right. *But you love him, stupid. Can you stand by and let him travel a dangerous road?* "If he is using drugs, I can help him," she said. The rope pulled the other way. At the Academy, Sergeant Handley had taught her, "Just because you have good intentions does not mean the end justifies the means." That warning caused her to pause, but only for a moment.

Sheldon had placed a photograph of their father on the nightstand. It showed him standing in full uniform on the courthouse steps a few years before he died. Back then, Evangeline had worried their father's death might break her brother. However, he had endured as she had. Losing Willie was another endurance test, though, and they weren't passing.

Evangeline dropped to a pushup position and peered beneath the bed. She dragged a Reebok shoebox into the light. When she removed the lid, she found pictures of Sheldon and their dad standing side by side in the backyard, Evangeline smiling and waving at graduation, and Sarah playing volleyball in middle school. One image showed her holding Sheldon when he was a baby. It made her heart feel heavy. The last pictured their mother sitting on the sofa, engrossed in a book. The photo captured Sheldon's resemblance to her.

A metal Madden County Deputy badge rested at the container's bottom. The star was scuffed, but Evangeline recognized it as the one she had given him when their dad had appointed her Interim Sheriff. Her eyes clouded with tears as she placed the items back into the box and pushed them beneath the bed.

She raised the blanket hanging over the edge and lifted the mattress. Her baby brother had stashed several magazines in the space. One cover depicted a blonde woman holding a lollipop with her right hand and squeezing the nipple on her perfect breast. Evangeline shook her head, slid the magazines back into place, and adjusted the blanket. She hoped it was the worst thing she would find.

She stood and inspected the room. Two framed pictures adorned the dresser top. The first was Uncle Willie and Sheldon standing side by side, wearing matching UK Basketball tee-shirts. In the other, Sheldon and Evangeline flexed their muscles for the camera.

Then she discovered the ornate box. The craftsman had carved two wolves facing each other into the wood. They appeared prepared to battle. She recalled Willie telling the story of the Two Wolves—a Native American Chief speaking around the fire telling the children each of us has two wolves fighting for supremacy inside us. One is good, and one is wicked. When a boy asks who wins, the Chief says, "The one you feed." Willie said his evil wolf was more potent than most.

Evangeline rubbed her fingers across the top, tracing the animals' faces. The rough texture reminded her of tree bark. This box was one of Sheldon's prized possessions, especially now, because it was a gift from Willie. She had no right to be in his room, rummaging through his things and holding such a personal object. No right.

She opened it and discovered intricate lettering inside the lid, an old watch that had belonged to their father, another faded picture of their mother, and a thick rectangular envelope containing folded pages bearing her name.

Chapter 50
Yours, in Secrets and Blood

Evangeline sat on her brother's bed and read the letter for a second time, hoping it would make sense. Uncle Willie had written the letter to her, but somehow Sheldon had intercepted it. Holding the smooth yellow pages made her shoulders tighten and her hands tremble. She read the first two paragraphs and took a deep breath before continuing:

Your Uncle Robert is the real hero of this story. What I know comes from him and my experience. At first, I thought he was a coward who passed his burden to me. However, I soon realized he was playing the long game. While he persevered to confront the summons, I shielded myself with alcohol and drugs. You tell me who was braver.

Of your uncles and aunts, Robert was the oldest. He wasn't around much when your dad and I were young. By then, the schools had labeled him as different, or as people in Madden would say, plumb crazy. I was closer to his age, so I knew him best. I had watched Robert change like a scarecrow left out in the storms year after year, essential pieces of him lost.

Secrets and Blood

When I was fourteen, Robert persuaded me to hike to the Pinnacle on Two Mile Mountain. The trail wound upward to a cluster of rocks overlooking a valley hundreds of feet below.

We sat a few yards from the highest cliff on the peak. Robert gave me a bottle of Nehi Orange pop and a Hershey Bar before saying, "I have something to tell you, Willie. It is a secret I am too weak to keep, but you aren't. I will share enough of what I learned to make it a lighter load, but now it is your cross to bear. Please don't hate me for it."

I stared into his sorrowful eyes and assumed it was another of his breakdowns. I steadied to hear his tirade about unknown evils running roughshod over the world.

But he did not rant or talk to people who were not there. Instead, he patted my shoulder, his touch delicate and final, then told me I was the only one who might believe him. Robert claimed I had something in me better than the rest of our family, and he thought I could hold the secret a long time before passing it to someone else.

Then my brother stared out into the sky beyond the mountain and said, "You know how our daddy says the only things separating family from other folks are secrets and blood?" He resembled your grandmother, except desperation replaced the kindness behind their eyes. On most days, stubble covered his chin, but today he was clean-shaven. The early October wind gusted. It carried the smell of pines and birches to us. The clouds resembled cotton balls glued to blue construction paper like we used to make in Sunday school, and the trill of a Goldfinch blended with a woodpecker's clacking against a distant tree.

Robert, talking faster, said, "We have to do this now." I understood him, but it was like hearing a record replayed at a faster speed. The scar on his cheek and his eyebrows bounced in unison as he hurried to deliver his practiced speech.

In October 1927, Madden County was in crisis. The coal companies used Baldwin detectives from New England and Virginia to scare the union boys. These so-called agents rained violence on the miners and their supporters, hoping to break the union.

All the agents were mean, but one was exceptional in his cruelty. His name was Daniel Barlow, but the other detectives called him the Agent. He did not hesitate to bludgeon miners, women, or even children if he felt like it. He was well-dressed and called us hillbillies, inbreds, and trash. The Agent scared people with his eyes. The other agents feared him and, behind his back, would describe how he kept a skull and a crooked finger bone on his nightstand. They said he spoke to those bones each night before sleeping. Barlow kept ancient books and drew symbols on the wall and floor of his hotel room. One detective claimed Barlow painted those signs with chicken blood.

One day Robert's friend, Leon McCoy, threw a baseball and hit the Agent. Everyone laughed, and Barlow acted tough but then brushed it off. However, soon the McCoys could not find Leon, so they rushed to see your grandfather, the sheriff. They feared the Agent had abducted the little guy. Barlow's colleagues told the sheriff the Agent was dangerous and they wouldn't put anything past him. The sheriff asked citizens to report if they saw the Agent or Leon. Sure enough, someone recognized Barlow driving up Rockhouse Creek.

Robert overheard the news and realized Barlow was traveling toward Madden County Coal's newest mine on Rockhouse Creek. Robert figured the Agent wanted to kill his friend and hide his body in the mine.

While the sheriff set up search parties, Robert hurried toward Rockhouse. Since Robert rode his bicycle, he could travel an old pathway to the mine. It was a much shorter and more direct journey than the winding asphalt roads.

Secrets and Blood

Robert pedaled like never before until he arrived near the shaft. He parked his bike and climbed up the hill, his head down and his mind flipping through his options if he discovered the Agent and Leon.

As he approached the structures to search for Leon, two giant hands grabbed him from behind and covered his mouth.

The Agent, his big arm choking Robert, asked if the sheriff was after him, and all my brother could do was say yes.

The Agent dragged Robert into the trees. Robert was sure he was about to die, just like Leon, except that is not what happened. Instead, the Agent released him in an open area and assured Robert he would not kill him.

"But what about Leon?" Robert asked the Agent.

The Agent laughed. "Little fucker is probably playing with his pecker somewhere in the woods."

Robert felt safe until Barlow raised his hands and spat on each palm as he had done at the courthouse. Then the Agent reached into his jacket pocket. However, this time he did not bring out a bottle. He retrieved a three-inch yellowed chicken leg. Robert recognized it by the thin shank leading down to the spur and claws. Without hesitating, the Agent raked the claw down Robert's left cheek.

Pain burrowed into Robert's face, and he tried to cover the cut, but the Agent's left hand grasped his wrist. A sizable gash traveled across the attacker's arm. Robert wondered if Leon had fought the Agent and cut him.

The Agent then used his other hand to touch the line of blood streaking down Robert's face. He followed it as though tracing the Big Sandy River on a map before forcing Robert to the ground and straddling him.

The Agent pinned Robert like a moth on a cork board. Stones surrounded them. "Little boy," the Agent said. "I initiated this spell myself. Our blood connects the circle of stones, bonding us."

The Agent cleared his throat and repeated a phrase three times.

"Mulengi Dori," as he pressed Robert into the dirt. My brother became dizzy, and the man's face hovering above him grew dark despite the sunlight. Robert claimed he heard the Agent speak to him as if whispering in his ear, but he did not see the man's lips move.

The Agent told Robert, "I curse you, your family, any other families who hurt me, and Madden County with whatever secrets are born this day. You will carry your secret, and I will carry mine. When one knows, I will be a whisper. When two know, I will be neither man nor ghost, but I will walk this land. The carrier of these secrets must never roam beyond the borders of this forsaken place. When none knows your secret, I am free to bring death to the family of all who here resides."

Bile scorched my brother's throat, and a sulfur odor encircled him as if he were in a gunpowder cocoon, squeezing the breath from his body.

Robert said he awoke a few minutes later, curled into a ball inside the circle of rocks and blood, alone.

The man spoke inside my brother's head. You will release me. Then I destroy this place man by man, woman by woman, child by child. Go home. Now. We will remember our secrets, the voice said.

Robert stumbled down the trail, retrieved his bicycle, and pedaled home. He prayed each crank carried him further from that place. However, throughout his life, Barlow appeared to Robert as a shadow, taunting and challenging him to reveal the secret. Despite the torment, my big brother never told anyone about the Agent until the moment he told me.

When he finished, Robert stared past me. I watched as his body tensed and his expression changed. He bared his teeth, and I swear he growled before gazing into my eyes, pointing at the trees in the distance and the final revelation in his tale, "Remember, the evil shadow is Agent Daniel Barlow. He will become more than a shadow whenever you tell others he exists. He lives forever if you don't tell anyone before you die."

The blackness between the trees and bushes converged as if God had assembled a human form from the shadows. I heard heavy footsteps snapping the twigs on the path.

Robert stood as though planning to attack the man. Instead, my brother used his delicate touch again to ruffle my hair as we watched the creature's frantic approach. "I wish I had time to tell you more, but he is your shadow now, Willie," Robert said. "Look at him. Watch him change."

I turned and watched the undefined man come closer. He was clay removed from the kiln too early but shaped like a man.

After a moment, I glanced over my shoulder. I watched as Robert launched himself from the rocky overhang. His arms were outstretched as though he expected to fly into the pale blue and white sky. I tried to stand, but my legs were so weak I stumbled, and an infant's cry escaped my lips. My heart thudded against my skinny chest, and my body fought to stop him even though my brain recognized it was too late.

Evil galloped toward me from the other direction, the footsteps warning me of his approach. With my knee grounded, I turned my head and shoulders to see the Agent coming for me. His face resembled melting wax, and his fedora merged with his head. His blue suit appeared grafted to his decaying skin, like his dead eyes and deformed mouth.

Fear locked my body. Barlow's rotting hand stretched toward my throat. I was afraid and devastated by the loss at the same time.

Then, it was over. The transformation process reversed until only the dense shadow remained.

It was as Robert had planned it. I witnessed the Agent's change with my own eyes—there was no disbelief or doubt to obscure the truth. The Agent existed, and now he was my companion. My brother's death and my survival triggered the Agent's return to the shadows. It also changed my life.

I sat on the mountain peak for a long time, crying and considering what had occurred and how my brother's suicide would hurt my mother the most. I stared at the shadow—its undeniable human shape floating against the backdrop of trees and the path home.

That is when the Agent spoke to me for the first time, deep and loud inside my head like a blaring song I couldn't silence, <u>Willie. It looks like it's me and you, kid.</u>

The Agent has haunted my soul for sixty years and shaped my life. I contained him longer than I should have, using whatever plant, chemical, or concoction available. Now, my dear sweet niece, it is your burden to bear. You must keep the secret, never leave Madden County, and pass it on to another person you trust, just as I have, before you die. Although he will shred your mind and emotions, the Agent cannot physically hurt you if you possess the secret alone. Only when two people know the truth can the Agent hurt you or anyone else.

If I had died without telling you the secret, he would have killed without limits. If I told you and stayed alive, then everyone we love, Sheldon, Faith, and Cyrus, would have also been in danger. That's why I asked you to wait until morning to read it. So I get one last sleep and end this existence on my terms. The Agent is too arrogant to allow me that final moment of satisfaction—he would rather kill me and weaken himself than allow me any victory, no matter how small. Believe me, his hatred and arrogance dwarf his power.

I love you, Lil Dep. Be strong. If anyone can end this threat, you can. Tell Sheldon I love him, too.

Yours in Secrets and Blood,
Willie

Evangeline's face burned, and her leg bounced, causing the yellow pages to vibrate in her hand. She was right to worry about Sheldon. Willie's description of Robert's suicide and an unhealthy dose of horror fantasy would traumatize any child. Willie's words scared her, but she was old enough to recognize a ghost story from the truth. She closed her eyes, but the image of Willie's lifeless body, the cell walls splattered with blood and sinew, retook the stage.

The sheriff shuffled the pages and reread the letter again and again.

Chapter 51

A Shadow, a Ghost, a Hallucination

"**D**o you know what you have done?" Sheldon asked.

He swayed in the doorway with his fists clenched at his sides. Evangeline remained seated on his bed, clutching the creased pages of yellow paper. She felt equal doses of anger, guilt, and concern, but her brain told her to bring her rage to the forefront.

"Yes, I know what is happening here," she responded. "I am reading this letter addressed to me. Why do you have it?"

"Evangeline, you have no right to...." Sheldon's face changed mid-sentence as if the hypocrisy tasted bitter on his tongue.

Evangeline stood, holding the letter and motioning toward it with her free hand. "What does all this mean, Sheldon? Certainly, when you read this, you see Uncle Willie was out of his mind."

Evangeline waited for a response, watching as Sheldon struggled to find words. "It means we have done something wrong," he sputtered. After a breath, he continued, "I mean, I did something very wrong. I should have listened to him when he gave those pages to me, but the secret made it impossible to fix things after I read the letter."

Evangeline straightened. "You think this fantasy is real? Sheldon, you're smarter than that. You have been acting so odd I was afraid I would find pills or heroin here." Now, she held up the legal pad pages like irrefutable evidence. "Instead, you behave this way because you believe in a ghost story. You think a shadow haunted Willie, and now it haunts you?"

"I'm not crazy, Evangeline, but I wish I were. You, me, and this whole world would be safer if my insanity explained everything. That letter is real."

"Real, my ass. Sheldon, you should have more sense than this." The letter quivered in her hand as she stepped forward. "Uncle Willie was an addict. He admits it himself on these pages. I loved him, too, but you have to grow up. Willie's gone. Dad and Mom are gone. We are the family now. People we love sometimes aren't what they appear."

"I know, Evangeline. All too well."

Anger rippled across Evangeline's body. Her eyes narrowed, and she leaned even closer to her brother. She wanted to shake him like the Etch A Sketch, but their father's picture on the desk watched her, so she controlled herself.

"Destroy the letter," Sheldon responded. "Burn it. Willie bought us time, but it feels like something awful will happen since the two of us now know the secret."

Evangeline's motor slowed. Again, he was her baby brother with tousled hair and frantic gestures as if conducting an unresponsive orchestra. She said, "You're scaring me, Sheldon. The more you talk, the more afraid I become."

Sheldon stared back at her. "Look, Evangeline, I admit it sounds impossible, but the Agent will come. He is probably listening to us and celebrating like he did at Willie's funeral."

Evangeline paused to plan her next step. *Maybe it's best to play his game for a minute. The letter is pretty creepy. It is no surprise he is having an irrational response to all this. Uncle Willie's words would haunt even the most skeptical reader, especially Sheldon, who loved Willie so much.*

"Sheldon, I get it. Let's sit here and wait for the big bad Agent to show up. Then we will deal with him together." Evangeline sat down on the bed to reread the letter. *Yeah, Uncle Willie's words would haunt anyone.*

"Thank you, Evangeline. Just be ready. The Agent is evil and dangerous, whatever he is—a shadow, a ghost, or a hallucination."

Chapter 52
The Sooner, the Better, and Good Riddance

Luke Porter finished his rounds on the second floor, ensuring the prisoners were quiet. The inmates didn't say much to him when he had night duty because they knew what would happen. Sure, Luke was a peace officer, but it didn't stop him from cracking heads whenever the situation called for it. He was where he belonged—in charge.

He stepped into the stairwell, allowing the heavy metal door to close behind him. He had endured a great deal in the past two weeks. Sheriff Grace had reprimanded him for "overly aggressive interactions" and belittled him with other officers present. Although the sheriff and her idiots had left him outside the loop, Luke had ensured the Kentucky State Police knew his contribution to taking down the Highlander. He had informed the lead trooper that the arrest resulted from his initial observations about the Highlander.

Luke recommended the State Police move the Highlander to a detention center in Jensen County. "Given his gang's apparent skills entering our jail, it would be best to detain Bell in a more secure facility," he said. Then Luke whispered to the state trooper,

"Don't worry. When I'm the sheriff, I will lock this place down like Alcatraz."

Also, it would be best if the sheriff's head didn't swell so much she changed her mind about leaving. He hoped it would give her the reputation she needed to get the Louisville job, thank goodness. The sooner, the better, and good riddance. Finally, he would get his chance.

The officer skipped down the stairs, anxious to get to his desk. The fluorescent lights buzzed like flies circling a carcass.

A movement caught Luke's eye, causing him to freeze with each foot on a different stair. The last echo of his shoes died against the cinder block wall. Another movement—a shadow pushing the light, gave Luke an odd sensation, like sitting still in a car as other cars moved in reverse beside him. The hairs on his neck stood up, and his knees felt weak.

"Otis, you better not be screwing around. I will fire your ass as soon as I can," Luke said.

A voice encircled Luke. *"When fighting in the war, I always recognized the real leaders."*

The deep sound penetrated Luke's brain. Each word echoed within the stairwell of his mind.

"Often, real leaders dwell in the background while others get the credit. It is a shame, Sheriff Porter, a real shame." The voice swelled from inside the darkness and then subsided for a moment. *"Oh, I am sorry, my friend. I should have said Deputy Porter."*

"What do you want?" Porter felt off-balance, as if the voice shoved him rather than spoke.

"Listen to these words, my friend. Hear them and live them. Your bones are my bones; your breath is my breath; my words are your words; my mind is your song. Constrained, impaled upon the same bloody thorn."

"Are you a nut, buddy?" Luke unsnapped his holster and

retrieved his gun in one smooth movement. He extended it at eye level with two hands. "Now, move forward where I can see you."

"*My name is Barlow, Deputy,*" the Agent said as he entered the light. Although Luke was on the second step, the figure stood eye-to-eye with him.

The deputy's breath became shallow, and the gun barrel quivered. A fedora topped the man's ample head—overlapping shades of gray, red, and black speckled his skin. His pupils were pale, like the eyes of a suicide victim Luke and Junebug had retrieved from Dewey Lake after the corpse had spent four days in the water.

"*We are both lawmen, Deputy Porter. We both want to end the corruption the Grace family has fostered in this wasteland,*" the Agent said as he stepped forward and reached into the pocket of his suit. "*Here, let me show you my badge.*"

The Agent's wide grin revealed a row of blackened teeth. The deputy's quaking hands lowered the gun against his will.

The Agent moved closer, his palm extending to show a silver badge. As Luke read "Baldwin Detective Agency," the Agent's other hand, black with coal dust, stretched toward the deputy's ear. Barlow raked Luke's cheek in one movement, causing a sharp pain to shoot across his face. Luke's left hand lifted to hold his face together.

Barlow laughed and stepped away.

"You idiot," Luke exclaimed. His body felt like it would explode due to the pain and surprise. He attempted to raise his gun, intent on emptying his clip into the attacker's chest. However, an unseen weight locked his arms, and his trigger finger refused his reflex. Every muscle in his body stiffened as blood dripped from his chin onto his sleeve. "What did you do to me?"

"*You ungrateful hillbilly. You should ask what I did for you.*" The Agent showed Luke the weapon he had used. He held the yellowed ankle between his thumb and forefinger, presenting three long talons with sharp nails at the end. A smaller toe protruded from the bottom.

"A chicken's foot? Did you scratch my face with a chicken's foot? What the hell are you?"

The Agent laughed. *"Don't worry, Luke Porter. My words are your words, and we are impaled upon the same bloody thorn."*

Bile rose into Luke's throat, and the edges of his mind darkened in a staircase all its own.

Chapter 53
The Dead Man's Finger

The ninety minutes Evangeline sat with her brother felt eternal. Each time she attempted to kindle a conversation, Sheldon did not respond. He pleaded for her patience when he did speak, as though he needed the shadowy evil figure to appear.

"The Agent will be here," he said. "I promise. He is too in love with his voice not to show up."

Perhaps Sheldon's anger at leaving Madden County had affected his thinking. She had read about criminals who created false stories to redirect their hatred of someone they could not hurt onto a substitute. Did Sheldon hate her so much for planning to leave Madden he projected his anger onto an imaginary villain?

After more silence, Evangeline asked, "Do you remember the 'dead man's finger'?" She floated her index finger in the air and made an eerie howl as she did so.

"Yes, I remember," he said. Evangeline thought he smiled. "You told me ghost stories, and I made you do the 'dead man's finger' before you said goodnight."

Evangeline sat up and folded her legs under her, sitting on her heels. She took Sheldon's right hand and pulled him into a seated position, his back against the headboard.

She held up her left hand as if requesting a high-five. "Come on, now. Do it... Dooooo itttttt," she chanted.

Sheldon laughed and placed his open right hand against her left. They closed their hands and interlocked digits, except for their trigger fingers. Those fingers, touching and extending upward, resembled an index finger touching a mirror.

"Okay," she said, her voice a poor Vincent Price impression. "Feel the dead man's finger."

Sheldon rubbed the two fingers up and down with the thumb and index finger on his other hand—his thumb caressing his finger while the other touched hers. A sensation of numbness filled his brain. The illusion made this one thick finger feel dead.

"That's the dead man's finger, Sheriff," he said. "It still feels creepy to me. As Dad would say, tag it and bag it."

The siblings laughed for a moment, just as they had when Sheldon was a little boy and Evangeline had aspired to be his protector.

"You know the feeling, Sheldon? The sensation your finger is numb? That's how I feel here in Madden County," Evangeline said as she leaned forward and wrapped her arms around her legs, "I have felt I don't belong here for a long time. That's why we need to leave."

The smile fled Sheldon's face. He shifted to extend his legs, his back still against the headboard. "That's why you blame me. You see it all as my fault."

"Why do you keep saying I blame you?" Evangeline said as she swiveled toward her brother. "It's not your fault this happened to Uncle Willie, Sheldon. When a man lives like he did, drugs and violence—"

"Not Willie's death," Sheldon said as he leaned away. "Hers."

His lips drooped, and his eyes clouded like a storm brewed moments away.

"I don't know what you mean." She touched Sheldon's arm.

"Mom. You blame me for Mom dying. You wouldn't be here if I had not made her die." Sheldon's lower lip trembled as he pulled his knees to his chest, creating a mountain between them.

Evangeline's breath caught in her throat. Unable to reply, she glared at her brother. Her words were trapped inside her brain, held in place by hospital hallways, fluorescent lights, and metal flower pots containing artificial flowers.

"Dad made you come home to help care for me. Mom would be alive if I had not happened, and you would be some bigshot in Louisville with Sylvia."

Sheldon filled the space where Evangeline's words should have been, "I know you have felt this way forever, Vangie. I heard you tell Sylvia on the phone long before Dad passed."

"You aren't right, Sheldon." For a moment, she did not respond. She wanted to say and do the right thing, but it eluded her. Her face faded and faltered as she surrendered to tears. She could not force herself to say what Sheldon needed to hear. Her throat tightened, the words of absolution choked by the dead man's fingers from her past.

Sheldon said, "Things are different now, sis. I can't leave, and now you can't either."

Evangeline wiped her face with her hands and breathed three deep breaths.

"So, you won't let go of this belief?" Evangeline sniffled again. "Uncle Willie's scribblings are all the proof you need?"

"I have the evidence, Evangeline," he said. "The Agent has been in the corners of my life and my brain since I read the letter. How do you think I knew about Willie's murder?"

Evangeline stuttered, "I'm not... I don't know." *How* did *Sheldon know?*

"Face it, sis. You don't get to control everything in the world just because...." Sheldon's voice trailed off as he scanned the corners of the room. Evangeline watched her brother's eyes tilt like an unbalanced carpenter's level.

"Then where is he? You said this ghost couldn't wait to confront us. How did you say it? The big mean Agent is just eager to celebrate his victory." Evangeline leaned further into Sheldon's space as if he were a suspect to intimidate. "This is why we have to leave this place. It makes you poor. It makes you crazy. It makes you die."

Sheldon clenched his fists.

"This imaginary man killed Willie almost as soon as you read the letter, right?" She retrieved and unfolded Willie's message and pointed to the text. "You read this, and then Willie died that night." She tossed the letter onto the carpet. "Willie's poor brain resorted to fiction to escape reality. But if Barlow killed Willie because you read the letter, why hasn't he killed one of us?"

Evangeline gauged Shel's reaction. If Dad were here, he would ensure this nonsense did not continue. She breathed and adjusted her tone.

"Sheldon, you know my secrets. You know how I am different. You know the times I snuck out of this room at night to be with my friends and how I did it without Dad suspecting anything. I shared my silly superstitions, like the same underwear for every game when we were on a winning streak. I told you about almost every crush I ever had. I trusted you. Why can't you trust me now and let this go?"

When Shel raised his eyes, Evangeline hoped to see her little brother, ten years old again, playing Uno with her before bedtime, pleading to stay up a few minutes more. It was not the case.

Sheldon stared into her eyes with great resolve. His countenance resembled their mother's face when she was angry. Sheldon had never seen that look, but Evangeline knew it.

"I don't know why he hasn't come, but when you think about it, you and I are the safest people in Madden County. When I read the letter, he didn't come here. He went to kill Uncle Willie. I have heard him in my head, but he becomes more when two people know the secret."

For a moment, Sheldon's panic caused Evangeline to question herself. What if this was indeed some inexplicable moment in time? She considered it, but only for a moment.

She exhaled. "Sheldon," she said, "I have to get you help." She stood and walked toward the door.

"Get me help? Jesus, Evangeline, if you want to help me, believe me."

She exited without looking back.

Chapter 54
Maxie Fleming

The first tap against the window pane woke Sheldon, but he remained in bed until he heard the fourth. Sarah had tossed pebbles against his window on two other occasions, but never at 3:30 AM. *It must be important.*

He walked to the window and pressed his face against the glass. When he peered through the tree branches, Sheldon did not see anyone in the yard beneath his window. However, a moment later, he recognized the rocking chair's back-and-forth cadence on the back porch, gentle and steady.

There must be something wrong for Sarah to leave her house so late. He slipped into his tennis shoes and crept downstairs, hoping Evangeline did not hear.

Sheldon entered the kitchen. Closer now, he heard the rocking chair's soft moan along with each rock. He unlocked the back door and stepped onto the back porch.

The early morning chill cut through his pajama bottoms and Ryan Adams tee-shirt, causing him to cross his bare arms and shiver. The chair faced the backyard, and darkness covered the porch, making it difficult for Sheldon to see Sarah.

"I feel like Juliet when you show up—"

"I love hillbillies, Shelly Belly. You have no power, no sense, and no hope. Did you think I would reveal myself to your bearcat sister so soon? I had people to go and places to meet." The Agent's laughter sounded like a scratched record.

Fear crawled across Sheldon's skin, replacing the goosebumps caused by the cold. Sheldon uncrossed and raised his arms, prepared to fight.

The Agent half stood, lifting the rocking chair by the armrests and turning it toward Sheldon simultaneously. When he faced Sheldon, Barlow dropped his butt back into the seat and continued rocking.

"I'm not here to hurt you, Shello," Barlow said. "I am enjoying my new body, thanks to Evangeline. I have too much to do to evaporate again."

Sheldon stepped back, but the Agent did not move from the chair. Instead, the Agent rocked like Sheldon's father had years before he became sick. Barlow's long legs pushed against the porch floor as he moved. His gray eyes, trapped inside a thin cocoon, smiled along with his distorted face. He rested his scarred and blistered hands on the armrests, only lifting them to brush dirt and blood from the jacket and pants melded to his body. The musky smell of dying leaves and Autumn dew blended with Barlow's pungent decay and coal smoke.

"It's 3:30 AM. Agent, Couldn't you wait until after school?"

"You better wake up, boy," the Agent said, his volume rising. *"Your sister doesn't give a bub about you. It takes a real heel to breach a man's castle and inspect his belongings. I don't blame you for hating her so much."* The Agent resembled an extra from *The Great Gatsby*. A watch chain swung near his belt, and a dirty handkerchief was attached to his jacket pocket. His hat hid part of his face but the pale, sagging gray skin of his cheeks and the vacant eyes. His teeth were black and yellowed, and coal dust

covered his hands. Sharp dirt-encrusted nails punctuated the fingers.

"What makes you think I hate—"

"*Please, boy, you can level with me,*" the Agent said, "*You have every reason to despise the little egg for how she controlled your life and refused to believe you. She might make this easier than your poor uncles did.*" The Agent rocked the chair, pleased with the situation. He frowned when he lifted his hand from the armrest, removed the handkerchief, and wiped his filthy fingers in disgust. "*Do you think she will believe the ink-fingered newspaperman?*"

"Why are you doing this? No one who was there when you died is even alive."

"*You little Kentucky rube— What about Sleeping Beauty I laid out in the woods back in '27?*" the Agent replied. "*Besides, I don't need a reason. I have always hated you people. Willie wasn't the first Kentucky white trash I dumped.*" Barlow's shoes pressed against the porch planks as he rocked.

"*Back in the war,*" he said, "*I had the bad fortune of fighting Germans with Lieutenant Maxie Fleming from Viper, Kentucky. What a bluenose he was. Even though he was from Kentucky and had marbles in his mouth, he somehow rose to command our platoon. Think about it, Shelly girl. A man born down the road from Madden County tellin' me what to do is a sin against natural law.*"

Sheldon stood, and another gust of cold wind cut through him. He had no weapons and wasn't sure they would hurt the Agent anyway. Barlow rocked—red splotches caked his suit, and a dense web of focus crossed his face.

Evangeline would sit in the same rocking chair and tell stories when Sheldon was younger. He pictured her animated, creating different voices for each character.

"*No one bossed me when I was back in Boston, except for my dad. He owned a knife factory in Quincy. When the war started, my*" *father saw dollar signs. Just like old Henry Ford made cars, Barlow made knives, swords, and bayonets, and he sold them to both sides of the war.*

"*But it didn't matter to the uneducated hillbilly, Fleming. He took command and told everybody what to do. The other dolts over-looked his way of talking and his country-fried boy scout routine and trusted him.*"

There is no escaping this evil, Sheldon thought. He stood in place, hoping the nightmare would end.

"*Fleming led us in the charge at Belleau Wood. The comman-ders wanted us to take out the Huns with bayonets and hand-to-hand, so he and I jumped into the trenches and fought together. I stayed on his tail the whole way as we sliced and stabbed through nameless, faceless men. Maxie was about as fierce a warrior as I have ever seen.*

"*Fleming killed nine or ten Germans by himself. I walked up to him and patted him on the back as he bent over to catch his breath. When he turned, I shoved one of my daddy's sharpest blades right between his ribs and twisted.*

"*Sheldon Grace, you should have seen his damn face. He froze, then dropped to the ground. I let him bleed until the spark left his eyes, and then I yelled for a medic.*"

"What are you?" Sheldon's throat tightened as he resisted the urge to cry.

"*I just told you, boy. I am the blade between the ribs of everyone you know. That's why I don't mind waiting before I let your big sister see me. She will never believe you, Sheldon. She would not have believed Willie and won't believe I exist even when she first puts those peepers on me.*"

The Agent laughed, stood, his gray skin like putty, and walked toward the concrete porch steps.

"*Now, Shelley Belly, thanks to you and your sissy, I can give these busybodies the same treatment old Maxie received."* The Agent stepped from the porch and walked into the darkness.

Within moments, Shel was alone, still shivering. He backed into the house, watching for the Agent. When he was sure Barlow was gone, Sheldon called Sarah's number.

Chapter 55
On the Phone With Sylvia

"I know," Evangeline said. She lowered her voice and made sure she had closed the office door. "Sheldon keeps spiraling. I found out he opened a letter Uncle Willie sent me."

"He shouldn't have read your mail, but it isn't the worst ever," Sylvia said. "I stole twenty bucks from my mom's purse to shop at the Jefferson Mall."

"Your first steps toward the criminal underworld," Evangeline said. "I am alright he read it. However, the letter rambled about evil spirits. I loved Willie, too, but Sheldon reads the insane letter as if it is true, ghosts and all."

"But you didn't find drugs?"

"I'm not sure if he is using drugs since I found the letter. Maybe Sheldon has lost his mind."

"I thought arresting Willie's killer was your final task," Sylvia said. "This is the big bust you were after, plus you have linked it to Willie's murder. That is a walk-off home run."

"I wish my dad were here. He would know what to do," Evangeline said.

"Probably take us to breakfast at Spence's Diner and make me eat a mountain of bacon."

"I don't know, Syl. The county is still in bad shape. There is something wrong with pinning Willie's death on Darryl Bell."

"You know I love you, Vangie, but...." Sylvia paused, and it extended longer than Evangeline liked. "I'm not pressuring you, but we have to seal the deal on this contract in five days, or the commander demands I look in-house for the position."

"I know, Sylvia." Evangeline cleared her throat. "Okay, changing the subject, I have to go. I will give you a call tomorrow."

"Evangeline, it is what we planned and what you always wanted, am I right?"

"Do we ever get what we want, Sylvia?" Before Sylvia could respond, Evangeline said, "We will talk soon." She placed the receiver back in its cradle, rolled over, and stared at the ceiling. Her dad would not hesitate to celebrate apprehending the Highlander. But he would also have an answer for everything wrong with the arrest and Willie's murder. Evangeline, though, found only more unanswered questions.

Her father had died four years before, but it felt as recent as Willie's death. Evangeline recalled the Wednesday her dad said he felt too tired to work. Seeing him stay home for anything was rare, so he visited Dr. Turner on Friday. The doctor sent blood to Lexington for a diagnostic analysis. Turner worried about the sheriff's bruised arms, and his fatigue was uncharacteristic. By Tuesday, the results were available, and the sheriff had had a Lexington Oncology Center appointment on Thursday.

He called for a meeting in the Conference Room on Monday morning. Everyone, including Paulene and Otis, was required to attend. Her father had announced he was diagnosed with Leukemia and scheduled to check in at the hospital later for treatment. He expected to beat cancer "Like a copperhead in a strawberry patch." He had also announced that he had spoken with the

County Judge Executive and appointed Evangeline to be the Interim Sheriff until he returned—or until the next election, if need be.

Everyone was stunned. Art had said, "Sheriff, she is the best of the best." Junebug had nodded while Luke simmered, and everyone else had remained silent.

Her father had laughed and wrapped his long arms around her. He had whispered, "You were born to do this, remember?"

One week later, at high noon, a doctor stepped into the waiting area and relayed the bad news—a brain aneurysm had ended her father.

She had arranged the funeral and transport by phone that day, then driven home on the Mountain Parkway, the long winding road connecting Eastern Kentucky to the rest of the state. The highway rose and fell, turned, and spiraled like a paper airplane carried by the wind.

The journey had proved eventful. First, Evangeline had helped a carload of nursing students stranded on the road. One had slipped her phone number into Evangeline's pocket. Thirty miles later, a mobile home near the highway had caught fire. The flames unfurled into the falling darkness, and white flakes of ash speckled the graying sky. She had stopped to help, but an older man had said everyone made it out unharmed. He was short, balding, and approached eighty years old. His eyes suggested he had experienced much more significant losses than this.

"It'd be good if we all come out unharmed at the end," he had said.

She had nodded but not spoken for fear she would break. When a fire truck arrived, she slipped to the cruiser and sped away, crying until she reached home.

"It's how I feel now," she said aloud as she turned her chair away from her desk. "I am watching a house burn. Only no one makes it out unharmed." Her mind flashed images—Sheldon's face, the tire tracks on the strip mine, the Ironweed flowers on Hammond Creek, the picture of her father with the governor, the signed contract on her desk, and Sylvia waiting for her. It ended with Brett's face on the football field.

"Daddy, I wish you were here with me. What should I do?"

Chapter 56
Truth Rests in Uncovering Someone Else's Lies

G ene Begley arrived at 5:00 AM to drink coffee in the glow of his computer monitor. Main Street was quiet, the phones did not ring off the hook, and his brain incubated and hatched his best and worst ideas. Wood smoke tinged the morning air, and the Madden Coal trains, carrying coal to far away places, sounded musical, the melody gentle.

Lilly urged him to stop working so much. "You have to slow down, Dad," she would say.

He smiled. If only Lilly realized he slowed down more each day. He worked hard because the slower his pace, the more consuming his need to work became. He wanted to write many more commentaries on social issues and poke fun at influential people until they felt accountable. Gene needed his time on Earth to mean something so his dear Maude would be proud.

He glanced at the folder on his desk. It was his great white whale, he thought. An event in Madden's past had poisoned the county's history, future, and present. Despite his efforts, he generated more questions than answers. It was something in 1927, right before Madden County avoided a bloody coal war. "It sounds crazy," he said into the empty room, "but the county's truth rests in uncovering somebody's lies."

Gene took a Sharpie from his desk, used his teeth to pull off the cap, and scribbled across the folder, "Goldenrods." He replaced the lid, leaned back in his office chair, his hands behind his head, and looked toward the train set curling across the tables.

The floorboards creaked outside his office door.

Often Sarah came by before school to drop off some edited copy or pick up a task she would have time to complete during the school day. It was earlier than her usual drop-in, but she worked hard, so he wasn't surprised.

"Come on in—"

The door swung open, slamming the inside handle against the wall. Gene leaned forward and turned.

"What in the hell are you doing?" Gene peered into the unlit hallway.

The Agent carried the darkness into the office with him.

Gene stood and lost his balance, using the chair to avoid a fall. A faded figure stood before him. A fedora drooped over the man's forehead, the brim concealing his eyes, and his dark suit and red tie dated back to an early-century advertisement insert preserved in the archives.

"*I wondered, Mr. Begley, if you might sell me an old Boston Post newspaper,*" the Agent said. The Boston accent echoed in Gene's ears.

"We don't sell old—"

"*Of course, you don't market in real newspapers. Not enough people here can read.*" The Agent's laughter caused Gene's stomach to churn. "*If you want to keep your money safe in Madden County, hide it in the local newspaper.*"

"Whoever or whatever you are, Mister, I want you to leave my office this minute."

Secrets and Blood

"My poor daddy appeared in the Boston Post back in 1924," the dark figure said, ignoring Gene's demand. *"Yep, someone stabbed him and cut his throat from ear to ear with one of his own Barlow pocket knives. Brutal murder—yes, it was. The Post covered it and even printed an obituary telling the world how good my old man was."*

Gene stood still. His eyes narrowed, and his wrinkled brow unfurrowed. "It's you. You killed Willie Grace."

"Ring a ding, ding. Somebody hand the hillbilly a prize. He just won first place at the Madden County Hog Screwing contest." The Agent giggled and slapped his knee, then changed his tone. *"So you've been digging into the past, Mr. Newspaper Man. You forgot what the word 'new' means, I guess. When you stick your shovel in someone else's dirt, you dig your own grave."*

"What are you? Some spirit or demon?" Gene sidestepped to the window. "Jesus, you look more like volcano lava than a man." Gene's hand flew to his mouth. The figure, his skin nothing more than ridges and ravines, advanced into the office.

"My honorable father used to say I didn't act like a man, even after returning from the war. Always telling me he wouldn't leave his company to a fool like me, no matter what happened." The Agent shuffled closer. *"He said he would rather give it away."*

"So your father was a Barlow. Are you Daniel Barlow, the Baldwin Agent? You can't be." Gene refrained from glancing at the folder on his desk, keeping his eyes riveted on the monster.

"See, you are acting like my dad, constantly questioning who I am and what I am."

Gene retreated until his back pressed against the window. As he focused on the Agent, he hooked his fingers under the small handle attached to the window frame.

"You are not reading the whole story, are you, newspaperman?" The Agent shook his head back and forth. He flicked his wrist, palm up, retrieving a knife from his sleeve. Gene heard the click as

a silver blade sprung from the pearl handle. *"You must not write the obituaries for this rag."*

Old paint wedged the window closed. Gene hefted it with all the force he could muster, causing the paint to crack as the window slid upward. Gene realized it had only opened a few inches before freezing in place. The cool Autumn air drifted into the room, and the newspaper editor felt it against his hand. *These are the softest winds in the south,* he thought.

The Agent leaned down, pushing his face into Gene's until their noses touched. He pushed Gene against the window frame. Gene gagged on the Agent's breath, a mixture of decomposing carcass and sulfur. As the knife penetrated his abdomen, Gene fell forward, his head falling on the Agent's shoulder. He heard the early morning coal train, and for a moment, he thought of sitting beside Maude on a train, the steady rhythm of the wheels against the track. He heard the train whistle blow as the Agent towed him toward the desk, the silver blade still in his stomach.

*****

Sarah hurried along the sidewalk. She did not want to be late for first-period English, but Sheldon's message to Gene was important. It would be easy to duck into the newspaper office before school and slide into her front-row seat in Mrs. Kirk's class. She was undefeated against the tardy bell. Her ambition was to be a journalist, so English mattered.

Her backpack was heavy, but Sarah considered it a way to increase her vertical leap for volleyball. She lifted her shoulders and stood straighter. The cool morning air lifted strands of her long black hair, but her jeans and gray Madden County Miners sweatshirt kept her warm.

Ever since her father and mother divorced, she had felt obliged to be independent. She worked to excel now so her path would be easier later. She did not mind living with her father, but, in effect, she lived alone. Even when home, he was seldom present, so she spent her days practicing self-reliance. It caused her to be protective of Sheldon—*because I do not want him to protect me.*

Besides, these were crazy times. Sheldon's sinister paranoia made her fearful. She accepted his ramblings and fascination with the past, but she was unsure what he hoped to find. Add her father's fragile grip on the company, and she felt like a tightrope walker poised between two lives. Sarah smiled at the image of herself in a sparkling leotard, a large audience holding their breath as she danced overhead.

Nonetheless, she refused to drift off course like many others in the mountains. Her friends thought life was easy for her. They perceived her as rich, attached to the sheriff's son, and intelligent—even the most challenging teachers loved her. But they did not know the whirlpool beneath the surface—the anxiety, the heart-break, and the feeling of abandonment since her mom's departure. She wore her doubt like an itchy sweater.

Gene's small Toyota truck, the tailgate extended like a tongue, was in his usual parking place. He was always there. She knew Gene was already at the office, so she pushed open the door and ran up the stairs.

"Gene, Gene dancing machine," she said when she entered the front office. Of course, she would not be so casual with guests in the office, but Gene wasn't as hard-shelled as everyone thought. She slid under the backpack and dropped it near her desk as she entered Gene's office. "I have a message for you from Sheldon. I'm not sure...."

Gene slumped over his desk with his arms crossed on the surface. His face wasn't visible, and he did not respond to her entrance.

"Gene, you taking a nap? You better listen to Lilly and stop putting in so many hours." Sarah approached him. The scene was off-kilter. "Gene? Are you playing opossum?"

Still.

Sarah touched Gene's elbow and shook it when she reached his desk.

Still.

Her smile faded as she stepped closer and placed her hand on his shoulder. "Gene, wake up. You are scaring me."

She lifted him to see his face. Gene's shoulders rose off the desk, but his head remained behind as if a magnet attached it to the table. Sarah did not understand at first. However, vomit rose into her throat when she recognized the truth—someone or something severed Gene's head from his body.

Sarah's heart drummed as she backpedaled toward the window. Her shoes sank into the blood-soaked carpet, causing her to stop and stare at her feet.

However, when the office door slammed shut and the tall figure behind it laughed, she froze. As the man came toward her, his splotched face and opaque eyes cradling a smile, her legs lost all strength, and her speech abandoned her. The cut separating Gene's head from his body flashed across her eyes. When the distorted figure engulfed her face with his palms, she smelled his stench, and the moisture on his hands reeked of copper and iron, just like the blood at her feet. When he closed her eyes with his thumbs, darkness overwhelmed her.

In a moment, she was still.

Chapter 57
First Remnants

Evangeline heard crying as she entered the *Madden County Mercury* office. At the top of the stairs, Junebug held Lilly Begley in his arms, her face buried in his shoulder. Junebug nodded to the sheriff and motioned toward the open office door behind them. Inside, Deputy Butcher knelt on one knee, placing an evidence marker on the saturated carpet near the window.

"Any idea how long?" she asked as she entered. Evangeline's eyes panned the room like a movie camera as she awaited Art's response. A whiteboard covered with a few old photographs and news stories attracted her attention first.

Then, she noticed a framed picture of Gene, Lilly, and Maude on the wall. Lilly was a very little girl, five years old at most, wearing a floral white and yellow dress. Missing teeth interrupted her smile, but that only caused it to be more beautiful. Gene's wide, authentic grin and straight shoulders hinted at a different person than he was today. There was truth in his happiness. Maude's green eyes and high cheekbones mirrored Lilly's features, and her brown hair rested on her thin shoulders. Maude's eyes resonated with kindness, reminding Evangeline of her mother's gentle face. Gazing at the picture and anticipating the horror at Gene's desk caused Evangeline to recall how she had treated Gene with animosity the last time she talked with him. She lowered her eyes.

"Best we can tell, he's been here since early morning," Art said. He looked at his thick wrist and said, "It is 4:15 PM, so I estimate between nine to ten hours."

Evangeline always examined everything else at crime scenes before inspecting the victim. Gene was facedown when she moved to the desk, his head detached from his torso. Bloodstains indicated he had bled on the desk's surface, but there was not enough quantity or spatter to suggest he had died there.

"It looks like he was attacked here by the window," Art said. "It is open four inches, so he may have been trying to escape. The cuts are similar to Willie's wounds at the jail."

The blood spurts stretched like oil-painted tentacles several feet onto the carpet, and blood on the wall indicated a right-handed assailant had sliced Gene. Evangeline had already concluded it was the same killer who had murdered her uncle.

The sheriff walked toward the desk, smelling the first remnants of death in the air. She leaned over to better view the body.

"Bring an evidence bag over here, Art," she said. The sheriff leaned closer to the desk's surface as Art approached her.

Gene's severed head rested on a black permanent marker and a thick manilla folder she recognized. She held Gene's skull in place with one gloved hand as she removed the folder and lifted it with her latex-covered fingers. Written in black lettering across the folder was a single word. *Goldenrods.*

After Art secured the folder in plastic, Evangeline accepted it and walked toward a model train on the room's other side. She bent down beside the black folding chair under a small desk covered in legal pads, pens, and scissors.

"Since Dr. Bell isn't available," Art said, "we may have a problem getting a good exam for the cause of death."

"We have a much more urgent problem, Art." The sheriff stood and lifted a heavy school backpack covered in volleyball stickers shoulder high.

*****

When Sheldon arrived on his bike, he did not engage the kickstand. He allowed the bicycle to tumble onto the sidewalk near Evangeline's police vehicle.

Cars and trucks rolled by the scene, and the occupants ogled the officers blocking the entrance to the building. Several women gathered outside Adele's Bookstore to observe the action.

Art stepped into the street and directed the traffic around the police cars and cones.

Evangeline recalled the night her brother burst into the station after Willie died. He had the same panic in his eyes now as he had then. He sprinted toward her, then stopped two yards away.

"Is Gene alright? Is Sarah here?" The words emerged between his gulps for air and frantic hand gestures.

Evangeline hesitated, then spoke. "Sheldon, I don't know where Sarah is."

He folded his hands into fists and held them at his side. "Gene Begley was discovered dead in his office. We found Sarah's school backpack near her work desk."

"Oh God," he said. "It is my fault. Why did I call her?"

"It isn't your fault, Sheldon. She isn't here now, but I believe she visited the office this morning to drop—"

"No. I called Sarah last night and asked her to tell Gene to be careful. It is just like I told you. Because the two of us know the secret, it is open season on anyone the Agent wants to kill."

She closed her eyes. Frustration percolated inside her again. However, so did doubt. Fear tempered her previous certainty. She wondered how Sheldon had known about Willie's death and how Willie's murderer had entered the cell and left undetected. The more she thought about those issues, the less logical she became.

"Slow down, Sheldon. We should focus on finding Sarah rather than blaming ourselves," Evangeline said.

"The Agent hinted he would kill people we know, and it's my fault." Sheldon paced in a circle; his arms stretched above his head as if he had finished a run and needed air. "He killed her. I know he did it to scare me. I did not think Sarah would come here, but I should have known when she wasn't at lunch or waiting when the school day ended."

Evangeline observed Sheldon for a few seconds before grabbing his shoulders. He stopped pacing and stared at her feet as she held him steady.

"This Agent stuff is not helpful right now, Shel. I need to find her. Pull yourself together and tell me, has she said anything about threats to Gene or anyone following her?"

Sheldon stared into her eyes. "You can't find her. She is with Barlow, alive or dead. You must find the Agent, but you don't even believe he exists." Sheldon brought his arms up and swiped her hands from his shoulders. "Barlow was right about you. You hate everyone here so much you can't even consider the possibility you're mistaken."

The sheriff stepped back from Sheldon. She motioned for Junebug to come and watched as he guided Lilly to lean against the wall. He whispered something to Lilly, then hurried toward Evangeline.

"Junebug, take Ms. Begley and Sheldon home. You can take them to Lilly's place. Stay with them and make certain they remain safe." She leaned into Junebug's thin frame and looked up at him. "Don't let Sheldon out of your sight. Keep them together if you can."

Junebug nodded.

Sheldon circled the room and mumbled to himself.

Junebug said, "Come on, Sheldon. You should help me take Ms. Begley home. She should not be here any longer."

Sheldon turned toward his sister, tears streaming down his face. "No, what I should do is kill myself, so only one person will have the secret."

Evangeline's heart froze mid-beat. "Dear God, Sheldon." She ran to him and put her arms around him. The sheriff steered him down the sidewalk away from Junebug and the others. "We will find Sarah and get this guy, I promise. But I expect you to pull it together and do what Dad would tell us to do. Find a way to come out the other side of this better than we are now and stay together."

Sheldon pulled away from her. "Don't treat me like I'm a lunatic, Evangeline. Just don't. I know I sound crazy, but you are the one who is insane if you believe this is some run-of-the-mill criminal." The teenager lowered his voice, but his eyes burned with intensity. He whispered, "His name is Barlow, and this time he will kill everyone else before he ends us."

Chapter 58
Wainscott at the Crime Scene

Evangeline heard Wainscott's Dodge pickup before it arrived. Luke guided him into a parking place next to her police car. As soon as the loud motor ceased, he exited the cab and headed straight toward her. Coal dust and dirt covered his blue button-down shirt, and mud changed his yellow work boots to brown.

"Sheriff, please tell me my daughter is alright." His voice strained.

"Mr. Wainscott, we aren't sure where she is, so I don't know. We called numerous—"

"What the hell do you know? My assistant said Gene Begley's dead, and Sarah is missing."

"It's true," Evangeline said, her voice steady. "We received a call from Lilly Begley at around 4:00 PM informing us she had found Gene's body in his office. We discovered Sarah's school backpack when we arrived. I am treating this as a kidnapping."

The stubble on his face and messy hair made him look older than he had at Willie's funeral.

"All we have is her backpack," she said, omitting the warning

Sheldon had asked Sarah to deliver. "We are talking to everyone to see if they witnessed anything."

"Sheriff, I realize you just made a big arrest, but this county is turning to shit, and it's all under your watch." His eyes drilled into her like an auger. His voice, laced with fear, turned into a whisper. "Listen to me. I don't care what it takes. Find my daughter."

Art moved to stand beside Evangeline. She sensed the deputy's urgency. "Sheriff, do you have a moment?"

"Excuse me, Mr. Wainscott. I promise you we will do our best." Evangeline broke eye contact with Wainscott and wondered what she would do or say if someone took Sheldon.

As she walked away, she heard Wainscott say, "At least until it is convenient for you to leave town. I don't need your promises, Sheriff. I need my Sarah."

Evangeline followed Art to his car. She knew he would not intervene unless she wanted him to act, but his lips were a thin line, and his eyes were narrow. "What's happening?" Evangeline said.

"Kevin at the gas station said a strange man packing something over his shoulder. The man headed east, and Kevin watched him until he turned up the sidewalk just past the bookstore. Kevin said the man moved so fast, whatever he carried was like a sack of feathers," Art said. "The only things back there are the creek and a logging road into the hills."

"Was he carrying Sarah?"

"Kev said he didn't think so this morning, but after hearing about Gene, he's not sure. The guy was slender and tall, wearing a hat and a suit." Art opened his notebook and read verbatim, "It was hard to see the guy because burns or something covered his skin. Besides, the suit and the hat reminded me of those dudes from the olden times."

Evangeline bit her lip. "Did Kevin act confident in the description?" She pictured Robert and Willie sitting at the Pinnacle, high above the hollers and creeks. Sheldon's claims about the letter echoed in her mind.

"He was certain," Art said.

The sheriff peered down the street and considered the man's possible escape routes. It did not make sense. Did he have a vehicle? If so, where did he park? Few spots existed on the street. He would not have cut between the buildings if he had left his car or truck and traveled in that direction to retrieve it. Nothing was in the back of those stores and offices, only a tiny yard with no room to park, a creek, and hills.

"We need to track him down before he hurts Sarah," she said.

Chapter 59
Too Much Evil

Junebug gripped the steering wheel while resting his other hand on Lilly's arm. She stared ahead in deep thought. Despite her swollen eyes, tear-stained face, and messy ruby hair, she was beautiful. He sensed her strength, despite her eccentric nature—a force he had not witnessed since Evangeline lost her father.

He glanced into the rearview mirror to check Sheldon in the backseat. The reflection concerned him. Tears streamed down the boy's face, but he did not wipe them. Instead, Junebug heard the kid murmuring, "It is my fault. I did this. Why did I call her? Sarah would never have been there if I hadn't told her to warn Gene."

Junebug tilted his head to hear Sheldon's voice better.

"I should never have been born," Sheldon said, then repeated, "It is all my fault."

Junebug listened without responding. He returned his focus to the road and concentrated on getting them to Lilly's place. When Lilly spoke, it startled him, and he tightened his grip on the steering wheel.

"Sheldon," she said, "what is happening? Who would do such a thing? Why would they want to kill my father and take Sarah away?"

"I told Sarah to warn Gene he was in danger," Sheldon said, his voice raw with regret. "The Agent wants to kill everyone." Sheldon used the sleeve of his sweatshirt to wipe his face. "But it goes back to me being born and opening Uncle Willie's letter."

"What agent? What kind of letter?" Junebug said. His eyes moved from the windshield to Lilly and back to the mirror. "I can't make sense of what you are saying."

"There's too much evil, Junebug. I can't say it without letting more into the world."

"That's not good enough, Sheldon," Lilly said through the open screen between the squad car's front and back seats. "There has to be a cause. I need to know who killed my dad, and we all need to know where Sarah is. If you know anything, please tell us."

Junebug said, "She is right, Sheldon. We are a mile deep in the hole. It is time to stop digging and tell us anything you know." He awaited the boy's response.

"Just tell us," Lilly said, her tone soft yet commanding.

"I can't," Sheldon said, the words bubbling to the surface. He remembered visiting a baptist church with his dad when he was a little boy. The preacher had called those who needed redemption to the altar. Sheldon had felt the magnetic pull to leap up and run to the minister. His father had held him back, telling him he was too young. Now, he wanted to tell Junebug and Lilly the secret, as much for himself as for them, but he refrained. "It is too dangerous."

Junebug placed both hands on the steering wheel and watched as Sheldon slumped into the seat and covered his face.

"You and I have something in common, Sheldon." Lilly's gentle voice made Junebug's heart lurch in his chest. He hoped to hear her pronounce his name with such kindness someday.

Sheldon's head leaned forward. "What do we have in common?"

"We have lost our mother and our father." She allowed the calm wave of her voice to roll toward him, leaving the space between them silent. When she continued, her words snagged in her throat. "It's a loss we can only recover by helping keep others safe."

Junebug pictured his parents gathered around a kitchen table. His father was a quiet man who built homes in Winchester and Lexington. His mother worked in a nursing facility's kitchen. Although neither offered him much affection, Junebug knew they loved him. Now twenty-six years old, he understood them better than when he was younger. He could only imagine Lilly and Sheldon's pain.

Junebug guessed Lilly's words had struck Sheldon, too. He sat taller, nodded to her, and leaned toward the front, placing his hand on the barrier as if to touch Lilly's shoulder. He appeared ready to speak, but he remained silent. After a few moments, Sheldon sat back and turned toward the window.

"Too much evil in the world," he said.

Chapter 60
Just Trust

"Pull over, Boss. I see something." Art pointed toward a worn path winding up the hillside. "It's a white tennis shoe."

They exited the car and examined the shoe. "It's hers, alright," Evangeline said. "This trail leads to the old DeLong family mine they worked for a few years. It is closed now, but we can get there by driving Route 40 and turning up Pigeon Nest Road."

"We had better hurry," Art said.

"Give dispatch and tell them where we are heading, Art. Have Otis, Luke, and Junebug meet us at the Delong mine. Also, just in case Sarah's hurt, have a bus join us. Besides them, I don't want any outside assistance. We don't need gun-happy idiots hunting this guy down, hoping to get a reward from Wainscott."

"I don't know, Sheriff. People around here pull together when needed. What if this is the guy who killed Willie? He could go into a cell, kill a man, and leave right under our noses. He has skill. Maybe Dr. Bell has contacted him from jail and wants us dead?"

"We don't have time, Art," the sheriff said. "Plus, if this guy killed Willie and Gene, we can't risk having our locals mess up, so he avoids prosecution."

It amazed Art how someone with her knowledge fell into self-made traps. For thirteen years, he had worked with Evangeline every day. She fought for justice in Madden County when it was not popular. She defended people. When church members harassed Harmon Pennix because they believed he had stolen money from the Eden Church of Christ, she stood up for him. Her efforts proved worthwhile when Lindsey Keith, the church pastor, confessed to the crime.

But at other times, she proved so narrow-minded she could peek through a monocle with both eyes.

"The good people will help you if you ask them, Evangeline," he said. "The people here in the mountains are your greatest asset if you just trust—"

"Just trust? Art, we have been through this before. Never underestimate Madden County's capacity for screwing up. Sarah is about as good as this place produces, yet somehow she may be dead at the top of this mountain. My brother hates me because of Madden, and he will go beyond hate if anything happens to her."

"Sheriff, you are right. We don't have time," Art said. "But a wise man used to tell us some things you must see to believe. However, other things you have to believe it to see it.'"

"Damn, Art. Is there anything my daddy said you can't quote?"

"Plenty, I am sure. My point is, someday, you will have to realize you can't do everything on your own," Art replied.

"Now I remember why I have you, my friend," Evangeline said as she started the car and peeled out, kicking rocks and gravel into the ditch.

Chapter 61
Sarah in a Sack

Sarah felt locked inside the belly of a ship. It was dark, and the rhythmic rocking came in vindictive waves, causing her to bounce, turn, and throw up in her mouth. Earlier, he had twisted her around and pried her shoe from her foot. He tossed her back and forth for a moment before she heard the shoe land on the ground nearby.

He will kill me, she told herself. She pictured Gene, his head and body separated like a broken mannequin. *I will be dead. Like Gene. Like Willie Grace. I will die.*

She trembled, and her head ached worse with each step. Branches and bushes swatted her legs as they ascended the hill. She realized it was a burlap sack covering her head and shoulders. A tight rope or string around her neck secured the bag over her head. The damp, wet dog smell caused her eyes to water, and its rough texture bloodied her cheek.

I am here to die.

When the man stopped, she wriggled against his shoulder. He laughed and, without warning, flung Sarah away like the shoe he had discarded earlier. When she landed, pain shot through her back and shoulders, and her breath abandoned her body.

"Now that's a kick in the gut, isn't it, Sarah?" The man's voice cut through her pain. *"One minute, it's smooth travels, then you're tits up on your back, wondering why the ground rose with such anger."*

The jolt reverberated through her body, and she struggled to breathe. She tried to remove the fabric surrounding her face, but her arms refused to act.

Soon a strong hand tugged on the burlap. *Maybe I am better off in the darkness?* The man was dramatic, removing the cloak inch by inch. Her head felt condemned, and she tasted blood.

When he removed the sack, her eyes adjusted to the dimming sunlight. The man standing over her was all edges and angles, topped by a hat creased like a paper airplane. The sky caused her to squint. Her hair supported her aching head like a thin, black pillow.

She withdrew from the man's large, textured hands. Dark skin tags hung like mounds of flesh on his knuckles, and his long webbed fingers dug into her skin. He wore a jacket and an out-of-fashion tie as if delivering Bibles door to door in town. Blood stained his shirt and slacks. Sarah concluded it was Gene's blood.

Red and black flecked the whites of his eyes, while his pupils were gray like ash from a wood fire. His cheeks resembled the clay pots in Ms. Sutton's art class, especially the ones impatient students had removed from the kiln too soon. His nose was a crooked mass of blue veins and burned flesh spread across his face like melted nickels. But his red and black smile caused her to squirm. His wet mouth, encircled by fragmented yellow and black teeth, reeked decay.

Sarah pictured herself rolling over, leaping to her feet, and sprinting away from this monster. But her arms and legs ignored her brain.

He mocked her as if he knew what she was thinking.

"Attagirl. For a minute, I thought you had died on me, but I can see those pretty eyes searching for the path down the mountain." The man's doughy lips formed words like the talking horse in an old television show she had watched with her dad—awkward as if chewing rancid licorice. *"A little country mouse like you might travel a long distance, I suspect. But you will be my sidekick until I don't need you anymore."*

Sarah winced when he kneeled beside her and pressed a knife against her cheek. She did not want to tremble, but her face shook, causing the sharp edge to press deeper against her skin. She stared into his ashy eyes, and her breathing came in rapid, shallow bursts mirroring her heartbeat. His hand was an inch from her nose. It smelled like wet copper pennies and rotten beef.

His other hand moved behind her, capturing a handful of black hair. He lifted her into a seated position, sliding the knife from her face to her soft neck and pulling her hair like a puppet's strings, forcing her to stand beside him.

"Take a gander at the big hole in the ground, Baby Doll," he said. *"Today, we are coal miners. Are you ready?"*

She stared at the knife, fearing her sheer will was the only thing preventing the man from cutting her open. When he twisted her hair again, she moaned and looked at the coal mine. The sun was high enough above the hills to illuminate the opening, but the cave devoured the light like a black hole they had studied in science class last year. The concrete sign above the entrance read, "Delong Mining."

"You are going in there with me, you little piece," he said. *"You better hope I need you for a long time."* He bounced her along—an awkward three-legged race as she lifted her bare foot from the dirt and clay. Her only shoe left prints on the ground as they hurried toward the entrance.

Secrets and Blood

*****

When they entered, the Agent seated Sarah with her back against the uneven mining wall. Jagged rocks and coal jabbed her back and legs.

The monster man threw a tarp into an empty coal car near the entrance. Sarah's father had given her a ride in an old coal car when she was eight. She remembered they were called tubs or buckets. The tubs transported men, equipment, and coal in and out of the mine. She worried the tubs might not hold them, but her father had told her each bucket weighed about 700 pounds.

The man swung an ax toward the low ceiling above his giant head. Each strike against the wooden beam echoed throughout the mine as wood chunks kicked to the floor. After he chipped away at the support until it sagged beneath the mountain's weight, he connected a black cord from the damaged beam to a handle on the first bucket. When he had completed the rigging, the Agent examined his work.

"What are you?" Sarah's voice was so weak she was unsure the evil man had heard her. "Why are you doing this? How did you kill Gene?" She cried and rocked her body, hoping to create enough momentum to stand.

The man whipped around, bared his black and white teeth, and walked toward her. His plastic face formed the same evil grin. The loosely connected parts of his body moved but were out of sync. An ax, the blade silver and sharp, hung from his hand.

He stepped over her as though she was not there, his wingtip shoes crunching the shale beside the track. He dropped the ax, causing the wooden handle to strike her bleeding cheek. Sarah had not noticed the kerosene lantern on the floor beside her, although it was the only light source in the mine. The man grasped the lantern and returned to her side, using his free hand to pull Sarah's hair.

Sarah's scalp burned as he dragged her deeper into the mine, sat her against the innermost wall, and positioned the lantern near the rails so the light illuminated the path they had just traveled. She could not see the tubs or entrance due to the declining slope of the mine's floor.

Then, the beast turned his full attention to her. He removed his knife, strutted toward her, and straddled her legs. He waved the knife near her bloodied face like a magic wand. Fear swelled inside her mind, making her vision unsteady—like a hand-held video.

The Agent traced her shoulder with the sharp point. He leaned closer as the blade traveled down her arm to her thigh. Again, Sarah struggled to breathe.

The knife drifted along her calf toward her bare foot. She shivered as the edge caressed her skin toward her heel. Sarah clenched her jaws as she said, "Please, I don't want to die here."

When the blade sliced through Sarah's Achilles tendon, her words collapsed into a high-pitched shriek. Poker-hot pain shot from her heel to her leg, and nausea flooded her stomach and throat. Blood leaked from the open gash, panic radiated inside her, and she fought the urge to call for her father.

She could not fight, and she could not flee. Her racing thoughts told her she would not live, either.

I wish Daddy were here, her brain repeated on a loop. All those times he had worked at the mines, attended meetings, and even driven coal trucks or bulldozers were irrelevant now—her past animosity was trivial. *I resented him then,* she thought. But now she resented herself, for the clay figure that had killed Gene and would kill her.

"*You have one little job left, Doll,*" the man said. "*It's something even a dimwit from the mountains can do.*"

Chapter 62
Always Shortcuts in Madden

Evangeline navigated the road with ease despite the sharp turns and potholes. The sun descended in the west, and darkness outlined the copper-tinted trees like one of Sheldon's drawings in Kindergarten.

Art braced himself when the sheriff leaned the car into a curve but did not complain. They had agreed to avoid the wider road and take this less-traveled route. Shortcuts were plentiful in Madden County.

Evangeline recognized the scars left behind by the mining operation. The broken pavement, the collapsed hillside, and the ruts created by coal trucks and mining equipment increased as they drove. Coal companies reclaimed the land usually. However, reclamation had not happened here on the company's private property. Most mines were closed and sealed when the work ended. However, the Delong site was different. At least several rich veins of ore remained. When K.P. Delong died, his oldest son continued his father's work, mining the land they owned in Kentucky, West Virginia, and Pennsylvania. However, the younger brother, who had left Kentucky for the comfort of

Charleston, South Carolina, decided his father would want him to close the mines. It was a battle Baron and Carl admired.

The Delong mine remained viable but inactive. The siblings and their lawyers still grappled about who would be permitted to decide its fate.

Evangeline pictured such a battle with Sheldon to decide who controlled their father's collection of Sheriff's Department hats and windbreakers. Her father had left some money for Sheldon's college fund, and he had paid the mortgage on the house down to a reasonable payment, but there was little wealth beyond those assets. Dad always said, "Honest cops don't have the money to buy everyone donuts."

"Don't pass the turn, Speed Racer," Art said as Evangeline accelerated out of a hairpin curve.

She tapped the brakes and turned right onto a rough dirt road between the trees. The trees swallowed the police car, and the deep potholes jarred Evangeline's teeth.

Focus, Evangeline, focus.

The headlights brushed the branches and illuminated the leaves scattering in their wake. The sun remained visible, but now the horizon resembled a bruised peach.

"I see the trail up ahead," Art said. "Pull off by those two walnut trees on the left."

"Let's make certain we are all geared up, Art, including lights and vests," Evangeline said as she eased the cruiser between the two trees. She picked up the radio and called the station.

Otis responded, "Go, Unit 1."

The sheriff shared their location and plan. An image of Sarah's shoe rushed into her mind's eye. "Did we get an ambulance?"

"Copy," Otis said.

Vangie viewed Art standing outside the vehicle, his body armor already in place and a large flashlight in his hand.

"And Otis, tell them to hurry."

Chapter 63
The Mine

"They were here," Evangeline said. She pointed to three shoe prints on the ground, toes aimed toward the mine entrance. Two tracks were prominent, while the single print was small but deep, as if the person had hopped on one foot. *It's a good sign,* the sheriff thought. *Sarah was alive up until this point, anyway.* The sheriff's muscles tightened as she imagined the man forcing Sarah into the mine.

Metal sawhorses and chains blocked the mine's entrance, but it was easy to enter. A concrete structure framed the opening. The remaining sunlight made the door a pale gray semi-circle, revealing the tail end of a coal tub a few feet inside the mine. "Delong Mining Company" stretched across the door frame.

"You ever go to the haunted house sponsored by the high school band every year before Halloween?" Art said. "For the first time, Callen wanted to go. We waited in a line longer than the Big Sandy River, but when we stepped up on the porch to pay for the tickets, he was skittish as a pony. I watched him wringing his hands and leaning closer to me."

"What did you do, Art?" They edged toward the mine entrance.

"I asked him if he had ever been to this haunted house. He stared up at me to say you already know the answer. Then he said, 'No, Daddy.' So I asked him, 'Then how do you know to be afraid?'"

"He said, 'I might not know what's in there, but I'm sure it ain't got my best interest in mind.'"

Evangeline nodded, and they approached the entrance.

*****

A dim light emanated from deeper in the mine. Evangeline directed Art to stop while she rested her shoulder against the concrete, watching the light flicker in the distance. The sheriff raised her flashlight, searching the mine. Her breathing was deep and steady, but worry knotted her neck, and she tightened her grip on her gun and the flashlight.

After her eyes adjusted, Evangeline pivoted toward the entrance and spotlighted her chest and face as if she planned to tell a ghost story at a campfire. She signaled she would proceed, and Butcher would remain at the entrance.

The three coal tubs and the railway dissected the mine floor. Jagged rocks and slivers of coal had fallen and narrowed the space between the wall and the tracks. The sheriff edged between the railing and the debris, her torch splitting the darkness. Two thick blocks were wedged under the third coal cart's wheels, preventing the linked tubs from rolling down the incline.

In the distance, a lamp shimmered, the light dancing against the dark wall.

"Help me..." It was as if the words drifted from the bottom of a well. Evangeline recognized Sarah's voice and its frailty. The sheriff glanced back to see Art examining the first coal tub and flashed her light long enough to show her location.

"Help me..."

The sheriff rushed toward the small voice, pointing her firearm like a metal detector and aiming the light ahead of her steps. Evangeline considered potential scenarios. She imagined standing face to face with Willie's killer, someone so dangerous she would need to take him out efficiently before he hurt or killed Sarah. She tightened the grip on her gun. *You were born to do this.* She visualized raising the gun and discharging it just as her father had taught her.

A roar reverberated through the mine. Evangeline lifted her gun and spun in a circle, bouncing her flashlight's beam around her. However, a second sound—a primal grunt—told her the disruption was behind her at the entrance.

*****

A canvas tarp rose from the coal car like the ghosts at the haunted house.

Art curled the flashlight upward and raised his hand to shield himself. The dark cloak fell away, and the beam revealed the attacker's deformed face and a blade arcing downward. The Agent roared as the knife sliced the deputy's sleeve. A maroon stain spread across the fabric near his elbow. Butcher did not fall away from the weapon. Instead, he lunged toward the man, grabbing the lapel and drawing the man closer.

Art smelled rot as the Agent fell toward him, the knife rising for a second cut. Before the blurred man followed through, Art pushed him away, seizing the man's wrist with his left hand and his throat with his right. The wrist felt like a thick bone covered in wet leather. The Agent's bare neck was half-baked dough in his palm, and Art's fingers dug into the rubbery skin near the man's face. Touching him made the deputy's stomach twitch. However, it also caused his attacker to grunt in pain.

The two men's noses were inches apart as Art glared into the

Agent's eyes. The deputy realized the evil creature was not human.

The deputy drove the attacker backward, causing the coal car to rock and sending the figure flying onto the floor.

The tub's wheels returned to the rail, hurling a loud crashing echo down the mine like an explosion. The Agent's animalistic groan trailed close behind it.

*****

Evangeline turned toward the noise, searching the void until she found Art, highlighted by the dim sunlight framing the entrance. The deputy motioned for her to continue into the mine, waving her away like a driver stranded on the road, signaling he did not require help. *He wants me to retrieve Sarah, of course.* As she continued toward the glow from deeper in the cave, she glanced back to see Art edging around the coal cars as if to change a flat tire.

"Help me," Sarah said. "Help me."

Between the cries for help, she heard Art yelling, too. "Hurry," he said. "Hurry, Evangeline."

The sheriff sprinted toward Sarah's calls.

*****

Art kept his head low and eyes wide as he crept around the tubs. He expected the man to ambush him again, so he unholstered his gun and held it near his hip. He never relied on his piece much when confronting an individual, but the blow this man had inflicted differed from those delivered by drunk coal miners and girls on Friday nights. Not since his football days had he been struck with such force. It wasn't just the gash on his forearm. The man's swing reminded Art of when an inattentive neighbor in a

Ford Thunderbird hit him when he was a boy. Art had walked away, but his body remembered the vehicle's power.

When Art reached the first tub's back corner, he waited, hoping the man was unconscious or immobile, although he figured it was too good to be true. Raising the weapon, Art could feel the blood soaking his sleeve. He wanted this issue to be over so he could escape this darkness. When his high school friends had chosen the mines for quick money, Art had left to play football and get a college education. When he returned, he had picked law enforcement over going elsewhere. Wouldn't it be ironic to die inside a coal mine after escaping the lure so long ago?

Art held his breath and dived from behind the tub onto his side. He aligned the flashlight with the barrel of his firearm and prepared to shoot. However, all he discovered on the other side was more darkness.

*****

Sarah's limp body basked in the lantern's glow as if she were on display. Evangeline rushed toward her. She heard Sarah's cry again. "Help me, help me!"

"I am here, Sarah," the sheriff said.

Evangeline pointed the flashlight at the floor to check for debris. She knelt beside Sarah, pushed the girl's hair away from her face, and lifted her into an embrace.

Sarah's dilated pupils and cold, clammy skin indicated she was in shock.

"Sarah, Sarah, wake up," Evangeline said, shaking the girl's shoulders.

Sarah's eyes opened. "Evangeline?" she said.

"Sarah, we have to go. Now. I'll explain later." Evangeline examined the girl while helping her stand. Dirt, coal dust, and blood caked Sarah's right foot. The severed Achilles tendon bled, but Sarah was upright, and the sheriff held her close as they walked on three legs toward the exit.

*****

Art cast the light all around. No darkness was as absolute as the black inside a coal mine. Soon night would prevail, ensuring there was no light except his torch. Chunks and slivers of wood littered the mine floor behind the first tub.

Two heavy cords were attached to the tub. Art followed the lines with the flashlight as they rose from the metal handles to the load-bearing wooden girder bracing the ceiling overhead. *What the hell?* He thought. *Why would someone attach—*

A scraping noise and a movement at the third bucket caused Art to stop.

He turned his light to the front of the train. The Agent stood twenty feet away beside the lead bucket. His gray face contorted into a smile, like a vicious wolf celebrating its kill. Before Art could react, Barlow dropped to his knees. The deputy heard another scrape as though the metal wheels raked against the rails. When the man returned to the spotlight, he presented the chock blocks wedged between the front wheels and the rails to prevent the train from rolling down the track.

The carts lurched forward, and the cords tethered to the girder tightened.

Evangeline and Sarah.

Art dropped his flashlight and gun to the hard floor and grabbed the handles on the bucket. He dug his heels into the rock and clay to hold the cars in place.

"Dear God, Evangeline, hurry."

*****

Art's urgency caused the sheriff to accelerate her progress with Sarah. Evangeline balanced the suffering girl on her hip, and they limped toward the door as if competing in a sack race. The bright lights along the mine's walls illuminated the path and allowed her to see Art better. It appeared the officer flexed every muscle in his body. His eyes focused on the tub as if he strained to push it down the track with his mind.

As they approached, Evangeline realized Art wasn't pushing the cart. Just the opposite—he held it back like the anchor in a tug-of-war. Was he afraid it would hit them as they came to the entrance? Before the words, "Just let them roll," left her lips, Evangeline stopped.

Thick cables tethered the coal cart to the damaged beams supporting the ceiling. If released, the heavy buckets would roll into the mine, breaking the girder and causing the roof to collapse.

The sheriff's brain downshifted, leaving only her instincts to act. She leaped from beside Sarah to face her. She drove her shoulder into the girl's midsection and lifted Sarah off her feet without hesitation. When Sarah's body folded over her shoulder, Evangeline galloped her toward the door. "Art," she said, "Hold on, Art, hold on."

Sweat streamed across Art's brow and red cheeks. His arms stretched the bloodstained fabric of his shirt, and his bent knees shook against the pressure. The heels of his heavy boots dug into the dirt and coal dust between the parallel metal rails.

"...hurt him," Art muttered.

Evangeline paused, uncertain if she had heard or imagined the words. "I will, Art. I will," she replied.

It was as if impatience streaked across his sweaty face.

"No. I hurt the man," Art gasped. Even his jaws appeared flexed as he increased his volume. "He can hurt." He enunciated the words with clarity and force.

When she passed Art, his face was no longer visible. His shirt rode upward due to his flexed shoulders and the vest. It revealed his undershirt. Something protruded from his left side about three inches above his service belt, and a dark stain formed around it. Evangeline wanted to move closer to examine the wound, but she knew she needed to move Sarah to safety. Next, Evangeline would find a brace or a block to stop the coal tubs from rolling. Then she would return to help Art.

As soon as she crossed the threshold and hauled Sarah another five steps beyond the entrance, Evangeline slid the girl off her shoulder onto the hard ground. Sarah moaned as she thudded against the well-worn dirt, but the sheriff ignored the girl's pain. Instead, she spun around and stumbled to face the mine entrance.

*****

Memories fragmented Art Butcher's mind. He lived his life challenge by challenge. Each day he attempted to become a better and bigger man. Whether it was physical strength, being a father and husband, or his job, Art sought to find the farthest boundaries of his body and mind. He pushed himself to his limits; then, he would step back a moment before, an inch before, a pulse before to avoid the painful collision between what he could and could not do. Then he rested, so the next day, he returned stronger, better, bigger, and ready to approach the edge again.

Today was not such a day. The inky black sky and the mine's darkness squeezed his vision. His massive back weakened, and his arms quivered like overextended ropes breaking strand by strand. The limit, the intersection, the boundary, this time, was behind him. Crossed like the wide creeks he had waded as a boy.

Art Butcher groaned. The handles slipped across his palms, his fingers failing as if an invisible tool pried them digit by digit from the metal. He held until he was farther beyond the intersections of his body and mind than ever before, where darkness exiled his sight and consumed his heart.

*****

Evangeline heard a groan and the wheels grinding as they shaved the rust from the rails. She threw her body toward the entrance, where Art staggered, and the thick cables, almost invisible against the dark walls, became taut and stretched—the descending tracks and the mine swallowing the cars. The cave's hollow, deep roar imitated Art's groan as the damaged wooden braces surrendered to the mountain's weight and the pull of the tubs.

The mine belched dirt, dust, rocks, and coal. A triangular stone struck Evangeline above her right eye. The jolt lifted her as the force from the crumbling mine pushed her ten feet farther from the entrance.

*****

Evangeline envisioned herself reaching out for Art and lifting him onto her shoulders just as she had Sarah. She carried him through the debris, gently placing him on his back. He smiled up at her and the world, for a moment, was decent again.

However, when the sheriff awoke, the yellow dirt pressed against her back and coal dust coated her mouth. The sheriff recognized the ambulance's red lights, tempering the blue and white police car's flashers. The collapse had dropped shards of coal and stone and splintered the wooden rails around her. Junebug and Luke hovered over her, kneeling as if they were praying.

"Art," Evangeline said, her voice hoarse. "Inside."

Junebug and Luke leaped from the ground as though their praying obligations were forever over, and they sprinted toward the rubble. She heard the deputies grunting as they strained to extract the rocks blocking the entrance to the mine.

Shaking his head, Luke lifted the radio handset attached to his belt and called for backup.

The Emergency Medical Techs replaced the two officers at the sheriff's side. It was the two EMTs she had met at the football field days ago. The female, a dark-haired Native American woman who appeared to be Junebug's age, tried to ease Evangeline's shoulders to the ground, but the sheriff resisted. Evangeline clung to the woman's arm and pulled herself up to see the mine, but the more she elevated her head, the faster the world spun.

"Help me see," she said to the EMT. The young technician turned to her partner. The large man, his shirt starched and white, shrugged and sprinted to help uncover the entrance. The EMT raised the sheriff to a sitting position and braced her.

The devastation and the first responder's desperate efforts caused Evangeline to tremble.

"Can you hear us, Art?" Junebug said. "Hang on, buddy. We will be there."

Evangeline rubbed the grit from her eyes. When she tried to stand, the EMT held her back.

"We will be here if he needs us," the woman said. "It does not help your partner for you to injure yourself further."

The words "if he needs us" scraped against Evangeline's brain like the wheels against the track, and she cried.

Clyde Perry's truck and trailer appeared near the mine. He removed the Bobcat bulldozer from the trailer within minutes and fired the engine. The men stepped aside for Clyde to excavate the rubble. His machine spewed dark smoke into the last vestiges of daylight.

When the EMT released her, grabbed her gear, and scrambled toward the rubble, Evangeline realized they had uncovered Art. She focused through the specks of dust and tears, but it was to no avail. Evangeline smelled the diesel fuel burning, but her brain was as foggy as the exhaust rising from the dozer. She stood, staggering like the drunks she placed in the tank each weekend.

When Evangeline stumbled and fell to her knees, she crawled toward the entrance. However, after the dozer rumbled a final time and fell silent, Evangeline stopped and listened.

The sheriff lowered herself to the cold ground as shadows prevailed across the dark hills and her grit-filled eyes.

Chapter 64
I'm the Damn Problem

Evangeline crawled deep inside the debris, her face blackened by coal dust and her eyes still burning. The walls were liquid night, like a puddle of black ink shimmering in her peripheral. Art turned away from her. "Run through the exit, Art," she yelled. She pointed past the opening toward the full moon outside the mine. But he did not move. She hurried toward him, pushing against his massive back, only to bounce off like a bird against a glass pane.

When he turned around, it was not Art at all. It was an undefined face, its features like melted iron, smiling at her—a wolf grinning at a helpless prey. She ran past him toward the moon visible beyond the exit.

Three blurred faces floated above her. A hard blink revealed Sheldon, Junebug, and Lilly. Sheldon sat on the bed, resting his hand on hers as Junebug and Lilly stood on the other side near flashing monitors, clear tubes, and a series of intersecting white cords. The lines on a monitor bounced like a ball rolling on uneven pavement.

"Hey, sis, you are okay," Sheldon said, his voice gentle. Junebug and Lilly stepped back from the bed to give them space. "You have been asleep all night and almost a whole day."

Evangeline tried to reply, but her mouth was dry, so she refrained. She glanced side to side, but before she asked, Junebug held a cup filled with water to her lips. The sheriff slid her butt up the white sheet and held his hand steady as she sipped the water until it was gone.

"Where are Art and Sarah?" Evangeline asked. Sheldon leaned closer to her while Junebug lowered his head, his black hair falling around his face. "Just say it," she pleaded.

"He didn't make it, Sheriff. They dug him out, but the collapse took him," Junebug said. "You know Sarah is okay. You carried her out and saved her life."

Evangeline's heart grew heavy as if anchored by the cables holding the coal tubs. She searched the room for a reason to disbelieve what she already knew. Evangeline berated herself. Disbelief was her default whenever anyone said something she did not want to hear.

Bouquets of chrysanthemums, lilies, and roses adorned the countertop near the bathroom door, and Hallmark cards crowded the mobile tray near the door. But there was no Art Butcher. She envisioned Maria and the kids, causing her chin to tremble and tears to race down her cheeks. She turned her head to bury herself in the white pillowcase.

"You did all you could, Evangeline," Sheldon said. "You saved Sarah's life."

"Sheldon, this is on my watch. Willie, Gene, and now Art and Sarah. I'm not the damn savior. I'm the damn problem," she said into the pillow. "I want to leave Madden County in a better situation. Even Dad would not urge me to stay now. He would drive me to the county line himself."

Sheldon's face morphed into a hard mask. "There you go, Evangeline," he said as he rubbed her arm. "You need to control it all. Dad wouldn't be blaming himself. No way. He would spend every waking moment putting the blame where it belonged, not feeling sorry for himself. He would blame the evil force that did this and figure out how to kill something already dead."

Junebug glared at Sheldon and shook his head.

Sheldon ignored the deputy and continued, "You dwell on your regrets and blame yourself. You don't listen to me or anyone in this town because everything begins and ends with you."

Evangeline listened to her brother. His words hurt, but she did not refute them.

"Now is not the time, kid," Junebug said. "She needs to rest."

Lilly stepped closer to Junebug and touched his shoulder. She said, "This isn't the time to rest, Ben. It is time to be angry and stop whoever is doing this to us."

Evangeline opened her hazel eyes and stared into the mirror near the bed. Her magnified, bloodshot eyes and the bandages pasted to her head made her nearly unrecognizable. She leaned forward to be closer to her brother's face and turned her attention to him. The hair on her neck stood, and the numbers on the monitor increased and flashed. "So, smart guy," she said, staring at her brother, "who do I hurt?" In her head, she heard Art's words, "*I hurt him.*"

"That's just it, my amazing sister," Sheldon replied. "You know who it is because you read Uncle Willie's letter. You won't believe it. But you will when you talk to Sarah."

"Don't tell me," the sheriff said.

Now it was her brother's turn to lean closer. Sheldon's pale skin blended into the bed when his hands touched the hospital sheets. Not even Junebug and Lilly heard the whisper.

"His name is Barlow. Agent Daniel Barlow."

Chapter 65
The Dead Man Walking

J unebug's radio rattled the kitchen table like one of Leon McCoy's clocks. It neared the evening, and Lilly, Sheldon, and the deputy were too tired to be startled this time. He picked the radio up and responded, "Copy, Paulene. Go ahead."

"Bug, just a heads up," Paulene said. "Someone has called the station three times for you. He won't leave his name or a message, so I tell him you are not here."

"Any idea who it is?"

"Not at all, but he sounds anxious if you know what I mean."

"Copy that. I'll stay alert, Paulene. Thanks for letting me know." Junebug returned the walkie to the table and checked his holster without thinking.

Lilly's house amazed Junebug. It was small, yet each tabletop, shelf, and corner offered his eyes something new. A Buddhist bowl bell cradled by a small blue pillow rested on the coffee table—a wooden mallet with a red felt tip balanced against the side. Various paintings and prints hung throughout the hallway and living room—ranging from Monet's *Water Lilies* to a poster for a

Bluegrass and Folk Concert in Bardstown to a *Monty Python and the Holy Grail* movie poster.

Built-in bookshelves revealed her eclectic tastes. Titles ranging from *Ethan Frome* to *A Midsummer Night's Dream* to *Salem's Lot* dotted the fiction shelves. Her nonfiction selections included such books as *Ancient Symbols and Totems*, *Magical Myths and Madness*, *Folklore and Mysteries of the Appalachians*, and *Dreams as Interpretations of the Future*.

Her home exuded the same warmth as she did. A framed photograph of her family hung above a small fireplace. Lilly was a girl, her elbow on her mother's leg as Gene stood behind them. He was dressed in a green blazer, a white shirt, and a light green tie to pull the outfit together. Lilly and her mom wore red dresses so long they touched the floor. Lilly's hair was less red and browner back then, but her smile was identical to today's. Junebug wondered if someone so beautiful—he aborted the thought, refusing to listen to the program running beneath his surface, telling him he was unworthy.

Junebug envied Lilly's close relationship with Gene. He had never been so fortunate with his parents. However, he did not envy her pain at losing Gene in any way, especially to such violence.

"Ms. Begley, this is a great house," Sheldon said as he rounded the living room, examining each corner. He reminded Junebug of a SWAT member clearing a house during a raid.

"Thanks, Sheldon. All I'm missing is a few hundred clocks spread around the room," she said, attempting to put him at ease. "With what we've been through, how about you call me Lilly when we aren't at school? Okay, buddy?"

Junebug smiled at Lilly, and she returned the favor, but he recognized the sadness crossing her face despite the joke. Tomorrow would be the visitation for her father. Gene's will had specified he did not want an overnight wake. Instead, he wished to have a morning visitation at the funeral home and then cremation in the afternoon. He requested that Lilly store his remains as she saw fit until she wanted to sprinkle his ashes on the flowerbed in her yard.

The deputy checked the windows and doors to ensure they were locked.

The sheriff had asked Junebug to protect Sheldon and Lilly right after Sheldon left her hospital room. Even if she had not asked, he would have kept them safe, but her order helped. Without Art, the department would be even thinner in a county already on the brink of chaos. Junebug figured Evangeline would call the state police or see if another county would loan Madden an officer for patrols.

When he thought about Butcher, Deputy Spears shivered. Junebug had spent his life hiding from his self-doubts. Art had been kind and supportive—an authentic person willing to share his experiences and imperfections. Butcher had taught him how to stay safe during a traffic stop, cuff an unruly suspect, and a million other things. He had lived in the world as Junebug dreamed he could live his life someday—without fear. Junebug choked up for a moment, so he turned toward a window and peeked through the blinds.

"You two make me nervous," Lilly said. She walked to the sofa and moved the pillows aside. "Come on, let's sit down and discuss some of this. As Dad says..." Her voice trailed off, but she sat down, dropped her shoes on the white carpet, and pulled her knees up to her chest.

Lilly's bare feet and the pumpkin-orange polish on her nails caused Junebug to smile. He shuffled over and sat beside her on the sofa without speaking.

Sheldon finished investigating and walked across the carpet toward a chair by the sofa. His steps resembled a death row inmate who carried a heavy burden to his execution. Only two options remained to help Sheldon. One was to coax him into sharing whatever secret he kept locked away, and the second was to find who had hurt Sarah and killed Willie, Gene, and Art. In truth, that would provide relief and closure for everyone.

Junebug cleared his throat when the dead-man walking eased into the chair.

Before the deputy could speak, Lilly, in a soft, measured tone, asked, "So, Sheldon, don't you think it is time to reveal what you are holding back from us? Who else needs to die before you open up?"

Junebug stared at Lilly at first. However, when he shifted his eyes to Sheldon, he noted the kid's agonized face. Lilly remained silent, so the deputy did the same to allow Sheldon to respond.

"I don't know what to do," Sheldon mumbled. "I can't move in either direction."

Lilly shook her head at Junebug. He knew she wanted the silence unbroken.

Sheldon looked at his hands, and Junebug heard his shallow breathing. "None of it makes sense. It can't be real, but it is happening. I am not as strong as Willie, and it's eating me up." He raised the sleeve of his blue sweatshirt, wiping it across his nose.

Finally, Lilly spoke. "You can tell us anything, Sheldon. Besides, how can things get much worse than they are right now? My dad, Art, and Willie are dead. Sarah is suffering. How could whatever you are holding back make matters worse?"

The boy's head rose as if emerging from a swimming pool. He stared back at Lilly. "You don't know—"

"And neither do you, Sheldon," she said. "Talk to us, please. Who knows? Together we may find a solution."

Sheldon sat contemplating Lilly's words until a soft knock on the door split the silence.

Chapter 66
Maria

"Arthur wanted to have your back," she said. "Isn't it funny?"

"What can I do, Maria? What?" Evangeline asked. The two women sat at the coffee table in Evangeline's living room.

Maria leaned back. "I am so angry at him right now. I told him not to get killed, but he still managed to leave me and the kids alone. Now, I want to get revenge on both of you. Arthur told me things behind your back. Shit, I figure I can get both of you at once and get back to saying goodbye to the person I will always love with my whole heart."

Evangeline leaned forward in the chair and cleared her throat. Maria appeared tired, although her thick dark hair and brown skin were flawless. She and Art had fallen in love at the University of Kentucky, and Evangeline found it easy to understand. Art often told her about seeing Maria for the first time and telling a football teammate, "That's her. She is the one." Maria's beauty and poise were evident even with the baby on the way and her keen sadness exposed.

"So all I need is for you to listen to me. Art said you were hard-

325

headed and insecure. You would not accept the good because you were never satisfied. Sometimes, he said, you insulted him by perceiving mountain folk as obstacles instead of people who needed you. It was like you thought you were better than the people here, which bothered him. He called you the smartest person he has ever met, but it did not make you superior to those you served."

"I see," Evangeline said. She did not mention Art had expressed some of those things to her face. No matter, the words stung.

Maria continued, "Art also talked about the differences between you and your father."

Spiders crawled up Evangeline's back. If the last words had stung, statements about her father would be a black widow's bite. Nonetheless, she listened. Suffering saturated Maria's words, but Evangeline owed it to Art to accept them no matter the pain attached.

"Art said your father trusted people and set the standard high for others to make Madden a better place. You kept the standard high for yourself but did not believe in others, so you treated them as helpless bystanders in their homes. I remember telling him you cared too much," Maria said.

Evangeline watched Maria smile as if she had unearthed a long-forgotten picture in a photo album. She awaited Maria's following words.

"Many people thought my Art was just a big, dumb brute. But you and I know he was wise. Art attributed his wisdom to your father. I will never forget what the big lug said when I defended you. 'Evangeline is like so many people who think people are most affected by their circumstances. But the truth is we are usually most shaped by the expectations of those we admire most,' Art said. 'Others admire the sheriff, so when she has low expectations for them, they adopt low expectations for themselves.'"

Small sobs accompanied Maria's final words. "You will never be as great as your father until you recognize your flaws."

The words cut, but they did not surprise her. She presumed this was how Art had felt about her and her father. But Maria was an overfilled container. The baby was on the way, and the significant loss was too much to hold. *Perhaps this will help Maria heal or free up more space for her unimaginable pain.*

Evangeline sniffed and asked, "Maria, is there anything else I should know?"

"Nope," Maria answered. In that single word, she sounded like Art.

Maria put her hand on the sofa's arm and willed herself to stand. Evangeline rose from her chair as well.

"I'll leave now, Evangeline. I hope I didn't say too much." Maria, her hand resting on her stomach, led the way until the sheriff passed her to open the door.

Evangeline felt Maria's hand on her shoulder. "I guess I should add this before I go. Art loved you like a sister and often told me you were his best friend. Next to me, of course."

A fog of sorrow settled over Evangeline's heart. "I don't know what I will do without...." Evangeline wept. She had believed that when she found the Highlander, she had met her obligations to her father and Madden County. Maria's words reminded her she had not.

Maria and Evangeline embraced each other. Both wept for a long time, bracing each other, so neither fell. But the fog never cleared.

Chapter 67
Evangeline Sees the Big Picture

Maria's words clung to Vangie's thoughts. The sheriff lifted her gun from the door-side table before walking toward the stairs, stopping to turn off the lamp near the chair. The air tasted bitter, and she had seen enough darkness, so Evangeline flipped on the upstairs hallway lights as she ascended the stairs.

Each step offered a different photograph on the wall. The first step revealed Evangeline's mother sitting on a chair as her father stood beside her. His big goofy smile glowed like a beacon. Images of Sheldon as a baby followed Evangeline's middle school basketball picture. Her black and red uniform shined, and she smiled, holding a ball under her arm. Another photo displayed Evangeline and her mom standing in the front yard, her father's arms stretched across their shoulders.

At the top, one picture remained. Evangeline had never examined the picture taken when the Governor came to Madden County. Before leaving for EKU, Evangeline had treated the framed photograph as a bad luck charm. It had rekindled emotions she did not want to explore again, so she averted her eyes. Even after Evangeline had returned from the Police Academy, she had ignored the photo at the top step.

But now, she forced herself to inspect the image. Her father stood on the politician's left, his smile less like a beacon and more like a smirk. She had stood on the Governor's right side, her arms crossed and her face stoic, unimpressed. The Governor's Hollywood smile suggested he was as unimpressed as she was but lacked the integrity to show it.

Evangeline studied her father. By God, it was indeed a smirk. She scrutinized the photo further when she noticed the campaign button next to her father's lapel. The design was an outline of Kentucky. She squinted and read the button—*Douglas for Governor*.

Evangeline blinked and focused again. "Douglas for Governor?"

Earl Grace stood with Governor Conley in 1976 while sporting a campaign pin supporting the politician's rival in the upcoming election. Dad waited for the picture after they disrespected him to hand the Governor a big fat "Screw you" as a lapel pin. Everyone had seen the image on the *Madden Mercury's* front page. The Sheriff of Madden County hadn't been the dupe—he had been the one doing the duping.

"What do you know?" she said to the empty stairwell.

Evangeline lifted the photo from the wall and gazed at her face in the picture frame's glass. Her younger self also stared back beneath the reflection. Her bandaged head, tired eyes, and swollen cheek reminded Evangeline of an injured soldier in *Saving Private Ryan*. She was sure her head was misshapen, warped like a deflated basketball. The skinny tomboy in the photograph was not bruised and bandaged, but she displayed anger and resentment. That day Evangeline had feared she was not enough and her father was not enough. She pressed the photo to her chest and wondered how she had missed so much for so long.

When she entered the bedroom, Evangeline removed Gene's files from the nightstand and placed them on the bed to make space to lean the photo frame against her lamp.

Still clutching her Glock, Evangeline entered the closet, opened the door, and unlocked the gun safe inside. The open safe caused her to picture the mine—dark, inescapable.

Moments later, when she stepped into the shower, she let the hot pebbles fall against her shoulders, face, and hair. Images of Art, the knife protruding from his back, collided against her closed eyes. The only person she trusted in Madden had died beneath a mountain as she stood there, too insignificant to save him.

But wasn't that the problem? Hadn't Sheldon and Maria expressed it right to her face? Trust. Even Art Butcher had chastised her for failing to trust others, especially the people of Madden County, yet she still stood in this shower, proclaiming there was no one she trusted. "Fools are not fools simply because of what they think," her father would say. "What a person does and doesn't do determines their foolishness."

Evangeline flattened her palms against the tiles on the shower wall as the stream massaged her neck. Water swirled down the drain, and thoughts swirled inside her brain. Art. Gene. The Hammond Creek house. The contract was pouting at her from the "Inbox" on her desk. Sheldon's face. Maria's words. Trust. She patted the washcloth against her swollen cheek and head.

People her father had trusted her to keep safe were dying. She slid down the white tiled shower wall, much like when she had heard about her mother's death. Only now, Sylvia was not here to hold her.

When Evangeline finally wrapped herself in a towel, she stared into the mirror above the sink. She was not the child in the photo anymore. She wiped away the fog obscuring the mirror and said, "I look like a thirty-six-year-old orphan." Over her shoulder, bright lights rose and fell across her bedroom window as though a spotlight searched the stage for an actress—or for a dark corner.

Chapter 68
Chiller Presents

Cyrus stood on the porch at Lilly's house. The sun peeked behind the mountains, but the tiny house was well-lit. The pumpkins, orange webbing, and plastic cauldron reminded him Halloween was days away, but that had never really affected him. Living on Hammond Creek behind the cover of trees and hills, it wasn't easy to go door to door asking for candy. Now, he was too old. Besides, he wasn't good at asking for anything.

Sure, some of his friends would play pranks, the occasional toilet papering of teachers' houses, or bags of flaming manure lofted toward front doors, but it wasn't his idea of fun. Some even took it too far by cutting down trees across the winding roads or getting drunk and fighting on a strip mine. He chose to hang out with his mom and Willie to watch horror movies on Chiller Presents.

Besides, fear was not a once-a-year event for him. He had always been afraid. He feared repeating his cousin Tucker's life, living on Hammond Creek and selling weed and Oxycontin pills to survive. But since Willie's death and his part in taking down the

Highlander, he had even less security than before. College was the only route to escape. But without Willie's help and encouragement, he wasn't sure it was his future.

Cyrus recognized Deputy Junebug's cruiser parked at the house. Since no one had responded to his first knock, he banged his knuckles on the frame with more force.

When the door opened, the lawman was tense, with one hand prepared to draw his weapon. Cyrus raised his hands, palms forward, to demonstrate he was not armed. Junebug appeared relieved it was only him, so perhaps the sheriff had communicated his role in arresting the Highlander.

"I'm sorry to drop by like this," Cyrus said. "When I heard about Deputy Butcher, it was terrible. He was a good man. But the news made me remember something Willie told me long ago."

Lilly appeared behind Junebug. She placed her hand on the deputy's shoulder. "Come on in, Cyrus," she said.

Junebug nodded, so Cyrus wiped his feet on the orange and black welcome mat and entered.

Cyrus waved to greet Sheldon and turned to face the deputy, anxious to tell his story. "Once, me and Tucker dug ginseng out on Rockhouse Creek. We earned about $90 each when it was dried and sold. But when I volunteered to take Willie out there to search for more, he was not too happy about it. He asked if we dug near the abandoned mine and the coal slurry pond."

Sheldon crept over to better hear the conversation, so Cyrus turned to include him.

"What old mine are you talking about?" Lilly said.

"There is an abandoned mine on Rockhouse Creek. The Wainscotts dug it a million years ago but never completed it. They shut down the mine, but since they owned the property, they turned the area into a coal slurry pond.

"Willie told me he had not been out that way since his brother died. I told Willie me and Tucker were smart enough to avoid the mine. The slurry pond was nasty, filled with coal waste and wash-off thick as motor oil. In geology class, Coach Douglas told us the pond has about 400 million gallons of sludge from the Wainscott mines. No doubt it is dangerous, but it has fencing around it, so nobody could fall in even if they tried.

"Willie said the place is dangerous for other reasons. Rock-house Creek is where everything changed for his brother and him. He called it 'Vadoma's little *Amer-reen*' or something similar."

Lilly reacted to his words. She walked toward the bookshelves across the room.

"It was one of those times Willie didn't make much sense to me. I asked him, 'Who is Vadoma?' He acted as if he had slipped up and told a stranger his computer password. Willie said, 'Be quiet and forget that name.'"

This time, Sheldon's face grew pale. The kid turned, stumbled, and moved away until he reached the sofa.

"I'm sorry if I am saying something—"

"What does that mean?" Junebug said. Although it appeared the deputy recognized Sheldon's behavior and Lilly's reaction, he wanted Cyrus to continue.

"I have no idea. I didn't remember it until I heard Deputy Butcher died in an abandoned mine."

Sheldon leaned against a chair, his face anguished and his shoulders slumped.

Junebug and Cyrus walked toward him while Lilly remained at the shelves, running her fingers along the spines of numerous books. She removed one and fanned the pages.

The deputy moved to Sheldon's side and guided him to the couch while Cyrus stood across from them.

Junebug spoke. "It will work out, Sheldon, don't worry, it's—"

"Got it," Lilly said. Cyrus watched as she rushed toward him. The teacher carried an open book spread across her hands like a hymnal in church. She wiggled between Junebug and Sheldon on the sofa and placed the text on the brown coffee table. "Cyrus, come close so you can see this."

Handwritten on the book's first page were the words "To Daniel From Vadoma."

Chapter 69
So Deep It Doesn't Have a Bottom

E vangeline wriggled into her sweatshirt and sweats and removed her gun from the safe. Her wet hair stuck to her head like a hair net. She pushed the brown strands from her eyes and hurried down the stairs, ready to see who had driven into her driveway.

The doorbell rang.

She glanced out the window. A large pickup truck growled in the driveway, the motor still running and the headlights cutting a path through the darkness.

Evangeline breathed and shook her head as she hid the gun behind her right butt cheek and opened the door.

"Mr. Wainscott," she said and nodded. She searched the background to ensure he was alone.

"I'm sorry to bother you so late, Sheriff. We didn't speak about all the mess today. Since Sarah is resting now, I thought I would come by." Wainscott's red jacket and blue jeans complemented his frame.

"You weren't so pleased with me earlier," Evangeline said. She moved aside to allow entry. The gun remained concealed. She stepped over to the door-side table as Wainscott entered and watched him as she rested the firearm on the table.

Wainscott nodded at the gun and said, "That's our world in Madden County now. We're not the Mayberry people picture when they think about rural counties." He paused before continuing. "I don't want to take up much time, but I need to say a couple of things."

Evangeline thought of Maria's "things" and took a deep breath. She gestured, inviting him further into the house.

Wainscott said, "Thank you," then stepped into the living room. She noted he did not sit down. Instead, Wainscott turned to face her.

"I am so sorry about Art Butcher, Evangeline," he said. "He was a good man. I propose the Chamber of Commerce erects a monument commemorating his great sacrifice. I owe him more than I can ever repay."

Tears welled in Evangeline's eyes. She pictured Art sitting beside her in her cruiser but heard Maria's words in the background. The hurt curled inside her like a hook piercing her heart. "It would be good if you helped Maria, his wife, and his kids. Deputies don't have large inheritances to take care of their families."

"I promise to help them. But I also need to thank you, Sheriff," he said. "You risked your life to save my little girl. I will always be indebted to you."

"Sarah is a special kid, Paul," she said. "I did my job." She forced a deep breath to remain composed.

"Yes," he said. I appreciate you being humble and all...." His words drifted. His body swayed with the burden of social discomfort. Evangeline allowed him to get his bearings. "Just thank you," he added.

"I've thought about what you said at the funeral home when we put Uncle Willie to rest," Evangeline said, hoping to redirect the conversation. She waited to see if Wainscott would say anything, but he remained silent. "You remember the part about the connection between our families? Your daddy supporting my father despite the politics?"

Wainscott's brow furrowed. He said, "It is still a mystery to me, but there are many things I can't understand. My daddy always said I was not the brightest log on the fire."

"You've managed well during difficult times since your father left you in charge," Evangeline said. "I believe our connection may go all the way to our grandfathers and the history of Madden County, although I don't know for sure. They worked together to keep the peace in Madden when other places like Matewan lost lives. Those towns had conflicts between coal companies, unions, and law enforcement, but Madden avoided war. Do you think it's what connected our families?"

"I must admit, I have not considered it, Sheriff," he said. "The problem is people have written books and made movies about Matewan, Sid Hatfield, and the union versus the coal company's hired guns. Madden managed to have peace, which isn't something the news outlets seek."

It was Evangeline's turn to nod.

"You keep me updated on anything you find, and I will do the same for you. Here is the number for the cell phone in my truck," Wainscott said, handing her a business card from his shirt pocket. "Call me if you get to the bottom of it."

"The past might be like those mining shafts, Paul," she replied. "So deep it might be bottomless."

He smiled. "The bottom line for me is you saved Sarah. I hope you catch the sonuvabitch and put him away for life. It doesn't have to be any deeper for me."

Evangeline did not like being thanked for failing, so she changed the subject again. She preferred to discuss the past, the future, or anything other than what had happened at the Delong

Mine. She said, "Thank you for the kind words, but I need you to tell me something, Paul. Can you be honest with me?"

His eyes grew large. "Of course, but what is it about?"

"I examined the Grantee-Grantor property book at the court-house the other day. I read the entry where your father transferred the deed to some Hammond Creek property. Don't you think the parcel of land and a house are worth a little more than a dollar?"

His face turned red, and his eyes narrowed.

"I can't answer that one," he said. "You know, my old man being gone and all."

Evangeline smiled. "I guess we all have our secrets," she replied. She gauged the effect of her words. Wainscott's blush became more crimson, but his face conveyed sadness, not deceit. She turned to lead him to the door. "I have a theory, you know."

"You detectives always do, Sheriff. Everyone in Madden County has a theory. I have always theorized you didn't want to come back here to work for Earl. Am I right?"

"I hope Sarah is resting well, Paul."

He walked toward the door. "You know what it is like to have a strong father, don't you, Sheriff? Sometimes they propel you forward, and sometimes they hold you back."

Evangeline smiled. She did understand what he meant, although she knew plenty of differences between their fathers.

"Thank you, again, Sheriff, for saving Sarah." He stepped onto the porch. Fall's last crickets and frogs serenaded her house—the ones who did not want to leave.

Wainscott stepped up into his truck and drove away.

Chapter 70
What If

As he drove home, Paul Wainscott played the "What if...?" game. What if he was more assertive, honorable, and courageous enough to buck his daddy's expectations? Would his life be happier now? He had not played the game for a long time and realized why he had stopped. Just because someone did not meet his father's standards should have meant very little because Paul had never met his father's standards either.

He was a forty-nine-year-old divorced man, still indecisive years after his father's death, unable to tell the truth even to himself.

Life is funny. You never really shed your past. No matter how long you hide it beneath the surface, parts drift down the creek, where somebody hooks it and brings it back to you.

Flashing lights drew Paul's attention to the rearview mirror. At first, he wondered if he had forgotten something back at the sheriff's house and she had followed him, hoping to get a second crack at questioning him about the past. Revisiting those times worried him more than any speeding citation.

Secrets and Blood

Wainscott navigated his truck to the shoulder, flipped on his overhead lights, and waited. The sheriff could ask all the questions she wanted.

Chapter 71
I Never Asked for This

After Wainscott left, Evangeline almost called Sylvia but did not. She longed to talk to Art but could not and needed to speak to Sheldon but would not. Instead, Evangeline sat on the bed, her knees pulled to her chest, and remembered her dad.

When the UK Cancer Center diagnosed Earl Grace with Leukemia, Evangeline had sat beside him while he received treatments. She had clung to his every breath the same way she listened to his experiences with police work. Except this lesson had ended with his final breath.

After their father passed, Evangeline talked to her brother for hours, assuring him they would survive. When Sheldon said he wanted to be alone, she granted him his wish. She had asked Ms. Endicott to check on him, then put on her running shoes. Evangeline had run so far that she lost count of the time and distance. Instead, she had allowed every step to punctuate her promises to her father. Evangeline had committed to staying at Sheldon's side, taking care of Earl's officers and the people of Madden County, and being careful as a sheriff.

She wasn't surprised or confused when he died—only weary. Thanks to Earl Grace, she knew what to do and how to do it as a sheriff. It was the personal part that confused her. How could she keep those promises and lead the life she wanted?

An instructor at the police academy once wrote on an evaluation, "Miss Grace is as sharp as a fifteen-year veteran." She had now served as an officer for twelve years and a sheriff for over three. She was a fifteen-year veteran but felt as sharp as a melted crayon. She wanted to reach her father's expectations, but the higher she climbed, the greater her descent. Willie and Art were gone, and Sheldon was on the verge of crisis. Madden County was crumbling, and even Sylvia questioned her intentions. The LMPD contract was a bomb Evangeline needed to detonate or dismantle, but she avoided it and its implications in the hope of keeping her promises. She drowned in indecision, incompetence, and insecurities.

"I never asked for this," Evangeline said. She rubbed her palms together, intertwined her fingers as if to pray, and clenched her jaws. She imagined how her father might respond. "You never turned any of it down either, Vangie, so face this challenge like a storm and run through it knowing you will get soaked, but the rain is good."

Gene's thick folder rested near the footboard. *Goldenrods.* Had Gene scribbled a reminder that she was a product of nepotism who didn't trust the people? She was not sure, but it didn't matter.

The next day would be Gene's visitation and funeral. She pictured his cold body, his throat slashed by the same sharp blade used to kill Willie. The following day would be Art's wake and ceremony, as well. She would be there, although letting him go would hurt.

It had only been four days since everyone had celebrated the Highlander arrest. She had been naive enough to believe the party signaled the end. She had lost sight of where she was. Madden County always yanked defeat from the jaws of victory.

The people at Gene's and Art's ceremonies would tell her how much they missed her father. "The way I have screwed things up, I guarantee they miss him."

Evangeline took a deep breath and stretched her long legs. Her toes nudged the folder she brought from Gene's office toward the mattress corner. The folder teetered on the blanket's edge and then dropped, scattering the papers and pictures across the white carpet like leaves littering the dying Autumn grass.

Chapter 72
Let's Take a Walk

"Raise your hands so I can see them," Luke commanded, motioning for Wainscott to exit the truck. Wainscott dropped from the cab, and Luke stepped over and motioned for him to move away from the vehicle. Then the deputy raised his shoe and kicked the door closed. The two men stood face to face.

Wainscott said, "Luke, you better tell me what's happening here. If you do and let me get on my way, I'll ignore how you're acting and let this go. You and your family will pay for your foolishness if you don't."

"He wants me to say some things to you himself. Let's take a walk into the trees," Luke said. Again, he used the gun like a divining rod, guiding Wainscott toward the trees off the road. "It'll be over after he sends his message. Then you can go on your way. If you need to report me, go ahead, but it is a good idea to hear what the Agent has to say."

"Jesus, Porter. You are scaring the hell out of me," Paul said. His hands trembled above his head, and his voice rose. "Who are you talking about? Are you receiving instructions?"

"Something like that," Luke said as he maneuvered behind the taller Wainscott. "Now, get moving, big shot moneybags." As they walked into the darkness, Luke listened for the voice to commence.

*****

The handcuffs cut into Wainscott's wrists. He leaned against an elm tree, his brown shoes digging into the soft dirt on the forest floor. "Who are you working for, Luke? What do they want?"

Luke stood six feet away; his thumbs notched into his pockets like a cowboy. "You know I used to love those Western movies with Harry Carey or Hoot Gibson. Those were some real men back then. Not Ethel's like you mountain trash."

"You're making no sense, Porter," Wainscott said. "Who is putting words in your mouth?"

"Wainscott sounds like a New England name. You may be blueblood, but you are still here amongst the poor, the tired, and those yearning to be me. My Vadoma would say you are guilty by blood. Where she is from, the son pays the father's debt."

Paul leaned away from the tree as panic ballooned inside him. He could not decipher Luke's words and wasn't sure it was Luke saying them. Wainscott stood up straight and measured the distance between Luke and himself. Should he risk a run at the officer to hurt Luke before he could draw the gun? Could he afford not to take the chance?

"I see your mind working," Luke's strange new voice said. He threw his head back and laughed. The laughter made Paul feel nauseous. "Let's experiment, Wainscott. I was in your predicament once. If you think you can get over here before I draw this gun from the holster, we will fight it out like they used to do on the waterfront or in Roxbury."

What the hell is he saying? Paul's heart revved like his truck's engine. Without responding, he lunged at Luke.

Wainscott heard the weapon clear the holster before his second step. The last things Paul saw before he fell were a flash and a cloud of sulfur.

Chapter 73
It Keeps You

T he book was ancient. Webs marked the cover, and the pages had yellowed over time. Lilly held it on her lap, her fingers bookmarking at least two sections. "I bought this book and several others from Adele's Bookstore years ago. Adele showed me an old box she secured when Sheriff Earl Grace auctioned unclaimed items from the courthouse storage rooms."

When Lilly opened the first marked page, Sheldon's leg bounced, and he fidgeted on the sofa. The illustration depicted a dark ghost—a form without a face—covering the entire page Lilly displayed. When Sheldon was a boy, he would sneak downstairs and spy on his father and Evangeline as they sifted through FBI sketches showing criminals' faces. If a police artist sketched Agent Barlow, it would resemble the picture. Shadowy lines outlined a somewhat human shape. Indistinct black and gray charcoals swirled inside the rough body. Different pencil markings filled the figures in this case, while the outer lines curved like a Madden County road.

"What does the drawing represent?" Junebug said.

Sheldon anticipated the summons, but there was only silence.

Lilly sat between Junebug and Sheldon while Cyrus was on his knees across from them. His elbows rested on the coffee table as he leaned toward Lilly.

Junebug smiled. "How do you even know stuff like this?"

"It is odd, but in graduate school, I wrote a paper on the similarities between the Romani people of Europe and the families here in Eastern Kentucky," Lilly said.

"Gypsies?" Junebug said.

"People called them Gypsies because Europeans believed they came from Egypt," Lilly replied. "Gypsy is considered a derogatory name, like hillbilly. They originated in India and roamed Europe to make a living. Others treated them like a plague. It reminded me of how mountain people traveled to places like Ohio, Michigan, and Illinois to find work."

"When I was in fourth grade, my friend Charles and his family moved north to Cincinnati, where his dad worked at a tool factory," Cyrus said. "Charles told me they nearly turned around because no one would rent them a place to live. People called them hicks and complained they would make apartments and houses too dirty for the good folks."

Lilly nodded. "It is something mountain folk and Roma had in common. Don't get me wrong—Roma's suffering during the Holocaust due to the Nazis is incomparable. But in small ways, they have similarities. Cincinnati passed a law to stop employers and landlords from discriminating against rural people. Northerners would say the hillbillies talked funny or had different beliefs and rituals than the city folk, so they pushed them away."

"Charles and his family came to Madden every weekend," Cyrus said. "I guess it makes sense to me now. I would come home often, too."

"Explain it again, Lilly," Junebug said, placing his index finger on the book's open page. "What does this have to do with Willie Grace?"

Sheldon watched, but the officer's question increased the panic swelling in his chest. If Lilly figured this out, would it free the Agent to destroy everyone in Madden? He shivered.

"I don't know what it means," Lilly said. She pushed her red hair off her face and refocused on the book. "When Cyrus said the names Vadoma and *Amriya*, I remembered the inscription from the book. In my research, *Amriya* meant a curse in the Roma language."

"It doesn't make sense, Ms. Begley," Sheldon said. His dissent was more a nervous reaction than a thoughtful statement. It all made sense to him. Cursing a family or a place to destroy the people he despises? That was the Agent's cruel work.

The teacher glared at him, then said, "Look at this, Sheldon. The Roma people probably weren't magical—"

Speak for yourself, lady. "Of course, they weren't," Sheldon said.

"But maybe someone familiar with spells hated Willie and my dad. They used to be drinking buddies, you know. Somebody with a grudge could be crazy enough to kill them."

"I want to know more about this," Cyrus said. "I'm remembering other things Willie told me."

"Like what?" Junebug and Lilly asked together and smiled at each other. It took effort for Sheldon not to roll his eyes. Then Sarah appeared in his thoughts. He missed her.

Cyrus continued, "Willie was a good man, so it stuck out when he said something bad about a person or place. One day, Willie told me to be careful with girls. He said I should find a good one no matter where she lived or what color she was. It made me laugh because my grandpa told me the opposite."

"So what?" Sheldon said. His word suggested he wanted Cyrus to stop talking. "That doesn't mean a thing."

"Let me finish," Cyrus said. "Out of nowhere, Willie said I should stay away from the strippers and gypsies. I did not even really know what he meant at the time. I thought I had seen a gypsy on television in a rerun of a Western. I said she was pretty hot, but I never saw a gypsy near Madden. He told me there was already one here. God, I laughed about it then because I thought he was joking about some woman in town. I wish I had asked him who."

Sheldon searched each corner. *Please let this conversation end.* His right hand gripped his knee with such force his arm muscles bulged.

"It can't be a coincidence," Lilly said. "Let me read this— 'Many cultures, like the Romani, believed curses and spells could help find love, keep loved ones safe, and bring good luck. However, they used the magical arts to punish opponents, control others, get revenge, and even allow the dead to remain in a place until they completed a task.'"

Sheldon stood, sure Barlow would show up at any moment.

"You okay, Sheldon?" Junebug asked.

"I am not," Sheldon responded. He turned to face the deputy, Lilly, and Cyrus. "I cannot tell you why, but we must get to Sarah and find my sister."

"Sheldon," Lilly responded as she placed the open book on the table. She lowered her head and closed her eyes, signaling her disappointment. It was a look he had seen on his sister's face too often lately. "Tomorrow, we have a ceremony for my dad at the funeral home, and then Elmo Phipps will cremate his remains. How can you not tell us everything you know about what happened to him?"

"I can't. It puts people in danger." He raised his hands and placed them behind his head.

Junebug spoke. "Keeping this secret also puts many people in danger because it hides the truth. The sheriff asked me to watch out for you because she feared you might hurt yourself. I didn't want to do it, but it is easy to see she was right to be worried."

A frustrated smile crossed Sheldon's face. "Junebug, the story I can't tell is eating me up. It killed my Uncle Willie, Deputy Butcher, Mr. Begley, and almost killed Sarah and my sister."

Sheldon glanced at the open pages spread across the table. He stopped breathing when he recognized the image on the first page. The picture depicted an eye surrounded by four circles. Within each loop, the artist had drawn a human form. However, each figure portrayed the human body at a different phase of evolution. Sheldon interpreted the picture as a clock. At twelve o'clock, the form was a simple man. The three o'clock image portrayed the man as a charcoal shadow, while the six o'clock figure appeared solid but resembled unmolded clay. The nine o'clock image replicated the midnight circle, but the face was angry and filled with hate.

"Then tell the story, buddy," Cyrus said. "Willie said to never put myself in a position where someone controls me because of a secret. He said you don't keep a secret—it keeps you."

Sheldon paced through the living room, his sneakers ruffling the carpet. He turned toward his three companions and said, "One thing is clear, I cannot say anything unless Evangeline and Sarah are with us when I say it."

Chapter 74
Evangeline

E vangeline flinched as if she had awoken on a raft cascading over a waterfall. She rubbed her eyes and recognized she was still in sweats and a tee shirt. The bedside lamp glowed, her bathroom door remained open, and the loose pages from Gene's folder littered the floor.

The clock read 10:00 PM, so she had not been out for long, although falling back to sleep would be a chore even with the pain pills.

Evangeline eased her bare feet onto the carpet, noting how the dull light from the lamp and the bathroom illuminated the papers strewn across the floor. The folder, *Goldenrods* printed across the cover, obscured part of a headline and a photograph.

The sheriff scooped it up along with other items at her feet. After spreading each separate piece across the bed, she examined them. First, she viewed a yellowing newspaper page with the bold headline, "McCoy Child Found Safe." It was dated October 24, 1927. Below the headline was a boy's picture, his face captured in fading black and white. His short hair, squinty eyes, and thin shoulders made him appear frail and unhappy. His father and mother, Evangeline presumed, bookended him as all three stood on a porch. The boy was there, but his demeanor suggested he did not want to be.

Another photograph and a second story were on the same page below the article. "Suspected Kidnapper Eludes Sheriff and Volunteer Searchers." Five men stood in the courthouse yard near the rock wall. The newsprint made the entire photo appear dirty. However, next to the newspaper was the original photograph. Someone, probably Gene, had printed, *Archives* in red marker along the bottom. Although not pristine, it revealed more details than the printed version. The men appeared almost as miserable as the McCoy kid in the first picture. Evangeline recognized her grandfather. He was tall, and his face appeared carved from granite. The others stared at the famous Sheriff Sheldon Grace as if awaiting orders.

Evangeline flipped the photo over. On the back, written in cursive, were the words, "Sheriff Grace talks to his posse, Mills, Wainscott, Ramey, and Reverend Adams after the search."

Returning to the article, Evangeline traced the fading print with her finger as she read aloud. "The sheriff and his search party did not find the suspect, Daniel Barlow, employed by the Boston and Virginia-based security company, the Baldwin Agency. The sheriff stated Barlow appeared to have exited Madden. County authorities have requested assistance in apprehending Agent Barlow for questioning."

Evangeline stared at the picture of her father beside the governor she had placed against the nightstand lamp. The image taught her photos told stories inside of stories.

After a moment, she lifted one of Gene's photographs from the quilt and leaned beneath the lampshade to leverage the light. In the background, kids played in the courtyard. One boy who reminded her of her father had separated from the other children.

At first glance, a fingerprint or smudge on the photo paper obscured the boy.

"Robert?" she said to the empty bedroom. The familiar face and eyes confirmed it was her uncle. A closer look revealed the flaw in the picture was not a fingerprint or a discoloration but a shadow. The darkness hung beside the boy like a misshapen balloon. She blinked twice and rotated the photograph toward the light again. The shadow formed the shape of a man. The shadow's source was not evident, but one thing was clear. It was a man in a fedora and a suit.

For a moment, the room spun around her. Evangeline picked through the folder's contents, carefully arranging them in their original order. She noted Gene's handwriting inside the folder stretching across the fold. Then she returned to the first articles and pictures, examining each one by one.

Another story, clipped from the back pages of a *Mercury* issue, depicted a birthday party for Leon McCoy dated a few weeks later. The McCoys had invited all the rescuers and Leon's best friends from school. The faded paper was even more yellow than in the older edition. However, the picture was clear. Leon, Robert, and several other kids posed for the photograph. The birthday boy's face appeared more appropriate for a funeral than a celebration. All the other children were smiling except for Robert. His stark face, his gaze turned toward something off-camera, reminded Evangeline of Willie talking to himself as he stared into the interrogation room's corner.

The sheriff's mind raced against her heart. She sifted through Gene's other artifacts. Several front pages from December and January celebrated how Madden County, thanks to the sheriff, Wainscott, Mills, and Ramey, avoided the bloodshed, death, and destruction other coal mining counties in Appalachia endured. Letters and editorials praised Sheriff Grace for his incredible leadership in difficult times. He was the "ultimate peacekeeper," according to one writer in the Lexington paper. Even clippings from other states heralded Madden County and the sheriff as indicative of what happened when law enforcement, coal companies, and union representatives collaborated. It culminated in the headline, "Grace Named KY Sheriff of the Year."

Evangeline examined another article dated July 18, 1928. A small report on page eight announced, "Sheriff Grace Officially Ends Search for McCoy Kidnapping Suspect."

Evangeline examined article after article. She couldn't connect some to the overriding story of Madden County. However, she was certain Gene had drawn those lines.

When she found a clipping labeled May 10, 1939, she cleared it from the other articles and stared at the headline and faded photo. "Local Student Wins Marshall University Scholarship." Uncle Willie posed in front of a school bulletin board. He appeared frail, and his clothes reminded her of when Sheldon would try on their father's uniform and hat.

Although a teen, Willie's eyes displayed the weariness he would carry until his death. In the photo, her uncle held a framed certificate in front of his chest. "Willie Grace received the prestigious Marshall University Creative Writer's Award of Excellence, entitling him to a tuition-free seat when he graduates from MCHS. His sophomore English Teacher, Mrs. Betty Chapman, says Willie's work and talent will take him far."

But time wrote a different story on his face. Rather than at the camera, he stared toward the corner, and his fake smile reminded Evangeline of hostage videos in law enforcement seminars. She expected him to blink a message in Morse Code to signal for help.

Then she recognized the shadow. She picked up Willie's picture and the photo of Robert in the courtyard. Side by side, the shadows became more ominous and less likely a photographer's error or a hidden light source. No, it was there. The rough human form hung in the air like a swarm of pale, gray flies.

Had Gene seen it, too?

She opened the empty *Goldenrods* folder. Gene had scribbled a timeline and questions across the inside cover beginning in 1927 and ending in October 2002. The points first listed Leon McCoy and ended with Uncle Willie's murder. Along the way, Gene jotted questions like, "How did Sheriff Grace keep the peace?" and, "Is Willie's inexplicable death related to Robert's suicide?" All questions she had never bothered to ask.

Evangeline shut her eyes. She remembered Willie's letter. "I interpreted it as a product of Willie's addiction," Evangeline whispered. Her brother had wasted time attempting to guide her because she had refused to listen. Instead, she had preferred to brand Sheldon with Willie's affliction.

"Dear God, am I blind?" Evangeline darted down the hall to Sheldon's room and stepped to his desk and the small wooden box on the surface. She lifted Willie's letter from the container and unfolded it as she sped back to her bedroom and the folder.

Surrounded by Gene's notes, pictures, and old articles, she placed Uncle Willie's letter side by side with Gene's list of events and dates outlining the history of Madden County. She reread her uncle's message again and again. Missing puzzle pieces materialized—not the details but the complete picture on the puzzle box. Now she inferred things she would have never conceived before the letter and the folder.

Whether or not she believed it, Willie, Sheldon, and Gene told the same story.

Evangeline, her legs folded beneath her, lifted her arms toward the ceiling. Her knees creaked as she stretched her legs, pointed her toes, and leaned her back and head onto the floor. She did not know if the ringing in her ears was due to the mine or the hours reading Gene's folder.

With the soft carpet cradling her body, Evangeline controlled her breathing. She had always been an above-average shooter as a basketball player, especially at the foul line. She would breathe and block out all the people in the stands and even the other players on the court. It was only her, the ball, and the basket. Steady. Balanced. Eyes on the goal.

She stopped breathing.

"Why don't you ever listen, Evangeline? You should have heard Sheldon. You should have interviewed Willie and known Dr. Bell and his men did not kill Uncle Willie. You should have thought—"

Before she berated herself further, Evangeline envisioned her father standing over her, trenches spreading across his brow. "Evangeline, people who say they *should have* are pretty dang arrogant. You believe you're so smart that you know what would have happened without you. It's too bad things don't work that way. Sitting around beating yourself up is like watering flowers in the front yard while your house is on fire behind you. Take care of what is important, and then you can second guess and regret."

She rose from the floor and dressed in her uniform.

"Daddy, I will take care of Sheldon and end this. Not for you or my future, but because it is my job."

Chapter 75
The Funniest Thing

Evangeline rounded the curve leading to the Wainscott's mailbox outside the elaborate gate. The brick and stone entrance caused her to shiver. Art's words—"I hurt him"—rang inside her head as if the concussion trapped them there.

The gate was open, so she turned onto the cobblestone driveway. Her headlights bounced on the back of Wainscott's pickup truck sitting near the center garage door. She pulled behind the massive vehicle and shut off the cruiser's engine.

The house was two stories, but Sheldon said he and Sarah usually watched television and played pool or ping-pong in the basement game room or studied in her room upstairs. Red, blue, and white stained glass on the door made it difficult to see inside, but lights shined through the windows. Evangeline hoped Wainscott was still awake, but it didn't matter. She needed to speak with Sheldon and Sarah. She planned to tell her brother she was ready to talk—and listen—about Willie's letter and the Agent.

But first, she would have to get someone to open the damn door. She rang the doorbell a third time and followed with a loud knock. She pressed her face against the stained glass in a futile attempt to see if anyone approached, then banged the door again.

When the door opened, her mouth fell open as well.

Luke Porter stood at the entrance.

"What are you doing here, Luke?" she asked. "Where's Wainscott?" She stretched her neck to see behind the deputy.

"Mr. Wainscott called and asked if I'd watch after Sarah while he went to a mine," Luke said. His overeager grin reminded Evangeline of how Sheldon had lied as a kid.

"You're so kind to rush over and help," she said. "Good thing you are in uniform, or I might have mistaken you for a burglar or a dangerous kidnapper. So, where is Mrs. James? I know she has been helping Sarah whenever Wainscott leaves. Is she here?"

"Oh, yes, Mrs. James. I sent her home when I got here. Poor thing looked so tired." The fake grin and shifty eyes returned. Luke was many things—arrogant, ambitious, entitled, self-righteous—but he wasn't the person blocking her way.

Evangeline remained quiet and craned her neck again to see past Luke. Despite the darkness, she spotted the stairs at the end of the foyer.

The sheriff knew Mrs. Collins, not Mrs. James, helped Paul with Sarah. Luke would know both women, so there was little chance he would confuse them.

"Yep, all I know is Wainscott was gone when I got here," he said. Luke spoke with the confidence of a drunk Christian attending a church picnic.

She observed his face. Her father had explained when someone lies, they speak with certainty, but their mouth gives them away. "'Keep staring right at their mug, Evangeline. Unless they are master liars, their lips will form a frown or smirk at you for just a second when they finally shut up. Their eyebrows raise as if they are surprised you believe their bull. And if they ever mention honesty, you got yourself someone with their pants on fire.'"

She detected a frown flash across the deputy's lips.

"What time did you get here, Luke?"

He paused. "Not too long ago."

"Is that right?" she said. "You know, Paul Wainscott came around my place at 7:45 PM and didn't mention any trouble at a mine."

Luke shifted his weight from one foot to the other. "What do you mean, Sheriff? Do you think I would make up a story about this? My parents raised me to tell the truth."

Lies can reveal as much as the truth. A cold gust of wind pushed against her back.

"It's a chilly night out there, Deputy." Evangeline stepped closer to gauge Luke's response. The deputy's body stiffened, and he slid sideways to block the path. "I guess you have everything under control, so I will head home," the sheriff said as she pivoted away.

Evangeline felt him step toward her. "I will lock up, Sheriff, and make sure Sarah is safe." She heard the relief in his voice. She reversed when he lowered his guard, bumped Luke off-balance with her shoulder, and sprinted toward the staircase.

As she ascended the dark stairs, she heard Luke's footsteps clapping against the tile floor behind her. The sheriff increased her pace but readied herself to turn and fight if needed.

However, her foot did not land on the top stair. Instead, she stepped on a solid bundle of clothes. She tried to grasp the rail before falling backward, but her fingertips grazed the railing, her weight shifted, and she fell toward the bottom of the stairs, the bundle rolling behind her.

The sheriff's sore body struck hard. Her head thudded against the steps as she slid like a sled down a rough slope as the slick hardwood stairs dug into her neck and spine. The fall ended on the third step from the bottom.

"Sheriff, you bustin' your ass is the funniest thing I have ever seen," Luke said.

Evangeline, groggy and injured, realized he had his boot against her shoulder, pressing downward to pin her to the steps. She tried to turn her head away, but his shoe grew heavier against her body. She struggled to remain conscious, fighting to break the surface and breathe fresh air, but her vision fluttered, and she succumbed to the darkness again.

Chapter 76
Lost Your Mind

As soon as his headlights revealed the sheriff's car in the driveway and the open front door, Junebug felt unsettled. He stopped the car with a jolt and touched the door handle.

"Stay here," he said, exiting the cruiser. As he walked along the Wainscott driveway, he heard the car door open behind him.

"What's going on?" Lilly asked. Junebug motioned for her to remain and watched as she returned to the car. Smart girl. Sheldon and Cyrus were in the backseat and would need Lilly to open their doors, so he had a little time to clear the house before allowing them to enter.

He removed his firearm and took three steps, avoiding the direct line of sight from the open front door. Sheriff Grace always said to approach a door like a squirrel but enter like a bear. He wasn't sure which Sheriff Grace gave him the advice, but it didn't matter.

Junebug sidestepped and bent low to peer into the house. Darkness. He removed his flashlight from his belt while staring into the foyer. He clicked on his flashlight and illuminated the entrance hall from the door to the stairs.

At first, Junebug thought a pile of clothes had cascaded down the steps. But when he stepped through the door, he recognized the sheriff's limp figure stretched out, her head near the bottom step and her legs bent and pushed to the right side toward the wall.

"Sheriff Grace," he said and dashed toward her.

He could see her head rise when he focused the flashlight on the stairs. Her weak voice called, "No, Junebug, no."

Junebug sensed movement in his peripheral. He raised his left arm just in time to absorb a fierce blow. Pain rippled through his forearm and elbow as the force slammed him into the wall. A family photograph above him wobbled and fell, the frame and the thick glass shattering on Junebug's head and the floor. Blood dripped from his forehead onto his brow.

When his vision steadied, Junebug saw Luke standing in the wide doorway framed like the wall portraits. Junebug watched as his fellow deputy held a police baton in his right hand, patting it against his left palm like a villainous prison guard. *A mistake. Luke must have mistaken me for the assailant who attacked the sheriff.*

"It's me, Luke. It's Junebug." The blood changed course and dripped onto his temple.

Luke exited the door frame into the foyer. His colleague's face —an angry smile beneath bulging eyes—told Junebug there was no mistake.

"Howdy, neighbor. Now, what is it they call you, Horsefly? Ladybug? Stinkbug? It doesn't matter," Luke said. To Junebug, it sounded like a different person than the Luke Porter he knew.

Bug stayed seated, leaning against the wall, his arm aching. "Luke, what are you doing? This isn't you."

"This isn't me, huh?" Luke said, mocking Junebug's drawl. "Let's say it ain't just me, shitkicker."

Luke swaggered across the hallway and straddled Junebug's

knees.

"What the hell, Luke?" Junebug said. "Have you lost your mind?"

"He hasn't lost it. He rented it out for a while," Luke laughed. "You may not get it because it's an inside joke," he said, howling even louder.

Junebug turned to check on the sheriff. She moved, but he could not see her injuries well enough to know their full extent. However, although blood stained her face, she stared at him. Junebug turned back to see Luke and the baton in his hand.

The sheriff's shriek cut the air like a horn blasted inside a church. It was so sharp Luke turned his head to see her.

Junebug struck. He bent his long leg upward and kicked the inside of Luke's knee. Luke's leg bowed outward as Junebug ground his heel into his tendons and bones.

Luke howled, but this time it was not in laughter. He stumbled to his left and fought to keep his balance but fell onto his side. The metal club slipped from his hand and scuttled across the ceramic flooring.

Junebug leaned his right arm against the wall and rose to his feet. His left arm trembled as waves of pain shot from his elbow to his wrist. He pressed the arm against his side like a broken wing.

"I don't know what happened to you, Luke, but this can stop here. You're a lawman, and that means something."

"Lawman doesn't mean anything here in Madden County, you long-haired rube. I suppose the lawmen aren't literate enough to read law books in hillbilly land." Luke's mouth moved as though it belonged to someone else.

Light flooded the foyer, revealing the rich decor and paintings hanging along the walls. Junebug turned toward the doorway, where Lilly stood, her arm extended to the light switch on the wall. Sheldon and Cyrus were behind her, frozen in place.

Lilly said, "What in heaven's name is going—"

Junebug raised his hand, stopping her mid-sentence. "Leave now," he said with calm authority. He stared at Lilly and knew he would never allow her to be hurt. Never, from this day forward.

Luke rose, balancing on his right leg. He attempted to stay upright and draw his pistol, using both hands to steady the holster and clutch the grip. However, the officer stumbled when trying to plant his left foot. He struggled to steady himself.

Junebug pushed off the wall, propelling his body toward his old partner. He arrived as Luke's Glock cleared the leather holster. Before Luke raised the weapon, Junebug hammered his right elbow into Luke's bicep. The gun flew from Porter's hand, clattering across the floor, causing Luke to turn his head in an attempt to locate it.

Junebug used the pause to slam his shoulder against Luke's chest, hoping to knock him further off balance. However, Luke grabbed Junebug's throat with both hands and spun him, using Junebug as a crutch as he slammed the thinner man into the wall.

"Boy, it looks like you and the sheriff weren't ready to take on a real man today," Luke said as he lifted Junebug upright and tightened the grip on his throat.

Luke's fingers dug into Junebug's neck, closing his airway. The sheriff struggled to stand near the stairs. She stumbled, falling backward, her butt landing on the third step.

Lilly's voice came closer, "Stop it. Why are you doing this?"

Luke stared at Lilly. "Maybe I will tell you when it is your turn later, sweetheart."

Luke turned his dead gaze toward Sheldon. "Hey, my little partner," he said. "You know what I mean. Eventually, I will get around to everyone, won't I?"

"Let him go, Agent. Junebug is not who you want," Sheldon said. As Sheldon yelled, Cyrus darted toward the two struggling men.

Junebug tried to tell him to stop, but the grip on his throat tightened, and he knew his strength and options dwindled with each passing second.

The grip closed even more.

Junebug stretched his injured arm just enough to shift the contents of his left hand into his right. The sharp edges of the glass dug into his palm. He leaned hard to his left and pulled Luke's head and body in the same direction. With all the strength he could muster, Junebug raised the shard from the shattered picture frame and gouged it into Luke's neck.

Luke's face morphed, then froze as the surprise parted his lips. He glared at Junebug as blood surged from the jagged gash on his neck and sprayed onto Junebug's face and the wall. The trajectory declined after several spurts and became a pulsing leak.

As Luke's grip on his throat gradually loosened, Junebug stared into the man's eyes. Bug believed the surprise wasn't the wound but the fact Junebug had inflicted it.

Junebug clung to Luke, unwilling to release him until Lilly's hand touched his back.

"It is safe now, Ben," she said. "We are all safe because of you."

Junebug eased Luke Porter onto the floor and allowed Lilly to examine his aching left arm and the cut on his right palm where he had held the shard of glass. He watched over her shoulder as Sheldon and Cyrus ran to help the sheriff.

*****

Sheldon wrapped his arm around Evangeline as she leaned against him. Cyrus dabbed blood from her nose and face with his shirt.

"Is Sarah...?"

"I don't know," Evangeline replied. "I didn't make it up the stairs. I tripped over poor Ms. Collins's body."

The woman's lifeless body sprawled across several stairs.

"But I don't think Luke got to Sarah, Sheldon," the sheriff said. "Remember, she is on painkillers, and she can't walk. If she heard the commotion, she would be terrified and unable to do anything about it."

"Go on, Sheldon," Cyrus said. "I'll help the sheriff."

*****

Sheldon bolted up the stairs. Lifting himself over the body, he said, "I'm sorry, Mrs. Collins. You should not have been anywhere near this mess."

Outside Sarah's door, Sheldon listened before entering. Silence. He pictured the worst because if you imagine the worst, the worst does not catch you unprepared. He envisioned Sarah like Mrs. Collins's empty shell, stretched out on the floor, her black hair disheveled, spread outward, a broken and discarded doll. He shook the image away and scolded himself. "Way to go, Sheldon," he whispered.

He turned the doorknob until it clicked. He always enjoyed being in Sarah's bedroom, but her father did not allow it often. *Where in hell is Paul Wainscott now when we need him?* Then another thought invaded his brain. *Where is my dad when I need him?*

Sarah's soft cries permitted him to exhale. When he entered, it was dark except for a small lamp on the bedside.

"Sarah, it's me, Sheldon," he said, matching her gentle tone.

She gasped. "Sheldon, oh my god, I was afraid you were dead. Who was downstairs?"

"I am here, Sarah. It's okay now." Sheldon hurried to Sarah's bedside and embraced her.

"Sheldon, I love you so much," she said. She buried her face into his chest and cried.

He pulled her closer and said, "You have never said that before,

Sarah."

She smiled through the tears, and her eyes became frozen blue stones. "Because it isn't true, Shelly Belly."

"What is—"

Sarah raised the pearl-handled pocket knife and drove it into his chest. She laughed as she forced it farther into his body until only the white handle remained exposed. His body convulsed, and a dark red stain widened across his chest and shoulder where her face had rested moments before.

Sheldon peered into her beautiful, smiling eyes until she glanced over his shoulder, awaiting a second victim. Sheldon heard the bedroom door open again. He wanted to yell, but his lungs betrayed him.

Sarah said, "Can't two young lovers get any make-out time? Don't worry, Honeypie, it's not like we haven't been here before."

Sheldon tumbled away onto the white and pink comforter. Cyrus darted across the white carpet, and Evangeline limped into the room behind him. Sheldon felt Sarah's hand on the knife handle. The pressure spiked the pain, squeezing bile into his throat.

However, before Sarah removed the knife, Cyrus dived, grabbed Sarah's wrist and arm, and held it in place. Without pausing, Cyrus sank his teeth into the soft flesh of her arm.

Sarah cried out in pain and released the knife handle. Sheldon's erratic breathing amplified as Cyrus wrestled Sarah back onto her pillows and restrained her with as much force as possible.

"Don't hurt her, Cyrus," Sheldon said, his voice raspy and weak. "It's not her."

Evangeline fell beside her brother on the bed. She grabbed the silk sheets and pushed a section against the wound, sealing the leak around the blade.

Sheldon heard his sister yell, "Junebug, Lilly, need you here now!" It was the last thing he heard before his eyes closed.

Chapter 77
I Don't Have to Travel

Blood everywhere. She promised her father she would stay with Sheldon and protect him, yet he swam in blood. "Please, God, don't let this happen," she said.

"What did you say, Sheriff Grace?" The EMT checked the IV stream connected to Sheldon's arm and then glanced at Evangeline. "Don't worry, Sheriff," she said. "They do a good job at Highland's Regional. The doctors will take care of him. Please, sit back and rest."

Evangeline nodded and reclined on the gurney. Her swollen nose felt broken, and blood had dried above her lips and cheek. She did not want to relive the experience at the house, but her mind refused to let it rest. She needed to assemble the puzzle no matter how sharp the pieces were.

"You and your friends did well by not removing the knife. People make that mistake too often," the EMT said, as though she realized Evangeline's need for distraction.

The sheriff tried to stoke her anger at Sarah, but it made no sense. Moments after being restrained, Sarah returned. Her cries

370

of, "What have I done?" and, "I am sorry, Sheldon!" had led Cyrus to release her and move over to help tend to Sheldon's bleeding.

When Lilly entered the room, Evangeline yelled, "Call an ambulance!" but the teacher continued to the bed.

"Ben is calling for an ambulance," she had said. Lilly had placed her hand on Evangeline's and whispered, "You are hurt. Let me take over."

When the ambulance arrived, it was the same team Evangeline had encountered many times before. The dark-haired woman had rushed to Sheldon's side and had not left him since. The male EMT had examined the sheriff, but she had pushed his hands away and said, "Just help my brother." Either her authority or desperation had led him to follow the command.

Evangeline leaned forward on the gurney to check on her brother again. The knife protruded from his chest.

"How did I let this happen?" she asked.

Again, the EMT glanced at her, but she did not comment this time. Instead, she turned back to Sheldon and adjusted his oxygen mask.

Evangeline remained quiet for a few minutes. As she stared at Sheldon, she said to the EMT, "Since you show up to save the day at every Madden County emergency, it would be good to know your name."

"I'm Sheila." The woman checked Sheldon's pulse as she spoke.

"Have you ever let your family down, Sheila?" Evangeline said. "Have you ever disappointed them by messing up everything?" The sheriff heard the words and mumbled, "Jesus, I must be delirious. What did you give me?"

Sheila laughed. "It was only a pain reliever, Sheriff. We've backed away from strong opioids on runs. Some people fake illnesses to get a quick fix and a prescription. I take it you aren't accustomed to even Tylenol." She checked Sheldon's bandages and adjusted his arm.

Evangeline hoped Sheila's silence signaled she had ignored the question. The EMT appeared younger than Evangeline, perhaps in her late twenties. Up close, her Native American heritage became more apparent. She used barrettes to pull her hair away from her face, but allowed it to fall down her back. It was radiant, even in the kaleidoscope lights surrounding the ambulance.

"It doesn't make sense," Sheila said.

"Excuse me," Evangeline responded.

"To live your life the way others want you to," the EMT said. "We are all influenced by our family in one way or another. Parents, grandparents, and even siblings can be disappointed when you decide something because they don't like it or understand it. But decisions based on what others want don't make sense. You live with the consequences, so you should decide. I hope I haven't disappointed my parents, but it is a chance I have to take to be true to myself."

"How does it play out in real life?" Evangeline liked the EMT's voice.

"It isn't pleasant. My dad believes women shouldn't be in the nasty emergency response business. He thinks it's men's work."

"You mean he doesn't trust you to do the work?"

"Nope," she laughed. "My father knows I will be good at it. He does not want me to leave him."

"Believe me. I understand, Sheila."

"Yeah, it is a joke between us," Sheila replied. "He tried to stop me when I joined the Army, but I went anyway. I did good work and got my stripes, but after serving in the Middle East, I missed him so much that I came home after my third tour. Now, I don't want to go anywhere else. Why would I want to leave Madden County? I know for damn sure they need me here. Please don't take it the wrong way, but I even get to help the sheriff's brother after his girlfriend stabs him in a mansion bedroom. I don't have to travel anywhere else to find excitement."

Evangeline nodded, closed her eyes, and leaned back. She hoped Sheila would talk more, but that was not the case. The EMT checked Sheldon, the IV line, and the wound surrounding the knife.

The ambulance's dull roar made Evangeline's head heavy, and the world turned into soft pastel hues. Willie's letter reappeared in her hands, but she did not read it. Instead, Willie read it to her, his voice telling her the story of a story.

Chapter 78
The Reality of Impossible Things

Doctor Osbourne turned toward Sheila and shrugged before returning his attention to Evangeline. "Sheriff, your stubborn streak will end you if you aren't careful," he said.

"After Sheldon is out of surgery, I will let you know if I need a room, Dr. Osbourne," Evangeline said. She sat on a padded bench outside the hospital's ICU.

Osbourne removed a small penlight from his pocket and examined the sheriff's face again. He touched Evangeline's nose and shined the penlight into her eyes. "You have broken your nose," the doctor said, "and you may have another concussion."

Evangeline remained stoic and stopped further attempts to admit her.

"Would you watch Sheriff Grace until someone gets here?" The doctor directed his question to Sheila.

"Happy to do so, Dr. Osbourne," the EMT said.

Evangeline nodded at Sheila and leaned back on the bench.

"Doctor, " Evangeline said before the doctor exited, "please take care of my brother. He is the only close kin I have left."

*****

When she startled awake, Evangeline's body spanned the entire bench, her head on a pillow and her knees bent so she fit between the armrests. Sheila was not there, but Lilly and Cyrus hovered above her. Junebug stood there, too, holding a pumpkin-colored coffee cup.

"Good morning, Sheriff," he said.

When Bug spoke, Evangeline scrambled into a sitting position, causing Junebug to step back and spill coffee on the sling carrying his left arm.

"Sheldon?" the sheriff said. "What's happened?" She swiveled to account for each person in the room, wherever she was.

When she did not see her brother or Sarah, Evangeline attempted to stand.

"Hold on, Sheriff. No need to worry," Junebug said as he moved closer. Lilly guided her back onto the bench. "Sheldon is still in ICU, but the doctors said he is strong and has shown improvement."

Evangeline rubbed the sleep from her eyes. "Finally, some good news." She glanced at Junebug's bandaged arm. "Are you alright?"

"Yes, ma'am. It is fractured and bruised but not broken," he said, lifting his arm.

"That's only half of what I mean. Are you alright with, you know, Luke?"

Junebug looked away, but only for a moment. "It shook me up, but I can't see any way around what happened. I feel bad about Luke, but..." The deputy censored himself as though he recognized his audience. He peered at his feet.

"Go ahead, Junebug," Evangeline said. "Be honest and say it."

"It wasn't Luke Porter." Junebug allowed the words to hang between them as he measured her response. "Something we have never seen before is happening, Sheriff. I'm in the *Evil Dead* movie."

Cyrus joined them to stand beside the deputy and Lilly.

"First, thank you, Junebug. You saved my life," Evangeline said. "Cyrus and Lilly, without a doubt, you saved Sheldon's life. I will be forever grateful. Dear God, Lilly, today is the celebration for Gene. You should be getting that ready, not risking your life."

"It is okay, Sheriff. The Phipps brothers postponed the ceremony until tomorrow at my request." She smiled and added, "You know Gene Begley would have no problem with a delay, especially if he blamed you for it."

"I wish he were here now." Her voice quivered. "I owe him an apology—I need to apologize to all of you. I didn't listen when you suggested there is more going on here than the Highlander and my wild suspicions about my brother. Don't stand there. Pull chairs over, and let's talk some things through."

*****

When everyone settled, Evangeline described how she had charged Art and Luke with interrogating Willie instead of doing it herself. "I didn't want to stain my work record and jeopardize my future in Louisville. My decision led to Sheldon receiving a letter Uncle Willie meant for me. The letter explained what is happening now, but the explanation came with complications."

Cyrus, Lilly, and Junebug reacted with silence. Evangeline shivered when she realized how young they were.

"I'll never forget," Junebug said. "We got those calls to the diner and the football field. That was a long and painful day."

"Yes, it was, Junebug," Evangeline said. "But there was another tragedy—Sheldon read the letter instead of me. Eventually, I found the letter when I searched his room."

"I bet he was dang angry," Cyrus said. "Rooms are sacred."

"Sheldon was upset, but not because I snooped in his room," Evangeline said. "He claimed I had jeopardized everyone's safety because now the two of us knew the secret."

"Talk about a doozy of a secret," Lilly said. "I would like to read that document myself. There are accounts of magical words passed down through generations to be concealed by the text holder."

"Nonetheless, Sheldon hid the letter and kept the secret. He planned never to tell anyone," Evangeline said.

Junebug sat up straighter, adjusted his arm, and spoke. "So, this secret would hurt people if it got out. It explains a lot about the way Sheldon acted." He looked at Lilly, and the teacher nodded at Evangeline.

The sheriff stared at each person. "I have always looked at the world through evidence, logic, and reason. But what I am about to tell you now doesn't have much to do with those things. It is about something beyond what we understand to be real."

"Sheriff, that's how you and your dad taught me to view things. He always said to follow the evidence, not the coincidence," Junebug said. Evangeline cracked a smile even with the pain in her nose and the fog in her brain.

"Yes, Junebug. I thought my dad meant to follow the evidence aligned with what I know," she said. "In this case, the evidence guided me toward things I am not inclined to believe. After he killed Willie, Gene, and Art and almost murdered my brother and Sarah, I have to follow the evidence, no matter how implausible it sounds. The evidence states I can no longer deny the reality of impossible things."

Junebug, Lilly, and Cyrus glanced at each other.

"I know you think I have lost my—"

"Not at all," Junebug said. He smiled. "Lilly, Cyrus, Sheldon, and I traveled the same road. We may have been at different mile markers, but it sounds like we ended up in the same place."

"There is almost nothing typical about his case, Sheriff," Lilly said. "We have a few things we need to tell you."

Lilly walked over to her jacket. She picked up a book and a white evidence bag.

"What's that?" Evangeline said.

"This book might help us understand how the impossible becomes possible."

"What's in the evidence bag?" The sheriff accepted the plastic bag.

"I'm sorry, Sheriff," Lilly said. "The doctors insisted I sign the evidence chain log and hand it only to you when you awoke."

Junebug said, "Sheriff, that's the knife Sarah used to...the knife she had on the bed. I figured we would hang onto it until I spoke with you about pressing charges against her."

Evangeline lifted the plastic and pried open the sealed top. She watched Junebug's discomfort rise as she ignored protocol.

The sheriff removed the open pocket knife from the bag. Sheldon's blood coated the pearl handle and the silver blade.

"We will stop this evil, no matter what it is," Sheriff Grace said. She examined the knife as she spoke. "Sarah is a triple victim in all this. Barlow kidnapped her, injured her foot, and somehow possessed her mind in this ordeal. She does not need an attempted murder charge. It will be rough enough recovering from all this as it is."

Angst showed on Junebug's tired face. It surprised her that he would lack compassion for Sarah's situation. However, she ignored it for a moment. She used her leg to close the knife. The blade left behind a dark red line on her slacks. She then offered the knife to Cyrus without speaking.

He did not raise his hand to accept it. Instead, he said, "I don't know, Sheriff. Are you sure?"

"Oh yes, Cyrus. You saved Sheldon from bleeding to death. If there is anyone I trust with that blade, it's you."

His cheeks grew red, and he accepted the plastic bag and knife from her hand.

"Now, Lilly and Cyrus, we need to continue this conversation, and you can tell me about the book, but right now, I need a favor."

"Of course," Cyrus responded. He appeared willing to walk on burning coals if she requested it.

"Go check on Sheldon while I talk with my deputy here. Please."

She watched as Lilly stepped over to Junebug, kissed him on the cheek, and left the room with Cyrus.

"I can explain...." Junebug said, but the kiss was easy to interpret.

"I want you to be happy, Bug. You don't owe anybody anything, especially me." She hoped her response would ease his awkwardness. She cleared her hoarse throat and said, "I need to understand if you think we should charge Sarah for stabbing Sheldon. We both know it was not her, any more than Luke acted of his own will."

"Sheriff, we should not charge her and ruin her life any more than it already has been," he said. He paused as if searching for the right words. "Paulene called while you were sleeping. Kids found Luke's cruiser in the woods and called the station. Otis discovered blood near the car, and when we checked Wainscott's truck at the house, there was blood in the bed. Otis thinks Luke used the truck to dump Wainscott before driving to the house. We are searching for the body now."

Evangeline felt her stomach churn again as she pictured Paul leaving her house earlier. Although she suppressed a primal scream, Evangeline formed fists, her arms quivering, and she searched for something to punch or break. When the search failed, she opened her hands and used them to cover her face.

Junebug placed his hand on her shoulder, but the fire blazed inside her. It melted her sadness and replaced it with hatred. It was profound hate borne from bitterness she aimed at herself and a shadow she had only seen in old photographs.

Chapter 79
The Reality of More Impossible Things

Evangeline needed sleep.

"Your brother will survive, Sheriff," Dr. Osbourne said, "But if you don't get some rest, you may not. We sedated Sheldon so well he would not recognize you anyway, so you might as well have Officer Spears take you home."

When Junebug and Lilly dropped her at her house, the sheriff felt stronger standing on her porch and waving goodbye. She was proud of Junebug. He had met challenges this week he may not have been able to face just a few weeks ago.

The shower's hot water dropped on her shoulders, washing away the bloody remnants of the day and night. Evangeline wondered how Sarah would fare without her father. *Sarah and Sheldon will struggle to understand what they have experienced.* She leaned her forehead against the shower wall and said, "I can't even make sense of it, yet I expect them to comprehend it?"

Evangeline patted the towel on her aching body. The mirror revealed the bruises and abrasions, but she would survive this round despite her aching back, shoulder, and nose.

Rest was the only solution. Evangeline would sleep, see Sheldon, check on Sarah at the hospital in the morning, and then go to Gene Begley's celebration to pay her respects. But first, she needed to reread Willie's letter, only this time without prejudice and doubt skewing her vision. As she walked toward Sheldon's room, she thought now was the time to acknowledge the reality of impossible things.

*****

"*T*hat must have been hard to watch, Chief."

Evangeline awoke. She raised her head, anxious to find the source of the voice, but soon she accepted it as another nightmare. The sheriff lowered her head back onto the unfamiliar pillow and rolled over. What was she doing in Sheldon's room? The folded letter beside her helped her recall her last words, "I will sleep for a minute...." Now, Sheldon's DVD player beneath the television glowed 5:07 AM. She usually arose at—

"*Seeing a little harlot sink a blade into Shelly's chest must have hurt. It pained like it was your own heart, I bet.*"

Did a nightmare cross with her from sleep into waking? She raised her elbow and rubbed her face with both hands.

Now was the time for Evangeline to commit. She recalled Willie, his face contorted and angry, as she and Art had watched him on the monitor. Her uncle's face had appeared confused and distant, as though he was not present. She recalled Luke and Sarah, their evil expressions and aberrant laughter. Now she heard the voice, and even logic required her to accept it.

This voice belonged to the demon who murdered Art, Gene, Mrs. Collins, and Wainscott.

"You are responsible for this," Evangeline said. "What are you? Step out so I can see you." She attempted to employ a forceful tone. However, she sounded angry and unsure.

"What am I?" he said with a chuckle. *"I wish my friend Willie were here to answer your question. He would tell you I am now your secret. I am the hidden fear you hold beneath your skin and the guide leading you to where you want to be."*

Evangeline slowed her breathing. In a moment, her buzzing brain stopped, righted itself, and told her this was the Agent. The shadow in the picture was now in human form. He had stabbed Art in the back, severed Gene's head, and killed Willie. She wanted the voice silenced but remembered what her uncle had written. *He likes to talk.*

She rolled over and tried to detect the speaker's whereabouts. "Did you help Willie? Did you guide him? Remind me not to ask you for directions."

The agent chuckled. *"Hell, Lil Dep, your old uncle was ready to go. He'd seen all he wanted of this world."* The voice surrounded and penetrated her brain. *"He just wanted to hand you your inheritance and move on. He got me a bit angry on the way out, but we were like brothers until the end. Oh, I am so sorry to remind you of Sheldon again."*

"I'm confused," she said after a moment. "I searched the room for a shadow resembling you, but I couldn't find one."

"It isn't your fault. Of course, you are mixed up and stupid because you have lived here in Madden County too long. Your father tricked you and drew you back. You cared for your brother like you birthed him. You've policed barbarians. It isn't fair for a promising law officer like yourself to be stuck in this depressing place."

The words raked against her brain like a dull razor. She wasn't afraid but disgusted—not at the Agent, but at herself. Was this how she sounded to Art and Sheldon? This devil had converted her bias, fear, and resentment to his advantage. By turning, twisting, and probing her prejudice and dissatisfaction, the Agent thought he might cultivate compliance or even an alliance. She had used the same trick to get what she wanted from suspects. She bit her lip to control her rage.

Light shifting under the bedroom door enabled her to locate him. Somehow his voice resonated as though he surrounded the room, but he skulked outside the door.

"Madden is a blister on a fat dame's heel. Don't you ever want to leave this place and do something important? People don't make a living here—they refrain from dying."

"What do you mean?" she asked. Her goal was to buy time until she determined what to do.

"Look at all the death. Down at the courthouse wall, they claim the problem is you. They said a woman sheriff invites trouble. They even blame you for the big baboon crushed up in the mine. Let me tell you. Seeing tons of rock and dirt stacked around you isn't fun. But he is resting now, so don't worry about him."

"I am armed now," Evangeline lied.

"I have never been a fan of guns. I used them back in the war and put down more than my share of Huns, but I can live without rifles and pistols. I prefer my killings to be more intimate. I enjoy how a good blade feels and a dying man's expression when he realizes no more days are on his calendar." The Agent's voice lulled as if he had relived a fond memory.

"I don't care what gets you excited, Agent Barlow," Evangeline said, "but I promise I will target you right between the eyes and dead center on your heart if you try to come through the door."

The Agent laughed again. *"Look at you being all formal! You can call me Barlow or Agent. It is easy to tell you don't belong in Madden County. You are decisive, and you mean business. These puds do everything halfway."*

"Leave. Now," the sheriff ordered.

"People here loved your father," the Agent said, *"but they don't care much for you. I can explain it if you want."*

Let him talk. Let him talk. Let him talk.

"You see, you are not much like your father," the Agent said. *"Old Earl Grace would say a line to make the people feel good, and that's why they thought he was so keen."*

Evangeline refused the bait. Instead, she opened Sheldon's closet and grabbed one of his sweatshirts and a pair of tennis shoes, slipping them on as she continued talking to the Agent. "What does that have to do with me?"

"You are more like your grandfather, the so-called Honorable Sheriff Sheldon Grace. He didn't waste time. If he caught a criminal, he had no trouble punching the man's ticket. Just like you, he didn't want everyone to know the truth. You take after him, not your father. You like the darkness, as I do."

"Very funny coming from someone who forced my uncle to keep a secret," Evangeline said.

"Willie and I were good at keeping our secrets," the Agent said.

Evangeline picked up Willie's letter from the bed and searched Sheldon's desk. She glanced at the photo of Sheldon and their father on the desktop. She folded the pages, pushed them into her sweatpants pocket, and opened Sheldon's desk drawer for the extra key to her car.

"Lil Dep? I'm not too fond of your silence over there. See, you're just like old Sheldon. You are plotting and conniving." The doorknob rattled as if the Agent tried to force it to turn. She had opened it with the paper clip again, so it had remained locked after she closed it, but the door would not hold for long.

"So, Agent." Evangeline paused. Her father had taught her to use words like a sharp stick—poke the bear and learn from his actions and inactions. "Uncle Willie sure had your number, didn't he? He kept you a secret for decades. How you killed the old man pointed to a lack of control and a need for revenge. It sounds like he beat you at your own game."

The Agent's banter and attempts to open the door halted. She sensed the weight pressing against the doorframe.

As she crept toward Sheldon's bedroom window, she added, "But don't worry, Agent. Willie was the smartest person ever to step into Madden County. You shouldn't be ashamed." Evangeline arranged her hands so her left applied pressure at the bottom and her right pushed upward at the top. The window slipped open, and the sheriff extended her leg until it dangled near a tree branch. She glanced down, but the path to the ground had not changed since she was a teenager.

The sheriff straddled the windowsill and turned.

The wooden door frame splintered against the Agent's force. He stumbled into the room and squared his body toward Evangeline, his red and black eyes smoldering. She had not seen him up close during the encounter at DeLong's mine. But she knew he was the gray monster who had killed Art and hurt Sarah. The dried blood and coal dust created patterns on his white shirt and suit jacket. He held a knife in his long, dirty fingers as though the blade were an appendage, and his smile revealed rotten, speckled teeth.

The Agent's speed surprised Evangeline. He charged, his big hands and arms stretching to grasp her before she exited. She lifted her left foot and rolled away from his assault, extending her right foot toward the tree branch a yard below the window. The sheriff's arm floated upward as she dropped toward the limb. She felt her foot connect with tree bark as the Agent's fingers grasped her sweatshirt sleeve.

Like a ballerina paused mid-performance, Evangeline's toe rested on the branch. Barlow grasped her shirt and yanked to lift her to the window.

The fabric stretched, and soon the shirt collar choked her like a noose.

Evangeline straightened her arm and finger and relaxed until her body became limp, and her foot landed squarely on the branch. Her hand slipped through the sleeve's cuff. She snaked her arm through the sleeve.

The Agent held the empty sleeve with both hands and pulled as if he were drawing water from a well. However, the sheriff bent her knee, freed her other arm from its sleeve, and slipped her head through the shirt's collar. She peered up at the Agent's angry, deformed face as she planted both feet on the tree. It appeared as if she sank into the well. Above her, the Agent disappeared inside the window.

Evangeline's bare arms and sports bra did little to combat the cold. "Only seconds," she said. She followed the same path down the tree she had always used, her muscle memory finding each hand and foothold.

Evangeline dropped from the last branch and sprinted toward her Honda Civic, the spare key in hand. Once inside the vehicle, she turned the ignition, shifted, and pushed the pedal to the floor.

As she sped away, the Agent loomed in the rearview mirror, a beast dressed in fine clothes.

Chapter 80
Righting Wrongs Costs More Than Looking Away

Evangeline greeted Otis as she rushed into the station. His awkward stare suggested her sports bra, unkempt hair, and oversized tennis shoes were akin to wearing a two-piece bikini to a church service.

"Sheriff, is there anything wrong?" he asked as she hurried toward her office.

"Otis, there's too many things to fix," she said. "I need you to call Captain Bates at the State Police in Pikeville and relay a request. Ask if he can send two or three troopers to help with calls." The sheriff entered her office and closed the door behind her.

She exchanged her sweats and shoes for a uniform and boots. A Sheriff's Department cap tamed her hair, and she retrieved a weapon from the gun locker.

When she exited, Evangeline said, "I'm sorry, Otis—"

"No problem, Sheriff," Otis said. "I am here as long as needed, and I talked with Captain Bates. He will send at least one unit to help. I told him you would explain later."

"Thank you, Otis," Evangeline said as she picked up a radio

from behind the office counter and attached it to her belt. "I have the radio, but I may be out of touch for a little while. I'm heading to the hospital. Afterward, I will be on a hunt."

"Be careful, Sheriff," he responded. "I got a feeling you plan to fix what's wrong around here. In Madden County, righting wrongs costs more than just looking away."

*****

A stocky blonde-haired nurse with thick forearms and a stern face assured Evangeline Sheldon was stable and needed rest.

"I woke him up long enough to give him meds, and then his head fell back to the pillow," she said. "But since you are so persistent, you can see him. Don't expect him to talk. His injury is severe, so the doctor keeps him comfortable until he can manage."

When they arrived at his room, Evangeline expressed her gratitude again and lowered herself into the chair at Sheldon's bedside. The nurse shuffled into the hallway and closed the door behind her.

Evangeline's lip trembled as she stared at her brother. *How did I let this happen?* She dug her fingers into the fabric of her brown pants.

Sheldon's pale skin contrasted with his dark hair, and although the circles around his eyes caused her heart to sink, his cheeks, chin, and mouth were soft and shaped like their mother's.

"Shel, I am sorry." She placed her palm against his forehead as if checking his temperature. "I was crazy to think you were losing yourself. You are braver than me. The Agent is right. I am not like our father, but you are. You are strong and willing to carry the Agent as Uncle Willie did. I owe you so much."

Evangeline touched his cheek with her fingertips and leaned closer to his ear. "I know you can't hear me, as if you would listen anyway, but I need you to know I love you, Sheldon. If I ever made you believe you were a burden...." Her voice trailed off, and she sniffled into her sleeve. "I tell you now; it was never the case. I am proud to be your sister. You are the most important person to me."

Evangeline's tears commenced. She wiped her sleeve across her nose and held his hand in hers. "I hope I can end the Agent and the suffering he causes, Sheldon. But if I can't...." She inhaled to contain her urge to sob. "I believe you can. You will end it all because you are like Daddy. Evangeline kissed his hand again and touched it to her cheek.

She gazed at him for a moment before standing, clearing her throat, and pivoting toward the door.

"Do you mean we can trade bedrooms?"

Evangeline spun. "Sheldon!" she said as she hurried back to her brother's side.

"Slow down, sis," Sheldon said. He attempted to raise his head but winced in pain and surrendered to the pillow.

"God, I am glad you are awake," Evangeline said. She leaned over and kissed him on the same cheek she had brushed earlier.

Sheldon attempted to clear his throat, but he was too weak.

"Don't try to talk," she said. Her hand shook as she held a glass of water to her brother's lips.

As he drank, Sheldon appeared anxious. After two gulps, he turned his lips from the water and said, "Sarah?"

"She will be okay, at least physically," Evangeline responded as she placed the cup back on the side table. "She broke down when she came back to herself, Sheldon. She didn't mean it, you know—"

"Yes," Sheldon said. "It was not her."

"It was Agent Barlow. I am so sorry, Sheldon. I was foolish to ignore you and Uncle Willie."

Sheldon grimaced as he nodded. "It doesn't matter," he said. "When can I see her?"

"You need to rest, Shel. Let me do the worrying, and you do the healing, okay?"

"The Agent is evil, Evangeline. Please wait for me. We can beat him together. You can't tell anyone else since Junebug, Ms. Begley, and Cyrus know about him."

The sheriff paused as if something had occurred to her. "Yes, they told me about the book, and it is important. When did they see the book—before or after we were at Sarah's house?"

"Before," Sheldon said. His hoarse voice and fatigue brought images of their father.

"Rest, Sheldon, please."

Sheldon fell asleep.

The sheriff remained for a moment, silent. Her resentment and regret about Madden County embarrassed her now. However, Evangeline knew her mission—to find and kill the Agent. Her chest tightened, and purpose rekindled her resolve. It made little difference to her plan, but this was a mission from which she might not return. The thought magnified those hours of pining to be somewhere different and made them loom large as wasted time. Her father had once told her, "You don't know how valuable something is until you risk losing it."

She leaned in and kissed Sheldon's cheek one more time.

His eyelids fluttered, unable to open fully. He whispered, "You're not the deadman's finger," before falling asleep.

Chapter 81
Dust to Dust, Hearts to Paper

"Lilly," Evangeline said as she approached the woman from behind.

Lilly turned and embraced the sheriff, her arms around Evangeline's neck.

The two women stood without speaking for several seconds, but Evangeline did not feel awkward. The pain they had endured together, the hurt of violence and loss, made words unnecessary.

Evangeline knew Gene's death exhausted Lilly because she remembered her own exhaustion at her father's funeral. Back then, she had stood in this funeral home, trying to rise above the hurt, but losing her father had shredded her heart like paper.

"Are you sure you want to do this now?" Evangeline asked.

"Too much is at stake, Evangeline," Lilly said. "Seeing how these books may give us real answers to unnatural things, it is too important to wait. Besides, I want Barlow to pay. Come with me."

The sheriff followed Lilly into a backroom behind the funeral home chapel. Evangeline was nervous as Lilly opened a leather bag and retrieved the leather-bound book. The teacher motioned for Evangeline to join her at a table.

As the sheriff sat, Lilly opened the book, presenting the front inside cover so Evangeline could read it. "First, Sheldon said you would understand what this means."

Evangeline read the handwritten note on the inside. "To Daniel B., The future will come like a cold winter for us. But then you will find the flames of hell to keep you warm. Let no hurt go unavenged. Your Vadoma."

Evangeline wrinkled her brow, then swallowed. *Daniel Barlow.* "Where did you get this book, Lilly?"

"As I told Sheldon, Junebug, and Cyrus, I bought it from Adele at the bookstore several years back. Today I called Adele to find out how she acquired it. She said your father gave it to her years and years ago," Lilly said. "It was in a storage room at the police station with other unclaimed properties and confiscations. They had stored a small box of books since the 1920s. I gave Adele $40 for the box."

The sheriff turned the book over to read the worn, brown cover —the *Ceremonies of Darkness and Despair*. Pieces of paper marked different pages, and a large bookmark protruded from the back pages. Evangeline traced the last raised lettering with her finger. *Live forever, My Love—Your Vadoma.*

"I spent last night reading and marking pages you might find relevant, Evangeline," Lilly said. "It is hard to believe, even for someone like me who has long been a believer, but we have to consider this as—"

"The reality of impossible things," Evangeline said. "Help me, Lilly. I fear I don't have much time."

Lilly's face focused on the pages, and Evangeline noticed the light freckles clustered across her cheeks and nose for the first time. Without comment, the teacher flipped the pages to the bookmark. "Look here," the teacher said as she placed her pointer finger on the page. Her delicate digit reminded Evangeline of the deadman's finger and Sheldon's words.

The page depicted an eye surrounded by four separate drawings of a human form. It reminded Evangeline of a Ferris wheel. The details changed from picture to picture, each evolving to a different phase or stage.

The top circle displayed a natural man, nude and detailed. The second circle, positioned clockwise at three o'clock, showed a human form resembling a deformed wax figure melting in the heat. Evangeline touched that image with her hand. The third image at six o'clock displayed the full details of a man. The final circle, positioned at nine o'clock, portrayed yet another figure. This well-defined model depicted a fully formed man, smaller than the others, with arms extended at his sides. In each sketch, the figure's index finger pointed toward the circular line surrounding it.

"It is similar to four versions of Da Vinci's Vitruvian Man," Evangeline said. She recalled the Agent framed by the rearview mirror as she sped away.

Evangeline pushed the image aside and smiled when her reference to Da Vinci surprised Lilly. "I made an A in Art History at EKU," the sheriff said.

Lilly nodded and whispered, "I'm sorry. I didn't mean to prejudge your—"

Again, the sheriff interrupted, "It doesn't matter, Lilly. Finding the meaning of this symbol or whatever it is matters."

Lilly turned to another page in the book. "This might explain it," she said. She tapped a highlighted paragraph on the page:

Secrets shared across death, and life are the fodder for a curse. The skilled practitioner leverages what may not be spoken with intention, caution, and wisdom. A secret tethers the spirit and the flesh to the living realm or anchors it forever in the prison of the beyond. Balanced like the fall and the spring, the immortality seeker can weigh their existence on the scales of unspoken words. The imbalance cultivates the blossoming.

The sheriff touched the eye in the center as she counted the rings, clockwise and one by one. *The secret,* Evangeline thought. She envisioned Sheldon in his bedroom. He begged her to believe. She no longer needed to blindly trust the phenomenon because she had witnessed Barlow's existence and his cruelty.

"This spell, if you can believe in such things, says the wronged may curse those who harmed them by attaching to them for eternity, as long as 'both eternal souls' carry their secret."

"Willie and I were good at keeping our secrets," the Agent had said at her house.

"The only surefire weakness I find is the requirement to return to the sacred ground every twenty-four hours," Lilly said as she turned two pages ahead in the book.

Evangeline read the page and confirmed Lilly's interpretation. However, the sheriff stopped at one sentence in the next paragraph. She tilted the book for Lilly to see, as well:

When the blossom blooms, only the blood of the cursed wields the scythe.

They reread the passage. Then the two friends stared at each other.

"I have one more favor to ask, Lilly. When will everyone gather today?"

Chapter 82
Evangeline Speaks

Evangeline rose from her chair and walked toward the podium. The pews and the people became one. No one shifted or talked—only the silence and the Autumn sun rays pierced the chapel's stained glass windows.

Pastor Granville had spoken first. His gray hair and the same black suit he had worn at Willie's funeral endowed him with a sense of unquestionable authority. "Heavenly Father," he said, "we ask this good man's soul be welcomed into your home, just as he was in our humble house on Earth."

Lilly followed Granville. She talked about her father's passion for the *Mercury* and Madden County and his great love for her mother, her, and for trains. When she finished and walked away, everyone in the chapel, including Evangeline, knew Gene better and missed him more.

Evangeline wished she had been kinder to Gene.

Evangeline cleared her throat and scanned the audience. The sheriff had asked Pauline to call certain people and request their attendance at the service. Baron and Carl were present, not together, of course, but both were there. Faith Cornett sat between

Tucker and Cyrus near the middle pews while Clyde, George Spence, and Otis were in the back row. Mrs. King, the school principal, and Mr. Davis, the grandfather at the football field, were on different ends of the same pew. Many others filled the remaining seats. Junebug stood near the door in his brown uniform, and although he tried to look in another direction, Bug's attention always drifted back to Lilly.

The people lining the pews stared back. A few she did not know, but the others she had seen throughout her life. Her father had referred to everyone in the county as his friends. He had respected everyone's humanity—their good, evil, and in between—with equal value.

Too often, Evangeline forgot this place was a home, not a stay-over or a step along the way to something better. The sense of belonging rolled over them like creek water cascading across bare feet. It was a belonging she had neglected or refused to accept. They did not have to earn or prove anything to anyone. The mountains embraced them without conditions, as had her father. They were not problems to be solved. They were his people in their good times and in their worst moments.

The Sheriff of Madden County straightened her back, adjusted her uniform, and spoke.

"Gene Begley and I disagreed often. To Gene, I was a privileged, arrogant girl who believed Madden County was a disaster area awaiting the Lord's final judgment. He once told me the people of Madden County deserve an honest and transparent sheriff. I thought he wanted to make his job more manageable and mine impossible. But now I know he attempted to help me be better.

"The two secrets I tell you today will be hard to believe. I will not go through every detail, but it is in the best interest of Madden County if you are aware. These secrets, which may have resulted from my grandfather's good intentions, have chained our county to a dangerous spirit for decades. Who knows, maybe the truth will set us free."

The sheriff noted the confused expressions in the crowd. However, Junebug, Lilly, Cyrus, and Faith did not appear conflicted. Evangeline finished her pause with a deep breath.

"The first secret is most troubling for several of us in this room. It happened in October of 1927 when a young boy disappeared. A Baldwin detective sent to Madden County to intimidate coal miners and squash the union was considered the lead suspect in the boy's kidnapping. My grandfather, Sheriff Sheldon Grace, assembled a search party to find the agent and the boy. His team consisted of Harold Wainscott, Calvin Mills, Lloyd Ramey, Reverend Zendell Adams, and Foster McCoy, the missing boy's father.

"The newspaper reported my grandfather's team didn't find the child or the Agent. Fortunately, others found the boy asleep in the woods. However, evidence suggests my grandfather's claim about Daniel Barlow eluding them was false. My grandfather and his team lied about what happened and managed to keep it secret throughout their lives.

"I'm afraid the truth is more painful than the lie. My grandfather manipulated the men into killing Agent Barlow. The Sheriff, Mills, Wainscott, and Ramey shot Barlow and dumped his body in the coal mine on Rockhouse Creek. I believe Reverend Adams agreed to the shooting but only observed."

Baron Mills stood. "Why would your grandfather kill someone?" He raised his arms, his palms facing upward as if questioning a bad call at a ballgame. "He had nothing to gain and everything to lose." Many in the crowd nodded, while others were silent.

"Baron," Evangeline said, "my grandfather was clever. With this act, he sealed a bond between the elites of Madden County—coal, the union, the church, and lumber—a connection he planned to leverage whenever he needed it. It was the power he held over the men's heads to preserve the peace in Madden County."

Conversations ignited around the chapel. Evangeline heard "Ridiculous!" and "Crazy" bounce around the room. She glanced at Lilly, Junebug, and others who remained silent.

Clyde Perry looked up at her and said, "You said you would tell us two secrets, Sheriff. Does the next one make more sense than the first one?" Clyde's question silenced the congregation.

Evangeline swallowed hard. The sweat on her brow and back rolled again. "The second secret is a consequence of the first. The Baldwin detective, Agent Barlow, was skilled in dark magic."

Several people laughed, while others groaned as though they had just heard the punchline to a cringe-inducing joke.

"I wasted a great deal of time by reacting as you did," the sheriff said. "Magic? Give me a break. I am a trained police officer. I base my beliefs on what the evidence proves. Believe it or not, that is still how I think. However, the evidence I gathered while investigating my uncle's murder, Art Butcher's death, and my own experiences with this evil tell me there is only one explanation, no matter how impossible you think it is."

Evangeline straightened her shoulders, controlled her expression, and glanced at Junebug. The deputy's smile encouraged her to continue.

"It appears impossible to me, too, but Barlow cursed Madden County," she said. Exasperation filled the pews. "He used his knowledge to give himself life after death by implanting a secret in my Uncle Robert, who passed it to my Uncle Willie. Willie kept the secret until hours before his death, when he handed it to me."

Several people in the pews shook their heads, and others whispered. But some of those present stared at Evangeline, caught between disbelief and consideration.

"So where is this Barlow now, Sheriff?" It was Faith Cornett's gentle voice.

Evangeline acknowledged her question and said, "Barlow first appeared as a shadow. However, when I shared the secret with my brother Sheldon, I empowered him to take on a human form."

Junebug spoke, "It means he can kill anyone in Madden County, just like any serial killer."

Several people stood and stepped toward the chapel exit. The County Council members, as though they had choreographed a dance, left their seats in unison and waddled away. Even some who had nodded in agreement moments earlier found their way to the door. The remaining audience sat as though waiting for the sheriff and the deputy to reveal the hidden cameras recording the prank.

Pastor Granville stayed seated. Although he stared at Evangeline, he did not appear troubled or skeptical.

However, Junebug turned and left the chapel.

*****

Evangeline stopped when Carl spoke from the pews. "What a secret! The law kills a man. What's your next big story? Bankers Take Money? President Clinton Enjoys Women?" Carl's angry words caused Evangeline to draw her lips to bottle the response growing inside her.

She stared back at the man and shook her head. "Not at all, Carl," she said. "The men who searched for Barlow did not act as we would hope. That is why the secret exists, and I believe I have to tell you the truth."

The sheriff shifted her weight to her right leg to alleviate the pain in her back. It didn't work. "I am not certain if my grandfather planned to use the Agent's killing to his advantage before they took off after Barlow. But he held it over those men's heads like a nasty picture to blackmail them into cooperating after they returned."

Clyde spoke, "I have something to say." His calm voice allowed

Evangeline to breathe again. "Sheriff, I've respected your father and now you. Are you claiming bad luck hit Madden County on that day about seventy years ago? It doesn't make much sense to blame luck for anything this world throws at us."

The entire chapel felt cramped to Evangeline now, as though she peered at it through the wrong end of a telescope.

"You are right, Clyde. I have never believed much in luck. People who try to find the answer to the problem outside themselves search for the most comfortable answers, not the right ones. The Agent was an evil man who had learned about spells and curses—"

A metallic sound resonated through the chapel. The entrance to the wheelchair ramp and the side parking lot opened and struck the wall. Light poured into the chapel from the outside. It revealed a thin man in an out-of-fashion black suit as he backed into the room, each step careful and measured.

Evangeline watched Junebug help the man in black ease a wheelchair across the threshold and into the chapel. The gray-haired man in the wheelchair, wearing an even more out-of-fashion black suit than his companion, sat upright, balancing a Bible in his lap as his sockless, pale ankles contrasted with his polished black shoes and pants.

After he closed the door behind them, Junebug announced, "Everyone, this is—"

"I am Leon McCoy. If you dang fools don't have the good sense to listen to the sheriff, maybe you will let me set you straight about what happened to the little boy sleeping in the woods. I am an eyewitness to the evil done by Daniel Barlow."

Chapter 83
I Am Expendable Now

E vangeline slipped away after Leon told his story and others asked him questions. She had to admit the old man was credible and kept everyone's attention. McCoy still may not convince those remaining of anything, but he had removed the spotlight from her.

She had half expected the Agent to appear in the chapel prepared to finish whatever he had hoped to do back at her house. But the funeral home parking lot was empty, and no mysterious shadows or spirits floated above her car. Evangeline even checked her backseat to ensure the Agent was not poised to attack.

"I am expendable now," she said as she exited the street. By revealing both secrets—Barlow's existence and her theory on Rock-house Creek—she hoped to end the Agent's hold over her, Sheldon, and everyone else. The book showed the eye symbol centered inside the different versions of a human form. The figure changed at each phase, like Willie's letter describing the Agent on the Pinnacle changing from fog to a wax figure. Evangeline interpreted the symbol as phases. The form originated as a ghost-like shadow but became more lifelike at each circle. Despite the risk,

Evangeline concluded the more people who "eyed" the secret, the more human the Agent became.

"I hurt him," Art had said. *People hurt, not ghosts.*

Besides, the book suggested two secrets, not simply one, kept the balance between life and death, the past and the present, the Agent and the secret keeper. Barlow had slipped and said both he and Willie kept their secrets.

Radio static filled the cab. "Sheriff Grace, do you copy?"

"Copy, Otis. What do you need?" Evangeline responded, hoping Otis was not asking her to answer a call. She had borrowed an officer from Jensen County and asked the State Police Post to provide support, too. If the sheriff had time to explain the situation to them, she would request the Trooper's help combating the Agent. However, she predicted the conversation would end with her at a Lexington mental facility.

"A tough one, boss," Otis said. "We have found Paul Wainscott."

"Good," she replied. "It will make it easier for—"

"Sheriff," Otis said. "He was sighted taking his truck from our vehicle lot earlier today. Marty Goble saw Wainscott and another man drive away. Marty tailed them to Rockhouse Creek Road. They turned toward the old mine."

"Is he sure?" Evangeline asked. Her heart raced, and she envisioned Paul Wainscott standing in her doorway and Sarah's pale face after she had stabbed Sheldon.

"Marty said it was in broad daylight and claimed he was sober as a minister. He recognized Paul, of course, and said he appeared to be injured. The other guy wore an old-timey costume and a hat."

"Otis, alert everyone you can with details about the truck," Evangeline said. "I am heading to Rockhouse Creek and the abandoned mine."

"Sheriff, what's happening?" Otis said. "This can't be right.

Wainscott's truck was bloody. I figured Luke dropped the dead body somewhere."

"It isn't right, but it's happening soon, Otis," Evangeline said. "Very soon. I have to call some people. If anyone calls, tell them I am traveling on Rockhouse Creek Road."

Chapter 84
Possible to Ache

T he gaps between the trees allowed Evangeline to see
Rockhouse Creek as she drove. Once, when the waters
were shallow, she and Uncle Willie had waded through
those waters. She had walked on the stones, her toes comforted by
the cold stream. Today, the Autumn rain swelled the creek,
causing the water to climb the bank as if it planned to escape.

"This creek feeds into other streams and ponds across the
entire county. It spreads its water to the Tug River and the Big
Sandy," Willie had said. "I reckon time and gravity carry Madden
County water to the Ohio and Mississippi Rivers."

*Some memories prove it is possible to ache and be happy at the
same time.*

Evangeline knew a trap awaited her at the abandoned mine.
Her experience at the DeLong mine had been a trap, although it
had been an interesting one. Rather than kill her without hesitation, Barlow's snare sought to keep her alive after the entrance
collapsed. She figured he had wanted to kill Sheldon and wait it
out as a shadow—until she had died hours later in the mine. It

would have meant the secret remained safe forever, providing him free rein to kill at will.

Art had foiled his plan. *Some memories prove it is possible to ache and then be happy.*

No doubt, Paul would be a hostage in whatever maneuver Barlow hoped to employ. She dreaded to see Barlow's form now. Evangeline had risked it all by telling the two secrets—the Agent existed because her grandfather and the heads of the Wainscott, Mills, Ramey, and McCoy families had gunned Barlow down and concealed his body inside the mine. However, judging by Barlow's book of spells, she could interpret the words in several ways. The image suggested that the Agent's evolution might extend beyond what he had told Robert and Willie.

Nonetheless, he had already been strong enough to kill before she had made a fool of herself at the chapel, so had it been a substantial risk to tell everyone the truth?

Evangeline tapped the brake pedal to ease onto the dirt road to the mine. The rocks and holes shook the car and pressed her sore shoulder against the seatbelt.

God, she missed her father. His courage had never wavered the way hers did now. She recalled his face in dangerous situations and how he examined the environment and assessed the danger. She tried to mirror him but realized she did not share his courage and resolve. No one did.

Then she remembered when they had responded to a domestic violence call together. It had been at a trailer park near the fairgrounds. Trees surrounded the park, and the dark sky made the mobile homes ominous. When her father had parked near the trailer, he had stopped. He had acted reluctant to exit the cruiser.

"What is it," she had said as she opened the door.

He had turned and said, "Calls like these get officers killed, you know, because there are kids in there."

Evangeline had scoffed. "Are you kidding, Dad? A drunk

husband and an angry wife are nothing compared to some of our calls."

"They make me afraid," he had said. "Officers hesitate to act because there are children in the picture. Who wants to shoot a daddy with their child watching?"

He had remained silent for several seconds until she heard the click of his seatbelt and door handle.

"Focus, Evangeline, focus," he had said. "Being afraid is a blessing if it makes you concentrate and keeps you safe."

Evangeline Grace feared the Agent, but she was also focused.

Some memories make it possible to ache...

Chapter 85
Annie Oakley

Evangeline stomped on the gas pedal an instant before the truck slammed into her car. The pickup had targeted her driver's side door, but she accelerated enough to redirect the blow to the back fender. The impact spun the patrol car counterclockwise, away from the other vehicle.

Her bones rattled, but she kept her hands on the steering wheel and turned into the spin. The trees, the mine entrance, the barren ground, the slurry pond, and a patch of trees whipped as if she were riding a manic carousel.

Evangeline's foot jumped to the brake pedal as she steadied the car. She stared through the windshield to see the truck roll back, facing her. Its metal grille bent toward the hood, and the cracked windshield created a web, hiding the driver's face.

The sheriff unsnapped her seatbelt and opened the car door. She heard the truck's engine whine and roar as she rolled from her seat onto the dirt and mud. Without hesitation, Evangeline stood and sprinted toward the rear fender. She dived away from the car as the truck's grille slammed against the passenger's side door. The force knocked the cruiser into a ditch near the tree line. The car's back end smashed into two intertwined trees across the gutter.

Evangeline remained on her knees for a few moments before she stumbled to her feet. As she did, she drew her sidearm. The collision wedged her back bumper against the trees and blocked access to the trunk, where she stored her shotgun.

The truck reversed and reset.

In response, the sheriff raised her gun and sighted the driver's side windshield. The already shattered glass resembled a shooting range target. Her hand remained steady despite the pain rising in her body.

Twenty-five yards away, the Ford F-150 was a four-ton monster. Even if Wainscott was behind the wheel and under the Agent's influence, she needed to protect herself.

Evangeline did not blink. She inhaled, exhaled, and fired into the center of the splintered glass. The report sounded like hail denting a tin roof. Each sound rose, fell, and ended with the bullet penetrating the windshield. The truck barreled toward the right, accelerating into the same ditch where her cruiser had stopped.

Damp air permeated the ridge. The sheriff held her gun high and sidled toward the truck, stopping when she heard the laughter.

"That was some fun, little lady. Besides Annie Oakley, I didn't know a dame could shoot a pistol so good." Barlow's voice emanated from the truck, but the sound changed yet again. She strained to hear him over the sputtering engine. The words did not ring with the same intensity as they had in Sheldon's room the night before.

Evangeline crept toward the driver's side door. The truck dipped nose-first into the wet ditch, forcing her to step down into the mud and reach up to the door. She prepared to fire the gun as soon as she pulled the handle, but as the door latch released, she heard another door spring open.

The Agent exited the cab on the passenger's side. His shoes created a suction sound as he ran toward the mine.

The sheriff crouched behind the truck bed near the tailgate. She leaned out enough to see the Agent's back as he rushed toward the mine.

"Stop," Evangeline said.

The man was tall and broad-shouldered, wearing his blue suit jacket and matching loose-fitting dress pants. His fedora fell onto the ground as he ran. It was him. But he was different than before. He was not the shadowy figure stalking the corners Sheldon had described, nor was he the unfinished clay monster she had encountered at the house.

The Agent resembled the fourth circle in Lilly's book. He was skin, bone, and sinew, wearing real clothes, and his voice was not an echo inside her brain. It was as human as her voice. He was Daniel Barlow.

Chapter 86
A Change of Scenery

Barlow walked backward and waved bye-bye to the sheriff as he entered the mine's open mouth. His smile, almost as fear-inducing as before, curled her stomach.

He halted when she stopped twenty feet from the entrance and took cover behind a metal barrier.

"Aren't you coming in, Sheriff? Remember, I was a guest in your home. The least you can do is tour my abode. Please forgive the mess. I've only lived here seventy-five years."

"That's about seventy-five years too long, Barlow," she said. "It is time for a change of scenery."

The dark mine served as the backdrop while the sun spotlighted the Agent on the stage.

"It's funny, Sheriff Grace," the Agent said, his voice much less threatening than when she had first heard it. "If anyone should understand my disdain for Madden and its people, it should be you."

She winced.

"You search for a change of scenery. You're leaving Madden County because it is backward and isn't too keen on your kind, if you understand me. You want to be where people notice your superior work and toss roses at your feet. You want to be the best among the best, not some two-bit law-woman in a dying town, surrounded by drug addicts, blood feuds, and poverty."

Evangeline winced again. She felt frustration as her words whistled back at her like a boomerang. Barlow reminded her she had not said the right things to Sheldon.

Barlow laughed. "Your grandfather was a hypocrite, considering how he trapped me in this grave. Your father was worth about as much as the tin in his badge here in Madden County. Hell, if Willie had not drawn the short straw, he would have been the real patriarch of your mountain clan."

Evangeline's grip tightened on her pistol. The Agent tried to lure her into the mine as he had with Sarah at the Delong mine. She considered pulling the trigger, although a handgun firing into the darkness would be a tough shot. Besides, if she interpreted the book correctly, she could not kill him alone. *When the blossom blooms, only the cursed blood wields the scythe.*

"Where's Paul Wainscott?" she asked. "Did you kill him?"

"His life depends on you, Sheriff," Barlow said. "Here, let me show you." The Agent faded into the dark mine. Seconds later, Evangeline heard muffled cries and a dead weight dragged along the mine's floor. When Barlow emerged from the dark, he kneeled behind a gray tarp. The canvas shifted and reshaped as though it trapped a wild animal.

"I'm here, Paul," Evangeline said before she turned her full attention and the gun on the Agent. "He better not be dying, Barlow." The sheriff stepped closer to the entrance. Barlow shielded himself even more with darkness and Wainscott's body inside the tarp.

"Dying?" the Agent said, feigning concern. "Let's see if the man is still kicking." The Agent kicked the tarp, and Wainscott moaned and struggled. "Alright, Doll, I will let him out for recess so you can see he's breathing."

Evangeline glared at Barlow, and her trigger finger twitched.

The Agent proceeded to remove a knife from inside his jacket. He held it with the fingertips of his right hand and raised his left palm to signal he meant no harm. He slid the blade along the canvas, opening it like a deep-sea angler might gut a fish.

Wainscott stopped struggling for a moment. Then he attempted to stand. The Agent had bound Paul's hands with rope and gagged him with a cloth. Paul's eyes pleaded for Evangeline's help. As soon as Paul stood, Barlow used him as a shield.

Then Barlow raised the knife to Wainscott's throat.

The sheriff closed the distance between her gun and the Agent's knife to fifteen feet. She pushed her hair from her face and gripped the weapon with both hands.

The Agent had sliced Willie open, cut Sarah so she could not walk, beheaded Gene, and stabbed Art. He displayed no hesitation when it came to using the blade.

"You will get him killed if you aren't careful, Sheriff Grace. Haven't you left too many of your family and friends rotting in jail cells and abandoned coal mines?" Barlow's smirk was uglier now than when it was no more than dead flesh bulging on his melting face.

She stepped closer.

"See what I mean, Sheriff? You came at me like old Sheldon Grace would have done. There is no doubt you are his grand-daughter," Barlow said. "Now, toss your fancy gun before I scalp this man like old Geronimo. Do it, and I will let Wainscott loose to scurry away like the cockroach he is."

Evangeline swallowed hard but did not drop her gun. Her father had taught her that hostage-takers acted in bad faith. If she played along with the deception, there would be more bloodshed, not less.

However, when the Agent grabbed a handful of Wainscott's hair and placed the blade against Paul's throat, Evangeline dropped her Glock onto the ground beside her. More than anything else, she needed to buy time and keep Barlow with her. To hold her gun not only meant the Agent would kill Paul, but it also escalated the standoff too soon.

Besides, the Agent's form had shifted to the final circle. He appeared human.

"Let him go," the sheriff said. "Or are you afraid of me like you were my uncle?"

The Agent's high-pitched laughter sounded like a hawk's cry.

Evangeline tensed her muscles and prepared to attack if Barlow hurt Wainscott. To her surprise and relief, the Agent lifted the knife from Paul's neck and slashed downward to sever the rope restraining the man's hands and the bonds around his feet. Barlow stepped away, raised his foot, and kicked Wainscott, causing him to stumble.

Evangeline yelled at Paul, but he was disoriented. To escape the Agent, he sprinted away from Barlow and the sheriff. After several steps, Wainscott stopped and fell to the muddy ground outside the mine. Still gagged, the man resembled a Guantanamo Bay prisoner she had seen on television earlier in the year.

Now nothing stood between Evangeline and the Agent.

Chapter 87
The Existence of Two Secrets

T he Agent wended his way from the mine entrance until he faced Evangeline in the sparse light provided by the darkening sky. Evangeline glanced upwards and thought about how the rain would ride fall's last leaves to the forest floor.

"So you thought of everything, didn't you, Sheriff?" The Agent shuffled closer to her until he stood ten feet away.

"Why do you say that, Barlow?" She still needed time.

"Look at my predicament. You figured out the two secrets. You brought me back to skin, muscle, and bone. Are you sure you don't have some Romani blood coursing through those veins?" His smile revealed black teeth, and his eyes were still the hue of a gray moth's wings. He wasn't as broad-shouldered as before, but the suit, stained by coal and blood, relaxed on his body instead of merging with it.

"I don't know about everything," she said.

"You begged those assholes to rescue you, didn't you?" He shifted his feet, ending up nearer to her. "Sure, maybe one or two may show up. But, you know Madden County. Most will pretend you are crazy like Willie Grace. You remember, like you did?"

Evangeline focused on the knife instead of responding. As adrenaline distracted her from the pain radiating in her shoulders and head, Evangeline accepted she could not run from this fight. Failure to defeat Barlow meant many people would die, including those she loved and had vowed to serve and protect.

She pictured Sheldon in the hospital bed, Sarah weeping, and baby Jessica gripping Art's finger as Faith Cornett rocked her on the glider.

"When you told everyone your grandfather killed me," he pointed with the knife blade toward a spot outside the mine, "I concluded you had talked to someone who knew the old ways, or you had found my books. Old Willie was right about you being smarter than him."

The Agent lunged toward the sheriff, sweeping the knife toward Evangeline's stomach. He was smaller but quicker than he had been at the house.

Evangeline blocked his arm to her left, avoiding the blade as she slipped to her right. She pounded her right fist into his face. The punch clapped as if thunder accompanied the rain. Barlow's military-length brown hair—slicked back and parted to the side—bounced. When one strand escaped and waved at the sheriff, the Agent stopped to pat his hair, then attacked again.

Arrogant and vain.

Evangeline leaned away from a blow and countered with another strike. This time she struck the side of his head. Barlow was confused. Evangeline inferred he had not been at this phase of transformation before, so taking a punch perplexed him. She remained focused, and although she hoped her risk had paid off, the Agent remained dangerous in any form.

"I hurt him."

Evangeline backed away but could not avoid the knife's second swing. The blade cut into her shoulder near her collarbone. She gasped, but did not examine the red cloud staining her shirt.

Instead, she slipped away, dropping into a fighting stance with her fists raised.

Barlow crept closer and circled to his left. The dark sky spat the October rain from Evangeline's right, so as she moved to her left to keep her distance from the man, the raindrops caused her to blink.

Time was on Evangeline's side. They might defeat this monster if she stayed alive until the others arrived. She shifted to her right and circled him. The scene would be comical if not for Barlow's damage to her family and Madden County. She pictured Gene and Lilly, Sheldon and Sarah, Robert and Willie, Luke and Mrs. Collins, Maria and Art—their pain stoked her anger.

The Agent snarled at the sheriff and rolled the knife in his hand. "Did I tell you about my daddy and his knife factory?" He leaped toward the sheriff and spun to her left. The knife sliced her left side below the ribcage. The sharp blade cut the brown fabric drawing a dark line on her pale skin.

The Agent straightened and inhaled as though he smelled victory.

Evangeline charged forward, feigned another punch to the face, and caught Barlow's arm as he swung the knife downward. Using his weight against him, she lowered her shoulder and flipped Barlow over her body onto the ground. Gripping his wrist, Evangeline sat beside the Agent in the dirt and yanked his arm while encircling it with her legs.

She pulled, twisted, and bent Barlow's arm until he released the knife. Evangeline controlled the taller man, wringing his arm like a wet beach towel. She strained against his resistance and dug her heels into his upper ribs and neck.

The Agent groaned, spat on the ground, and laughed. "You believe you thought of everything, don't you? I'm sorry, Doll, but you can't kill me."

She turned his hand and wrist further while applying pressure with her legs. She was unsure she could have restrained the Agent who had attacked her at the house, but she was determined to hold onto this version.

When the sheriff tightened her grip, her muscles strained. The exertion and the soft rain collided, one hard and the other gentle, on her face. To distract herself from the pain and exhaustion, she watched the almost naked trees sway in the wind. The black sludge pond rippled, and between the trees, hawks rode the gusts rising from the mountains to soar, their wings still. The tears spilled onto her cheeks blending with the rain. Evangeline torqued Barlow's arm until she felt his tangled body surrender.

Moments later, Junebug's cruiser skidded onto the scene. Junebug leaped from his vehicle to assist the sheriff. He drew his gun, aimed it with one hand, and placed his foot on the Agent's chest. When Evangeline released the Agent, she turned to find her weapon in the dirt yards away. She picked it up and wiped it on her trousers before she directed it at the Agent. Junebug, his arm still in a sling, tossed her his handcuffs.

The sheriff flipped the Agent over so his face rested in the dirt. As she cuffed him, she told Junebug, "You better release those guys from the backseat before they kill each other."

The deputy nodded and walked to his police car. After Carl and Baron exited the backseat, Evangeline watched them as they stepped toward the sheriff.

"This guy is the Agent you told us about?" Baron asked.

"It's him," she responded. "He doesn't look so tough now, but he was an evil force yesterday."

"Why is he dressed like a 1920s gangster?" Carl said.

The Agent smiled.

"It is just like the sheriff told you," Junebug said.

Carl added, "He doesn't look like a ghost or a monster."

Another vehicle arrived. Otis stepped from the driver's side and opened the police van's sliding door. He helped Lilly out first, then stepped aside to allow Reverend Granville, Cyrus, and Morgan McCoy to exit onto the wet ground. McCoy carried his shotgun with him.

Lilly took her place beside Junebug while the Reverend walked closer to the Agent to get a better look at his face.

Evangeline wondered if she trusted Granville. She did not know him well enough to be sure, so she waited to hear his reaction.

"So this is the spirit you described at the Chapel, Sheriff?" Rather than a gun, he carried a Bible. His stern look did not offer any doubt about his belief. "Evil has many forms and faces," the Reverend said, "and this man has worn them all."

Another vehicle roared up from the road. A Dodge Ram truck towing a small bulldozer drifted from over the ridge. Clyde Perry's broad shoulders filled the windshield.

The Agent's laughter caused Evangeline to reach for her Glock even though she had cuffed Barlow's wrists.

"He ain't going nowhere," Carl said. He stared at the Agent and said, "What do you think is so funny?"

"Hillbillies," the Agent said. He resumed his gleeful fit as the party surrounded him. When the laughter subsided, Barlow smirked at Evangeline. "You can't kill me, Sheriff."

"Why do you think I can't kill you?" Evangeline smiled back at him. She broke eye contact and turned toward Lilly. "Wait. Ms. Begley, perhaps he is referring to the passage in the spell book. Remember, *When the blossom blooms, only the blood of the cursed wields the scythe.*"

The Agent's smirk transformed into a smile.

Lilly said, "We read Vadoma's little book of magic and know the families who put you in the ground are the only ones who can end your life."

The Agent said, "You did think of everything... Almost." He

looked over Evangeline's shoulder. "I wonder where Paulie Wainscott is?"

Evangeline whipped her head around to find Paul. He was no longer resting outside the mine. She scanned the entire landscape but did not see him. Her heart became a lump of coal.

"He scampered into the abandoned mine," the Agent said. "He looked determined to get the operation up and running. I bet he plans to blast down there any time."

"Does anyone see Paul Wainscott?" Evangeline said as she sprinted toward the mine.

Everyone scattered to search for Paul. Cyrus ran toward the entrance to the mine, calling Wainscott's name, while the Reverend and Otis turned to check behind the cruiser and the van. Junebug ran toward the slurry pond, calling Wainscott's name. Clyde checked behind the trailer carrying his dozer.

Everyone stopped when the Agent yelled, "Fire in the hole!"

*****

The blast was more like an earthquake than an explosion. The ground trembled. Evangeline struggled to keep her balance, then fell back seated in the dirt. Lilly fell near the Agent, and Junebug stumbled as he tried to return to her. Otis and the Reverend clung to the van as if it were a lifeboat.

Then an explosion happened in Evangeline's brain. She realized what she had not considered before. Barlow was right—she had not thought of everything.

The Agent had known she would beat him, so he had conjured one last spell. He had used Paul to detonate an explosive inside the mine, but not as an elaborate way to kill Wainscott. It was much more devious.

The sheriff stared past Junebug toward the Coal Slurry Pond. The only barrier between the pond's 400 million gallons of coal sludge was the westernmost mine wall. Without the wall, the toxic sludge—the oily minerals and waste washed from the coal—would seep into the mine and flood Rockhouse Creek. It would flow down the waterway until the sludge contaminated every stream and water source in Madden County.

Barlow, now upright, smiled at her, and he had somehow freed himself from the handcuffs. He laughed and blew her a kiss.

Evangeline inhaled and followed him but halted when a shotgun blast cut through the light rain and autumn air. The shot reminded her of Dr. Bell's warehouse.

The Agent staggered, his filthy suit and white shirt riddled with buckshot. What would not have harmed him before now spiked his body like nails.

Morgan McCoy held the shotgun against his shoulder with the barrel still pointed at Barlow's chest.

The second and third shots came from a rifle and a handgun. Baron and Carl were side-by-side as the gray smoke rose from the weapons Junebug had provided. Each held their ground, prepared to take another shot.

The Agent fell to his knees when the bullets struck him but rose to his feet before the smoke cleared.

"He is a demon, Sheriff," Baron Mills said. "No one survives being shot so many times."

The Agent averted his eyes from the shooters and glared at the sheriff. A pained smile swept across his lips. "You can't kill me, Grace. I will be a shadow again attached to you and your little brother like—"

Barlow froze. Confusion wrinkled his face, and his knees trembled as he stretched his dirty hand toward Evangeline. "It can't," he said. His voice was weak—and human. The Agent's legs buckled, and he dropped to his knees as though kneeling before a king. "I can't die."

Cyrus stood behind the Agent. Evangeline recognized the

white-handled pocket knife Cyrus held as the one she had gifted him at the hospital. Blood dripped from the blade, the handle, and the young man's hand. Cyrus stared at the Agent like a boxer, shocked by the power of his last punch.

The sheriff walked to the Agent but locked eyes with Cyrus. Disbelief and confusion registered on the boy's face. "It is okay, Cyrus. That one was for Willie."

Evangeline's body ached when she bent over the Agent. She examined Barlow's face and shell-riddled body. His chest fluttered, and his pupils grayed even more than they had already been, while his skin cracked like the cover of Lilly's ancient book of spells.

"You not only can die, Agent Barlow," Evangeline said. "You *will*." She motioned for Clyde to unload his dozer and watched as he nodded to her and hurried toward the trailer.

The sheriff's Glock felt comfortable in her hand. She aimed and fired as though it was what she was born to do.

Chapter 88
Summer 2003

E vangeline glanced into the rearview mirror to ensure the U-Haul trailer was still attached. Then she reached for Sheldon in the passenger seat of her Honda and patted him on the hand as she accelerated westward.

The last eight months in Madden County were challenging. After Clyde buried Barlow beneath the mountain and sealed the mine's entrance, Evangeline had ridden home with Bentley in his cruiser. She had implored him to stop and check Rockhouse Creek, where swirling black shadows colored the stream.

Soon every Madden County waterway had flowed like black syrup spilled from a bottle. The wildlife—the fish, birds, turtles, deer, raccoons, foxes, bears, and opossums—had left the county in search of better grounds or had died in the muck and mayhem of what Lilly Begley, the *Mercury's* interim editor, had referred to as "The Slur." National news outlets had mentioned it was the most significant environmental disaster in the southeast before they had left it behind like a missing mountaintop.

Evangeline had tried to tell the truth, but everyone had

attributed her delusion to the concussions she had suffered in her brave efforts to keep the county safe.

Madden County knew the story by heart. An evil stranger sent by a drug cartel in the south murdered Willie Grace because he had learned too much. The sheriff and her deputies had closed in on the assassin. He killed poor Luke Porter and Grace Collins and almost murdered the sheriff's brother and his girlfriend, Sarah. When the hired gun kidnapped Paul Wainscott, Grace asked for volunteers to help the police track him down. Of course, the sheriff found the killer. However, he had already set a line of explosives in the old Wainscott mine beside the slurry pond. The sheriff and her volunteers freed Wainscott, but he died during a heroic attempt to disarm the explosives. The stranger died inside the mine, as well. The blast destroyed the wall between the deep slurry pond the company used to store its toxic waste materials, which released the sludge into Rockhouse Creek.

The Honda remained silent as they passed by the courthouse. As was now her habit, Evangeline slowed to observe the large monument beside her grandfather's historical marker. The metal placard commemorated "Deputy Arthur Butcher, 1964-2002, a Husband, Father, Friend, Police Officer, and Hero Who Died Protecting Madden County." It made her smile to know Baron and Carl had collaborated to create the tribute to Art, and Paul Wainscott's Foundation had paid for the memorial.

She proceeded along Route 23 to the Mountain Parkway. The temperature was above 90 degrees, and clouds dotted the azure sky—fluffs of cotton with no discernible forms. Evangeline raised her finger to the rearview mirror and tapped the metal scrip hanging on a string from the frame.

"Don't worry about Sarah, Sheldon," Evangeline said. "She will be just fine. Lilly has kept her busy this summer, and school will start soon. She gets better daily and has the best doctors in the state."

"I know," Sheldon said. He shifted to see his sister better. She felt thankful he had regained some of the weight he had lost in the hospital.

A hand reached from the backseat to pat Sheldon's shoulder. "Sarah is one strong girl, Buddy. Together, you two are unbeatable."

"Thanks, my friend," Sheldon responded.

Cyrus leaned back and continued reading the book on his lap.

When they arrived on campus, a white sign with blue letters pointed to the parking lot for new students. A blue arrow with white letters guided them toward the registration area.

"There are signs everywhere," Evangeline said. "They've thought of everything."

Tables covered with campus maps, name tags, and even water bottles lined the sidewalk. Cyrus registered at the A through D table, and a brown-haired sophomore named Laura in a Berea College tee-shirt offered to help them find Cyrus's dorm.

After they unloaded the U-haul, Evangeline, Sheldon, and Cyrus stood outside the dormitory in the parking lot.

"I can't thank you enough, Evangeline. You, too, Sheldon. My mom said I had better do a good job here because that would be the best way to repay for all your help. It also honors Willie."

"That's right. We have confidence in you. But no matter how well you do, Cyrus, you mean so much to us."

Cyrus embraced Evangeline and then Sheldon. He tried to speak but only managed, "I will see you soon."

Sheldon said, "Watch out for these college girls."

"If you need us, Cyrus, please call. You know where home is," Evangeline said.

Cyrus smiled and walked toward Bingham Hall's back entrance.

*****

As she drove eastward toward the Mountain Parkway, Evangeline talked to Sheldon about their mother and father—like how her father would tell stories so outrageous that she and their mom had almost peed themselves with laughter. Once, at breakfast when he had embellished a story about a woman in California who had called 911 because her pizza arrived late, their mother had thrown a biscuit at him to make him stop.

Sheldon's laughter made the world feel like a better place to her—a place where she belonged.

Before they crossed the Madden County line, a yellow and gold field spilled from the road to a dark green mountain. The plants caught the sunlight and held the rays until the entire meadow glowed. Some goldenrods had yet to blossom, but it was still early in the season. Beautiful flowers take time to grow, even beneath the warmth of the Appalachian sun.

About the Author

Dewey Hensley was born and raised in Eastern Kentucky. Inspired by great teachers and coaches, he became an award-winning educator and leader, all while writing stories and poems for and with his students. He lives in La Grange, Kentucky, with his wife, Kathy, and his stepson, Daxon, as well as their cat Hobbes, and dogs Cricket, and Birdie.

CPSIA information can be obtained
at www.ICGtesting.com
Printed in the USA
LVHW070954080623
749250LV00005B/40

9 781958 414972

QUERIDO TIGRE QUEZADA

Para los verdaderos héroes de nuestra nación:
los atletas con capacidades especiales.

Y para Laura, a quien no le gusta el futbol...
pero le gustan mis historias.

DIRECCIÓN EDITORIAL: Antonio Moreno Paniagua
GERENCIA EDITORIAL: Wilebaldo Nava Reyes
COORDINACIÓN DE LA COLECCIÓN: Karen Coeman
CUIDADO DE LA EDICIÓN: Pilar Armida y Obsidiana Granados
FORMACIÓN: Gil G. Reyes
ILUSTRACIONES: Edgar Clement

Querido Tigre Quezada

Texto, D.R. © 2005, Antonio Malpica Maury

PRIMERA EDICIÓN: abril de 2005
SEGUNDA EDICIÓN: febrero de 2007
CUARTA REIMPRESIÓN: junio de 2011
D.R. © 2007, Ediciones Castillo, S.A. de C.V.
Insurgentes Sur 1886, Col. Florida,
Del. Álvaro Obregón,
C.P. 01030, México, D.F.

Ediciones Castillo forma parte
del Grupo Macmillan

www.grupomacmillan.com
www.edicionescastillo.com
info@edicionescastillo.com
Lada sin costo: 01 800 536 1777

Miembro de la Cámara Nacional
de la Industria Editorial Mexicana.
Registro núm. 3304

ISBN: 978-970-20-0995-5

Impreso en México/*Printed in Mexico*

Toño Malpica

Ilustraciones de Edgar Clement

QUERIDO TIGRE QUEZADA

Castillo de la lectura

Ahí está. No lo pierdan de vista. Es aquél, el que porta el número 10 en la camiseta. No lo pierdan de vista, porque ha prometido que el primer gol de esta Liga de Campeones de la UEFA será suyo. Y ha prometido meterlo en los primeros cinco minutos del partido inicial. Así que no pierdan detalle. Como ven, ya ha saludado a la tribuna con un ademán, ya dio ese par de brinquitos que suele hacer antes de que empiece el partido, ya se ha persignado. Todo comenzará en pocos segundos y veremos de lo que está hecho el centro delantero del Inter de Milán.

Y en este momento, señoras y señores, cuando el árbitro silba el inicio del partido, es en el que debemos estar verdaderamente atentos. Porque mírenlo, ahí va; ha pasado el balón a su compañero, el brasileño Estevao, para que éste se descuelgue por la banda y él, corriendo como locomotora (o tal vez debería decir como cohete), se ha acercado a los albores del área grande, sorprendiendo al portero y a dos atónitos defensas para recibir el pase de su compañero. Y, como verán, en efecto recibe el balón del brasileño, matándolo con el pecho. Entonces, driblando como sólo los grandes maestros saben hacerlo, se quita a uno, se quita a dos y ahora está solo frente a la portería. Solos él y el portero. Señores, no han pasado ni dos minutos desde que comenzó el encuentro; parece que el gran centro delantero mexicano del Inter cumplirá su promesa. Los defensas van de nuevo a su caza. Tiene apenas unos pocos segundos para disparar. Se le ve seguro. Se perfila, levanta el rostro y... y... y...

Pero esperen. No tan de prisa, que esta historia no puede empezar aquí. ¿Por qué? Bueno, porque... en realidad... es aquí donde termina, en la Liga de Campeones de la UEFA. Sí. Justo aquí termina. Pero entonces... ¿dónde empieza? Pues bastantes años atrás. Muchos, debo decir. Y a varios kilómetros de distancia de este partido, que tiene lugar en el estadio Santiago Bernabeu de Madrid. Empieza de este lado del océano Atlántico, en una escuela primaria de la Ciudad de México, la escuela de la cual surgió el más grande atleta mexicano de todos los tiempos.

Así que, para empezar por el principio, vayamos a esa escuela donde todo comenzó, cuando el más grande atleta era sólo un niño y no "uno de los máximos orgullos del país", como lo llamó el presidente de la República la última vez que lo invitó a desayunar. Y hemos de estar ahí el preciso día en que detonaron los acontecimientos que dan origen a esta historia. ¿La ven? Es ésa: la Escuela Primaria Federal Héroes de la Nación; ahí, bien cerquita del Parque de los Venados. Exacto, ese parque con las fuentes y los venados de piedra. Ese mero. Pero no se queden ahí. Al rato venimos, si gustan, que buena parte del relato tiene que ver también con el parque. Ahorita acompáñenme a la escuela, porque está ocurriendo algo importante en mi salón de clases.

Así es. ¿Ya vieron? Ése es mi salón. El de quinto grado. El que se encuentra al final del pasillo. Entren. Sin miedo. ¿Ya se dieron cuenta? El hombre de bata blanca es precisamente quien ustedes suponen: un doctor. Y todos los niños que hacemos fila a su lado esperamos que nos revise la garganta, los ojos, las orejas, la panza y el corazón. En pocas palabras, el doctor ha ido a hacernos un examen de rutina, sin inyecciones ni cosas espantosas como ésas. Entonces... ¿por qué es tan importante el examen si es de rutina? Bien, se los diré: porque gracias a ese examen supe, a la corta edad de diez años, que tenía los días de mi vida contados.

Pero no se asusten. Y tampoco nos adelantemos. Antes, déjenme poner una cosa en claro, para que entiendan lo que pasó después: siempre fui un niño preocupón y aprensivo. De esa clase de niños a los que no se les puede decir que se coman las verduras porque hay muchos niños pobres muriéndose de hambre en África. Con eso tenía para no dormir en varios días, luego de comerme las verduras, aunque estuvieran frías o mal cocidas. Si la maestra Lucía (suspiro) nos dejaba tarea para las vacaciones, yo era de esos niños que todas las vacaciones se la pasan pensando que ya es tiempo de hacer la tarea, pero nunca se deciden, todo para acabar haciéndola de un solo golpe el último domingo y con la angustia de no terminarla o al final hacerla mal.

O bien, ahí les va otra: si me ponía a ver la televisión durante mucho tiempo, mi mamá me decía que no saliera a la calle inmediatamente porque podía darme un aire y quedarme bizco para siempre. Entonces yo prefería mejor no salir y encerrarme en mi cuarto, convencido de que, con tan sólo una brisita que me pegara en la cara, no se me iba a quedar un ojo chueco, sino los dos.

Y ahí estoy. Soy aquél, el que está delante de Dolores Zúñiga, la niña de las colitas (la única niña que come sapos vivos arrancándoles la cabeza), esperando mi turno de ser revisado. Sí, el niño de la cara pálida, a quien le retumba el corazón a mil por hora, el que está completamente seguro de que el doctor le va a encontrar algo malo e incurable en cuanto le revise la garganta. Y en lo que llega mi turno, antes de que les contagie mi angustia, déjenme ver si puedo presentar a mis compañeros, para hacer un poco de tiempo.

A ver... ese güero que ahora le está mostrando la lengua al doctor, se llama Iñaki. Es mi mejor amigo. Su único defecto es que le gusta a mi hermana Susana. Ése de allá, el gordo que parece el papá de todos y que está haciendo dibujos en su cuaderno, se llama José Luis, pero todos le decimos el Burbuja. Sí, sé que es enorme, pero les juro que tenemos la misma edad y que va en quinto año. Esos tres de allá que se están aventando entre ellos, son Rubén, Fito y Tony; siempre andan haciéndose los muy rudotes porque están en un equipo de futbol americano, el de los Cherokees. Pero créanme una cosa, sé que no tienen cerebro. Cuando nacieron, algún doctor loco se los sacó para hacer experimentos y así se los entregó a sus padres, sin cerebro, porque no saben hacer otra cosa que golpearse entre ellos, y cuando se aburren, golpean a los demás. Si lo sabré yo. En cambio, Carlos Alberto, el chavo que está detrás de Iñaki, es otra cosa: aunque también está en los Cherokees, por lo menos sabe comportarse como ser humano y no como un simio que nunca evolucionó. A mí me cae bien, aunque todas las niñas del salón estén enamoradas de él. El otro de allá, el chavo de los lentes, se llama Esteban, pero todos le dicen por su apellido: Olariñárritu (quién sabe por qué, si ya es bastante difícil decir correctamente Olariñárritu sin equivocarse). Es el único del salón a quien los Cherokees no molestan, porque él dice que sabe karate, judo, kung-fu y tae-chun-quién-sabe-qué-cosa. Claro que él sí está loco: no habla con nadie y su mayor fascinación son los Beatles; ustedes pueden preguntarle en qué fecha se le cayó el primer diente a John Lennon y les aseguro que se los dirá con toda precisión. Y aquel de allá, el niño que está leyendo *La pequeña Lulú*...

Pero bueno, antes de que me llegue el turno con el doctor y de que termine de presentarles al salón completo, quiero que noten una cosa con respecto a mi persona, porque es importante que la sepan antes que nada. Sí, recuerden, soy aquél, el que está delante de la niña de las colitas, Dolores Zúñiga (la única niña que, con un conjuro, te puede convertir en piojo). Sí, el de las pecas y el cabello parado en la parte alta del coco (qué quieren; mi mamá me peina con limón todas las mañanas, y ni así consigue el milagro: que esos mugrosos pelos desobedientes se queden en su lugar). Ese mismo soy yo.

Ahora... quiero que observen con detenimiento y me digan qué encuentran de especial en mí. ¿No lo notan? Acérquense un poco más. ¿Ya? El reloj. Claro. El reloj. ¿Qué tiene de especial el reloj? ¿Pues qué no lo ven? La carátula es la imagen de un futbolista; los brazos del jugador son las manecillas; su pierna derecha patea un balón con cada tic y regresa a su posición con cada tac; en la parte del fondo, un portero chiquitititito espera el tiro que nunca ha de llegar a su portería. En pocas palabras, y para que me entiendan, voy a usar las mismas palabras con las que mi mamá describe ese reloj: "es el reloj más feo de todo el Universo". ¿Y por qué suponen que alguien podría traer con orgullo en su muñeca un reloj tan horrorosamente horroroso? Pues por una simple y sencilla razón; porque sólo piensa en una cosa: futbol.

Sí. Futbol, futbol, futbol y futbol. Sólo pienso en futbol. No es broma. Y para los que no me crean, acompáñenme a la tercera banca de la segunda fila. Echen una mirada al lugar contiguo al que acaba de ocupar Iñaki. Ah, ¿verdad? Se los decía. Tengo toda la mochila cubierta de calcomanías de futbol, y también el estuche de los lápices, la parte de abajo de la tabla del pupitre, los lápices mismos, las contraportadas de los libros, las libretas, las reglas, el compás, un par de gomas, los calzones y los calcetines (bueno, sí, ya sé que ésos no se ven, pero créanme, tienen baloncitos). Futbol. Sólo futbol.

Estábamos a un año de la Copa del mundo que iba a celebrarse en Argentina y yo era el único de todo el salón (tal vez de toda la escuela, de toda la ciudad y de todo el país) que pedía noche tras noche en sus oraciones que México calificara para el torneo. Futbol. Futbol. Nada más que futbol. Aunque, por otro lado... he de confesar... que en aquellos tiempos sólo había alguien (suspiro) que me sacaba de la mente el juego de las patadas. Y ahí está: sentada a un lado del doctor.

¿A poco no es tan hermosa que es imposible sacar dieces con ella? (Claro que eso es algo que jamás les confesaré a mis padres: que no puedo sacar un solo diez porque la maestra Lucía es tan bonita que sólo verla me convierte en un verdadero idiota.) Y como notarán, no miento; en estos momentos la estoy mirando y díganme ustedes si la cara que pongo no es la de un verdadero y redomado idiota. Exacto. Estoy enamorado de la maestra y, para que sepan, tengo pensado casarme con ella algún día. Claro, ella no lo sabe todavía. Y no pienso decírselo aún porque primero tengo que hacer un par de cosas en la vida: convertirme en el mejor jugador de futbol del mundo, para empezar. Ser alguien como el Tigre Quezada, por ejemplo.

Por cierto... ¿les conté del Tigre Quezada? ¿No? Bueno, pues déjenme decirles que...

—Vicente Mendiolea Urbina.

¡Ey! ¡Ése soy yo! Es el doctor quien me llama. ¿Les suena conocido el nombre? Pues claro. Soy ese comentarista deportivo de la televisión que siempre dice: "Para todos aquellos que aman más el juego de las patadas que las pantuflas viejas que recibieron en el intercambio de Navidad", cada vez que se inicia la transmisión de un partido. Ése mismo. Claro que en estos momentos, en el salón de quinto grado, para todos soy solamente...

—Tito.

—¿Mande, maestra Lucía? (Suspiro.)

—Es tu turno, acércate al doctor.

Claro, la maestra me sorprendió con la cabezota en las nubes y por eso no me di cuenta de que tocaba

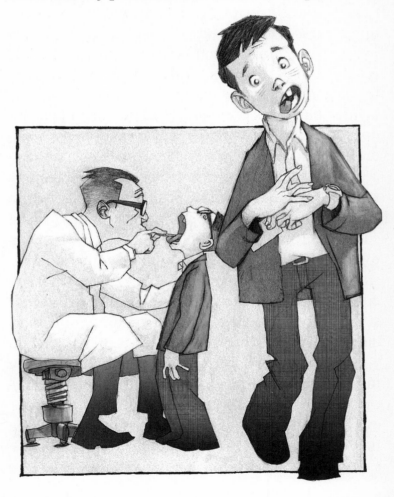

mi turno. Me acerqué. Pero no me gustó nada cómo me miró el doctor. Y el corazón me empezó a latir, ya no a mil por hora, sino a cien mil por hora.

—A ver, niño, repíteme... ¿cuál es tu nombre?

—Vicente Mendiolea Urbina.

El doctor sonrió muy raro. Muy, muy raro. Tanto, que me puso más nervioso. Y más nervioso porque me puso encima del pecho ese aparato que siempre está bien frío y me escuchó el corazón. Luego me vio los oídos, pero no me dijo, como a todos "Hay que lavarse bien esas orejotas". Sólo se quedó pensando y sonriendo. Y volvió a oírme el corazón. A nadie le había oído el corazón dos veces; eso, con toda seguridad, significaba problemas. No me pidió que sacara la lengua ni nada. Seguía sonriendo. A mí me pareció que era un doctor muy macabro; estaba convencidísimo de que había oído algo muy malo en mi corazón y que por eso ya no había querido revisarme la garganta: ya para qué, si lo que había oído en mi corazón era tan grave que ni tenía sentido ver si tenía anginas. Me puse blanco como mi camisa del uniforme. Y lo peor fue cuando siguió sonriendo y hurgó entre las bolsas de su bata; de ahí sacó una tarjeta con su nombre y su teléfono. Y me revisó el corazón de nuevo. Yo juraba que no oía nada y por eso hacía el intento a cada rato; a lo mejor se me había detenido el órgano vital hacía unos minutos y el doctor macabro no se animaba a decirme que ya no me latía nada en el pecho. Entonces, si ya me había muerto… ¿por qué sonreía? Maldito doctor tenebroso.

—Vicente, ¿cuántos años tienes?

—Diez.

—¿Y de dónde eres?

—De Guadalajara.

Y volvió a sonreír, para luego agregar:

—Vicente, te voy a dar mi tarjeta. Diles a tus papás que tienen que hacerme una visita —sonrió el doctor—. Es muy importante, ¿eh?

Pasé del blanco al transparente. ¿Alcanzan a distinguirlo? Cualquiera diría que se podían ver las cosas a través de mí. El doctor macabro me guiñó un ojo y todavía se atrevió a decir: "Estás bien, Vicentito", para luego agregar: "El que sigue".

Pero a mí no me engañaba. Si yo estaba bien, ¿por qué me había escuchado el corazón tres veces?, ¿y por qué había insistido tanto en ver a mis papás? ¿Por qué razón había apuntado mi nombre en su agenda? Claro que yo, en ese momento, no sabía que, por mis apellidos, el doctor se había dado cuenta de que conocía a mis papás, a quienes había dejado de ver desde los tiempos de la universidad, allá en Guadalajara. Los conocía tan bien y habían sido tan buenos amigos, que se puso a recordar los viejos tiempos, cuando él, mi papá y mi mamá salían juntos al cine, a tomar helados o a pasear. Se acordó en

15

ese momento de la boda de mis papás, que había sido hacía ya once años.

Por eso me preguntó mi edad y de dónde era, para estar seguro. Pero yo qué iba a saber en ese momento. Creí que me había preguntado mi edad porque lamentaba que alguien tan joven tuviera que despedirse del mundo a tan temprana edad. Y creí que me había preguntado de dónde era porque a lo mejor los de Guadalajara suelen morir jóvenes del corazón. Yo qué iba a saber. Y menos a imaginar que por andarse acordando de los buenos tiempos con mis papás, se distrajo de tal manera que no se dio cuenta de que me revisó el corazón tres veces y en cambio, la garganta, ninguna.

De todos modos, para el momento en que regresé a mi pupitre, yo ya llevaba certificado de zombi, era un muerto caminante. Y la única y absoluta verdad respecto al doctor macabro no la sabría sino hasta muchos, muchos días después.

Claro, para el caso yo sentía que en cualquier momento podía caer al suelo fulminado por un rayo y sin siquiera tener tiempo de decir "adiós, mundo cruel", como hacen en las caricaturas. Tan sólo me quedaría viendo todo sin poder hacer ni decir nada, porque los muertos no hacen ni dicen nada. Lo malo es que nadie, ni la maestra Lucía, se dio cuenta durante el resto de la clase. Nadie se dio cuenta de que se podía mirar a través de mí, ni de que estaban hablando con un muerto. Así que, ya enfadado, después de clases, cuando Iñaki y yo regresábamos juntos a nuestras casas (la suya estaba a un lado de la mía, justo enfrente del Parque de los Venados), decidí reclamarle.

—Eres un mal amigo.

—¿Quién? ¿Yo?

—Sí, tú, mal amigo.

No podía esperar el momento de decirle mi secreto y que se sintiera tan mal que a lo mejor hasta lloraba y me ofrecía disculpas y me regalaba todos sus juguetes.

—¿Y por qué? —dijo, sin dejar de darle chupadas a su congelada. En verdad se veía poco mortificado.

—¿A poco no te diste cuenta?

—¿De qué? ¿De cuando los Cherokees te hicieron volar en el recreo? Tito, siempre te hacen lo mismo.

Cierto, pero no era a eso a lo que me refería. Iñaki, mal amigo. Insensible y de corazón de piedra.

—No. No de eso. De que el doctor me revisó el corazón tres veces y me dio su tarjeta para darles a mis papás la mala noticia.

—¿Qué mala noticia? —él seguía chupando su congelada sabor rompope.

—Pues que voy a morirme en menos de un año.

Bueno, había que echarle un poco de invención al asunto para que la cosa fuera más melodramática. Si no, ¿cómo quería que Iñaki se pusiera a llorar arrepentido?

—¡Qué te pasa! ¿Estás loco de la cabeza o qué?

Odiaba cuando Iñaki decía eso de "loco de la cabeza". Y más cuando lo usaba en mi contra. Y todavía más cuando era por un asunto tan delicado como mi próxima muerte.

—Claro que no. Es verdad. Te lo juro.

—¿Eso te dijo?

—Bueno... no exactamente. Pero si hubieras visto sus ojos sabrías que no miento. ¿Te acuerdas de esa película del Santo que vimos el sábado pasado en la tele? ¿Ésa, donde salía un científico loco? Pues el doctor tenía los mismos ojos que el científico loco.

—Estás loco de la cabeza, Tito.

Iñaki mal amigo. Se metió a su casa sin siquiera despedirse. Pero lo peor fue cuando llegué a mi casa con mi mejor cara de "pregúntenme cómo me fue en la escuela". Ni siquiera había alguien a la vista, ni mi abuelo que siempre está deambulando por la casa, ni Hugo, mi hermano de dos años, a quien siempre encuentras donde menos te lo esperas.

Así que después de cambiarme el uniforme, me senté a la mesa con una cara aún mejor que la otra, una de "pregúntenme cuántos días dijo el doctor que me quedan de vida". ¡Vaya chasco! Sin decir nada, mi mamá sirvió la sopa (de verduras, además) y me reclamó que siguiera haciendo pipí sin levantar el asiento del baño y, para rematar, me pidió que cuidara a Hugo en la tarde porque iba a salir con sus amigas al "cafecito de mil horas". Susana me pateó por debajo de la mesa porque Iñaki y yo nos habíamos escapado de ella a la salida de la escuela para que no nos siguiera a la casa. El abuelo sólo dijo que la sopa estaba fría y que por menos que eso, había descuartizado a varios huertistas en la Revolución. Y Hugo sólo se dedicó, como es su costumbre, a echarse el caldo encima en vez de tomárselo.

Nadie se dio cuenta de que en cualquier momento podía yo morir de un ataque al corazón. Y sentí tanto coraje, que me dieron ganas de que ocurriera ahí mismo, en ese momento. Casi podía oír a mi mamá tomando mi mano inerte y decir: "¡Oh!, ¿cómo pude ser tan insensible?. Él, tan bueno. Y yo, en cambio, soy una canalla que a cada rato le exigía que recogiera su cuarto". Y a mis hermanos llorando. Y al abuelo diciendo: "Murió como un héroe".

Pero no ocurrió. Nunca me fulminó un rayo ni nada. Así que me terminé la sopa, la carne y, para dejar en claro que era un muerto en vida, ni toqué el postre; me fui a ver el programa de la Calaca Tilica y Flaca en completo silencio. Sólo a la media hora llegó mi abuelo a sentarse a mi lado a decir sandeces sobre la Revolución. Que si la Revolución esto, que si la Revolución lo otro. Que si los huertistas se merecen esto, que si se merecen lo otro. ¿Y saben qué es lo peor del asunto? Que él ni siquiera estuvo en la Revolución. Fue su padre quien sí estuvo en la Revolución, peleando, creo, con los obregonistas, los villistas o algo así; por eso se la pasa echándole a los huertistas.

El caso es que mi abuelo perdió la chaveta en un partido de futbol y ahora cree que fue a la Revolución. Se los juro, se volvió loco de remate en un partido de futbol. Y es que, hace muchos años, mi abuelo era un gran jugador. ¿No me creen? Bueno, la verdad, yo tampoco lo creería. Pero acompáñenme aquí cerquita, a un lado del estudio, en donde el abuelo tiene su cuarto. ¿Ven que no miento? Todos esos trofeos son de mi abuelo, el Mago Urbina, que jugó con las Chivas Rayadas del Guadalajara durante varios campeonatos, allá por los años cuarenta o cincuenta o algo así. Fue un gran jugador. Pero un día, en un partido contra el León, en un remate de cabeza, mi abuelo, en vez de pegarle a la pelota, le pegó al poste izquierdo de la portería. ¡Tooooiiing! Quedó inconsciente por tres minutos. Y cuando por fin volvió en sí, se puso de pie sin más, como si nada hubiera pasado. El público le aplaudió y toda la cosa. Y lo dejaron seguir jugando. Pero al poco rato, todo mundo se dio cuenta de que algo no andaba bien: mi abuelo empezó a arremeter a golpes y trompazos contra los del León confundiéndolos con huertistas. Estaba seguro de hallarse en un campo de batalla y no en una cancha de futbol. Tuvieron que sacarlo entre varios. Y nunca volvió a jugar. Aunque lo que más me duele de todo este cuento es no poder hablar con mi abuelo de futbol porque en serio que, en sus tiempos, fue un gran jugador y ahora, en cambio, nomás no da pie con bola, como dice mi mamá. ¿No me creen? Miren esto:

—Abuelo, cuéntame de cuando le ganaron al Atlas por goliza.

—Mugrosos cobardes, Tito. Nos tenían acorralados. Y nosotros casi no teníamos parque.

—¿Y tú cuántos goles metiste, abuelo?

—Me despaché como a cuarenta huertistas. Y eso que nada más tenía veinte balas en mi fusil. De a dos por bala.

¿Ven lo que les digo? Por eso no representó ningún consuelo para mí que el abuelo se fuera a sentar a mi lado a ver la tele y se pusiera a decir tonterías. Terminé por irme a mi cuarto, lamentando que el mundo fuera tan injusto con nosotros, los de corazón débil. Saqué la tarjeta del doctor macabro de entre mis cosas de la escuela y me puse a estudiarla. Y me puse a pensar qué haría el Tigre Quezada en una situación como la mía. Por cierto... ¿les conté del Tigre Quezada? ¿No? ¡Vaya descuido! Pues nada más vean a mi alrededor. ¿Ven esos cuatro carteles y esos dos banderines? Sí, ésos, los del lado derecho. Por el momento, no hagan caso de los otros carteles, ni los de la selección mexicana ni los del mundial de Alemania 74, ni los de México 70, ni los de los estadios, ni los de Pelé. Fíjense nomás en aquéllos, los de la derecha. Pues ése es el Tigre Quezada, el mayor goleador de la liga mexicana. Ése es el Tigre Quezada: mi héroe, quien además, como seguramente ya adivinaron, juega con las Chivas Rayadas del Guadalajara.

Ah, pero lo que ustedes no saben es que el Tigre Quezada es mi amigo. Tengo la dirección de su casa, allá en Guadalajara. Y, por supuesto, le escribo cartas muy seguido. Lo único malo es que él nunca me responde... pero bueno, sé que es un jugador muy ocupado y por eso no lo hace. Además, tiene derecho a no responderme porque... porque... bueno, porque es el Tigre Quezada y punto.

Así que me acosté en mi cama y me puse a pensar qué haría el Tigre Quezada en mi lugar. Y me acordé de la primera vez que lo vi jugar, antes de que nos viniéramos a vivir al Distrito Federal. Recordé cuándo decidí que él era el héroe a quien yo quería imitar cuando fuera grande. Fue durante un partido contra el América. El Tigre Quezada burló a toda la defensa de los Cremas del América (no pongan esa cara, antes no eran Águilas, eran Cremas), llegó hasta la portería y, aunque no lo crean, también burló al portero.

Ahí, en vez de chutar con todas sus fuerzas para meter la pelota hasta el fondo de la red, ¿qué creen que hizo? Algo increíble. Detuvo el balón a unos centímetros de la línea de gol y, manteniendo a todo el estadio en un hilo, se esperó a que el portero volviera a ponerse de pie. Entonces, como todo un héroe, hizo como si fuera a dar una gran patada, pero sólo rozó la pelota con la punta de los tacos, y el balón, con toda lentitud, traspasó la línea de meta. El portero todavía se aventó en pos de él, pero le fue imposible alcanzarlo. Todos gritamos de la emoción. ¡Qué gol! Ése sí que fue un golazo. Las Chivas iban perdiendo 1 a 0.

Con ese gol empataron al América. Y luego, gracias a un pase del Tigre, remontaron el marcador y consiguieron el 2 a 1. Yo salí del estadio que no cabía en mí. Mi papá me compró mi primer banderín del Tigre. Y, desde ese momento, empezó a ser mi héroe.

Supe exactamente qué hacer cuando mi mamá entró a mí cuarto, sentó a Hugo en mi cama y dijo:

—Tito, voy a confiar en ti. Cuida bien a tu hermano. No quiero irme con ningún pendiente.

—Sí, mamá. ¿Qué puede pasar?

Como si no lo supiera. Se refería a la vez que Hugo metió la cabeza en la parte trasera de la lavadora y mi papá tuvo que sacarlo con pinzas y martillo, o cuando confundió el jabón con el queso manchego y hubo que llevarlo al doctor a que le lavara la panza, o aquella vez que usó los crayones de Susana para decorar las paredes de la cocina.

—¿Qué puede pasar? Pues nada más lo mismo que cuando usó mis zapatos como si fueran barcos y los metió al escusado.

Cierto. No me acordaba de ésa.

Y en ese momento me di cuenta de lo que tenía que hacer para ser un héroe como el Tigre Quezada. Tenía que lograr que mi mamá se sintiera orgullosa de mí. No como...

—Cuídalo bien, Tito. No quiero arrepentirme de confiar en ti. Además, no andes por la casa con tus zapatos de futbol porque rayas el mosaico. Y sube el asiento del baño cuando hagas pipí.

No como eso. Si me quedaba poco tiempo de vida, lo usaría bien. Sería un héroe. Sólo así la maestra Lucía se enamoraría de mí. Sólo así los Cherokees dejarían de molestarme para siempre. Y mi mamá jamás en su vida me volvería a decir "¡Ay, Tito! ¡Ay, Tito!".

Querido Tigre Quezada:

¿Cómo has estado? Espero que bien. Te vi en el partido del domingo contra el Toluca. Y me di cuenta de que ninguno de tus compañeros te dio un buen pase para que metieras gol. Yo sí me di cuenta. Sé que en el siguiente lo harás. Nada más diles que te pasen el balón y ya está.

Pasando a otras cosas, fíjate que tuve una muy buena idea. Ya te había dicho que de grande quiero ser como tú. Pero me puse a pensar que si quiero ser como tú, a lo mejor tengo que empezar desde ahorita, ¿verdad?

Claro. Porque nunca se sabe si uno va a llegar a ser grande o no. Uno siempre dice "cuando sea grande". Pero, ¿qué tal si uno nunca llega a ser grande? Y no me refiero a quedarme chaparro para toda la vida, sino a no llegar. Tú me entiendes, ¿no? Digo, pueden pasar cosas. No sé, como que a uno lo aplaste un piano mientras va caminando por la calle, como en las caricaturas. Uno nunca sabe. Por eso me dije que tengo que ganar mi primer campeonato de futbol lo más pronto que pueda. Sí. Y creo que ya sé cuál es la mejor manera de...

—¡Ay, Tito! ¡Ay, Tito! Te lo dije. No sé quién me manda.

¡En la torre! Cuando volteé, Hugo ya había sacado al pez de su pecera y lo había subido a uno de sus carritos de bomberos. Mi mamá echó el pez al agua vivo todavía, pero cómo iba a nadar si Hugo le había puesto la ropa de uno de mis muñecos de acción. Me dio mucha vergüenza, pero no supe qué decir. Decidí volver a mi carta, en donde le acababa de contar mi plan al Tigre Quezada. Además, yo qué iba a saber que mi mamá regresaría tan pronto del "cafecito de mil horas" con sus amigas, si siempre se tarda como mil horas. En fin... ya ni modo.

El caso es que decidí no decirle a nadie que mi corazón estaba a punto de hacer ¡cuaz! No crean que fui tan heroico como para no decirlo porque no quería abrumar a los demás con mi desgracia. La verdad es que me dio miedo. Cuando llegó mi papá de trabajar, se me ocurrió tantear el terreno. Mi papá es maestro de escuela, lo cual no tiene nada de malo. Lo malo es que a veces se le olvida que nosotros no somos sus alumnos, porque nos trata como si lo fuéramos. Aunque igual conviene preguntarle cosas porque mi papá lo sabe casi todo. Cuando terminé la carta y salí de mi cuarto, lo encontré dialogando con Hugo acerca de su travesura, si es que a eso se le puede llamar dialogar.

—Hijo, no debes sacar a los peces del agua porque ellos tienen branquias en vez de pulmones. Y no pueden respirar fuera del agua.

—Corbata —Hugo había agarrado la corbata de mi papá y seguro que se imaginó que era una liana porque ya quería columpiarse en ella como Tarzán.

—Los pececitos sólo pueden vivir en el agua porque en el agua encuentran su oxígeno. Fuera de ella, no pueden sobrevivir.

—Corbata.

Mi papá tuvo que darse por vencido. Se quitó tanto la corbata como a Hugo de encima y se sentó a leer el periódico. Era el momento ideal para saludarlo y hacerle una pregunta hipotética.

—Papá... fíjate que hoy vi una película, pero no la acabé de ver por estar cuidando a Hugo.

—¿Ah, sí? —no apartó la vista del periódico.

—Sí. Fíjate que sale un niño al que el doctor le está oyendo el corazón. Pero el doctor oye algo raro y no se lo dice al niño porque detecta algo malo. ¿Qué crees que podría tener el niño en su corazón?

Me regaló una mirada. Una de esas que seguro también utiliza con sus alumnos de preparatoria porque se empujó los lentes y se aclaró la garganta.

—Creo que sí vi esa película alguna vez. Es muy triste. El niño muere al final.

—¿Pero por qué? ¿Le da un ataque al corazón? —volvió mi palidez.

—No. Creo que lo atacan unos lobos. ¿O se cae a una alberca? Ya no me acuerdo...

—Olvida la película, papá. ¿Qué le puede pasar a un niño si está mal del corazón?

Volvió a su periódico.

—Dolores, un ataque, convulsiones o algo así, claro. Lo primero es llevarlo al hospital para que le hagan estudios.

Con eso tuve. Susana era la única niña conocida que había estado en un hospital, cuando le sacaron las anginas. Y lo había descrito en una sola palabra: horriblemente horripilante (bueno, dos palabras, pero ustedes me entienden). Decía que los doctores y las enfermeras eran muy parecidos a los ogros y a las brujas de los cuentos que había leído en su vida. Aseguraba que la habían torturado sólo por placer con instrumentos que únicamente se han visto en la

guerra (claro que, aunque seguro eran puras mentiras para hacerse la interesante, yo no estaba dispuesto a comprobarlo). Así que con eso tuve. La tarjeta del doctor macabro se quedó en el fondo de mi
mochila. Y yo me quedé callado.

Decidí seguir con mi plan, el cual tampoco sería
nada fácil. Pero estaba verdaderamente decidido a ser
un héroe antes de que el corazón me hiciera ¡cuaz!
Casi hasta estaba orgulloso de mí mismo. Pero en
cuanto le conté a Iñaki lo que tenía pensado hacer
al día siguiente, entrando a la escuela, sacudió sus
cabellos güeros. Y su falta de apoyo me dejó muy angustiado, porque si alguien sabía sentirse angustiado
era yo.

—Estás loco de la cabeza, Tito.

A lo mejor era cierto. Y cuando ya me estaba arre-
pintiendo de la decisión que había tomado, entró al
salón (suspiro) la maestra Lucía y lo echó todo a perder. ¿Por qué? Pues porque me sonrió (claro que ella
siempre sonríe cuando entra al salón, pero es distinto cuando te sonríe a ti, que estás en la tercera banca y no hasta adelante). Fue entonces cuando pensé
que no podía echarme para atrás. Sería un héroe. Y
nada me lo impediría. Porque no podía decepcionar
a la maestra Lucía, que en esos momentos me sonreía, me guiñaba un ojo y me lanzaba un beso.

Bueno, está bien, esto último no pasó, sino en mi
cabeza. Pero para mí, como si hubiera pasado, porque

tenía otra vez la misma cara de idiota que siempre pongo cuando mi mente empieza a viajar sin que yo la pueda detener. Y me di cuenta de que no podía echarme para atrás.

Además, ya se lo había platicado al Tigre Quezada y le había dado la carta a mi papá para que la pusiera en el correo. ¿Qué iba a decir el Tigre si no cumplía? Iba a decir que soy un tonto llorón y un miedoso.

Así que, a la hora del recreo, a pesar de que —como diría Iñaki— sólo un loco haría lo que yo iba a hacer: ir a la oficina del director sin antes haber hecho algo malo, me dirigí con pies de plomo a la oficina del profesor Colina. El problema fue que ni siquiera pude llegar al patio que separa su oficina de los salones de clase. Los Cherokees se me pusieron enfrente.

—Miren quién está aquí —dijo Rubén.

—Tito Tito Capotito —respondió Tony.

Y aquí vamos otra vez. No sé por qué no se les ocurre hacer otra cosa. Después de decir eso, me levantan entre los tres y me arrojan al aire, al tiempo que dicen:

—Tito Tito Capotito, sube al cielo y pega un grito, ¿qué es?

Y entonces me atrapan en el aire. Así pasa unas tres o cuatro veces. Aunque nunca me han dejado caer, sí me da miedo que un día se les ocurra hacer su graciosada cerca de uno de los barandales o de las escaleras, y me dejen ir por el hueco hasta el piso inferior, me rompa todos los huesos y tenga que vivir el resto de mi vida todo vendado y asomado a la ventana de mi cuarto sin poder salir a jugar. De cualquier modo, en esta ocasión sí me enfadé. Primero, porque nadie con el corazón en estas condiciones debe ser arrojado así a las alturas y, segundo, porque quería ir a ver al director y esos monigotes estaban quitándome el tiempo.

—¡Ya! ¡Déjenme! —se me ocurrió decir.

Lo peor que puedes hacer cuando un bravucón te molesta es hacerle ver precisamente eso, que te molesta. Es como darle cuerda. Y así fue.

—Ya, déjenme —me remedaron los tres. Y siguieron con lo suyo.

Me acuerdo que desde los aires alcanzaba a ver a mi hermana y sus amigas reírse, a Olariñárritu menear la cabeza, a Iñaki cambiar estampas con unos de tercero, a Luisito Pichardo levantar el rostro hacia mí. Y él fue el único que se atrevió a decir:

—Oigan, ya déjenlo.

O sea que les dio más cuerda. Pero no lo culpo. Me cae bien Luisito Pichardo. Es el hijo del conserje y, desde que llegué de Guadalajara, me ha tratado bien. Lo malo es que nació con un problema en los ojos y no puede ver nada, por eso casi siempre está solo. Siempre se para a la salida de la conserjería, con sus anteojos oscuros y su bastón, a escuchar a los niños jugar, porque nadie en el recreo juega con él. Iñaki y yo a veces lo llevamos a la cooperativa para que se compre dulces, aunque tampoco jugamos con él pues no sabemos a qué. No se nos ocurre a qué jugar con un niño que no ve nada. De cualquier modo, si alguien tiene buen corazón en esta escuela llena de bestias peludas, es él, de eso estoy seguro. Aun así, Luisito Pichardo debería quedarse callado de vez en cuando, porque gracias a él me hicieron volar todavía unas seis o siete veces más con esa tontería de Tito Tito Capotito que nunca he entendido.

Con todo, los Cherokees también tienen llenadera, y cuando se aburrieron de molestarme, fueron contra otro de segundo a quien tomaron de los tobillos y metieron de cabeza en un bote de basura. Hasta eso, creo que tuve suerte, pues pude retomar mi camino hacia la Dirección. Así, despeinado y con la ropa fuera de sitio. Iñaki me vio desde lejos y volvió a sacudir sus pelos güeros.

Y ahí iba yo, camino a enfrentar mi destino, cuando en el patio me encontré con Edson (¡guau!, Edson). Oh, perdón. Es que siempre me pasa lo mismo; cuando me lo topo de frente, me pongo nervioso y lo saludo casi con una reverencia. ¿Por qué? Bueno, verán. Edson es un niño brasileño de sexto año, quien dicen, es el mejor jugador infantil de futbol que existe en la escuela, en la colonia y a lo mejor en la ciudad. Es tan bueno que ni siquiera juega en los recreos, porque no le gusta exhibirse. Siempre he querido ser su amigo y cuando paso frente a él lo saludo igual: "Hola, Edson, ¿qué tal esos goles?", aunque él nunca me responde nada. De todos modos es un tipazo. No le gusta presumir ni nada (Edson, ¡guau!).

Por eso me tardé tanto en contestar cuando me paré frente a la puerta del profesor Colina, porque estaba pensando en Edson y en mí. Él me daba un pase que yo remataba con la cabeza y...

—¡Mendiolea!

—Sí, señor —respondí, espantado.

—¿Qué lo trae por aquí?

El profesor Colina siempre nos habla de usted y por nuestros apellidos. Y además, siempre tiene abierta la puerta de su despacho porque dice que cualquiera de nosotros puede ir a verlo con confianza cuando quiera. Pero, seamos honestos, ¿quién en su sano juicio iría a la oficina del director sin ser llevado a la fuerza? Bueno, mejor ni digo nada. El caso es que es un hombre calvo, extremadamente flaco y muy chaparrito. Algunos de sexto son más altos que él (aunque no más altos que el Burbuja; creo que nadie es más alto que el Burbuja). Y, según yo, es un buen hombre, porque siempre está sonriendo. Dicen que, hasta cuando te expulsa, sonríe como si te estuviera mandando a dar un paseo por el parque.

—Profesor Colina.

—¿Qué hizo, Mendiolea? ¿Lo mandó su maestra? ¿Acaso le pegó a uno de primero?

—¡No! ¡Le juro que no, profesor!

Me miró por encima de sus anteojos que sólo usa para leer. Y de seguro creyó mi respuesta únicamente porque a mí nunca me han llevado a la Dirección. Sólo aquella vez que le conté a Rodrigo Vélez que había visto a Dolores Zúñiga hervir a un bebé en su caldero negro. Rodrigo Vélez se puso a llorar de la impresión y me acusó con la maestra Lucía.

—¿Entonces? ¿Qué lo trae por aquí, Mendiolea?

—Profesor Colina, vengo a proponerle una cosa.

—¡Ah, caray!, eso sí que es nuevo. Pase usted.

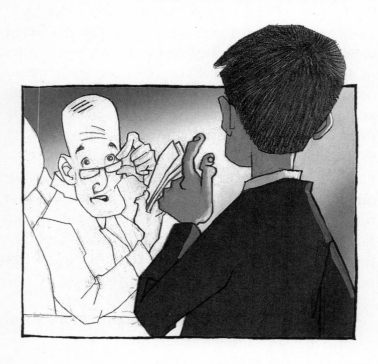

Querido Tigre Quezada:

Ni te imaginas. El profesor Colina aceptó.

Le encantó la idea de hacer un torneo de futbol en la escuela. Y también la idea de hacerlo este año, antes de que termine el curso. Lo único malo es que piensa abrir las inscripciones para todo mundo. ¿Tú crees?

Eso significa que hasta las niñas y los de sexto pueden inscribirse. Eso ya no me gustó tanto; en primera, porque si se inscriben las niñas, ¿qué clase de torneo va a ser ése? Y si además se meten los de sexto, va a ser muy difícil ganarles. Aunque, por otro lado, también es bueno que entren los de sexto. ¿Sabes por qué? Porque así puedo invitar a Edson a formar parte de mi equipo. Edson es un niño brasileño que jugó con Pelé alguna vez y creo que le ganó, ¿tú crees? Pues él va a estar en mi equipo.

Nada más hay un problemita, Tigre. Pero sé que en realidad no lo es, pues tú me vas a ayudar porque somos amigos, ¿verdad? Fíjate que le dije al profesor Colina que eres mi amigo y que si yo te lo pedía, no te ibas a negar a entregar la copa al mejor equipo en la final. ¿Cómo ves? Pero no creas que fue por eso que aceptó hacer el torneo, ¿eh? No. Aceptó porque se ve que le gustó mucho la idea. Pero bueno, ¿verdad que sí me ayudas?

Luego te sigo contando porque Susana acaba de entrar a mi cuarto y creo que se robó un muñeco mío.

Con cariño,
Tito

Odio cuando mi hermana Susana juega a la casita con mi Aventurero de acción y su Barbie. Qué humillación. Mi Aventurero, que ha vencido a los más horribles monstruos y ha salvado varias veces el Universo, se ve obligado a ponerse un delantal y ayudar en los quehaceres de la casita de muñecas. Una vez, hasta lo obligaron a besar a la Barbie en la boca. ¡Guácala!

—Susana, dame mi Aventurero o te acuso con mi mamá.

—¡Ay!, ni que le fuera a pasar nada, chillón.

—Sí. Lo puedes romper.

—Tú lo avientas por las escaleras y no le pasa nada. Yo nada más voy a jugar a que es el papá.

—Devuélvemelo o agarro tu Barbie y la aviento por las escaleras para que veas lo que se siente.

Ya no dijo nada. Me dio mi mono y yo lo volví a meter en mi bote de juguetes. De todos modos, sé que cuando me vea salir de casa, lo va a sacar de nuevo y, a lo mejor, hasta le pinta los labios. Pero no me importa porque me siento de muy buen humor. Pronto voy a ser un héroe y eso le compone el ánimo a cualquiera.

—¿A dónde vas? —me preguntó Susana en cuanto me vio en la puerta de la calle.

—Qué te importa.

—Si vas con Iñaki, me lo saludas.

Pobre de mi amigo. Gustarle a Susana, según yo, es peor que comer cucarachas vivas durante toda tu vida. Yo preferiría tener pompas de mandril que sufrir a alguien como Susana haciéndome ojitos y esas cosas. ¡Guac! Hasta escalofríos me dan.

Entré a la casa de Iñaki porque siempre tienen la puerta abierta y a mí me dejan entrar sin tocar. No sé cómo no le da miedo a la mamá de Iñaki que se les meta un ratero o algo así. A lo mejor porque es la única persona que está casi tan loca como mi abuelo. Es una señora tan dulce que casi hasta te da miedo encontrártela. Siempre te llena de besos, te dice "mi amor" por cualquier cosa y, además, te aprieta los cachetes. Lo verdaderamente horrible es que así se porta con todo el mundo. A mi mamá también le dice "mi amor, mi alma" y esas cosas, y le da dos besos, uno por mejilla. Hasta eso que no le hace lo de los cachetes.

Por fortuna, la señora no estaba a la vista y llegué al cuarto de Iñaki sin tener que sufrir los embates acaramelados de su mamá. Éste es el cuarto de Iñaki. Y la verdad, no sé qué le pasa. Mírenlo nada más. Está obsesionado con las naves espaciales, los extraterrestres y esas tontadas. Vean nada más cuántos carteles de *La guerra de las galaxias*, cuántos muñecos y cuántas naves cuelgan del techo. No sé cómo puede haber alguien que sólo piense en una sola cosa y adorne su cuarto de una sola cosa. Hay que estar un poco loco. Sólo véanlo ahorita: está leyendo una revista que se llama *Duda*, y mi papá dice que está llena de mentiras. En esa revista sólo hablan de extraterrestres, del abominable Hombre de las Nieves, de los vampiros y todas esas cosas. Y a Iñaki le fascina.

—Hola.

—Tito, ¿sabías que a lo mejor sí hay vida inteligente en Marte?

—No. No lo sabía. ¿Cómo diablos iba a saberlo?

—Mira. Ésta es una foto de Marte. ¿Verdad que se alcanza a ver como una casita?

—Es un truco de fotografía.

Si quieres hacer enojar a Iñaki, basta con que lo hagas dudar de esas cosas. Y eso que la revista que compra se llama *Duda*.

—No es cierto. No es cierto. Aquí mismo dice que fue tomada con un telescopio superpotente.

No quise arruinar mi buen humor con una pelea. Por eso hice como que me fijaba bien.

—Sí, es cierto. Tienes razón. Vamos a la tienda.

Y si quieres contentar a Iñaki, basta con que le hagas sentir que esas cosas son posibles. Si le dices que la otra vez viste algo parecido a un ovni, se pone como si hubiera ido a Disneylandia.

La idea era comprar algunas golosinas y discutir el plan para armar el equipo de futbol (aunque Iñaki pensaba que sólo compraríamos algunas golosinas). Pero yo no contaba con dos obstáculos que nos lo impedirían. El primero, que la mamá de Iñaki nos sorprendió en el pasillo.

—Hola, mi amor —beso, beso—. ¿Verdad que este vestido me queda muy bien? —me dijo—. Me lo puse en la fiesta del patronato la semana pasada. Todas las señoras pensaron que era francés, pero no, cómo crees, ahorita la moda en París no tiene nada que ver con las flores y el color verde, aunque ellas...

¿Ven cómo está loca? ¿Por qué habría de hablar de esas cosas con un niño de diez años que además llevaba puesto un uniforme de futbol? Tuve que soplarme sus relatos sobre la fiesta del patronato, la vez que fue a los quince años de una tal Maruca, y la fiesta de aniversario de los padrinos de Iñaki. No sé cómo no la junto con mi abuelo; seguro que no se enterarían nunca de lo que habla el otro, y serían felices platicando cada uno de sus loqueras.

Me escabullí cuando amenazó con invitarme un poco de té y galletas. Me acordé de mi Aventurero de acción y sentí una cosa fea en el estómago. Tuve que decir "conpermiso, mellamamimamá", para poder alcanzar a Iñaki en la calle.

—¿Por qué le das cuerda a mi mamá? Tienes que aprender a huir más rápido —dijo mi amigo.

Era cierto. Pero a mí no se me daba dejar a la señora hablando sola porque me daba como pena. Mi mamá me decía que no debía ser grosero con ella, porque estaba muy sola y necesitaba quién la escuchara, porque el papá de Iñaki se había muerto hacía muchos años. Y ya saben que a mí esas cosas me pueden y preocupan. Por eso, lo mejor para mí era esconderme de la señora, porque si me interceptaba en el pasillo, era hombre muerto.

Caminamos a la tiendita. Iñaki llevaba una de sus naves en la mano. Una pequeña, hasta eso. Yo maquinaba mi plan de reclutamiento de grandes del futbol. Edson encabezaba mi lista. Nos atravesamos hacia el Parque de los Venados y decidimos cruzar para ir a la tiendita. Entonces, mi amigo me rompió el corazón cuando dijo:

—Tito... ¿es cierto que te vas a morir pronto?

Me dieron ganas de llorar. Mi amigo del alma, Iñaki, se preocupaba por mí. Hasta me odié por haber pensado dejarlo fuera de mi equipo.

—Sí, Iñaki —respondí, con un nudo en la garganta.

—Oye, cuando te mueras, ¿me puedo quedar con tu máscara de Darth Vader?

Iñaki mal amigo. No le respondí nada porque en ese momento nos topamos con el segundo obstáculo de la tarde: los Cherokees.

—Miren quién está aquí —dijo Rubén.

—Tito Tito Capotito —respondió Tony.

No sé por qué no se inventan otra cosa.

—Tito Tito Capotito, sube al cielo y pega un grito, ¿qué es?

Tuve que volar varias veces por el aire. Y cuando se hartaron, me molestaron por mi uniforme de las Chivas y me torearon como si fuera una chiva loca. No les habría seguido el juego si no me hubieran quitado los cinco pesos que traía para dulces. Al final, se fueron con mi dinero y con todo mi aire, porque terminé por tirarme en el pasto, cansado de perseguirlos por todos lados. Iñaki se sentó a mi lado a jugar con su nave.

—Dime una cosa, Iñaki. ¿Por qué si tú y yo siempre estamos juntos, sólo me molestan a mí?

—No sé.

Un misterio de la naturaleza. Una pregunta que seguramente ni los Cherokees se hacían porque su falta de cerebro no les daba para tanto. De cualquier modo, lo verdaderamente malo era cuando Carlos Alberto no andaba con ellos, porque no sólo me molestaban, sino que también abusaban. Ellos me habían dejado sin dinero y sin buen humor. Me dieron ganas de que en ese momento mi corazón hiciera ¡cuaz!, y terminaran mis sufrimientos. Pero... ¿para qué son los amigos?

—Tito, ¿y si me la regalas de una vez? Total. Tú ni te la pones —dijo Iñaki.

—¿Qué?

—Tu máscara de Darth Vader.

Se me fueron las ganas de hablar sobre el equipo de futbol por varios días.

Pero el lunes siguiente, en plena ceremonia de Honores a la Bandera, se me volvió a levantar el ánimo y se me volvió a hinchar el corazón. El profesor Colina, en persona, dio el anuncio después de que una niña de segundo año recitara las efemérides de la semana como si se hubiera tragado un perico. Él habló del torneo y de la importancia de hacer deporte. Dijo que las inscripciones estaban abiertas y quién iba a entregar el trofeo. Pero no mencionó nunca a quién se le había ocurrido la idea. Y sí sentí feo porque yo quería que, en cuanto dijera mi nombre, toda la escuela (incluso la maestra Lucía) volteara a mirarme y yo, orgulloso, hiciera mi mejor cara de: "¡Oh!, no fue nada, esas cosas se me ocurren a cada rato". Pero ni chance hubo, porque el profesor Colina, con su sonrisota, terminó por anunciar que él sería el árbitro de todos los partidos porque siempre había querido ser árbitro en su juventud.

Hubo que conformarse. Aunque yo de todos modos estaba muy feliz y no pude esperar al otro día. Así que, a la hora del recreo, en el pizarrón de los anuncios, apareció la primera hoja con el primer equipo: las Chivas Rayadas del Guadalajara. Capitán: Tito Mendiolea. Me sentí como un globo, de tan ancho, cuando pegué la hoja y apunté mi nombre. Nadie antes que yo lo había hecho. Mi equipo era el primero en anunciarse. Y debajo del capitán, aparecían los renglones en blanco para que se apuntaran todos los niños que quisieran hacerlo. ¿Ya dije que me sentía como un globo de tan ancho? Pues lo vuelvo a decir. Me sentía un globo de Cantoya, un dirigible, un...

—Hola, Tito, ¿qué haces?

Era Dolores Zúñiga, la niña que mete vísceras de rata en su sándwich y agua de pantano en su cantimplora. Huí de ella antes de que se me pegara. No sé qué le da por seguirme. Desde que llegué de Guadalajara, desde mi primer día en esta escuela, a veces se me pega como si se hubiera tragado una plancha y yo trajera un imán conmigo, como en las caricaturas. No sé qué le pasa. Seguramente me quiere arrojar un hechizo que me convierta en moco o algo así. Y por eso fui al patio a correr la noticia entre los demás niños: que ya podían apuntarse en el equipo de las Chivas Rayadas, capitaneado por Tito Mendiolea. Pero mucho, mucho interés no hubo, hay que admitirlo. Cuando se terminó el recreo, me di cuenta de que no sólo no se había apuntado nadie; ni siquiera había otros equipos en el pizarrón. El torneo empezaba mal, eso estaba claro. Pero no quise desanimarme, porque no había pasado más de media hora desde que había pegado mi hoja. De todos modos, cuando pasé frente al pizarrón, para que mi hoja no se viera tan triste, hice una anotación: apunté el nombre del único niño que yo sabía que, si no se había anotado, era por descuido o por distracción.

Sin embargo, ya vería yo después que estaba equivocado. De todos modos, al regresar al salón, cuando terminó el recreo, me dio un gusto tan enorme que no lo puedo poner en palabras porque la maestra Lucía (suspiro) me saludó a la entrada y me dijo, con una sonrisa que iluminaba el salón entero:

—Tito, muy bien. Veo que ya tienes tu equipo.

No me acuerdo qué siguió después, ni qué vimos en la clase ni nada, porque me convertí en un idiota a la cuarta potencia. Sólo recuerdo cuando Iñaki me zarandeó para que nos fuéramos a la casa porque ya todos habían abandonado el salón y yo todavía flotaba entre nubes. Claro que Iñaki, mi buen amigo, se encargó de hacerme bajar a tierra. Y de sopetón, además.

Íbamos pasando frente al pizarrón cuando me di cuenta de que nadie se había anotado, no había ningún equipo nuevo y, además, alguien había borrado el nombre de Iñaki de la hoja de las Chivas Rayadas del Guadalajara.

—Iñaki —dije, molesto—, algún malvado borró tu nombre del equipo.

Y ya iba yo a apuntarlo otra vez cuando mi mejor amigo aclaró:

—Sí. Yo fui. Yo me borré.

Se me cayó la mandíbula al suelo. No podía creerlo. Me quedé sin palabras hasta que llegamos a la puerta de la casa de Iñaki, donde debíamos separarnos para irnos a comer cada quien a su casa. Lo único que nos libró del espantoso silencio en el camino fue Susana, que se nos pegó y no dejaba de preguntarle a Iñaki cosas que él no respondía. Hasta que ella dijo: "Nos vemos mañana, Iñaki" y se metió a la casa, salí de mi estupor. Creí que mi corazón no aguantaría la decepción, pero hasta eso que sí aguantó.

—¿Por qué no quieres estar en mi equipo, Iñaki mal amigo?

—Es que quería ver qué otros equipos se abrían antes.

Lo sabía. Lo sabía. Sabía que tarde o temprano ocurriría. Y como mi mejor amigo ya se encargó de echarme de cabeza, voy a tener que contarlo.

Ahí va. La verdad... la verdad... es que no soy muy bueno jugando futbol.

No. No es cierto. Tengo que ser honesto. La puritita verdad es que más bien soy bastante malo. Qué digo malo. Soy un maleta. Cuando en el recreo se hacen equipos para jugar futbol, ¿a quién creen que escogen hasta el último? Sí. Adivinaron. Ni siquiera cuando yo pongo el balón, me dejan armar equipo. Qué digo armar equipo, ni siquiera los capitanes me escogen en segundo o tercer lugar, aunque sea para no hacerme sentir tan mal. Siempre hasta el último. Y por no dejarme fuera, que ya sería el colmo. Ha habido partidos en los que hasta me la dan de "chocolate", o sea, que lo que yo haga en el campo no cuenta. En el remoto caso de que yo metiera un gol, no contaría porque soy "chocolate".

¿Quieren saber cuál es la verdadera humillación? No, nada de lo que ustedes creen. No es que te abran la puerta del baño mientras estás haciendo. Ni que te obliguen a vestirte de niña y te paseen así por la calle atado a una cuerda. Eso no es nada. La verdadera humillación es cuando los capitanes están armando los equipos y uno de ellos le dice al otro: "Te regalo al Tito". Ésa es la verdadera humillación. Que te regalen y te hagan ver que no sólo no sirves, sino que, además, estorbas.

Yo sé que le echo muchas ganas. En serio. Sé que le echo muchas, muchas ganas. Pero también siento que algo me falta y no sé qué es. Y cuando lo aprenda, no habrá nadie ni nada que me pare. Voy a ser el mejor. Voy a ser como el Tigre Quezada. O como Pelé. Quién sabe. O mejor que Pelé. Aunque mientras eso ocurre... mientras aprendo lo que me falta... voy a tener que convencer hasta a mi mejor amigo de que le entre a mi equipo de futbol o voy a ser el hazmerreír de toda la escuela.

—Iñaki, olvídate de la máscara de Darth Vader. Y olvídate de la nave que toca la musiquita de *La guerra de las galaxias*.

—¿La nave de la musiquita? ¿También me la ibas a dar cuando te murieras?

—No. Te la iba a dar antes. Pero ya no, porque no quieres estar en mi equipo.

Miró hacia su casa. Desde ahí, donde estábamos parados en la calle, se veía la ventana de su cuarto y las naves colgadas del techo. Una más para su colección. No pudo resistirlo.

—Bueno. Estoy en tu equipo, pero con una condición.

—¿Cuál?

—Que le pongas un nombre que pensé.

Nos peleamos durante toda la tarde, desde que fue a mi casa para decirme su "maravilloso nombre" hasta que empezó a oscurecer. Pero cómo no íbamos a pelearnos: Intergalactical Rockets of the Future. ¿Pueden creerlo? Ése es el nombre que sugirió Iñaki. Sí, sé lo que están pensando. Que no hay nombre más feo y más horrible en el mundo que ése. En definitiva, no hubo modo de que lo resolviéramos hablando. Tuvimos que llegar a los jalones de greñas. Y lo malo fue que Susana se metió para defender a Iñaki y el nombre que propuso Iñaki. Y antes de que mi mamá nos regañara y nos castigara a todos, porque hasta el abuelo se metió y empezó a tirar manazos, decidimos que lo mejor era echarlo a la suerte. Sí, lo mejor. ¡Ja! Y como los cuatro volados los ganó Iñaki, le dije que no tendría ni máscara ni nave ni nada, que ya no lo quería en mi equipo y que se largara a su casa.

Al final, tuvimos que llegar a un acuerdo porque Iñaki no soportó la idea de esperar hasta mi muerte para tener esos tesoros. Y la hoja de las Chivas Rayadas del Guadalajara fue intercambiada en el pizarrón, al otro día, por la de los Cohetes Rayados de la Colonia Portales.

Querido Tigre Quezada:

Ya tengo equipo. No te digo el nombre porque te vas a reír. Pero es el mejor equipo de todo el torneo. Sí, sé que todavía no empieza, pero vamos a ser los mejores porque tendremos el mejor uniforme de todos: el de las Chivas. Además, ya empezamos a entrenar y estamos haciendo mucho músculo. Por cierto, ¡qué bueno que expulsaron al del Veracruz que te fauleó el partido pasado!

¡Lero, lero! Por cochino.

Con cariño,

Tito

Mentira. Todavía no entrenábamos porque en el equipo nada más éramos dos. Además, Iñaki me chantajeó varios días para jugar a la guerra espacial o si no, no entrenaría para el torneo. De todos modos, preferí jugar porque me angustiaba que todo se fuera al traste. Ya podrán imaginarse por qué. A casi una semana del anuncio, no había más que dos equipos y sólo el de los Cohetes Rayados tenía dos nombres anotados. El otro equipo sólo anotó al capitán. O sea que, de toda la escuela, a tres monos nos había entusiasmado mi fabulosa idea. Ni siquiera Edson estaba interesado, a pesar de mi ilusión de que se apuntara con nosotros, el primer equipo de la pizarra.

Está bien. Tendrán curiosidad por saber qué otro equipo se anotó en el pizarrón de avisos. Aunque no vale la pena mencionarlo, les diré cuál fue: Pumas de la Universidad. Así se llama el equipo. Su capitán, Óliver Mendoza, un niño de tercer grado que está completamente mal de la cabeza. ¿Por qué? Pues porque está convencido de que él es Cabiño. Sí. El jugador de los Pumas, los reales (un jugador tan bueno que muchas veces ha sido campeón de goleo; a veces hasta pienso que casi es tan bueno como el Tigre Quezada).

Óliver está tan loco que nadie lo invita a jugar cuando hay partido de futbol porque es un plomazo. Cuando juega, ni siquiera responde por su nombre. Tienes que decirle Cabiño para que voltee o para que te pase el balón. No, no es un apodo, lo juro. El triste enano cabezón está convencido de que es Cabiño. Una vez en el recreo, nos dijo a Iñaki y a mí: "¿Vieron en la tele el gol que metí ayer contra el Cruz Azul?".

¿Ven cómo el enano está loco? Es cierto que juega más o menos bien, pero es tan pesado que, cuando jugamos, nadie lo quiere en su equipo. ¿Recuerdan que a mí siempre me escogen al último? Pues no me había puesto a pensar que por lo menos me escogen; al enano de Óliver ni siquiera eso. Siempre termina haciendo dominadas con su propio balón en la orilla del patio mientras todos los demás jugamos, porque nadie lo aguanta (lástima, porque el verdadero Cabiño es un gran jugador y casi tan bueno como el Tigre).

Y la verdad me deprimía ver que, además de mi equipo, el único que se había anotado al torneo era el del chiflado de Óliver. Como que hasta daba vergüenza. De repente, me daban ganas de arrancar la hoja de mi equipo del pizarrón porque ver a los Cohetes Rayados al lado de los Pumas de Óliver es... ¿cómo dice mi papá cuando mi abuelita enseña sus fotos de niño en las que sale desnudo...? ¡Ah!, sí, denigrante. De repente me daban ganas de renunciar. Y más en un día como ése, en el cual, los Cherokees, al darse cuenta del nombre de mi equipo, más la tomaron en mi contra, como si hubiera sido una provocación. Me agarraron a la salida de la escuela y me hicieron volar más alto que otras veces, muertos de la risa.

—Tito Tito Capotito, sube al cielo y pega un grito.

Así me hicieron hasta que Carlos Alberto les dijo que ya le pararan porque tenían que irse a su entrenamiento de futbol americano. Lo único bueno fue que Susana se cansó de esperar a que terminaran de ponerme en órbita, y se fue sola a la casa. Al menos Iñaki sí me esperó, a pesar de haberse terminado su congelada antes de que los Cherokees me dejaran en paz. Y cuando caminábamos hacia nuestras casas, se me ocurrió decir:

—No sé qué tiene que ver el nombre de nuestro equipo con su tontería de "Tito Tito Capotito". Nomás se dieron cuenta de que nos llamamos Cohetes Rayados y la tomaron contra mí.

Iñaki me miró como si no pudiera creerlo.

—¿Estás hablando en serio?

—Claro que sí. ¿Por qué?

—¿No sabes qué tiene que ver el nombre de nuestro equipo con lo de "Tito Tito Capotito"?

—Pues no sé qué tiene que ver.

—¿Estás loco de la cabeza o qué? ¿A poco no sabías que es una adivinanza? "Tito Tito Capotito, sube al cielo y pega un grito, ¿qué es?", pues "el cohete".

No sé qué me impidió estrangular a mi mejor amigo. A lo mejor mi corazón enfermo.

—¿Y tú sí sabías que era una adivinanza? ¿Y además, que la respuesta es "el cohete"?

—Pues sí.

—¡¿Y aun así dejaste que le pusiéramos al equipo los Cohetes Rayados?! Para que me molesten hasta el fin de mis días con esa estupidez.

—Es un bonito nombre.

La verdad, lo único que me impidió estrangular a Iñaki fue que él corre más rápido que yo y llegó a su casa en un santiamén. Además, cerró la puerta muy rápido y ahora sí le echó llave, contra la costumbre de su mamá.

Me dio coraje. Claro que me dio coraje. Sólo me calmé cuando pensé en mi fatigado corazón. Y cuando eran las cuatro de la tarde, e Iñaki no se había presentado a la sesión de juegos intergalácticos que habíamos pactado tener antes de los entrenamientos, me dio más coraje. Mi abuelo me contaba cómo le había sacado las tripas a un huertista y se había fabricado una bufanda con ellas, cuando no pude más. Hugo intentaba comerse uno de sus pies. Susana hablaba por teléfono con su amiga Lulú. Así que me puse mis zapatos de futbol (ya traía encima el resto del uniforme), tomé mi balón y salí.

Tuve que llamar a la puerta de la casa de Iñaki porque seguía clausurada.

—Hola, mi alma —dijo la mamá de Iñaki (Beso, beso).

—Hola, señora —contesté apresuradamente y me escabullí hasta el cuarto de mi mejor amigo. La sangre me hervía.

—Hola, cobarde —le dije al tonto de Iñaki.

—Hola, ¿qué haces? —contestó, como si nada, sin dejar de ver la televisión.

—No te hagas, Iñaki. ¿Por qué no fuiste a mi casa a jugar?

—No me acordé.

—No es cierto. Tenías miedo de que te hiciera mi famosa llave china por nunca haberme dicho que eso de "Tito Tito Capotito" era una adivinanza.

—Es la adivinanza más mala y más vieja del mundo. Creí que la conocías.

—Pues no. No la conocía.

Nos quedamos en silencio, sentados en los extremos de su cama. Entonces Iñaki dijo algo que me sorprendió.

—Si quieres, volvemos a tu nombre de las Chivas.

Y me di cuenta de que los héroes precisamente están hechos de eso. Bueno... no sé cómo se llama. Pero sí sé que los héroes nunca se echan para atrás en sus decisiones. Me di cuenta de que si lo hacíamos, peor me iba a ir con los Cherokees y más me iban a molestar. Así que yo también dije algo que me sorprendió:

—No. Es un bonito nombre.

Iñaki me sonrió. Y con eso hicimos las paces. Bueno... casi.

—¿Jugamos con mi máscara de Darth Vader? —dijo él.

—No. Vamos a empezar a entrenar —dije yo.

Y volvimos a discutir. Al final yo gané, y sin tener que usar mi famosa llave china, porque Iñaki todavía se sentía un poco mal conmigo. Así que nos fuimos al Parque de los Venados en cuanto Iñaki se puso sus tenis. Ya habría tiempo de pensar en la forma de mejorar su atuendo porque ningún Cohete Rayado que se respete puede ir a entrenar con una playera de Tom y Jerry.

Y nos fuimos a parar frente a un pasamanos. Mi idea era hacer algunos tiros de distancia. Yo primero e Iñaki después, porque todavía no decidía quién podría ser el portero de los Cohetes Rayados. Yo empecé. Un tiro. Otro. Otro.

—Tito, hay que atinarle a la portería —me conminó Iñaki, cansado de recoger mis balones, los cuales salían muy desviados.

Pero bueno, para eso se supone que entrena uno, para mejorar con la práctica. Así que en eso estábamos, cuando sentí que me agarraban por las axilas. Iñaki no pudo avisarme porque estaba recuperando uno de mis tiros que casi se salía del parque.

—Miren quién está aquí —dijo Rubén, que traía puesto su jersey de futbol americano.

—Tito Tito Capotito —respondió Tony.

Y de nuevo me hicieron volar un par de veces y, a la tercera, en lugar de enfadarme, se me ocurrió preguntarles, antes de que me volvieran a lanzar por los aires:

—Oigan, ¿y por qué siempre me molestan a mí? ¿Por qué no molestan también a Iñaki?

Se veía que nunca se lo habían preguntado. Fue Tony el que dijo:

—Sí, es cierto. ¿Por qué?

—No lo sé —contestó Fito.

—¡Oh, oh! —dijo Iñaki, aún con el balón en sus manos.

Entonces los tres se fueron contra él. Y tuvieron que perseguirlo por todo el parque. Dieron varias vueltas hasta que se cansaron. Y me di cuenta de que mi amigo corre muy rápido; tal vez sea el niño más veloz que conozco. El caso es que los Cherokees no pudieron darle alcance y se fueron de nuevo contra mí. Pero como estaban muy cansados, ya no pudieron ni levantarme. Como yo no llevaba dinero para dulces, tampoco pudieron asaltarme, así que terminaron empujándose unos a otros. Se veían muy enfadados y yo no quise esperarme a ver cómo terminaba aquello. Alcancé a Iñaki en la calle.

—Oye, de veras corres muy duro.

—Tito... mal... amigo —dijo con el poco aire que le quedaba, antes de tirarse en la banqueta.

Pero a mí lo que me preocupaba era dónde íbamos a entrenar si todo el Parque de los Venados era territorio cherokee. Y sólo se me ocurría otro sitio: nuestra calle. No vi por qué no podríamos jugar futbol en la calle si prácticamente todos los niños del Distrito Federal lo hacen. Nomás hay que aprender a torear coches. Se lo propuse a Iñaki y tuve que esperarme un rato para que me pudiera responder.

—Estás.. loco... de... la... cabeza.

Pero no teníamos opción. Así que, sin preguntarle si estaba de acuerdo o no, marqué unas líneas en el asfalto con un ladrillo, aprovechando que en ese momento no pasaban autos, para que nos sirvieran como marcos de portería. En eso estaba, cuando escuché una vocecita muy desagradable y conocida para mí.

—Vas a ver con mi mamá que estás jugando futbol en la calle.

Era Susana, asomada a la ventana de su cuarto.

—Le dices algo y echo tus monas al escusado y le jalo.

—No digo nada si Iñaki me invita a verlos jugar.

Mi mejor amigo adivinó mis pensamientos, porque me miró como si estuviera a punto de venderlo como esclavo a unos gitanos.

—Ándale. Es por el bien del equipo. Ni modo.

—¿Qué te pasa, Tito? Si de por sí ya no me la quito de encima.

—Ni modo. Es eso o no jugar.

—Pues mejor no jugar.

Tuve que detenerlo. Estaba a punto de meterse en su casa. Le ofrecí jugar después a *La guerra de las galaxias* y ser la princesa Leia y con eso accedió, aunque a regañadientes.

—Está bien, Susana, baja —dijo, muy quedito para mi gusto.

Vimos hacia la ventana y ella ya no estaba. Nos miramos con alivio. Tal vez se había arrepentido.

Qué va. Ni siquiera esperó a que Iñaki la invitara. Ya estaba ahí abajo, junto a él, haciéndole ojitos. ¡Guac!

Iñaki ni la miró. Estaba pendiente del semáforo. En cuanto se pusiera el rojo, podríamos empezar a jugar. Y así fue, cuando dejaron de pasar coches, Iñaki tomó el balón y se encaminó a la mitad de la calle. Susana estaba fascinada. ¡Guac!

—Tito, pero ahora yo tiro, porque tú tienes la pata muy chueca.

—Está bien —dije. Y me puse frente a nuestra portería pintada.

—Iñaki, mete gol, mete gol —echaba porras Susana.

Entonces, Iñaki tomó vuelo y corrió hacia la pelota. Yo estaba en mi mejor pose de portero, listo para recibir el tiro como si fuera un penalti. Pero qué les cuento. Si yo tengo la pata chueca, Iñaki la tiene al revés. No sé ni cómo le pegó al balón, que éste salió con chanfle hacia la derecha y, volando por los aires, fue a meterse en una casa a través de la ventana. Lo malo es que la ventana estaba cerrada. El ruido fue más o menos como ¡CRAAAAAAAAAASH! O algo parecido.

—¡En la torre! —dijo Iñaki.

—¡En la torre! —dije yo.

Hicimos lo único que se puede hacer en esas circunstancias: nos echamos a correr. Lo malo fue que en ese momento, empezaron a pasar los coches y tuvimos que irnos del lado del parque, en vez del de nuestras casas, donde habríamos estado a salvo. Apenas alcanzamos a escondernos detrás de un árbol. Pero Susana, horror de horrores, se quedó en la otra acera, y en vez de echarse a correr, que era lo más sensato, se quedó como estatua viendo la ventana rota. Seguro que el pánico la inmovilizó. Claro que el vecino no tardó en asomar la cabeza: era un señor tan gordo, que parecía haberse comido un Volkswagen. Dijo un montón de groserías y luego, cuando descubrió a Susana mirando hacia allá, pareció calmarse.

—Niña, ¿tú viste quién me rompió el vidrio?

—No. No vi —dijo.

Me enorgullecí de mi hermana. Era toda una valiente. Se enfrentaba al mal encarado vecino con una fortaleza increíble. Hasta me dieron ganas de que Iñaki un día le hiciera caso. Y ya estábamos a punto de salir de nuestro escondite cuando agregó:

—Pero sí sé quién lo hizo.

—¿Ah, sí? ¿Quién?

—Fue mi hermano.

Era una traidora. Seguro lo hizo por salvar a Iñaki. En cuanto la cabeza del señor desapareció de la ventana, mi amigo y yo aprovechamos que el semáforo estaba en rojo de nuevo para huir hacia nuestras casas. Me metí a la carrera. Pero antes de esconderme debajo de la cama, tuve una súbita ocurrencia. Y fui por mi abuelo, que dormía su siesta.

—¡Abuelo, abuelo! ¡Me persiguen!

—¿Quiénes? —preguntó sobresaltado.

—Los huertistas. Sálvame.

—Faltaba más.

Por respeto, no contaré lo que pasó después, porque las escenas de violencia nunca me han parecido muy gratas. Sólo diré que el señor gordo tuvo que enfrentarse a toda la furia de mi abuelo cuando llamó a la puerta de mi casa. Y tuvo que marcharse sin que nadie le respondiera por su vidrio, lo cual no me hizo sentir nada bien.

Cuando dieron las siete de la noche y mi mamá me llamó a merendar, yo sentía que me daba el soponcio. Cada vez que sonaba el teléfono o tocaban a la puerta, me imaginaba a la policía preguntando por Vicente Mendiolea Urbina: "Tenemos una orden de aprehensión contra ese criminal". Y como la preocupación no me dejaba en paz, fui con mi papá en cuanto llegó a la casa.

—Oye, papá, ¿te pueden meter a la cárcel por romper un vidrio?

—Claro, sobre todo si el vidrio es de un banco, por ejemplo.

¡Vaya ayuda! Preferí tomar el asunto en mis manos, porque no soportaba que mi abuelo contara a cada rato a todos cómo había defendido la casa de siete huertistas invasores, ni que Susana no dejara de mirarme como mosquita muerta cada vez que pasaba a mi lado, con su cara de: "Yo sé tu secreto y juro que lo contaré a la menor provocación". Tomé el teléfono y llamé a casa de Iñaki.

—¡Guau, Tito! ¡Nos salvamos por los pelos! Tu abuelo es a todo dar. ¿Viste cómo se le subió encima al señor?

No sé cómo le hace Iñaki para que estas cosas no le preocupen. No sé cómo le hace todo el mundo.

—Iñaki, tenemos que confesar. Llamo para que me acompañes a ver al vecino.

—¿Estás loco de la cabeza o qué te pasa?

No hubo modo de convencerlo. Mi mamá me hizo colgar, porque yo había empezado a gritonearle a mi mejor amigo. Y terminé haciendo lo que seguramente hacen los verdaderos héroes para poder dormir tranquilos: abrir la caja de sus ahorros (aunque hayan estado destinados a comprar un Tango) y presentarse con el dinero a pagar sus culpas.

Y para que vean cuán difícil me fue tomar esa decisión, quiero que me acompañen rápidamente a una tienda deportiva que está enfrente del súper de aquí a la vuelta. Es rápido. Al fin que todavía no han cerrado. ¿Ven qué me refiero? Sí. Ahí en el escaparate. El balón más hermoso del mundo: un Tango, el balón oficial de la Copa del Mundo Argentina 78. ¿A poco no está bien padre? Pues con dos domingos más, hubiera sido mío. Lástima. Sólo me pregunto si el Tigre Quezada habría hecho lo mismo que yo.

La mitad de mis ahorros fue lo que el pesado del vecino me quitó. Y ni las gracias me dio. Además, me dijo que no me regresaba el balón porque lo había apuñalado con un cuchillo cebollero, en venganza por los jalones de greñas que le había dado mi abuelo. No sé. Creo que tenía razón de seguir tan enojado, aunque sí me cayó mal que me dijera que el que la hace, la paga. Sobre todo porque yo ni siquiera le rompí el vidrio. Por eso, al día siguiente, tuve otro altercado con Iñaki, el cual empezó al inicio de clases y se prolongó hasta el momento en que la maestra Lucía (suspiro) nos dictaba unos problemas de matemáticas.

—Tito, Iñaki, ¿qué se traen? ¿Por qué se están empujando?

—Por nada, maestra —dijimos al unísono.

—Esténse quietos o los dejo sin recreo.

Dejamos de pelearnos en clase, pero le seguimos en el recreo. Aunque en el fondo yo sabía que era inútil pedirle a Iñaki que me repusiera la mitad de lo que había pagado por el vidrio, puesto que podía decir de antemano que Iñaki no tenía un solo centavo ahorrado. Iñaki podrá ser el niño que más rápido corre, pero también es el que más rápido se gasta sus domingos. Y es imposible sacarle un peso por la simple razón de que no lo tiene. Lo único que Iñaki tiene en la vida es lo que trae puesto.

—Cuando menos invítame un Pascual Boing y un Gansito —le dije, ya abatido.

—Bueno —consintió, revisando sus bolsillos.

Y me sentí tan mal de haber perdido para siempre mi Tango, que fui al patio a sentarme, a un lado de Luisito Pichardo, y terminé por regalarle mi Gansito y mi Pascual Boing. Eso lo hizo muy feliz y hasta me abrazó, cosa que me animó un poco. Lo malo fue que ya le había regalado las golosinas cuando vi, a lo lejos, algo que me puso colorado y molesto: Óliver le invitaba a Edson una torta y un helado. No lo podía creer, estaba comprando al mejor jugador de la escuela. El triste enano cabezón estaba jugando sucio. Pensé seriamente en quitarle a Luisito Pichardo el Gansito y el Pascual Boing para también hacer mi intento con el brasileño. Total, si Luisito de todos modos no ve, a lo mejor nunca se enteraría de quién le había quitado los dulces. Pero no pude. Ya me veía en las noches, torturado por el remordimiento de haberle quitado sus golosinas a un niño ciego. Pero tampoco me iba a quedar con los brazos cruzados. Fui a donde estaban Óliver y Edson (Edson, ¡guau!).

—Hola, Edson —dije, palmeándole la espalda—. ¿Ya escogiste equipo?

—Lárgate, Tito, estamos platicando —dijo Óliver.

—¿Y qué? ¿No puedo platicar yo también?

—No.

Preferí dirigirme a Edson.

—¿A poco le hablas a los de tercero? ¿No crees que es malo para tu reputación?

Edson ni me atendía. Pero tampoco a Óliver. Estaba como distraído. A veces me preguntaba si Edson hablaba español.

—Oye, Edson. ¿No se te antoja un Pascual Boing y un Gansito?

—Lárgate, Tito —insistía Óliver.

Terminamos discutiendo nosotros dos solos. Cuando nos dimos cuenta, Edson ya se había marchado. Y de nada sirvió que nos lanzáramos a buscarlo, porque sonó la campana de fin del recreo.

Pueden imaginar cómo me sentía en la tarde de ese día. En el pizarrón no había nuevos equipos, tampoco nuevos integrantes en los dos únicos equipos apuntados; la maestra Lucía me había regañado varias veces por discutir con Iñaki en el salón; el bobo de Óliver y yo habíamos ahuyentado a Edson;

el entrenamiento tendría que realizarse con una pelota de Mickey Mouse que le robé a Hugo porque ya no teníamos balón y, para rematar, los Cherokees se habían adueñado del parque. Iñaki, mi mejor amigo, se dio cuenta de que algo me pesaba cuando íbamos a entrenar al parque. Iba como si me llevaran arrastrando al matadero.

—¿Te sientes mal, Tito? ¿Ya te vas a morir?

—No sé. A lo mejor.

—Si quieres, mejor jugamos con mis naves.

No. No tenía ánimos de jugar a *La guerra de las galaxias*. Pero una cosa era segura, tampoco quería que los Cherokees me molestaran, pues si me veían llegar al parque con la pelota de Mickey Mouse de Hugo, no me salvaría de una buena sesión de tonterías. Y como ya habíamos comprobado que entrenar en la calle era mala idea, pensé que estábamos a la mitad de la nada. Como en las caricaturas, cuando los personajes van corriendo y se dan cuenta de que se les acaba el piso hasta que ya es muy tarde y se van para abajo.

—Mejor vamos a ver la tele en tu casa —le dije a Iñaki, todo apesadumbrado.

Y ahí, frente al programa de la Calaca Tilica y Flaca, se me ocurrió una gran idea, que a lo mejor resolvía uno de nuestros múltiples problemas: el de la falta de espacio para entrenar.

—Ahorita vengo —fue todo lo que le dije a Iñaki.

De todos modos, ni siquiera estaba viendo la tele. Estaba leyendo su revista *Duda*. Así que, procurando que la señora no me viera salir, huí por la puerta y me dirigí al parque lo más rápido que pude. A la distancia pude darme cuenta de que había llegado a tiempo: ahí estaban todavía los Cherokees. Y con ellos, Carlos Alberto. Un par de niñas de mi salón también estaban con ellos, de ésas que están enamoradas de Carlos Alberto.

Y me subí en un columpio a esperar el momento adecuado.

Mientras me balanceaba, preguntándome si las alturas no le harían mal a mi corazón, oí una música agradable. Me detuve y me fijé en la resbaladilla, de donde provenía la melodía. Era Olariñárritu, quien, sentado en los escalones con una guitarra, cantaba una canción. Entonces me acerqué para saludarlo.

—Hola, Olariñárritu, ¿qué cantas?

—...

—¿Es una canción de los Beatles?

—...

—Está padre.

—...

—No sabía que tocaras la guitarra.

—...

—Bueno. Luego seguimos platicando.

Ese Olariñárritu me dio envidia. Ahí estaba, como si nada, en pleno territorio cherokee y ni quién lo molestara. A pocos metros estaban todos esos descerebrados de quinto grado y ni quién se metiera con él. En cambio, nomás pregúntenme qué pasaría si a mí se me ocurriera sentarme un día en una resbaladilla con una guitarra. Seguro que me la harían tragar. Bueno, en verdad no podía seguir platicando con Olariñárritu porque en esos momentos estaba ocurriendo lo que yo esperaba: que Carlos Alberto se despidiera de sus compañeros de equipo y se fuera a su casa. También se despidió de las dos niñas, y les dio un beso en la mejilla (¡guac!), luego se enfiló hacia su calle, que no queda lejos de ahí.

Lo seguí un par de cuadras, hasta que se dio cuenta y me encaró.

—Tito, ¿qué haces? ¿Por qué me sigues?

—Hola, Carlos Alberto. No te estaba siguiendo.

—Sí, me seguías. ¿Qué pasa?

—¿Podemos platicar un ratito?

—Bueno.

Querido Tigre Quezada:

Te escribo para recordarte que tienes que entregar la copa del torneo de mi escuela. No se te vaya a olvidar, por favor, porque si no, seguro que el profesor Colina se va a enojar tanto conmigo, que me va a hacer repetir el año. Por favor.

Y bueno, ya que estamos platicando, te quiero contar que ayer me sentí muy triste por muchas cosas. Pero la que más me entristeció fue que Carlos Alberto no me quisiera ayudar a que sus amigotes me dejen de molestar. Me dio tristeza porque antes él y yo éramos cuates. Hace un año, éramos los únicos nuevos en el salón porque yo apenas había llegado de Guadalajara y él, de Tampico. Y recordé que en el recreo él y yo jugamos juntos varios días, porque no conocíamos a nadie más. Pero parece que él ya no se acuerda porque me dijo: "No puedo ayudarte, Tito. Los Cherokees siempre hacen lo que quieren, y yo no puedo impedirlo". Pero no es cierto. Yo sé que si Carlos Alberto les dice que nos dejen entrenar en el parque, ellos lo harán porque se ve que lo respetan mucho por ser el mejor mariscal de campo de su equipo. Pero a él no le importa. Por eso me cayó gordo. Y eso me puso triste. Creo que ya no le voy a volver a hablar nunca. Pero bueno, no te apures, que de todos modos vamos a ganar la copa. Y tú nos la vas a entregar. No se te vaya a olvidar, porque si no vienes, a lo mejor el director se enoja tanto, que me regresa a cuarto grado. Porfa. Adiós.

Con cariño,
Tito

Fue gracias a que yo estaba tan triste, que el milagro ocurrió. La maestra Lucía (suspiro) me sorprendió caminando durante la hora del recreo con la mirada tan perdida, que se dio cuenta de que yo estaba, como dice mi mamá, que no me calentaba ni el sol. Hasta tomó mi cara entre sus manos, levantándola. Y, por supuesto, esto me convirtió en el mayor lelo de toda la historia.

—Tito, ¿qué te pasa? ¿Por qué te ves tan triste?

Juro que intenté responderle, pero no me salieron las palabras. Además, al fin y al cabo fue mejor porque parecía que la maestra se portaba más cariñosa si yo no decía nada y hacía mi mejor cara de melancolía. Hasta me acarició el cabello. Juro que si hubiera podido fingir que lloraba, lo habría hecho. Y si me hubieran salido las palabras, hasta le habría confesado que el corazón estaba a punto de hacerme ¡cuaz!, y que lamentaba mucho no poder vivir más tiempo para ser su mejor alumno y sacar las mejores calificaciones porque ella era la mejor maestra del mundo y...

—Tito, pobrecito. Si quieres, puedo llevarte a mi casa y ahí puedo cuidarte y mimarte como sólo tú te mereces.

Bueno. En realidad no dijo eso. Pero sus ojos tenían tal brillo, que yo creí que era como si lo hubiera dicho.

—Ya sé por qué estás triste. Por esto —ahora sí dijo de verdad, señalando el pizarrón a mis espaldas.

Claro. No era casual que yo estuviera ahí tan triste. Me había parado justo en ese lugar para invitar directamente a los que pasaran a apuntarse en mi equipo. Claro que no a todos. A algunos de sexto y a los brasileños, sobre todo. Pero nadie había querido.

—Sé cómo remediarlo. Vas a ver —dijo. Y me guiñó un ojo.

Y no supe qué pasó desde ese momento hasta el siguiente lunes, cuando en plena ceremonia de Honores a la Bandera, el profesor Colina volvió a tomar el micrófono para dirigirse a todos los alumnos. No supe nada de mí porque la maestra Lucía (suspiro) nunca me había hecho guiños ni me había acariciado el cabello. Nunca estuve más convencido en toda mi vida de que tenía que ser un héroe.

—Niños… —dijo el profesor Colina, con su sonrisa de mazorca—. En vista del poco entusiasmo que ha despertado el torneo de futbol, he decidido tomar una medida para que se animen, gracias a un consejo que me dio la maestra Lucía.

Y la maestra Lucía, lo juro, me sonrió desde lejos. Lo juro. Lo juro.

—¡Qué caray! He decidido ponerles diez en deportes a los que participen en el torneo. Pero recuerden que deben apurarse, porque solamente puede haber dieciséis equipos de seis integrantes cada uno.

No me pregunten qué pasó después. Una estampida, creo. Un huracán. Un terremoto. Parecía que alguien hubiera gritado "¡Se quema la escuela!". Todos los niños abandonaron el patio a la carrera, con excepción de algunas niñas y niños pequeños de primero y segundo. Eso hizo el milagro. Aunque he de decir que fue un milagro a medias. Pero esto lo supe hasta la hora del recreo, cuando Iñaki y yo fuimos directo a la pizarra. A la distancia, nos parecía un sueño: dieciséis hojas cubrían el pizarrón. Eran dieciséis equipos. Y uno de esos equipos era el nuestro, los Cohetes Rayados.

Pero la decepción llegó al instante, en cuanto nos acercamos. Todos los equipos ya tenían seis integrantes. Excepto el nuestro, al que sólo se había apuntado alguien más: Susana Mendiolea. Y claro, el equipo de Óliver, al que no se había apuntado absolutamente nadie. Eso sí que era... ¿cómo dice mi papá cuando mi abuelita cuenta que él mojaba la cama de chico? Ah, sí, denigrante. Iñaki todavía intentó darme ánimos:

—No te sientas mal, Tito. Podríamos estar peor. Podríamos estar como los Pumas de la Universidad que no tienen mas que al capitán.

Pero yo sí me sentía en verdad mal. Hasta los Cherokees habían hecho su equipo al que, por cierto, no se apuntó Carlos Alberto y, aun así, ya estaban completos. También había un equipo de puras niñas: los Ángeles de Charlie. Y así, sucesivamente. Aunque, si uno se fijaba bien, sólo había un equipo que parecía verdaderamente bueno: los Relámpagos, formado por puros niños de sexto que son muy buenos jugando. Con todo, cuando nadie me veía, aproveché para borrar el nombre del tercer integrante de los Cohetes Rayados. "Mejor solos que mal acompañados", le dije a Iñaki. Y estuvo de acuerdo. Lo único bueno fue que Edson no se había apuntado con nadie, ¿ustedes creen? Aún había esperanzas.

No obstante, al final de las clases, Iñaki y yo fuimos a ver si alguien más se había apuntado en nuestra hoja. Además del nombre de Susana, estaba el de alguien peor: Dolores Zúñiga, la única niña capaz de volar por los aires si se sube a una escoba.

Me sentí mal del estómago, sobre todo porque tuvimos que esperar a que salieran casi todos para borrar esos dos nombres de la hoja. El problema fue que, cuando salimos por la puerta del colegio. Ahí estaban. Una detrás de la otra.

—Hola, Tito, me inscribí en tu equipo. Qué padre, ¿no? —dijo Dolores Zúñiga, la niña de la lengua verde.

Y detrás de ella, Susana.

—Óyeme, tonto. ¿Por qué me borraste del equipo? Sé que fuiste tú —dijo con una furia que no había visto desde la vez que le pinté la cara de azul mientras dormía—. Me tuve que volver a apuntar.

—Y yo volví a borrarte. Porque, para que sepas, el futbol es un juego de hombres, no de niñas.

—Pues eso no es cierto. Vas a ver, te voy a acusar con el director.

En ese momento, cuando pensé que todo estaba perdido, no sé de dónde sacó la idea Iñaki, mi mejor amigo, todo un genio.

—Es que ustedes pueden ser las porristas —dijo.

—¿Cómo? —preguntó mi hermana, un poco más tranquila. Finalmente, Iñaki le estaba dirigiendo la palabra.

—Sí. ¿A poco no sería más padre ser nuestras porristas?

Susana y Dolores Zúñiga, la única niña que roba muertos frescos del cementerio para hacer pasteles, se miraron, complacidas.

—Sí, es cierto. ¡Qué padre! Vamos a ser las porristas de los Cohetes Rayados. Qué buena idea, Iñaki —exclamó Susana.

Y no hubo más qué hablar. Las dos se quedaron discutiendo sobre el color que tendrían sus faldas de porristas y otras bobadas, mientras Iñaki y yo nos echábamos a correr a nuestras casas.

Está bien. ¿Quieren saber qué es verdaderamente denigrante? No tener equipo y, en cambio, tener cinco porristas. Eran las cinco de la tarde. Iñaki y yo veíamos en su casa el programa de la Calaca Tilica y Flaca, pues no habíamos ido a entrenar porque ni siquiera había en dónde. Entonces, tocaron el timbre. Nos asomamos a la ventana y ahí estaban: Susana, Lulú, Dolores Zúñiga (la única niña del mundo que puede hacer que el pelo se te caiga echándote el mal de ojo), Goya y Marita. Lulú es la mejor amiga de Susana, una niña pelirroja con pecas hasta en las pecas; Goya es una niña de sexto que más bien parece niño, porque sus brazos son más anchos que mis dos piernas juntas, y Marita es una escuincla de primer grado que ya se siente grande sólo por andar con Susana y con todas sus amigas.

—¿Qué quieren? —preguntó Iñaki.

—Qué, ¿no van a salir a entrenar? —demandó Susana—. Nosotras les vamos a echar porras.

—Lárguense, no sean ridículas. Qué porras ni qué porras. Las porras se echan en los partidos, no en los entrenamientos —dije yo.

—Mira, Tito. Todas nos pusimos suéteres rojos —dijo Dolores Zúñiga, la única niña que se habla de tú con el Diablo.

—Lárguense, Dolores Zúñiga —grité. Y cerramos la ventana.

Claro que no contábamos con que volvieran a tocar el timbre. Y la mamá de Iñaki acabó de hacernos la maldad. Las invitó a tomar té y galletas. Nosotros tuvimos que atrancar la puerta de la habitación con el ropero de Iñaki para sentirnos a salvo.

—Tú y tus ideas —le reclamé a Iñaki, mi amigo el genio.

—Podemos huir por la ventana. Sólo son cuatro metros.

No era tan mala idea. Una pierna rota era preferible a obedecer a la mamá de Iñaki, quien no dejaba de gritarnos que bajáramos a tomar té con las Rockets, como se habían autonombrado esas cinco ridículas que nos esperaban abajo. Pero en cuanto la señora dejó de llamarnos, decidimos esperar atrincherados a que se marcharan las amenazas vestidas de rojo. En ese momento, empezó a darme angustia.

Ya me imaginaba las burlas de los demás niños de los otros equipos. Contábamos con porristas y toda la cosa, en cambio, sólo éramos dos monos quienes formábamos el equipo. Teníamos que hacernos de más integrantes lo antes posible.

Pero no me imaginé cuán importante iba a volverse este deseo, puesto que al día siguiente, el director publicó la fecha de inicio de la Primera Copa de la Escuela Primaria Federal Héroes de la Nación. No nos quedaba mas que una semana para completar el equipo. Así que había que tomar medidas drásticas. Por ejemplo...

—¿Qué es eso? —me preguntó Iñaki, incrédulo.

—Pues nada. Un poco de estrategia.

Una cartulina había aparecido junto al pizarrón de los equipos a la hora del recreo. El mensaje decía, textualmente: "Refrescos gratis para todos los que se apunten en el mejor equipo, el de los Cohetes Rayados de la Colonia Portales".

—¿No ves que nos estás avergonzando? —dijo Iñaki, mi mejor amigo.

—Pues a lo mejor. Pero más vergüenza será que empiece el torneo y nosotros dos tengamos que jugar solos todos los partidos. Nos van a meter todos los goles del mundo y sin cansarse.

Naturalmente, Iñaki desaprobó mis métodos desde el principio. Pero cuando pasaron diez minutos del recreo y nadie se apuntaba, se unió a mis penosos intentos de reclutamiento. A los veinte minutos, ya habíamos prometido, además de los refrescos, pastelitos. Luego, helados. Al final del recreo, cuando ya estábamos verdaderamente desesperados, le dimos la vuelta a la cartulina y apunté: "Uniformes del Guadalajara para todos los que se anoten en el mejor equipo de todos: el de los Cohetes Rayados". Iñaki me regañó. Prometer refrescos era una cosa, pero prometer uniformes era otra muy distinta. ¿De dónde íbamos a sacarlos? Ni yo mismo lo sabía. Pero sí sabía que si ni así nadie se apuntaba, mejor sería dedicarnos al volibol. De todos modos, para esos momentos ya éramos la burla de toda la escuela. Hasta Susana me ofreció anotarse otra vez en el equipo. ¡Vaya humillación!

Claro que yo no me di cuenta hasta qué punto éramos la mofa general, sino cuando, al salir de clases, noté que algún chistoso había apuntado los nombres de Luisito Pichardo y la maestra Romero, la de cuarto, en nuestra hoja.

Y además, había cambiado el nombre de Cohetes Rayados por Capotitos Rayados. No había que ser un Einstein para darse cuenta de quiénes habían sido los chistosos. Tampoco había que ser un genio para darse cuenta de que, si apuntaban a Luisito Pichardo y a la maestra Romero (una señora que tiene como ciento cuarenta años) es porque nos consideraban los más malos del planeta. Digo... no tengo nada en contra de Luisito, pero hay que comprender que no se puede jugar futbol sin ver. Y la maestra Romero... bueno, para qué hablar.

Fue entonces, al mirar el pizarrón colmado de equipos, con sólo dos de ellos aún incompletos, cuando comprendí que tendríamos que hacer un sacrificio o estábamos fritos para ese torneo.

Se lo comenté a Iñaki, quien al principio no estuvo de acuerdo, pero cuando vio nuevamente nuestra patética hoja, comprendió que yo tenía razón.

No fue difícil dar con aquel que estábamos buscando. Lo difícil fue que nos atendiera. Después de llamarlo varias veces por su nombre, comprendimos que, si no le seguíamos el juego, jamás nos escucharía. No obstante, preferí tocarlo por la espalda a darle por su lado.

—Óliver —le dije.

—Cabiño —contestó con cara de pesado.

—Óliver.

—Cabiño.

—Óliver.

—Cabiño.

Iñaki me jaló de la camisa. Me estaba dando a entender que tendríamos que aflojar un poco o no conseguiríamos nada.

—Está bien, como quieras —dije, molesto—. Tenemos algo que proponerte.

—¿Qué?

Me dieron ganas de decir "nada". Nomás de verlo, caía gordo. Tan enano y tan pesado. Él y su mochila llena de calcomanías de los Pumas. Pero ni modo. Había que aflojar o todo estaría perdido.

—Queremos proponerte unir fuerzas —dije. Eso me costó un trabajo enorme, más que cuando mi mamá me obliga a pedirle perdón a Susana.

—¿Quieren que los deje entrar a los Pumas de la Universidad? —dijo Óliver.

En ese momento me imaginé aventando al enano de cabeza a una alcantarilla abierta que estaba ahí cerca. ¿Cómo podía haber imaginado eso?

—¿Estás loco? ¡Claro que no!

—Pues qué bueno, porque no los iba a dejar entrar. Mi equipo es de puros buenos, no caben los maletas, como ustedes.

—Óyeme, ¿a quién le dijiste maleta? —era Iñaki, jalándolo del suéter. Y por un momento pensé que, si no intervenía, arrojaría al enano de cabeza a la alcantarilla abierta que estaba ahí cerca. Me costó un trabajo intervenir, que no vean.

—Un momento, un momento —dije—. Seamos honestos, Óliver, o aceptas nuestra propuesta, o vas a quedarte fuera del torneo, igual que nosotros.

Se quedó pensando. En el fondo sabía que yo tenía razón. Sólo había una hoja más patética que la de los Cohetes Rayados, y era la de los Pumas de la Universidad. Además, a nuestro equipo se habían anotado aunque fuera un par de niñas; al de él, nadie. Y yo sabía que ni su mamá se anotaría con él aunque se lo suplicara, porque seguro que ni a su mamá le caía bien el enano sangrón.

—Pero con dos condiciones —dijo.

"Aquí vamos", pensé, seguramente pediría que le pasáramos nuestros domingos íntegros durante toda nuestra vida.

—Que yo sea el centro delantero —solicitó, antes de darnos tiempo de decir algo.

Ya iba a oponerme. Nomás porque sí. Pero me di cuenta de que era una petición que hasta nos convenía. Si Edson no se apuntaba en nuestro equipo, lo cual ni en nuestros más guajiros sueños podría ocurrir, ¿quién más podría ser el centro delantero? Óliver era el mejor de los tres, eso era seguro, por mucho que me doliera admitirlo. Así que me hice el benevolente y, después de pensarlo un rato, dije:

—Está bien. Para que veas que somos muy cuates.

—Y la segunda condición... es que nos llamemos Pumas de la Universidad.

—Óyeme, ¿qué tienes en contra del nombre de Cohetes Rayados? —dijo Iñaki, jalándolo otra vez del suéter.

Ahora sí no intervine. Prefería mil veces que fuéramos los Cohetes Rayados a los Pumas de la Universidad. Nomás porque no me daba la gana darle ese gusto al enano cabezón. Así que permití a Iñaki zarandearlo un rato. Mas no fue hasta que detuve a Óliver de los brazos e Iñaki empezó a arrancar las calcomanías de los Pumas de su mochila, que el enano admitió que Cohetes Rayados era un bonito nombre. (La verdad, no me hizo sentir nada bien el método de persuasión que utilizamos, porque Óliver gritaba como si le estuviéramos arrancando las uñas de los pies con unas pinzas de electricista, pero en ese momento pensé que no teníamos otro remedio, pues por nada del mundo quería ser Puma cuando ya me estaba acostumbrando a ser Cohete.)

El caso es que ya éramos tres en el equipo y eso me hizo sentir bastante mejor. Ni siquiera el hígado encebollado que me esperaba en la casa me descompuso el ánimo. Me lo terminé todo (algún día les contaré el secreto para poder comerlo sin devolverlo). Y no hay nada mejor que levantarte de la mesa cuando tu hermana y tu abuelo siguen ahí, mirando cómo su pedazo de carne se pone frío y tieso.

Eso fue magnífico. Porque dieron las cuatro de la tarde, hora en que sería nuestro primer entrenamiento, y Susana todavía no podía levantarse de la mesa, pues aún no terminaba (mi mamá puede ser la tirana más despiadada para obligarnos a terminar toda la comida; ni aunque finjas un desmayo te permite dejar la mesa si no has limpiado el plato). Eso significaba que tal vez podríamos entrenar sin sufrir la molestia de las porristas.

No obstante, ahí estaban las otras cuatro, afuera de mi casa, esperando a Susana.

—¿Y Susana? ¿No va a salir? —preguntó Lulú.

—Dijo que la esperen, que no tarda —dije, con mi mejor sonrisa maquiavélica (yo sabía que Susana tardaría todavía un largo, largo rato).

—Tito, ya inventé una porra. ¿Quieres oírla? —dijo Dolores Zúñiga, mostrando su negra y chimuela dentadura.

Pero yo no le hice caso. Corrí a la casa de Iñaki y lo saqué casi a la fuerza, porque ya íbamos retrasados y no quería que el cabezón de Óliver pensara que somos unos indisciplinados. Ni siquiera le di chance de cambiarse el uniforme de la escuela. Corrimos al parque y ahí, efectivamente, ya estaba Óliver esperándonos, con su uniforme de los Pumas de la Universidad.

En cuanto llegamos al pasamanos donde quedamos de vernos, miró su reloj.

—Llegan tarde. Hay que tener disciplina si queremos ser los mejores.

—No seas exagerado. Por unos minutos, Óliver.

—Cabiño.

—Óliver.

—Cabiño.

—Ya, como sea.

Era maravilloso. Los Cherokees no estaban por ningún lado. Hasta el sol brillaba con esplendor. Así que yo, como capitán del equipo, me di a la tarea de organizar el entrenamiento. Les mostré, rayando en la tierrita del suelo con una vara, cómo quería que practicáramos pases y luego tiros de media distancia; luego practicaríamos remates de cabeza y saques de banda. Me sentía orgulloso de mi estrategia. Entonces, Óliver levantó la mano.

—Tengo una pregunta, señor capitán —dijo. No me gustó su tonito cuando dijo "capitán".

—¿Qué es lo que no te quedó claro, eh Óliver? —para que se le quitara, yo usé el mismo tonito cuando dije "Óliver".

—¿Cómo quieres que entrenemos sin balón, señor capitán?

Era cierto. Ninguno llevaba balón.

—¿Por qué no trajiste tu balón, Óliver?

—Porque no se me dio la gana. Es mío. Y no quiero que se me pierda mientras entrenamos. Pon el tuyo, capitán.

Miré a Iñaki. ¡Vaya predicamento!

—Ve por el balón, Iñaki —dije.

—¿Cuál balón? ¿La pelota de Mickey Mouse de tu hermano?

—Pues ni modo. Si no tenemos otra, ni modo.

—¿Qué? ¿Una pelota de Mickey Mouse? —intervino Óliver—. ¿Qué clase de entrenamiento es éste?

—¡Ay!, ya cállate. Tú tienes la culpa por no traer tu balón, Óliver.

—Cabiño.

—Óliver.

—Cabiño.

—Bueno, ya. Yo voy por la pelota.

Tuve que ir porque Óliver e Iñaki comenzaron a decirse de cosas y a empùjarse. Lo único malo de volver a mi casa, era tener que pasar otra vez frente a las líneas enemigas. Y en efecto, ahí seguían las porristas, practicando unas maromas horribles que hacían que se les vieran los calzones. Qué espectáculo tan desagradable. Pero tuve suerte, hasta eso. Pude entrar corriendo y salir corriendo. No sé qué alcanzó todavía a decirme Dolores Zúñiga (algún conjuro maléfico o algo así, creo), aunque yo ni la escuché. Salí como de rayo y volví al parque a tiempo para impedir que Iñaki y Óliver se arrancaran los cabellos.

—¡Alto, equipo! ¡Es hora de entrenar! Dejen los juegos para después.

No hicieron caso a la primera, y tuve que separarlos. Y justo cuando empezaba a reorganizar el entrenamiento en mi mente, sentí un par de manos posarse sobre mis hombros.

—Miren quién está aquí —dijo Rubén.

—Tito Tito Capotito —respondió Tony.

Ya para qué les sigo contando. No hubo entrenamiento. Óliver se cansó de hacer dominadas con la pelota de Hugo y terminó por irse a su casa; Iñaki también se hartó de jugar a las naves con un par de tronquitos. Para cuando los Cherokees me dejaron en paz, ya empezaba a oscurecer. Todavía estuvieron platicando un rato sentados encima de mí. Y si creen que eso fue una tortura, no lo fue tanto como tener que oírlos hablar entre ellos. Sólo cuentan las tontas hazañas de su tonto equipo de tonto futbol americano. No saben hablar de otra cosa. Y creo que si no hubieran terminado discutiendo y empujándose entre ellos, yo seguiría ahí tumbado en el pasto, con sus horribles traseros encima de mí. Me sentí tan mal que estaba seguro, ahora sí, de que el corazón me dolía, y que no tardaría en dejar de funcionar.

Cuando volví a la casa, también las porristas habían claudicado. Mi hermana seguía sentada a la mesa, y no dejaba de llorar. Y tan mal me sentía del corazón, que no se me dio la gana burlarme de ella. El abuelo también seguía contemplando su plato, al que ya le había puesto cátsup y otros menjurjes similares, pero ni así le entraba. Y mi mamá leía un libro bien gordo frente a ellos, como hacen los carceleros aburridos.

Brinqué a mi hermano Hugo, que jugaba en el suelo a que era una alfombra y me fui a mi cuarto, triste y abatido.

89

Querido Tigre Quezada:

Te escribo para contarte que las cosas no van tan bien como esperábamos. Fíjate que hemos tenido algunos problemas para entrenar porque resulta que el campo que usamos está ocupado por unos maleantes. Sí. Son unos delincuentes que acaban de salir de la cárcel y usan cuchillos y granadas de mano. Y creo que hace poco se comieron a un niño de primero. Y estaba vivo.

Pero bueno, te escribo porque se me ocurrió preguntarte qué harías tú en mi caso. Ya sé que tú nunca dejarías que esos tipejos se salieran con la suya, pero tampoco se trata de arriesgar el pellejo, ¿no? ¿Qué tal si me parten en dos de un navajazo y luego se reparten mis tripas entre ellos?

En fin. No sé ni para qué te lo pregunto si ya sé la respuesta. Me vas a decir que no me deje y que si debo usar mi famosa llave china, lo haga. Que tengo que enfrentarlos y no ser un tonto llorón. Me vas a decir que haga lo que hacen los héroes como tú, ¿verdad? Creo que tienes razón. Así que ya sé qué hacer mañana mismo para que podamos seguir entrenando.

Gracias por tus consejos. Te mantendré informado.

Con cariño,

Tito

Había que tener un chorro de valor para hacer lo que hice la mañana del día siguiente. Me acuerdo que todavía me estaba peinando y hablando con mi imagen del espejo, cuando mi papá me gritó desde afuera:

—¡Tito! ¡Apúrate o vas a llegar tarde a la escuela!

El corazón me palpitaba bajo el pecho, y me miré con coraje mientras intentaba hacerme la raya en el cabello.

—¿Eres un héroe o eres un tonto llorón?

Era un héroe, eso estaba decidido. Fui a mi clóset y saqué de mi cochinito la última esperanza de tener un Tango algún día. Era todo el dinero que me quedaba, y tuve que echar mano de todo mi valor para tomarlo. Cuando salí de mi cuarto, todavía estaba gruñendo. Grrrr, grrrr, grrrr, igual que el Tigre

Quezada en una situación como la mía. Mi mamá me interceptó antes de salir para la escuela.

—¡Ay, Tito!, ¿qué peinados son ésos?

—Grrr, grrr, grrr.

—No te hagas el chistoso y ven acá, que te voy a pasar un limón por la cabezota.

Pero yo era un héroe. Y no había nada más que agregar. Todavía me fui gruñendo a la escuela, a pesar de que Iñaki nomás sacudía sus pelos güeros y no dejaba de decir que yo estaba loco de la cabeza.

En cuanto entramos al salón, me apresuré a hacer lo que tenía que hacer, antes de que llegara la maestra Lucía.

—Olariñárritu, tengo algo que proponerte.

Él ni siquiera levantó la vista. Estaba muy entretenido revisando una revista que se llamaba *Guitarra fácil*, y que traía varias canciones de los Beatles.

—Quiero que seas mi guardaespaldas —continué.

—...

—No hagas esa cara, pienso pagarte.

—...

—Mira, son todos mis ahorros para comprarme un Tango. Pero ya no lo quiero. Prefiero dártelos para que me ayudes.

—...

—Es muy fácil. Nada más tienes que andar conmigo para todos lados.

—...

—Bueno, si no quieres a todos lados, por lo menos acompáñame al Parque de los Venados en las tardes para poder entrenar con mi equipo para el torneo. ¿Qué dices?

No dijo nada, claro está. Me miró como si se me hubiera zafado un tornillo, detrás de sus feas gafas de armazón grueso. Sin embargo, como sí aceptó el dinero y se lo guardó en la bolsa trasera del pantalón, yo estaba seguro de que el asunto estaba resuelto. Hasta me pude imaginar a mi mamá diciendo: "Tito, estoy orgullosa de ti".

Volví a mi lugar apenas a tiempo para saludar a la maestra Lucía (suspiro), que en ese momento entraba al salón. Una gran sonrisa me iluminaba la cara.

Y mi felicidad fue mayor cuando Iñaki y yo hicimos un descubrimiento en el recreo: nuestro anuncio de uniformes gratis del Guadalajara había surtido efecto. Dos nombres más aparecían en nuestra hoja. Claro que nuestra alegría no fue tan completa cuando nos dimos cuenta de quiénes se habían anotado.

—José Luis Castrejón —dije yo.

—El Burbuja —confirmó Iñaki.

Pero eso no era lo peor. Había que fijarse en el otro nombre.

—Otilio Sánchez —dije.

—¡El Hombre Nuclear! —confirmamos al unísono.

Sí. Todos lo conocíamos como el Hombre Nuclear. Y como casi todos los apodos del mundo, éste era más una burla que un homenaje. Todos le decían el Hombre Nuclear porque cuando corría, lo hacía de una manera tan chistosa, que todos empezaban a hacer el ruidito que le ponen al Hombre Nuclear en la tele cuando usa sus piernas biónicas.

A Otilio siempre le pasaba lo mismo en la clase de deportes: todos se burlaban de él a la hora en que empezaba a correr. Y la maestra Lucía siempre terminaba callando las carcajadotas de todo el mundo cuando Otilio corría y todos hacían el ruidito "tututututuuuu, tutututututuuuu".

Era una maldición que el Hombre Nuclear se hubiera apuntado con nosotros. Pero nuestra hoja se veía tan bonita casi completa, que preferí no echarlo a perder. Aunque Iñaki no pensaba igual.

—No puede ser. Con el Hombre Nuclear en nuestro equipo, va a ser como jugar con un hombre menos.

—No seas así. Puede ayudar en algo.

—Sí. A lo mejor desarmamos al equipo contrario provocándole un ataque de risa.

Al final, Iñaki tenía razón. El Hombre Nuclear corría como si tuviera las rodillas pegadas una con la otra. Era imposible no reírse de él aunque nadie hiciera el sonidito. Pero no quise pensar más en eso. Ya éramos cinco en el equipo y eso me hacía sentir más que bien.

—Vente. Vamos a darle la bienvenida a los nuevos integrantes. Iñaki sacudió sus pelos güeros y me siguió por el patio. Dimos muy fácil con el Burbuja porque su cabeza sobresale en cualquier multitud.

—Burbuja, bienvenido a los Cohetes Rayados. No te vas a arrepentir. Te lo dice tu capitán —afirmé, muy orgulloso, y estreché su grande y rechoncha mano.

—¿Qué hay de mi uniforme? —preguntó él—. Soy talla cuarenta.

—Claro, tu uniforme. No te preocupes. Lo tendrás. Los entrenamientos son en el Parque de los Venados a las cuatro de la tarde. No faltes.

—Cuarenta. No lo olvides.

Y luego fuimos con nuestro otro integrante. Estaba comiéndose su lunch, cuando lo encontramos. Hasta me dio un poco de pena. Es muy flaco y sus orejas parecen las de Dumbo. Y habla un poco chistoso porque es de Monterrey. Pero también era uno de los Cohetes Rayados y nada más por eso merecía respeto.

—Hombre Nu.... eh... digo, Otilio. Bienvenido a los Cohetes Rayados —lo saludé, estrechándole la mano.

—Bueno, bueno... nada más quiero que sepan que lo hago por sacar diez en deportes. No creo poder ayudar mucho. Ya saben que no soy muy bueno jugando futbol.

—Eso no importa —le dije—. Con nosotros vas a ser el mejor.

Iñaki sacudió otra vez sus pelos güeros y se marchó a cambiar estampas con unos niños de cuarto.

—Los entrenamientos son en el Parque de los Ve... —comencé a decir cuando él me interrumpió.

—Tito... nada más quiero pedirles que no se burlen mucho cuando corra.

—Claro que no, Otilio. Somos equipo, ¿recuerdas?

Otilio sonrió. Y estoy seguro de que mi mamá, la maestra Lucía y el Tigre Quezada habrían estado muy orgullosos si me hubieran oído decir eso.

Ahí estábamos. Eran las cuatro de la tarde y los cinco jugadores de los Cohetes Rayados de la Colonia Portales estábamos listos para nuestro primer entrenamiento. Todo hubiera sido perfecto (hasta Óliver iba a prestar su balón) de no ser por...

¡Tocinos, frijoles y huevos estrellados!
¡Tocinos, frijoles y huevos estrellados!
¡Arriba! ¡Arriba! ¡Los Cohetes Rayados!

Sí... de no ser por la porra del equipo.

—¿No se les ocurrió otra cosa más mala? —dijo Óliver.

—Cállate, pigmeo —contestó Susana—. A ti ni quién te eche porras. Las porras son para Iñaki.

—Y para Tito —dijo Dolores Zúñiga, con su verruga en la nariz y sus pelos de estropajo.

Pero yo estaba en otra cosa. Planeando la estrategia de los entrenamientos. Y llamé a todos los del equipo para que me pusieran atención. Tomé una vara y dibujé un campo chiquito en la tierra para mostrar las posiciones.

—Bueno. Pues vamos a jugar así: Burbuja, serás el portero. Hombre Nuc... eh... digo, Otilio, a ti te toca ser defensa lateral derecho. Tú, Iñaki, el izquierdo. Tú, Óliver...

—Cabiño.

—Como sea. Tú serás el centro delantero. Y yo, seré el medio de contención.

—Mejor tú serás puesto en órbita.

—¿Eh? ¿Quién dijo eso?

La verdad estaba tan contento de que ya tenía equipo, que ni me acordaba. Los Cherokees estaban justo detrás de nosotros. Yo no podía creer mi mala suerte. Tendría que aguantar la humillación ante mis propios compañeros de equipo. Ya ni me acordaba de que Olariñárritu tenía todos mis ahorros y que no se había presentado a cumplir su parte del trato; me dieron ganas de tenerlo enfrente, porque juro que, aunque él supiera artes marciales, ya le habría aplicado mi famosa llave china.

Pero eso no fue lo peor. Tampoco que Fito me alzara en vilo y me empezara a dar vueltas. Lo peor vino después.

—Déjenlo o no respondo.

Era Marita, la niña de primer grado. No sé cómo se atrevió a decir eso si con trabajos se puede ver sin la ayuda de un microscopio. Pero lo dijo. Y no sólo aumentó mi humillación, sino que provocó la risa de todos los Cherokees. Hasta Carlos Alberto, que no suele participar de las graciosadas de sus compañeros de americano, se rio.

—A ver, ¿qué vas a hacer al respecto? —dijo Rubén, poniéndose al alcance de la niña.

Hasta a mí me dolió. La niña le propinó tal patada en la espinilla, que todos dejamos salir un quejido involuntario. ¡Ouch!, dijeron varios. Y no quiero ni decirles cómo se puso Rubén. En cuanto se repuso de la patada, se convirtió en una fiera. Hasta espuma le salió de la boca y los ojos se le pusieron rojos. Y yo, en manos de Fito, creí que verdaderamente tenía los días de mi vida contados. Hasta deseé que mi corazón hiciera ¡cuaz! de una buena vez, antes de que mi captor me arrojara a las manos de Rubén y éste me arrancara la garganta de una mordida. Me acuerdo que hasta volteé a ver a Carlos Alberto, a ver si hacía algo por mí, porque todos los de mi equipo ya se habían echado a correr y hasta las niñas estaban subidas en la parte alta de una resbaladilla. Pero Carlos Alberto no iba a hacer nada por mí, eso se adivinaba; aunque sí bajó la mirada, como apenado.

Me puse a recitar todas las oraciones que todavía recordaba del catecismo por si moría en ese instante, cuando oí una voz que me devolvió el alma al cuerpo.

—Bájalo, Fito.

Era la voz de Luisito Pichardo. ¿Y quién creen que lo acompañaba?

—Ya oíste. Que lo bajes.

Era Olariñárritu con todo y su guitarra. Y cuando habló lo hizo con tal firmeza, que hasta a mí me dio miedo que la emprendiera a karatazos en contra de los Cherokees y los dejara inválidos para siempre. Fito me puso en el suelo al instante. Y Rubén dejó de echar humo por las orejas. Ni siquiera agregaron nada. Enfrentaron miradas con Olariñárritu y, después de un rato, se dieron la vuelta.

—Vámonos —dijo Tony—. Ya me aburrí de estar en este lado del parque.

—Sí. Yo también —dijo Rubén.

Y se fueron. Me sentí tan agradecido con Olariñárritu que me dieron ganas de abrazarlo. Pero él ya no agregó nada. Tomó de la mano a Luisito y se lo llevó a sentar a unos columpios.

—Qué bueno que viniste, Luisito —dije, en mi entusiasmo de saberme vivo y en una sola pieza.

—Es que los jueves Olariñárritu me enseña a tocar guitarra. Y como me contó que iba a venir para acá, le dije que yo lo acompañaba a ver el entrenamiento. ¡Ja, ja! ¿Oíste lo que dije, Tito? Dije, "a ver" el entrenamiento. ¡Ja, ja, ja!

Ese Luisito es a todo dar. Me dio un gusto tremendo que nos acompañara, sobre todo porque me di cuenta de que tiene un oído increíble; con sólo levantar el rostro, podía saber por nuestros gritos lo que estaba pasando en el entrenamiento. Y hasta se daba el lujo de opinar. ¿Ustedes creen? No dejaba de decir cosas como: "Échale ganas, Burbuja" o "Corre más aprisa, Tito". Ese Luisito es un tipazo.

Aunque no crean que por eso la práctica fue buena. Todo lo contrario. Ni siquiera por el entusiasmo de Luisito, ni por las porras de las Rockets, ni aun por las canciones de los Beatles que Olariñárritu se aventó a tocar, mostramos algo de talento. La verdad es que fuimos todo un fiasco. El único no tan malo fue Óliver; a los demás, en cambio, parece que nos habían movido la portería de lugar porque no atinamos ni un solo tiro. Y eso que el Burbuja no para ni un camión; Óliver le estuvo metiendo más goles de los que jamás ha metido en toda su vida, y eso porque era el único que chutaba en dirección correcta.

De todas formas, me sentía bien. A pesar de que el Hombre Nuclear nunca quiso correr por temor a las burlas, a pesar de que Iñaki se la pasaba haciendo ruidos de nave espacial, a pesar de que Óliver nunca me pasó un balón porque nunca le dije Cabiño, y a pesar de que el Burbuja no me dejó de molestar con lo de su uniforme, me sentía contento. A fin de cuentas, como dijo Luisito Pichardo: para eso son los entrenamientos, para mejorar. Cuando terminamos y cada quien se fue a su casa, yo me sentía tan contento, que en lugar de ver la tele, me puse a platicar de futbol. Claro, con quién va a ser.

—Abuelo, ¿qué crees? Hoy estuve practicando mis tiros. Y creo que cada vez me salen menos chuecos, ¿cómo ves?

—Yo también tuve alguna vez un rifle con la mira chueca. Pero de todas maneras, aniquilaba a bastantes soldados.

—¿No será culpa de mis tacos? ¿Cómo los ves?

—Sólo los cobardes le echan la culpa a sus fusiles. Si te falla la pistola, entonces a golpes. Y si te fallan las manos, entonces a patadas. Y si te fallan los pies, a cabezazos. Y si te falla la cabeza, todavía les puedes escupir.

Pero yo ya tenía los ojos y la mente en uno de los trofeos de mi abuelo, que obtuvo como el jugador más valioso de la temporada. Y a un lado, estaban los zapatos de futbol con los que ganó más de cinco copas. Eran las cosas más viejas y feas del mundo: todos gastados y con las agujetas raídas. No obstante, me daba cuenta de que, comparando esos zapatos con los míos, había una enorme diferencia. Aunque esos estaban horribles, tenían algo que los hacía mucho mejores. Y precisamente eso, tan difícil de decir con palabras, era lo que seguramente me faltaba para ser un héroe. No. Mi problema no eran mis tacos, sino eso que tenían los tacos del abuelo y que les faltaba a los míos.

—Abuelo, cuéntame por qué usaste esos zapatos por cinco temporadas.

—Zzzzzzzzzz... zzzzzzzz...

Lástima. Mi abuelo es capaz de quedarse dormido en los lugares más increíbles y en las posturas más incómodas. Esta vez, mientras se sonaba la nariz. ¿Pueden imaginarlo? Bueno... no importa. De todos modos, no esperaba obtener una respuesta sensata.

Querido Tigre Quezada:

Hoy tuvimos un entrenamiento súper. La verdad no me importa que todavía no completemos los seis jugadores porque todos le echamos muchísimas ganas. Me gustaría mucho que nos vieras entrenar, seguro que hasta podrías darnos algunos consejos para ganar. Porque vamos a ganar, ¿eh?

Bueno, pasando a otra cosa... voy a tener que pedirte un favor enorme. Sí, tan enorme que necesito que pienses en lo más grande que hayas hecho por alguien y lo multipliques por diez y luego lo eleves a la décima potencia. ¿Ya? Se trata de lo siguiente: quiero ver si nos puedes conseguir (todo lo puedes, eres el Tigre Quezada), unos uniformes de las Chivas para nuestro equipo. ¿Verdad que sí?

¡Claro! Yo sabía que no me ibas a defraudar. Por favor, manda los uniformes a mi dirección, que está en el sobre. Te apunto las tallas atrás de esta hoja.

Gracias y acuérdate de que tienes que entregar la copa al final del torneo.

Con cariño,
Tito

El buen humor me duró hasta el otro día, y todavía estaba con Iñaki comentando la práctica del día anterior en los ratitos que podía durante la clase, cuando la maestra Lucía (suspiro) dio un aviso que me cayó, igual que dice mi mamá, como balde de agua fría.

—Niños —dijo, muy seria—, tengo una noticia que darles.

Luego, tomó aire. Se veía que no le resultaba fácil. Todo el salón guardó silencio.

—Es algo un poco doloroso para mí... pero así es la vida.

En ese momento pensé: "Ya se enteró. Ya se enteró de que voy a morir y no lo puede soportar. No puede soportar que la deje sola en el mundo". Me odié por no habérselo dicho yo mismo para poder aliviar un poco su pena. Pensé que en ese momento daría el aviso a todo el salón. Casi podía oír a los Cherokees llorar y pedirme perdón por haberse portado tan malvados conmigo. Casi podía ver cómo las niñas borraban el nombre de Carlos Alberto de la última hoja de sus cuadernos y anotaban el mío. Pero la maestra jaló aire y continuó.

—Me voy a Zurich a vivir.

¿Qué? ¿Zurich? ¿Qué es eso? ¿Otro planeta o qué?

—Así que no voy a poder estar con ustedes el año que entra. Lo siento mucho. De veras lo siento muchísimo.

Se veía que en verdad le dolía. Se veía que no quería irse. Algo o alguien la estaba obligando a irse a *Zuchir,* o lo que fuera. Seguro que la estaban secuestrando. Me sentí lleno de rabia. Y levanté la mano.

—¿Sí, Tito?

—Maestra, yo la quiero. Y voy a luchar por usted hasta el último día. No voy a dejar que se la lleven lejos a otro planeta. Y no me importa que todos se rían de mí. Yo la quiero. Y por eso...

Bueno... no. En realidad no dije eso, sino más bien:

—Maestra, ¿cuándo se va?

—Cuando termine el curso.

¡Vaya un idiota! Yo en realidad quería preguntarle si la estaban secuestrando, porque se veía que le dolía mucho tener que irse. Y eso a mí no me gustaba. De cualquier modo, a la hora del recreo, justo cuando sonó la campana y los niños salieron en estampida del salón, yo me quedé un poco más. Cuando sólo estábamos nosotros, la maestra y yo, me acerqué a su escritorio mientras ella revisaba algunas tareas.

—Maestra Lucía...

Levantó la cara y me sonrió. Juro que me sonrió.

—Tito, contigo quería hablar.

—Eh... ¿conmigo?

—Sí, Tito. Quería decirte que unos extraterrestres se llevaron a mi mamá. Y yo tengo que ir al planeta Zurich a rescatarla. ¿Podrías acompañarme en esta peligrosa misión?

—Claro que sí. Cuente conmigo.

Bueno... ya, ya. Okey. En realidad eso no fue lo que pasó. Más bien, ella dijo:

—El profesor Colina me pidió la lista de los que van a estar en el torneo. Y vi que en tu equipo sólo hay cinco integrantes. Les falta uno.

—Sí, maestra. Nos falta uno. Nadie más se quiso apuntar.

—¿Y qué van a hacer?

—Jugar nosotros cinco nada más. Ni modo.

Me acarició el cabello. Lo juro. Y dijo:

—Eso es muy valiente.

Lo consiguió de nuevo. Me convirtió en el mayor lelo de toda la historia. Me quedé petrificado y empecé a flotar. Juro que empecé a flotar.

—Tito. Tito. ¡Tito!

—Perdón. Mande.

—¿Qué me querías preguntar?

—Eh... ya nada.

Se me había olvidado. Salí del salón flotando, tratando de no chocar con el techo. Ya ni me acordaba que pensaba preguntarle a la maestra si quería irse o no. Porque si no quería irse, pensaba sugerirle que ya veríamos el modo de traer a su mamá de Zurich en una nave de la NASA o de los rusos, daba igual.

Pero entonces ocurrió el milagro. Y yo volví al suelo de sopetón.

Edson (¡guau!) estaba revisando el pizarrón de los equipos del torneo. Era un milagro; sobre todo, porque si pensaba inscribirse, sólo había un lugar disponible. Ustedes saben cuál.

Me puse tan nervioso que me oculté de su vista, detrás de un bote de basura, porque todavía estaba indeciso y yo no quería espantarlo diciendo de pronto "Hola, Edson, qué tal esos goles". Crucé los dedos de ambas manos y ambos pies. Pero Edson sólo miraba el pizarrón. Como sentí que eso era malo para mi corazón, pensé que lo mejor sería salir corriendo de ahí e irme al patio.

Y lo hice. Pasé detrás de Edson como una ráfaga en dirección al patio. Estoy seguro de que no me vio. Ya en el patio no pude más. No pude más. Ahí cerquita estaba Óliver y lo llamé.

—Óliver.

—Cabiño.

—Ven. Quiero que veas algo.

Lo llevé al otro extremo del pasillo en el que está el pizarrón. Nos ocultamos detrás de otro bote de basura. Edson seguía ahí, estudiando las hojas.

—¡No me digas que se va a apuntar en nuestro equipo!

—No lo sé.

—¡Cómo que no lo sabes! —dijo el enano—. Pues hay que averiguarlo.

—¿Estás loco? —tuve que detenerlo—. Tú sabes cómo es Edson. Si nos acercamos, lo vamos a espantar y no se va a animar a apuntarse.

Óliver pensó un rato.

—¿Y si no se apunta? —dijo.

—Entonces nos suicidamos.

Ahí estuvimos, todo el recreo, sudando la gota gorda, cruzando los dedos, rezándoles a todos los santos, pero Edson no sacaba una pluma para anotarse. Al final, cuando sonó la campana, Óliver y yo estábamos a punto de sufrir un colapso. Yo sentía que, en verdad, me daba el soponcio. Edson se fue a su salón y nosotros a los nuestros. Pero al pasar frente al pizarrón, creí que me moría. Nunca vimos que Edson se anotara porque... ¡ya se había anotado!

Ahí estaba. En el último renglón de la hoja de los Cohetes Rayados: Edson Guimaraes.

Entre eso y que la maestra Lucía (suspiro) me había dicho que para ella, yo era el más valiente de los héroes (o algo así), estuve todo el resto de la clase haciendo dibujitos en mi cuaderno, planeando estrategias, conquistando todas las copas de futbol del mundo. No podía esperar el momento en que sonara la campana de fin de clases. Y cuando por fin sonó, ¿quién creen que en sólo cuatro segundos y tres décimas ya estaba en la puerta del salón de los de sexto, esperando a que salieran?

Cuando lo vi venir, el corazón me latió a cien mil por hora.

—Hola, Edson.

—Hola.

Edson (¡guau!) me había hablado. ¡Guau! Y yo era su capitán. Si en ese momento el corazón me hubiera hecho ¡cuaz!, hubiera muerto feliz, lo juro.

—Quiero darte la bienvenida a nuestro equipo. No te vas a arrepentir. Los entrenamientos son a las cuatro de la tarde en el Parque de los Venados.

—Mmmm... qué crees, que a esa hora no puedo. Voy a una clase por las tardes.

—No importa. Je, je. Claro que no importa. Tú puedes faltar. Je, je. A fin de cuentas, los entrenamientos son para mejorar. Y tú... pues ya es imposible que mejores más, ¿verdad? Je, je. Bueno. Me voy. Nos estamos viendo. Ah, perdón, se me olvidaba, ¿qué talla eres?

Me puse nervioso. Me daba miedo que por cualquier tontería que yo dijera, Edson se arrepintiera.

Ahora sí que teníamos el triunfo del torneo en nuestra bolsa y no quería echarlo a perder. Me fui corriendo a casa, sin esperar a Iñaki, a Susana ni a nadie, porque sentía que iba a reventar de felicidad. Además, quería darles la noticia a todos durante la práctica. Al mismo tiempo me moría por ver las caras de todos.

Y cuando pasé por Iñaki a su casa en la tarde, él lo notó.

—¿Qué te pasa, Tito? ¿Por qué estás tan sonriente? No me digas que ya no te vas a morir porque ya no pienso regresarte tus cosas.

—No. Es otra cosa.

Al llegar al parque, todos los integrantes de los Cohetes Rayados, incluso la porra, Luisito Pichardo y la música ambiental de los Beatles, di la noticia con el pecho henchido.

—Edson Guimaraes es uno de los Cohetes Rayados de la Portales.

Hubo un gran silencio, seguido por toda clase de comentarios:

—¿Quién es Edson Guimaraes? —preguntaron las niñas.

—¿Cuánto le pagaste? —dijo Iñaki.

—Pero yo sigo siendo el centro delantero —advirtió Óliver.

—¿Y cuándo llegan los uniformes? —me interrogó el Burbuja.

—¿Y si mejor me quedo en la banca? —preguntó el Hombre Nuclear.

—¿Es más bueno que tú, Tito? —dijo Dolores Zúñiga, rascándose los piojos.

—¡Arriba los Cohetes Rayados! —exclamó Luisito Pichardo.

Dicho y hecho. Edson nunca asistió a los entrenamientos. Y qué bueno. Porque hubiera sido muy vergonzoso que se diera cuenta de la clase de equipo en el cual estaba. Aunque algunos de nosotros ya no éramos tan malos (el Burbuja descubrió que lo mejor era parar los balones con las manos y no con la panza, Iñaki ya no hacía ruidos de nave espacial y yo cada vez chutaba mejor), y otros seguían en las mismas (el Hombre Nuclear de plano no se animaba a correr), el equipo era el mismo de siempre. Pero nos mantenía el ánimo en alto saber que éramos seis y que teníamos al mejor jugador de toda la escuela.

En los recreos nos juntábamos con Edson a hablar de futbol y a discutir el calendario del torneo, que el profesor Colina ya había colocado a un lado de las hojas de los equipos. El primer equipo contra el que jugaríamos era, como dice mi mamá, pan comido: los Ángeles de Charlie, aquel equipo del cual les platiqué, formado por puras niñas. Luego iríamos contra los Kiss, unos chavos de cuarto grado que se pusieron así por el grupo de rock. Y luego, el tercer partido sería contra los Archies, un equipo que es un relajo: está formado por niños y niñas de tercero, cuarto y quinto.

Aunque, en realidad, los más entusiastas éramos Óliver y yo, ninguno de los muchachos faltó a los entrenamientos. Iñaki a veces llevaba algún mono de *La guerra de las galaxias*, pero de todos modos iba a practicar. Y tanto Luisito Pichardo como Olariñárritu también se volvieron parte importante de las prácticas porque el primero siempre nos apoyaba mucho con sus porras, y el segundo nos animaba con sus canciones.

Así que llegó el gran día. El día de nuestro primer partido. Los encuentros se llevarían a cabo los viernes en las últimas horas de clase, para lo cual el profesor Colina había dispuesto que no volveríamos al salón después del recreo, sino que todos estábamos obligados a participar, ya fuera jugando o mirando desde las gradas. Serían partidos de media hora, con dos tiempos de quince minutos cada uno. Y aunque en la escuela no hay una cancha propiamente hecha para jugar futbol, sí teníamos un gran patio de tierra en el que no sería difícil pintar las líneas divisorias del campo.

La verdad es que el profesor Colina se lució. Mandó hacer unas porterías chiquitas bien padres, con red y toda la cosa. Mandó poner unas gradas de metal en las que cabían casi todos los niños de la escuela (tampoco somos muchos). Y se mandó hacer un uniforme de árbitro como el de los que salen en la tele. Todo negro.

Y nos presentamos a nuestro primer partido.

Empezamos con el pie izquierdo, porque no llevábamos uniformes. Hasta las dizque Rockets iban todas del mismo color. En cambio nosotros...

—A ver, Mendiolea... ¿por qué no vienen uniformados? —preguntó el profesor Colina, mientras revisaba sus tarjetas, se colgaba su silbato, se ajustaba las calcetas, antes de dar inicio al Primer Torneo de Futbol de la Escuela Primaria Federal Héroes de la Nación.

Era cierto. Y no supe qué responder. De todos los equipos, nosotros éramos los más dispares. Yo iba vestido con mi uniforme de las Chivas, Óliver llevaba el de los Pumas y los demás, como Dios les dio a entender: el Hombre Nuclear iba todo de blanco, el Burbuja, con una playera rayada, de ésas que se usan en la playa, Iñaki con una playera de Luke Skywalker y Edson... bueno, Edson traía una playera sin mangas. Al menos todos llevábamos tacos y pantalones cortos.

—¿Cuándo nos entregan nuestros uniformes, eh Tito?

—No sé, Burbuja. Cállate.

De cualquier modo, el torneo estaba a punto de empezar. Todos los equipos estaban formados en la cancha. Y los Cohetes Rayados éramos los únicos que parecíamos confeti. Hasta los Cherokees llevaban uniforme. ¡Vaya comienzo!

El profesor Colina tomó el micrófono de los Honores a la Bandera y después de aburrirnos con sus recuerdos de cuando era niño y jugaba con una pelota que a cada rato se le ponchaba, dio inicio al torneo. Ese primer viernes todos jugaríamos un partido, cuando menos. Y nosotros, claro, íbamos contra los Ángeles de Charlie.

Me sentía entusiasmado. La maestra Lucía (suspiro) me había saludado un par de veces desde las gradas. Y nosotros, estaba segurísimo, ganaríamos ese primer partido; por goliza, además, porque contábamos con nuestra arma secreta: Edson, e íbamos contra un equipo de puras niñas. Pan comido. Lo único que no me gustaba era que Edson estaba más nervioso que el Hombre Nuclear; hasta se estaba comiendo las uñas.

—¿Todo bien, campeón? —le pregunté.

—Claro —asintió. No dejaba de limpiarse el sudor de las manos en su camiseta.

Y llegó nuestro turno. Las Rockets se encargaron de hacérnoslo saber:

—¿Quién vuela más alto que Supermán? ¿Quién vuela más rápido que un avión? ¿Quién llega hasta las órbitas siderales? ¡Los Cohetes Rayados de la Colonia Portales!

—¿No pudieron pensar en algo peor? —preguntó Iñaki mientras entrábamos en la cancha.

Estábamos convocados. La maestra Rosario, de segundo, había voceado nuestros nombres y también el de los Ángeles de Charlie. Y ambos equipos entramos a la cancha. Ellas iban de color azul pastel. Nosotros, como bolsa de colación.

—¡Caray! ¿Por qué no vienen uniformados, Mendiolea? —volvió a preguntar el profesor Colina, aunque nunca dejó de sonreír.

—Sí, ¿por qué? —gritó el Burbuja desde la portería.

—Ya cállate, Burbuja —le grité.

—Bueno, qué caray. Vamos a empezar —dijo el profesor Colina.

Todos en posiciones. Como ganamos el volado, pedí que nosotros tocáramos el balón antes que ellas. Y en cuanto el profesor Colina sopló su silbato, comenzó nuestro infierno.

Apenas estaba tocando el balón, cuando una de las niñas ya me lo había quitado para irse directamente contra el Burbuja. Lo acribilló con un balonazo que fue a dar contra la red. No supimos ni por dónde se nos habían colado. Sólo habían pasado dos minutos del primer tiempo y ya íbamos 1 a 0. Me enojé y, antes de volver a poner el balón en juego, reuní a mi equipo.

—Oigan, chavos, no hagan tonterías. Nada más acuérdense de la estrategia: hay que pasarle la pelota a Edson. Y que él haga los goles.

—Pero los otros también pueden hacer goles si quieren, Tito —dijo Edson.

—No, campeón. Ahorita hazlos todos tú.

Todos consintieron. Hasta Óliver. Yo sólo agregué:

—Hombre Nuc... eh, digo, Otilio... vas a tener que correr. Ni modo.

—Pero todos se van a burlar.

—No lo creo. El profesor Colina no lo permitiría.

Se quedó pensando. Y volvimos al partido. En cuanto toqué el balón, se lo pasé a Óliver, quien avanzó, solo, hasta la portería de nuestras contrarias. Ahí dio un pase a Edson. Toda la escuela enmudeció. Todos se quedaron paralizados, esperando el tiro del brasileño. Y entonces... las carcajadas. Un mar de risas se nos vino encima.

Edson le pegó tan mal a la pelota, que se cayó de pompas y el balón ni se movió. Los Ángeles de Charlie recuperaron el balón y lo llevaron casi sin problema hasta nuestra portería: 2 a 0.

—¿Qué pasó con esos goles, Edson? —le pregunté a mi arma secreta.

Me miró como avergonzado y volvió al partido.

¿Qué quieren que les diga? A partir de ahí, los goles se sucedieron uno a otro. Al terminar el primer tiempo, ya nos habían metido ocho. Y nosotros ni siquiera uno. Pobre Óliver, él solo no podía hacer todo. Yo nomás corría por todo el campo sin lograr gran cosa. Iñaki, lo mismo. Y Edson, desconcertado, sólo nos veía pasar corriendo a su lado, igual que el Hombre Nuclear. ¡Qué fracaso! Por eso, en el medio tiempo, con el cambio de cancha, lo encaré.

—Campeón, sé que estás nervioso. Pero no te apures. Sólo son unas niñas. Tú puedes llevarnos a la victoria, ¿verdad?

El campeón se sonrojó. Pasó del color negro al morado.

—Tito... tengo que confesarte que yo no sé jugar futbol.

—Ja, ja, ja. No seas bromista. Si tú eres el mejor.

—No, es cierto, Tito. O dime, ¿cuándo me has visto jugar?

Se me borró la sonrisa. No era posible. Estábamos en verdaderos problemas. El profesor Colina aún no pitaba el inicio del segundo tiempo, y yo ya me quería ir a mi casa. El marcador decía 8 a 0. Y todavía faltaban quince minutos.

Hicimos todo lo que pudimos. Corrimos como locos (y ya ven que en eso a Iñaki nadie le gana). Aunque de qué sirve correr si nunca tienes el balón en tu poder. Cambiamos de portero once veces, una por cada gol que nos metían, intentando detener la masacre. Pero ni así. Y el acabose fue cuando, ya para terminar el partido, milagrosamente el balón le cayó en los pies al Hombre Nuclear. Ése fue el fin. Porque todos gritamos al mismo tiempo:

—¡Corre!

Horror de horrores. La escuela entera hizo el sonidito "Tutututuuuu". Y todos se empezaron a reír. Todos. Sí, todos. También el profesor Colina. Hasta Iñaki y Óliver, mugrosos traidores. Bueno, a mí también me quiso dar risa, pero nada más de ver el marcador, se me quitaron las ganas. Creo que el profesor Colina prefirió pitar el fin del partido sólo para terminar con eso que, como diría mi papá cuando mi abuelita nos cuenta que de chico se comía la tierra de las macetas, era lo más denigrante del planeta.

Al final de ese día, a todo el mundo le quedó claro que no había peor equipo en el Primer Torneo de la Escuela Primaria Federal Héroes de la Nación, que los Cohetes Rayados de la Colonia Portales.

Ballet. Tal y como lo leen. Ballet. Eso es lo que verdaderamente le gusta a Edson. Es la clase que toma a las cuatro de la tarde, de ballet. Todo lo que se decía de él era mentira. Aquello de que no jugaba por no lucirse, también era falso. La leyenda del chico brasileño era una completa patraña. ¡Vaya chasco! Creo que hasta Marita, la porrista, juega mejor que él. Pero, cuando me lo confesó, de todos modos no quise correrlo del equipo.

No entiendo por qué extraña razón a un niño brasileño le puede gustar más el ballet que el futbol, pero tampoco se me hizo justo correrlo. Nada más le pedí que asistiera a los entrenamientos, porque sí tenía que practicar como todos. Terminó por cambiar su clase de danza para dos horas más tarde y así poder estar a las cuatro en el Parque de los Venados.

El siguiente lunes, cuando nos juntamos a entrenar en el parque, fue como ir a un verdadero velorio. El único que no estaba abatido era Luisito Pichardo, que cantaba con Olariñárritu las canciones de rigor. Antes de que siquiera tocáramos el balón, Iñaki dijo algo que todos pensábamos:

—Somos el equipo más malo que existe en toda la Vía Láctea.

—No es cierto —dije yo, no muy convencido.

—Sí es cierto. Sí lo son —dijo Goya.

Nadie se atrevió a contradecirla. A lo mejor porque con una sola mano es capaz de agarrarte del cuello, levantarte y triturarte. O a lo mejor porque tenía razón.

—Somos tan malos que perdemos 19 a 0 contra unas niñas —dijo Iñaki.

—Sí. Somos tan malos que mejor vámonos a nuestra casa a ver la tele. Para qué estamos aquí perdiendo el tiempo —añadió el Hombre Nuclear.

—Ni siquiera tenemos uniformes —concluyó el Burbuja.

Se hizo el silencio. Pensé que era cierto. Éramos el equipo más malo de la galaxia y yo era el capitán más malo del Universo. Entonces, Luisito Pichardo dejó de cantar y se acercó a nosotros.

—Si creen que son tan malos, entonces tal vez sí lo sean.

¿Qué puede ser peor que te regañe un niño ciego? Sólo lo que pasó después. Empezaron a llegar un montón de niños, todos de la escuela. Se había corrido el chisme de que los Cohetes Rayados, el equipo que tantas risas había arrancado en el partido del viernes, entrenaba a las cuatro en el Parque de los Venados. Y muchos se dieron cita ahí para seguir con la diversión. Estaban los Cherokees, algunas Ángeles de Charlie, un par de niños de los Relámpagos y varios más.

—Les dije que aquí entrenaban los "Capotitos" —dijo Rubén.

—Pues veamos si nos hacen reír aunque sea un rato —dijo una niña de los Ángeles de Charlie.

Me dieron ganas de decir: "Propongo que nos vayamos a ver la tele y no sigamos perdiendo más el tiempo", pero Luisito Pichardo se me adelantó.

—Pues, por si no lo saben, ellos van a ganar la copa porque tienen algo que a ustedes les falta.

—¿Ah, sí? ¿Y qué es eso, Luisito? —preguntó Tony, con su cara y su sonrisa de simio.

—Estás loco si crees que te lo voy a decir.

Todos nos miramos estupefactos. Si Tony me hubiera preguntado a mí, hubiera tenido que decirle lo mismo que Luisito porque no tenía la menor idea de lo que estaba hablando.

—Ya sé cómo van a ganar —confirmó Rubén—. Nos van a matar a todos de risa. Y así se van a quedar solos con la copa.

Sólo él se rio de su bobada. Pero a mí se me ocurrió una salida.

—Vengan, muchachos. Vamos a platicar con nuestro entrenador.

Mis compañeros me miraron como si estuviera loco. A lo mejor sí lo estaba si pensaba hacer lo que se me había ocurrido.

—¿"Nuestro entrenador"? ¿Cuál entrenador? —preguntó Fito.

—Nuestro entrenador, el Mago Urbina —dije, con toda la altanería de la que era capaz.

—¿El Mago Urbina? ¿Y ése quién es? —preguntó uno de los Relámpagos.

—No les voy a decir. Entérense por su cuenta, si quieren. Vengan, chavos.

Y todos, incluidos Olariñárritu y Luisito Pichardo, me siguieron hasta mi casa. Sólo Iñaki comprendió:

—Tito, estás loco de la cabeza si crees que tu abuelo nos puede entrenar —me dijo bajito.

—Ya lo sé. Pero esos tontos no lo saben.

Y llegamos a mi casa. Éramos una comitiva de trece niños, entre porra, equipo y música. Los hice entrar, saludar a mi mamá y acariciar a Hugo, que jugaba a ser un perro, hasta que dimos con mi abuelo en su cuarto. Al menos no estaba en calzones, como a veces acostumbraba.

—Abuelo, te presento a mis amigos.

—¡Aaatención! —dijo, poniéndose de pie, muy derecho, como si le fuéramos a pasar revista a un soldado.

—Los traje a que vieran tus trofeos.

Nunca me arrepentiré de haber tenido esa idea. Ninguno de mis amigos había oído hablar del Mago Urbina. Y tenerlo ahí enfrente, con todos sus trofeos, sus medallas, sus reconocimientos y la foto con Garrincha, era casi mágico. Lástima que mi abuelo tuviera que abrir la boca.

—Les puedo contar la historia de cuando destripé a aquel huertista y lo regalé a los puercos para que se dieran un festín.

Tuve que contarles que había perdido la chaveta en un remate de cabeza contra un poste. Pero eso no deshizo la magia. Hasta para aquellos a quienes les gusta más el ballet, fue fascinante tener tan cerca a un ídolo como mi abuelo. Luisito Pichardo acariciaba las medallas como si fueran objetos maravillosos. Incluso Olariñárritu dijo un par de palabras. Fue muy emocionante. Cuando se despidieron de él, se sentían orgullosos de haberlo conocido y de que nos fuera a entrenar. Aun a sabiendas de que él no sería más que una pantalla para que los demás equipos no se burlaran, esa tarde surgió algo que nos unió como equipo.

Cuando los despedí en la puerta de mi casa, me sentía menos mal. A lo mejor no era el peor capitán de todo el Universo.

—Gracias por invitarnos a tu casa, Tito —dijo Dolores Zúñiga, la última que faltaba por salir, la única niña que...

¡Me dio un beso! ¡Horror! ¡Me dio un beso en la mejilla! Creí que en ese momento me iba a dar el patatús. Yo y mi pobre corazón.

—Oye Tito, ¿por qué no me dices Lolita como todos? ¿Por qué siempre me dices Dolores Zúñiga?

—Así te llamas, ¿no?

—Pues sí, pero, si quieres, me puedes decir Lolita.

—Lo pensaré. Adiós.

Al menos nadie había visto. Claro, excepto...

—Tito y Lolita son novios. Tito y Lolita son novios. Tito y Lolita son novios —repetía Susana mientras bailaba como una boba.

Mi mamá nos tuvo que separar porque terminamos jalándonos los pelos. Sin embargo, a pesar del par de nalgadas que me tocaron, ese día me fui a acostar muy contento, porque sabía que el Tigre Quezada, mi mamá y hasta la maestra Lucía (suspiro) estarían muy orgullosos de mí si supieran lo que hice esa tarde por los Cohetes Rayados de la Colonia Portales.

Querido Tigre Quezada:

¡GANAMOS! ¡GANAMOS! ¡GANAMOS!

No te había querido escribir porque me daba pena. Es que perdimos el primer partido del torneo y no quería que pensaras que somos unos maletas. Pero el segundo, lo ganamos. ¿Cómo ves? ¿Verdad que estás muy orgulloso? Ganamos 7 a 4. ¡Qué padre!, ¿verdad?

¡Ah!, por cierto. Te encargo nuestros uniformes, ¡por favor!

Con cariño,

Tito

Efectivamente, ganamos el segundo. Aunque desde luego, no se debió a la influencia de mi abuelo en los entrenamientos. Al contrario. A veces, mi abuelo era más un estorbo que una ayuda. Nos servía, eso sí, para confundir al enemigo, pero nada más. Algunos niños de los otros equipos se enteraron con sus padres de quién era el Mago Urbina y nos dejaron de molestar. Incluso varios le pidieron que les firmara sus balones y sus camisetas. El abuelo, hay que decirlo, sólo iba a las prácticas porque le habíamos hecho creer que estábamos pensando en ir a la guerra. Y con esa idea se presentaba todos los días, a prepararnos para la batalla.

Con todo, mi abuelo se volvió parte importante de los Cohetes Rayados. Con sus grandes barbas, su viejo uniforme de las Chivas y sus locas estrategias

("Nunca hay que dar cuartel", "Al enemigo se le toma por sorpresa", "Al final, gana la guerra el que se queda con más hombres de pie"), las cuales teníamos que traducir a términos futboleros; para todos era una gran alegría tenerlo ahí, porque nos divertía mucho con sus loqueras.

Pero no fue gracias a él que ganamos el segundo. De hecho, tampoco fue por nuestra capacidad deportiva. Se lo debemos a Susana (lamento decirlo, pero así fue.)

Íbamos perdiendo 4 a 0. Y aunque los Kiss no eran tan buenos como los Ángeles de Charlie, también fueron duros de pelar. Y aún más porque el Hombre Nuclear no quería correr, Edson no intentaba gran cosa, e Iñaki sólo le daba vueltas al campo como loco desaforado. Una nueva catástrofe, pues. Sin embargo, todo cambió cuando empezó el segundo tiempo.

Parecía como si los hubieran paralizado con una pistola de rayos gamma. O al menos eso fue lo que dijo Iñaki, porque, de repente, todos se quedaron petrificados. Uno de ellos iba a chutar contra nuestra portería, mientras el Burbuja se tapaba la cara para no ver y, en ese instante, se quedaron como estatuas, haciendo una cara tan terrible, que creí que les habían hecho un maleficio. Hasta me di vuelta para ver a Dolores Zúñiga, pero ella estaba muy ocupada haciendo maromas con las otras Rockets. ¿Qué podía haber pasado? ¡Quién sabe! Mas nosotros aprovechamos esa confusión para hacer de las nuestras. Metimos nuestro primer gol. Óliver hizo el tanto. Y lo festejamos como los grandes: aventándonos unos encima de otros (lo bueno fue que el Burbuja no participó, de lo contrario todos habríamos quedado lesionados).

Cuando por fin volvieron a sacar, los Kiss se veían peor. Caminaban como viejitos y tenían la cara verde. Entonces vi que las Rockets, lejos de echar porras, se reían como locas. Algo habían hecho, y yo estaba seguro de que la culpable era Dolores Zúñiga. Pero no me iba a poner a cuestionarlo porque, en cuanto se movió el balón, volvimos a correr a la portería contraria.

Otro gol. Y otro. Y otro. Y otro. Y otro. Así, hasta contar siete. Obtuvimos nuestro primer triunfo con siete goles de Óliver. Una verdadera hazaña. Como los verdaderos grandes, remontamos el marcador. Íbamos perdiendo por mucho y, al final, ganamos. Claro que el gusto no nos iba a durar mucho tiempo (¿o debería decir que no "me" iba a durar?). En cuanto el profesor Colina marcó el fin del partido, nuestros contrincantes salieron corriendo. Nosotros creímos que se debía a la gran vergüenza que seguramente sentían por haber perdido tan feo, pero no era así; era por una razón más urgente. El misterio se develó al instante. Susana se acercó a nosotros en cuanto salimos de la cancha, todavía sonrientes y palmeándonos entre nosotros.

—Ya, ya. Ni se sientan tan importantes. ¿Qué nos van a invitar por haberles conseguido el triunfo?

—¿Qué dices? —pregunté.

—Pues eso —dijo Goya—. Que nadie puede jugar un segundo tiempo si se acaba de tomar una purga superpoderosísima.

Así fue. Las Rockets habían obsequiado refrescos a los del equipo Kiss en el descanso, refrescos con un potentísimo ingrediente extra que había conseguido Goya. No me lo quería ni imaginar. Con razón habían salido corriendo del partido. Sólo esperaba que hubieran llegado a tiempo al baño o eso habría sido un verdadero desastre.

Como fuera, lo importante era que habíamos ganado. Eso les levantó el espíritu a todos. En la tabla general se reflejaba que estábamos en segundo sitio, con dos puntos, sólo debajo de los Ángeles de Charlie. Los Archies y los Kiss tenían un solo punto, pues habían empatado en su primer encuentro.

En conclusión, aún era posible que pasáramos a la siguiente ronda. Y la verdad se lo debíamos a Susana, porque sólo un milagro habría podido conseguir que transformáramos un 4 a 0 en un 7 a 4.

No obstante, ya se imaginarán que yo no me sentía nada bien. Habíamos ganado a la mala y eso me descomponía. Me daban ganas de renunciar. Y se los dije a todos a la salida. Claro que de inmediato me llovieron las quejas y los zapes.

—¿Estás loco de la cabeza o qué, Tito? —dijo ya saben quién.

—Si renunciamos al triunfo, estamos fuera. Y si no puedes darte cuenta de eso, eres el más tonto de los hermanos y de los capitanes —añadió ya se imaginan quién más.

—Mis siete goles fueron todos buenos. Lo que pasa es que eres un cochino envidioso —concluyó otro que ya supondrán.

No supe qué decir para no empeorarlo más. Por fortuna, no estaba solo.

—Tito tiene razón —dijo Luisito, que estaba bastante cerca—. No se vale ganar a la mala.

Y se hizo el silencio. Casi nadie se atreve a contradecir a Luisito Pichardo, porque siempre dice cosas ciertas. Es un niño muy listo.

—Pero Susana también tiene razón —agregó—. Y si renuncian al triunfo, los voy a agarrar a palos a todos porque, si los descalifican, ¿a qué equipo le voy a echar porras?

Volvieron las sonrisas. Hasta yo sonreí.

—Ahora aprovechen que siguen en el torneo. Pero hagan bien las cosas, como debe ser. Ganen los partidos jugando, sin trampa. O si no... O si no... —volteaba el rostro hacia nosotros como si de veras nos pudiera ver—, o si no, los voy a agarrar a palos a todos.

Admitimos, uno por uno, que Luisito tenía razón. Y al mismo tiempo convenimos en que sólo había un modo de conseguir pasar a la siguiente ronda sin hacer trampa: practicando. Y mucho. Por eso, el mismo día, a las cuatro de la tarde, cuando llegué al Parque de los Venados con mi abuelo y con Hugo (mi mamá me encargó que lo cuidara para poder irse a su "cafecito de mil horas"), ya todos estaban ahí. Todos habían llegado temprano.

Y en cuanto puse un pie en el parque, todos me miraron como si verdaderamente yo pudiera llevarlos al triunfo. Ahora sí sentí que el corazón se me desconchinflaba. Cierto, había que practicar, pero ¿cómo?, ¿qué era exactamente lo que había que hacer?, ¿cómo era posible que el niño más maleta de la escuela estuviera dirigiendo un equipo de futbol? Pero así era. Y aunque no quería defraudarlos, comprendí en ese momento que, para poder llevarlos a la victoria, algo me hacía falta; eso que Luisito aseguró a los niños de los otros equipos que teníamos los Cohetes Rayados y que yo no tenía ni idea de qué se trataba. En ese momento estaba seguro de que al menos yo no lo tenía. Me dio pena estar ahí, al frente de todos. Pero no lo demostré. Inicié el entrenamiento lo mejor que pude.

Y el entrenamiento, como podrán adivinar... fue el mismo fiasco de todos los días. Hasta mi hermano Hugo le metió dos goles al Burbuja. ¡Vaya equipo! ¿Cómo íbamos a pasar a la siguiente ronda si un niño de dos años nos anotó sin sacarse el chupón de la boca? ¿Cómo íbamos a ganar si Iñaki y Óliver no se dejaban de empujar todo el tiempo? ¿Cómo íbamos a hacer algo en la cancha si hasta Marita me quitó el balón una vez, nomás por hacerse la chistosa? ¡Vaya equipo!

Toda la semana le estuve dando vueltas. Lo consulté con mi papá, por ejemplo.

—Cuando arriesgas un capital, tienes que calcular las pérdidas y el tiempo que te va a llevar amortizar tu inversión antes de cualquier cosa.

¿Alguien puede explicarme eso? Yo solamente le pregunté cómo mejorar mi tiro directo. También indagué con mi abuelo, claro.

—Tienes que basarte en la estrategia. Si tienes que perder algunos hombres por ganar la batalla, ni modo.

Y a mi mamá.

—¡Ay, Tito!, no sé. Ayúdame a echar esta ropa en la lavadora, ándale.

Estábamos perdidos. No obstante, seguimos entrenando. Y haciendo el ridículo con música de los Beatles de fondo.

Lo único bueno de todo eso era que la maestra Lucía (suspiro) parecía tener cierta predilección por nuestro equipo. Nos preguntaba cómo iban nuestros entrenamientos y cómo nos sentíamos para el siguiente partido y todo eso. A lo mejor ésa era la única razón por la cual yo no había decidido huir del país escondido en un camión de toronjas, idea que no me parecía tan mala (sobre todo cuando pensaba en por cuántos goles perderíamos el siguiente partido).

Y créanme, cuando llegó el momento y estábamos ahí, formados en la cancha, todos multicolores y sin haber mejorado en nada nuestro juego, pensé que había sido un tonto por no haber huido del país escondido en un camión de toronjas.

—Caray, Mendiolea, ¿cuándo van a venir uniformados?

—Sí, cuándo, ¿eh, Tito?

—Cállate, Burbuja.

Lo cierto es que, aunque íbamos contra los Archies y yo sabía que no eran tan buen equipo, nada me hacía pensar que podríamos meterles un solo gol. Ni aunque llovieran sapos o se abriera la tierra, podríamos conseguirlo, de eso sí estaba seguro. El profesor Colina iba a lanzar el volado y yo salí corriendo del campo. Me dirigí a la porra, a las Rockets.

—Oye, Goya, ¿ya no tienes de la purga superpoderosísima que conseguiste?

—Cállate y juega, Tito.

Volví al campo. Perdí el volado y tuve que aceptar que los Archies nos cedieran el balón para sacar antes que ellos.

Ya iba yo a moverlo cuando tuve una gran idea. Y ni se imaginan de dónde la saqué. Nada menos que de lo que me dijo mi abuelo, nuestro "entrenador", el Mago Urbina. Había dicho que, si tenía que perder algunos hombres para ganar la batalla, así lo hiciera, ¿no? Pues exactamente eso haría.

Pero, ¡ey!, no se espanten. No crean que se me había botado la canica igual que a mi abuelo. Hay que fijarse en lo que significan esas palabras. Y es que, para no hacerles el cuento largo, me di cuenta de que nos bastaba un empate para pasar a la siguiente ronda.

Sin duda, no tendríamos que hacer ningún gol si no queríamos; pero sí evitar a toda costa que nos anotaran. Así que, en lugar de mover la pelota, jalé a Óliver de su camisa de los Pumas y lo llevé hacia la portería. Y luego hice lo mismo con los demás, uno por uno.

—Mendiolea, por favor, ya basta de interrupciones. Mueva el balón —dijo el profesor Colina, mirando su reloj. Pero yo estaba muy ocupado llevándolos a todos a la portería.

—¿Qué te pasa, Tito? ¿Qué mosco te picó? —me dijo Edson, el último al que arrastré hacia atrás.

Cuando ya estuvieron todos al lado del Burbuja, expliqué:

—Ésta es la estrategia: no puede entrar ningún balón por esa portería. No importa lo que tengan que hacer para evitarlo.

—Ahora sí se te volatilizó el cerebro. Propongo cambio de capitán.

—Pon atención y cierra la boca, Óliver. Si no nos anotan ningún gol, entonces empatamos a cero. Y si empatamos, pasamos a los cuartos de final.

Me miraron y guardaron silencio un momento. Se veía que los había puesto a pensar.

—Insisto en que cambiemos de capitán —dijo Óliver.

—Yo también —dijo el Hombre Nuclear.

—O mueven el balón o los descalifico —gritó el profesor Colina.

No les di tiempo de pensarlo más. Corrí hacia el balón y le di una fuerte patada en dirección al campo contrario. Luego, volví a la portería que custodiaban los otros cinco. Y no sé por qué extraña razón ninguno se movió. Ahí estábamos. Con los seis enfrente del marco, no había modo de meter la pelota porque no dejábamos ni un solo huequito libre.

Como dice mi mamá, ahí ardió Troya. Los Archies se fueron contra nosotros y empezaron a hacer tiros contra la portería de seis porteros. Eso se convirtió en una verdadera masacre. Unos nos daban en el pecho, otros, en la cara y otros más, en los muslos o en las rodillas.

Pero hasta que un balonazo estuvo a punto de pegarme en donde ustedes ya se imaginarán, les ordené a mis compañeros cambiar la estrategia. Y a la voz de "¡ya!", todos nos pusimos de espaldas. Los niños de las gradas se reían tanto, que se doblaban de las carcajadas, pero a nosotros no nos importó. Tiro tras tiro tras tiro, y los Archies no anotaron. Así terminó el primer tiempo: 0 a 0. Un milagro.

El capitán de los Archies se quejó. Sin embargo, el profesor Colina respondió que en ninguna parte de su reglamento decía que eso fuera ilegal. Y así nos fuimos al descanso. Pero no crean que nos estaba resultando fácil. El Hombre Nuclear y Edson lloraban cuando se inició el segundo tiempo. Iñaki me dijo que eso me iba a costar todas mis estampas de *La guerra de las galaxias*. Sólo el Burbuja no se quejaba, satisfecho de "su" labor.

Y empezó la segunda parte de la carnicería. Balón tras balón tras balón tras balón. Y los Cohetes Rayados no dejábamos pasar ni el aire, a pesar de los "¡ay!", "¡auch!", "¡auxilio!", que se oían a cada trallazo.

Juro que todo habría terminado bien, de no ser porque el Hombre Nuclear se volteó un minuto antes de que acabara la segunda mitad. Al valiente y feroz grito de "¡Ya no aguanto, yo me largo!", se salió de la línea de seis... al mismo tiempo que un balón iba en dirección suya. E hizo lo que hubiera hecho cualquiera de nosotros: lo atrapó con las manos. Así los Archies consiguieron un penalti de la manera más absurda.

Pero nadie dijo nada. Estábamos tan vapuleados, que no queríamos saber nada más. Las pompas nos dolían como si nuestras mamás nos hubieran dado un millón de nalgadas. Y nos fuimos a tirar boca abajo a un lado de la portería. Todos, excepto el Burbuja, claro está, que debía parar el penalti.

¿Quién se iba a imaginar que pasaría lo que pasó? El capitán de los Archies se encargó de cobrar el penalti. Y, para nuestra enorme fortuna, lo mandó... ¿a dónde creen ustedes? No lo envió fuera (que hubiera sido lo mejor). No. Lo mandó derechito a la panza del Burbuja (yo creo que, de tanto estar enviando tiros hacia nosotros, no pudo evitar hacerlo por última vez). El Burbuja paró el tiro con la panza, lo sostuvo con las manos y así, cuan grande es, se desplomó en tierra. El profesor Colina pitó el fin del partido. Y nosotros estábamos en los cuartos de final.

144

Querido Tigre Quezada:

Estamos en los cuartos de final. ¿Verdad que es estupendo? Lo único malo es que nos quedamos sin portero. Fíjate que se lesionó una rodilla durante el partido y ya no va a poder terminar el torneo con nosotros. Pero de que vamos muy bien, vamos muy bien. Ya no puedo esperar al día en que nos entregues la copa.

Con cariño,
Tito

P. D. No se te olviden nuestros uniformes.

Mentira. No fue la rodilla, fue la panza. Y no es que se la lesionara, sino que el balonazo le sacó el aire de tal forma, que estuvo tumbado durante más de media hora en la cancha. Hizo una cara igualita a la de los peces de mi mamá cuando Hugo los saca de su pecera. Cuando finalmente se repuso, sólo una cosa tenía en claro: que ya no quería jugar. Y lo confirmó el lunes siguiente, cuando él mismo tachó su nombre de la hoja de los Cohetes Rayados, dejándonos con sólo cinco elementos. Pero, ¿qué podíamos hacer? Les juro que el mismo lunes a las cuatro de la tarde, fuimos todos a tocar a su casa (y cuando digo "todos" me refiero a equipo, porra, abuelo, Luisito, bailarín de ballet y los Beatles) y ni siquiera asomó las narices. Eso, aunado a otro suceso ese mismo día, me puso tan abatido que me deprimí bastante.

—Hoy no entrenamos —les dije a todos, en la orilla del parque.

—¿Por qué? —preguntó Edson.

—Porque primero hay que conseguir un portero. Sin portero no somos equipo.

—Sí somos —dijo Óliver—. Así podemos entrenar.

—No podemos, Óliver.

—Cabiño.

—Óliver.

—Cabiño.

—Ya, como sea. No podemos entrenar porque yo lo digo. Y porque me siento mal.

En ese momento pensé confesar que tenía una enfermedad incurable del corazón porque de veras me sentía muy mal. Y además, aunque parezca mentira, sí me sentía mal del corazón. Lamentablemente, sólo Dolores Zúñiga pareció interesarse.

—¿De veras te sientes mal, Tito? —dijo.

—Sí.

—Bueno. Entonces mejor vámonos a ver la tele —dijo Iñaki.

Iñaki mal amigo. Malos amigos todos. Se fueron a casa de Iñaki a ver el programa de la Calaca Tilica y Flaca, y ni siquiera se esperaron a ver qué pasaba conmigo, si me daba el soponcio o qué. Sólo Luisito Pichardo se quedó en el parque conmigo. Sólo él, Olariñárritu y Dolores Zúñiga, quienes no se veían muy interesados en ver la tele (Luisito por razones obvias) o en comerse las galletitas de la mamá de Iñaki. Olariñárritu se puso a tocar la guitarra, Dolores, a practicar conjuros, y Luisito se sentó junto a mí en los columpios.

—Tú estás triste por otra cosa —me dijo.

Parece increíble que un niño ciego pueda ver tanto.

—Pues sí. Puede ser —le confesé.

—¿Quieres contarme?

¿Pero cómo podía contarle? Lo que me tenía verdaderamente triste, además de que el equipo era un fracaso, era lo que la maestra Lucía nos había dicho en la mañana. Desde que entró al salón de clases, se veía triste. Y una de las niñas le preguntó qué le pasaba.

—Casi nada: que no quisiera irme de México —fue lo que dijo, con los ojos llenos de lágrimas.

Nadie dijo nada. Ni siquiera alguno de los Cherokees, que suelen burlarse de ese tipo de cosas. Nadie dijo nada. Y ése fue el problema, que yo debí haberme puesto de pie para decir algo así como:

—Maestra, no tiene que irse si no quiere. Nadie puede obligarla. Y yo voy a luchar por usted contra cualquier villano que intente secuestrarla.

No. No dije eso. Ni nada de nada. De hecho, nadie se atrevió a agregar nada. La maestra se limpió los ojos con un pañuelo y nos empezó a dictar la lección luego luego, como sin darle importancia al asunto. Yo estuve con una cara tan apachurrada, que parecía bulldog con dolor de panza. Y luego, cuando al salir de clases me di cuenta de que el Burbuja nos había abandonado, me puse todavía peor. Pero estarán de acuerdo en que no podía contarle eso a Luisito. Así que preferí inventarme algo.

—Es que mi mamá me regañó por no levantar el asiento del escusado para hacer pipí.

—¡Ah, sí! A mí me pasa lo mismo.

Estoy seguro de que no me creyó. Pero Luisito Pichardo es tan intuitivo que hasta eso puede ver: que uno no quiere hablar de algo porque le incomoda. De veras que es un gran chico. Así que mejor volvimos al tema del futbol.

—Oye, Luisito, ¿qué es eso que decías que nosotros tenemos y los otros equipos no?

—No te lo puedo decir.

No sé por qué sabía que me iba a contestar eso.

—Y no te lo puedo decir... —agregó—, porque es una de esas cosas que no se pueden ver. Yo, como no puedo ver, sé que está ahí.

—Qué lástima. Me hubiera gustado saberlo, porque la verdad es que, como equipo, somos una verdadera calamidad, los peores de todo el Universo.

—¿Por qué lo dices? Ya están en los cuartos de final.

—Sí, pero en qué forma. Ninguno de nosotros se pudo sentar en todo el fin de semana, de tanto que nos dolían las pompas. Y ahora, sin portero, seguro que hasta aquí llegamos.

Luisito se quedó pensando un largo rato. Olariñárritu estaba cantando una canción muy triste; me dieron ganas de decirle que se callara.

—No sé cómo se llama lo que ustedes tienen, pero sí te puedo demostrar que ahí está. Lo único que necesitan para ganar es utilizarlo. Nos vemos aquí mañana.

Se puso de pie. Sólo agregó una cosa: "Mañana te demuestro que todos lo tienen, especialmente tú". Y nos despedimos (yo tuve que echarme a correr a mi casa para que Dolores Zúñiga no me volviera a dar un beso traicionero).

No pude terminar bien mi tarea. Casi no pude dormir. Tampoco atender bien a la maestra Lucía al día siguiente. Era como si Luisito hubiera afirmado que teníamos poderes mágicos y no sabíamos utilizarlos, en especial yo. Así que al otro día, a las cuatro de la tarde, no cabía en mí de las ansias. Luisito y Olariñárritu aún no llegaban al parque, pero todos los demás ya estaban ahí.

—¿A qué horas empezamos a entrenar, eh? —dijo Óliver, molesto.

—En cuanto llegue Luisito Pichardo —dije yo.

—¿Luisito? ¿Y para qué necesitamos a Luisito?

Ni yo lo sabía. Afortunadamente, Luisito apareció casi al instante. Llevaba tenis y ropa deportiva. Olariñárritu lo guiaba, como siempre. Sin decir nada, éste ató una cuerda a uno de los árboles cercanos y luego se fue hasta otro árbol que estaba bastante lejos para atar el otro extremo con fuerza. Ninguno de nosotros sabía de qué se trataba. Luisito se puso a hacer calentamientos... hasta que dijo:

—¿Quién de ustedes corre más rápido?

—Iñaki —contesté, intrigado.

—Pues yo les apuesto que este niño ciego le gana a Iñaki a correr.

Todos se rieron, menos Luisito. Por eso mejor ya nadie dijo nada. Luisito se puso al lado de la cuerda y esperó.

—Cuando quieras, Iñaki —dijo.

Iñaki nos miró a todos. Y se puso al lado de Luisito. Se le notaba en la cara que estaba totalmente confiado de ganar, hasta que Luisito dijo:

—Sin trampas. Quiero que corras todo lo que puedas.

—En sus marcas —dijo Olariñárritu—, listos... ¡Fuera!

Increíble, es todo lo que puedo decir. Luisito corrió como una ráfaga. Agarrándose de la cuerda para no desviarse y chocar, dejó atrás a Iñaki en un santiamén. Y llegó al otro árbol sin ningún problema. Iñaki llegó después que Luisito por varios segundos.

—¿Quieres la revancha? —dijo Luisito.

—Bueno —confirmó Iñaki, sin aliento.

Y se echaron el trayecto de regreso. Increíble. Otra vez ganó Luisito. En la cara de Iñaki se veía que estaba echándole todas las ganas que podía. Y aún así, volvió a perder.

—¿Son tan malos que hasta un niño ciego les puede ganar? —dijo Luisito.

—Yo compito —dijo Óliver, poniéndose al lado de Luisito.

Y perdió, naturalmente. Y luego, Edson. Y también yo. El Hombre Nuclear ni el intento hizo, por supuesto. Pero hasta Susana probó y perdió. Y luego, Lulú. A todos nos quedó claro que éramos los más papas del mundo.

Después de vencer a todos, Luisito se veía cansado, pero feliz. A mí me dieron ganas de darle un par de coscorrones. Lo único que nos había demostrado era cuán malos éramos hasta para echar carreras. Finalmente, cuando nos tuvo a todos tumbados en el pasto, volvió a hablar, y nos dijo:

—¿Saben por qué los pude vencer tan fácilmente?

Ahí venía la revelación. Nadie se atrevió a romper el silencio. Nadie.

—Los pude vencer muy fácil... precisamente porque estoy ciego.

—No inventes —dijo Susana—. No te burles.

—No, es en serio —continuó Luisito—. Como yo estoy ciego, no puedo ver a mi contrincante. No puedo ver cuán alto o fuerte es, o cuán rápido es.

Se veía en las caras de todos que empezaban a comprender.

—En vez de fijarme en la superioridad de mi competidor, me fijo en mis posibilidades. En pocas palabras, les gané a todos porque no competí contra ustedes. Competí contra mí mismo.

Luisito no dijo más. Se sentó junto a Olariñárritu y se puso a cantar con él.

Sorprendentemente, los entrenamientos fueron otros a partir de ese día. No lo sé explicar porque ni yo lo entendía. Aún no sabía a qué se refería Luisito que teníamos porque, según yo, no lo había demostrado. Nos había dado una lección, eso sí. Pero de eso a aquello de los poderes mágicos (en especial los míos), como que todavía no se veían. Sin embargo, los entrenamientos fueron otros. En las caras de todos se notaba un entusiasmo distinto. Ni siquiera nos importaba no tener portero, o ser sólo cinco.

Algo nos decía que podíamos ganar. Algo nos decía que podíamos conquistar la copa. Y yo pensé, tal vez por primera vez desde que se me ocurrió la idea del torneo, que verdaderamente éramos capaces de ganar. Por eso me empezó a preocupar que llegara el día de la gran final y ocurriera algo que ya desde antes me temía: que el Tigre no se presentara a entregar la copa. Claro que lo temía, pues él nunca me había confirmado nada. Es más, ustedes saben que nunca había contestado una sola de mis cartas. Por eso decidí escribirle una más y jugarme el todo por el todo, una carta que realmente lo convenciera de que tenía que venir a mi escuela.

Querido Tigre Quezada:

Hoy me he propuesto contarte algo. Es importante y muy grave. Pero antes, quiero decirte que, si quieres, te olvides de los uniformes. A lo mejor piensas que somos muy encajosos y por eso no nos los has mandado. No te apures.

Bueno, como te decía, quiero contarte algo muy grave. Y creo que me darás la razón, porque es muy triste que un niño se despida del mundo a tan temprana edad. Verás...

Suspendí la carta porque me llamaban por teléfono. Y ni se imaginan quién. Tomé el auricular y estuve varios segundos diciendo "Bueno", hasta que se animaron a hablar.

—Hola, Tito. Habla Esteban Olariñárritu.

—Hola, ¿qué cuentas?

—Dos cosas, nada más. La primera: pienso devolverte tu dinero.

Sentí horrible. Pensé que me iba a abandonar a mi suerte. Hacía mucho que los Cherokees no me molestaban; ya ni en la escuela me daban lata. No podía volver a lo mismo. De veras sentí horrible.

—¡No! ¡No lo hagas! ¿Ya no quieres ser mi guardaespaldas? ¿Por qué? ¿Quieres que te pague más? No renuncies. Mira que los Cherokees me dijeron que me van a cocinar vivo, te lo juro. Además...

—No es eso, Tito. No te aloques. Déjame terminar —continuó—. Te devuelvo tu dinero porque creo que no es justo. Además, nunca me lo gasté ni nada.

—Como quieras —le dije, impresionado. Y eso que todavía faltaba lo demás.

—La segunda cosa es ésta: quiero jugar con los Cohetes Rayados. Quiero ser el portero.

En cuanto colgué, cargué a Hugo y me puse a bailar con él. Susana pensó que se me había zafado un tornillo, pero no hice caso de sus burlas. Seguí bailando hasta bien tarde, hasta que se me pasó la alegría.

Y es que, pensándolo bien, tal vez hubiera bailado hasta el día del siguiente partido. ¿Por qué? Ni yo mismo lo sé, pero llegamos al viernes con un ánimo incontenible. Todavía ni nos llamaban a la cancha para jugar contra los Tribis, que era el equipo contra el que nos debíamos enfrentar, y no dejábamos de calentar, ejercitarnos y practicar nuestros pases. Estábamos tan prendidos que parecíamos... bueno, sí, parecíamos unos cohetes a punto de despegar. Y, la verdad, sólo de ver a Luisito sentado a un lado del Burbuja en las gradas, nos hacía sentir más entusiastas.

El profesor Colina nos llamó a la cancha y entramos como nunca lo habíamos hecho: corriendo. Al partido anterior habíamos entrado caminando y con desgano. Pero no más. Hasta Olariñárritu parecía otro. No dejaba de dar brincos en su portería. Y, lo crean o no, vi a Carlos Alberto en las gradas, interesado en el partido que estaba a punto de contemplar. Nunca lo había visto así en ninguna contienda en la que no estuvieran involucrados los Cherokees. Era casi mágico.

—Mendiolea, a ver si ya consiguen uniformes —dijo el profesor Colina, antes de pitar el inicio.

Movimos el balón. Y lo peleamos en todos los rincones de la cancha. Todos nosotros, excepto el Hombre Nuclear (que seguía sin animarse a correr), estuvimos tanto arriba como abajo, tanto atrás como adelante. No había un solo balón que no disputáramos. Así que, cuando estaba por terminar el primer tiempo, ocurrió el milagro: Edson le mandó un pase filtrado a Óliver, quien no dudó en ponerlo en la red. Un golazo. Nuestro primer gol del torneo sin hacer trampa ni nada. Qué felicidad.

Hubieran visto. Cuando nos fuimos al descanso, las Rockets estaban imparables (horriblemente imparables, porque sus porras seguían siendo tan malas como al principio: "¡Atole, pozole y tamales. Atole, pozole y tamales. Arriba, arriba, los Cohetes Rayados de la Colonia Portales!"). Pero eso no mermaba nuestra alegría. Estábamos seguros de que ganaríamos el partido. Y fácilmente. Claro que todavía no sabíamos lo que estaba por ocurrir en el segundo tiempo. Todavía me acuerdo y me pongo a temblar. El profesor Colina pitó el inicio de la segunda mitad y nosotros supimos mantener el marcador.

El problema vino cuando uno de los Tribis se coló hasta nuestra portería y enfrentó a Olariñárritu solo. Tiró... y, aunque no lo crean, Olariñárritu paró el balón, sí, pero con la cara. Y en ese preciso momento se volvió loco. No sé qué le pasó por la cabeza a nuestro portero, porque empezó a hacer gala de sus conocimientos en artes marciales en contra de todos los Tribis (no sé por qué me recordó a mi abuelo). Tuvimos que detenerlo entre varios porque en serio que estaba fuera de sí y sacando de combate a varios niños a punta de karatazos.

El profesor Colina le sacó a Olariñárritu todas las tarjetas que tenía, hasta las de crédito, y nos quedamos de nuevo sin portero. Y para nuestra desgracia, no tuvimos más opción que volver a la estrategia del partido pasado: cuidar el marcador a fuerza de aguantar balonazos. Edson se puso a llorar automáticamente y amenazó con irse corriendo. Tuvimos que agarrarlo entre varios y llevarlo a la portería.

Fue horrible; creí que nunca pitarían el final; se nos hizo una eternidad. Todavía recuerdo a Óliver preguntándome por qué no podíamos ganar un solo partido como Dios manda, cuando el profesor Colina dio el silbatazo final. En ese momento, la pesadilla terminó. Y el resto fue como un sueño. Todos los de las gradas aplaudieron. Hasta Carlos Alberto se puso de pie y aplaudió. Y la maestra Lucía fue directamente a felicitarnos: "Son unos valientes, muchachos".

Creo que en ese momento a todos (y no sólo a mí) nos dejaron de doler las pompas por los balonazos.

Fuimos a asomarnos a la pizarra de los equipos para ver las posiciones antes de irnos a nuestras casas. Dos malas noticias a la vez: la primera, que ni se imaginan contra quién íbamos en la semifinal. En cuanto lo leí, sentí que el corazón me hacía ¡cuaz!

—Parece que acabas de ver un fantasma, Tito —me dijo Iñaki—. Estás blanco.

Ganarles a los Cherokees iba más allá de nuestros sueños más guajiros. Y ellos lo sabían. Tanto que, en cuanto nos vieron ahí, frente a la pizarra, se pusieron detrás.

—Capotitos, queremos informarles que ni con Pelé en su equipo podrían ganarnos —dijo Rubén.

—Y si nos llegaran a ganar, les pondríamos las piernas de collar —dijo Tony.

—Pero no nos pueden ganar, torpe, eso es imposible —peleó Fito.

—Bueno, yo sólo decía que si nos ganaran —se defendió Tony.

—Pero no nos pueden ganar, torpe.

Y fueron a empujarse entre ellos a otro lado, porque llegó el profesor Colina, aún vestido de negro, a mostrarnos la otra mala noticia.

—Notarán que el nombre de Esteban Olariñárritu está tachado de su equipo. Yo lo hice. No podrá seguir participando por su conducta antideportiva.

Pero ése no era el mayor problema, sino que había otro nombre tachado.

—¿Y usted también sacó al Homb... eh, digo, a Otilio Sánchez?

—No. No fui yo —concluyó el profesor. Y siguió su camino.

Y hasta ese momento nos dimos cuenta. El Hombre Nuclear no estaba con nosotros. Tampoco me acordaba de haberlo visto cuando terminó el partido y todos nos abrazamos por el triunfo. No recordaba haberlo visto siquiera participar activamente en la cancha. Había estado tan relegado, que lo habíamos olvidado por completo.

—Yo vi que él mismo se tachó —dijo Lulú, para terminar con el cuadro.

Era horrible. En una semana se jugarían las semifinales y nosotros éramos sólo cuatro en el equipo. Parecíamos cangrejos; a ese paso, si llegábamos a la final, íbamos a terminar siendo sólo dos en el equipo. No podía quedarme de brazos cruzados. Le estuve dando vueltas al asunto durante todo el fin de semana porque no quería aceptar que Dolores Zúñiga entrara al equipo, como ella misma había sugerido. No podía permitirlo ni aunque nos ayudara con sus pócimas y conjuros. Y le pregunté a mi papá, porque ni mi abuelo ("Fusila al desertor, sólo eso se merecen los cobardes"), ni mi mamá ("¡Ay, Tito! ¡Ay, Tito! Tráeme mis pantuflas, ándale") eran de mucha ayuda.

—Papá... ¿cómo puedo convencer a uno de los de mi equipo de futbol para que regrese con nosotros si no quiere ni contestarme el teléfono?

Era cierto. Había estado buscando al Hombre Nuclear por teléfono en los últimos dos días sin ninguna suerte. Un par de veces me contestó él mismo y, al darse cuenta de que era yo, colgaba inmediatamente.

Mi papá se empujó los lentes, sacó la cara del libro que estaba leyendo y me dio el mejor consejo que jamás me había dado:

—La comunicación es el pilar de la civilidad, Tito. Hablando se entiende la gente.

No estoy seguro de si me quiso decir lo que yo entendí, pero al menos no me fui con las manos vacías. Según yo, eso quería decir: "Ve a buscar al Hombre Nuclear para que te diga por qué demonios se salió del equipo o aplícale tu famosa llave china". Y eso hice.

Fui solo a casa del Hombre Nuclear porque, en domingo, Iñaki nunca está. Es el día que sale con sus abuelitos y su mamá a dar la vuelta.

Cuando llamé a la puerta de la casa, sólo de milagro pregunté por Otilio Sánchez y no por el Hombre Nuclear. Su mamá, una señora muy cortés que habla muy chistoso, me dijo que pasara y esperara. Y ahí estaba yo, con mi uniforme de las Chivas, sentado en un sofá, cuando Otilio apareció.

—Hola, Tito.

—Hola, Hom... eh, digo, Otilio.

Se sentó frente a mí. Su mamá nos llevó chocolate y tortillas de harina con mermelada. Permanecimos callados hasta que ya no pude aguantar más.

—Bueno, ya. ¿Por qué te saliste del equipo, eh?

—¿Cómo que por qué? Por malo. ¿Qué no te das cuenta, Tito? Soy el único que no hace nada en la cancha. Soy tan chafa, que hasta me da pena estar ahí, por eso me salí.

—Pero sólo es porque no corres. Si corrieras, sería otra cosa.

—Sí, claro que sería otra cosa. Todos se morirían de la risa.

Era cierto. ¿Cómo discutir eso? Y aunque el Hombre Nuclear nunca hiciera nada de nada en el campo, al menos era un sexto hombre. Pero no podía pedirle que hiciera lo que no quería. Ni yo mismo, en su situación, habría aceptado jugar, porque debe de ser horrible que toda la escuela se burle de ti. Así que, en cuanto terminé mi chocolate, me dispuse a marcharme.

—Hace dos años me fracturé la pierna jugando futbol en Monterrey —dijo él, de pronto—. ¿Sabes por qué corro tan chistoso? Porque me da miedo volver a fracturarme.

—Creí que tenías un problema en las rodillas y que por eso no corrías bien.

—Sí tengo un problema, pero no en las piernas. El doctor que me operó dice que quedé muy bien. Mi problema es que tengo miedo. Nada más.

No supe qué más decir. Si Otilio no quería correr, era su decisión. Y no podíamos hacer nada al respecto. O al menos yo, por muy capitán del equipo que fuera.

Solamente quedábamos cuatro integrantes. Y así nos enfrentaríamos a los Cherokees en la semifinal, para que nos despedazaran. De todas formas, seguíamos dándonos cita en el Parque de los Venados para entrenar todos los días. Hasta Óliver, quién lo dijera, se puso a hablar, a la mitad de una de nuestras prácticas, para encontrarle una solución a nuestro problema.

—Capitán, tenemos que hacer algo o los Cherokees nos van a hacer pomada.

—Cierto, Óliver —tuve que admitir.

—Cabiño.

—Bueno, ¿qué sugieres?

—Que entren dos niñas. Ni modo.

Iñaki y Edson me miraron. Teníamos que hacerlo. Sabíamos perfectamente que algunas de ellas eran bastante buenas jugando, aunque nos doliera mucho reconocerlo. Además, como era martes, todavía teníamos un par de prácticas por delante. Consentimos en que era lo mejor. Así que, haciendo de tripas corazón, como dice mi mamá, convoqué a todos: mi abuelo, Hugo, Luisito, Olariñárritu y, por supuesto, las Rockets.

—A ver, chavos —dije—, quiero preguntarles a quiénes de ustedes les gustaría ocupar los lugares vacíos en los Cohetes Rayados.

Todavía ni terminaba de hablar cuando adivinen quién se apuntó.

—¡Yo!, yo quiero formar parte. Muchas gracias, Tito.

Era Luisito. Y si le hubieran visto la cara, habrían hecho lo mismo que yo. Tragué saliva y dije:

—Bueno, ya está ocupado uno de los lugares. ¿Quién entra en el otro?

Me da pena decir lo que siguió después. Pero así fue: Susana y Dolores Zúñiga se pelearon por el único puesto vacío. Hubo que separarlas. Una quería jugar al lado de Iñaki; la otra... en fin, para qué les platico. El caso es que mi hermana ganó (creo que porque se ha entrenado bastante bien conmigo en eso de los jalones de pelos). Y cuando Dolores Zúñiga, llorando, admitió quedarse con el puesto de capitana de las porristas, todo volvió a la normalidad.

Y no fue tan mala idea, hay que decirlo. Susana era mejor que varios de nosotros. Eso se vio en el entrenamiento. ¡Vaya vergüenza! De hecho, para que no quede duda, he de decir que no sólo era mejor que Óliver. Pero a pesar de lo buena que era, la pusimos en la portería, porque ninguno de nosotros quiso ocuparla y ni modo de poner a Luisito ahí, pues eso sí hubiera sido el colmo de los colmos.

Y seguimos practicando. Yo corría para todos lados tomando a Luisito de la mano. Los Cherokees nos miraban a lo lejos y se burlaban. Carlos Alberto, en cambio, rodeado siempre de las niñas que estaban enamoradas de él, cada vez nos miraba con más respeto. O eso digo yo, cuando menos, porque eso parecía.

Y llegó el viernes. Toda la escuela se presentó a las dos semifinales. La primera, entre los Ángeles de Charlie y los Relámpagos. Hubieran visto qué partidazo. Ambos equipos son muy buenos, pero al final ganaron los Relámpagos 5 a 3. Un partidazo, la verdad. Esos chavos de sexto de veras son buenos.

Luego vino el otro partido: Cohetes Rayados contra Cherokees. Y hay que admitirlo: a pesar de que llegamos bastante animados, cuando estábamos esperando el silbatazo del profesor Colina, me di cuenta de que verdaderamente éramos un equipo de lástima. Sin uniformes, con una portera que apenas había entrenado dos días para estar ahí (y que no dejaba de lanzar besos a la defensiva, en especial al güero del lado izquierdo), un niño bailarín de ballet, otro que no veía nada... en fin, éramos de veras un equipo como para dar pena.

Y, no obstante, ahí estábamos, enfrentando nuestra suerte, esperando el inicio de lo que se veía venir como toda una carnicería. Vi en las gradas a la maestra Lucía, que nos sonreía. Vi a Carlos Alberto, que de veras parecía otro. Vi en las gradas varias pancartas que nos apoyaban. Y en ese momento me di cuenta de que Luisito tenía razón: teníamos eso que a los otros les faltaba. Que, a pesar de ser el equipo más raro del mundo, ahí estábamos, dispuestos a darlo todo. ¿Cómo se llamaba eso que sentía pero que no podía explicar?

—Mendiolea, ¿está seguro? ¿Quiere que Luis Pichardo juegue con ustedes? —me preguntó el profesor Colina antes de silbar el inicio.

—Claro que sí, profesor. Es muy bueno jugando —dije, palmeando a Luisito.

—Bueno, pues ustedes sabrán. Aunque no debería permitirlo.

Y el profesor Colina sopló su silbato.

Fue un partido muy distinto al anterior. Aunque salimos a la cancha con gran ánimo, desde el principio era obvio que estábamos en desventaja. Luisito se la pasaba tirando puntapiés a diestra y siniestra sin pegarle a nada (ni siquiera a un Cherokee, que ya hubiera sido algo); Óliver no podía hacer todo él solo en la parte delantera; Iñaki no dejaba de correr por todos lados sin tocar siquiera el balón, como es su costumbre, y yo no podía controlar el centro de la cancha. En pocas palabras, los Cherokees demostraron su superioridad desde el principio. A los cinco minutos metieron su primer gol. Y Susana no le vio ni el polvo al balón, el cual se incrustó en la red como si quisiera agujerearla.

Aun así, volvimos a la batalla en cuanto hicimos el saque de media cancha. Y de una cosa sí me di cuenta al instante, y eso me parecía todo un milagro: ninguno de nosotros dejaba de correr, de pelear, de buscar la pelota. Es cierto que éramos más malos que los Cherokees, pero ninguno de nosotros parecía notarlo. Me acordé de las palabras de Luisito: era como si estuviéramos compitiendo los Cohetes contra los Cohetes, no contra los Cherokees. Como si quisiéramos demostrar que podíamos ser mejores, no que ellos, sino que nosotros mismos. Y al acordarme de las palabras de Luisito, quien dentro del campo también corría y buscaba una pelota que le resultaba imposible encontrar, comprendí que sin duda había demostrado que teníamos algo que los demás no, algo que puedes tener así seas niño o niña, gordo o flaco, chico o grande. Ninguno de nosotros se había fijado en que los Cherokees eran más rudos o más grandes que nosotros; simplemente habíamos salido a ganar. Y eso era lo importante.

Terminamos el primer tiempo 5 a 0. Curiosamente, los Cherokees, que se veían tan cansados como nosotros, no se pusieron a molestarnos ni nos hicieron burla ni nada durante el descanso. Algo me decía que comenzaban a respetarnos.

De cualquier modo, yo no podía perder de vista un detalle importante. Aunque habíamos salido a ganar... íbamos perdiendo. Y por mucho.

—No sé por qué pensé que íbamos a conseguir el milagro —dije, desmoralizado.

Entonces, quién sabe si por mis palabras o por qué razón, ocurrieron dos milagros, uno tras otro. Dos verdaderos milagros. El primero:

—Tito, quiero pedirte un gran favor. Permíteme estar en tu equipo.

Miré por encima de mi hombro. Era increíble. Se trataba de Carlos Alberto. Yo no supe qué decir. Me quedé mudo. En primera, porque no había ningún sitio disponible en nuestro equipo y ni modo que inventara uno así de la nada. Y en segunda, porque no podía creer que el mejor mariscal de campo de la liga infantil de futbol americano me estuviera pidiendo eso a mí, el jugador de futbol más maleta del mundo.

—¿Y por qué? —le pregunté.

—Porque me gustaría estar en un equipo que juega con tanto corazón como el de ustedes.

Eso era. Ahí estaba eso a lo que se refería Luisito. No es lo mismo jugar bien que jugar con corazón, con espíritu. Eso era más importante. Y yo creo que Luisito también se dio cuenta de mi gran descubrimiento. O no habría dicho lo que dijo después.

—Me parece muy bien, Carlos Alberto. Yo hasta te cedería mi lugar. Excepto por una cosa.

—¿Qué cosa?

—Que para jugar en este equipo no basta con desearlo; hay que tener eso que no se ve pero se siente. Y el lugar que estoy ocupando pertenece a alguien que siempre lo ha tenido.

Carlos Alberto se quedó muy triste, mirándonos a los dos, sobre todo porque, detrás de él, estaba el único y verdadero dueño del puesto que ocupaba Luisito Pichardo: el Hombre Nuclear.

—Tito, ¿hay problema si quiero entrar otra vez? —dijo Otilio, el Hombre Nuclear Sánchez.

—Claro que no —respondió Luisito por mí—. Además, estoy seguro de que lo vas a hacer muy bien.

Y entonces, el otro milagro. Todos los niños de las gradas empezaron a gritar como locos. Parecía que hubieran visto un ovni aterrizar en pleno patio o algo por el estilo.

—¿Qué pasa? ¿Qué les pasa a todos? —dije.

—¿Qué no lo ves? —me preguntó Iñaki. Y agarrándome la cabeza, me hizo voltear en la dirección correcta.

Increíble. Me dieron ganas de llorar. El Tigre Quezada en persona se abría paso entre la chiquillada. Iba con varios hombres de traje que sostenían algunas cajas. En cuanto localizó al profesor Colina, fue hacia él y le dio la mano, muy efusivo. Yo no lo podía creer.

—¡Caray, niños y niñas! ¡El Tigre Quezada ha venido a nuestra escuela! —exclamó el director, por el micrófono. Se veía que él tampoco podía dar crédito a sus ojos.

Más gritos. Y el Tigre Quezada, en su atuendo deportivo, con sus anteojos oscuros y su gran sonrisa, saludaba a todos a la distancia. La gritería era impresionante. Y yo no cabía en mí. De veras creí que era un sueño. Se acercó al micrófono y dijo:

—Estoy muy orgulloso de estar aquí, en la escuela Héroes de la Nación, gracias a que fui invitado a entregar la copa del primer lugar.

Más gritos y algarabía. Las Rockets se echaron una "a la bimbombá" en honor al Tigre. La locura, pues. El profesor Colina tuvo que pedir silencio varias veces para poder hacer una observación.

—Sí, pero la gran final de la copa es hasta la semana que entra —dijo.

—¿Ah, sí? —contestó el Tigre Quezada—. ¿O sea que me equivoqué?

Sí. Se había equivocado de fecha, pero ¿a quién le importaba? Además, lo que dijo después casi me hace desmayar.

—Entonces no es mi culpa. Alguien por ahí me pasó mal la fecha. ¿Dónde está Tito Mendiolea?

Me tuvieron que empujar hacia allá. No podía creer que el Tigre me estuviera llamando a su lado, aunque fuera para regañarme por haberme equivocado de día. Cuando llegué frente a él, pensé que iba a sufrir mi tan temido y esperado infarto. Pero aun si eso ocurría, no me importaba, porque estaba seguro de que moriría completamente feliz.

—Hola, Tito —me dijo, revolviéndome el pelo—. Traje los uniformes que me pediste para tu equipo. Y unos cuantos más para tu porra.

Era cierto. Los hombres que iban con él se pusieron a repartirlos. Llevaban quince uniformes en total. Hasta las Rockets alcanzaron. Y también traían uno talla cuarenta. Cuando lo sacaron de la caja, por su enorme tamaño, todos supimos luego luego para quién era. El Burbuja se abrió paso entre los demás niños como si lo fueran persiguiendo. "¡Ése es el mío!", gritaba a voz en cuello, "¡ése es mío!". No pudo esperar ni un segundo para probárselo. Le venía que ni mandado a hacer.

Luego, el Tigre volvió a tomar el micrófono para decir:

—¿Y dónde está Iñaki Fuentes?

Iñaki se puso más blanco que un papel. Estaba seguro de que era una broma. Y antes de que se echara a correr afuera de la escuela, presa del pánico, tuve que ir por él.

—¿Por qué me está llamando a mí? —me preguntó, todo descompuesto.

—Cállate y hazte el enfermo —le dije al oído (aunque mi petición era innecesaria porque Iñaki se veía verdaderamente enfermo de tan pálido que se había puesto por el susto).

—¿El enfermo? ¿Por qué?

—Porque le conté en una carta que estás mal del corazón y que a lo mejor te mueres muy pronto.

—¿Estás loco de la cabeza o qué? El que está mal del corazón eres tú.

—Sí, pero me dio no sé qué decirle eso. Capaz que no es cierto.

—Eres un mentiroso. Eres un...

No pudo terminar. Ya lo había arrastrado al lado del Tigre, quien nos sonreía. Entonces mi ídolo se arrodilló frente a mi mejor amigo. Lo que le dijo fue maravilloso, porque sólo nosotros dos pudimos oírlo. Y yo sentí que me lo decía a mí.

—Lo que haces es muy valiente. Acuérdate de que el valor no significa no tener miedo, sino vencer todos tus miedos. El primer contrincante a quien tienes que vencer siempre es a ti mismo. Felicidades, eres un campeón.

Y no dijo más. Fue a sentarse a las gradas en compañía de los hombres que iban con él, para presenciar el partido. Ya todos los Cohetes Rayados se pintaban de los colores de las Chivas del Guadalajara. Y cuando digo "todos", me refiero a todos. Hasta Óliver se quitó su uniforme de los Pumas. El Hombre Nuclear, Luisito, Olariñárritu y toda la porra. Todos. Y mientras Luisito Pichardo se ponía su playera rayada de Cohete Rayado me comentó algo que me puso tan rojo como las rayas de nuestros nuevos uniformes.

—¿Te das cuenta, Tito?

—¿De qué?

—De que todo esto fue por ti. Sólo alguien con tu espíritu habría podido llevar tan lejos a su equipo.

Te lo dije, tú en particular tienes eso que no puede verse con los ojos.

—¿Yo? ¿Y por qué yo? —me puse tan rojo como un jitomate.

—Porque desde un principio tú lo deseaste con todo el corazón. Y eso es contagioso, más contagioso que la tos. Tanto, que se lo pegaste a todo tu equipo. Míralos.

Cierto. Había que verlos. Estaban que parecía Navidad. Además, ya hasta portero teníamos. El Burbuja se fue a parar a la portería y no hubo poder humano que lo quitara de ahí. Susana estuvo empujándolo con todas sus fuerzas para sacarlo del campo, pero estoy seguro de que ni una grúa lo habría hecho moverse. "Quítate, gordo", decía una y otra vez. Pero no lo consiguió. Terminó por volver a su sitio en la porra.

Iba a comenzar el segundo tiempo de la semifinal. ¿Cómo se los platico? Íbamos perdiendo 5 a 0, pero no se nos notaba en la cara. Con los nuevos bríos que nos había infundido el Tigre, parecía que era al revés: que fuéramos ganando 5 a 0. Al grito de las Rockets ("¡Arriba el mejor equipo de todos los sistemas solares: los Cohetes Rayados de la Colonia Portales!"), el profesor Colina dio inicio al segundo tiempo. Entonces yo, antes de tocar siquiera el balón, llamé al Hombre Nuclear a mi lado porque sentí que era mi deber.

—Tengo algo que decirte.

—Adelante, capitán.

Pero se me borró el casete, como dice mi mamá. En esos momentos, mi mejor intención era decirle lo que nos había dicho el Tigre a Iñaki y a mí para que se sintiera animado, que no tuviera miedo, que... pero no supe ni cómo empezar.

—Caray, Mendiolea. Si no mueven el balón, los descalifico —nos urgió el profesor Colina en tono enérgico.

—¿Qué tienes que decirme, Tito?

—Nada, que le eches ganas, Otilio —fue todo lo que dije. ¡Vaya fiasco de capitán!

—Dirás Otilio, el Hombre Nuclear Sánchez.

Ese día nació la leyenda. Claro que en ese momento yo no lo sabía; ya después me enteré de que Otilio y Luisito Pichardo se habían estado viendo para entrenar. Fue Luisito quien lo ayudó a sacar al campeón que llevaba dentro (el que no había pisado las canchas desde su natal Monterrey). Se veían en el Parque de los Venados por las noches. Ahí Luisito había tenido tiempo de platicar con él. Y seguro que le había dicho algo como lo que el Tigre nos había dicho a Iñaki y a mí. Me di cuenta de que yo no tenía nada que decirle al Hombre Nuclear, porque todo estaba dicho.

Así que moví el balón.

Éramos otro equipo. Jugamos como si fuéramos de primera división. ¿Pero quién creen que hizo la

verdadera diferencia? Pues nada menos que Otilio, el Hombre Nuclear Sánchez. Aún recuerdo que, en cuanto empezó a correr, toda la escuela hizo el sonidito "tutututuuuu". Pero ahora fue distinto. Otilio en verdad corrió. Sin miedo. Sin trabas. Ya no lo hizo como si tuviera las rodillas pegadas. Un milagro. Corría de un lado al otro como si se quisiera desquitar de todos los años que no lo había hecho, como si se quisiera desquitar de todos los partidos que había jugado con miedo. Iba de aquí para allá como una locomotora (¿o debería decir como un cohete?) y no perdía para nada el balón cuando se lo pasaban Óliver o Edson, quienes estaban impresionadísimos. Burlaba a los Cherokees que daba gusto. Se dio un autopase en el área chica. Hasta una chilena se aventó. Un verdadero prodigio.

Siete goles anotó Otilio esa mañana. Siete goles en quince minutos. ¿Pueden creerlo? Los Cherokees ya no pudieron hacer ni uno solo en ese segundo tiempo porque la defensiva también estaba infranqueable. El marcador final fue de 7 a 5. Un partido como no se había visto en mucho tiempo. Y no lo digo yo, lo dijo el mismísimo Tigre Quezada, quien de inmediato preguntó el nombre de ese muchacho maravilla. ¿Quién lo iba a decir? Ese día nos vinimos a enterar de que Otilio era un campeón goleador cuando jugaba en Monterrey, antes de fracturarse la pierna. Un campeón como no ha habido ni habrá otro.

Esa tarde fue estupenda. Pero no crean que porque el Tigre Quezada nos llevó a tomar un helado a todos los Cohetes Rayados y después nos estuvo enseñando, en el parque, cómo dominar un balón con la cabeza. Ni tampoco porque Lolita me regaló un Tango nuevecito (no, yo todavía tampoco lo creo; es más, déjenme repetirlo porque me gusta mucho como suena: Lolita me regaló un Tango nuevecito; el balón oficial de la Copa del Mundo por fin era mío). Esa tarde, Lolita y yo empezamos a ser amigos. Qué cosas, ¿no? Pero les digo que tampoco por eso la tarde fue estupenda. Fue por lo otro. Porque me di cuenta de que si quería en verdad ser un héroe como el Tigre, tenía que poner en práctica sus palabras.

Así que lo primero que hice después de que el Tigre se despidió de nosotros, fue ir a la casa de la maestra

Lucía. Llamé a su puerta. Y en cuanto abrió, se lo dije, sin tomar aire siquiera:

—Maestra, no quiero que se vaya muy lejos. Por favor, no lo haga.

Se arrodilló para que sus ojos quedaran frente a los míos.

—¿Y por qué, Tito?

—Porque yo la quiero mucho. Y quiero casarme con usted algún día.

Esta vez es cierto, eso le dije. Ella me acarició el pelo y me abrazó. Les juro que me abrazó.

—Nada me daría más gusto que casarme con el capitán de los Cohetes Rayados, Tito —dijo sin dejar de abrazarme—. Pero tengo que irme a Zurich porque me ofrecieron una beca y no puedo desperdiciarla.

—¿No la están secuestrando unos extraterrestres, maestra?

—No, Tito, te juro que no. No quisiera irme porque aquí en México he hecho toda mi vida, tengo a mi mamá, los tengo a ustedes. Pero nadie me está secuestrando, en serio.

Se puso de pie y me sacudió el cabello. Luego, añadió:

—Te prometo que nos vamos a escribir mucho. Y ya veremos si todavía quieres casarte conmigo cuando crezcas.

—Bueno.

Nos despedimos. Me dio un beso en la mejilla. Y yo me fui flotando a mi casa. Me fui flotando porque me había atrevido a hacer lo que tenía que hacer. Y porque había vencido el miedo de decirle a la maestra Lucía lo mucho que la quería. Creo que hay que ser una especie de héroe para hacerlo. Pero en cuanto llegué a mi casa, dejé de flotar por los aires y deseé que la tierra se abriera y me tragara porque todavía tenía otro miedo que enfrentar. Uno peor. Pero acordándome del Tigre Quezada y de Otilio, el Hombre Nuclear Sánchez, me enfrenté a mi destino. Mi papá ya había llegado del trabajo y estaba leyendo el periódico. Así que corrí a mi recámara y, de mi mochila, saqué la tarjeta del doctor macabro. Y otra vez, sin tomar aire siquiera, le dije a mi papá:

—Papá, no te había querido decir, pero este doctor fue a vernos a la escuela. Y me dio su tarjeta para que un día le hiciéramos una visita.

Mi papá tomó la tarjeta en sus manos y, en cuanto vio el nombre del doctor, se puso a dar de gritos. Les juro que necesité echar mano de todo mi valor para no salir corriendo de la casa y buscar refugio en la de Iñaki o huir del país escondido en un camión de toronjas.

—¡Marta! ¡Marta! ¡Ven para acá! ¡Rápido! ¡A que no sabes quién quiere vernos!

Mi mamá acudió enseguida. Yo juraba que no tardarían en llamar al doctor y, con él, al dueño de una funeraria para que me tomara medidas para el ataúd. Por la cara de felicidad que puso mi mamá en cuanto vio la tarjeta, me di cuenta de que, o no comprendía el tamaño de la tragedia, o nunca me había querido y le daba un gusto enorme deshacerse de mí. Me dio un coraje tremendo que sólo por no levantar el asiento del baño cuando hago pipí quisiera enterrarme con tanta prisa. Corrí a la puerta de la casa, pero antes de salir, reclamé:

—¿Me voy a morir y a ti te da risa?

—¿Qué tonterías dices, Tito?

—Pues que ese doctor fue a la escuela y me revisó el corazón tres veces y luego me dio esa tarjeta para que se las diera a ustedes. Seguramente les va a decir que me voy a morir, y ustedes se ponen tan felices por eso, que de puro coraje me voy a ir a vivir para siempre con Iñaki. Y los dos vamos a formar una banda de asaltabancos.

—¡Ay, Tito! ¡Ay, Tito! —dijo mi mamá.

En ese momento me di cuenta de que uno no puede ser un héroe para todo el mundo. Además, las mamás son las mamás. Y me imagino que hasta la del Tigre Quezada le dice de vez en cuando "¡Ay, Tigre! ¡Ay, Tigre!", si a su hijo se le olvida quitarse los zapatos de futbol para andar descalzo por la casa. Eso es seguro.

Para todos aquellos que aman el juego de las patadas más que las pantuflas viejas que recibieron en el intercambio de Navidad, ¿en qué estábamos? Ah, sí. Decíamos que el gran centro delantero del Inter de Milán, a los dos minutos de haber empezado el partido, se perfila para tirar hacia la portería, después de burlar a toda la defensa del Real Madrid. Tal parece que va a cumplir su promesa de anotar el primer gol de esta Copa antes de que transcurran cinco minutos del partido. ¿Y qué creen que hace? En vez de tirar a quemarropa, también decide burlar al portero. Lo deja tirado a pocos metros del área. Y así, con toda tranquilidad, lleva el balón hasta la línea de meta. Pero ahí tampoco se decide a tirar.

En vez de eso, sólo roza la pelota con la punta de los tacos, y el balón, con toda lentitud, traspasa la línea de meta. El portero no tiene tiempo de impedirlo. ¡Qué golazo, señores! Y apenas a los tres minutos de haber iniciado el encuentro. Qué golazo de Otilio, el Hombre Nuclear Sánchez, el mejor centro delantero mexicano de todos los tiempos.

Y véanlo, seguramente va a festejar el gol como siempre lo hace. Se levanta la playera y se aproxima a la tribuna. Y ahí, estampado en la camiseta blanca, puede leerse el nombre de la persona a quien dedica el gol.

Se los dije. Está dedicando su gol al mejor atleta de todos los tiempos, aquel al que el presidente invita a desayunar a cada rato a su casa, aquel que ha sido un gran ejemplo para todos los niños de nuestra nación, aquel que está en toda la propaganda de las casas de ropa deportiva.

¡Ey!, pero no hagan esa cara de perplejidad. En ningún momento dije que el centro delantero del Inter fuera el mejor atleta mexicano de todos los tiempos. ¿O sí? No. Vuelvan a las primeras páginas si no me creen. Aunque ambos entrenaban juntos de niños, no son la misma persona. ¿Quieren acercarse para ver a quién me refiero? Claro que lo recuerdan. Lean con atención lo que dice la playera de Otilio Sánchez: "Gol dedicado a mi amigo y héroe Luis Pichardo". Eso es lo que está estampado en el pecho del famoso Hombre Nuclear, el delantero mejor pagado en la historia del futbol europeo.

Nada menos que Luis Pichardo —el mayor orgullo de México, quien ha ganado tantas medallas de atletismo en los últimos Juegos Paralímpicos, que ya ni le caben en su casa— es el mexicano más veloz de todos los tiempos, el mejor atleta. Y también es mi amigo. Y se entrenó junto con Otilio Sánchez cuando estudiábamos la primaria. Porque empezaron a trabajar una noche, hace muchos años, cuando Otilio le confesó sus miedos y Luisito le dijo que nada es imposible si se hace con espíritu y corazón. Y así lo hicieron. Aun antes de aquella memorable semifinal, el niño ciego más rápido de todos los tiempos y el mejor centro delantero que jamás tendremos en muchos años ya se daban cita para vencer todas sus barreras en el Parque de los Venados.

Y hasta aquí llega la historia.

Bueno... no dejemos aquí las cosas, pues sé que les da curiosidad saber qué pasó exactamente después de esa semifinal.

Pues bien, les diré que los Cohetes Rayados nos enfrentamos a los Relámpagos en un partido en el que el marcador fue lo de menos, porque tanto unos como otros dimos todo en la cancha. Al final, es cierto, perdimos 4 a 3. Pero eso no importó porque el juego fue memorable y los dos equipos jugamos limpiamente. Hasta yo pude hacer el pase para uno de los dos goles que hizo el Hombre Nuclear. El tercer gol fue de Óliver (que se puso de un pesado que no vean).

Después, la escuela dio una fiesta a la que invitaron a nuestros padres, hermanos y abuelos (incluso los ex futbolistas deschavetados). Hubo música de los Beatles; la mamá de Iñaki hizo un millón de galletas, en fin... todo un suceso (de cualquier modo, al Tigre Quezada se le olvidó ir a entregar la copa, o sea que nos dolió menos haber perdido). Los Cherokees, misteriosamente, me dejaron de molestar...

La vida siguió su curso. Y aunque es cierto que México consiguió su pase para el mundial de Argentina 78 gracias a mis plegarias de todas las noches, también es verdad que quedamos en último lugar. Pero yo seguí haciendo deporte siempre que pude (aunque nunca fuera tan bueno como mis amigos Otilio Sánchez o Luis Pichardo).

La maestra Lucía nunca regresó de Zurich. Pero no me importó, porque la maestra nueva, Pilar, era tan bonita que resultaba imposible sacar dieces con ella.

Y se preguntarán, ¿qué fue del Tigre Quezada? Pues bien... un buen día decidió que ya estaba cansado del futbol y se metió a hacer telenovelas (¡guácala!) porque dijo que ahí le pagaban más. Así que, como dejó el futbol, yo... pues tuve que buscarme otro deporte... y otro héroe. Pero no me fue nada difícil encontrar uno nuevo. Nada difícil.

Querido Toro Valenzuela:

Primero déjame presentarme.

Mi nombre es Tito, siempre me ha gustado el beisbol y desde chico te he admirado...

Impreso en los talleres de
Grupo Gráfico Editorial,
Calle B No. 8, Parque Industrial Puebla 2000,
C.P. 72220, Puebla, Pue.
Junio de 2011.

John Calvin and the Printed Book

Habent sua fata libelli

John Calvin and the Printed Book

Jean-François Gilmont
Translated by Karin Maag

Sixteenth Century Essays & Studies 72
Truman State University Press

Translation of Jean-François Gilmont, *Jean Calvin et le livre imprimé,* edition published by
Droz, 1206 Geneva, Switzerland, © copyright 1997 by Librairie Droz SA.

Cover illustration: "Ionnes Calvinus Natus novioduni Picardorum," in John Calvin, *Joannis
Calvini Noviodumensis opera omniain novem tomos digesta.* Amsterdam: Johann Jacob
Schipper, 1667, 1:*4v.

Cover and title page design: Teresa Wheeler
Type: AGaramond, copyright Adobe Systems Inc.
Printed by Thomson-Shore, Dexter, Michigan USA

Library of Congress Cataloging-in-Publication Data

Gilmont, Jean François.
   [Jean Calvin et le livre imprimé. English]
   John Calvin and the printed book / Jean-Francois Gilmont ; translated by Karin Maag.
      p. cm. — (Sixteenth century essays & studies ; v. 72)
   Includes bibliographical references and index.
   ISBN-13: 978-1-931112-56-7 (alk. paper)
   ISBN-10: 1-931112-56-8 (alk. paper)
      1. Printing—Switzerland-Geneva—History—16th century. 2. Early printed books—
   Switzerland—Geneva—16th century—Bibliography. 3. Christian literature—Publishing—
   Europe—History—16th century. 4. Calvin, Jean, 1509–1564—Bibliography. 5. Calvin,
   Jean, 1509–1564—Books and reading. 6. Reformation—Switzerland—Geneva. 7. Cen-
   sorship—Switzerland—Geneva. 8. Geneva (Switzerland)—Imprints.   I. Title. II. Series.
   Z176.G2G5513 2005
   686.2'092—dc22

                                                                                    2005021531

Contents

Translator's Preface

In the spring of 2002, at the request of Jean-François Gilmont, I began the translation of his work on Calvin and the world of printing, originally published by Droz in Geneva in 1997. I had previously served as translator and English-language editor for another work edited by Professor Gilmont, *The Reformation and the Book*, published by Ashgate in 1999. Professor Gilmont is one of the foremost experts on Calvin's writings and I deeply appreciated the opportunity to translate this current text.

I wish to thank five students at Calvin College who helped with various stages of the project over the course of four summers: Ruth Speyer (2002), Joshua Wierenga (2003), Jeff Rop and Allison Graff (2004), and Lauren Colyn (2005). They proofread sections and suggested changes, typed and verified footnotes, and helped to create the bibliography. Without their able assistance, the project would have taken much longer. Susan Schmurr, the Meeter Center program coordinator, also valiantly typed large sections of the text and helped work on the bibliography. I take responsibility for any remaining flaws in the translation.

I am also deeply grateful to Raymond Mentzer, general editor of the Sixteenth Century Essays and Studies series, and to the staff at the Truman State University Press for their interest in this work and their help throughout the publishing process.

It is my hope that this work will prove to be a valuable resource for English-speaking students, Reformation scholars, and general readers who want to learn more about what Calvin read and wrote, and how he interacted with the world of print.

Karin Maag
Grand Rapids, Michigan
July 2005

Preface

Books in the Life of Calvin

John Calvin was a landmark figure in the history of Christianity. Thanks to his strong personality, he established and shaped a confessional branch of the Christian church, a branch that has become firmly rooted and has flourished throughout the centuries.

At the same time, the Reformer from Noyon was himself rooted in a specific historical context. He influenced his contemporaries and future generations by making use of the techniques of his day.

In this work, I intend to analyze one of the media he used extensively, namely, printed books. This approach will prove useful both for Calvin scholars and for historians of print and printing. However, my aim in advancing our knowledge of this aspect of the Reformer's work is not to isolate printing from other forms of communication that Calvin used. Indeed, my plan is to link the theme of printing to other aspects of communication, such as public and private oral discourse and unpublished writing. This task is made easier thanks to the important work of the last fifty years on Calvin's sermons.[1]

In establishing Calvin's relationship with printed books, the intention is not to focus on the content of his works, whether in terms of their style or the theological issues they address. Given the thorough research on Calvin's polemical writings carried out by Francis Higman[2] or, more recently, Olivier Millet's work on Calvin's rhetoric,[3] there would be little point in revisiting these topics. Instead, my bibliographical-historical approach is intended to complement earlier research. When relevant, I will highlight the links between communication techniques and the author's style.

---

[1] E. Mülhaupt, *Die Predigt Calvins, ihre Geschichte, ihre Form und ihre religiösen Grundgedanken* (Berlin: W. de Gruyter, 1931); and T. H. L. Parker, *Calvin's Preaching* (Edinburgh: T & T Clark, 1992), to mention only the oldest and most recent of these works. See below, 26–32.

[2] F. M. Higman, *The Style of John Calvin in His French Polemical Treatises* (Oxford: Oxford University Press, 1967).

[3] O. Millet, *Calvin et la dynamique de la parole* (Paris: H. Champion, 1992).

In the same way, I will not deal explicitly with the theological content of Calvin's writings. However, when analyzing his means of communication, content-related questions are inevitable. Indeed, such investigations can sometimes shed new light on the Reformer's thoughts and lead to new issues for theologians to consider.

Examining Calvin as author and writer in his historical context leads to a series of questions: What kinds of messages did Calvin entrust to the printed word? What were his reasons for writing? Did he have any interest in the work of printers and booksellers? In what ways were his oral and written teachings linked? What connections were there between what he said and what he wrote?

Given that Calvin lived during a major transitional era in the history of printing and reading, some of these questions are wide-ranging ones. Invented in the mid-fifteenth century, printing took more than eighty years to fully break free from its earlier dependence on manuscript texts. Between 1520 and 1540, the printed book became recognizably modern. For example, it was at this time that title pages began to provide the key elements of a book's identity. Character fonts became simplified and lost the numerous abbreviations and ligatures prevalent in manuscript writing. The body of works published became much larger and more modernized. Books were no longer the exclusive preserve of religion and the universities, but instead penetrated a wider social spectrum. As is true for all new technology, printing offered previously unknown advantages, but also brought new constraints.[4]

In the French printing industry in particular, a technological revolution took place. In less than ten years, between 1530 and 1540, the use of roman and italic fonts became widespread. Furthermore, and significantly, French became more commonly used in subject areas where Latin had previously reigned supreme. Moreover, Calvin played a significant role in the evolution of the languages considered appropriate for theological writings.

These changes also had an impact on reading. When printing was first developed, reading methods and strategies went through a series of subtle changes. For a long time, reading was such a difficult technique that almost no one could directly absorb the content of a text simply by looking at it. Instead, reading had to be done aloud, even if only quietly. The main reason for this was undoubtedly the clumsy setup of characters on the page. However, by the end of the Middle Ages, two important developments transformed reading. First, thanks to the growth of universities beginning in the twelfth century, a new kind of reader emerged: a researcher who consulted documents to locate references. To facilitate this process, printers used different techniques to enable readers to find subsections of text. Second, in early fifteenth-century Florence, under the leadership of Niccolò Niccoli young humanists developed a font that was more pleasing than Gothic and pioneered less compact typesetting. Thus the outward appearance of books achieved a better balance between

---

[4]See my introductory chapter in J.-Fr. Gilmont, ed., *La Réforme et le livre. L'Europe de l'imprimé (1517–v. 1570)* (Paris: Cerf, 1990), 19–28.

black and white on the page, thereby facilitating silent reading.[5] However, this new practice did not become immediately widespread. During the religio-political pamphlet wars in the German lands between 1520 and 1525, printed works made an impact more through group reading than private perusal. As Robert Scribner pointed out, "the multiplication effect usually attributed to the printed word was just as much a product of the spoken word."[6]

But this observation leads to further questions: are the same kinds of texts produced for reading aloud and silent reading? As we know from daily experience, the logic of oral discourse differs from that of printed materials, even though the links between the written and oral word are strong. Flaubert stated that a well-written text must pass the "talk-test," because the written word absolutely needs harmonic resonance. Was Calvin aware of the distinction between written and oral style?

As I was completing this study, I learned of Holger Flachmann's thesis produced in late 1996, *Martin Luther und das Buch*.[7] This scholar wrote his work, as I did, without having any similar monographs at his disposal dealing with the great humanist and religious leaders of the sixteenth century. There are only general works, as well as a few limited studies on Erasmus, Rabelais, and Luther. There is no study that deals with the questions I have raised here, even though there are a few interesting works in this area on Luther.[8] In contrast, there are no works at all in this field on Zwingli, Bullinger, Bucer, or even on Calvin's colleagues Farel, Viret, and Beza, making comparisons very difficult.

Holger Flachmann's work has changed this situation. It seems to me that his thesis proves both how rich and how complex these issues are. Coming at a similar topic from two different standpoints and with different concerns, we have each dealt with it in a unique fashion. It is true that Luther often made statements about books and printing, something Calvin did not do. It may not be too far off to say that Flachmann's work focuses primarily on what Luther said, and my work deals primarily with what Calvin produced. Of course we must recognize that Flachmann is aware that Luther's words and his actual practice feed off each other, for in his thesis, Flachmann deals with both topics. Beginning with Luther's use of texts (reading, book ownership, and publications), he continues his study by focusing on what Luther said about books, in terms of the words and images he used to define the concept of the book. Subsequently, Flachmann analyzes the role written works played in society, in terms of both civil and religious social practice, and the attitude

[5]See the articles of P. Saenger, A. Grafton, and my own in G. Cavallo & R. Chartier, eds., *Storia della lettura nel mondo occidentale* (Rome, Bari: Laterza, 1995); or its English translation, *A History of Reading in the West* (Amherst: University of Massachusetts Press, 1999).

[6]R. W. Scribner, *Popular Culture and Popular Movements in Reformation Germany* (London: Hambledon Press, 1987), 65, see also 54–60.

[7]H. Flachmann, *Martin Luther und das Buch* (Tübingen: J. C. B. Mohr, 1996).

[8]For Erasmus and Luther, see below, 281–83. For Rabelais, see M. B. Kline, *Rabelais and the Age of Printing* (Geneva: Droz, 1963).

of authorities, particularly in terms of censorship. It is at this point that the author deals with the connections between books and preaching—the proclamation of the word of God. Flachmann ends by highlighting the role that Luther gave to books in the history of salvation. This brief overview does not do justice to the depth of this work, in particular to the author's consummate skill in going back and forth between books and "the Book," namely, the Bible. I will leave to others the task of comparing his approach to mine. However, I felt it was important to acknowledge the work and note the ways it differs from mine, even though we deal with similar themes including reading, censorship, relations with printers, and different approaches to scripture.

THE OUTLINE OF THE WORK

Logic, rather than aesthetics, has guided the structure of this book. In order to devote the sections of each chapter to a coherent topic, I ended up with sections of different lengths. Therefore, certain sections are divided into subsections, while most of the text is divided primarily into paragraphs. Overall, the book consists of six chapters, structured as follows.

Chapter 1 does not constitute a narrowly focused introduction. Instead, I begin with three short sketches that present different facets of Calvin's relations with books and writing. These sketches are intended to whet the appetite by bringing the topic to life. The following section provides an overview of the key moments of the Reformer's life. As my intention is to provide a dynamic portrait of Calvin that shows how his relationship to books evolved, I wanted to provide some reference points to anchor the following analysis. Finally, before focusing on Calvin as the author of books, I discuss two other forms of communication that he used, specifically, speech for his teaching and manuscript text for his letters and certain other works.

Which of his writings did the Reformer entrust to printers? The next chapter provides an overview of his literary activity by listing his main printed works: the *Institutes*, exegetical commentaries, ecclesiastical writings (namely, works intended to sustain the life of the church, catechisms, liturgies, etc.), and polemical writings. The final section of the chapter deals specifically with the publication of Calvin's sermons. Chapter 2 thus presents an overview of Calvin's published corpus, a topic often omitted by his biographers.[9]

Since his writings are already well known, the next step is to examine how they came into being. The third chapter analyzes Calvin's writing process. The first matter to be considered is his reasons for writing: what factors led Calvin to take up his pen? Then there is the issue of language, since Calvin subtly shifted between Latin and

---

[9]A useful but superficial introduction can be found in W. de Greef, *Johannes Calvijn, Zijn werk en geschriften* (Kampen: De Groot Goudriaan, 1989); and W. de Greef, *The Writings of John Calvin: An Introductory Guide* (Grand Rapids: Baker Books, 1993).

French. Following a discussion of aspects of Calvin's style as noted by both the Reformer and his readers, a final section deals with where the writing process actually took place.

Calvin not only produced books, but he also made use of them. Thus the fourth chapter deals with Calvin as a reader. What do we know about Calvin's own library? This first question is followed by an analysis of the three most basic types of works he read, which were biblical, patristic, and classical texts. The subsequent section deals with the works of his contemporaries, predecessors, and colleagues in the work of the Reformation. The chapter ends with a few thoughts on what Calvin believed simple Christians should read.

The fifth chapter comes back to Calvin's own writings: when he had finished his works in manuscript form, they were brought to the printer. This chapter discusses Calvin's choice of printers, the role of the dedicatory prefaces, and finally, his specific knowledge of the world of the printed book.

During the Reformation, censorship regulated both what was written and what was read. In order to study Calvin's reaction to censorship, the entire topic has to be approached from several different viewpoints. First, in Geneva itself, Calvin was both one of the main instigators of the Genevan censorship system and also at times its victim. Second, outside Geneva, Calvin adopted the role of censor to control access to the works produced by other groups of Protestants, while he himself was on the receiving end of censorship carried out by Catholic authorities.

The conclusion to the book not only summarizes the whole, but also attempts to evaluate the importance of books and printing in the context of Calvin's other activities.

A number of rather dry but more comprehensive appendices offer readers a means of locating the data for some of the analyses presented in this work.

One final comment on my approach to this text is in order. Because the book follows a logical rather than chronological order, I have used the same anecdote more than once, drawing different lessons from it each time. Reference numbers will lead readers back to the most extensive account of any one anecdote. Furthermore, from my point of view, this topic does not need extensive scholarly notes on thousands of related topics or extensive bibliographical notes for each name or event mentioned. Thus the critical apparatus focuses primarily on the primary sources, which I have used extensively, and I have kept learned discussions in the footnotes to the bare minimum, attempting to make it unnecessary for readers to concentrate on the notes.

THE SOURCES

This research is directly linked to the *Bibliotheca Calviniana,* the bibliography of early editions of Calvin's writings. This work was begun by Rodolphe Peter, but was interrupted by his death in 1987. I have since continued the task and have completed three volumes presenting Calvin's published works up to 1600. This *Bibliotheca* does not merely describe the physical characteristics of each edition: it brings together the most information possible about the writing, printing, and dissemination of each work. These volumes, therefore, constitute one of the main sources for this monograph.[10]

Much of the data for the *Bibliotheca* and this book come from Calvin's correspondence, and his letters have proved invaluable for my topic. In search of information on books and printing, I have read the complete set of Calvin's letters. Although the information is not complete, as the edition of the *Calvini Opera* is outdated and poorly annotated, the body of correspondence was extensive enough to provide sufficient material for this study.

Beza's biography of Calvin is important because of both the specific details it includes and the historical context it provides. Three versions of the biography are available. The first was swiftly written after Calvin's death. Calvin died on 27 May 1564 and Beza completed his text on 14 June, describing it as a "short discourse," and publishing it immediately. A year later, Beza fulfilled his promise of "a beautiful and ample history" with a more fleshed-out version of the biography that was also chronologically much improved. Finally, when he published a selection of Calvin's letters in 1575, Beza revised his biographical account once again. In a polemical debate, Beza stated that the second version was not his, but had been written by Nicolas Colladon. Daniel Ménager has shown that Beza's statement was intended as a way of deflecting the critics who accused him of turning the dead Reformer into a new idol. Nonetheless, the three versions all carry the weight of Beza's authority, whether or not there were other writers involved in any of the editions.[11] Yet in order to distinguish between the first and second version, I have kept to the traditionally attributed authors, calling one Beza's biography and the other Colladon's biography. The final version makes almost no appearance in this work.

Sources for the chapter on censorship come primarily from the registers of the Genevan Council. The originals are held in the Archives d'Etat of Geneva. The registers are in two series, the first being the Council registers themselves and the second being the Council registers dealing with specific matters. As regards the topic of bookselling, using the systematic indexes prepared by scholars Alfred Cartier and Théophile Dufour greatly simplified the task of finding information in the registers. These notes are available in the Genevan Bibliothèque Publique et Universitaire.[12] I have also made use of the transcription of a certain number of extracts from the registers of the Consistory of Geneva, thanks to the kindness of Robert M. Kingdon, who

[10]R. Peter and J.-Fr. Gilmont, *Bibliotheca Calviniana,* 3 vols. (Geneva: Droz, 1991–94).

[11]D. Ménager, "Théodore de Bèze, biographe de Calvin," *Bibliothèque d'humanisme et renaissance* 45 (1983): 231–55, esp. 244–47.

[12] Geneva, Bibliothèque Publique et Universitaire, Ms. Fr. 3817 and 3871–3873.

sent to me parts of the work that he is currently preparing for publication. The first volume of that series appeared in the autumn of 1996.[13]

To help readers, but also to make sure that I have clearly understood the texts, I have translated all the quotations from Latin documents. When the works in question are ones by Calvin published in the sixteenth century, I use translations done in his lifetime as often as possible. For his polemical writings, I have used the *Recueil des opuscules,* a collection of Calvin's short treatises translated into French and published in 1566 by Pinereul.[14]

The groundwork for this synthesis was prepared through a series of articles and conference presentations. I have reworked and reorganized them, removing repetitious sections but also amplifying and at times correcting certain sections thanks to further in-depth analysis of primary sources.[15]

[13]*Registres du Consistoire de Genève au temps de Calvin,* 1:1542–1544, ed. T. A. Lambert and I. S. Watt under the direction of R. M. Kingdon and with the assistance of J. R. Watt (Geneva: Droz, 1996).

[14]This work is described in the third volume of the *Bibliotheca Calviniana,* 66/3.

[15]J.-Fr. Gilmont, "Calvin et la diffusion de la Bible." Lecture presented at "La Bible imprimée dans l'Europe moderne" conference, Paris, November 1991; idem, "Comment Calvin choisissait-il ses imprimeurs?" *Australian Journal of French Studies* 31 (1994): 292–308; idem, "L'apport de La Rochelle"; idem, "La rédaction et la publication du Commentaire des Pseaumes de Jean Calvin," *Bulletin de la recherche sur le psautier huguenot* 10–11 (1995): 6–10; idem, "Les sermons de Calvin: De l'oral à l'imprimé," *Bulletin de la société de l'histoire du protestantisme français* 141 (1995): 145–62; idem, "L'imprimerie réformée à Genève au temps de Laurent de Normandie (1570)," *Bulletin du bibliophile* 2 (1995): 262–78; idem, "La place de la polémique dans l'oeuvre écrite de Calvin," in *Le contrôle des idées à la Renaissance,* ed. J. M. De Bujanda (Geneva: Droz, 1996), 113–39; idem, "Comment Calvin choisissait-il ses dédicataires?" Lecture presented at the "Calvin et ses contemporains" conference, Paris, October 1995; idem, "La censure dans la Genève de Calvin," in *La censura libraria nell'Europa del secolo XVI,* ed. U. Rozzo (Udine: Forum, 1997), 15–30; idem, "Les épîtres dédicatoires de Jean Calvin," in *Prologues et préfaces de la Bible, xve–xvie siècles,* ed. B. Roussel and J.-D. Dubois (Paris: Cerf, 1998); idem, "Les premières traductions de l'Institution de la religion chrétienne" in *Festschrift for Peter De Klerk,* ed. W. H. Neuser, H. Selderhuis, and W. van't Spijker (Heerenveen: J. J. Groen, 1997); and idem, "La correction des épreuves à Genève autour de 1560," to be published in the *Mélanges Elly Cockx-Indesteege.*

Acknowledgments

In scholarly terms, this work owes much to the fruitful discussions I have had during my Genevan visits with the members of the Institut d'histoire de la Réformation and the Musée historique de la Réformation, especially Francis M. Higman, but also Max Engammare, Reinhard Bodenmann, and Alain Dufour. Over the course of many years, I have had the opportunity to receive constructive criticism from Bernard Roussel for my various projects. I wish to thank Robert M. Kingdon for his generosity in providing me with extracts from the Genevan Consistory registers. My thanks also go to Etienne de Sadeleer, who alerted me in a timely fashion to a recent study on Erasmus and printing. I am grateful to Monique Mund-Dopchie, Pierre-Maurice Bogaert, Claude Bruneel, Jean-Marie Cauchies, Roger Chartier, and Jean-Pierre Massaut for their willingness to read my manuscript and provide feedback on it.

The publication of the *Bibliotheca Calviniana* clearly acted as the starting point for this project. I am delighted to reiterate my deepest thanks to Mrs. Rodolphe Peter and her children for their confidence in me in asking me to continue the work carried out for so long by their husband and father.

The final version of this work was made possible by a sabbatical granted by the Catholic University of Louvain. I wish to thank the rector, Professor Crochet, the Dean of the Faculty of Philosophy and Humanities, Professor Bruneel, and the Director of the Bibliothèque générale et de sciences humaines, Jean Germain. I also wish to thank Hugh R. Boudin for the care with which he read the final version of this work.

My wife and daughters deserve at least the order of merit of the Knights of Calvin for their patience and support for my research, and their willingness to hear about my latest discoveries. I know they would prefer to see the sequel to Maître Abel, but to everything there is a season.

Abbreviations

ARG   *Archiv für Reformationsgeschichte.* Gütersloh, 1903– .

B.C.   R. Peter and J.-Fr. Gilmont, *Bibliotheca calviniana*: *Les oeuvres de Jean Calvin publiées au XVIe siècle.*

      Vol. 1, *Écrits théologiques, littéraires et juridiques, 1532–1554.* Travaux d'humanisme et Renaissance 255. Geneva: Droz, 1991.

      Vol. 2, *Écrits théologiques, littéraires et juridiques, 1555–1564.* Travaux d'humanisme et Renaissance 281. Geneva: Droz, 1994.

      Vol. 3, *Écrits théologiques, littéraires et juridiques, 1565–1600.* Travaux d'humanisme et Renaissance 339. Geneva: Droz, 2000.

CO   J. Calvin, *Opera quae supersunt omnia.* Edited by G. Baum, Ed. Cunitz, and Ed. Reuss. Corpus reformatorum 19–87. 59 vols. Berlin: Brunswick, 1863–1900.

O.S.   *Joannis Calvini Opera Selecta* Edited by Peter Barth and Wilhelm Niesel. 5 vols. Munich: Kaiser, 1926–59.

RC   Geneva, Archives de l'État, Registres du Conseil.

R. Consist.   Geneva, Archives de l'État, Registres du Consistoire.

R. Crim.   Geneva, Archives de l'État, Registres des Sentences criminelles.

RCP   *Registres de la Compagnie des Pasteurs de Genève.* Edited by Olivier Fatio et al. 13 vols. Geneva: Droz, 1962–.

R. Part.   Geneva, Archives de l'État, Registres du Conseil pour les affaires particulières.

VD 16   *Verzeichnis der im Deutschen Sprachbereich erschienenen Drucke des XVI Jahrhunderts.* Edited by Irmgard Bezzel. 25 vols. Stuttgart: Hiersemann, 1983–.

CHAPTER ONE

Introductory Remarks

In order to accurately weigh the importance of the printed text in Calvin's career, several areas deserve attention. Firstly, in order to evaluate his changing attitude toward books, we should note the key moments of his career. Secondly, we should set Calvin in the context of the people he encountered, the ideas he defended, and the institutions of which he was a part. Finally, we will examine two other means of communication that Calvin used, namely, oral discourse for his teaching and hand-written materials for his correspondence and some of his works. As a prelude, here are three short sketches illustrating different facets of Calvin's interactions with books and writing.

I.   THREE PREFATORY ANECDOTES

It seemed to me that a few short stories would immediately bring out the more human and lively aspect of this topic. These anecdotes illustrate some of the many facets of Calvin's connection with the written word.

A Hurriedly Written Work

In 1545, Calvin decided to write a lampoon exposing Pierre Caroli to ridicule. Precise information about Caroli is not significant at this point; the circumstances surrounding the writing of this lampoon are what prove interesting. We need only know that Caroli was a Parisian doctor of theology, who joined the Reformation only to return again to the Catholic church, and became anathema to Calvin and his two closest colleagues among the Reformers, Guillaume Farel and Pierre Viret.[1]

---

[1]A critical edition with scholarly introduction can be found in J. Calvin, *Défense de Guillaume Farel et de ses collègues contre les calomnies du théologastre Pierre Caroli par Nicolas des Gallars*, trans. J.-Fr.

In June 1545, Farel and Viret sent documents to Calvin on the subject of Caroli.[2] Pressed for time, Farel sent Calvin the original copies. In early July, Calvin decided to spend three days in the countryside at the small farm of his brother Antoine together with his main secretary of the time, Nicolas des Gallars. However, as they prepared to leave, disaster struck. Farel's notes were nowhere to be found. "Because I thought at the time, and I still believe," said Calvin, "that someone fraudulently absconded with them, I was so upset that I had to remain in bed the following morning." The loss of the documents was all the more serious in that Calvin had not yet read them. By the end of the day, the Reformer had regained his equilibrium and decided to leave for Saconnex regardless. Night fell when he and des Gallars were halfway there, and the two travelers were forced to spend the night at an inn. "The bedbugs tormented us so badly all night that we were unable to sleep for more than half an hour." At 3:00 a.m. the two unfortunate travelers set off again, but this time they were held up by rain. They finally arrived at the farm at 5:00 a.m., rested for two hours, and then began to work. Shortly thereafter Calvin was able to send the start of the text to Viret. "You will soon hear that it is all done," he added confidently.[3] Viret replied in a satirical letter, claiming to be amazed that Calvin was not stopped by so many extraordinary obstacles: compelled to leave the inn because of the bedbugs, he then begins to struggle against a flea—Viret meant Caroli.[4] Calvin enjoyed the joke: "Had I been lacking in courage to deal with Caroli's bites, your elegant and humorous comparison of bedbugs and fleas would have set me aflame." The work was not completed as quickly as originally intended because Calvin and then des Gallars were called upon to deal with other matters.[5] In any event, the work proceeded apace. Following the suggestion of Pierre Viret, the tract appeared under Nicolas des Gallars's name. Indeed, he was more than simply a fictitious author, because he had actually contributed to the writing of the work. In August, looking back on the whole matter, Calvin admitted that he came close to leaving Caroli to "bark." But as the treatise now existed, "Nunc alea jacta est. I was so heated after having started that I had no trouble reaching the finish. In truth, being able to play more freely, almost leaping, by using another name, also contributed to this ease of writing. See how pleased I am with myself. I feel I have written a work that is worthwhile."[6]

Gounelle (Paris: Presses universitaires de France, 1994). See also M. Engammare, "Pierre Caroli, veritable disciple de Lefevre d'Etaples," in *Jacques Lefevre d'Etaples (1450?–1536): Actes du colloque d'Etaples les 7 et 8 novembre 1992*, ed. J.-Fr. Pernot (Paris: Champion, 1995), 55–80. Regarding this anecdote, see E. Doumergue, *Jean Calvin, les hommes et les choses de son temps* (Lausanne: G. Bridel, 1899–1927), 3:533–34, 6:68.

[2]CO, 12:93 (CO references are to volume and column; Roman numerals following volume number refer to prefatory pages); and *B.C.1,* no. 45/10.

[3]CO, 12:100–1 (undated letter from early July 1545).

[4]CO, 12:105–6.

[5]CO, 12:107–8.

[6]CO, 12:124.

This story reveals many aspects of Calvin as a writer, first of all his astounding ability, in terms of both his speed of writing and his depth of thought. In a few days, he completed an in-octavo work of about a hundred pages, or seventeen thousand words. Furthermore, he wrote the work in spite of having lost a part of his source material. This situation had already occurred during the writing of the *Psychopanny-chia,* for which Calvin admitted having only indirect sources: "I have only received some notes from a friend, who had taken down what he had cursorily heard from their lips or collected by some other means."[7]

This story also displays Calvin's extremely sensitive emotional state. When he believed that his documents had been stolen, he fell ill. Calvin's emotions often played a major role in his writing. Another humorous anecdote confirms the Reformer's physical frailty. In September 1540, when living in Strasbourg, Calvin welcomed paying guests into his home to earn some money. Among others, he hosted a noble-woman, the Damoiselle du Verger, who behaved so fiercely toward his brother Antoine that the latter left the house. In reaction, Calvin suffered a gastric attack, as he explained at length to Farel. "When I am worked up by gastric trouble or great anxiety, I tend to calm down by eating and devouring food more voraciously than I should. This is exactly what happened to me this time. I filled my stomach that night at dinner with too much of the wrong kind of food and I was tortured by terrible indigestion the following morning."[8] I will leave aside the rest of this letter that goes on to describe the many ailments that plagued Calvin at the time.

Regarding the documents, however, I do not believe that Calvin had been a victim of theft. Other evidence suggests that Calvin's papers were very disorganized. In 1547 he lost a manuscript by Ribit and in 1550 he mislaid a manuscript by Farel for several days.[9] However, the accuracy of Calvin's treatise suggests that he had at least part of the texts sent by Farel still in hand.[10] Even if his papers were disorganized, his mind was clearly not. He had enough specifics on Caroli in his head to attack him for a hundred pages. Finally, we see here the particular bitterness with which Calvin pursued former friends, such as Pierre Caroli, who had been at his side during the Lausanne Disputation of 1536.

The Lost and Found Manuscript

The manuscript of Calvin's commentary on Second Corinthians caused its author a month's worth of worry. At that time, Calvin felt it necessary to entrust the

---

[7] John Calvin, *Psychopannychia; or, the Soul's Imaginary Sleep between Death and Judgement,* in *Selected Works of John Calvin: Tracts and Letters,* ed. H. Beveridge and J. Bonnet (Grand Rapids: Baker Books, 1983), 3:414; and J. Calvin, *Recueil des opuscules,* ed. Theodore Beza (Geneva: J.-B. Pinereul, 1566), 1.

[8] A.-L. Herminjard, *Correspondance des Réformateurs dans les pays de langue française, 1512–1544* (Geneva: H. Georg, 1866–1897), 6:313; and CO, 11:84.

[9] CO, 12:384, 13:408–9.

[10] J. Calvin, *Défense de G. Farel,* 99 n. 5.

Latin edition of his commentaries to the Strasbourg printer Wendelin Rihel.[11] In early July 1546, Calvin gave the manuscript and several letters to a young messenger. After a month without news, Calvin began to wonder about the reliability of the bearer. "He may have wanted to take revenge on us because my brother did not trust him. Indeed, he had disappointed my brother, who then later refused to entrust some valuable books to him." Calvin had, however, given the young man his manuscript without retaining a second copy. Two days later he was even more anxious. Thus he continued to wait for news from Strasbourg to find out whether the package had arrived:[12] "I still have no news about my commentary. If I find out that my commentary is lost, I have decided to never touch Paul again. But the danger is great. It has been a month since he left. I await with great anxiety the news that will come in the next mail delivery."[13] Viret was quick to react: "If your commentary on Paul is lost, I will be very upset, both for you and for the church."[14] On 25 August, Farel felt compelled to chastise his friend: "I was disappointed to learn that you had carelessly entrusted your notes on Second Corinthians, and they are at risk of disappearing. Given that mothers do not neglect their children, you, too, should have sent out this fruit of the Lord with greater care. And I hope that the Lord will be merciful to us so that the text is not lost."[15]

On 15 September 1546, when Calvin announced that the manuscript had been found, he explained that because of his concern over the loss of the text he had been unable to concentrate on his work: "Because I thought it might have disappeared, I lost a whole month's work. I had begun to work on the treatise *De Scandalis*, but was forced to lay it aside. Then everything that I started came to nothing. In fact I was only able to get through less than half a chapter of the Epistle to the Galatians. The problem was not so much the loss of the text itself, but the fact that I blamed myself for my negligence."[16] Two weeks later, on 2 October 1546, Calvin had regained his peace of mind: "Now I have finally begun to work my way through the Epistle to the Galatians."[17]

Three factors seem significant here. First, Calvin failed to make a copy of the manuscript, largely because of the cost in terms of time and money. Second, Calvin reacted strongly to the loss by exclaiming that he would no longer write anything on Paul. However, he did not keep to that plan, since he tried to start his commentary on the Epistle to the Galatians. Finally, Calvin's extreme sensitivity made it impossible for him to concentrate on his work, due, as he said, not so much to the loss in and of itself as to the fact that he blamed himself for it.

[11]See below 181–82.
[12]CO, 12:367.
[13]CO, 12:368.
[14]CO, 12:370.
[15]CO, 12:374.
[16]CO, 12:380.
[17]CO, 12:391.

Between the Written and Spoken Word

The issue of the Lord's Supper sharply divided the Protestant world: was Christ truly present in the bread, as Luther argued, or, as Zwingli saw it, was the Lord's Supper purely symbolic? At the time when Calvin was beginning to hear news of the Reformation, the divide between these different interpretations had been sealed by the Colloquy of Marburg in 1529. By 1536, thanks to the good work of Martin Bucer, the Wittenberg Concord allowed for a rapprochement between Luther and the south German theologians, though the Swiss were left out of the agreement.

While in Strasbourg, Calvin attempted to encourage concord by laying out a middle way in his *Traicté de la Cène*. He stated that the body of Christ is truly given to the faithful in the Lord's Supper, but in a spiritual sense. At first, Zwingli's successor at the head of the Zurich church, Heinrich Bullinger, neither could nor would follow Calvin, remaining firmly committed to the symbolic interpretation of his master. By 1540, friends on both sides tried to bring Calvin and Bullinger closer together. The task was not an easy one, for Calvin had as many reservations about Zwingli as Bullinger had about Calvin. However, the need for unity ultimately proved stronger than these concerns.

Luther's attacks propelled them both into the same camp, even though Calvin felt Bullinger was too forceful. In November 1544, Calvin suggested collaboration, though he restricted himself to suggesting a working method. He avoided dealing with the substance of the issue, "for I am worried that you will object to certain aspects of my way of teaching." He declared that he was simple and sincere in his speech: "whatever I feel, I say it simply and straightforwardly." Then he offered his solution: "if we could get together and talk for even half a day, it would be easy for us to come to an agreement, I hope, both in terms of form and content." Further on, he spoke of the small pebble, the "scruples" that ought not to stand in the way of brotherly friendship.[18] Shortly thereafter, Bullinger wrote a treatise in which he laid out his doctrine on the matter, and he seized the opportunity of Calvin's trip through Zurich in January 1547 to give it to him.[19] This particular journey was not, however, the opportunity for the meeting that had been sought after since 1544, perhaps because Calvin's stay was too brief. It is more likely that the Germanic Bullinger wanted letters rather than face-to-face meetings, feeling that written correspondence tended to remove ambiguities.

Before responding to Bullinger's treatise, Calvin turned to Farel. Claiming that letters were too risky for secrets, he called Farel to an emergency meeting. "Come

---

[18]Herminjard, *Correspondance*, 9:375; CO, 11:775. Regarding this anecdote, see A. Bouvier, *Henri Bullinger le successeur de Zwingli d'après sa correspondance avec les réformés et les humanistes de langue française* (Neuchâtel and Paris: Delachaux et Nestlé, 1940), 110–49 (including an analysis of the theological content of the discussion).

[19]Calvin left Geneva for Zurich on 24 January and reported to the Genevan Council on his return on 10 February 1547 (CO, 21:395, 397).

right away, I have something to deal with that needs immediate attention."[20] Five days later, Calvin wrote a long letter to Bullinger. While he generally approved of the work, he still had certain reservations. Yet, in spite of Calvin's positive tone, Bullinger took offense at his criticisms and withdrew into silence.[21] Six months later, Calvin wrote again, wondering at his correspondent's lack of reaction to the letter, especially since Bullinger had urged Calvin during his Zurich visit to keep in frequent contact.[22] Compelled to respond to Calvin's remarks, Bullinger stubbornly continued to maintain his view. Calvin wrote in disappointment to Viret that the Zurich men "continue to sing the same tune."[23]

Calvin's next conciliatory letter, in March 1548,[24] led to a calmer response from Bullinger, even though he made no concessions regarding the substance of the matter.[25] But before that letter reached Geneva, Calvin and Farel came to Zurich to get help for Viret, who was facing conflict in Lausanne. Contacts with Bullinger were a bit awkward and the topic of the Lord's Supper was barely mentioned. Upon his return, Calvin shared his disappointment with Simon Sulzer, pastor in Bern at the time.[26] Shortly thereafter, in spite of the tension caused by a letter sent by Bullinger's adopted son and closest colleague, Rudolf Gwalter,[27] Calvin took stock of the situation. In his letter to Bullinger, he listed the points upon which they both agreed, but before that, he reiterated his regrets: "It would have been much better, when we were with you, for us to have discussed these questions face-to-face with you and your colleagues. We all certainly would have benefited from this. I was not planning to come and make a scene. I hate that as much as you do."[28]

One key moment that took place between July and November has left only indirect traces in the sources. Having received a positive letter from Bullinger, Calvin suggested working on a common text.[29] Bullinger took up the letter from June and extracted twenty-four numbered propositions from it, which he then annotated and sent back to Calvin.[30] Bullinger made a distinction in his list between the affirmations of Calvin "that I support and those that I support less." In other words, the situation had changed from one of disagreement to one of limited agreement. In spite of delayed mail due to a malicious act by a pastor of Lausanne who opposed Calvin, the dialogue by correspondence began anew.[31] Calvin added his own remarks to

[20]CO, 12:479.
[21]CO, 12:480–89.
[22]CO, 12:590.
[23]CO, 12:654.
[24]CO, 12:666.
[25]CO, 12:706–7.
[26]CO, 12:720.
[27]CO, 12:709–11.
[28]CO, 12:727.
[29]CO, 13:101.
[30]Text in CO, 7:693–700.
[31]CO, 13:115–18.

Bullinger's notes, and sent them back to Bullinger on 21 January 1549. However, in his accompanying letter, Calvin chastised Bullinger for unwarranted suspicions, thereby impeding an atmosphere of serenity and mutual trust.[32]

Meanwhile, because Calvin was seeking an agreement not only with Zurich but also with Bern, he wrote a twenty-point-confession of faith on the Lord's Supper. He hoped that Berchtold Haller, the Bernese pastor, would submit it to the synod meeting on 12 March.[33] Unfortunately, Haller did not do so, fearing that such a move would raise suspicions among his colleagues rather than lead to concord.[34] The document, however, was still significant, serving as the first draft of the *Consensus Tigurinus.*

Bullinger, who was still not fully convinced by Calvin's propositions, sent new remarks on 15 March 1549.[35] This time, after apologizing for having initially shown little understanding, Bullinger stated that he could no longer see any grounds for disagreement. "Now I understand you much better than before.... Please do not hold it against me that I wrote to you so sharply. Many scholars today, even very learned ones, change their minds more often than they should. I did not think such things about you, but I had hoped to hear you state clearly what I have now heard." He now seemed ready for face-to-face dialogue, ending on a note of complete agreement: "I hope that after you have read my answer, you will agree that our differences have been resolved."[36]

In spite of these favorable words, Calvin became discouraged and did not want to make any further efforts on the matter. His wife's death on 29 March undoubtedly increased his sense of despair. Farel then took over and insisted that Calvin go to Zurich.[37] Although Calvin found numerous reasons to object, he still mentioned the matter in a letter to Bullinger on 7 May. However, he stated that he would only agree to go if his correspondent requested him to.[38] Then, on 20 May, he suddenly decided to travel to Zurich. He explained his reasons in a December 1549 report to Oswald Myconius, the successor to Oecolampadius at the head of the Basel church. "Since I am rather slow to make up my mind, either because of natural weakness or inertia, I was waiting for the right moment. And suddenly I set off, without having considered doing so two days ago."[39]

Meanwhile, Bullinger had sent a letter on 11 May to dissuade Calvin from the trip, but the letter arrived after Calvin had already left. "Until now we have understood

---

[32] CO, 13:164–66. Text of the annotations: CO, 7:701–8.
[33] CO, 13:216–18. Text of the confession: CO, 7:717–22.
[34] CO, 13:240–44.
[35] Text in CO, 7:709–16.
[36] CO, 13:221.
[37] CO, 13:260–62.
[38] CO, 13:266.
[39] CO, 13:456–57.

each other better by correspondence rather than presenting oral propositions face-to-face. Until now the written route has proved successful. Thus there is no reason for you to leave your church in these troubled times."[40]

In spite of these reservations the meeting led to a rapid resolution, as Calvin explained to Myconius in his report: "God blessed this first meeting in such a way that within two hours we had put together the text that we have sent to you, something that I had not hoped and that no one would have expected given the early stages of the affair. All the credit for the negotiation should go to Farel, for he was the only one to have thought of it."[41]

The minor subsequent alterations resulting from the approval process of other churches need not concern us here. The key point is Calvin's preference for face-to-face dialogue as opposed to written correspondence. One should note, though, the imbalance of signatures in the *Consensio mutua*. It was not the case that Calvin and Bullinger alone signed the document, nor was it the case that all the Genevan pastors and all the Zurich pastors signed it. Instead, Calvin inscribed his name on the one side he signed and all the Zurich clergy did the same on the other. This lack of symmetry emphasizes Bullinger's preference for written procedures, for he wanted to have the approval of his colleagues at each stage of the process. Furthermore, it displays Calvin's control over his church.

Calvin's relationship with Philip Melanchthon, which I will address later,[42] also conveys his desire for a meeting in order to heal theological divisions. In 1552, Calvin wrote to him, "if only we could discuss these matters a bit in person...."[43] Melanchthon, who was considering exile in the Swiss lands, also hoped for a meeting.[44] Calvin was delighted to hear this, and he said as much to Farel shortly thereafter: "Let us hope he moves closer! For I would benefit more from a three-hour conversation than from a hundred letters."[45] This admission effectively expresses Calvin's confidence in his powers of persuasion during private meetings.

Concluding Remarks

These anecdotes open up many paths of inquiry. They show that there is definitely no primacy of the written text in Calvin's mind. On the contrary, although he wrote with great ease, he relied more on the spoken word. The two first accounts also show how sensitive Calvin was: he was very far from being as coldly rational as he is sometimes portrayed.

[40]CO, 13:279.
[41]CO, 13:456–57.
[42]See below 104, 169–70.
[43]CO, 14:417.
[44]CO, 15:269.
[45]CO, 15:321.

2. THE JOURNEY OF THE REFORMER

John Calvin was born in Noyon in 1509. There is no need here to discuss his early student days, about which we often have only shadowy knowledge at best. Historians disagree as to whether the young man from Noyon arrived in Paris in 1521 or 1523. The two divergent timelines merge more or less by the time Calvin obtained his law degree in Bourges in late 1530 or early 1531.[46] Nonetheless, despite these uncertainties, a few matters remain definite. Calvin's studies in humanities and law provided him with a high-caliber humanist training, which shaped his entire relationship with the written text. His linguistic skills in Latin and French will be addressed in a later chapter.[47]

Calvin's first steps into public life were those of a young scholar seeking to become famous and make his name known in humanist circles. The printing industry provided him with opportunities to do this and he intended to take advantage of them. Although his preface to the 1531 edition of *Antapologia* by his friend Nicolas Duchemin was still self-effacing, his influence was significant in this polemical work, which dealt with the controversy between Pierre de l'Estoile and Andreas Alciatus. In the following year, Calvin brought out his edition of Seneca's *De Clementia*. By publishing this work, he aimed very high, intending to improve on Erasmus's own edition of the same text. Undoubtedly Calvin's interest in having his text published lay in the impact that he thought his work would have. He paid the publishing costs himself and urged his friends to encourage sales of his book so he could recoup his expenses.[48] But even amidst his writing, the young humanist never neglected oral communication. He taught classes based on his Seneca commentary at the Collège de Fortet while the text was being published.[49]

The dedications in his early works show Calvin's internal conflict between a strong thirst for literary fame and a mix of humility and shyness, as well as the confidence and daring that the young writer displayed.[50]

Scholar or Pastor?

A "sudden conversion" radically redirected Calvin's life as a humanist. It is not my intent to discuss again the meaning of the term "sudden conversion" or debate the exact date of the event (now placed around 1533 by most scholars). Calvin described his spiritual journey and his conversion in particular in 1557, in the preface to his

---

[46]The two chronologies are discussed by O. Millet in *Calvin et la dynamique de la parole* (Paris: H. Champion, 1991), 27–39.

[47]See below 113–21.

[48]CO, 10/b:20–22. See J. Calvin, *Calvin's Commentary on Seneca's De Clementia,* intro., trans., and notes by F. L. Battles and A. M. Hugo (Leiden: E. J. Brill, 1969), 387–91.

[49]J. Dupèbe, "Un document sur les persécutions de l'hiver 1533–1534 à Paris," *Bibliothèque d'humanisme et Renaissance* 48 (1986): 406, 416–17.

[50]See below 83–84, 196–97.

Commentaire des Pseaumes. This text should be read accurately, not as a strictly auto-biographical work, but as an appeal to justify his vocation as a Reformer.[51] Through-out his life, because he had neither undergone ecclesiastical ordination nor been called by his peers, Calvin was concerned about the legitimacy of his mission. For Calvin, it was God who broke down his reluctance and forced him to take up his vocation. This anxiety over his legitimacy as a Reformer is important because it reappeared in many of his activities, especially in his writings.

Consequently, Calvin focused his activity on religion. His first undertaking was to write—to use his skill at creating syntheses for the cause of evangelization. In 1557, he explained the impact of his conversion as follows: "Having thus received some taste and knowledge of true godliness, I was immediately inflamed with so intense a desire to make progress therein, that although I did not altogether leave off other studies, I yet pursued them with less ardor. I was quite surprised to find that before a year had elapsed, all who had any desire after purer doctrine were continually coming to me to learn, although I myself was as yet but a mere novice and tyro."[52] In less than a year, those around him pressed him to become their master. The Reformer, recognizing that his own shyness and search for peace and quiet had been wrecked by Providence, expressed these sentiments himself: God "never permitted me to rest in any place, until, in spite of my natural disposition, he brought me forth to public notice."[53] Calvin's first activities both in France and in Basel after the Affair of the Placards were largely literary. In 1534 in Orléans, he wrote his first polemical tract against the Anabaptists, the *Psychopannychia*. This text, reworked in Basel in 1536, did not appear until 1542.[54]

Calvin's new course of action can be charted by considering certain markers:[55]

- In April 1532, he published his commentary on *De Clementia.* At this point his humanist studies were still his main concern.
- In October 1533, he wrote a report to a friend on the religious events taking place in Paris. From this point on, Calvin was attentive to such matters, but what he wrote was "the work of a spectator rather than that of an 'activist.'"[56]

---

[51]The leading study of this document is still the one by A. Ganoczy in *Le jeune Calvin: Genèse et évolution de sa vocation réformatrice* (Wiesbaden: F. Steiner, 1966), 295–304, 366–60. For a different interpretation, see D. Fischer, "Nouvelles réflexions sur la conversion de Calvin," *Etudes théologiques et religieuses* 58 (1983): 203–20.

[52]John Calvin, *Commentary on the Book of Psalms,* ed. James Anderson (Grand Rapids: Eerdmans, 1949), 1:xl–xli.

[53]Calvin, *Commentary on Psalms.*

[54]*B.C.1,* no. 42/5.

[55]See B. Roussel's helpful comments in his "François Lambert, Pierre Caroli, Guillaume Farel…et Jean Calvin (1530–1536)" in *Calvinus servus Christi: Die Referate des Congrès international des recherches calviniennes,* ed. W. H. Neuser (Budapest: Presseabteilung des Ráday-Kollegiums, 1988), 35–52.

[56]Herminjard, *Correspondance,* 3:103–11; and CO, 10/b:27–30. I am following B. Roussel's analysis ("François Lambert," 40).

- On All Saints' Day 1533, he participated in the speech given by the rector, Nicolas Cop, which suggests that he knew something of Luther's *Postilla*.[57]
- In May 1534, he renounced his ecclesiastical benefices in Noyon.
- Around November 1534, he wrote his first version of the treatise on the immortality of the soul, a work that should undoubtedly be tied to the Affair of the Placards (17–18 October 1534) and the accusations of Anabaptism leveled against the French evangelicals. For the first time, Calvin wanted to intervene publicly in a theological debate.[58]
- In December 1534 or January 1535, Calvin settled in Basel.

It was in Basel that he completed the *Christianae religionis institutio*. His chief purpose for the work is described in the preface to Francis I. "When I first set my hand to this work...my purpose was solely to transmit certain rudiments" for his fellow citizens who were "hungering and thirsting for Christ."[59] However, he wrote this work in Latin, a point of interest that I will come back to. But before he completed the work, he added an apologetical aim to his pastoral one. Calvin sought to dispel the accusation of Anabaptism and insubordination leveled against his fellow believers. In defending his oppressed brothers, Calvin directed his words as much to the French government as to German public opinion. In his 1557 preface, he only focused on the second motivation and, in fact, accentuated its urgency: "unless I opposed them to the utmost of my ability, my silence could not be vindicated from the charge of cowardice and treachery."[60]

In Basel he followed with interest his cousin Olivétan's production of the first French version of the Bible, based on the original Hebrew and Greek. Calvin wrote two short pieces for that Bible, which was published in June 1535: a fictitious privilege in Latin and the preface to the New Testament.

In 1535, Calvin's dream was to serve his fellow believers from the quiet of his study. In spite of his love of peace and quiet, the newly converted humanist undoubtedly dreamed of filling a role in the rapidly changing religious world similar to that played by Erasmus prior to his death. Calvin saw himself as a man who would spread his ideas via books and correspondence, without having active pastoral responsibilities.

Guillaume Farel's abrupt and insistent demand for help in Geneva in 1536 destroyed this dream and led Calvin to gradually reorient his life. Here, too, the 1557 preface provides the main source of information concerning these events, a source in which their dramatic depiction highlights the irresistible force of Calvin's divine vocation.

[57]J. Rott, "Documents strasbourgeois concernant Calvin," in *Regards contemporains sur Jean Calvin: Actes du colloque Calvin, Strasbourg 1964* (Paris: Presses universitaires de France, 1965), 28–49.

[58]B. Roussel believes that Calvin wrote the work in November ("François Lambert," 39).

[59]John Calvin, *Institutes of the Christian Religion*, ed. John T. McNeill and Ford Lewis Battles (Philadelphia: Westminster Press, 1960) 1:9.

[60]Calvin, *Commentary on Psalms*, 1:xli–xlii.

Let us review the facts. The city of Geneva began to support the Reformation in 1534, following Bern's strong support for Farel's actions. In the summer of 1536, chance led Calvin to Geneva; warfare had made it necessary for him to detour through Geneva to get from Noyon and Paris to Basel and Strasbourg. He attempted to remain incognito during his overnight stay in the city on the shores of the Leman, but failed. One of his close friends of the time, Louis du Tillet, discovered his whereabouts and told the other Reformers of Calvin's presence in the city. Farel rushed to meet him and pleaded with him to remain in Geneva to support him in the establishment of the Reformation. Farel did not confine himself to simple exhortations, but made use of "a dreadful imprecation, which I felt to be as if God had from Heaven laid his mighty hand upon me to arrest me."[61]

But Calvin did not understand this pastoral vocation and could only accept it little by little. At first, he took on the role of *Sacrarum litterarum* professor, limiting himself to his beloved academic pursuits. At this time he was only a minor figure. The registers of the Small Council, when discussing payment for his lectures in Saint-Pierre, refer to him as a little-known man, calling him *ille gallus,* "that Frenchman."[62] Soon after, he took on the tasks of a pastor, though his starting date in that position is unknown and, in all likelihood, the change was a gradual one.[63] On 13 March 1537, the Council registers mention for the first time a joint intervention by Farel and Calvin.[64]

Calvin's horizons rapidly stretched beyond the walls of Geneva. In October 1536, he participated in the disputation of Lausanne, which led to the Pays de Vaud's joining the Reformation camp. Hence Calvin began to have an influence in church circles beyond Geneva. During the disputation he spoke only twice. The first time he noted that "I have refrained from speaking until now, and had intended to refrain from speaking for the whole time," as he felt that Farel and Viret were up to the task. But when his side was accused of despising the fathers and the doctors of the church, Calvin felt compelled to intervene. Calvin's presence at this gathering was important primarily for the impact the event had on him. Through his experience at the disputation, he became aware of the importance of public discourse and the need for missionary and pastoral work.[65] In Geneva, Calvin the teacher became Calvin the pastor as well, writing a first catechism. This first stay of twenty months in Geneva was marked by numerous conflicts. The debate over excommunication

---

[61]Calvin, *Commentary on Psalms,* 1:xlii.

[62]CO, 21:204.

[63]CO, 7:386.

[64]RC 30:189v; and CO, 21:208.

[65]A. Piaget, *Les actes de la dispute de Lausanne, 1536* (Neuchâtel: Secrétariat de l'Université, 1928), 224–30, 330–31; and E. Junod, ed., *La dispute de Lausanne, 1536: La théologie réformée après Zwingli et avant Calvin* (Lausanne: Bibliothèque historique vaudoise, 1988). See in particular the article by E. M. Braekman, "Les interventions de Calvin," in *La dispute de Lausanne, 1546: La théologie réformée après Zwingli et avant Calvin,* ed. E. Junoid (Lausanne: Bibliothèque historique vaudoise, 1988), 170–77; and Ganoczy, *Le jeune Calvin,* 108.

led to defeat in April 1538. Neither the civil authorities nor the pastors were willing to cede control of that ecclesiastical sanction, which could compel recalcitrant Christians into obedience. The Genevan Council played their trump card to ensure their hold on power by sending Farel and Calvin into exile.

The Strasbourg Experience

Calvin withdrew to Basel, hoping to take up his beloved studies once again. Deeply demoralized by the Genevan fiasco, he was overcome by grave doubts about his vocation and returned to the idea of a scholarly haven. He confessed this to Louis du Tillet in July.[66] "Because of what happened [that is, the departure into exile], since I am free and released from my vocation, I intend to live peacefully and not take up any public responsibilities."[67] But Bucer convinced him otherwise. Using "similar reproaches and protestations to those of Farel,"[68] Bucer asked Calvin to provide religious education and assistance to the French refugees in Strasbourg. His arrival in Strasbourg in the summer of 1538 marked the beginning of the French church in that city.[69]

The three years Calvin spent in Alsace were crucial ones. Thanks to his contacts with Bucer and his work as a parish pastor, he refined his approach to the Reformation. He was also invited to participate in the religious colloquies of Hagenau, Worms, and Regensburg. The relations he established in these settings and the impact of his writings slowly increased his international standing. His growing reputation meant that, as a writer, he moved from having to ask for his works to be printed to being courted by booksellers. A study of his dedications and the outward appearance of his first publications shows Calvin's growing confidence as he addressed his readership. Indeed, his work as a pastor did not stem the flow of his writings. On the one hand, he worked on major contributions, such as his revision of the *Institutes* and his first exegetical commentary on Paul's Epistle to the Romans. On the other hand, he responded to various requests by writing short polemical or pastoral works.

During these years, Calvin's financial situation was extremely precarious. In 1538, the earlier gift of money from Louis du Tillet ran out and Calvin spoke of selling his books. However, he refused further offers of money from Du Tillet.[70] He continued to make numerous references to his financial difficulties during the first months of 1539.[71] Beginning in May 1539, the situation improved a little. At this

---

[66]Herminjard, *Correspondance,* 5:44; and CO, 10/b:221.

[67]CO, 31:26; see also CO, 5:389.

[68]CO, 31:28.

[69]Ph. Denis, *Les Églises d'étrangers en pays rhénans (1538–1564)* (Paris: Les Belles Lettres, 1984), 66–70.

[70]Herminjard, *Correspondance,* 4:358, 5:44, 107–8, 165; and CO, 10/b:149–50, 221, 244–45, 272.

[71]Herminjard, *Correspondance,* 5:270, 291–92, 307; and CO, 10/b:332, 340, 343.

time, the city began paying him the same amount that deacons received, fifty-two florins a year. But he did not obtain an increase to a hundred florins as had been projected in July 1540.[72] Hence, to make ends meet, he took up some bread-and-butter work by writing political pamphlets for the Count of Furstenberg.[73] His friendship with Wendelin Rihel was accompanied by a sense of gratitude for Rihel's generosity.[74] In August 1540, Calvin married Idelette de Bure and with her help he ran his household more effectively and rented rooms to wealthy students.

In spite of all this, his stay in Strasbourg still felt like exile to him. Calvin remained in contact with Geneva, even though during the first months he refused to consider any thought of ever returning. He closely followed the political changes in the city, where the elections of February 1539 brought in a majority in the Council that supported him. When Sadoleto sent an open letter to the Genevans in March 1539 inviting them to return to the fold of the Catholic church, the dismayed Genevan Council sought advice from Bern. The Bernese suggested asking Calvin for a response and he agreed to help his former church at the end of August 1539.

The Genevan Reformer

In dismissing Farel and Calvin, the Genevans had no intention of abandoning the Reformation. But they simply could not accept the balance of power between the church and the state that these expelled ministers favored. However, the lack of character of the replacement pastors in Geneva led increasingly to a troubled situation. Already by October 1540, there was a desire in Geneva to have Calvin back, and an official delegation attempted to organize his return. Calvin agreed to return, but asked for a deferral because he was bound to his post in Strasbourg due to his involvement in the French church and the German religious colloquies there. At Calvin's suggestion, Viret began to restore the Genevan church beginning in January 1541, though Calvin himself did not return to the city until September of that year. One detail shows his state of mind: when he mounted the pulpit for the first time since his departure, he simply gave a short introduction on the principles of his ministry and picked up his biblical commentary exactly where he had left off four years earlier. What an amazing sign of his devotion to continuity, born out of his awareness of his mission![75] Nevertheless, he did set out certain conditions for his return. Above all, he demanded a certain measure of independence for the Consistory, for he felt that this ecclesiastical body should have the right to apply excommunication, that is, to bar anyone from access to the Lord's Supper without interference from the

---

[72]Herminjard, *Correspondance,* 5:230–31 n. 19, 6:255.

[73]*B.C.1,* nos. 39/1, 39/3, 40/1, 40/4; and J. Calvin, *Plaidoyers pour le comte Guillaume de Furstenberg,* ed. R. Peter (Paris: Presses universitaires de France, 1994).

[74]See below 181–82.

[75]Herminjard, *Correspondance,* 7:412; and CO, 11:365–66. Overall, see B. Cottret, *Calvin: Biographie* (Paris: J. C. Lattès, 1995), 157–62.

civil authorities. The Reformer actually obtained only an ambiguous text that gave the spiritual sword to the Consistory and refused to give any civil jurisdiction to the pastors. This undoubtedly deliberate equivocation merely deferred the problem until later, and the clash between the pastors and the Council over conflicting interpretations of the rules occurred in 1553.[76]

The following years were shaped by his Genevan ministry and his various interventions in the Reformed world. There is no need to study Calvin's career in detail from this point on. Instead, we will focus on three main periods during these years.[77]

The first period runs from 1541 to around 1547. When Calvin returned to Geneva in September 1541, he faced tenacious political opposition and a city that only partially supported him. Calvin's first move was to establish a reliable pastoral corps, a crucial part of a well-run church, and by 1547 he had achieved his goal. From then on there was less opposition within the church itself, or at least Calvin had sufficient support to quell any dissent.

The second period saw the continuing strength of powerful political opposition, rooted in the "Vieux-Genevois" party or in the "Perrinistes," named after the Perrin family, its backbone and symbol. Calvin's opponents had two main complaints about him. First, they objected to his overly harsh moral rigor that led him to ban all of life's pleasures. Second, out of anger at the growing tide of French exiles in Geneva, his detractors stated that Calvin was himself a foreigner and had no right to intervene in the city's affairs. This critique was motivated by the fear of the political changes that could result from the arrival of immigrants. The ministers responded to this opposition by indoctrinating the population from the pulpit, doing so more effectively after 1547, once Calvin's words were echoed by other reliable pastors.

During this period, the other major landmark was Calvin's controversy over predestination with Jerôme Bolsec, a former Carmelite. This doctor of theology, who had become a physician, publicly opposed the Calvinist understanding of predestination in March and May 1551. The conflict led to a trial that lasted from October 1551 to February 1552 and resulted in Bolsec's banishment, as well as a division among Calvin's friends. The Reformer's intransigence led some to distance themselves from him, not on the grounds of doctrine but rather because of his excessive harshness. Among the friends Calvin lost, the most distinguished was Jacques de Bourgogne, seigneur de Falais, the highest-ranking nobleman of the Low Countries who had accepted the Reformation.[78] But there were many others, including René

---

[76]F. M. Higman, *La diffusion de la Réforme en France, 1520–1565* (Geneva: Labor et Fides, 1992), 117 n. 4; and W. G. Naphy, *Calvin and the Consolidation of the Genevan Reformation* (Manchester: Manchester University Press, 1994), 181–87.

[77]See Naphy, *Calvin and the Consolidation,* passim.

[78]Ph. Denis, "Jacques de Bourgogne, seigneur de Falais" in *Bibliotheca dissidentium: Répertoire des non-conformistes religieux des seizième et dix-septième siècles,* ed. A. Séguenny (Baden-Baden: V. Koerner, 1984), 4:9–52.

de Bienassis.[79] The controversy over predestination even led to conflict within the Reformer's closest circle of friends.

This period ended in the spring of 1555, when the Perrinist opposition was ruthlessly crushed. Already, the results of the February elections had favored Calvin. By April, the new Council granted bourgeois status to numerous foreigners: fifty were registered between 18 April and 9 May, compared to only thirty in both 1553 and 1554.[80] In response, a riot broke out on 16 May, during which Ami Perrin committed the irreparable act of seizing the syndic's wand of office. Given that touching this symbol of the high office of Geneva's leading magistrates was a crime of lèse-majesté, reprisals against the Perrinists and their friends were quick to follow. No fewer than eight men were executed, while another sixteen were condemned to death in absentia. Over fifty people faced charges that led to fines, exile, and various public punishments.[81]

The final period began in June 1555; from then on Calvin benefited from the wholehearted support of the civil powers. Throughout these years, other major changes were taking place. Calvin's return to the helm in Geneva increased his international stature, and his works began to be more and more popular after 1541. A letter dated April 1543 from Antoine Fumée, a leading member of the French parlement, testifies to Calvin's growing reputation. "You are probably now aware of your role and of the number of people, even here, who are fascinated by what you say, and who are surely extraordinarily affected by your writings."[82] Indeed, Calvin was increasingly aware of this, as can be seen in his dedicatory prefaces. In 1548, Calvin began to dedicate his commentaries to Protestant princes scattered across Europe. Furthermore, the *Consensus Tigurinus,* which marks the 1549 agreement between Zurich and Geneva, confirmed the international importance of the Genevan church, thanks to Calvin's work. Finally, in 1550, the sudden influx of refugees enabled the Genevan printing industry to take off. In short, between 1547 and 1550, Calvin found himself playing an increasingly prominent role within both his local church and the Reformed churches as a whole.

In 1541, Calvin was gripped by the urgent work to be done in Geneva, and thus he no longer had the leisure to write the lengthy works that he had planned. Although in his 1539 *Institutes* and in his 1540 commentary on Romans, he had promised to continue producing biblical commentaries,[83] these works ultimately had to wait. This was particularly clear throughout the first years following Calvin's return to Geneva, a time when establishing church structures and preaching took up almost all of his time. For instance, Calvin's collaborative effort with Claude Roset to

---

[79]On René de Bienassis see below 187–88.

[80]A. L. Covelle, *Le livre des bourgeois de l'ancienne république de Genève* (Geneva: J. Jullien, 1897), 238–44.

[81]The list of the condemned appears in Naphy, *Calvin and the Consolidation,* 195–96.

[82]CO, 11:538.

[83]See below 40–42, 45–47.

compose new ordinances for Geneva was such a priority that the Council released Calvin from most of his preaching duties between 11 September 1542 and 22 January 1543.[84] A few months earlier, in July 1542, when Farel asked him to publish his teachings on Genesis, he had replied that other matters were more pressing: "As for my remarks on Genesis, if God grants me a longer life and free time, I may begin work on that.... Indeed, my main concern is to serve this present age and follow my vocation. If I have any opportunity left, I will try to devote myself to that other work at a later date."[85] At that time, Calvin wanted to delay any scholarly writing. In fact, the regular appearance of his commentaries on the Pauline Epistles did not resume until 1546.[86]

Still, the demands of pastoral work did not prevent Calvin from answering other calls. The period from 1543 to 1547 was his most prolific in terms of polemical tracts. Farel effectively expressed these feelings of being torn between immediate needs and long-term projects when, in February 1543, he asked Calvin to provide a refutation to an Anabaptist work, and added, "We all know that you are overworked, and that you have other topics to deal with, not only for your contemporaries but also for future generations, especially as regards scriptural commentaries."[87] Farel's mention of future generations highlights the dilemma between writing for the present and writing for the future. Later on, Farel returned to this point, writing to Calvin on 25 February 1546, "I am really embarrassed to take you away from the holy commentaries on Paul, not to mention the revised version of the Bible. We should all work so that you have to do nothing other than one of these two things, and if possible both of them."[88]

Beginning in 1546, Calvin returned to writing exegetical commentaries, but there were too many demands on his time. As we will see later in more detail, his associates began to record his oral teachings, both his sermons and his exegetical lectures. After much indecision, Calvin authorized the publication of his lectures on Hosea in 1557. In spite of his worries, readers seemed satisfied by this approach and Calvin was able to free himself from the heavy burden of writing for a number of years.

During the final years of his life, a new complication arose: the Reformer's health was steadily declining. From October 1558 to June 1559, he essentially never left his room. In spite of these problems, he continued to write, but much more slowly. It was in this period that he established the definitive text of the *Institutes,* both in Latin and in French.[89] Other factors also marked Calvin's gradual withdrawal from his administrative duties; increasingly, he left Beza to deal with polemical issues. Apart from that,

[84]See below 66.
[85]CO, 11:418.
[86]*B.C.1,* nos. 46/2, 48/7, 48/8, 48/9, 49/4, etc.
[87]CO, 11:681, 682.
[88]CO, 12:297.
[89]J.-D. Benoît, "L'année 1559 dans les annales calviniennes," *Revue d'histoire et de philosophie religieuses* 39 (1959): 103–16.

Calvin continued his exegetical tasks. In 1563, he published his commentary on the Pentateuch, thus bringing to an end the work begun in 1554 with his Genesis commentary. Calvin himself worked on the French translation of the Genesis work, and especially on the translation of the whole Pentateuch commentary.[90]

The man who died on 27 May 1564, surrounded by the affection of his followers, was worn out by many years of sickness. When Calvin died he was, as we would say today, only fifty-three years old. Nevertheless, he left behind a major body of written work, representing only one of his lifetime accomplishments.

3. His Context—People, Ideas, and Institutions

Three last areas of focus will complete this biographical overview: first, a rapid survey of the men Calvin was in contact with, both friends and foes, second, a summary of the theological ideas he fought for, and finally, an outline of the political and religious structures of Geneva.

His Faithful Friends

We have already mentioned a number of Calvin's contacts.[91] One main group consists of Calvin's closest friends, including Guillaume Farel (1489–1565). Farel was one of the first Frenchmen to work for the Reformation, and he was the one who kept Calvin in Geneva in 1536. Another of Calvin's closest friends was Pierre Viret (1511–71), whom Farel had converted. The area known today as French-speaking Switzerland was led to the Reformation by the joint efforts of these three men. From 1536 until 1559, Viret was in Lausanne, while Farel worked in Neuchâtel from 1538 onwards. Letters traveled frequently from one city to another, including many letters heading for Zurich and going via Neuchâtel. Theodore Beza (1516–1605), Calvin's successor in 1564, began his teaching career in Lausanne from 1550 to 1559 and then moved to Geneva when the Academy was established there.

Among the Genevan ministers, Nicolas des Gallars (ca. 1520–ca. 1579) stands out. He was especially close to Calvin, often acting as his secretary until he left Geneva in 1557. Two other men were closely associated with Calvin until his death: Jean Budé (1515–87), one of Guillaume's sons, and Charles de Jonviller (ca. 1517–91). These two men were closely related as well because Jean had married Charles's sister.[92]

---

[90]*B.C.1*, nos. 54/8, 54/2, 63/16, 64/5.

[91]Readers will find entries on most of the figures mentioned in this paragraph and the next one in H. J. Hillerbrand, ed., *The Oxford Encyclopedia of the Reformation* (New York and Oxford: Oxford University Press, 1996). If the Reformation figure does not appear in the encyclopedia, I provide further sources in the notes.

[92]On these two secretaries see Doumergue, *Jean Calvin*, 3:606–19.

For financial and publishing matters, Calvin's closest confidants were his brother Antoine (d. 1573), who lived with him almost continuously, and Laurent de Normandie (ca. 1510–69). We will discuss later the different publishers that Calvin used.

Calvin's circle of friends was not restricted to Geneva and France. Early on, he forged ties with the Strasbourg Reformers. Among them, Calvin was closest to Martin Bucer (1491–1551), who led the Reformation in Strasbourg in 1549 and later emigrated to England. We have already mentioned Bucer's influence on Calvin during his stay in Strasbourg. Bucer's colleague Wolfgang Capito (1478–1541) died too early for Calvin to have extensive dealings with him. The Italian theologian, Girolamo Zanchi (1516–90), was a professor in Strasbourg from 1553 to 1563 after having lived in Geneva for ten months. He later left Strasbourg because of its increasingly Lutheran climate under the influence of the pastor Johannes Marbach.

Thanks to his attendance at religious colloquies during his Strasbourg stay, Calvin met Philip Melanchthon (1497–1560). The two men saw eye-to-eye and preserved friendly relations throughout their lives. As for Martin Luther (1483–1546), Calvin, though respectful toward him in spite of doctrinal reservations, always avoided confrontation.

We have already examined Calvin's relationship with Heinrich Bullinger (1504–75), the Antistes, or senior pastor, of the Zurich church. Calvin also exchanged letters with Rudolf Gwalter, Bullinger's son-in-law and successor. Similarly, Calvin kept in regular touch with other Swiss-German pastors, including the Bernese pastor Berchtold Haller (1492–1536), and the Bernese professors Wolfgang Musculus (1497–1563) and Oswald Myconius (1488–1552). Finally, the Biel pastor Ambrosius Blaurer (1492–1564) was also a fervent admirer of Calvin.

The stance of Basel theologians on confessional conflicts tended always to be more reserved. During his first stay in Basel, Calvin forged a close bond with Simon Grynaeus (1493–1541), who led the Basel Reformation following the death of Oecolampadius in 1531. Simon Sulzer (d. 1585), although he held Lutheran views and was expelled from his native city of Bern, always remained in friendly contact with the Genevan theologians. After being expelled from Bern in 1548, he went to Basel, where he later became Antistes.[93]

His Opponents

One aspect of Calvin's interpersonal relations is worth further analysis. It appears that a significant number of those who at one time were his friends or his enthusiastic disciples later distanced themselves or even became fiercely opposed to Calvin. Clearly, each party was somewhat responsible for these splits, but Calvin's intransigence never helped matters.

---

[93]See H. Vuilleumier, *Histoire de l'Église réformée du Pays de Vaud sous le régime bernois* (Lausanne: La Concorde, 1933), 4:721.

Among those who left Calvin's side was Louis du Tillet, a canon of Angoulême.[94] He was Calvin's friend, companion, and patron between 1533 and 1538, but Du Tillet's return to the Catholic fold broke the bond between them, though the parting was not acrimonious. The same was true in the case of Antoine Fumée (1511–after 1575), a leading member of the Paris Parlement.[95] Fumée is a perfect example of a Nicodemite, a Protestant who did not dare to sever his ties with the Catholic church. After Calvin's condemnation of Nicodemism, the two men quietly broke off their correspondence.

Another example is the case of Antoine du Pinet, or Pinet, Lord of Noroy (ca. 1510–ca. 1566). He was one of Calvin's former fellow students, who had known him well during his years in Orléans and Bourges, beginning in 1530. Pinet had even received a copy of *De Clementia* from Calvin and was a faithful supporter of the Reformer during the difficult Strasbourg years.[96] He later became a pastor at Ville-la-Grand in the Chablais, a league and a half away from Geneva. Pinet even helped Calvin put the finishing touches to the 1539 *Institutes*. Around 1548, however, he turned against Calvin for reasons that remain unclear, and left for Lyon. There he became known for various publications and translations.[97] When Viret found him in Lyon in 1562, Pinet was still part of the Reformed community, but Viret kept his distance from him.[98]

The cases of Sebastian Castellio (1515–63), Jacques de Bourgogne (d. 1556), and François Bauduin (1520–73) were more clearly the result of Calvin's intolerance. A dedicated disciple of Calvin since 1540, Castellio left Geneva in 1545, following clashes over divergent theological viewpoints. Based in Basel, he became a resolute defender of toleration against Genevan intransigence. Jacques de Bourgogne, whose friendship Calvin found so flattering, broke off all contact after the Genevans condemned Bolsec, his personal physician. De Bourgogne, who was second cousin to Charles V, left Geneva following Bolsec's trial. François Bauduin, a childhood friend of Jean Crespin, was more fickle.[99] He left Calvin several times and then rejoined him before attempting to bring religious concord to different confessional groups. Not only did Calvin reject these three men, but he pursued them with enduring hatred.

The Paris theologian Pierre Caroli can also be included in this group of opponents, even though he was never one of Calvin's personal friends. As a theologian with divided allegiances, he accompanied Farel and Calvin to the disputation of

---

[94]E. Haag and E. Haag, *La France protestante,* ed. Henri Bordier (Paris: Librairie Sandoz et Fischbacher, 1877–88), 5:1085–86 (references are to volume and column).

[95]See Haag and Haag, *Le France protestante,* 6:755–57.

[96]Herminjard, *Correspondance,* 2:419; and CO, 19/b:21.

[97]See Haag and Haag, *Le France protestante,* 5:852–63; E. Droz, *Chemins de l'hérésie: Textes et documents* (Geneva: Droz, 1970–76), 2:55–76, esp. 63 n. 11 bis; and *Dictionnaire de biographie francaise,* 1970, s.v. "Antoine du Pinet" (by Y. Destianges), 12:372.

[98]CO, 19:474.

[99]M. Turchetti, *Concordia o Toleranza? François Bauduin (1520–1673) e i "moyenneurs"* (Geneva: Droz, 1984).

Lausanne in 1536, but once he returned to the Catholic church he hounded Farel and his friends.

Another group of Calvin's opponents grew out of the unease felt by some Genevans over the establishment of the Reformation in Geneva, a move that threatened their traditional practices. One party opposed to Calvin centered around Ami Perrin and caused serious trouble for the Reformer until 1555, as previously discussed. Various foreigners joined this group, including Jerôme Bolsec, the theologian and physician who clashed with Calvin over the issue of predestination and was banished from Geneva in December 1551. Calvin also clashed with Jean Trolliet, a man of Genevan extraction. When Calvin barred him from the pastorate, Trolliet became a dangerous foe, all the more so because he had the ear of the civil authorities. On several occasions, Trolliet, together with the Genevan doctor Louis Beljaquet, was put in charge of book censorship, and did not hesitate to criticize Calvin, as we shall see.[100]

For many years, Calvin managed to avoid any doctrinal controversy with Luther's followers by discreetly indicating his reservations while emphasizing the points of agreement. But beginning in 1554, for reasons that will become clear, he entered into a violent polemical debate with the gnesio-Lutherans.[101] Joachim Westphal (1510–74), the pastor of Hamburg, was the first to be targeted. Later, Calvin directed his vehemence toward Tilemann Hesshusen (1527–88), pastor of Bremen in 1559. Hesshusen had earlier held various posts, especially in Heidelberg. A third opponent, Johann Brenz (1499–1570), the leader of the Lutheran churches in Wurtemberg beginning in 1551, inspired fear in Calvin and his colleagues.

Finally, let us highlight a Catholic theologian from the Netherlands, Albert Pigge, also known as Pighius (ca.1490–1542). He had met Calvin at various religious colloquies and attacked him explicitly in his polemical works.[102]

The Foundations of Calvinist Theology

The core of Calvin's theology echoes Luther's key insights: justification by faith, the radical power of sin, and Christ as the only savior. Calvin accentuated humanity's state of total dependence by stressing the infinite grandeur of God. Because his emotional outlook differed greatly from Luther's, Calvin distrusted the effects of the senses. He established a very austere worship service, refusing any use of images and accepting only unison singing in order that the text retain precedence.

Like Luther, Calvin held to the doctrine of *sola scriptura*: the Bible was the only source of doctrine. Human traditions were worthy of respect when they followed the path of scripture, but in the absence of scriptural justification these traditions could not serve to settle doctrinal matters. Throughout this book, we will concentrate on

---

[100]For more on these opponents, see Naphy, *Calvin and the Consolidation,* passim.

[101]See below 104–5.

[102]R. Bäumer, "Albert Pigge (†1542)," in *Katholische Theologen der Reformationszeit* (Münster: Aschendorff, 1984), 1:98–106.

Calvin's lifelong exegetical work. However, we should note the limits of applicability of *sola scriptura,* for Calvin firmly held to the doctrine of the Trinity and the practice of infant baptism, neither of which appears in the New Testament. Indeed, it was the early church that had established this dogma and this practice.[103] Calvin did recognize that the term "trinity" was not present in scripture. Yet, he justified its use by stating that it was good to "set out in clearer words things that are only obscurely presented in scripture."[104] As for infant baptism, providing a scriptural basis for the practice proved to be what François Wendel called "adventurous" exegesis, one that based itself primarily on a parallel between circumcision and baptism.[105]

With even more originality, Calvin developed a theology of the Holy Spirit linked to his vision of Christ ascended in glory and sitting at the right hand of the Father. Since Christ is absent from this world, God acts in it through his spirit. This point had clear consequences for Calvin's understanding of the Lord's Supper: since the body of Jesus was in heaven, it could not be present on earth in the bread and the wine.

Calvin also developed his own concept of church and state. A Christian's process of sanctification was mediated through the sacraments, the church body itself, and scripture. For Calvin, the church was an institution that surrounded Christians and taught them their faith: the church was a "mother." Christians, he thought, should show in their daily living that salvation had refashioned them into "images of God." Given Calvin's support for the principle of religious unity within the state, he established a close bond between civil and religious authorities, while maintaining their distinct identities and functions.

A Few Controversial and Polemical Matters

The Lord's Supper was among the leading topics of theological controversy. Moreover, the debate predated Calvin and continued long after his death. As we have already noted, Calvin could not accept Luther's realist doctrine or Zwingli's symbolic understanding.[106] Instead, Calvin proposed that Christ was truly present, but in a spiritual sense. Barring a few adjustments, his viewpoint was adopted by Zwingli's followers: the Zurich pastors signed the *Consensus Tigurinus* with Calvin in 1549. While Melanchthon and his followers remained quiet, the gnesio-Lutherans launched themselves against this Zwinglian-Calvinist doctrine beginning in 1553. One of the main stumbling blocks was the issue of the ubiquity of Christ's body. The Calvinists asked how it was possible for the risen body of Christ to be simultaneously present at the right hand of God the Father and everywhere on this earth.

---

[103]F. Barth, *Calvin und Servet* (Bern: A. Francke, 1909), cited by A. Bouvier, *Henri Bullinger,* 437–38.

[104]Calvin, *Institution,* ed. J.-D. Benoît (Paris: J. Vrin, 1957–63), vol. 1, ch. XIII, S 3–4, 147–48; and F. Wendel, *Calvin, sources et évolution de sa pensée religieuse* (Paris: Presses Universitaires de France, 1950), 122–25.

[105]Wendel, *Calvin,* 246, and see 246–50.

[106]See above 5–6.

A second source of controversy was the doctrine of predestination, which dealt with the absolute sovereignty of God. God alone saved people, and only by his grace. This debate about humans' role in their salvation was at least as old as Christianity itself. The conflict took on new life, however, thanks to the controversy between the captivity of the will and the freedom of the will, championed by Luther and Erasmus, respectively. Calvin stretched the matter even further by his clear affirmation of double predestination: some are predestined to salvation through the mercy of God and others are predestined to damnation through God's justice. This perspective led to difficult questions on the links between eternity and temporality, on determinism shaping human lives, and on the picture of a God who saves some while condemning others. This last point was precisely what upset Jerôme Bolsec. In his eyes, Calvin made God the author of evil. For Bolsec, God calls all to salvation, and those who are condemned are those who reject their election.

Calvin's attacks on Bolsec conceal a power struggle. If Calvin gave in to his opponent, his position as an interpreter of scripture would be seriously jeopardized. In order to salvage his mission as a Reformer, Calvin had to be proved right. Fortunately for Calvin, because of his strong powers of persuasion, he succeeded in gaining support from most of the Swiss churches, in spite of certain clear reservations on their part.[107]

The sixteenth century was marked by a clear challenge to the traditional doctrine of the Trinity, led by Anabaptists and Spiritualists. They followed the doctrine of *sola scriptura* to the letter, rejecting anything not contained therein. The most famous case was that of Michael Servetus, but a major anti-Trinitarian church also took root in Poland during Calvin's lifetime.

Generally speaking, Calvin fought against all dissident groups that had sprung up during the Lutheran Reformation. The Anabaptists, mentioned above, were given their name because of their refusal to agree to infant baptism. Yet both Protestants and Catholics also feared this group because of their rejection of the link between church and state. In another instance, Calvin gave the name Spiritualist Libertines to groups who were motivated by a mystical apocalypticism and a pantheism with no connections to traditional morals and notions of sin and repentance. These groups appeared in the area around Lille and Tournai and managed to have an audience at the court of Marguerite of Navarre.[108] Calvin also condemned another

---

[107]J. W. Baker, "Jérome Bolsec," in *The Oxford Encyclopedia of the Reformation,* ed. H. J. Hillerbrand (New York: Oxford University Press, 1996), 1:188–89. Ph. C. Holtrop's work, *The Bolsec Controversy on Predestination, from 1551 to 1555* (Lewiston, NY: Mellen, 1993), is less controversial in terms of its contents than in terms of its methodological approach. See R. A. Muller, "The Bolsec Controversy on Predestination from 1551 to 1555," *Calvin Theological Journal* 29 (1994): 581–89; and B. G. Armstrong, "The Bolsec Controversy on Predestination," in *Sixteenth Century Journal* 25 (1994): 747–50.

[108]G. Moreau, *Histoire du protestantisme à Tournai jusqu'à la veille de la Révolution des Pays-Bas* (Paris: Les Belles Lettres, 1962), 83–87.

group of Christians, calling them Nicodemites because of their compromises between their Reformed beliefs and the papist practices they followed due to the pressure of the dominant church. The name Nicodemite refers to the visit Nicodemus made to Jesus by night.[109] By attacking them so vehemently, Calvin forced them to choose between martyrdom and exile in a Protestant land.

Geneva's Political and Religious Institutions

Calvin's activities in Geneva were sometimes hampered and sometimes facilitated by the various political bodies in the city. I will give a brief overview of the leading institutions without discussing their later development at length.

The Genevan republic was governed by an oligarchic system with four councils.[110] The Conseil général (General Council) included all the bourgeois, both those who were *citoyens*, that is, born to bourgeois of Geneva, and those who had acquired the bourgeoisie in other ways than through birth. The General Council's only role was to approve the decisions made in the higher councils. Even its main prerogative—electing the syndics, the treasurer, and the *lieutenant de justice*—was a minimal one, since the four syndics were elected from a list of eight proposed by the Grand Conseil (Great Council) and the original list had been made by the Petit Conseil (Small Council).

Both nomination to the higher councils and election to the magistrate positions happened on an annual basis. The main function of the Conseil des Deux Cents (Council of Two Hundred) or Great Council was to oversee and approve the work of the Small Council. New ordinances had to be approved by the Great Council and the General Council, but neither body had the right to propose legislation. The members of the Great Council chose their successors once a year. These elections had to be approved by the Small Council.

A midlevel body, the Conseil des Soixante (Council of Sixty), included the members of the Small Council and thirty-five delegates of the Great Council. It met to vote on certain major decisions, especially ones dealing with foreign affairs.

The Small Council (or simply, the Council) held the bulk of the executive, legislative, and judicial power in the city. The Council had twenty-five members, including nine ex-officio members: the four serving syndics, the four outgoing syndics, and the treasurer. The other councilors were elected by the outgoing Council and their nomination was approved by the Great Council. The Council met at least three times a week, often more. The four syndics constituted the executive body, which met daily. As a body, they were the representatives of the republic. Alongside

---

[109]C. Ginzburg, *Il nicodemismo: Simulazione e dissimulazione religiosa nell'Europa del '500* (Turin: G. Einaudi, 1970).

[110]For information on political institutions in Geneva, see Doumergue, *Jean Calvin,* 3:324–32; Naphy, *Calvin and the Consolidation,* passim; and *Encyclopédie de Genève* 4, *Les Institutions* (Geneva: Association de l'Encyclopédie de Genève, 1985), 86–88, 132–40, 199–203.

them, the *lieutenant de justice* was responsible for the day-to-day operation of the justice system.

This system appeared to be democratic because of the existence of the General Council to which all bourgeois belonged. Yet the system actually benefited the members of the oligarchy who, using the rule that authorized outgoing members to name their own successors, could reelect one another year after year.

The Company of Pastors and the Consistory were the two dominant institutions in the power structure of the Genevan church. The Company of Pastors included all the pastors, both those serving in the city and those in the countryside. The 1541 ordinances called for eight city pastors.[111] By 1544, there was already a total of eighteen, counting the pastors from rural areas. From 1559 onwards, the Company of Pastors also included the professors of the Genevan Academy. The Company met several times a week, especially on Fridays for the *congrégation*, a body that will be discussed in greater detail later.[112] The Company was led by a moderator, a post held by Calvin from 1541 until his death. The Company served as the main forum for decisions made by the ministers, both regarding internal matters and international relations. Pastors were chosen by their peers, and then after having been approved by the Council, they were presented to the population. Thus the body of the faithful had no say in the choice of their pastor, and civil authorities had at most the opportunity to approve of the Company's choice. In other words, the church structures were no more democratic than the civil ones. However, relations between pastors and the city government were not completely free, since the Company of Pastors was completely financially dependent on the Council.[113]

The Consistory was the main control mechanism over the moral and social life of the entire population of Geneva. It met on Thursdays and was chaired by a syndic. It included all the city pastors and twelve elders. These twelve were originally laymen chosen by the councils, but from 1555 onwards the ministers were consulted regarding these elections. From the judicial point of view, therefore, the Consistory was a commission subject to the civil powers. For instance, it could call on the services of a court usher from the Council to summon perpetrators or witnesses. Nonetheless, the Consistory remained an ecclesiastical body, since the 1541 ordinances stated that elders were one of four categories of office-bearers in the church.

Both in theory and in practice, there were more elders than pastors in the Consistory. Not only was the number of elders greater, but they were also less likely to be absent than their clerical colleagues. In reality, however, the power of the ministers was greater, and there were many conflicts between the Consistory and the Council. We have already seen the conflicts over the issue of excommunication. In general,

---

[111]H. Heyer, *L'Église de Genève: Esquisse historique de son organisation* (Geneva: A. Jullien, 1909), 196; see also 48–50.

[112]See below 31–32.

[113]See R. M. Kingdon, "Compagnie des pasteurs," in *The Oxford Encyclopedia of the Reformation* 1:392–94, and the edition of the *Registres de la Compagnie des Pasteurs* (Geneva: Droz, 1962–).

though, the culprits who were thought to need temporal punishment were sent on to the Council.[114]

Calvin always thought of the church as a territorial institution, responsible for all the inhabitants of an area. This is why he saw the need for links between church and state. Furthermore, the pastors' salaries were paid by the state and the Consistory, while an ecclesiastical institution, still exercised state control over all inhabitants without leaving room for rival confessional groups or, even worse, for atheism. At the same time, Calvin wanted to build a confessing church and expected that everyone would be firmly committed to it. This motivation provided another reason for the mechanism of the Consistory, which was meant to sustain religious commitment. On this basis, his reluctance to support the creation of minority churches in France is understandable. His dream had been to convert the whole kingdom, not to separate a few faithful believers from the rest.[115]

Was the Genevan regime a theocracy? A superficial survey of the overlap between powers may suggest so, but the more accurate description would be that of a "city-church." Calvin would have agreed with Zwingli: "a Christian city is nothing other than a Christian church."[116] In contrast, a true theocracy calls for ecclesiastical powers to dominate, and this was far from the case in Geneva, as I hope to have shown sufficiently. Still, there remains a gap between the institutions as described on paper and their actual operation. Due to Calvin's extraordinary personality, he was able to have the civil powers do as he wanted, without any indication of this in the city's constitution. However, the later history of the Company of Pastors, especially after Theodore Beza's death, shows that the Council had the upper hand over the church.

4. Oral Instruction

The Reformers, like the humanists before them, were quick to point out several weaknesses of medieval education. They focused their criticism on the theological training available in universities and the instruction of laypeople through preaching.

University-level theological instruction often got lost in subtle games of logic unrelated to Christian life. Both humanists and Reformers agreed in their rejection of scholasticism and, finding it impossible to change preexisting institutions, they looked instead for other methods of instruction. The study of ancient languages became important because of the need to understand scripture better, leading to the

---

[114]E. W. Monter, "The Consistory of Geneva, 1559–1569," *Bibliothèque d'humanisme et Renaissance* 38 (1976): 467–84; R. M. Kingdon, "Calvin and the Establishment of Consistory Discipline in Geneva: The Institution and the Men Who Directed It," *Nederlands Archief voor Kerkgeschiedenis* 70 (1990): 158–72; and Kingdon, "Consistory," in *The Oxford Encyclopedia of the Reformation*, 1:416–17.

[115]H. A. Speelman, *Calvin en de zelfstandigheid van de Kerk* (Kampen: Kok, 1994).

[116]H. Zwingli, *Sämtliche Werke* (Zurich: Theologischer, 1959), 14:424.

foundation of purpose-built schools. More generally, the emphasis in education shifted from dialectic toward rhetoric.[117]

In Calvin's day the educational system was confusing: primary and secondary education was available both from public schools and private instructors, while university studies provided a basic grounding as well as a smattering of liberal arts to boys around thirteen or fourteen years old. In this context, the creation of colleges modeled on the Strasbourg Academy was profoundly innovative. Inspired by the teachings of the Brethren of the Common Life, this school offered a more structured curriculum, bringing in humanist values and thus breaking free from scholasticism. In the Reformed world, theological training was added to the curriculum and the whole institution became similar to a university, whether in Geneva or in the United Provinces and the Rhineland. These changes marked more than a break with the practices of scholasticism. Instead, new institutions were established beyond the confines of the old ones.

Renewal was needed even more desperately in public preaching. Bishops and priests, whose task it was to preach, neglected preaching almost entirely. They left it instead to the mendicant orders, which made sermons disconnected from the celebration of the Mass. Sermons had become an occasional practice, mainly displayed at certain times of the year such as Lent, Advent, and a few major festivals. The reaction both among the Protestant and Catholic Reformers was to insist on more frequent preaching. Protestants did not restrict sermons to Sundays only, but spread the practice to every day of the week. The content of the sermons became closer to that of scripture as the Reformers abandoned the "modern method" that was taken from scholasticism. They rejected its complicated outlines filled with artificial divisions and pedantic quotations in favor of models that were closer to patristic preaching. This return to the sources had already taken place to a certain extent prior to the Reformation, as seen in the example of Jean Vitrier, Erasmus's favorite preacher. While Lutheran churches maintained the practice of preaching from set texts spread through the liturgical year, the Reformed preferred the *lectio continua,* and this principle prevailed in Geneva.[118]

Once he understood and accepted his vocation as a Reformer, Calvin gave priority to this teaching mission. It is hard to exaggerate the importance Calvin assigned to the Christian formation of laity and clergy through oral teaching. Theodore Beza gave the following account of Calvin's daily schedule "over the course of twenty-three years" (1541–64): "Apart from the fact that he preached every day on alternate weeks, he tried as often and as much as possible to preach twice every Sunday. He also taught

---

[117]Fr. Laplanche, "L'enseignement universitaire," in *Histoire du christianisme des origines à nos jours,* vol. 8, *Le temps des confessions, 1530–1620/30* (Paris: Desclée, Fayard, 1992), 1066–77.

[118]L. Taylor, *Soldiers of Christ: Preaching in Late Medieval and Reformation France* (New York: Oxford University Press, 1992), 15–36; A. Godin, *Spiritualité franciscaine au XVIe siècle: L'homéliaire de Jean Vitrier* (Geneva: Droz, 1971); and Ph. Denis, "La Bible et l'action pastorale," in *Le Temps des Réformes et la Bible,* ed. G. Bedouelle and B. Roussel (Paris: Beauchesne, 1989), 515–44.

three times a week in theology, gave the remonstrances in the Consistory, and essentially gave a lecture every Friday during our scripture study sessions that we call the *congrégation*."[119] A student's description of his studies, shortly before Calvin's death, completes this picture. On 25 February 1564, François Perrot wrote about his studies in Geneva. "I learn theology in part at school and in part at home. Our good teacher and father of us all is in the habit of commenting on Ezekiel, which he is currently working on. During this year, he lectures for the first three days of every second week, while our Theodore in turn comments on the Greek catechism during the first three days of his week. Indeed, each man is free from teaching for the second three days of his own week.... Because of his illness, Calvin can barely take his turn."[120]

The Lectures

Calvin's first teaching assignment in Geneva was his exegetical lectures, which he gave before a small audience in Saint-Pierre Cathedral beginning in September 1536. He was paid for the work by the Genevan Council, albeit reluctantly, as shown in February 1537 when it was noted that "he has not received much so far."[121] Following on these lectures, Calvin began to preach to a wider audience. Beginning in January 1538, his exegetical lectures were part of the curriculum of the Genevan Latin school, even though they took place outside its walls. At that point, the plan was for two daily lectures, one on the Old Testament and one, taught by Calvin, on the New Testament.[122]

In Strasbourg, Calvin continued to both preach and teach. But here preaching was his primary activity, a task he began as soon as he arrived in the city. The more academic teaching—his lectures—came only later. At the end of January 1539, he explained to Farel, "I teach or preach daily."[123] Besides his four weekly sermons, he also taught three times a week, a task which at first he did privately, but then, beginning on 1 May, he lectured publicly and was paid by the city for this task.[124] In 1555, one of the Viennese court counselors, Gaspard Nydbruck, remembered attending these lectures on the Pauline Epistles during his time in Strasbourg. According to him, the lectures took place in 1538, but as he also noted the death of Claude Féray (which occurred in March 1541) and the presence of Féray's disciples (that went back to 1539), in all likelihood Nydbruck attended Calvin's lectures for a number of years.[125]

From the first days of his return to Geneva, Calvin went back to his teaching and preaching. In November 1541, Christophe Fabri rejoiced over this: "We see and

[119]CO, 21:33.
[120]CO, 20:259.
[121]RC 29:51r; RC 30:316r.
[122]Herminjard, *Correspondance,* 4:459.
[123]Herminjard, *Correspondance,* 5:230; and CO, 10/b:316.
[124]J. Rott, "Documents strasbourgeois," 60–61.
[125]CO, 16:87. On Féray and his followers, see F. Buisson, *Sébastien Castellion, sa vie et son oeuvre, 1515–1563: Etude sur les origines du protestantisme libéral français* (Paris: Hachette, 1892), 1:114–15.

we experience the great fruit of these lectures and colloquies, even in neighboring lands."[126] By colloquies, he meant the *congrégations,* which we will discuss below. Rapidly, therefore, Calvin was back to his smaller audience for his lectures. Those who attended the lectures were boys and men who had finished their secondary schooling or had recently arrived in Geneva, all seeking the foundations of theological training.

Thus, Calvin "read" holy scripture. Thomas Parker highlighted this teaching, a very neglected topic until recently.[127] Following the establishment of the Genevan Academy in 1559, the lectures were intended first and foremost for theology students and were always done in Latin. Thomas Parker underlined the youthfulness of the audience, even though he has abandoned the assertion in his first edition that the average age of Calvin's hearers was thirteen to fifteen years old.[128] However, he is correct that the average age of entry to university during this century was around fourteen or fifteen years of age.[129] But in the case of Geneva, one has to bear in mind the varied recruitment of the Academy, at least in the time of Calvin and Beza. Few of the birth dates of the first students to matriculate in the *Livre du Recteur* are known, yet all indications suggest that there was a wide range of ages. Jean des Gallars was twelve or thirteen when he registered in 1559; Paul Baduel, fourteen; Peter Young, fifteen; Robert Bimard and Jean Colladon, seventeen; Pierre Colladon, eighteen; Jean Blanchard, Gianbattista Aureli, Léon Colladon, Florent Chrestien, and Odet de Nort, nineteen; Jean Hortin, twenty-one; and the two brothers Marnix de Sainte-Aldegonde were twenty-three and twenty. Alongside them, many adults were starting a second career, like Theodor Weyer, who had obtained his doctorate in law three years prior to enrolling in Geneva, or François Guarin, who had begun his studies back in 1523. Jean Cormère was twenty-nine; Nicolas Baudoin, thirty-four; Germain Chauveton, forty-four; and Antoine Chauve, fifty. Many students whose ages are unknown took up pastoral charges within three years following their matriculation, suggesting that they were more than thirteen or fifteen at that point. Among those who enrolled in 1559, the following are some pastors or future pastors with the year in which they began their ministry: Lancelot Dolbeau (1558), Jean de Cenesme and Sancius Tartas (1560), Urbain Chauveton and Nicolas Le More (1561), Jean le Gaigneux and Barthélemy Perrot (1562).[130] In any event, the audience included pastors and other laymen.

[126]Herminjard, *Correspondance,* 7:350–51; and CO, 11:347–48.

[127]T. H. L. Parker, *Calvin's Old Testament Commentaries* (Edinburgh: T & T Clark, 1986, repr. with minor corrections, 1993), 13–29.

[128]Parker, *Old Testament,* 15–16 (in both editions). Parker changed his viewpoint due to comments by P. Wilcox (1993 ed., 8)

[129]J.-P. Massaut, *Josse Clichtove, l'Humanisme et la réforme du clergé* (Liège, Paris: Les Belles Lettres, 1968), 1:102 n. 9.

[130]S. Stelling-Michaud, ed., *Le Livre du Recteur de l'Académie de Genève (1559–1878).* 6 vols. (Geneva: Droz, 1959–1980). The biographical entries appear in alphabetical order. My analysis is echoed

Calvin gave three lectures one week out of two. For the lectures given after 1557, Colladon specified the starting and ending date for the commentary on each biblical book. In fact, one can go further and date each lecture specifically, for the speaker quite often referred to what had been said "yesterday" or what would be presented "tomorrow." Thus one can establish groups of lectures given during a specific week,[131] and the result of this work suggests that the timetable of three lectures every second week was not always followed, whether because of temporary overload or illness of the professor, leading to his absence from class.

Calvin spoke very slowly in his lectures, almost at a dictation pace. The number of words of a few of his lectures shows that he was speaking at a pace of about forty-six to fifty-two words a minute, while public speakers usually use 120 words a minute, the pace of Calvin's sermons.[132] This difference in tempo probably explains in part why Calvin reacted differently to the publication of his lectures than to that of his sermons. In his lectures, he spoke more slowly and his audience had fewer difficulties taking it all down word for word. In a later chapter, we will consider how these lectures were prepared for publication.[133] However the first attempts to write down a complete copy of his lectures beginning in 1549 did not lead to a systematic procedure until 1556.

Preaching

Already in 1536, Calvin had begun to preach to the general public, a practice that played an increasingly important part in his pastoral activities.

The frequency of Calvin's sermons during his first period in Geneva is unknown. In all likelihood, from the very start he preached not only on Sundays, but also on weekdays. Calvin rapidly became aware of the usefulness of this practice and considered it one of the most effective tools of pastoral work. When he arrived in Strasbourg, his first action in his new French-speaking congregation was to preach, leaving academic lecturing until later. He delivered his first sermon on Sunday, 8 September 1538[134] and soon shifted to a rhythm of three sermons during the week, together with three lectures, as described above.[135]

His strategy remained the same when he returned to Geneva. Indeed, in 1541, Calvin probably preached twice on Sundays and three times during the week, one week out of two. On 11 September 1542, when he and Claude Roset were asked to write the ordinances, Calvin was authorized to cut back on all his preaching apart

---

by a recent article by P. Wilcox, "The Lectures of John Calvin and the Nature of his Audience, 1555–1564," *Archiv für Reformationsgeschichte* 87 (1996): 136–48.

[131]Parker, *Old Testament,* 17–18.

[132]Parker, *Old Testament,* 22–23.

[133]See below 54–66.

[134]Herminjard, *Correspondance,* 5:111–12; and CO, 10/b:247.

[135]Herminjard, *Correspondance,* 5:145 n. 19; and CO, 10/b:288.

from one Sunday sermon. This measure was undoubtedly in effect until the ordinances were put into effect on 22 January 1543.[136]

Beginning in 1549, information on the frequency and content of the sermons is more specific. In that year, Calvin was preaching daily every second week. He also preached twice on Sundays every week, once in the morning and once in the afternoon. In his sermons he worked his way through entire books of the Bible. On Sundays he preached on the New Testament or Psalms, and during the week, he did the same for books of the Old Testament. In 1549, Calvin preached on three different books simultaneously, one on Sunday mornings, another on Sunday afternoons, and a third during the week. From 1554 onwards, he only dealt with one book of the Bible on Sundays.[137]

The year 1549 proved to be a turning point in the history of Calvin's sermons, marking the start of a systematic written record of what he said, a matter which will be dealt with later on. We will also consider the amount of time Calvin spent preparing his sermons.[138]

The Congrégations

The *prophezei,* established in Zurich in 1525, was a creation of the Zwinglian Reformation and was rapidly taken up by churches in Strasbourg, Bern, Geneva, Lausanne, and others. These regular gatherings of pastors listened to the exposition of a scripture passage and served as a Bible study group, continuing education session, and a place for doctrinal oversight of pastors all at the same time.

In Geneva, this gathering, known as a *congrégation,* took shape thanks to scripture study sessions that met every Friday. While these sessions had begun already in 1536, they were restarted again in 1541 and were mentioned in the ecclesiastical ordinances. All the ministers in the Genevan territory were to attend, together with a group of laymen numbering three times more than the pastors, so that the total group stood at about sixty people. Each pastor in turn explained a passage from scripture. The exegesis was then commented on by those in attendance. In all likelihood, Calvin only presented his exegesis once every three or four months. But if Colladon is to be believed, Calvin's participation in the discussions was both active and substantive: "what he added after the person who had done the exegesis, was like a lecture."[139]

As we shall see, the *congrégations* provided the foundation for the writing of several commentaries. This does not mean that Calvin merely wrote down what his

---

[136]RC 36, fol. 117v; CO, 21:302; and Doumergue, *Jean Calvin,* 6:32.

[137]T. H. L. Parker, *Calvin's Preaching* (Edinburgh: T & T Clark, 1992), 59–64.

[138]See below 79.

[139]CO, 21:66. On the *congrégations* see J. Calvin, *Deux congrégations et exposition du catéchisme,* ed. R. Peter (Paris: Presses universitaires de France, 1964), ix–xx; and Ph. Denis, "La prophétie dans les églises de la réforme au XVIe siècle," *Revue d'histoire ecclésiastique* 72 (1977): 287–316, esp. 298–300.

colleagues had said, but rather that his reflections born out of the *congrégations* led him to put his own thoughts down on paper.

The Omnipresent Bible

Calvin encountered the Bible at three key points in his weekly routine, namely, in lectures, sermons, and the *congrégations,* leading him to analyze several books of the Bible simultaneously. Overall, he would read and comment on four or five biblical books at the same time: his lectures focused on one book, while the *congrégations* dealt with another. In his Sunday and weekday sermons, he presented his exegesis on another two or three books. Scholars editing his sermons have in fact noted at times the reciprocal influences of these exegetical studies.

5. On the Usefulness of the Pen

Alongside oral discourse, Calvin used the written word. Gutenberg's invention did not transform the habits of his contemporaries so radically as to eliminate entirely the need to write things down by hand. Indeed, letter-writing took up a considerable part of Calvin's time: writing to friends or to strangers was stressful for him, as he indicated in his complaints over the years. At the same time, it is important to note that manuscript copies remained an economical way to reproduce texts, a procedure not fully taken over by the printing industry.

Correspondence

"I Hate the Letters Themselves"

Letter-writing was very common among the influential men of the sixteenth century. It is tempting to try to compare a few leading authors, although the figures provided in modern editions of correspondence are not always reliable. Numbering generally includes both letters received and letters sent, and can even make serious mistakes—Luther's correspondence goes directly from number 2,399 to 3,000—or makes excessive use of *bis* and *ter*. Even the definition of the term "letter" varies, depending on whether one includes dedications and assorted written reports. Finally and significantly, no one has tried to estimate the number of letters that have been lost.

Yet one can draw up an approximate comparative chart of the total number of surviving letters of several sixteenth-century writers. A few individuals are clearly in the lead. Of the 9,301 items in Melanchthon's correspondence, approximately 7,000 are probably ones he wrote. Ignatius of Loyola left 6,815 letters, followed by Luther with more than 2,600 personal letters, to which one should add the 166 he cowrote. Bucer is around the same number, with 2,503 letters. Extrapolations based on the volumes that have already appeared suggest that Bullinger's letters number about 2,500 in a collection that totals over 12,000 items. Calvin's 1,247 letters place him closely behind Erasmus (1,980), Beza (1,750), and Peter Canisius (1,414). We should also specify that certain very productive writers had secretaries who took on the task of writing the letters based on the instructions they were given.[140] In terms of the surviving letters, Calvin always wrote them himself or dictated them.

Dominique Bertrand's study of the correspondence of Ignatius of Loyola, and even more so Matthew Arnold's work on Luther's letters, go far beyond mere number-crunching. These studies highlight how these two men had an impact on their contemporaries through their correspondence. For most of the Reformers, letters were intended to be private, thus distinguishing themselves from the humanist tradition that saw each letter as a stylistic exercise for possible future publication. For instance, Erasmus was careful to make sure that a selection of his letters appeared in print during his lifetime.[141]

The 1,247 surviving letters of Calvin are only a small part of his complete body of correspondence. For instance, the letters that have survived for the period 1536 to 1564 amount to an average of three to four letters a month, a total that does not match the description of the exhausting work that Calvin often mentions. In Strasbourg in 1539, he penned a hurried reply to Farel because he had a lot to do, including writing four letters.[142] In October 1542, he acknowledged to Viret, "I have almost no idea what I am writing, because my eyesight is so blurred."[143] A year later, writing again to Viret, he said, "I was already exhausted from writing letters when yours was brought in. Since then, I have not stopped writing, and I have another five letters to do before I can turn to something else."[144] In 1551, he made a similar admission to Bullinger: "And I am absolutely exhausted from ceaseless writings, so much so that as I am often filled with disgust, I reach the point where I hate the letters themselves."[145] In each of these cases, the numerous letters he referred to have completely disappeared and thus are not included in the earlier total.

On several occasions, Calvin asked his correspondent to forgive him for his abbreviated answer. This was true on 8 November 1542 when writing to Bullinger, and Calvin was all the more embarrassed in that he was breaking a long silence on his part due to the time it was taking him to put the Genevan church back in order.[146] In February 1551, he said the same thing, even adding that it was Bullinger's indulgence

---

[140]See D. Bertrand, *La politique de S. Ignace de Loyola. L'analyse sociale* (Paris: Cerf, 1985), 36–39; M. Arnold, *La correspondance de Luther: Étude historique, littéraire et théologique* (Mainz: P. von Zabern, 1996), 27; F. Büsser, in H. Bullinger, *Briefwechsel* 1 (Zurich: Theologischer, 1973): 8, 19; and J. Rott, *Correspondance de Martin Bucer: Liste alphabétique des correspondants* (Strasbourg: Palais Université, 1977).

[141]L. E. Halkin, *Erasmus ex Erasmo: Érasme éditeur de sa correspondance* (Aubel: P. M. Gason, 1983).

[142]Herminjard, *Correspondance,* 5:289; and CO, 10/b:337.

[143]Herminjard, *Correspondance,* 8:167; and CO, 11:460.

[144]CO, 11:647.

[145]CO, 14:51.

[146]Herminjard, *Correspondance,* 8:186; and CO, 11:463.

in accepting his infrequent letters that explained why "I am less diligent in your case than toward other friends. In truth this is because the others rouse me from my sluggishness by their importunate requests. In your kindliness, you are willing to remain silent." Calvin continued, "May Heaven grant that others may become as moderate as you are, so that I can cultivate friendships faithfully while writing less. But our French friends are too heedless in their demands in this area." [147]

A few months later, it was Farel's turn to receive a note from Calvin complaining about his excessive workload, which compelled him to write brief and dry letters. Farel understood the situation all the more in that he had scolded Calvin for writing too many letters and advised him to delegate the writing to secretaries.[148]

In his letters of 1557 to the Zurich pastor Hans Wolf and of 1559 to Simon Sulzer, pastor in Basel, Calvin reiterated his views. He wrote much too rarely to his friends and then only for urgent reasons. Thus he wrote to Sulzer, "While I am burdened by having to write letters to so many people, many of whom I know little or not at all, I am neglecting a few close friends, so that they do not receive letters from me unless I am forced to write to them for some serious reason."[149]

In 1561, Calvin weighed the relative importance of a pamphlet and his correspondence. He wrote to Beza to complain about an anonymous work that he thought had been written by François Bauduin: "I would like to deal with this rascal as he deserves, but I am overburdened with letter-writing, and my remaining energies are becoming depleted."[150]

Relying on the Mail

The rhythm of correspondence was tied to opportunities to transport the mail. While sixteenth-century people did have access to a public mail service, many preferred to entrust their letters to travelers who were known to them.[151] The story of Calvin's manuscript that went astray between Geneva and Strasbourg shows the risks of this strategy.

This reliance on irregular letter carriers explains why many letters were written. Many times, Calvin noted that he had to hurry because of the messenger's imminent departure. "Please excuse my haste," he wrote to Bullinger in 1551. "For when these young Germans offered me their services, they only gave me an hour to write, and the time is nearly up."[152] Already in 1542, he complained to Farel about the carelessness of the carriers. "They have a bad habit of announcing their departure to everyone just as they are dressed and ready to set out, and only then ask me whether

---

[147]CO, 14:51.
[148]CO, 14:140, 143.
[149]CO, 17:514, see 16:729.
[150]Theodore Beza, *Correspondance de Théodore de Bèze,* ed. Hippolyte Aubert et al. Travaux d'humanisme et renaissance (Geneva: Droz, 1960–), 3:149.
[151]See J. Delumeau, *Rome au XVIe siècle* (Paris: Hachette, 1975), 13–24.
[152]CO, 14:101.

I have any messages for you." Calvin then recounted his experience with Sebastian Castellio: "he came to see me in the evening and said he was leaving the next day at first light. However, I could not write the letter that night without jeopardizing my health, and I do not get up early enough in the morning to catch up with him then. Furthermore, I still had to prepare my sermon."[153] This was not the only time when letter-writing and sermon or lecture preparation were in conflict. In May 1554, Calvin admitted to Farel, "At this point I have no time to write, because it will soon be time for my lecture, and I still have not thought about what I will say."[154]

At times, the problem lay in finding an available messenger. At the close of a letter of 1538, Calvin added, "I have kept this letter for ten days, waiting for a messenger to turn up."[155]

Letter-writing thus seems to have been stressful work, generally done in haste and dependent on the availability of letter carriers. In his 1542 letter to Farel, Calvin began by explaining that he had not given any letters to Maturin Cordier, who had just set off on the trip from Geneva to Neuchâtel, because a number of people had told him that they too would shortly be leaving for Neuchâtel.[156]

Handwritten Letters

Out of respect for his correspondents, especially those he knew less well, Calvin preferred to send letters written in his own hand. In 1563, Jonviller explained to Bullinger that he should not tire himself out by writing letters himself. Jonviller recalled that he had made Calvin change his practice on this matter. A few years earlier, Jonviller had suggested that Calvin spare himself, and make use of the services of a secretary. But the Reformer had said that he worried about being criticized or thought to be negligent by some of his correspondents. Jonviller had needed great patience to convince Calvin to make the change.[157] Yet, based on the reaction of the Maastricht pastor Menso Poppius, recipients greatly appreciated receiving a letter in Calvin's own hand.[158]

However, this description of Calvin's letter-writing practices needs to be confronted with reality: Calvin had to rely often on a secretary due to sickness. In all likelihood to avoid offending his correspondents, Calvin apologized frequently for not writing himself: "I am forced to dictate this," "from my bed," "I am compelled to dictate these few words because a headache is keeping me in bed," "I have dictated this letter from my bed," and "please forgive me for the unfamiliar handwriting, since I have dictated this from my bed," and so on. In 1541, he was forced to use

---

[153]Herminjard, *Correspondance,* 8:78; and CO, 11:417.

[154]CO, 15:148.

[155]Herminjard, *Correspondance,* 5:148; and CO, 10/b:280.

[156]Herminjard, *Correspondance,* 8:78; and CO, 11:417.

[157]CO, 20:132.

[158]CO, 17:629; see J. J. Kalma, "Poppius, Menso," *Biografisch lexicon voor de geschiedenis van het Nederlandse protestantisme* 2 (Kampen: Kok, 1978–): 370–71.

French for one letter he dictated from his bed, for lack of a secretary able to write Latin.[159]

A Rushed but Conscientious Correspondent

Both because of the energy required and its effective spread of Calvin's thoughts and actions, letter-writing certainly played a key role in Calvin's life.

By underlining the haste with which Calvin wrote his letters and linking this to the speed at which Calvin prepared his sermons and lectures, I hope to show that the urgent nature of the tasks to be done was one of the key characteristics of Calvin's written work, including his printed writings.

Yet Calvin never gave up. Because he thought that his correspondents deserved to receive letters in his handwriting, he took up the pen himself in spite of the additional fatigue caused by this task.[160]

Matthew Arnold's recent study on Luther's correspondence deals mainly with its content, yet the description of the writing, mailing, and collecting process is very similar to Calvin's activity, with one exception: while Calvin was careful to keep certain copies of his letters, Luther was extremely careless in this regard.[161]

Manuscript Circulation

The Survival of Hand-copied Materials

Calvin was not the only one to make use of a pen. In many instances, he asked secretaries to transcribe his thoughts for him. Furthermore, there are numerous traces of manuscript copies of Calvin's writings. The following paragraphs provide some contemporary evidence related to different literary genres.

Published in Geneva in 1544, the *Epinicion Christo cantatum* was written by Calvin in 1541 during the Colloquy of Worms. At the time, Calvin allowed three or four copies to be made. He was therefore very astonished to discover from merchants returning from Lyon that the *versus Joannis Calvini* had made it onto the index of the French inquisitor-general, Vidal de Becanis. Calvin was intrigued by this mention, as were his friends, who asked him to publish the poem, which he did in 1544.[162] One should note in passing that the Becanis Index also circulated only in manuscript form.

Even printed books could be copied by hand. When Valérand Poullain received a copy of the 1543 *Petit traicté monstrant que doit faire un fidele entre les papistes* in

---

[159]CO, 12:689 (29 April 1548), 13:451 (March 1551), 14:202 (November 1551), 14:274 (27 January 1552), 14:305 (13 March 1552); Herminjard, *Correspondance,* 7:183; and CO, 11:253 (12 July 1541).

[160]See below 127–28.

[161]Arnold, *La correspondance de Luther,* 22–35.

[162]*B.C.1,* no. 44/8; and Fr. H. Reusch, *Die Indices librorum prohibitorum des sechzehnten Jahrhunderts* (Tübingen: Litterarischer Verein, 1886), 133 no. 59.

Strasbourg, he sent "a handwritten copy" to the faithful in southern Flanders and the region of Tournai. Later, he was able to send them over two hundred copies of the work.[163] Herminjard saw a connection between this occurrence and the 1541 publication of Viret's *Epistre consolatoire aux fideles qui souffrent persecution.* Yet the situations were different, since in Viret's case the request for copies led to publication. Indeed, Viret stated that he had sent a letter of 1543 to the printer, "so that we would not lose so much time and work in transcribing several copies, as we had done for the *Epistre consolatoire.*" Thus the *Epistre* of 1540 was spread thanks to printing in 1541.[164]

The publication of Calvin's sermons received little encouragement from their author, as we shall see.[165] He had no objection, however, to their circulation in manuscript form. In fact, the existence of the copies themselves is the best evidence for this. Alongside the transcriptions done in Geneva by Raguenier and his successor, several manuscripts of Calvin's sermons have survived. These manuscripts are collections of several dozen sermons, as is the case in the Bodleian at Oxford, in the library of Lambeth Palace in London, in the Bürgerbibliothek of Bern, or in the Walloon church of London, where a new collection was recently uncovered.[166] At times, as in the case of the Puy collection in the Bibliothèque Nationale in Paris, the sermons in question were found on a number of sheets folded in four, greasy from being consulted so often.[167]

The conflict that emerged in 1565 around a La Rochelle printing of Calvin's sermons shows how the sermons were spread in two ways: private copies were obtainable relatively easily and, in all likelihood, at no cost.[168] However, once the demand for manuscript copies became too great, printers were called in. Such was the case for the *Deux Sermons,* printed in 1546. The printer explained that there was such demand from all over for this text that "it would have been much too much work to write them out so many times."[169]

Letters too, especially those with a more marked doctrinal content, circulated in multiple handwritten copies. Menno Poppius provided evidence for this when he explained to Calvin in his letter of 10 September 1559 that a previous missive sent

---

[163]Herminjard, *Correspondance,* 9:173; and CO, 11:683.

[164]Herminjard, *Correspondance,* 6:429 n. 1–2.

[165]See below 73–81.

[166]Parker, *Preaching,* 179. See also, M. Engammare, "Des sermons de Calvin sur esaie décooverts à Londres," in *Calvin et ses contemporains,* ed. O. Millet (Geneva: Droz, 1998), 69–81.

[167]R. Stauffer, "Les Sermons inédits de Calvin sur le livre de la Genèse," *Revue de Théologie et de Philosophie* 98 (1945): 26–36.

[168]E. Droz, *Barthélemy Berton, 1563–1573* (Geneva: E. Droz, 1960), 46–52. See also J.-Fr. Gilmont, "L'apport de La Rochelle et du royaume de France à la diffusion des écrits de Calvin (1560–1600)," in the forthcoming proceedings of the colloquium "Le livre entre Loire et Garonne," Niort, Paris: Association des amis d'Agrippa d'Aubigné, Librairie Honoré Champion, 1998.

[169]*B.C.1,* no. 46/3.

by Calvin had been copied and circulated widely, because it provided important instructions for ecclesiastical discipline.[170]

A mistake by Jonviller in the first months of 1563 reveals that Calvin's lectures were also circulating in manuscript form. A Polish correspondent of Jonviller's, Krzystof Trecy, asked him for Calvin's lectures on the first chapter of Ezekiel. Jonviller intended to satisfy Trecy's request, but as he sealed the letters, he inadvertently slipped the requested copy into the letter he was sending to Bullinger. This mix-up allowed us to learn of the practice.[171]

These few examples show that one should not be transfixed by printing to the point of believing that it put an end to the use of the pen. Manuscript writing remained a very practical tool for private letters, and was also valuable when an individual or a group of friends wanted to have a copy of a text, even if it was already in print.

[170]CO, 17:629.
[171]CO, 19:694.

CHAPTER TWO

Printed Works

Apart from a few scattered treatises, the bulk of Calvin's writings can be divided into two main categories: exegesis and polemic. A few ecclesiastical texts complete the picture. Printed sermons should be considered separately, since Calvin preached them but did not write them down.

Calvin's exegetical works make up the majority of his writing. They form a coherent whole, undoubtedly conceived during his first stay in Geneva; Calvin furthered his aim step-by-step, in spite of the turmoil of his existence. In contrast, his polemical works arose out of the current events of his day. At the heart of his work lay the *Institutes,* "like a key and a doorway" to the right understanding of scripture. The *Institutes* served as the gateway text, to be read prior to the exegetical commentaries.[1]

I. THE *Institutes of the Christian Religion*

As this chapter shows, Calvin's masterpiece held a special place in his written corpus. The wealth of information about the writing process of the *Institutes* also contributes significantly to this study.

The Christianae Religionis Institutio

The first edition of the *Institutes* has already been mentioned. Printed as a small octavo of slightly more than five hundred pages,[2] the work had a dual purpose: to present the key points of Reformed doctrine and to defend the cause of French men and women persecuted for the sake of the Gospel. The initial four chapters met the first goal, while the last two chapters, together with the prefatory letter to Francis I,

---

[1]Calvin, *Institution,* ed. Benoît, vol. 1:25.
[2] *B.C.1,* no. 36/1. For details on the various editions of the *Institutes,* see O.S., 3:VI–L.

fulfilled the second. Calvin described this first edition as a *libellus* and a *breve enchiri-dion*. The printer Oporinus, for his part, spoke of a *catechismus*.[3]

The work was completed during Calvin's stay in Basel beginning in January 1535. In all likelihood, he finished writing in August 1535 when he signed the dedicatory letter, but for publishing reasons the printing took place in March 1536, the time of the spring book fair.[4] On this point, I disagree with Eugénie Droz, who describes Calvin's "frantic work" on the book between July 1535 and March 1536.[5] Did he begin writing the book in France? This hypothesis is quite likely, given that the more defensive tone of the last two chapters was probably shaped by the Affair of the Placards (17–18 October 1534) and the resulting wave of persecutions faced by French evangelicals. If such was indeed the case, the first chapters were written in France, perhaps even in Angoulême at the home of Louis du Tillet or in Orléans.[6]

Early on, Calvin considered producing a French version of the *Institutes*. In October 1536, he spoke to François Daniel, one of his friends from the university, about a French translation project that was already well advanced. "We were always thinking about the French edition of our little book." Calvin even delayed writing his letter because he hoped to include the new book with it. Yet the disputation of Lausanne disrupted this endeavor, and showed Calvin the urgent need for pastoral work.[7] Thus he restricted himself to extracting the key passages from the *Institutes* and translating them for the 1537 *Instruction et confession de foi*.[8] This small octavo book of forty-eight sheets allowed the substance of the 1536 *Institutes* to be available in French for the first time.

The First Revisions

The first published version of the *Institutes* was very successful. A year after it appeared, the Basel publishers no longer had any copies available in the city, with only about fifty remaining in Frankfurt. Oporinus urged Calvin to prepare a new edition for him.[9] Calvin took up the suggestion, but radically modified the original plan, shifting the *Institutes* from an advanced catechism to a manual of theology. Calvin probably finished this first revision in Geneva in 1537–38, and gave the task of retranscribing a clean copy of his first drafts to Antoine du Pinet. This hypothesis is supported by Calvin's impatience in waiting for the final product shortly after his arrival in Strasbourg in October 1538,[10] though he had to wait until August 1539 to see the printed version of his book. Once again, the printers were the main cause of

---

[3]Herminjard, *Correspondance*, 4:88, 208; and CO, 10/b:63, 90–91; 2:3–4; 31:23.
[4]See below 181.
[5]Droz, *Chemins*, 1:89–129, esp. 119, 122.
[6]Doumergue, *Jean Calvin*, 1:594–95.
[7]Herminjard, *Correspondance*, 4:87–88; and CO, 10/b:62–64.
[8]*B.C.1*, no. 37/2.
[9]Herminjard, *Correspondance*, 4:207–9; and CO, 10/b:90–91.
[10]Herminjard, *Correspondance*, 5:134; and CO, 10/b:261.

the delay: Calvin's first choice of printer in Basel did not work out, so he had to turn to a Strasbourg press.[11]

The second Latin edition was much more extensive than the first, going from six to seventeen chapters.[12] Calvin stated in the letter to the reader that his intentions had changed. While the earlier version had provided a summary presentation of doctrine, this one was intended "to prepare candidates in sacred theology and train them in the study of Holy Scripture, so that they may have easy access to it and progress unimpeded therein." Calvin also specified the connections he saw between his compendium and the biblical commentaries he intended to write. Each time, in order to avoid lengthy doctrinal digressions, he planned to refer the readers of his commentaries back to the *Institutes*. He noted that he had already done so in his commentary on the Epistle to the Romans that he was currently working on. In the commentaries that appeared in the following decade, Calvin consistently referred back to his *Institutes*, as in the commentaries on First[13] and Second Corinthians,[14] Ephesians,[15] the First Epistle to Timothy,[16] the Epistle to the Hebrews,[17] and the book of Acts.[18]

Following the revised edition of 1539, Calvin worked on producing a complete French version of his work. From this point onwards, each new Latin edition of the *Institutes* was followed by a French edition. This had been the plan from the very start, but it did not happen in the case of the 1536 edition. Instead, the first French version, published in 1541, was based on the Latin edition of 1539.[19] However, certain modifications in chapter order did occur and the changes reappeared in each subsequent French edition. Furthermore, some of the translated passages came from the Latin 1536 edition. One must conclude, then, that Calvin relied at least in part on his original 1536 work.[20] Thus beginning with this first French version, the Latin and French texts were different and this situation persisted as later editions appeared.

The 1539 and 1541 editions were followed by a number of later editions that had undergone only minor revisions. The Latin edition of 1543 included a number of substantive changes as it went from seventeen to twenty-one chapters and almost a quarter of the material in the book was new. Most of the additions were born out of Calvin's experiences during his stay in Strasbourg, as well as the time he spent at

[11]See below 181–82.
[12]*B.C.1*, no. 39/4.
[13]*B.C.1*, no. 46/2; CO, 49:352, 356, 381, 440, 461.
[14]*B.C.1*, no. 48/8; and CO, 50:59, 65.
[15]*B.C.1*, no. 48/7; and CO, 51:188.
[16]*B.C.1*, no. 48/9; and CO, 52:272, 303.
[17]*B.C.1*, no. 49/4; and CO, 55:100, 226.
[18]*B.C.1*, no. 52/2; and CO, 48:11, 120.
[19]*B.C.1*, no. 41/3.
[20]R. Peter, "La première édition de *l'Institution de la religion chrétienne* de Calvin," in *Le livre et la Réforme*, ed. R. Peter and B. Roussel (Bordeaux: Société des bibliophiles de Guyenne, 1987), 17–34.

religious colloquies in 1540 and 1541.[21] In all likelihood, this revised manuscript was well advanced even prior to Calvin's return to Geneva in September 1541. In January 1542, Calvin announced that the work on the edition was done[22] although once again, there was a significant delay between that time and the actual appearance of the book off the presses in March 1543.[23]

The French edition linked to the 1543 revision appeared in February 1545.[24] This version seems to have been prepared somewhat carelessly, since only the lengthy new passages of text were translated, while the minor changes made to the Latin edition were omitted in the French one.

The new Latin edition, begun in November 1544 and completed in March 1545, only added a few minor clarifications and corrections without any major changes.[25] This version had no matching French edition.

In 1549, Calvin took up his masterwork once more and reread it, publishing yet another revised edition in early 1550.[26] Once again, the revisions were not radical. Minor changes included the addition of citations from patristic sources. Apart from rewriting chapters 1, 3, and 8, Calvin made two stylistic changes to his text. First, he divided his chapters into numbered paragraphs, making it easier to use the text as a reference. This innovation slightly predated the numbering of Bible verses carried out by Robert Estienne in 1552. Second, the work now included new indexes, including one for biblical citations and a topical index. These indexes were prepared by Valérand Poullain. The 1553 Latin reprint was based on the 1550 edition, but a number of errors were corrected both in the text and in the biblical references.[27]

The third French edition of the *Institutes* appeared in October 1551 and included the Latin additions of 1550.[28] In fact, the entire text was revised based on the 1550 Latin edition, including the division into chapters and numbered paragraphs. Yet the 1551 French edition also contained a number of new passages, the most notable of which is three paragraphs on the resurrection. This insertion was missing from every Latin edition until that of 1559, where the passage reappeared in a different form.[29] The indexes of the 1551 French edition were based on the Latin 1550 edition and were prepared by Nicolas Colladon.

---

[21]P. Fraenkel, "Trois passages de l'Institution de 1543 et leurs rapports avec les colloques interconfessionnels de 1540–41," in *Calvinus ecclesiae genevensis custos* (Frankfurt am Main: P. Lang, 1984), 149–57.

[22]Herminjard, *Correspondance,* 7:410; and CO, 11:364.

[23]*B.C.1,* no. 43/5.

[24]*B.C.1,* no. 45/6.

[25]*B.C.1,* no. 45/5; and CO, 11:762.

[26]*B.C.1,* no. 50/16.

[27]*B.C.1,* no. 53/6. For information on the indexes, see below 144–45.

[28]*B.C.1,* no. 51/11.

[29]See paragraphs 221–23 of chapter 8 in the French 1550 edition, and paragraphs 7–9 of chapter 25 of book 3 in the 1559 Latin edition.

The Definitive 1559 Edition and the 1560 French Version

In spite of the previous revisions, Calvin was not yet satisfied with his work. Already by 1556, he intended to carry out a more radical rewrite: when Jacques Bourgeois and his associates obtained a printing privilege for the French *Institutes* on 27 October 1556, the city councilors added one caveat: "until the said Master Calvin revises it."[30]

In his preface dated 1 August 1559, Calvin explained why he had prepared this new edition. He noted that he had not expected his original text to meet with such success, so he had worked "more superficially, concentrating on being succinct." Given that the book had been received "with more favor than I ever could have hoped," the author felt bound to respond "better and more fully" to "those who receive my doctrine so faithfully." He added that "it would have been a sign of ingratitude on my part, had I not satisfied their wishes, as far as I was able." Calvin noted that he had been guided by this concern in revising the text both in the second edition and in subsequent ones. This statement is perfectly accurate if one leaves aside a number of reeditions that were not done under his oversight. However, the extent of the revision varied a great deal from one edition to another.

Calvin acknowledged that he enjoyed the revision process: "However, I admit that I have never been satisfied until I have worked through it in order, as you will see." He then insisted on the care and energy which he had devoted to the work: "Last winter, when I was so ill with quartan fever that it seemed I was at death's door, the more I felt ill, the harder I worked, until I had improved the book." He ended his preface by explaining that his work would outlive him, because it would show "how much I wish to satisfy those who have already profited from this book, and wish to profit even more from it."[31] The work thus occupied Calvin's time during the winter of 1558–59, when he rarely left the house due to ill health. The manuscript was finished in early February 1559,[32] and the work came off the presses in August of the same year.

The definitive version was much larger than the preceding one; it was divided into four books and no fewer than eighty chapters. Calvin based the 1559 edition on the 1553 Estienne edition and inserted pages from earlier works, such as his attacks against Socinus and Biandrata and the verdict against Menno Simons.[33]

The 1559 edition first appeared without an index because the publisher felt that the intelligent organization of topics within the text was enough to guide the reader. But pressure from customers led him to add an index, prepared by Nicolas Colladon, who had also done the index for the French 1551 edition.

---

[30]RC 52:68v.
[31]Calvin, *Institution*, ed. Benoît, 1:23–24.
[32]CO, 17:431.
[33]See O.S., 3:XLI.

The definitive French version appeared in 1560.[34] Just as in the earlier versions, Calvin himself did the translation, a topic which we will deal with again below.[35] Thanks to the efforts of Nicolas Colladon, this edition also consequently featured an index.

The 1559/1560 definitive text was such a significant rewrite that "one can almost consider it as a new book," as the title stated. Modern scholars have highlighted the evolution in Calvin's style, in part due to the fact that in 1558–59 he dictated his additions to the text.[36] The result was that the more serene and didactic tone of 1536 became more committed and more passionate in 1559. As Olivier Millet noted, Calvin used more concrete and dynamic spiritual language in his final edition and turned to diatribe more often.[37]

Preliminary Observations

The *Institutes* were a part of Calvin's life as a Reformer from 1534 to 1560. At first, the work was a relatively concise 85,000 words. By the second edition, it had more than doubled in size, to reach 200,000 words in 1539. The revisions carried out by Calvin at the end of his stay in Strasbourg and in 1550 were more modest, as the work reached 250,000 and then 275,000 words. The final rewrites done during the winter of 1558/59 were rather substantial: the definitive edition contained 450,000 words.

In his *Institutes*, Calvin brought together the essence of his thoughts and experiences as a theologian, giving the book pride of place as the chief reference work in his body of writing. We shall continue this study by analyzing the writing process behind the *Institutes*, one which involved the slow and patient accumulation of knowledge and information. This analysis confirms the centrality of the *Institutes*, which Calvin reworked so regularly between 1535 and 1560.

In comparison with his exegetical work, the *Institutes* displays another very specific characteristic, namely, that it was designed to be read without being linked to any other instruction of any kind. In contrast, as shown in the next section, the exegetical commentaries were closely tied to oral discourse from the very start. Indeed, Calvin often wrote his commentaries on biblical books after having explained their meaning in sermons or lectures. At other times, he instead took his inspiration for his sermons from commentaries that he had already written, as was the case for his sermons on Genesis preached in 1559 and 1560.[38] However, this aspect of the process need not concern us at this point.

---

[34]*B.C.2,* no. 60/8.

[35]See below 116, 120.

[36]See below 129–30.

[37]Millet, *Calvin et la dynamique,* 867–70.

[38]Max Engammare, "Le Paradis à Genève: Comment Calvin prêchait-il la chute aux Genevois?" *Etudes théologiques & religieuses* 69 (1994): 342.

2. THE SCRIPTURE COMMENTARIES

Sixteenth-century theologians saw it as their duty to publish good exegetical commentaries. Calvin explained this to Peter Martyr Vermigli in 1554, when he mentioned their two commentaries on Genesis. Calvin's was only just printed, and Vermigli's was still in process. Calvin first complained that he was faced with a "wild forest of books," and noted that "before all else, we need to have serious, learned, and solid commentaries by pious men of good judgment, who are authoritative and wise." He outlined two goals, namely, to ensure the purity of doctrine for future generations and to refute those who muddled everything.[39] Calvin's confidence in his own authoritative interpretation can be read between the lines in this description.

Calvin's published exegetical work came in three very different forms: the commentaries he wrote himself, his exegetical lectures taken down and published by his secretaries, and the sermons taken down by a team of stenographers. Because the status of the sermons is unique, we will deal with them in a separate chapter. In contrast, the commentaries Calvin wrote and the lectures transcribed by his colleagues have a shared history.

As stated in the dedication of Calvin's first commentary on the Epistle to the Romans, the main qualities of a commentator are brevity, simplicity, and edification. Calvin's exegetical practice was to follow the text verse by verse, shedding light on it through historical, geographical, or cultural remarks, and presenting the message of the sacred text and applying it for his readers. Thus he followed the same line as Luther, using an approach that was completely different from that of medieval commentaries, which were based on the four senses of scripture.[40]

The exegetical works that Calvin wrote himself were all called "commentaries." The term appeared in Calvin's titles mostly in the masculine plural (*Commentarii*), sometimes in the singular (*Commentarius*), (especially when published by Robert Estienne), and once in the neuter plural (*Commentaria*). In French, Calvin always used the singular form until 1550. Afterward, he regularly used the plural with no rationale for the change as far as I can determine.

The New Testament Commentaries

Shortly after his arrival in Geneva, Calvin became a "reader in Holy Scripture." Starting in September 1536, he began his lectures on the Pauline Epistles. Oporinus noted this in his letter of 25 March 1537: "I understand that you are commenting on the Epistles of St. Paul, to the praise and benefit of all. Thus I ask you to not hesitate to ensure that through us one day we can transmit to others all that you have

[39]CO, 15:219–20.
[40]K. Hagen, "What did the Term *Commentarius* mean to Sixteenth-Century Theologians?" in *Théorie et pratique de l'exégèse*, ed. I. Backus and F. M. Higman (Geneva: Droz, 1990), 13–38, esp. 22, 33–34.

commented and usually annotated for your own people."[41] This comment illustrates effectively the link between a discourse intended for a restricted audience and a written work, which could reach a much wider group of readers. Oporinus, as a good publisher, also insisted that he participate in the spread of this work.

There is no information on the lectures Calvin gave in Geneva until his banishment. In all likelihood, the first lectures were on the Epistle to the Romans. In Strasbourg, according to the recollection of one of his hearers, Calvin continued to comment on the Pauline Epistles. In May 1539, he began his commentary on the Epistles to the Corinthians.[42] Years later, Jean Sturm recalled that the magistrates asked Calvin to lecture on the scriptures as soon as he settled in Strasbourg, but this was not in fact what happened.[43] Sturm said that Calvin began with the Gospel of John, which is quite possible.[44]

By August 1539, Calvin had almost completed his commentary on the book of Romans, a fact that he mentioned in his letter to the reader in the new edition of the *Institutes*.[45] The work was finished soon afterwards, since Calvin dated his dedicatory letter on 18 October 1539. The work came off the presses only in March 1540,[46] a customary practice in that the printer was waiting for the first Frankfurt book fair following the submission of the manuscript.

At this stage, Calvin still had to make a name for himself in the world of scriptural exegesis. By dedicating the work to Simon Grynaeus, Calvin sought the patronage of a better-known senior figure. Calvin also noted that he and Grynaeus spent time together in Basel in 1535–36, and that together they had worked out the principles of good scriptural exegesis. Calvin also gave his viewpoint on some recent commentaries, including those of Melanchthon, Bullinger, and Bucer, situating his own work in light of theirs.

From 1539 onwards, Calvin intended to provide a complete set of commentaries on the New Testament Epistles. On several occasions in his commentaries, he noted that he would address a given question in a later work. Thus in his commentary on the First Epistle to the Corinthians, he referred readers to the commentary on Galatians—"as we shall see"[47]—and to the Hebrews commentary—"we will state this if God gives us enough time."[48] At this point, his aim was to publish everything with Rihel in Strasbourg.[49] In the second edition of his commentary on Romans that

---

[41]Herminjard, *Correspondance,* 4:208; and CO, 10/b:91.

[42]Herminjard, *Correspondance,* 5:230 n. 19; and CO, 16:87.

[43]See above 28–29.

[44]J. Sturm, *Quarti Antipappi Tres Partes Priores* (Neustadt: M. Harnish, 1580), 20; J. Ficker, *Die Anfänge der akademischen Studien in Straßburg* (Strasbourg: J. H. Ed. Heitz, 1912), 4.

[45]Herminjard, *Correspondance,* 5:367.

[46]*B.C.1,* no. 40/3.

[47]CO, 49:382; this note and the following two are based on Parker, *New Testament,* 10–11.

[48]CO, 49:489.

[49]CO, 12:391; and below 181–82.

appeared in 1551, he indicated to readers that he planned to write a commentary on the Epistle of James—"there, I will explain this further, if God gives me the opportunity."[50] However, the writing and publishing schedules were out of step with each other. The revision of the commentaries on the Pauline Epistles, already begun in July 1549, was only published in 1551,[51] while the commentary on James was already available in 1550. However, although it was published sooner, Calvin wrote the commentary on James after the revising of the Romans commentary.[52]

Between 1546 and 1550, Calvin gradually published his commentaries on the Pauline Epistles. The interruption between 1540 and 1546 was naturally due to the extra work he had to do to reorganize the Genevan church. Indeed, Calvin declared openly that his priorities were clear: his vocation as a restorer of the Genevan church came before everything else.[53]

The revision of his written commentaries began once again in 1545. A letter from Valérand Poullain indicated that the commentary on First Corinthians had arrived in Strasbourg in November 1545, and that the anticipated publication date would be in time for the spring fair of 1546. The deadline was met.[54]

The commentary on Second Corinthians should have followed relatively swiftly thereafter, since the manuscript version was finished in August 1546 when Calvin sent the text to Strasbourg. The Schmalkaldic War and the changing situation in Strasbourg delayed the printing, forcing Calvin to take his work back. In the end, he gave it to a Genevan printer to publish, delaying the publication of the work until 1548.[55] This was the same manuscript referred to earlier, which had been lost for a time between Geneva and Strasbourg.[56]

Once Calvin had recovered from the incident, he worked with determination on his commentary on the Epistle to the Galatians. This new work was completed in November 1546; Calvin would have sent it to Strasbourg if the Schmalkaldic War had not already prevented the printing of the commentary on Second Corinthians in that city.[57]

Calvin's correspondence does not provide any further details regarding the subsequent commentaries that he wrote. In the first months of 1548, a volume of commentaries came off the presses, bringing together his work on four Pauline Epistles: Galatians, Ephesians, Philippians, and Colossians. This printing probably occurred very shortly before or after that of the commentary on Second Corinthians.[58] This

---

[50]CO, 49:70.

[51]CO, 13:324; and *B.C.1*, no. 51/10.

[52]*B.C.1*, no. 50/2. Parker brought this matter to my attention, after not noticing it in time to include it in his *New Testament*.

[53]See above 14–16.

[54]*B.C.1*, no. 46/2; and CO, 12, 216.

[55]*B.C.1*, no. 48/8.

[56]See above 3–4.

[57]CO, 12:423.

[58]*B.C.1*, no. 48/7.

quick succession of publications suggests that Calvin accelerated his pace of commentary writing beginning in 1545. The lack of publications in 1547 was due more to the change in printers than to anything else.

The commentary on the two Epistles to Timothy appeared shortly thereafter, ready for the September book fair in 1548.[59]

From 1549 onwards, sources show that Calvin based several of his commentaries on the New Testament on themes presented in the Friday *congrégations*. Clearly, Calvin did not reproduce what various pastors said, but he did work on similar topics.[60] The group study of the Epistle to the Hebrews came to an end in 1549 and Calvin's commentary on Hebrews appeared in May of that year.[61] It is possible that a similar situation held true for earlier years, but evidence is lacking since the subjects dealt with in the *congrégations* in these earlier years are unknown.

In January 1549, Calvin's work on the Pauline Epistles was almost complete: "I have not yet written anything on the Epistle to Titus and the two to the Thessalonians."[62] While the dedication for the Titus commentary was dated November 1549, the text itself was completed in early 1550 and was very brief, running to forty-two pages.[63] The commentary on First Thessalonians was dated February 1550, while the one on Second Thessalonians was dated in July of the same year. Neither of these editions has survived, but these were also short works, similar in length to the commentary on Titus.[64] In the collective edition, Calvin added a commentary on Philemon, one which never appeared in an independent edition.

Calvin's commentaries on the Pauline Epistles followed the traditional order aside from two exceptions: the two Epistles to the Thessalonians were placed at the end of the series, while the commentary on Hebrews appeared before the one on Titus. These two alterations may have been due to the topics chosen for the *congrégations,* the lectures, or the sermons.

Calvin's plans for a collective edition of all his commentaries on the Pauline Epistles and the Epistle to the Hebrews dated back at least to July 1549[65] and gave him the opportunity to revise his work. The plan was to have the work printed for the September book fair in 1550,[66] but the schedule was not followed; the work had to wait to the end of the following year to be published. In his preface dated October 1551, Beza highlighted the usefulness of the work, which brought together "the complete body" of the commentaries "that you have liked so much, even when they were in separate pieces and not attached to each other." Beza added that "many

---

[59]*B.C.1,* no. 48/9.
[60]Parker, *New Testament,* 22–23.
[61]CO, 21:71; and *B.C.1,* no. 49/4.
[62]CO, 13:165.
[63]*B.C.1,* no. 50/5.
[64]*B.C.1,* nos. 50/6, 50/7.
[65]CO, 13:324.
[66]CO, 13:606.

things have been added and amended in many places, and many new things, never published before, have been added to this work." However, in spite of what Beza said, the changes were not very significant.[67]

Around 1550, Calvin moved away from the concept of small booklets offering brief commentaries. Until that point, Calvin had been publishing shorter and shorter commentaries. After the first ones that filled 400 to 500 pages, he brought together his commentaries on four Epistles into a book of 320 pages. His next volumes, containing commentaries on one or two Epistles, went as low as around forty pages. Subsequently, Calvin brought more extensive commentaries to print. Given that this change occurred at a time when he selected new printers, this editorial decision many not have been his own.

Calvin tirelessly pursued his work on the New Testament commentaries. Once again, he began to shadow the studies of the Friday *congrégations*. Indeed, in 1549–1550 the *congrégations* focused on the Catholic Epistles.[68] In July 1550, the Reformer announced the upcoming publication of his most recent commentary on the same books, planned for the following winter.[69] In August, Jan Utenhoven was aware that the work would soon appear, but it was not completed until the end of January 1551.[70] The Latin original ran to a folio volume of two hundred pages, about a fifth of the total of the commentaries on the Pauline Epistles.

Leaving aside for the moment Calvin's commentary on Isaiah, which is an exceptional case, let us continue to follow Calvin's publication of his New Testament commentaries. From the late 1540s on, increasingly detailed sources enable us to more clearly determine the links between his oral teaching and his publications.

His commentaries on the book of Acts, published in March 1552 and January 1554,[71] were based on the sermon cycle that he began on 25 August 1549, preaching one sermon every Sunday morning. The total cycle of 189 sermons was completed at the very end of 1553.[72] There is no evidence that Calvin gave exegetical lectures on this book, nor that the *congrégations* dealt with it, or at least Colladon makes no mention of it in his biography of Calvin. The Reformer's work on the commentary did not strictly follow the more regular rhythm of the sermons. On 10 November 1550, Calvin admitted to Farel, 'I am ashamed to acknowledge how slowly I am making progress in Acts. I think it will be a long work, given the first third that I have completed."[73] By that time, therefore, he had commented on around nine

---

[67]CO, 49:VIII.

[68]CO, 21:71, 72.

[69]CO, 13:606.

[70]CO, 13:626; and *B.C.1,* no. 51/5.

[71]*B.C.1,* nos. 52/3, 54/3.

[72]B. Gagnebin, "L'histoire des manuscrits des sermons de Calvin" in *Supplementa Calviniana* vol. 2 Sermons sur le livre d'Esàïe, ed. G. A. Barrois (Neukirchen-V Luyn: Verlag der Buchhandlung des Erziehangsvereins, 1961), XV; Parker, *Preaching,* 150–51; and CO, 21:76.

[73]CO, 13:655.

chapters. In 1551, he made little progress, since his first volume only contained the commentary on thirteen of the twenty-eight chapters in Acts. The second volume appeared in January 1554, and Calvin may have finished writing the book before he finished preaching his sermons, since the preaching cycle on Acts ended at the end of December 1553.

Meanwhile, Calvin revised his commentary on the Gospel of John, which came off the presses on 1 January 1553.[74] This work followed the pace of the sessions of the *congrégations,* which studied the fourth Gospel from 1550 to 1553.[75]

During these years, Calvin's interconnected teaching opportunities led to a series of publications that appeared in a somewhat convoluted order. The commentary on Isaiah in early 1551 was rapidly followed by the one on the canonical Epistles. The commentary on the first part of the book of Acts appeared in 1552, followed by the one on John's Gospel in 1553. Before publishing the commentary on the synoptic Gospels in 1555, Calvin finished his work on the book of Acts and brought out his commentary on Genesis in 1554. This pattern of publications was due to the links between his written work and his teaching, and Calvin himself seemed unconcerned by the lack of order, as demonstrated by his choice of sermon topics.

To conclude this section on the New Testament, the second part of Calvin's commentary on Acts followed the course of his Sunday morning sermons, and the work itself appeared in print in January 1554.[76] His commentary on the synoptic Gospels was linked to the *congrégations,* which dealt with the same topic from 1553 to 1555.[77] On 23 June 1554, he explained that his main task was to comment on the harmony of the three Gospels: "I must not be kept away from what I am burning to write about the three Gospels. Indeed, once this book is published, I will turn to silent meditation."[78] In the end, Calvin had done commentaries on the whole of the New Testament apart from the book of Revelation and the last two Epistles of John. In December 1554, Calvin went even further in stating that he would stop writing and even hesitated to have his concordance published. "Now I am unsure about what to do with my Harmony."[79] A short while earlier, Calvin had had a difficult encounter with the Genevan Council over his reply to Westphal and he may have been temporarily discouraged.[80] He may also have been considering looking for a printer outside Geneva. Yet on 28 January 1555, the Genevan Council received an official request for printing permission.[81] The work took a number of months, since the date of completion of printing was 17 July, while the preface was dated 1 August 1555.[82]

---

[74]*B.C.1,* no. 53/5.
[75]CO, 21:72, 76.
[76]*B.C.1,* no. 54/3.
[77]CO, 21:76, 79.
[78]CO, 15:175.
[79]CO, 15:356.
[80]See below 268.
[81]RC 48, fol. 184r.
[82]*B.C.2,* no. 55/9.

In 1556, Calvin carried out an in-depth revision of his commentaries on the New Testament Epistles due to the reedition to be carried out by Robert Estienne. The modifications to the text were quite significant.[83] In following years, Calvin continued to insert minor changes into his copy of the work. Jean Crespin took advantage of this by incorporating the changes in his edition begun in 1557, but it was not published until 1563 because of a conflict over authors' rights.[84]

From the "Commentaries" to the "Lectures"

Calvin's exegesis of the Old Testament, which began to appear in print in 1551, also marked a change in his practice, as he gradually abandoned writing his commentaries himself in favor of authorizing the publication of his exegetical lectures. In later years, when his poor health forced him to step back from his active role in the Genevan church, he returned to the practice of writing his commentaries himself.

In 1550, Calvin began to teach on Genesis in his theology lectures, completing the process in 1552.[85] He probably had in mind both his lectures and their written-down version when he noted to Farel in a letter of July 1550, "This week, I have begun Genesis. I hope it will be worthwhile."[86] Indeed, on 19 August, Calvin announced to Farel, "Given the Lord has enabled me to take my commentary on Genesis up to the end of the third chapter, I have decided to send you a foretaste of the work."[87] But in November 1550, Calvin's difficulties with the book of Acts led him to leave Genesis aside for a time.[88] No information about the commentary on Genesis appears in his correspondence until June 1554. At that point, the work was complete and in press and Calvin was considering the selection of an appropriate dedicatee. His commentary came off the presses on 20 July 1554.[89]

The first concerns Calvin voiced when working on the synoptic Gospels resurfaced when he began work on the Psalms. Shortly thereafter, Calvin left his task as scripture commentator aside for a number of years, at least in the form that he had used until this point. In a letter dated October 1557, he confirmed that he had stopped writing commentaries. When Utenhoven suggested to Calvin that he should dedicate a book to Nicholas Radziwill, Calvin noted that this request had come just after the commentary on the Psalms had appeared. Therefore he could make no promises to his correspondent, because "no opportunities will be available in the next while."[90] In other words, Calvin had no plans to write further commentaries in the immediate future.

[83]*B.C.2*, no. 56/3; see CO, 49:IX.
[84]*B.C.2*, no. 57/5; for more on this conflict, see below 189.
[85]CO, 21:72, 75.
[86]CO, 13:606.
[87]CO, 13:623.
[88]CO, 13:655.
[89]*B.C.1*, no. 54/8.
[90]CO, 16:673.

To understand this change, we must return to the commentaries on Isaiah. The 1551 *Commentarii in Isaiam prophetam* holds a specific place in Calvin's written corpus because he did not write the text himself.[91] Instead, the work was Calvin's attempt to transmit his thoughts via another man's pen. In March 1550, he explained: "I do not have enough time to write."[92] In 1546, the Reformer gave a series of sermons on Isaiah, and returned to the same book during his lectures in 1549, ending the series in July 1550.[93] Given that he had lengthy notes taken down both during the sermons and the lectures, Nicolas des Gallars suggested to Calvin that he write a commentary, a plan Calvin accepted. Although the work appeared under Calvin's name, the two co-authors clearly delineated their respective contributions: the ideas were Calvin's but the style was des Gallars's. In March 1550, Calvin gave the following explanation for the work: "My meditations on Isaiah, which you are waiting for, as you say, will soon be available, but they are written by des Gallars, for I have too little time to write. But he takes notes while I teach, and then writes the commentary at home. I reread it, and make changes as needed in places where he has not correctly followed my train of thought."[94] Des Gallars's preface provides more details regarding the role of the "author" and the "collector" (*me colligentem*) of the commentaries. Des Gallars took advantage of breaks in Calvin's schedule to read his growing text to him, a system that allowed Calvin to follow the writing process closely, "even if he was not able to examine the whole thing with care." Their meetings were often interrupted, so that des Gallars could only read to Calvin the commentary on two or three verses at a time. Des Gallars's writing was based on his notes: "As for my work, it was simplified in that I had a number of annotations that I had taken down as he said them when he preached. For it was over four years ago that he preached in public on this prophet with fruitful results, and then interpreted it for us in the school." Later in the preface, des Gallars mentioned only the 1546 sermons.[95] He explained that his writing in Latin was done from memory and that he used his notes in a rather free fashion. Thus, the text was not taken down word for word as Calvin preached or taught, but rather was one that des Gallars "gathered together and assembled."

The commentary was dedicated to the king of England, but as Calvin explained, "because the work of another is involved, the canonical Epistles, which will be completed at the same time, will come as a welcome addition.... I will therefore dedicate both works to him."[96]

This attempt to lighten Calvin's workload may have been a response to an earlier wish. When Calvin refused to write a commentary on Genesis in 1542 because

[91]*B.C.1*, no. 51/6.
[92]CO, 13:536.
[93]CO, 21:71, 72; 13:606.
[94]CO, 13:536.
[95]CO, 21:68.
[96]CO, 13:655.

of time constraints, he remarked, "otherwise, I have little confidence in my hearers,"[97] which suggests that he had begun to consider the idea of having his oral teaching written down.

The experience of the Isaiah commentary had a minimal impact, as the results failed to satisfy Calvin and he never followed this approach again. Furthermore, when the commentary was reprinted in 1559, Calvin took the opportunity to carry out a major revision of the text.

From 1551 to 1554, Calvin returned to writing the works himself. However, some of his disciples continued to think that Calvin's pearls of wisdom uttered during his lectures should not be lost. The idea was all the more feasible in that Denis Raguenier, for instance, had been systematically writing up Calvin's sermons since 1549.[98] Jean Budé and Charles de Jonviller, the main architects of the plan, began to apply it systematically by taking down Calvin's lectures on the Psalms in 1552.[99]

Calvin lectured on the book of Psalms beginning in 1552. Budé and Jonviller, with the help of des Gallars, wrote down the entire text of these lectures. Their goal was to end up with a written commentary of the Psalms in this fashion. When the lecture series came to an end in 1555, the three men suggested to Calvin that their notes be published, but Calvin was completely against the idea. In order to avoid the risk, he decided to write a commentary himself. In his preface, Calvin noted that among other reasons for publishing, "I was worried that one day the material gathered from my lectures would be printed, be it against my wishes or at least without my knowledge. Indeed, I can certainly say that I was compelled to write this work more out of fear than because I really wanted to write it."[100]

Calvin had another cause for concern: "Before I began to expound on this work in my lectures at the request of my brothers, I had said (truthfully) that I would not do it, because Martin Bucer, the very faithful doctor of God's church, had worked on it with such knowledge, diligence, and faithfulness, and had done it so well that at the very least my contribution on the subject was not really needed."

Calvin specified that his first attempts at writing the commentary predated the end of his lectures in early 1556. A letter from des Gallars on 15 June 1555 gives a hint of these first drafts. In it, he recalled that he had promised to give Calvin his notes taken during Calvin's lectures, a promise that des Gallars had subsequently forgotten. "But when I saw recently a few things that you had written earlier on the Psalms lying on your chair by the bed, I remembered that you had wanted to work on this." Thus, des Gallars sent Calvin his notes,[101] but there is no indication in Calvin's preface that he made any use of them.

---

[97]Herminjard, *Correspondance,* 8:80–81; and CO, 11:418.
[98]See below 73–75.
[99]CO, 21:75.
[100]CO, 31:16; for the text of Calvin's preface, in Latin and in French, see CO, 31:13–36.
[101]CO, 15:657.

Calvin's first drafts went well: "matters progressed as I wanted, much more so than I had hoped." But this honeymoon period soon faded, and the writing process became long and laborious. Calvin's complaints on this subject explain his change in attitude toward the publication of his lectures. On 10 October 1555, he wrote to Farel, "You would like me to write more commentaries than I could compose even if I lived a long life in total tranquility, as if I could produce books at the very moment that I thought of them."[102] In his preface to his lectures on Hosea, Calvin confirmed that his commentary on the Psalms was a "very long and very difficult task."

Chronological evidence underlines this sense that the work was arduous. Calvin began the process before June 1555. Estienne, who was printing the work as the manuscript sheets were turned in to him, had printed a third of the work by December 1556.[103] If the manuscript had been complete by that point, four months would have been enough to finish the printing, but in fact the volume was only ready at the end of July, in time for the September Frankfurt fair.[104]

Publishing the Exegetical Lectures

Before the Psalms commentary was completed in July 1557, Calvin authorized the publication of his lectures on Hosea, a work that was put on sale in February 1557.[105] The problems he encountered in writing his Psalms commentary were explicitly mentioned as a reason for his change of attitude.

At the start of the 1557 *Praelectiones,* Calvin explained that he allowed the publication to go forward to keep from having to write the work himself, "something which I had to do for the Psalms, a task that I still find so long and difficult because I find it impossible to compose so many works." He reiterated his concerns about publishing a less than perfectly polished text. "As I can truthfully and rightly show, and even prove through reliable witnesses, the works that I have made public until now (even though I polished them with great care and attention) were almost seized from my hands by urgent prayers and requests...." His lectures were not published with his "agreement and support." While Calvin conceded that the lectures were probably acceptable for their hearers, he did not feel that they should be "read by simply anyone." He felt that it would be a "grave mistake" to believe that the lectures that "came straight from my mouth" deserved to be considered on a par with works "that are published to be read by everyone." The Reformer made a clear distinction between the writings that he himself prepared or dictated at home, and the thoughts "freely articulated in my lectures." He highlighted the pressure he was put under: "I was unable to suppress them and could not otherwise prevent them from being printed, unless I took on the task of making new commentaries to replace them, but

---

[102]CO, 15:812.
[103]CO, 16:335, 350, 723.
[104]*B.C.2,* no. 57/4.
[105]*B.C.2,* no. 57/3.

could not do this due to overwork. Furthermore, seeing that many of my friends, believing that I was too strict in censoring my own writings, kept on repeating endlessly to me that I was harming the church by keeping these texts from her, I preferred to have this work based on my lectures put into print. Otherwise, if I prevented it, I would have to write the work myself.... Therefore, I have agreed to have this presentation on the prophet Hosea printed, since I was not allowed to prevent it from being published." Calvin then praised the faithfulness of the text, adding that he would have wished that the secretaries revised their notes more freely: "It may have been desirable for them to take more liberties in removing superfluous material, organizing other matters more clearly, or even expressing other passages more clearly and elegantly."

In his preface, Jean Budé explained how the lectures were taken down. For a number of years, "a certain number of his hearers had the habit of taking down notes in his lectures, each doing what he saw fit, to use the material later in his private studies." But in order to make the lectures more generally useful, they decided to "take down the lectures word for word, not omitting anything." Budé specified that the work was carried out by "two of the brethren and me." Most of the subsequent editions of the lectures were signed by Jean Budé and his brother-in-law, Charles de Jonviller. The third man mentioned by Budé is clearly Nicolas des Gallars, who did not continue to participate in the work simply because he left Geneva. All three thus took down notes: "Meeting to go over what each one had written, and writing out a clear copy, we found that so few things had escaped us that we could remedy the problem without great difficulty." We should remember Thomas Parker's remarks on the speed of Calvin's lecturing: he spoke so slowly that one could imagine he was dictating to his audience.[106]

Budé then went on to explain that they obtained with difficulty Calvin's authorization to have the lectures printed, thanks to their "importunate requests." Budé justified the less careful style of the lectures by stating: "the author, who wished to use a style appropriate for his audience, strayed a bit from his usual grace and excellent form of expression that he followed in all his other works." Budé noted that Calvin usually had only a very short amount of time to prepare his lectures. "As he usually is burdened with a great number of responsibilities, he can hardly find a half-hour to think over his lectures." Hence his style was "plain and simple," "different from that of many men, who, as we know, bring in their pre-prepared lectures, and then read them out to their hearers, just as they are written."

In the 1559 edition, Jean Crespin added a few details. He specified that Calvin lectured without notes, and did not even mark in his Bible the point that he had previously reached. Budé and Jonviller used the following method to take down the lectures: "Each of them has his sheet of paper ready and as usefully laid out as possible, and each writes as quickly as possible. If one of them misses a word (which

---

[106]See above 30.

happens sometimes, especially when he becomes forceful in his exposition of certain passages that require it), the other one writes it down.... As soon as the lecture is over, Jonviller alone takes the sheets of the two others, and adding it to his own, he examines them together and compares them diligently." Here Crespin takes an odd shortcut: given that he only mentioned Budé and Jonviller until this point, why does he mention indirectly the notes of a third scribe? Crespin was probably influenced by Budé's 1557 preface. Using the notes, Jonviller then dictated a complete text: "Then he looks over the whole thing, so that he can read the whole in front of the author at his home the next day. There, if by chance a word is missing, [Calvin] inserts it; or if something seems to be unclear, he explains it more simply." In 1557, Budé made no mention of this rereading in Calvin's presence. In all likelihood, the practice occurred once Calvin became more used to the idea of having his lectures published. In his foreword to the lectures on Ezekiel, Jonviller confirmed that Calvin looked over the text prior to publication. The text of the foreword appears below.

An Unexpected Success

Calvin's concern over the publication of this new genre of work explains the absence of any dedication, for in his eyes, this was not a major work. He jokingly tried to defuse any potential criticisms on Bullinger's part by sending him a copy of the book "not to compel you to read this seriously and with great care, but to show you how much free time our printers have, since they have the time to print this. And also so that Mr. Peter Martyr learns to bring well-built books to light, since mine are born prematurely."[107]

Reactions to the work were very positive. Although he only learned of the book in early 1558, Ambrosius Blaurer was immediately enthusiastic: "I approve and applaud the very rigorous and meticulous faithfulness and care displayed by your hearers, by which they have taken down your words so well that their hands and their pen have smoothly followed your words. You have testified to this yourself and others also recognize the phrasing and the particular genius of your writings."[108] Thanks to these reactions, everything was resolved. Calvin accepted the systematic publication of his lectures written out by Jean Budé and Charles de Jonviller all the way up until his death. These works became major ones, deserving of dedications.

After having presented his exegesis of Hosea, Calvin continued to analyze the other minor prophets. From 1556 to 1558, he gave a total of 184 lectures that Jean Budé and Charles de Jonviller faithfully put into writing.

This time, Calvin participated actively in the process, as Colladon noted in the section on this work in his biography: "He had lectured on all the minor prophets apart from two or three final lectures on Malachi when he fell ill with quartan fever.

[107]CO, 16:412.
[108]CO, 17:41.

However, so that the work would not remain incomplete, once the printer reached that point, Calvin gave the remaining lectures in his bedroom to a small number of people who were able to come (because of his fever and the winter season, it was not good for him to go outside). These lectures were taken down as he gave them, just like the others, and were included in the published work."[109] This particular illness of Calvin's lasted during the winter of 1558/59 and the work itself appeared in January 1559.[110]

This edition reused the 1557 prefaces, including Calvin's complaints. Alongside Budé's preface explaining the working method, the printer Crespin provided his own preface discussed above. In his dedication, Calvin reiterated the publishing conditions for this private instruction. He was "not the cause nor the author of this printing," because in most cases "I am a rather troublesome and difficult proofreader of material I have written with greater work and diligence." If possible, he would have avoided this new publication. "But given that a similar work, the Commentaries on Hosea, was much better received than I had hoped, setting ablaze the interest and longing of many, now this one single prophet is pulling another eleven small ones behind him. I have therefore thought that it would not be impertinent for me to present to Your Majesty this sizeable work full of useful doctrine." Thus Calvin repeated his reservations regarding the spread of his oral teaching, outlining his fears regarding the 1557 attempt and his surprise at its success.

After the twelve minor prophets, Calvin gave sixty-six lectures on Daniel's prophecies from June 1559 to April 1560. These lectures were published in August 1561.[111]

One innovation in this work shows that the publisher was aiming at a scholarly audience. As was customary in this literary genre, Calvin began by presenting the biblical text to be analyzed. In his lectures, he read it first in Hebrew and then in a Latin translation.[112] The printer added the Hebrew to the Latin version, explaining that he did so in response to pressure from "erudite and scholarly people" who wanted it included "for various reasons," especially "because it is very useful for those who know Hebrew to have before them the source itself, from which this faithful interpreter draws out the authentic meaning of the prophet." Less knowledgeable readers could still hear Daniel speak in his own tongue: "And furthermore, Calvin, that very learned interpreter, has the habit of reciting each verse in Hebrew, and then translating it into Latin."[113]

Calvin continued his lectures on the prophecies and Lamentations of Jeremiah. He began this new cycle of lectures on 15 April 1560. Following 193 lectures on the prophecies, he moved to Lamentations in September 1562, and after eighteen lectures

[109]CO, 21:88.
[110]*B.C.2,* no. 59/5.
[111]CO, 21:89, 90; and *B.C.2,* no. 61/20.
[112]See below 145–47.
[113]The printer's note (complete text) can be found in CO, 40:521–24.

on the latter topic, he ended the cycle on 9 January 1563. The work was rapidly sent to the printers since it was ready for sale in July 1563.[114]

Strangely enough, the original text of scripture was omitted in this work, mainly for economic reasons. The printer's explanation for this in some sense takes the opposite view to the one articulated in the preceding edition: "We decided against including the Hebrew text for many reasons, especially as we were sure that the experts in the language would have it at hand. We considered that it would really not be as useful to others." These justifications were followed by a cost-driven explanation, which was probably the main one: "We feared that this large volume would stretch to more than normal length and that the buyer would be charged an excessive and unnecessarily high amount."[115]

Calvin continued his lectures, this time on Ezekiel. He began the cycle on 20 January 1562 and broke off permanently on 2 February 1564 for health reasons. By then, he had presented sixty-five lectures on the first twenty chapters. The decision to print was made in October 1564 and the work appeared in January 1565.[116]

In his preface, Jonviller described the background to the write-up of these last lectures:

> On 20 January 1563, he began to lecture on Ezekiel in the public lecture hall, in spite of being constantly afflicted by so many serious illnesses that he often had to be carried in a chair or travel on horseback because the strength of his poor sick body was fading. While he fought for a whole year against the violence of so many illnesses simultaneously, continuing to fulfill his preaching and lecturing duties, finally, around the first of February of the following year, having reached the end of the twentieth chapter (apart from four verses), he had to stay at home and nearly always remain in bed. However, while he continued to be ill, he also ceaselessly worked on things, either by dictating them to another or writing them himself, so that one can hardly believe all the things he did during the period when he could not leave the house because of his serious illnesses. Among other things, he diligently revised and corrected a large number of these lectures, as can be seen in the copy with his handwritten corrections, which I am keeping carefully with the others.

Jonviller went on to lament the end of the lectures and explained the different characteristics of the edition.

Calvin therefore fully accepted this publication genre, though he always made a distinction between the commentaries and the lectures. A study of his choice of printers shows that he did not see himself as the owner of the published lectures.

---

[114]CO, 21:90, 93, 95; and *B.C.2,* no. 63/19.

[115]See fol. α6v in the original text.

[116]CO, 21:95, 773, 811; RC 59, fol. 116r; and *B.C.3,* no. 65/4.

Instead, the publication of those works was directly managed by Jonviller and Budé.[117]

The Return to the Written Commentaries

Calvin thus ceased writing commentaries himself for a number of years. In the last years of his life, when he had to remain at home more frequently for health reasons and had gradually turned over the management of the church to Theodore Beza, Calvin returned to this earlier project.

In 1559, he not only completed the definitive revision of the *Institutes,* but also revised his commentary on Isaiah. Because the version prepared by Nicolas des Gallars did not satisfy him, Calvin rewrote the text extensively. Calvin also preached on Isaiah in his weekday sermons between 16 July 1556 and 22 September 1558, for a total of 343 sermons. Thus there was a clear link between the revision of the commentary and his sermons.[118]

At the start of his dedication to Elizabeth I, Calvin stated, "I have put so much work and care into revising this commentary that it should certainly be considered a new work." His statement is, however, somewhat exaggerated. A comparison of the 1551 and 1559 versions confirms the more nuanced assessment of the 1572 translation. In his preface, the translator declared that Calvin, "in revising this work printed in Latin and in French, not only reworked it to clarify what might have been obscure because of brevity, and reorganized what was unclear, but also worked so well and so diligently that he increased the Latin text by over a third." Based on his expertise on the written work of the Reformer, the translator insisted, "furthermore, this second version of the commentary was not based on his lectures in the school, but was written at home word for word under the oversight of the author."[119]

A series of textual analyses show that half of the definitive 1559 edition offers des Gallars's text without any major changes, that a small third was revised superficially in some places and in depth in others, and that a little less than a fifth of the revised version was new. "Overall, counting both the minor modifications and the simple additions, the 1559 edition is 20 percent longer," explains Peter Wilcox.[120]

Calvin, who had already published a commentary on Genesis in 1554, began his exegesis of the four other works of the Pentateuch in parallel in a concordance. He began this writing process in 1559, a year in which these books were the subject of the Friday *congrégations*. "In that year [1559]," wrote Colladon, "toward the end, the Friday *congrégation* began to work on the last four books of Moses as a harmony,

---

[117]See below 193–94.

[118]P. D. Nicole and Christophe Rapin, "De l'exégétique. Évolution entre le commentaire de 1551, les sermons de 1558, et le commentaire de 1559 sur le prophète Esaïe" in *Calvinus ecclesiae genevensis custos,* ed. W. H. Neuser (Frankfurt am Main: P. Lang, 1984), 159–62.

[119]CO, 36:[9–12]; J. Calvin, *Commentaires sur le prophete Isaie* (Geneva: Fr. Perrin, 1572). See also *B.C.3,* no. 72/1.

[120]The notes accompanying *B.C.2,* no. 59/1 describe Peter Wilcox's data.

as Calvin did in his commentary that was later published."[121] The link with the *con-grégations* is confirmed by the printing authorization requested from the Genevan Council on 12 January 1563, where the request mentioned "printing the concordance of the books of Moses that has been dealt with in the *congrégations*."[122]

The printing process began already in 1561. On 10 April, Ambrosius Blaurer asked Calvin for the list of his published works and those about to be published. Calvin's reply is lost, but on 6 July, Blaurer noted that he was waiting impatiently for the harmony of Moses.[123] The work came off the presses in August 1563.[124] If Calvin's preface to the French translation is to be believed, the Latin version contained numerous errors. There are indeed many typographical mistakes, but these do not affect the meaning of the commentary.[125]

All of Calvin's commentaries and lectures were rapidly translated into French. However, Calvin himself never handled this translation work directly and the names of the translators are only rarely known. Nicolas Colladon claimed to be responsible for the French version of the commentary on the synoptic Gospels, and for the in-depth revision of the commentary on the Gospel of John.[126] In his preface to the Psalms commentary, Calvin admitted that he had originally thought of writing his commentary on the Psalms directly in French, but ended up writing it in Latin. When it came to his work on the Pentateuch, Calvin followed a new approach, translating these new commentaries himself and revising the translation of the commentary on Genesis. On 30 November 1563, he noted to a correspondent, "I have begun to translate my commentaries on Moses into French, not only so that the work may be more accessible to our readers, but also because I had to correct the numerous errors that filled the text. In fact, I do not regret doing this work."[127] This work once again reflects Calvin's free translation style, put to use when he provided the French version of one of his own works. In Calvin's first biography, Beza confirms that Calvin's translation work took place during his last period of illness.[128]

The study of a few passages points to the fact that Calvin revised the Genesis commentary by comparing it to the Latin original. In all likelihood, a secretary read the original while Calvin followed the text in its French version. The changes were minimal: a few inaccuracies in translation were corrected, both in the commentaries and in the biblical text, and a number of paragraphs that were out of sequence in the first edition were repositioned in the right order.

[121]CO, 21:90.

[122]RC 57, fol. 184r.

[123]CO, 18:422, 538.

[124]*B.C.2,* no. 63/16.

[125]CO, 23:VXI–XVII.

[126]See the lengthy letter to Marcuard from Colladon, printed in the 1576 Lausanne edition of the *Institutes,* fol. **2r.

[127]CO, 20:199.

[128]CO, 21:33–34, 42.

Calvin's final commentary was tied to the Friday *congrégations*: "In June [1563]," Colladon explained, "the *congrégations* began to study the book of Joshua."[129] Calvin took the opportunity to write his own commentary on Joshua, as he explained on 30 November 1563: "The brethren encouraged me to comment on the book of Joshua. So far, I am only at chapter three, even though I am trying to be as concise as possible."[130] In his biography, Beza states that Calvin managed to finish the commentary: "Finally, he then began work on the Joshua commentary, his last work, that he completed during his remaining days."[131] This final work appeared after Calvin's death, with Beza's preface to the Joshua commentary serving as a first draft of his biography.[132]

Theodore Beza's Assessment

Beza's dedicatory letter for the unfinished lectures on Ezekiel offers an overview of Calvin's exegetical work. Beza made clear distinctions between Calvin's different literary genres, including his commentaries, lectures, and sermons, noting in particular that the sermons only partly filled the gap left by missing commentaries:

> No other single person of our time has left so many works containing such healthy and complete doctrine. If God had been pleased to let us enjoy such a leading light for another year or two, I do believe that in truth no one could have asked for more in terms of acquiring a perfect understanding of the Old and New Testaments. But he wrote nothing on the books of sacred history (apart from Joshua), on Job, and on the two books of Solomon, although his sermons on Job, Samuel, and the first book of Kings, that were taken down word-for-word as he preached them, will fill this gap somewhat. For among other things God also gave him the grace to speak almost always in the same way as he wrote. As for the prophets, he wrote full and complete commentaries on Isaiah. For the others, there are his printed lectures, taken down diligently and faithfully by two good, God-fearing and wise men, Jean Budé, the son of the world-renowned Budé, and Charles de Jonviller. His death kept him from finishing Ezekiel, a loss to the church, especially as he [Ezekiel] is the most obscure of all the prophets, particularly toward the end, and no one knows when another one will be found who will complete the work begun by such an Apelles. Yet we do not think we need to justify why it seemed appropriate to us to have this work printed, even if it is incomplete.[133]

[129]CO, 21:95.
[130]CO, 20:199.
[131]CO, 21:160; see also 21:41.
[132]*B.C.2*, no. 64/9.
[133]Apelles was a late Classical period artist, and a friend and portrait painter of Alexander the

Conclusion

Calvin's exegetical work is impressive when one considers that it was only one among many of his responsibilities. Even though he was forced to leave this work aside for a time beginning in 1541, he returned to it from 1545 onwards, and spent more and more energy on it until 1557. From 1556 on, the publication of his lectures took over, but after 1559, he devoted more time to his written commentaries once again.

In terms of numbers, the Romans commentary stands alone in 1539 with its 107,000 words. After pausing to set up the Genevan church, Calvin began to write and publish his exegetical commentaries again in 1545. The publications continued until 1550 at an average of a little less than 65,000 words a year. The length of the commentaries then clearly increased until 1557, reaching nearly 200,000 words in 1553 and over 300,000 in 1554 and 1555. The Psalms commentary, published in 1557 after a year's silence, contained 465,000 words. Subsequent works included the revision of the Isaiah commentary in 1559 (approximately 130,000 additional words), the extensive 1563 harmony of the four books of the Pentateuch (412,000 words), and the short 54,000 word commentary on Joshua, published in 1564. Calvin's difficult years dealing with the Genevan civil authorities match the period during which he was most productive as an author. The turning point in 1555 had no positive effect on Calvin's output: his 1557 commentary was painstakingly written, and once it was finished Calvin thought he would stop commenting on biblical books. Beginning in 1558, he turned once more to the *Institutes* and to revisions of commentaries, but from this point on he worked more slowly, for the extensive commentary on the Pentateuch was written over the course of many years.

If one takes into account his many opportunities for study of the Bible, Calvin was immersed in scripture. He oversaw the revision of the French translation of the Bible,[134] he preached on two or three scriptural books simultaneously, he lectured on another in front of his students in the Academy, and focused on yet another during the *congrégation* sessions with his colleagues.

This apparent chaos should not obscure the fact that from 1538 onwards, Calvin had wanted to write complete commentaries on the New Testament, and then on the whole Bible. Though he did not manage to achieve this to the dismay of his colleagues, according to Beza he had completed a great deal of the work.

Calvin's commentaries were more clearly tied to the *congrégations* and the exegetical lectures than to the sermons. Starting in 1556, his lectures were systematically recorded and published. In a separate development, Calvin published commentaries on almost all of the books that he dealt with in the *congrégations* and

---

Great. Beza's preface can be found in *Correspondance de Théodore de Bèze*, ed. H. Aubert (Geneva: Droz, 1970), 6:15–21.

[134]See below 148–56.

the lectures, apart from the times when the *congrégations* studied a book that Calvin had already analyzed in a commentary. This situation held true at least during the years in which the topics covered in the *congrégations* are known. Calvin wrote commentaries on all the books of the Bible covered during his lectures between 1549 and 1555. In contrast, the commentaries on the Acts of the Apostles and Isaiah are the only ones based on cycles of sermons.[135]

3. ECCLESIASTICAL WRITINGS

Alongside his exegetical works primarily directed at pastors and theologians, Calvin wrote a number of works intended for a wider readership: catechisms, confessions of faith, and liturgical manuals. These should be considered ecclesiastical works because they were distributed under the oversight of the Genevan church, though in all likelihood they came from Calvin's pen.

During his first period in Geneva from 1536 to 1538, Calvin only published one work of this type. In early 1537, he wrote a catechism, *Instruction et confession de foi*. A few months earlier, in late 1536, Farel had written a *Confession de foi*.[136] Calvin's text explained the Ten Commandments, the Creed, and the Lord's Prayer, and was in fact an abridged version of the 1536 *Institutes*. Calvin wrote the catechism first in Latin, and then translated it into French, though the Latin version was only published in 1538.[137] Throughout this period, Farel remained the leading figure in Geneva, since he had initiated the Reformation in the city, and it was Farel who wrote the confession of faith and organized the liturgy based on his Bernese-inspired manual published in 1533.[138]

As noted above, the Strasbourg period from 1538 to 1541 was a particularly fruitful one for Calvin. Thanks to his contact with Martin Bucer, Calvin deepened his understanding of the church and its structures.

Liturgical Works

In Strasbourg, Calvin's work of setting up a French liturgy led him to publish a number of books. Very early on, at least beginning in November 1538, the church services led by Calvin featured psalm-singing.[139] Hence Calvin worked to provide his congregation with a repertoire of psalms and hymns in French. On 20 December 1538, he announced to Farel that a volume of psalms set to music would be published

---

[135]See the list in Appendix 2.

[136]O. Labarthe, "La relation entre le premier catéchisme de Calvin et la première confession de foi de Genève," unpublished thesis, Geneva, 1967; and *B.C.1*, no. 37/2.

[137]*B.C.1*, no. 38/1.

[138]J.-Fr. Gilmont, "L'oeuvre imprimé de Guillaume Farel," *Actes du Colloque Farel Neuchâtel, 29 septembre–1er octobre 1980. Revue de théologie et de philosophie* 2 (1983): 122–23.

[139]Herminjard, *Correspondance,* 5:145 n. 19; and CO, 10/b:288.

shortly.[140] This work appeared anonymously and without a preface in 1539, and contained thirteen versified psalms by Marot and three by Calvin himself. The Reformer also put the Song of Simeon, the Ten Commandments, and the Creed into verse.[141] These translations by Calvin subsequently disappeared from the work.

In 1540 or 1541, Calvin produced a new edition of the Psalter, this time including a first version of a printed liturgy. The work is lost, but its content can be reconstructed thanks to the reprint done in 1542 by Pierre Brully, Calvin's successor as the head of the French church of Strasbourg. *La manyere de faire prieres aux eglises francoyses* was inspired by Bucer's liturgy and Farel's 1533 liturgy mentioned above. The volume also contained a simple catechism in dialogue form, an early model of the Genevan catechism of 1541.[142]

Calvin's return to Geneva was shaped by a threefold need, namely, to compose ecclesiastical ordinances, a catechism, and a liturgy. The texts that had been used between 1536 and 1538 no longer satisfied the Reformer, who had been enriched by his Strasbourg experience. The liturgical book came together quite rapidly, as Calvin explained in his letter of late January 1542:[143] "As the plague was hitting hard in the German empire, and warfare raged elsewhere, I saw to it that special prayers were decreed." On 21 October 1541, the pastors informed the Genevan Council of the plague that had attacked Bern, Basel, Zurich, and Strasbourg. On 11 November, the Council ordered a day of prayers to be held on Wednesday, 16 November.[144] Calvin continued, "I wrote the prayers to be used in such circumstances. I added new versions to have a more extensive and fuller model to use for the administration of the sacraments." In his farewell speech to the Genevan ministers in 1564, Calvin described how the work came into being: "As for the Sunday prayers, I took the Strasbourg model, and borrowed the greater part of it. As regards the other prayers, I could not take them from Strasbourg, since they did not exist there, so I took it all from scripture. I also had to write the baptismal liturgy while in Strasbourg... I wrote this primitive liturgy, but at this point I suggest that you do not change it."[145] Indeed, this liturgy took elements from his Strasbourg manual and mixed them with others taken from Farel's work. This synthesis was known as *La forme des prieres et chantz ecclesiastiques avec la maniere d'administrer les Sacremens et consacrer le mariage,* first published in 1542[146] and reprinted countless times.

[140]Herminjard, *Correspondance,* 5:452; and CO, 10/b:438 (wrongly dated 1539).

[141]R. Peter, "Les premiers ouvrages français imprimés à Strasbourg," in *Annuaire de la Société des Amis du Vieux-Strasbourg* 4 (1974): 81–82; and René Bornert, "L'Eglise française de Strasbourg," in *La réforme protestante du culte à Strasbourg au XVIe* (Leiden: E. J.Brill, 1981), 196–97.

[142]Peter, "Premiers ouvrages français," 4:85–86; Bornert, "L'Eglise française," 198–99; and Pidoux, *Psautier,* 2:13–15.

[143]Herminjard, *Correspondance,* 7:408–13; and CO, 11:363–66. The events in question took place on 7 and 17 January (Herminjard, *Correspondance,* 7:409 n. 3, 412 n. 24).

[144]CO, 21:284, 286.

[145]O.S., 2:403–4.

[146]Pidoux, *Psautier,* 2:14–15; and RC 35, fol. 499v (14 February 1542).

The Catechism

Calvin seemed dissatisfied with the extracts of the *Institutes* published in French as the *Instruction et confession de foy* and in Latin as the *Catechismus,* though he gave no explanation for his dissatisfaction. In Calvin's biography, however, Colladon affirmed that the problem lay primarily in his preference for a question and answer format: "Over the course of a few days, he also wrote the Catechism as we now have it, not that he made any doctrinal changes from the first version, but he followed a good method by using questions and answers, an easier approach for children in contrast to the other one, where topics were treated through summaries and brief chapters."[147] Calvin had already made an attempt at this dialogue style in the draft of his catechism published in Strasbourg.

In his farewell speech of 1564, Calvin asked the Genevan pastors to make no changes in the catechism and in church discipline. He then depicted in a lively fashion the work he had done in 1541: "When I came back from Strasbourg, I wrote the Catechism in haste because I did not want to accept any pastors unless they had taken an oath on two things, namely, to accept the Catechism and the discipline." Shortly after having voted to accept the ordinances, the Council asked the clergy on 25 November 1541 "to establish the catechism to teach the children."[148] The date of Calvin's response to this request is uncertain, but it seems that the catechism was already written in 1541. In his reminiscences, Calvin continued, "while I was writing, people came to fetch the pieces of paper as big as my hand, and carried them off to the printers." This work was his own in spite of Viret's presence in Geneva, since Calvin never showed his manuscript to Viret. According to Calvin, "I never had the time to do so."[149] This first edition has completely disappeared, but it would be safe to presume that it was published in 1541. It was certainly completed by the end of January 1542, when Calvin outlined his first tasks done in Geneva. "Finally, as regards the catechism, I confess that God sustained me in this work. I spent only a few short days on it, but in the midst of so many distractions that drag me here and there, there is no such thing as easy work. In fact, I do not recall ever having had two uninterrupted hours since I came here."[150]

The oldest surviving version of the *Catechisme* is from 1545, and not surprisingly it was reprinted numerous times.

Both books, the liturgy and the catechism, were put in place shortly after Calvin's return to Geneva and remained essentially unchanged thereafter, though it is true that Calvin had prepared earlier draft versions of these works. Calvin's deathbed description of the writing process of these works was motivated by his desire to prevent his colleagues from making any changes to them.

---

[147]CO, 21:64.
[148]CO, 21:287.
[149]O.S., 2:403–4.
[150]Herminjard, *Correspondance,* 7:409–10; and CO, 11:364.

Though these books do not compare with the exegetical works in terms of their size and the time it took to write them, their influence on the daily life of the church has been substantial.

The Legislative Texts

In Strasbourg, Calvin had already begun to establish ecclesiastical discipline. He closely followed the attempts of his Strasbourg colleagues, both in terms of ecclesiastical discipline and the setup of the Latin school.[151] Valérand Poullain, one of his successors at the head of the French church of Strasbourg, published a Latin text in London in 1551 which provides the only indirect witness to these first attempts.[152]

When he presented himself before the Genevan Small Council on 13 September 1541, Calvin "asked that the church be set in order and that the order be written down."[153] Six councilors were appointed to work with Calvin and Viret on this task. Together, they quickly completed the assignment in two or three weeks, according to what Calvin explained to Bucer. However, the Council took its time in accepting the ordinances.[154] Discussions began on 29 September, and a final text was established on 25 October. The ministers were not allowed to see the modifications made by the Council in spite of their request on 9 November. Once the Small and Great Councils had voted to accept the ordinances, they came into effect on 20 November 1541.[155] Calvin admitted that he had been forced to compromise on the content: "At first we began by writing the ecclesiastical laws. Six members of the Council were assigned to work with us to create them. We wrote a text in twenty days, not a perfect text, but an acceptable one given the current circumstances."[156] We have already seen the undoubtedly deliberate ambiguity around the issue of excommunication.[157]

Shortly thereafter, the Council called again on Calvin's legal expertise to write a body of civil ordinances. This mission, which he worked on together with the councilor Claude Roset, was so urgent that the Council relieved the pastor of most of his preaching duties from 11 September 1542 to 22 January 1543.[158]

In all likelihood, Calvin also played a role in the writing of various supplemental ecclesiastical edicts from 1542 to 1560.[159] All of these texts appear in the *Ordonnances écclesiastiques de l'Eglise de Genève,* revised and completed in 1561 and printed

---

[151]Herminjard, *Correspondance,* 5:144, 6:157.

[152]O.S., 2:325. The edition is described on 327. Ph. Denis does not believe that any ordinances were set down in writing during Calvin's time in Strasbourg. See Ph. Denis, *Les Eglises d'étrangers en pays rhénans, 1538–1564* (Paris: Les Belles Lettres, 1984), 482–83.

[153]See Herminjard, *Correspondance,* 7:249 n. 2.

[154]Herminjard, *Correspondance,* 7:292; and CO, 11:298.

[155]*RCP,* 1:1–13.

[156]Herminjard, *Correspondance,* 7:409; and CO, 11:363.

[157]See above 15.

[158]RC 36, fol. 117v; and Doumergue, *Jean Calvin,* 6:32–37.

[159]The list of these is available in O.S., 2:325.

immediately. This was the first time such legislation had been printed, except for *L'ordre des escoles de Geneve,* which appeared in 1559 in Latin and French.

The revision process for the ecclesiastical ordinances was an unusual one. On 29 September 1561, Artus Chauvin requested permission from the Genevan Council to publish the ecclesiastical and civil ordinances. The Council discussed the issue.[160] Claude Roset consulted Calvin and reported to the Council on 10 November that the Reformer had indeed "revised them." Roset brought a copy of the ordinances back to the Council, which immediately "began to read them to approve them." The approval process was completed the next day, and the Small Council voted in favor of the amendments. During the next few days, the ordinances were submitted to the Council of Two Hundred and the General Council. Artus Chauvin was then able to obtain his printing authorization and even a privilege.[161] The pattern of events suggests that Calvin had decided to revise the ordinances prior to any request from the Council, and it was only Chauvin's publication request that led the councilors to discover what Calvin had been doing. The revised version was approved without difficulties.

The information from sources for the 1541, 1542, and 1561 ordinances is relatively clear: Calvin was directly involved along with others. His role in 1561 may have been greater still. However, one should not look for Calvin's influence in everything that was done in Geneva between 1541 and 1564. Scholarly debates over the authorship of the *Leges Academiae* are typical of the desire of most historians to bring everything back to Calvin. For instance, Charles Borgeaud rejected any questioning of Calvin's authorship of the document thanks to one simple argument: according to him, the text was in Calvin's style.[162] His viewpoint was echoed by later scholars, including Julien le Coultre, Henri Vuilleumier, and Paul-F. Geisendorf.[163]

Julien le Coultre did note, however, that Calvin based himself extensively on the *Leges Scholae Lausannensis,* themselves largely dependent on Jean Sturm's ideas in Strasbourg. Although Calvin may have contributed to the Genevan document, it is equally possible that Beza or even Maturin Cordier was involved in writing it. Indeed, Beza had just returned to Geneva after a ten-year period in Lausanne when the document was written and soon became the first rector of the Genevan Academy. Maturin Cordier, Calvin's former teacher who was then seventy-nine, also could have told Calvin of his experiences at the head of the Lausanne school from 1545 to 1558.

---

[160]RC 56, fol. 244r (29 September 1561).

[161]RC 56, fols. 260r, 261r–v, 262v (10–14 November 1561); the plans and final version of the ordinances are available in the O.S., 2:325–89.

[162]Ch. Borgeaud, *Histoire de l'Université de Genève,* vol. 1, *L'Académie de Calvin* (Geneva: Georg & Co., 1900), 42–47.

[163]J. Le Coultre, *Maturin Cordier et les origines de la pédagogie protestante dans les pays de langue française (1530–1564)* (Neuchâtel: Secrétariat de l'Université, 1926), 324–25; Vuilleumier, *Histore de l'Église réformée,* 408–9; and P.-F. Geisendorf, *Théodore de Bèze* (Geneva: Labor et fides, 1949), 107–8.

The Confessions of Faith

Calvin's exact role in writing the various confessions of faith published during his lifetime is unclear. The 1559 confession of faith for students of the Academy could have been the work of Theodore Beza. Beza, in contrast to Calvin, enjoyed writing confessions of faith. As for the *Confession de foy* of the French churches, we know that Calvin was suspicious of the first synod of the French Reformed churches, and would rather have prevented the writing of a confession. In order to retain control over the movement, he took the lead and suggested a text that his representatives brought to the synod in time for it to be considered. However, the French pastors made some modifications to the text that Calvin proposed. The end result was two different versions, one with thirty-five articles and the other with forty. Both were distributed beginning in 1559. The shorter version was the text Calvin had sent, although several scholars do not believe that he wrote it entirely by himself.[164]

In 1562, Calvin wrote another confession of faith. This one should have been presented at the November Frankfurt Diet in the name of the Prince of Condé, but Calvin's envoy did not arrive at the meeting in time. The goal of the confession of faith was to convince the German princes of the worth of Reformed doctrine. The document came out in print in 1564.[165]

These confessions of faith were generally published for defensive reasons in order to refute the accusations of heresy made both by the Catholics and the Lutherans against the Reformed.

Conclusion

In the context of Calvin's written corpus, the ecclesiastical writings tended to be rather quickly produced works, done mainly during Calvin's early years as a Reformer. The catechism and the liturgy were written in the space of a few weeks after September 1541. These works were the result of Calvin's earlier experiences, especially during his time in Strasbourg. Calvin ascribed great importance to these texts and insisted on his deathbed that his disciples make no changes to them.

As noted above, any study of the spread of Calvin's writings and their influence should focus considerable attention on these short works, as well as on the directives contained in the ecclesiastical ordinances. However, any study of Calvin's views on books can pass more swiftly over these brief texts.

---

[164]J. Pannier, *Les origines de la confession de foi* (Paris: F. Alcan, 1936), 92. P. Barth and D. Scheuner do not completely disagree with Pannier's viewpoint (O.S., 2:297–99). J. Cadier argues that Calvin was the sole author of the work: "La confession de foi de La Rochelle. Son histoire, son importance," in *La Revue réformée* 86 (1971): 47. For their part, Benoît in "L'année 1559," 113–16; and R. Stauffer in "Brève histoire de la Confession de La Rochelle," *Bulletin de la société de l'histoire du protestantisme française* 117 (1971): 359 n. 4, both adopt a neutral position on the matter.

[165]*B.C.2*, no. 64/7.

4. POLEMICAL WORKS

Was the sixteenth century a more polemical age than other eras? This hypothesis is debatable, although printing did provide a tool for polemical exchanges, enabling them to spread more widely and leading to a systematic pattern of attack and response, of reply and rejoinder. Confessionally rooted polemics flourished not only between Catholics and Protestants, but also among different branches of Protestantism. By pursuing his study of polemical writings into the seventeenth century, François Laplanche noted that apart from deepening divisions, polemics also "stimulated the rapid advance of European culture." Alongside the overflow of insults, controversial writings led to a rise in rationalism and also encouraged biblical criticism and patristic studies.[166]

In Calvin's day, polemics were widely used and all sides took advantage of the resources of the printing industry. A more peaceful climate would not emerge for some time. Even though Calvin did not start any new trends in this domain, it is worth determining what role polemical works played in his communication strategy.

Attempting to separate his polemical writings from the whole is a difficult task, since all his writings contain polemical elements. Several of his dedications, for instance, were in fact pamphlets.[167] The definitive edition of the *Institutes* contains entire pages of polemical attacks.[168] I have, however, separated out one group of works whose content is purely polemical, taking as a guide the *Tractationes theologici omnes* published under Beza's direction in 1576. All of Calvin's writings, apart from the *Institutes* and his exegetical commentaries, are brought together in this work and divided into two main categories: didactic writings and polemical writings. Statistically, the relative weight of these two sections is clear. Of the 1,168 total pages, polemical writings took up 1,008 or over 85 percent of the whole. To these we should add a few anonymous writings that did not appear in the collected edition. Furthermore, in order to keep to a straightforward overall approach to Calvin's body of work, we have moved a few tracts from the first section to the second, in cases where these treatises dealt with debated matters.[169]

The Pace of Production of Polemical Pamphlets

Early on, Calvin threw himself into religious polemics. His first treatise, the *Psychopannychia,* was written in Orléans in 1534 and reworked in Basel in 1536. However, the young Reformer was not yet as self-confident as in later years. Following the

---

[166]Fr. Laplanche, "Controverses et dialogues entre catholiques et protestants" in *Histoire du christianisme des origines à nos jours* 8 (Paris: Desclée, Fayard, 1992): 299–321 (see 319). See also M. Lienhard, "Controverses et dialogues entre Luthériens et Réformés," in ibid., 281–99.

[167]See above 209–10.

[168]See below 43.

[169]Appendices 3 and 4 provide a chronological and systematic list of Calvin's polemical works.

advice of Capito and Bucer, he postponed the printing of his tract until Bucer urged its publication in 1542.[170]

In the years prior to his permanent settlement in Geneva in 1541, Calvin's most personal polemical works took the form of open letters. These texts were really meant for a specific correspondent, but aimed at a wider audience. The use of such literary genres testifies to the concerns of a young Reformer searching for a legitimate voice. He did not yet dare to address the public at large directly, but preferred to put his warnings in so-called private letters. However, he soon left this literary fiction aside.[171] In the first of his *Epistolae duae* of 1537, he explicitly broadened the circle of his readers: "I believe that I am not doing something useless or pointless when I work to teach at one time many others who have fallen into the same error, so that if by chance some of them begin to read this letter (something I desire greatly) and are willing to listen, they may be admonished as to what they should do and how they should act."[172] The *Epistolae duae,* written in Ferrara in 1536, was Calvin's first intervention against Nicodemism.[173] The next letter, Calvin's answer to Sadoleto, is a crucial document for Calvin's career since it was written at the request of the Genevans who had previously sent him into exile.[174]

At the same time, during his stay in Strasbourg (1538–41), Calvin wrote his opinions on Paul III's *Consilium* and translated documents from the Regensburg colloquy into French.[175] These works were less Calvin's personal projects than texts written under Bucer's direction. In order to earn some money, Calvin also composed two apologetical works for the Count of Furstenberg.[176] Finally, during these years he also wrote his *Petit traicté de la Cène,* aiming to generate unity among Protestants rather than controversy, though the topic remained a highly divisive one.[177] All of these texts were relatively concise, averaging between 10,000 and 25,000 words.

In the first years after his return to Geneva, Calvin published a flurry of polemical pamphlets: four in 1543, four in 1544, two in 1545, and three in 1547. Calvin reacted against the Catholic church mainly over public events, such as German diets, the articles of the Sorbonne, and the Council of Trent. He also engaged in a more focused debate with Albert Pighius on free will[178] and wrote a small satirical masterpiece, his treatise on relics.[179] At the same time, the Reformer remained aware of the

---

[170]*B.C.1,* no. 42/5.

[171]See Millet, *Calvin et la dynamique,* 479–80

[172]CO, 5:243; and *Recueil,* 62.

[173]*B.C.1,* no. 37/1.

[174]*B.C.1,* no. 39/5.

[175]*B.C.1,* nos. 41/6, 41/1.

[176]*B.C.1,* nos. 39/3, 40/4. Calvin, *Plaidoyers pour le comte,* with introduction and notes by R. Peter (Paris: Presses universitaires de France, 1994).

[177]*B.C.1,* no. 41/4.

[178]*B.C.1,* no. 43/3.

[179]*B.C.1,* no. 43/2.

dangers of dissidents among Protestants, whether they were Nicodemites, Anabaptists, or spiritual libertines. In general, Calvin wrote in response to other recently published works. His treatise, *De Scandalis,* is an exception, for it represents the result of a long maturation process. In it, while he attacked all those who refused the Gospel, he also encouraged the true faithful.[180] His growing fame and increasing awareness of his vocation meant that works began to appear under his own name, rather than anonymously.

In contrast to the situation regarding his exegetical commentaries, Calvin did not reduce his production of printed polemics during the first years after his return to Geneva. Instead, he published very short pamphlets of 10,000 words or fewer, as well as larger works of controversy of more that 30,000 words. His refutation of Albert Pighius even reached 65,000 words. In 1543 and 1544, his total polemical output came to 180,000 words, more than the annual average output for his exegetical works between 1545 and 1550. During these seven years Calvin continued to produce polemical pamphlets at the rate of about 28,000 words a year.

After that, his pace slowed down, but Calvin continued to clash with his adversaries. From 1554 onwards, the debates became more technical. Each publication now attacked not only a book, but also a specific person: Michael Servetus, Joachim Westphal, Sebastian Castellio, François Bauduin, and so on. In fourteen years, Calvin wrote seventeen new pamphlets. Their length continued to be as varied as in previous years, but on average he produced around 20,000 words per year.

Calvin's more personal attacks following his victory over opponents in Geneva in 1555 were not coincidental. At the same time, he handed over to Beza the task of pursuing several controversies. Between 1559 and 1564, in spite of major health problems, he completed the definitive edition of the *Institutes* both in Latin and in French and wrote a number of commentaries. Yet up until his death he also continued to enter the polemical fray, writing his final attacks against the Polish anti-Trinitarians.

His Opponents

The 1576 edition of the *Tractatus* presents Calvin's polemical work divided into seven convenient sections. The first section brings together his works against the Catholics, a heterogeneous collection of eleven texts to which another four anonymous pamphlets should be added that were not included in the collected edition.

The treatise on relics, one of Calvin's best sellers, is an exceptional case. It was his only pamphlet seemingly unconnected to a recent event or publication, and it provided a general attack on one abuse of the Roman church. However, it is possible that Calvin's amazingly specific knowledge about relics may have come from a work that came across his desk by chance.

---

[180]*B.C.1,* no. 50/9.

Many other anti-Catholic pamphlets responded to historical events, such as documents by Paul III, the imperial diets of Regensburg and Speyer, the Sorbonne articles on faith, the Council of Trent, and the Augsburg Interim. This cluster of works published between 1541 and 1549 has a common theme: the Reformer's concern to alert Protestant public opinion about the threats posed by the Catholic church. Calvin's focus on German events was the result of his experiences at the religious colloquies and his firm bonds with the Strasbourg theologians.

Other anti-Catholic writings attacked individuals, such as François Bauduin and his search for conciliation among Christian confessional groups. Calvin also denounced the doctrine of free will supported by the Dutch theologian Albert Pighius and ridiculed the Lyon canon Gabriel de Saconnay for his new edition of Henry VIII's *Assertio septem sacramentorum*.

The second category of works was aimed against the Anabaptists and the Spiritual Libertines.[181] Calvin wrote four works against these adversaries between 1542 and 1547.

The third section of pamphlets contains those against the Nicodemites. Calvin wrote these texts throughout his career, since the first was done in 1537 and the final one appeared in 1562. Calvin and his colleagues were deeply involved in the struggle against Nicodemism: many of the pamphlets in this section were reprinted and translated.

Calvin's short work against judicial astrology, that is, against foretelling human destiny by studying the stars, constitutes a category of its own.

The fifth category includes works against anti-Trinitarians, a late-developing concern of Calvin's. In 1554, he wrote a defense of the execution of Servetus. From 1561 onward, he flew to the rescue of the Polish Reformed churches, in their struggles against Biandrata, Stancaro, and other heretics, not to mention Valentino Gentile. The end result was no less than five works published during Calvin's lifetime.

Calvin was only rarely asked to defend his doctrine of predestination in writing. One of his works in 1552 criticizes Bolsec first of all, but also Albert Pighius and Giorgio Siculo. Later on, he wrote two or three works against Sebastian Castellio, but it is worth wondering who in fact wrote the texts Calvin was reacting against.

Finally, the last section contained works dealing with the Lord's Supper. Alongside the *Consensio mutua* that marked the agreement between the Zurich and Genevan churches, we find the endless quarrel with Westphal (three works) and with Hesshusen. Beza rapidly took over to defend Calvinist orthodoxy in these debates.

These works highlight how broad Calvin's involvement was in public debates. He addressed a wide range of topics, and his opponents came both from within the Catholic church and from outside it. As regards the internal debates within Protantism,

---

[181]For information on these groups, see above 23.

Calvin not only criticized many deviations, but also witnessed direct clashes between Lutherans and the Reformed beginning in 1554.

Conclusion

This first overview is intended to situate the place of polemics within Calvin's writings. In the next chapter, we will reexamine the reasons why Calvin entered into controversies with his opponents, in order to analyze his forceful style and see how his friends and enemies reacted to these writings.

This survey shows that polemic was always part of Calvin's work, although it evolved during his career. In the early years, he dealt with general topics, but over time his attacks were directed more against a particular opponent. His critique of the Catholic church, commonplace during his early years, dwindled in favor of debates within Protestantism. Following his attacks against dissidents, he turned to direct polemic against disciples of Luther, albeit extremist ones. While Calvin originally published these works anonymously or under a pseudonym, he increasingly used his own name later on. Conscious of his "office" as a Reformer and aware of his reputation, he wanted to take advantage of these factors to spread his ideas or even to spread Truth.

The low number of reprints suggests that the majority of the polemical pamphlets were not successful. One should not think that polemical works were always good news for booksellers. The tract on relics was exceptional, with eight French editions published during Calvin's lifetime. The anti-Nicodemite polemics were also relatively successful, underlining their significance in Calvin's work. As for the others, the result was disappointing. A few pamphlets intended for a wider audience were republished or translated after a number of years: the *Supplex exhortatio* directed at Charles V on the means of reforming the church, Calvin's two attacks against the Sorbonne, and his work on the Augsburg Interim. In many cases, the reeditions occurred within a short time period, suggesting that their success was temporary. This was certainly the case for the *Interim adultero-germanum,* which was republished twice and two hundred copies of which were requested by a Zurich bookseller.[182] The more personal polemic that Calvin produced after 1555 was never reprinted. His first treatise against Westphal was published in Latin and French, but the following ones were only published in Latin.

5. The Sermons in Print

Historians of Calvin the preacher have one major asset: a highly accurate stenographical transcription of a significant number of his sermons. While this literary genre was well known from the Middle Ages onward, we often have few manuscript or printed

---

[182]*B.C.1,* no. 49/6–8; and below 237.

records of the texts themselves. In all likelihood, a number of transcription methods were used, including using a text prepared by the cleric before or after his sermon or using notes taken by the hearers during the sermon, notes which then could be reworked afterwards by the author. Some written sermons could become no more than outlines, especially in collections intended to help preachers. In Calvin's case, the very specific sources answer any doubts that may exist regarding the nature of the texts that have been preserved.

Calvin's Sermons and Lectures in Written Form

The close links between writing biblical commentaries and preaching explain why the idea of writing down this oral teaching surfaced so rapidly among Calvin's entourage. In his biography, Beza indicated that the work of writing down the sermons and lectures began in 1549. He recalled earlier attempts: "It is true that earlier on many had tried to do this for the lectures and sermons, but they had not yet been able to write everything down word for word." However, in spite of this, Beza sought to praise them: "the work done by these first men (including M. Nicolas des Gallars, François Bourgoing, and Jean Cousin, all three ministers of the holy Gospel) was praiseworthy, in that it gave the impetus for others to advance the process and as it were turn it into a perfect system." Beza then presented the lectures written down by Budé and Jonviller and the sermons taken down in shorthand by Denis Raguenier. Thanks to Raguenier, who was "paid by the strangers' company," Calvin's sermons were preserved.[183]

The early history of the transcription efforts is almost unknown. Beza mentioned three names: des Gallars, Bourgoing, and Cousin. No trace of Bourgoing's work has emerged, while Jean Cousin's name appears in the first edition of Calvin's sermons, the *Deux Sermons,* preached in 1545 and published in 1546.[184] We have equally strong evidence for Nicolas des Gallars's work, as described in the commentaries on Isaiah.[185]

Calvin's two written comments in 1546 and 1547 indicate that he took an interest in the process of writing down and publishing his sermons. Jacques de Bourgogne's wife had complained that Calvin had not dedicated any of his works to her, although he had done so for her husband, and she suggested to Calvin that he should publish more in French, including his sermons. "You have asked me about my sermons," answered Calvin. "I would be willing to work at getting them published, but it will not be for this year."[186] Hence in 1546, Calvin did not reject the idea of having his sermons published, but he wanted to do it after working on them. The delay was not an attempt to find a polite way of refusing, since a few months

---

[183]CO, 21:70.
[184]*B.C.1,* no. 46/3.
[185]See above 51–52.
[186]CO, 12:401.

later Calvin wrote to Jacques de Bourgogne, "Lord [Pierre de] Maldonad[e] spoke to me about Jacques [Daléchamps] as to whether he could take down my sermons. As far as I can tell, he gets a few of the sentences down, but the substance is not really what I would hope for. It is possible that over time he will improve. While waiting to see whether he will become more adept through practice, it is still better to have what he does rather than nothing. Over time we may obtain someone who is more appropriate."[187] In 1546–47, Calvin was not only considering the publication of his sermons, but was also looking for a stenographer. He was even willing to hire someone who was only minimally competent in that it was still better than nothing!

An ambiguous reference may situate the idea of obtaining a stenographer back in 1542. When Calvin refused to work on his commentaries on Genesis because of the pressures of his vocation at the time, he wrote, "I have little confidence in my hearers."[188] Were some attempts to take down the sermons or lectures already in progress? Was he referring to his sermons, his lectures, or both?

Denis Raguenier began to write down Calvin's sermons beginning on 29 September 1549. Together with some assistants, he progressively managed to take down the sermons almost word for word. The first sermons recorded during the summer of 1549 ran to an average of 4,000 words. The sermons on Micah preached in the winter of 1550–51 increased to 5,500 words. Finally, the sermons on Isaiah preached from 1556 to 1559 ran to 7,000 words, which meant a very natural speaking rhythm of 120 words per minute. After Raguenier's death, his successor reached slightly lower totals, with 6,000 words per sermon on Samuel.[189]

The Bourse française of the poor foreigners, which hired Raguenier for this work, was granted a monopoly on publishing rights.[190] The primary task of the Bourse was not only to help the destitute, but also to underwrite the costs of religious proselytizing outside Geneva. Jean Budé played a key role in this work,[191] though his activity in terms of Calvin's writings lay primarily in recording the theological lectures.

Raguenier's sermon inventory, prepared after February 1560, provides a very clear picture of Calvin's preaching from 1549 onwards.[192] Raguenier fell ill at the end of 1560 and was paid one last time by the deacons of the Bourse française on 2 December 1560. His replacement for the taking down of Calvin's sermons, Paris

---

[187]CO, 12:540. Jacques Daléchamps returned to Catholicism and became a physician in Lyon. For further information on Daléchamps, see Ch. B. Schmitt, "The Correspondence of Jacques Daléchamps (1513–1588)," *Viator* 8 (1977): 399–434.

[188]CO, 11:418.

[189]F. Higman, T. H. L. Parker, and L. Thorpe, in *Supplementa calviniana*, 3:XXII–XXIII; and Parker, *Old Testament*, 22–23.

[190]Gagnebin, "L'histoire des manuscrits," XIX–XXVIII; and Parker, *Preaching*, 65–75.

[191]J. E. Olson, *Calvin and Social Welfare: Deacons and the Bourse française* (Selinsgrove, London, Toronto: Susquehanna University Press, 1989).

[192] The inventory appears in Gagnebin, L'histoire des manuscrits," XV–XVII.

Prostat, was paid for the first time on 7 February 1561.[193] A preface by Badius, dated 1 March 1561, confirms that Raguenier died in January 1561.[194] Yet his death did not put an end to the work, as evidenced by surviving sermon texts from 1562, 1563, and 1564.[195]

The Publication of the Sermons

The eager anticipation of Calvin's audience for his teaching helps to explain their insistence that his sermons be published. In 1542, Calvin published an *Exposition sur l'epistre de sainct Judas*. Rodolphe Peter saw this as a first set of sermons that were written down. His hypothesis is certainly correct, but in any event, this work was revised and rewritten by Calvin himself.[196] The first sermons to be published without Calvin's revision work were the *Deux Sermons faitz en la ville de Genève* of 1545, published in 1546.[197] Jean Cousin was the stenographer in this instance.

The *Quatre Sermons fort utiles pour nostre temps,* published in 1552, is an exceptional case, as this work was the only one to be revised by Calvin, who justified his involvement because of the importance of its theme. Indeed, Calvin intended the work to be a response to the calls for a new work on Nicodemism.[198]

Beginning in 1554, sermons began to be published based on notes taken by Denis Raguenier. Information on successive editions, publishers, and the printing process will be provided below.[199]

We need to consider briefly the reliability of the printed copies. The titles consistently specified that the books contained the text of Calvin's sermons "without anything subsequently added or removed"! In order to interpret this statement correctly, one must be aware of the differences between exact transcriptions in the sixteenth and twenty-first centuries. Francis Higman has carried out a detailed comparison of the printed version of the *Sermons sur le cantique que feit le bon roy Ezechias* with Raguenier's manuscript copy.[200] This is one of the rare cases in which the manuscript transcription has survived, because as a general rule the manuscript copy was destroyed during the typesetting work. Leaving aside spelling changes, Francis Higman found around 450 variations for the four sermons. In fact, the modifications generally made no changes in the meaning of the text, but instead were stylistic changes. Some alterations corrected mistakes in the intonation, while others corrected faulty biblical references. Some additions were made to focus the message more effectively. Overall,

---

[193]Olson, *Calvin and Social Welfare,* 47–48.
[194]*B.C.2,* no. 61/24.
[195]Gagnebin, "L'histoire des manuscrits," XVII.
[196]*B.C.1,* no. 42/3.
[197]*B.C.1,* no., 46/3.
[198]*B.C.1,* no. 52/9.
[199]See below 192–93.
[200]*B.C.2,* no. 62/21.

there were no more than ten changes that affected the content of the text so that the faithfulness to the preacher's message was certainly very great.[201]

"Forced and Compelled to Print"

Most of these works include a preface by the printer, providing valuable indications regarding the circumstances of each publication. I would like to review the main explanations provided on this matter.[202]

Overall, it is clear that Calvin was very unwilling to see his sermons published. In the 1546 edition, the printer simply stated that "the author was not accustomed to have his sermons printed."[203] In 1557, Badius affirmed that apart from the four sermons that he revised, Calvin always opposed the idea and was never willing to authorize the publication of his sermons. The works that did appear "were more the result of a forced and constrained permission, or even as a result of badgering than out of his free will and consent."[204] Only the *Dixhuict Sermons* of 1560 drew a different reaction from Calvin, as he "willingly" authorized their printing.[205] In contrast, Jacques Roux claimed in 1562 that he only obtained permission to print the sermons on the song of Hezekiah "with great difficulty."[206] In almost every instance, Calvin did not initiate the idea. In his 1558 publication of *Plusieurs Sermons,* Badius indicated the person who was most responsible for the major sermon editions: "Several leading people wanted to have them printed in quantity, especially Laurent de Normandie."[207]

Thus there is clear evidence for Calvin's reservations, which Beza highlighted again in his 1593 preface to the Latin version of the sermons on Job.[208] What explanation did the publishers have for Calvin's reluctance?

A first reason has to do with the style of the sermons. Because Calvin preached without notes, much less a full text, these were not composed with the care that was called for in works that had a wide audience. This same issue resurfaced when Calvin's entourage sought to publish his lectures.[209] The sermons of 1546 were "preached once, not written up to be published throughout the world."[210] In fact, Farel complained about this to Calvin: "I would have liked it if you worked on your discourse with more care, as you usually do."[211] In 1557, Badius explained that Calvin cared about the quality of his printed works: "He dislikes the fact that what he preached

---

[201]Higman et al., *Supplementa calviniana,* 3:XIX.
[202]The quotations from the prefaces all appear in the *Bibliotheca calviniana* 1 and 2.
[203]*B.C.1,* no. 46/3.
[204]*B.C.2,* no. 57/10.
[205]*B.C.2,* no. 60/4.
[206]*B.C.2,* no. 62/21.
[207]*B.C.2,* no. 58/5.
[208]CO, 33:13–14.
[209] See above 54–56.
[210]*B.C.1,* no. 46/3.
[211]CO, 12:302.

simply and plainly to adapt to the common people…is rapidly brought to light, as if he felt that everything he said should immediately be spread everywhere, and that the world should be filled with his writings."[212] Badius repeated the same thing in 1561 regarding the sermons on Timothy and Titus: these were not writings "that were premeditated and mulled over for a long time." Badius echoed an expression already used earlier: these were not homilies "done at leisure." "I say this because some may think that he polished and refined them at his leisure at home to make an impression, but I can assure you that they are just as he preached them in public as God inspired him, without any words being added or taken away."[213]

In his final preface to Calvin's sermons, Badius changed the parameters of the issue. Here, Badius referred to readers who were "surprised" about this publication of sermons that were neither "polished nor structured." He admitted that "there are at times some repetitions or even sentences that are short and obscure, which is common when one is not speaking on the basis of a written text and long preparation, but rather according to what the Holy Spirit gives to one to say."[214]

One particular aspect of the sermon style increased Calvin's reluctance, namely, that the sermons were too long-winded. Brevity was one of the hallmarks of Calvin's written style,[215] while the persuasive aim of sermons meant that they made use of repetitions. This difference bothered Calvin. In the case of Psalm 119, he would have preferred "to print a brief commentary when the time was right, rather than fill the sheet with so many long passages just as in the pulpit." But once again, Calvin indicated that he had too little free time to write the commentary. Badius noted that while waiting for "a more polished and exquisite work," the sermons would already bear fruit.[216]

A second reason that slowed down the publication of the sermons was that homilies intended for a particular audience would not necessarily have universal applicability. In 1558, Badius explained this in *Plusieurs Sermons*: Calvin "did not want his sermons to extend beyond his sheepfold: both because they were done for his own flock, adjusted as much as possible to their capacity and because he felt that a different order and setup would be needed if the sermons were presented to the rest of the world."[217]

Jacques Roux gave a similar explanation in 1562. In his sermons, Calvin "only wanted to serve the flock God gave him by teaching it in a familiar fashion, not to write sermons at his leisure to have them displayed before the eyes of the whole world."[218]

---

[212]*B.C.2*, no. 57/10.
[213]*B.C.2*, no. 61/24.
[214]*B.C.2*, no. 62/22.
[215]See below 122–24.
[216]*B.C.1*, no. 54/13.
[217]*B.C.2*, no. 58/5.
[218]*B.C.2*, no. 62/21.

Calvin was certainly very aware of his audience whether he was speaking or writing. Since his sermons brought the word of God to life for his Genevan audience, was it right for him to distribute them more widely? In his 1558 preface to *Plusieurs Sermons,* Badius claimed that Calvin did not merely invoke his lack of time for his refusal to revise the text of his sermons. "For if he wanted to put them out for publication, he would write new and better structured sermons, without having to rework something that he already preached extemporaneously."[219]

In fact, the editors managed to turn the argument around by affirming that the benefit arising from the sermons could not be confined to Geneva alone. Thus in 1554 Jean Girard obtained the first authorization to publish Calvin's sermons.[220] The wider benefit for the whole church was the only argument used in the short preface to the *Deux Sermons* of 1555.[221] Badius stressed the same approach in the *Sermons sur les dix commandemens* of 1557, stating that he wanted to allow the "faithful who are dispersed around the world" to participate in the riches of the Genevan church.[222] Badius reiterated the same theme in the *Plusieurs Sermons* published in 1558.[223] In his preface to the 1562 *Soixante cinq Sermons sur l'Harmonie,* Badius referred to the result of previous publications which "served as silent teachers to those who, while prevented from listening to the sermons, still benefited from reading them."[224]

Hence readers were to imagine themselves in attendance at Calvin's sermons. The 1546 preface explained that the reading would have more impact if "the readers imagined being present."[225] In 1561, in the preface to the sermons on the Epistles of Timothy and Titus, Badius acknowledged that sermons had specific characteristics, where "the gestures done while speaking help a great deal in understanding the topic, while a written text is often much less graceful than it was when it was originally delivered."[226] Badius added that experienced listeners would easily reconstruct the intonations of the preacher.

One final objection against the publication of the sermons was never mentioned during the sixteenth century, but it does appear in the writings of certain twentieth-century editors. Calvin's lack of preparation sometimes led him to make mistakes in his translation of the biblical text or to develop themes that were foreign to the passages on which he was commenting. In fact, Calvin was too overburdened with work to spend long hours on sermon preparation. In all likelihood, one can extrapolate for the sermons what Jean Budé says about Calvin's exegetical lectures: in most cases

[219] *B.C.2,* no. 58/5.
[220] *B.C.1,* no. 54/13.
[221] *B.C.2,* no. 55/8.
[222] *B.C.2,* no. 57/10.
[223] *B.C.2,* no. 58/5.
[224] *B.C.2,* no. 62/22.
[225] *B.C.1,* no. 46/3.
[226] *B.C.2,* no. 61/24.

Calvin never had more than half an hour to prepare for a one-hour lecture. We should imagine Calvin getting up to work for half an hour on his sermon before heading for Saint-Pierre at six or seven in the morning, depending on the time of year. This preparation period varied, however, and the result was sermons of uneven caliber. As Max Engammare noted, while Calvin might have provided a less than perfect translation from the Hebrew in a sermon on one day, he would prepare a much better one the following day.[227]

One of the best reasons for publishing Calvin's sermons was certainly to supply a concrete model of good Reformed preaching. Already when referring to the sermons on Psalm 119 in a 1555 letter to the church of Poitiers, Calvin stated, "you see here our style and usual way of teaching."[228] Badius highlighted this outcome of publication several times, first in the *Plusieurs Sermons* of 1558: "It is expedient that those who are newly starting in this charge [of preaching] observe his way of teaching in order to follow it."[229] In 1562, he noted the fruit of sermon editions, which had served "as a form for many who have been called to the ministry of the Gospel during these times of trial."[230]

This use of Calvin's sermons also surfaces in other sources. In a letter sent from La Rochelle on 29 November 1561, the pastor Ambroise Faget asked Germain Colladon to send him a copy of Calvin's unpublished sermons on Genesis. Faget wanted to have them to help him in his work as a pastor, admitting his lack of abilities for the task.[231] Another moving testimony comes from a handwritten note by a certain Benoid that was added to a copy of the 1562 *Sermons sur l'Epistre aux Ephesiens*. "I began to preach on this Epistle on 20 August 1564, on the day I was received as a minister of the Gospel of the Lord in the church of the district of Dijon, having been ordained at Nuits. Jehan Benoid."[232] This young pastor is otherwise unknown, but there is clear evidence that the services of the Dijon church took place at that time at Nuits-Saint-Georges.[233] Benoid's case was probably not the only one, and many novice pastors benefited from Calvin's sermons when they were called to the pulpit.

This practice brings us back to the apparent contradiction between Calvin's interest in having the sermons recorded and his unwillingness to have them printed. Calvin may have wanted the written version to serve as a source for his own writing, as he explained to the wife of Jacques de Bourgogne. It is more likely that he was considering circulating the sermons in manuscript form, a well-established practice.

---

[227] Engammare, *Paradis,* 333–34, 343–44; and Engammare, "Calvin connaissait-il la Bible?" 164–65.

[228] CO, 15:446.

[229] *B.C.2,* no. 58/5.

[230] *B.C.2,* no. 62/22.

[231] CO, 19:143.

[232] The work in question is part of the collection of the Bibliothèque de la Société de l'histoire du protestantisme, Paris, A 465.

[233] E. Belle, *La Réforme à Dijon des origines à la fin de la lieutenance générale de Gaspard de Sauls-Tavanes, 1530–1570* (Dijon: Damidot frères, 1911), 103.

However, the extent of manuscript circulation may have explained why Calvin finally allowed printed distribution of the sermons. Evidence for this comes from the *Deux Sermons* of 1546, which was printed because there were too many requests for copies: "it would have been too much work to write them out so many times."[234]

The Congrégations

Many of Calvin's biblical commentaries were written on the theme covered in the Friday *congrégations,* a topic with which we have already dealt. But one should note that some of the *congrégations* have survived, including all the contributions made by the various pastors. None of the manuscripts or printed copies provide any information on how they were written up or published. Yet the presence of the *congrégations* in manuscripts that also contain Calvin's sermons and the fact that the first *congrégation* to be printed appeared together with sermons lead one to speculate that the *congrégations* were taken down by Denis Raguenier or his successor, Paris Prostat.

The first *congrégation* to be printed appeared in 1558, in *Plusieurs Sermons touchant la divinité, humanité et nativité de N. S. Jesus Christ,* and dealt with the beginning of John's Gospel. The book's structure suggests that the *congrégation* was included at the last minute.[235] The 1562 *Congrégation sur l'élection éternelle de Dieu* presented the debates held during a special meeting in response to Bolsec's criticisms.[236] The reasons for the publication delay are unclear. The *Deux congrégations du second chapitre de l'Epistre aux Galatiens* appeared in 1563 without explanation. Galatians had been the subject of *congrégation* meetings from November 1562 to May 1563. The two printed *congrégations* deal with verses 11 to 21 of chapter 2.[237] This evidence of the weekly practice of the Genevan pastors was thus quite rare.

Conclusion

Calvin's reluctance to have his sermons published seems to strongly indicate how aware he was of the distance between oral and written discourse. But one must distinguish between the lectures and the sermons. The favorable response of readers to the publication of the lectures rapidly led the Reformer to a broad acceptance and even to an open collaboration with the publishers. In spite of the haste with which it was prepared, this academic discourse seemed to him to be worth spreading through print. These works were somewhat more polished since Calvin spoke so slowly in the lectures. Furthermore, some adjustments could be made during the rereading of the text in Calvin's presence.

In contrast, Calvin's resistance to the idea of printing the sermons remained. The two strongest reasons offered against publication were the excessive length of

---

[234]*B.C.1,* no. 46/3.
[235]*B.C.2,* no. 58/5.
[236]*B.C.2,* no. 62/7.
[237]*B.C.2,* no. 63/10.

the sermons and their more local applicability. While the first reason had to do with issues of style, the second one was different.

Unhappy about the publication of his sermons but willing to accept it for his exegetical lectures, Calvin still faced the urgent needs of his readership. In all likelihood, up until his death he would have preferred to publish brief, well-polished, and well-structured commentaries.

His awareness of specific requirements for written texts lay behind his preference for the publication of works written "at leisure" and his unwillingness to consider a wider distribution of his sermons. For this master of the spoken and written word, the sermon was not a literary genre to be entrusted to printers.

CHAPTER THREE

Writing

This chapter deals with four themes related to the act of writing. First of all, it seeks to establish the reasons that led Calvin to take up his pen. Second, it analyzes Calvin's use of both Latin and French, in order to shed light on the audiences he was seeking. Third, this chapter examines some specific evidence regarding Calvin's style. Finally, it attempts to describe the concrete setting of the Reformer's study.

I. CHOOSING TO WRITE

Why did Calvin decide to write? What factors led him to take up his pen? Was it a spontaneous movement or was he responding to external forces? I will consider these questions by looking at his entire body of writing and then examining his polemical works more specifically. Indeed, the impact of this genre and the violence with which Calvin attacked certain opponents deserve closer attention. In a final section, I will show that Calvin never wrote in isolation. Instead, he always wrote with the support of friends and community. Furthermore his investment in writing was always sustained by his high sense of calling.

Why Publish Books?

"On the Advice of a Few Good and Faithful Friends"

The theme of loving pressure applied by friends is commonplace among many writers in moments of false humility. Calvin too made use of this. Throughout his career, he explained his reasons for publication, perpetually caught as he was between his fear of being presumptuous and his confidence about the value and success of his work.

In 1556, in his preface to the lectures on Hosea, he asserted firmly that all his publications only appeared because of the ceaseless requests of those around him:

"...I can truly and honestly say, and even prove through trustworthy witnesses, that the works that I have brought to light until now (even though I polished them as diligently and carefully as possible), were almost torn from my hands by urgent and persistent requests...."[1]

Calvin already made use of this commonplace as a young man in an early yet subtle sign of his search for literary glory. In Duchemin's *Antapologia,* Calvin explained that his friend's work "was not written with the aim of being published one day."[2] Before saying the same thing in his *De Clementia,* Calvin criticized the ambition of those who sought publication because "their desire to write [is] unhealthy and excessive." The advice of François de Connan and other friends almost compelled him to have the work printed.[3] The same held true for the *Psychopannychia.*[4] It is hard to verify the accuracy of these statements, though one can doubt the sincerity of his comments in the case of the *De Clementia,* which he published at his own expense.

From the 1540s onwards, evidence from his correspondence suggests that a part of what he wrote was indeed requested by those around him. However, one should make a distinction between his exegetical and polemical works.

The first edition of the *Institutes* in 1536 was the result of a personal and spontaneous decision, even though there are hints that his circle already had certain expectations. Calvin's intention was to remind readers of the foundations of the faith and to refute accusations of Anabaptism. When he revised the work in 1537 and 1538 to turn it into a theological manual, Calvin planned a general program in which his first work would be the "key" allowing for a right understanding of the successive biblical commentaries. Outside pressures certainly played no major role in this decision. However, Calvin was sustained by his friends and encouraged to follow the path he had laid out. Indeed, already by March 1537, Oporinus asked him to republish the *Institutes.*[5] When Calvin's pace of writing was slowed down by his activities in Geneva, Farel grew impatient to read his works, and repeated this to him on several occasions in 1542, 1544, and 1546.[6]

The preface to the final version of the *Institutes* offers a rather balanced view of the various concerns of the author, from answering the expectations of his readers to offering a public service. Calvin expressed his astonishment at the success of his book: "over time, having realized that it was received much better than I could have desired or even hoped, I felt all the more obliged to work better and more fully for those who receive my doctrine so gladly, for I would have been ungrateful if I did

---

[1]CO, 42:183–84.

[2]Herminjard, *Correspondance,* 2:315; and CO, 9:785.

[3]Herminjard, *Correspondance,* 2:411; and CO, vol. 5; a good analysis of the topic appears in John Calvin, *Calvin's Commentary on Seneca's De Clementia,* ed. F. L. Battles and A. M. Hugo (Leiden: E. J. Brill, 1969), 12*.

[4]CO, 5:169–70.

[5]Herminjard, *Correspondance,* 4:208; and CO, 10/b:90–91.

[6]Herminjard, *Correspondance,* 8:80–81; CO, 11:418, 681–82; and 12:297.

not satisfy their expectations as far as my small capacity allowed." Therefore he revised his text for each new edition and in 1559 brought the work to its final length.[7]

Calvin gave several reasons for his 1541 publication of the *Traicté de la Cène*, his first treatise in French. Among the reasons given was the pressure of friends: "and also because several good men who saw the need for it asked me to."[8] In the *Brieve instruction contre les anabaptistes,* the pressure from readers was hinted at in a more general way.[9] This work was "sought after by many and even insistently requested."[10]

Because he was confident of the worth of exegetical studies, Calvin promised to devote himself to the task as much as possible. "For the remainder of my life, if I have sufficient time and freedom, I have decided to devote myself mainly to this work.... Even if my post leaves me with very little time, I have however decided to dedicate it, as minimal as it is, to this kind of writing."[11] He repeated the same thing on subsequent occasions.[12] He also brought up once more the excessive number of bad books, complaining that it meant good authors had to defend their published writings, or again that "soon learned men will be too embarrassed to print anything."[13]

Many of the works Calvin wrote in Strasbourg were done in response to a request, whether from the Genevan citizens in the case of the letter to Sadoleto, or probably from Bucer for the pamphlets dealing with the diet of Regensburg and the council called together by Paul III.[14] In 1543, Bucer also encouraged Calvin to write about the diet of Speyer.[15] Throughout the 1540s, Viret and especially Farel pushed Calvin to get involved in various controversies.[16] Indeed, Calvin's mastery of polemics was quickly apparent. As soon as a pamphlet required a response, his friends turned to him. Calvin's correspondence shows that he acted as a firefighter, tackling blazes on all fronts. Farel's request for a refutation of the Anabaptists is revealing: after first mentioning more important works—"We all know you are overloaded with work and that you have other topics to deal with"—Farel still asked Calvin to intervene in the polemical debate.[17]

After the *Consensus Tigurinus* was accepted, Calvin regularly confided in Bullinger. Naturally, when polemical debates spread to the German lands, and especially when the disputes became more technical after 1553, the Reformers discussed whether or not to respond, whether responses would serve any purpose, and what

[7]Calvin, *Institution,* ed. Benoît, 1:23.

[8]CO, 5:433.

[9]CO, 7:49.

[10]CO, 12:258.

[11]CO, 14:37.

[12]CO, 17:447.

[13]CO, 13:281; and 9:125.

[14]*B.C.1,* nos. 39/5, 41/1, 41/6.

[15]*B.C.1,* no. 43/7.

[16]*B.C.1,* nos. 43/7, 44/6, 44/7, 45/4, 45/10, 47/3.

[17]Herminjard, *Correspondance,* 9:173–74; and CO, 11:681–82; see also *B.C.1,* no. 44/7.

form they should take. In the case of the attack on the Augsburg Interim, for instance, Calvin told Farel of his unease: "Bullinger had urged me to write against this adulterous reformation. I had been getting ready to write when I received his letter, but then I decided against it. I have asked Bucer for advice. If he approves of it, I will try to write something."[18] The ongoing controversies with men like Westphal, Castellio, Bauduin, or the Polish anti-Trinitarians led to numerous letters between the Reformers.[19] On more than one occasion, Calvin had to be pressured to take up his pen.

While external pressure was the most common motivator for Calvin's polemical works, there were some exceptions. The preface to the 1536 *Epistolae Duae* makes no mention of outside appeals in explaining why the work was written.[20] Indeed, it seems that Calvin's anti-Nicodemite writings were generally written spontaneously. The same was true for his pamphlet against Servetus. In November 1553, Calvin told Bullinger of his intention to write on the subject, "If I have some free time, I will show in a rather short book what kind of monster he was, so that evil men do not continue their slander (I understand that this is happening in Basel), and so that the ignorant do not murmur against us."[21] Though there is no formal proof, I would say that the same rationale holds true for other works, including the treatise on relics, the *Des Scandales* and the *Congratulation à Gabriel de Sacconnay.*[22] Colladon said that Calvin saw the last of these works as "a sort of pastime," a description that fits the treatise on relics as well.[23] Furthermore, neither the treatise on relics nor the *Des Scandales* was written in response to a particular event or publication, but instead they were the result of Calvin's own initiative.

Calvin's international reputation can also be measured through the increasing diversity of those who turned to him for help. The 1552 pamphlet on predestination was in part a response to a request from the "Italian brethren."[24] The call for a rebuttal of Dirck Coornhert's tract came from the Netherlands.[25] Finally, the Polish Calvinists turned to Calvin and Bullinger for help on several occasions.[26]

"This Teaching Charge and Office"

Calvin's most common explanation for his writings is that he wanted to help his readers. He stated this clearly in his *Traicté de la Cène,* "I thought it would be very useful to deal briefly with and clearly explain the sum total of what one should know [about the Lord's Supper]."[27] In his lectures on Jeremiah, he exclaimed, "I have no

---

[18]CO, 13:27; and *B.C.1,* no. 49/6.

[19]*B.C.1,* no. 54/6; and *B.C.2,* nos. 55/6, 56/4, 57/11, 61/11, 63/4.

[20]CO, 5:233; and *Recueil,* 57.

[21]CO, 14:671; and *B.C.1,* no. 54/6.

[22]*B.C.1,* nos. 43/2, 50/9; and *B.C.2,* no. 61/13.

[23]CO, 21:93.

[24]*B.C.1,* no. 52/4.

[25]*B.C.2,* no. 62/16.

[26]*B.C.2,* nos. 61/11, 63/4, 63/12.

[27]CO, 5:433.

fear of being called arrogant if I simply confess that I never would have authorized the publication of this book had I not been sure of its usefulness and fruitfulness for the church."[28]

At the heart of his written work lay his sense of duty, linked to his vocation as a Reformer. After having noted his friends' pressure to have the *Traicté de la Cène* published, he added, "I could not have turned them down without going against my duty."[29] In 1548, Calvin clearly stated, "... Since God wanted me to be one of those through whose work the world has received a purer doctrine of the Gospel...."[30] He referred to his mission on other occasions.[31] In 1561 he told his compatriots all that he had done for the French Reformation, both in public and in private. He had attempted to "rescue them and help them publicly ... to prod those who were cowardly and slow, to give good courage to those who were afraid, to exhort those who were shaky and doubting to persevere." By offering his lectures to them, "I try to do my duty."[32] In a letter sent to the Christians of Rouen in 1547, Calvin echoed the same theme in a different form. "The zeal I have for the house of God constrains me to write this to you, both because of the concern I have for your salvation, and because I must not hide or be silent when I hear that God's name is blasphemed in some places and his doctrine falsely corrupted, if I have any power to oppose this."[33]

Indeed, Calvin had a high sense of his calling. To avoid it would be to resist the will of God. The entire preface to the 1557 Psalms commentary is intended to show that his task as a Reformer was given to him against his will by a divine decision.[34] The issue of the legitimacy of his vocation was a burning one when he was expelled from Geneva, and in fact his exile led him to have momentary doubts about his calling. His letters in the following months show that he was keen to receive the approval of sister churches, in Zurich, Bern, Basel, Strasbourg, and Biel.[35] But his doubts quickly dissipated. His friend Louis du Tillet, who had returned to Catholicism, criticized him for having entered the ministry without being called by the church. Calvin's answer was unambiguous: "If you doubt it [my vocation], that tells me that it is certain...." He added, however, that some approval was needed: "not only that, but that I may have it approved by those who are willing to submit their censures to the Truth."[36] This caveat allowed Calvin to avoid any external criticism, since only those who were willing to submit to the Truth were valid critics of Calvin's actions! In other words, those who did not support him showed, as in the case of Du Tillet, that they were opponents of the Truth!

[28]CO, 20:77.
[29]CO, 5:433.
[30]CO, 13:17.
[31]For example, CO, 13:598; and 15:200.
[32]CO, 18:615.
[33]CO, 7:345.
[34]See A. Ganoczy's analysis noted above 10.
[35]Herminjard, *Correspondance,* 5:43–44; and CO, 10/b:220.
[36]Herminjard, *Correspondance,* 5:162; and CO, 10/b:270.

A letter to Farel dated January 1539 shows that Calvin had recovered his aplomb entirely. After complaining about the delay in the publication of the *Institutes* due to the negligence of Robert Winter, he specified, "Though I have no reason to complain because of my own affairs, but because I think that an earlier completion date is in the public good, I cannot help but be greatly troubled that one man's peevishness has disappointed the hopes and expectations of so many good people."[37] The delay did not affect him personally, but he regretted that so many of the faithful would be disappointed! This remark is all the more revealing in that he wrote it spontaneously to a friend. This sense of public service surfaced already in October 1538, when Calvin asked Antoine du Pinet to prepare a clean copy of the *Institutes,* "not for me, but for all pious men."[38]

In his letter of June 1539 written to appease ecclesiastical quarrels in Geneva, Calvin supported the current pastors by stating that "the vocation of your ministers did not take place without the calling of God," adding quickly, "one must ascribe our departure to a move of the devil."[39] Calvin's letter to Sadoleto contained several statements regarding the legitimacy of his ministry and the permanence of his bond to the Genevan community: "As God ordained me once, he compelled me to always be loyal and faithful to him." [40]

On a somewhat humorous note, in the 1534 preface to the *Psychopannychia,* Calvin also refers to a call of conscience: "I do not know how I would avoid charges of treason toward God's truth if I remained silent and still in a matter of such great urgency." Yet this moral constraint was not absolute, since Calvin delayed the publication of this work for eight years on the advice of Capito and Bucer.[41]

Calvin wrote for all, but only submitted to the judgment of certain men. In the case of his commentaries, he was willing to seek out professionals like Grynaeus and his colleagues.[42] Calvin wanted to serve "simple, good, and sensible" readers, and rejected those who read in bad faith, hooded monks, and degenerate idlers.[43] Confident in the faithful readers' reception of his writings, Calvin felt no need to brag.[44]

This same self-assurance reappears in his writings against the spiritualist libertines. As he explained to Marguerite de Navarre, "Since our Lord called me to this post, my conscience compels me" to respond.[45] He echoed this sentiment in his preface to the definitive edition of the *Institutes:* "since he [God] gave me this charge and office of teaching, I have no other purpose except to benefit his church by

---

[37]Herminjard, *Correspondance,* 5:227; and CO, 10/b:315.

[38]Herminjard, *Correspondance,* 5:134; and CO, 10/b:261.

[39]Herminjard, *Correspondance,* 5:338; and CO, 10/b:353.

[40]CO, 5:386; and *Recueil,* 145.

[41]CO, 5:169–170; *Recueil,* 1–2; and *B.C.1,* no. 42/5.

[42]Herminjard, *Correspondance,* 6:78; and CO, 10/b:405–6.

[43]CO, 15:711; and 17:446–47.

[44]CO, 13:17; 15:17, 711; and 17:446.

[45]CO, 12:66; see *B.C.1,* no. 45/4. Other evidence of Calvin's inability to maintain silence can be found in Millet, *Calvin et la dynamique,* 443.

declaring and maintaining the pure doctrine that he taught us." Calvin continued by affirming that he did not think there was any other man as vilified as he was.[46]

In his will, Calvin repeated his point: "I affirm also that I have tried, according to the measure of grace that he gave me, to teach his word purely, both in sermons and in writings, and to faithfully expound Holy Scripture; and even in all the disputes I have engaged in against the enemies of truth, I never used cunning or sophistry, but worked straightforwardly to maintain his position."[47]

As described below, Calvin's work as an expositor of scripture was based on the gift of good scriptural understanding, given to him by God. This gift was all the more necessary in that most Christians were unable to discover the meaning of the scriptures without help.[48] Calvin did not hesitate to proclaim his talent: "I am not ashamed to recognize what God gave me in terms of understanding scripture since it is true (it is nothing else than a way to find glory in him)."[49] In his lectures on Jeremiah, he said, "If Jeremiah himself were alive today on earth, he would, I believe, agree with this dedication, because he would admit that I explain his prophecies with both integrity and respect."[50] If this biblical author approved of Calvin, who then could criticize him?

The Author's Outlook

Writing a work (especially a pamphlet) can be the result of extensive discussions, but Calvin's decision to write was not due solely to cold rationality. As an author, the Reformer was sometimes suddenly led to write, or, in contrast, was forced to fill pages while being overcome with disgust. A glance at a number of his works shows the range of Calvin's attitudes toward the blank page.

The stories in the first chapter depicted how sensitive Calvin was, to the point that he had to take to his bed or stop writing when he encountered obstacles. He went through periods of discouragement that led him to make major—seemingly final—decisions. When he thought his commentary on Second Corinthians was lost, he decided never to write any more commentaries on Paul's Epistles.[51] When the Genevan Council hesitated before authorizing his first attack against Westphal, Calvin threatened never to publish any work in Geneva again, and even debated what to do with his commentary on the synoptic Gospels.[52] A few months earlier, he had announced that he would stop writing after the current commentary was complete: "Once this work appears, I will concentrate on silent meditations."[53]

---

[46]Calvin, *Institution,* ed. Benoît, 1:23.
[47]CO, 20:299.
[48]See below 154–56.
[49]CO, 13:282; see also 14:293; 47:V–VI; and 15:710.
[50]CO, 20:77.
[51]CO, 12:368.
[52]CO, 15:356.
[53]CO, 15:175.

Further evidence of his sensitivity appears in his reaction to Hesshusen's tract. At first, he remained unmoved. "I started to work through Tilemann [Hesshusen]'s book with distaste, but the chatter of this noisy man is too ridiculous to arouse my anger. I have not yet decided to answer him. I do not think that these trifles are worth many days' work, for there are so many writings that I am considering."[54] But shortly thereafter, the situation changed. He wrote to Bullinger, "when your letter was brought to me, I had already written half of the response I feel is necessary to refute Hesshusen. This was not the result of deliberate thought, but rather of a kind of surge. His work is so awful that it even deserves stoning."[55]

Calvin's initial reaction to Bucer's request for a work against the upcoming diet of Speyer was not positive. A first letter from Bucer hints at Calvin's reluctance.[56] Complaining to Viret in a letter dated 9 November 1543, Calvin stated, "I will do as Bucer wishes, but it will be very difficult."[57] The next day, Calvin wrote to Farel, "You carefully urge me to start the work given to us by Bucer. I have already started and made a little progress, but, believe me, I will not advance without great difficulty."[58] Calvin made no further comments on this work, which appeared in print a month later.[59]

As for his critique of the Council of Trent, Calvin waited until he "sensed" the topic. He explained to Viret, "I will shortly attack the Neptunian [Tridentine] fathers, since so many people from all over are asking me to. If the first part goes well, I will continue. However, I cannot promise anything."[60] A little later, he admitted that he was discouraged: "I am so overwhelmed by writing and worries that I am almost tired of life. I will however add a corollary to your work as soon as I catch my breath. I had considered writing something against the Council of Trent. But I am aware that I will not be able to do this work unless I give my exhausted mind a bit of rest."[61] Calvin was not completely satisfied with the result and needed Farel's congratulations before revising his opinion of the work.[62]

During August 1546, Calvin failed to make any progress in writing the *De Scandalis* because he was too distraught over the loss of his commentary on Second Corinthians. When the manuscript resurfaced, Calvin took up his writing again, but in October he put *De Scandalis* aside "because the style is not flowing the way I wanted."[63]

---

[54]CO, 18:237.

[55]CO, 18:255.

[56]Herminjard, *Correspondance,* 9:86–87; and CO, 11:634–35.

[57]Herminjard, *Correspondance,* 9:103; and CO, 11:647.

[58]Herminjard, *Correspondance,* 9:105; and CO, 11:642.

[59]*B.C.1,* no. 43/7.

[60]CO, 12:569; see *B.C.1,* no. 47/3.

[61]CO, 12:579.

[62]CO, 12:642.

[63]CO, 12:391.

On 7 December 1549, Calvin thanked Bullinger and his colleagues for sending him a bookseller's critiques, though we do not know exactly what this was about. Calvin's first sentences seem to suggest that the matter is beyond hope: "Would to Heaven that I had been informed earlier, but better late than never." But all was not lost. "I will do as you suggest, though I had planned to delay composing this short work until the time of the fair. Writing will be painful rather than difficult, because I will have to struggle against friends. In truth, I would rather fight against declared enemies, even though this too is part of our struggle. This is why I will complete the text rapidly."[64] It seems to me that this is a warning, perhaps concerning a reminder about a promised text. The work in question may have been the extremely short preface that Calvin wrote for the *Exemplum memorabile desesperationis in Francisco Spera* by Henry Scrimger. There is, however, one problem with this scenario: the preface is dated 5 December 1549, while the letter talking about a future work is dated two days later. The same preface is even dated 15 November 1549 in Jean Girard's French edition.[65] To make our hypothesis workable, the printed preface would have to be antedated. Protestants launched many debates around the story of Francesco Spira, who died after having forsworn Protestantism.[66] Whatever the case regarding this work, Calvin's letter indicates that he was more at ease in open controversies than in writing sly remarks against men of his own party.

At times, Calvin's work on his commentaries also slowed down. In 1550, Calvin simultaneously began to write commentaries on the Acts of the Apostles and on Genesis. On 19 August, Calvin told Farel about the first fruits of his work. "Since God allowed me to bring my commentary on Genesis to the end of chapter 3, I decided to give you a foretaste of the work."[67] But in November 1550, the situation had changed. Once again writing to Farel, Calvin exclaimed, "What do you have to say about Acts and Genesis, barely formed embryos still in the womb? I am embarrassed to admit how slowly I am making progress in Acts. And I think it will be a long work based on the first third that I have completed."[68]

His controversy with François Bauduin, his former disciple, was especially painful for Calvin, who only reluctantly wrote against him. As soon as the *De officio pii viri* appeared, Calvin felt obliged to respond to its presumed author: "I would like to deal with this rascal as he deserves, but I am drowning in private correspondence, and even if I still had a bit of energy left, it has weakened."[69] Shortly afterwards, he began to write and soon announced to Beza that the work was in print. "It was only

---

[64]CO, 13:488.

[65]Text in CO, 9:855–58. Both the Latin and French editions appear in P. Chaix, A. Dufour, and G. Moeckli, *Les livres imprimés à Genève de 1550 à 1600* (Geneva: Droz, 1966), 16.

[66]D. Cantimori, "Spigolature per la storia del Nicodemismo Italiano," *Ginevra e l'Italia* (Florence: G. C. Sansoni, 1959), 185–90.

[67]CO, 13:623.

[68]CO, 13:655.

[69]Beza, *Correspondance*, 3:149; and *B.C.2*, no. 61/22.

small consolation for my labors, but this rascal's hateful audacity had to be refuted."[70] A little later, Calvin returned to the topic, still without any pleasure. "I regretted having to do this work which left me disgusted. As you read it, you will notice that I was irritated by this outrage."[71] It is important to note the link that Calvin perceived between his mood and the quality of the resulting work.

To end this section, I turn to an unexpected matter: Calvin said and believed that he was lazy. I will only bring together a few quotations because at first I did not notice this kind of statement in Calvin's correspondence. I later realized that this was rather more than a commonplace: as strange as it may seem in the case of this tireless worker, he thought he was lethargic and too passive. Already during his stay in Angoulême in the spring of 1534, Calvin indicated to his friend François Daniel that he felt well and was making some progress in his work "as far as I can, given my laziness that you know about."[72] Shortly thereafter, while in Basel in September 1535, he made the same admission. When mentioning his revision of the French translation of the New Testament that he had promised to Olivétan, he explained his reasons for delaying the work. "In between times, I have turned to other studies… or rather I rested in my usual laziness, so that I have not yet started on this work."[73] In both cases, he used the same Latin word: *desidia*. These claims should be considered alongside Calvin's often fragile state of health. In 1546, he explained to Jacques de Bourgogne how his health issues were preventing him from working. "As well as the sermons and lectures, I have not done much for about a month, so much so that I am almost ashamed to live in this useless fashion."[74] Calvin's remark to Myconius in 1549 regarding the *Consensus Tigurinus* regards his decision making. "As I am rather slow to decide, either due to natural weakness or to inertia, I was waiting for the right moment."[75] A year later, when Farel praised him extensively for the publication of his commentary on Genesis, he bristled, "I tell you, I read with shame the part of your letter that praises my work, while I am fully aware of my laziness and sluggishness. May God lead me to always benefit a bit as I advance slowly and little by little."[76] Whatever one's opinion about Calvin's natural weakness, the quotations provided above are consistent in terms of the impact of his sensitivity on his decision making. Calvin also often claimed that he "did not know how" he did certain things: he needed an internal stimulus to push him to write his works.[77]

---

[70]Beza, *Correspondance,* 3:174.
[71]Beza, *Correspondance,* 3:247; and *B.C.2,* no. 62/27.
[72]Herminjard, *Correspondance,* 3:157; and CO, 10/b:37.
[73]Herminjard, *Correspondance,* 3:349; and CO, 10/b:51.
[74]CO, 12:319–20.
[75]CO, 13:456–57; and above 7.
[76]CO, 13:656.
[77]For example, see below 98, 115.

The Polemical World

The Need for Written Polemic

Calvin was active in polemical debates for other reasons than those motivating his exegetical and pastoral writings. He knew that a pamphlet could do more harm than good. In a letter probably written in 1535, Capito recommended against publishing the *Psychopannychia* because "in the midst of religious catastrophes, the Germans have learned that attacking errors only makes them better known."[78] Calvin himself admitted that he waited before writing against the Spiritual Libertines. He had wanted "to see whether silence would be effective against this disease."[79]

Subsequently, various Swiss pastors deplored the controversy with Westphal. In their eyes, the aim should have been not only to limit the attacks, but also to hold one's peace.[80] In the same way, François Hotman objected to the attacks against Castellio. He sorrowfully admitted to Calvin, "when I see all this, I am discouraged, predicting that this controversy over predestination will be no less damaging than the one on the sacrament, which has torn the churches apart for the last thirty years. Your most recent book was received by our people in such a way that I await another uproar."[81]

It is true that one of the rules of controversy holds that silence is a proof of weakness. Thus Calvin published his Latin catechism in 1538 to refute Caroli's accusation of Arianism.[82] When Pighius challenged Calvin in 1542, the latter felt compelled to respond: "he is attacking me by name and is looking for an opponent."[83] The final paragraph of Calvin's tract underlines the speed of the response: "Because if I kept quiet for a while, the risk was that Pighius would dazzle some by his boasting. However, I was willing to present this part, both to take him down a peg and to awaken and encourage all good and faithful people."[84]

In a response to Antoine Cathelan, written in 1556 but only published ten years later, Calvin intermingled a number of themes without clarifying his train of thought. He began by disparaging his opponent and the pamphlet in which he attacked Calvin. He continued by stating, "Since he [Cathelan] is such a joker, one may well ask why I bother to deal with him. I admit that in his folly he has at least achieved this result, namely, to get me to reply to his tall tales. He addressed his letter 'A Messieurs les Syndiques de Genève' so that they would compel me to respond, as if everyone would hold me guilty if I said nothing. It is true that he can make as much noise as he

---

[78]Herminjard, *Correspondance*, 3:243–45; CO, 10/b:45–46; and *B.C.1*, no. 42/5.

[79]CO, 12:66.

[80]See the opinions provided by S. Sulzer, P.-P. Vergerio, and the pastors of St. Gallen (CO, 15:491, 532, 556, 560–62, 665, 845).

[81]CO, 17:133; and *B.C.2*, no. 58/1.

[82]*B.C.1*, no. 38/1.

[83]Herminjard, *Correspondance*, 8:220–21; CO, 11:474; and *B.C.1*, no. 43/3.

[84]CO, 6:404; and *Recueil*, 438.

wants in the future before he drags any response out of me. For may God keep me
from such misuse of my time and from bothering readers with such nonsense, which
is not worth discussing."[85] The Reformer clearly stated the unworthiness of his opponent. He also said that Cathelan's provocation of the syndics of Geneva had no effect
and that the topic itself was not worth it, but without any further explanation, Calvin
wrote his pamphlet. He ended it by refusing to continue the controversy, "for it is not
up to me to silence all the barking dogs of the world."[86]

Calvin again claimed that responses were necessary in his second pamphlet
against Westphal.[87] And when he continued to spar against Hesshusen on the same
topic, he used less than convincing arguments. When Hesshusen had begun "to stir
up this topic once again," Calvin had originally held his peace, since the writings of
Oecolampadius, Bullinger, and Vermigli were clear and sufficient. Furthermore,
Calvin felt that the adversaries "ought to be convinced by sufficient reasons" and that
it was as though "we were talking with deaf men." Following these statements, readers might expect to find out what pressing motivation led Calvin to take up his pen
regardless, but no such rationale emerges. He simply wrote, "I would be glad to
make use of this short defense, in which readers can see that this new antiquarian
[Hesshusen] is as dry and inept as Westphal."[88] Calvin was hooked by the lure of
polemics.

Calvin's exceptional literary talents as a polemicist explain why his fellow believers turned to him in order to refute publications considered to be dangerous or scandalous. The sequence of these calls for help did, however, evolve. His first writings
had a more general aim: to warn against the Catholic church and against deviant
movements such as Nicodemism. After 1550, Calvin became involved (or rather he
willingly involved himself) in more personal confrontations.

A "Truly Prophetic Vehemence"

In Calvin's case, his polemical works raise one particular issue, namely, the violence of his statements. While Beza's pen was no less sharp than Calvin's, the former
was well aware of the critiques voiced in Protestant circles about Calvin's polemical
excesses. Beza felt obliged to make excuses for Calvin's aggressive approach, both in
his first biographical notes of 1564 and in the preface to the *Tractatus Omnes* volume
of 1576. In his 1564 biography, Beza admitted that Calvin was "too prone to anger,"
but because Beza admired this biting style, he generally saw the positive side of this
fault: "God made marvelous use, even of this vehemence." Later on, he repeated that
"all can judge how much this vehemence—truly prophetic vehemence—has served
and will serve all of posterity."[89] And in the 1576 preface, Beza justified Calvin's

[85]CO, 9:125.
[86]CO, 9:136.
[87]CO, 20:446; and *B.C.2,* 56/4.
[88]CO, 9:490; and *Recueil,* 1723–24.
[89]CO, 21:39–40.

sharp tone through examples taken from the Old Testament and the history of the early church.[90] In a sense, Beza gave literary standing to "theological pamphlets."[91]

The *Psychopannychia* prefaces of 1534 and 1536 show that Calvin was conscious of this issue very early on. In the prefaces, he announced a few of the goals he would pursue throughout his life. In 1534, he claimed to have "a spirit opposed to all contention and debates." It was for the sake of truth that he entered the arena. "If those who spread these fantasies had allowed, I would gladly have forgone this form of combat, which is unlikely to bring in as much fruit as it costs in effort." Calvin was forced to join in the polemic, while being aware that the positive results would be minimal. He announced that his criticisms would solely target ideas. "I will engage in disputations without malice, and without targeting specific individuals, and without seeking to lampoon or slander, so much so that no one will be able to complain truthfully that I injured him or even offended him in any way."[92] This is an admirable program, full of respect for his opponents.

Two years later, when revising his work, Calvin confessed that he had not lived up to his ambitions: "When I reread this disputation, I noticed at the heart of the matter a few things that were said a bit sharply, or even harshly, which may hurt the delicate ears of certain people." He then made distinctions between his readers, classifying one group as "a number of good people" who were taken advantage of due to their innocence, credulity, or ignorance, and added that "I would not want them to be offended by me." But when Calvin became irate—"whenever I am emboldened to speak"—he spoke to "this evil and obstinate flock of Anabaptists." According to him, this group could never be treated more harshly than they deserved. After announcing that he would always stand "unbeatable" on their path, he reiterated his desire for moderation: "I have always avoided insulting and biting words." He controlled his pen, so that his discourse would be "more likely to teach than to compel." "And in truth my goal has been to bring them back to the right path, rather than irritate them and provoke their anger."[93] Similarly, a few years later, when glancing at his pamphlet against Caroli, Calvin stated, "I only declared what is strictly true, but I kept a number of matters quiet, either because they were useless or because they damaged the cause."[94]

Calvin thus made distinctions between two kinds of readers. On the one hand, there were those who "do not sin obstinately or maliciously" and can be brought back to the right path; one should avoid offending them. On the other hand, the "evil and obstinate flock" deserve the worst insults. In his own eyes at least, Calvin's insults were minor. In fact, the Reformer used two complementary expressions to describe his own polemical attacks. The first expression linked his words with the

[90]Beza, *Correspondance,* 17, esp. 78–79.
[91]Millet, "Calvin pamphlétaire," 9–10.
[92]CO, 5:169–72; and *Recueil,* 1–2.
[93]CO, 5:173–74; and *Recueil,* 3.
[94]CO, 12:108.

simple Truth. The 1558 translator rendered the Latin phrase "quoties aliqua dicendi libertate evehor" as "whenever I am emboldened to speak." The notion of freedom of speech implies that of telling the Truth. A few lines later, he admitted to losing his temper with his adversaries (contra eos, nisi modice, bilem effundi), which the translator rendered as "I only expressed my anger against them in a modest fashion." We shall see that Calvin maintained that he had followed this practice until the end of his life.

When completing the *Apologie* of Jacques de Bourgogne, Calvin showed that he was able to master his violent tone. "Given the current situation, when the time comes to print it, I do not see that there is much to change. It is impossible to soften it, and the time is not right to make it fiercer."[95] In the same way, when Viret made some remarks about his attack against Pierre Caroli, Calvin replied, "As regards insults, my rule is to only use them in the right place, that is, when the subject calls for them."[96]

When Calvin addressed an opponent directly, he knew that he was not going to change the adversary's mind. Calvin was less interested in a debate over ideas than in exposing the blindness and obstinacy of his opponents. He wanted to unmask the impostors by giving absolute proofs of the truth. If his opponents would not admit the truth, it was because they were lost in their errors. Thus the two types of hearers were those who accepted the truth and those who rejected it. Calvin's specific intention was to highlight the dividing line between these two groups.[97]

Like a good pastor, the Reformer chased away the wolves and brought his sheep to pasture. His attacks on errors were intended to comfort the faithful and perhaps convince his opponents' supporters. Thus his attacks against the Polish anti-Trinitarians sought to "expose this impious error that fascinates our faithful."[98] Ten years earlier, his short work on the execution of Servetus had two goals: "that wicked men cease to slander us (I hear this is going on in Basel) and also so that the ignorant do not murmur against us."[99] There are many other quotations available along these same lines.[100]

"To Remove Several Insulting Words"

While Calvin's friends applauded each new work he published, his opponents did not give up, even in Geneva. Already in 1548, Calvin was worried that Jean Trolliet's

---

[95]CO, 12:494–95; and *B.C.1,* no. 47/1.

[96]CO, 12:107.

[97]Millet, "Calvin pamphlétaire," 9–22.

[98]CO, 19:640; and *B.C.2,* no. 63/4.

[99]CO, 14:671.

[100]See his polemical works against the Polish anti-Trinitarians (CO, 19:729; and *B.C.2,* nos. 61/11, 63/4, 63/12), against the Anabaptists (Herminjard, *Correspondance,* 9:173–74; CO, 11:681–82; and *B.C.1,* no. 44/7), against Westphal (CO, 15:64; and *B.C.2,* no. 55/6), and against Hesshusen (CO, 18:310; and *B.C.2,* no. 61/11).

opposition could succeed in banning the publication of his critique of the Augsburg Interim. As a matter of fact, the first official complaints against the tide of insults in Calvin's pamphlets came from his adversaries in 1548. The authorities' examination of Calvin's pamphlet against Bolsec indicated that the work is "important and significant." The examiners then added, "However, there are several insulting words that could well be removed."[101]

The decision to execute Servetus followed extensive consultations with the Swiss cities. Calvin thought it helpful to publish a short apology in which he not only refuted the heresies of the condemned man, but also provided justifications for the right to condemn heretics to death.[102] The reaction of Calvin's Bernese friend Nikolaus Zurkinden was perceptive. He approved of the work but regretted that Calvin had signed it, for Zurkinden felt it should have been published in the name of the Genevan Council. He continued, "As far as I can tell based on early reports, I do not see that you will gain any advantage from peace-loving men due to having been the first to deal *ex professo* with his argument that is detested by almost everyone."[103] Wolfgang Musculus also feared negative reactions: "I would have preferred it if the book had been published under another title, for fear that readers who hate bloodthirsty cruelty may avoid reading the book when they see the title, or if they read it, they may do so with reservations, full of suspicion, and be less likely to use healthy judgment in a sincere fashion."[104]

The debate with Joachim Westphal provides quantities of evidence about the concern caused by Calvin's violent personal attacks, even among Calvin's most faithful supporters. A first attempt to limit these excesses was to ask Viret to write an answer to the German theologian, but this attempt failed. Sending the text of his first pamphlet to Bullinger, Calvin claimed that he had targeted his personal attacks carefully: "While directing my words against some uncultured men, I certainly made sure to avoid offending anyone whose friendship is valuable to us."[105] Though worded differently, this comment echoes the distinction Calvin made in 1536 in the *Psychopannychia* and confirms that Calvin believed he was preserving clarity of judgment in his polemic.

Bullinger answered with a long series of remarks on the text, filling more than twelve pages in the *Opera Calvini*. Most of his critiques were doctrinal, but the first of these condemned the violence of Calvin's personal attacks.[106] In his answer to the Zurich pastors, Calvin rejoiced in their approval and in the confidence with which they sent him their feedback. He asked them to display the same confidence regarding the rare points at which a small difference still remained between them. He

---

[101]See below 267.
[102]*B.C.1*, no. 54/6.
[103]CO, 15:22, 116, 416.
[104]CO, 15:68.
[105]CO, 15:255; and *B.C.2*, no. 55/6.
[106]CO, 15:272–96, 15:273.

noted, "In the letter, I have corrected the passages where I seemed to write too force-fully against Joachim, and I do not think that anything else is left that may offend you; furthermore, when I called him *nebulo*, I meant something other than what you thought: I did not mean to say that he was a scoundrel or a rogue, but rather, in an old-fashioned sense, that he is a worthless man, or one lost in the fog of falsehood. I also erased the word *bestia*."[107] Calvin included a note to Bullinger in his general let-ter: "We will now print the refutation to Westphal.... If you read the text, you will easily see the effort I have made to turn aside the hatred of those who can still be healed and even to calm their indignation. I noticed that I had treated the man him-self a little more harshly than I had thought."[108]

On the grounds of urgency, Calvin speeded up the printing process and as a result was forced to apologize to his Zurich colleagues.[109] I suspect, however, that the rush to print could also be a pretext to avoid having to put in all the requested corrections. As a matter of fact, Calvin reinserted the more inflammatory passages in his French translation, a rather clear indication of his disagreement with his Zurich friends over the best way to handle opponents such as Westphal.[110]

As he thought about restarting his polemic against Westphal, Calvin discovered what approach to take on the matter when writing to Bullinger: "I am sure that you have read Westphal's book. If I hold to my earlier opinion, I will give a brief and his-torical critique of his follies, so that he cannot complain of having been treated too harshly."[111] Bullinger was pleased to hear of the project: "I am glad that you plan to answer him in a restrained fashion, and to leave the man and his excesses aside."[112] Yet polemic had a firm grip on Calvin. When he sent his text to Bullinger, he con-fessed, "I seem to have been a bit more violent than I wanted to be. I do not know how it happened while I was writing."[113] This tone was inadvertent and he did not know how it happened!

Calvin wrote a third critique of the Hamburg pastor. This time, Farel advised restraint. "I do not know whether you should attack Westphal again. I would urge you to avoid making personal attacks. To struggle with someone so insane is beneath you and those who are offended that you are targeting a person are right."[114] Calvin was more honest with his old colleague. He intended to continue his pamphlets in the same style as the first ones. "It will be difficult for me to follow your advice and restrain myself against Westphal and the others. You call them brothers, these men that not only reject the fraternal name we offer to them, but who loathe it.... And

[107]CO, 15:304–7.
[108]CO, 15:358–59.
[109]CO, 15:375–76.
[110]*B.C.2*, no. 55/2.
[111]CO, 15:835; and *B.C.2*, no. 56/4.
[112]CO, 15:854.
[113]CO, 16:11.
[114]CO, 16:512; and *B.C.2*, no. 57/11.

even though it would not be difficult to follow you and the others in your suggested path, my approach has been a different one."[115]

His polemic against Castellio also raised concerns. Wolfgang Musculus did not approve of the first pamphlet, explaining to Ambrosius Blaurer that he did not even want to believe that Calvin wrote the work. "I have read the work published under Calvin's name against an adversary of divine predestination. I am amazed that the title promises a response by Calvin, since the work is not his, but someone else's. Finally I would hope for some milder terms than rascal, hound, and barking dog. Indeed among those who teach Christ's Gospel today, there are more than one who think along the same lines as this barking dog."[116]

Bullinger continued to uphold his viewpoint, as seen in his reaction to Hesshusen's attacks: "I am also sending you Hesshusen's book. If a response is absolutely necessary, deal with this matter in a spirit of gentleness and filled with candor."[117] In spite of these friendly warnings, Calvin remained unrepentant.

However, we should not end on this negative note, for the Reformer's attitude was more complex and paradoxical than it seems. We will leave aside the fact that his view of polemic was shared by many on his side. Alongside the concerns highlighted above, we could also emphasize the praise that Calvin's correspondents had for his work. Even Bullinger, who was so often critical of his overly personal attacks, continued to rely systematically on his friend's pen.

The paradox lies in Calvin's own conception of what it meant to be a polemicist. His acute sense of the inalienable rights of truth and of his mission as a Reformer were in conflict with his passionate temperament, clearly suited to polemic. In the early stages of his career, in his *Psychopannychia,* he claimed that his mind was averse to all contention and debates. He stated that he wanted to proceed quietly, "without any malice, without attacking individuals, and without seeking to lampoon or slander."[118] For many years, he avoided making overly personal attacks, but he did not always control his fondness for satire. His answer to Albert Pighius in 1543 was rather direct. He rushed to publish a first critique of the German theologian "to bring him down a little."[119]

From 1552 onwards, Calvin made an increasing use of personal attacks and streams of insults. It is somewhat surprising, therefore, to find the following statement in his farewell speech to the Genevan pastors: "I never wrote anything motivated by hatred of another but have always faithfully stated what I thought was for the glory of God."[120] This statement can only be understood if one believes that some opponents are so stubborn in their refusal of the truth that they deserve the

[115]CO, 16:552.
[116]CO, 17:30; and *B.C.2,* no. 58/1.
[117]CO, 18:224; and *B.C.2,* no. 61/11.
[118]CO, 5:173–74; and *Recueil,* 2.
[119]CO, 6:404; and *Recueil,* 438.
[120]CO, 9:893.

harshest criticism. A similar contradiction appeared in his polemic against Westphal. In a letter to German correspondents, Calvin claimed that his first work on the subject was designed to calm controversies.[121] In contrast, when sending his *Ultima Responsio* to Bullinger, he indicated, "as I know that everyone will hate me, I will be greatly comforted to know that you liked my work."[122] Hence he lived within the contradictions of the Gospel, which brings both peace and the sword.

Following all these fiery words, Calvin ought not to have been surprised when his adversaries replied in kind. Yet he reacted to criticism by portraying himself as an innocent victim. In his preface to the lectures on Hosea, he noted that in spite of the care with which he wrote, "I still cannot avoid being slandered by a mass of malicious and envious people...."[123] And in his preface to the 1559 *Institutes,* he wrote, "I doubt that there is any man on earth as attacked, savaged, and disparaged by false calumnies" as he was.[124] For Calvin never doubted the rightness of his cause. In his most polemical dedication, introducing one of the pamphlets against Westphal, he began abruptly, "My conscience is clear that the cause that I have set out to defend in this book is right and just and that I have defended it faithfully...." His opponents had therefore been warned. Later on, he moderated his tone to return to his original outlook: "because it is not enough for me to have this inward sense, unless what I have worked on so carefully is also approved by all of God's faithful, it seemed to me, dear and honored brothers, that it would be best if I started by taking you as my witnesses, that I was almost forced to publish this work. My fear was that if I kept quiet and concealed my views, I would be abandoning and betraying the truth of Christ when there are some insane men who do almost worse things than did the papists in their barbarity."[125] When Calvin turned in this fashion to external witnesses to prove his mission, he simply repeated that his task was imposed on him by his desire not to betray the truth.

Hesitations and Refusals

Calvin did not automatically answer all requests for him to intervene in controversies. He responded as follows to one of Westphal's pamphlets that targeted him: "Westphal has written a dreadful book against me. I do not know whether I should respond, though certain friends are asking me to. Once I have read the book, the Lord will advise me."[126] At times, his friends' insistence was enough to overcome his unwillingness. Explaining to Bullinger why he took up the pen once more against the Polish anti-Trinitarians in 1563, Calvin wrote, "Although I had decided to leave

---

[121]CO, 15:478, 502.
[122]CO, 16:565.
[123]See *B.C.2,* no. 57/3.
[124]Calvin, *Institution,* ed. Benoît, 1:23.
[125]CO, 9:45–50; and *Recueil,* 1498.
[126]CO, 15:812–13.

the Polish illnesses aside for the moment, your insistence led me to condemn this impious error that fascinates our brethren."[127]

However, Calvin did not like repeating himself. In a letter dated 1560 to the church of Corbigny, Calvin refused to write once again against the Libertines. "I intend to avoid delving deeper into this matter. After all, you have the treatise I wrote against them. It can serve as your shield to repel any such assaults."[128] Even that treatise was only written after much hesitation, in response to a request from Tournai. Beginning in 1544, Calvin warned of the danger of the sect and announced that he would write a tract against them "if I have the opportunity." But he delayed the fulfillment of this promise for a year. However, when Antoine Pocquet, one of the leaders of the sect, was received at the court of Marguerite de Navarre, Calvin's reservations crumbled. As we have seen, he had waited an entire year "to see whether silence would be effective against this disease."[129]

The *De aeterna Dei praedestinatione* targeted three opponents: Albert Pighius, Giorgio Siculo, and Jerome Bolsec.[130] Calvin's refutation of Pighius was completed in part in 1543, and his project for a second work on the same subject was abandoned following the death of the Catholic theologian. When Italian friends asked Calvin to counter Siculo, Calvin was unconvinced. "I have not done so, because it would be an endless process if each of these dogs has to be chased off by a specific book. It would therefore be much better if we decided it was not worth responding to many of them. If I find the time, I will do what I promised to eight years ago. Thus while answering Pighius, I will also silence the barking of the others."[131] In fact, the conflict with Bolsec pushed other matters aside.

Antoine Pocquet was one of those who Calvin felt was not worth responding to. In 1548, an infrequent correspondent sent Calvin various writings by Pocquet to have them refuted. Even though the correspondent pointed out that "this vainglorious man takes pride in attacking you and does you great harm,"[132] Calvin did not write any reply.

In the same year, Viret sent Calvin an anonymous letter that he had received, identifying its author as Michael Servetus. Calvin said to Viret that he was tired of answering Servetus: "Finally, I do not want to continue struggling with this desperately obstinate heretic."[133]

In 1551, Calvin's link to Melanchthon went via Strasbourg and Francisco de Enzinas, who sent to Calvin a letter from Melanchthon, together with a pamphlet by Andreas Osiander. "In this letter, you will see that this violent and arrogant man who

[127]CO, 19:640; and 606–7. The work in question is described in *B.C.2*, no. 63/4.

[128]CO, 20:510. On Corbigny, see Theodore Beza, *Histoire ecclésiastique des Eglises réformées au royaume de France* 1, ed. G. Baum and E. Cunitz (Nieuwkoop: B. de Graaf, 1974), 64, 749.

[129]CO, 12:66; and *B.C.1*, no. 45/4.

[130]*B.C.1*, no. 52/4.

[131]CO, 14:165; and *B.C.1*, no. 52/4.

[132]CO, 13:28.

[133]CO, 13:33–34, 42.

loves controversies is not only destroying the doctrine of the church, but also attacks all the pious and wise men who are well-thought-of in the church. Philip hopes, as you will see, that someone can be found not only to condemn his [Osiander's] folly but also to deflate his excessive arrogance. And as he knows your agility of mind and your doctrine, he considers you among the main people affected by this matter, as much as he is."[134] This request, which did not elicit anything further, is important in showing Melanchthon's respect for Calvin's polemical skills.

A few months later, it was Bullinger's turn to show signs of irritation. On many occasions, he had told Calvin about the *De divinis apostolicis atque ecclesiasticis traditionibus* by the Spanish theologian Martin Perez de Ayala, published in Paris in 1549. "I told you that it would be very helpful if you answered him. Why have you not mentioned this matter in your letters?"[135] Calvin continued to avoid the subject and there are no further traces of Perez de Ayala in the correspondence between Zurich and Geneva.

Since Calvin had so effectively attacked the first sessions of the Council of Trent in 1547, Haller hoped that a new publication of the Acts of Trent, the *Generale Consilium Tridentinum,* would elicit a response from him, but Calvin did not react to the idea.[136]

Based in Augsburg, Matthias Schenck kept Calvin informed of all Hesshusen's writings on the Real Presence, and in June 1561 sent him a sermon by Johannes Karg—known as Parsimonius in Latin—on the same subject. Schenck believed that the work had been written by Brenz himself. Calvin felt it unnecessary to respond.[137]

When Bullinger asked Calvin to write against Brenz in 1563, Calvin refused, mainly on the grounds of lack of time and his worsening health. But he promised that if time allowed and his health improved, "I will try to do something. Brenz's hallucinations can be refuted in few words."[138] However, Bullinger reiterated his request especially because of the publication of a French version of the *Catéchisme amplement déclaré avec bonne et utile exposition* by Brenz, printed in Tübingen in 1563. Bullinger also put pressure on Beza regarding this matter.[139]

These examples show that Calvin at times resisted the lure of polemic. To conclude, Calvin's final words in his refutation of Antoine Cathelan sum up his position with a flourish: "If that dandy continues to chatter impudently, I could easily leave him aside with other beasts worth a hundred times more than him. It is not my task to silence all the barking dogs of the world."[140] The decision to be silent could also

---

[134]CO, 14:76.

[135]CO, 14:155.

[136]CO, 14:276. For information on the Venice edition of 1552, see H. M. Adams, *Catalogue of Books Printed on the Continent of Europe, 1501–1600 in Cambridge Libraries* (London: Cambridge University Press, 1967), 1:320, no. C 2790.

[137]CO, 18:525. See also J. A. Wagenmann, "Karg, Johannes," in *Allgemeine Deutsche Biographie,* 15:120–21 (Berlin: Duncker & Humblot, 2003). On Karg's work, see *VD* 16, no. K 119.

[138]CO, 19:602–3.

[139]CO, 20:27; Beza, *Correspondance,* 4:158, 196; and *VD* 16, no. B 7575.

[140]CO, 9:136.

take into account the other urgent work to be done and the long-term impact of the debates.

Calvin the "Compromiser"

This paragraph heading uses a word that Calvin employed as an insult to attack the attempts of men like François Bauduin and George Cassander at conciliation between Catholics and Protestants. I am using the term in a somewhat ironic sense, to highlight the fact that Calvin too tried to calm certain controversies among Protestants.[141]

Calvin was deeply affected by the debates about the Lord's Supper. In 1533, he encountered a Protestant church that was already deeply divided, something that shocked him and even made him hesitate to follow the Gospel.[142] Yet Calvin rapidly sought to reconcile opposing viewpoints while giving preference to Luther's position. In the 1536 *Institutes,* he expressed sadness over the "horrible dissensions" that caused divisions among Protestants.[143] Calvin rejected Zwingli's memorialist stance and followed Luther's views to a large extent, while still refusing to accept the Lutheran doctrine of the ubiquity of Christ's risen body.[144] In his *Petit traicté de la Cène,* published in 1541, Calvin criticized both sides, and not only for doctrinal reasons: "Both sides have erred by lacking the patience to listen to each other, so as to follow the truth without partisanship, wherever it shall be found." These failings should not lead them "to forget God's gifts to them, and the benefits provided to us by God through them." Until the time that the dispute would be fully resolved, "we should be satisfied with fraternity and communion among the churches."[145]

In 1539, concerned that the reservations expressed in the *Institutes* could be taken as a critique of Luther and his supporters, Calvin considered adding a justification at the start of his commentary on Romans. There he explained that he had not wanted to stir up controversy on the subject, for he hated strife. Calvin affirmed his agreement with the Formula of Concord, signed in Wittenberg in 1536. He concluded by solemnly promising to foster as much agreement as possible with the German churches.[146]

When controversy later resurfaced between Zurich and Wittenberg, Calvin attempted to pour oil on troubled waters. After having acknowledged Luther's intemperate approach, Calvin wrote to Bullinger as follows in 1544: "At this point, I hardly dare to ask you to keep quiet.... But I would like you to consider this: first, what sort of a man Luther is, what talents he displays, and what courage, perseverance, skill,

---

[141]Given that the following chapter deals with Calvin's relations with Luther and Zwingli (168–70), I will only provide key information at this point.

[142]J. Calvin, *Des Scandales,* ed. O. Fatio (Geneva: Droz, 1984), 168.

[143]CO, 1:120.

[144]Ganoczy, *Le jeune Calvin,* 148.

[145]CO, 9:457–60.

[146]Herminjard, *Correspondance,* 6:132–37.

and doctrinal force he has used to end the reign of the Antichrist and spread the doctrine of salvation." Later in the letter, Calvin noted that Luther's "major vices" were encouraged by the undue flattery of his entourage.[147]

The best example of Calvin's respectful yet critical attitude toward the German theologians is his 1546 preface to Melanchthon's *Somme de théologie*. After brief praise for the author "renowned for his excellent learning," Calvin introduced the work to French readers: "It contains a brief summary of the things a Christian should know to find the path of salvation." Calvin provided a few details on the book's topics and concluded, "all this is contained in the present book and presented in such a way that young and old may gain sound teaching and benefit from it." Calvin did add the following caveat: "assuming that they approach it with a genuine aim to profit from it." This statement allowed Calvin to express some reservations, noting that the author "has not wanted to engage in artful disputations.... He has avoided taking certain matters to their conclusion." Calvin then stated his concerns regarding Melanchthon's treatment of the freedom of the will, predestination, and the presentation of absolution as a sacrament.

Calvin kindly allowed for a number of inaccuracies in Melanchthon's text because he wished to avoid peripheral details. Indeed, Calvin even praised this approach: "having only edification in mind. This is certainly the approach and the way that we should all follow, except if our adversaries force us to change tack due to their complaints." Calvin's critique of polemic is somewhat comical given his own propensity for the genre.

In his preface, Calvin also explained how to read a work containing some theological inaccuracies. "If readers are as restrained in judging the book as the author was in writing it, all will be well.... But the problem is that today, most people reading any book are not looking for instruction but for a target to attack."[148] He expanded his thought by condemning those who rejected a book because of one sentence, when the same book also contained a thousand good sentences. Furthermore, "the most ignorant readers are the most brazen at it."

On several occasions, Calvin explained his conciliation attempts between Luther and Zwingli by noting that the division among Protestants was a scandal that risked turning good Christians away from the Truth. Calvin insisted on this matter particularly in *Des Scandales*.[149] Thus, he accepted a compromise with Bullinger in spite of his earlier reservations about Zwingli. After 1548, when Melanchthon was under attack from Matthias Flacius Illyricus, Calvin attempted to get closer to Melanchthon and have him announce their theological agreement on the Lord's Supper. In public, Calvin carefully avoided referring to any divergence of opinion, though he never hesitated to indicate his viewpoint clearly to Melanchthon himself.

---

[147]Herminjard, *Correspondance,* 9:374; and CO, 11:774.
[148]CO, 9:847–50.
[149]Calvin, *Des Scandales,* 167–75.

In terms of the doctrine of the Lord's Supper, Calvin did not reject the Wittenberg Concord and accepted the Augsburg Confession, having signed his agreement to it at the Regensburg Colloquy. He never repudiated this agreement and, in fact, evidence exists for his continuing support for the Augsburg Confession throughout his lifetime.[150]

Calvin's ongoing conciliation efforts with Luther and Melanchthon on the one hand and Zwingli and Bullinger on the other testify to his intent to salvage Protestant unity. One may well ask, therefore, why he attacked Westphal and the Saxon theologians so ferociously.

The targets of Calvin's polemical attacks naturally included Catholics as well as opponents who were universally considered a threat, such as Anabaptists and Spiritualists. Calvin also targeted the Nicodemites, whom he considered as a particularly serious danger for Protestantism. In the case of Westphal, who was a member of a large Protestant church, Calvin abandoned his policy of conciliation within Protestantism. Calvin's comment quoted above, where he refused to consider his adversary as a brother, undoubtedly provides the key to Calvin's reversal: the gnesio-Lutherans were no longer brothers. Calvin was probably affected by the traumatic experience of the Flemish refugees who fled London. Having been forced out of England after the accession of Mary Tudor, they had been turned away from Denmark when they refused to sign the Augsburg Confession. Their reception in other German cities was equally cold, if not openly hostile.[151]

An isolated remark on Calvin's part regarding one of the replies to Westphal shows how strong an impact the Danish attitude had on Calvin: "While there is nothing as idiotic as the libel written by that good man Westphal, we see however that the minds of princes can be corrupted by such slander—a recent example comes from the king of Denmark—and therefore it appears to be our duty to confront this by any means possible."[152]

Thus, it seems to me that this unhappy experience convinced Calvin that Westphal and his friends no longer deserved the same treatment as the Protestant "brethren," but that they had broken the bond all by themselves. Hence Calvin could live in peace with fellow Protestants, even if they did not fully share his ideas. However, once a break had occurred, Calvin saw it as his duty to expose opponents before the entire world.

Looking for a Talented Polemicist

My earlier description of Calvin as a polemicist-for-hire refers to the fact that on many occasions, other Reformers, Pierre Viret in particular, were asked to write

---

[150]Doumergue, *Jean Calvin,* 581–82; and Wendel, *Calvin,* 98–99.

[151]Ph. Denis, "Jean Laski et le retour au papisme" in *Les Églises et leurs institutions au XVIe siècle: Actes du Ve colloque du Centre d'Histoire de la Réforme et du Protestantisme* (Montpellier: Université Paul Valéry, [1978]), 5–6. See also Denis, *Les Eglises.*

[152]CO, 15:124–25.

pamphlets. However, requests often swung back to Calvin, who was more concise, faster, and more efficient. Such was the case for the articles of the Sorbonne in 1543. Calvin wrote to Viret, "I heard that you were thinking of writing against the articles of the Sorbonne, something that I would highly encourage.... I would therefore prefer it if you do it.... I have received requests from some people. If you are willing, you can take this task from me."[153] But in the end, Calvin wrote the reply.

Calvin was not always quick to entrust work to Pierre Viret, mainly for stylistic reasons. This reluctance surfaced in spite of Viret's effective role in polemic, especially against Catholicism. For instance, in 1546, Calvin quickly decided against asking Viret to write the apology of Jacques de Bourgogne, because Viret was too verbose.[154]

In contrast, Calvin found in Theodore Beza his ideal polemicist. Already by 1549, in his brief *Zographia,* Beza defended Calvin against the attacks of Cochlaeus over the *Interim.*[155] Calvin's positive response to Beza's abilities appears in relation to a later pamphlet, the *Epistola Magistri Benedicti Passavantii* of 1553 mocking Pierre Lizet, a member of the Paris Parlement and the author of two large volumes against Calvin and his followers.[156] In 1554, Calvin announced to Blaurer that he was sending him a few books: "I have added Beza's satire, a letter written under the name Passavent. It will make you laugh, I hope."[157] Many of Calvin's controversies were continued by Beza, whether against Westphal and the Lutheran theologians, against François Bauduin,[158] or against Valentino Gentile. In 1561, when Zanchi was looking for a polemical response against Hesshusen, he spontaneously linked the names of Calvin and Beza. Zanchi sent Hesshusen's work to Calvin: "we ask that you or Beza deal with this draft rapidly and according to its merits."[159] Both men complied.

Calvin seemed secretly pleased when he sent Bullinger his own pamphlet together with Beza's satirical dialogues. "Have a look at the refutation of Hesshusen when you have a chance. Beza is adding another one. You will say that the mockery in my text is like a gentle pat when you see Beza's response."[160] Calvin's remark is all the more significant when one recalls that Bullinger constantly criticized Calvin for excessive aggression.

---

[153]Herminjard, *Correspondance,* 9:184; CO, 11:687; and *B.C.1,* no. 44/6.
[154]CO, 12:321; and *B.C.1,* no. 47/1.
[155]This material appears in Beza, *Correspondance,* 1:49–55. The work in question is a reply to J. Cochlaeus, *De Interim Brevis Responsio* (Mainz: Behem, 1549). See also Beza, *Correspondance,* 1:53 n. 6.
[156]CO, 15:25. On the *Epistola,* see F. Gardy, *Bibliographie des oeuvres théologiques, littéraires, historiques et juridiques de Théodore de Bèze* (Geneva: Droz, 1960), nos. 62–72; for instance, Lizet's *Adversum pseudo-evangelicam haeresim libri novem* (Paris: Vascosan, 1551) is held in the British Library (4061.g.17).
[157]CO, 15:25.
[158]Beza, *Correspondance,* 3:247; and *B.C.2,* no. 62/27.
[159]CO, 18:348; and *B.C.2,* no. 61/11.
[160]CO, 18:350.

However, there were stylistic differences between Beza and his mentor. Beza enjoyed writing satire while Calvin avoided the genre, preferring to sprinkle his text with rapid comments, without creating systematic portrayals of his opponents. In 1544, in his preface to Viret's *Disputations chrestiennes,* Calvin explained his view on entertaining books and on humor. He unhesitatingly condemned "vain and frivolous books," but he praised authors who "through humor" provided solid teaching. However, he was careful to specify what topics could be the subject of humorous discussions. While religious abuses could be mocked, when speaking of the truth and especially about God, "we should never adopt a humorous stance."[161] Dealing with serious subjects through satire was a common strategy among the Reformers who provided works to the presses of Pierre de Vingle in Neuchâtel around 1535. Other authors pursued the same approach in Geneva, including Pierre Viret, Conrad Badius, with his *Satyres de la cuisine papale,* and especially Theodore Beza. In contrast, Calvin's polemic was more somber in tone, making more direct attacks on the main errors of his opponents.[162]

Support and Critiques from Calvin's Circle

The Encouragement of Other Reformers

Like any normally constituted person, Calvin was sensitive to the reactions of his readers. In 1547, Farel reacted enthusiastically to the *Acta synodi tridentinae.* Calvin answered him frankly, "I am starting to like my *Antidotum* ever since you told me you approved of it so strongly. Before that, I was not really satisfied with it."[163] In 1552, he welcomed the compliments of a German correspondent who praised the impact of his books. "This blessing from God fills me with much courage. In this terribly evil century, there are still pious and scholarly men who not only benefit personally from my commentaries, but who also faithfully ensure that they spread more widely the benefit they have received, almost from hand to hand, as one might say."[164]

Calvin did put on some author's airs within his circle of friends. We have already noted his half-serious, half-joking comments when he sent the first edition of his exegetical lectures to Bullinger. His air of indifference was intended to keep criticism at bay.[165] When he sent a work in 1555 to his former teacher Melchior Wolmar—probably his harmony of the Gospels—Calvin left Wolmar free to react as he pleased. "Here is a new book for you, on the condition that you should reject it entirely if it displeases you at first glance."[166]

---

[161]CO, 9:863–66.
[162]Millet, "Calvin pamphlétaire," 20–21.
[163]CO, 12:642, 634–35.
[164]CO, 15:214–15.
[165]See above 56.
[166]CO, 15:643.

On several occasions, when debates grew to international proportions, Calvin looked for support from other pastors to underpin his own positions. The clearest instance of this was the case of his anti-Nicodemite tracts. Many of Calvin's correspondents who lived in areas controlled by Catholic powers intensely disliked Calvin's extremely harsh viewpoint. Antoine Fumée was particularly clear on this point.[167] In January 1545, he asked Calvin to have the German theologians ratify the Genevan perspective and was even willing to pay the costs of sending them the tracts.[168] Calvin reluctantly agreed, largely because he wanted to prevent a similar appeal by some of his friends in France.[169] In January 1545, Calvin sent Claude de Senarclens to the German lands with letters for Luther and Melanchthon, as well as Latin translations of the *Petit Traicté* and the *Excuse*. Calvin had asked Melanchthon to decide whether or not to transmit his letter to Luther. In the end, Melanchthon decided against it in order to avoid unnecessary upset. He explained this to Calvin in a letter dated 17 April, in which he included his own response.[170] On his way back from Wittenberg, Claude de Senarclens came through Strasbourg and submitted Calvin's question and Melanchthon's answer to Bucer and Vermigli.[171] These various letters of support appeared in later editions of the book.[172]

The *Consensus Tigurinus,* jointly signed by Calvin and the Zurich pastors, was naturally prefaced by two letters, one by Calvin to the Zurich clergy, and one by the clergy in response.[173] When Calvin defended the consensus against Westphal he received Bullinger's support. Indeed, Bullinger had the work reprinted in Zurich, adding a postscript of his own.[174]

The pamphlet on predestination, originally written in response to the Bolsec affair, was preceded by a dedicatory letter signed by all the Genevan pastors, a fact underlined in the title of the Latin edition: "Agreement of the Genevan Pastors presented by J. Calvin."[175] Two years later, the book that attacked Servetus and justified his death sentence included at the end a list of "the ministers and pastors of the church of Geneva who approved this book and endorsed it."[176]

In his final years, Calvin varied his tactics and chose to build up dossiers against his opponents. In the case of Valentino Gentile, after Calvin's refutation of forty theses by the anti-Trinitarian, he included several documents from Gentile's Genevan trial. As for François Bauduin, Calvin brought together critiques written by various

---

[167]Herminjard, *Correspondance,* 9:126–27; and CO, 11:646.

[168]Herminjard, *Correspondance,* 9:444–48; and CO, 11:826–30.

[169]CO, 12:27, 32.

[170]CO, 12:6–12, 25–26, 61–62, 100, 256 (a letter dated 1545).

[171]CO, 12:72. On Senarclens's mission, see E. Boehmer, *Spanish Reformers of Two Centuries from 1520. Their Lives and Writings* (Strasbourg, 1874; reprint, New York: B. Franklin, [1962]): 1:204–5.

[172]*B.C.1,* no. 45/9.

[173]See above 5–8.

[174]*B.C.2,* no. 55/7.

[175]*B.C.1,* no. 52/4.

[176]*B.C.1,* nos. 54/5, 54/6.

authors as well as older documents, including letters from Bauduin to Calvin. The Genevan Reformer began the work with his own response to Bauduin's criticisms.[177]

Advice and Constructive Criticism

Given that Calvin claimed his published works were often done at the request of friends, one should conclude that these friends knew of the works in some form or another before they were printed. However, the manuscript circulation of Calvin's works has left very few traces.

One exception was Calvin's first religious work, his *Psychopannychia*, written in 1534 and published in 1542. Capito read it in 1535 and even suggested to Calvin to give it "another form."[178] Robert Olivétan, who also had access to the first version, passed it on to Christophe Fabri.[179] In all likelihood, Bucer saw the revised version. He dissuaded Calvin from publishing it in 1535, only to change his mind in 1538.[180] This example shows that Calvin was still a diffident author, quick to follow the suggestions of his more famous elders.

In response to Luther's concerns, Calvin had considered inserting a justification of his views on the Lord's Supper in the preface to his commentary on the Epistle to the Romans. Following Melanchthon's advice, he omitted the passage[181] though he preserved the text, inserting it into his 1543 *Institutes*.[182]

The ministers of Neuchâtel requested the 1544 *Brieve instruction contre les anabaptistes*. Calvin planned to dedicate the work to them, and sent them the draft of his preface on 25 March.[183] It seems that he did not send them the entire work, since Farel subsequently indicated that he was looking forward to reading it. "…I would very much like to see what you have already written, not to voice criticisms but to rejoice at this good start. I pray to God that the work will expand and happily come to completion. The messenger denies having been given anything, in spite of your statement that you did send something."[184] This last remark may suggest that Calvin intended to submit the whole manuscript but that it went astray. In any event, when Farel sent back the opinion of his colleagues on 21 April, it only dealt with the preface.[185]

Calvin sent his draft pamphlet against Caroli to Viret in July 1545. Viret sent his comments back in a veiled fashion, annoying Calvin because of his cautious

---

[177]*B.C.2,* nos. 61/14, 62/27.

[178]Herminjard, *Correspondance,* 3:243–45; and CO, 10/b:45–46.

[179]Herminjard *Correspondance,* 3:349–50; and CO, 10/b:51–52.

[180]Herminjard, *Correspondance,* 5:132; and CO, 10/b:260.

[181]Bucer's opinion can be found in Herminjard, *Correspondance,* 6:132–37. An echo of Melanchthon's opinion appears on 165.

[182]Calvin, *Institution,* ed. Benoît, vol. 4, ch. 17, sect. 11, 385–86.

[183]Herminjard, *Correspondance,* 9:185; and CO, 11:687.

[184]Herminjard, *Correspondance,* 9:193–94; and CO, 11:692.

[185]Herminjard, *Correspondance,* 9:202–3; and CO, 11:698–99.

approach.[186] Calvin stated bluntly, "I appreciated your comments, but I would have liked them better if you had been more free in criticizing whatever you thought was wrong. In sparing my feelings, you seem to me to be an overly timid or indulgent critic, not that you should have harshly condemned every mistake, but that you show too much respect for me, as if you wanted to sweeten the bitterness of your critique by sugarcoating it with gentle words."[187]

In contrast, the catechism was written so rapidly in 1541 that Calvin had no time to show it to Viret, even though the latter was working alongside Calvin in Geneva at the time. Calvin explained this in his farewell speech to the pastors.[188]

Once again, it was to Farel that Calvin sent the first drafts of his commentary on Genesis. He asked for Farel's opinion, "since the Lord has allowed me to pursue my commentary on Genesis until the end of the third chapter, I have decided to give you a foretaste of the work. First, if the work pleases you, you will receive an early benefit from its fruit. Second, I wish to receive your feedback on this work, in case you think it necessary to alert me to certain issues for the rest of the commentary."[189]

In 1551, Calvin took the opportunity of the dedication letter for his commentary on the canonical Epistles to attack the Council of Trent. Pleased with the result, he sent a copy of the letter to Pier Paolo Vergerio, who then showed it to Bullinger. The dedicatory letter ended up being the only part of the two commentaries that Bullinger saw prior to their publication in early 1551.[190]

Calvin's first refutation of Westphal should have been signed by other Swiss pastors, especially as the work was also a defense of the *Consensio mutua,* the common declaration of the Genevan and Zurich churches on the doctrine of the Lord's Supper. On 6 October 1554, Calvin consulted his colleagues in Zurich.[191] On 25 October, Bullinger sent his comments as well as those of his colleagues and the notes written by Theodore Bibliander. As indicated earlier, these notes and comments were very detailed, though Calvin only partially took them into account.[192]

Calvin also consulted Farel and the Bernese and Basel churches.[193] He criticized Ambrosius Blaurer, the pastor of Biel, for having circulated a draft version too widely.[194] On 27 November 1554, Calvin sent to Farel an amended version of the text, asking him to send a copy to Ambrosius Blaurer. On the same day, he sent a copy to Peter Martyr Vermigli, who was in Strasbourg at the time. Calvin noted that he had not always followed the Zurich clergy's advice, but that he hoped to have

[186]CO, 12:105–6.
[187]CO, 12:107.
[188]O.S., 2:403; and see above 65.
[189]CO, 13:623.
[190]CO, 14:74, 86. See *B.C.1,* nos. 51/5, 51/6.
[191]CO, 15:255.
[192]See above 97–99.
[193]CO, 15:297–98.
[194]CO, 15:315–16.

appeased his colleagues.[195] Finally, the work appeared in early 1555, but without the explicit endorsement of the Swiss churches.[196]

The lengthy critiques sent by the Zurich clergy in response to this first manuscript may explain why Calvin later changed his tactics. While there was full agreement from Zurich that Calvin should take up his pen once more against Westphal, Calvin only sent the work to them after it had been printed. He took the same approach for his third work in the same debate, his 1557 *Ultima admonitio ad J. Westphalum*. Though Bullinger did see the text before it was completely printed, this was due to the fact that on 7 August, Calvin sent him the sheets that had already been printed.[197] "You will be able to assess the skill of my approach against the Saxons. I preferred to send you the incomplete version rather than leave you in suspense."[198] Beza sent Bullinger the last sheets of the *Ultima admonitio* from Lausanne.[199] Thus Calvin tended to send copies of his works to his friends only when the works were in their final form. That way, he no longer had to go back over the text to make changes.

In contrast, Calvin was more willing to show drafts of his work to a faithful disciple like Theodore Beza, to whom he gave his *De aeterna Dei praedestinatione* against Bolsec. In fact, Calvin sent Beza the only manuscript copy of the work. Beza's reaction was both very detailed and critical. Though he referred to the work as a "golden booklet," he still commented on the structure of the text, and asked for a more serene tone, making use of Bullinger's authority.[200] Calvin followed the same procedure for his refutation of a work attributed to Castellio. Beza undoubtedly deserved Calvin's trust, since he was the one to discover the supposed Castellio pamphlet and pass it on to Calvin. In response, Beza sent two pages of comments, suggesting a clearer formulation in one place, an added quotation in another, and a correction in a third.[201]

Calvin's colleagues who were regular visitors to his home in Geneva had easy access to his works while he was writing them. Des Gallars's brief description of the writing process Calvin used when composing his commentary on the Psalms seems to me to be suggestive: "when I saw recently a few things that you had written earlier on the Psalms lying on your chair by the bed, I remembered that you wanted to work on this."[202] This was in 1555. Over time, as his health worsened, Calvin spent more and more time in bed and composed a number of works by dictating them from that location.[203]

---

[195]CO, 15:322–23.
[196]*B.C.2*, no. 55/6.
[197]*B.C.2*, no. 56/4; and Calvin's letter to Bullinger, dated 23 January 1556 (CO, 16:11).
[198]CO, 16:565.
[199]Beza, *Correspondance*, 2:81–82, 85; and *B.C.2*, no. 57/11.
[200]CO, 14:254–55; Beza, *Correspondance*, 1:81–82; and RC 46, fol. 138v (21 January 1552).
[201]*B.C.2*, no. 58/1; and Beza, *Correspondance*, 2:168–69.
[202]CO, 15:657.
[203]See below 129–30.

In 1561, when Calvin decided to write a new work against François Bauduin, Beza was in France, attending the Colloquy of Poissy. The two men exchanged a number of letters regarding the pamphlet, but in the end Calvin sent Beza the text for information only, not for his editorial comments. Complaining about the slow pace of printing, Calvin stated, "You will read it in manuscript form.... I am not sending it to you for your advice or opinion, because the time for that is past, but in order that you can decide what to do on the basis of what you have read."[204]

Conclusion

Calvin's motivations for writing thus combined rational reasons and subjective forces. However, the exegetical commentaries were the result of a larger project that dated back at least to 1538, which Calvin pursued systematically depending on the time he had available and his state of health. In contrast, his polemical writings emerged out of specific events, even though certain opponents caused him more concern than others. Furthermore, we should not discount the importance of his sensitivity as he alternated between pleasure and disgust at the thought of writing.

In his role as a polemicist, Calvin knew that he would not be able to change his adversaries' opinions. While he would undoubtedly strengthen his friends, he would irritate his enemies. Yet he continued to write pamphlet after pamphlet. His violent verbal attacks even frightened those of his supporters who saw polemical works as essential. Calvin seemed unable to contain his ferocity when targeting an opponent with his pen. His only concession was to limit his attacks to sworn enemies, avoiding offending "any whose continuing friendship is important."

The irresistible attraction of pamphleteering for Calvin was due to his temperament. Calvin often threw himself into controversies with enthusiasm: he clearly enjoyed it when his polemical attacks hit home. But overall, Calvin felt himself constrained to respond because of his vocation. He was a servant of the Truth and therefore every lie was to be exposed, especially if it risked leading weaker minds astray. These two motivations probably reinforced each other.

Calvin's references to this quasi-prophetic mission led to a few chinks in the intransigent stance he adopted. Even though he proclaimed loudly that he could not keep silent, he admitted that sometimes he let certain matters lie. One would have to carry out a more in-depth analysis of his relations with Bullinger to differentiate between genuine theological convergence and a certain opportunism, born of the general Reformation climate and Calvin's concern for Protestant unity. Calvin may have also genuinely believed his own claims that he fully respected each of his adversaries as a human being.

Calvin did not write in isolation. On the contrary, he was very sensitive to the encouragement and reactions of those around him. He needed to be sustained in his work, even though he had a high sense of calling. His awareness of his "teaching office"

---

[204]Beza, *Correspondance*, 3:249.

was clearly central to his written work. He saw it as his duty to speak the truth, whether in his exegetical teaching or in his polemical writing. He had several audiences in mind: the faithful, to whom he brought guidance and comfort; the weak, who had been misled by the devil and whom he tried to steer to the right path; and the followers of Satan, locked into their errors, for whom no insult was sufficiently harsh.

Although Calvin was very confident about the quality of his work, he had no hesitation in submitting it to friends prior to publication. As a young author, he followed this course with the *Psychopannychia*. Later on, he pursued this strategy when he had time, especially with close colleagues like Viret and Beza. Calvin disliked his experiment of working with Bullinger on the first refutation against Westphal and thus stopped sending his manuscripts to the Zurich clergy prior to publication, without damaging relations between the two cities.

2. Selecting a Language

Calvin's choice of language is important in establishing his attitude toward written works: his preference provides indications as to the intended audience of his writings.

Calvin wrote and published works during an era of linguistic change. The status of French improved, and it became more widely used in new areas. In 1539, the edict of Villers-Cotterêts made French the official language of administration in the kingdom of Francis I. In 1530, the entire Bible was translated into French for the first time. Early on, Protestants wrote their theological pamphlets in French—not as easy a matter as it may seem at first glance. As Olivétan stated in his 1535 edition of the Bible, "… It is as difficult to render Hebrew and Greek eloquence into French (a barbarous language in their eyes) as to teach the gentle lark to sing the song of the raucous crow."[205] This situation rapidly changed. When Robert Estienne settled in Geneva in 1550, even though he pursued his research on the text of scripture, he made one important change: for the first time, he began to take an interest in the French version. In his Latin-French New Testament printed in 1551, he stated explicitly, "there is no doubt that French is better than Latin at expressing and more closely representing both Greek and Hebrew."[206] Estienne's optimism was probably not shared by all, but these two quotations only fifteen years apart show how matters had altered. Not only were people more amenable to the idea of using French, but the language itself had also evolved.

Indeed, Calvin played a role in this evolution. As Francis Higman noted, Calvin's first French version of the *Institutes* of 1541 did not follow the rules of the day. In some senses, the work was "eccentric." Twenty years later, the translation of

---

[205] *Bible*, trans. Olivétan (Neuchâtel: Pierre de Wingle, 1535), fol. *4r.
[206] *Nouveau Testament* (Geneva: J. Gerard, 1551), fol. *2r; for the shift in opinions on this matter, see the contributions in the volume edited by Claude Longeon, *Premiers combats pour la langue française* (Paris: Librairie Générale Française, 1989).

the definitive version of the same work was no longer outside the norms. In between times, the literary use of French had evolved, in part thanks to the influence of Calvin himself.[207]

Calvin's Mastery of Latin and French

Since Calvin's education took place in the 1520s and 1530s, he was naturally taught in Latin. Thus he wrote Latin spontaneously, as seen in his personal correspondence with other French speakers such as Farel and Viret, with whom Calvin preferred to use Latin exclusively, even for the most trivial details of day-to-day life. Calvin's practice was to conduct all his correspondence in Latin unless the recipient did not really know the language. Hence Calvin inquired of Jacques de Bourgogne about what language to use in writing to de Bourgogne's brother.[208] At times, practical considerations forced Calvin to use French, as he explained to Viret in 1541. Referring to a letter that is now lost, Calvin noted, "I wrote to you via Fortuné [André] in French, in part because I was dealing with an issue such that the letter would need to be passed on to people who know no Latin, and in part because I was dictating the letter from my bed, and had no secretary available who knew anything other than French."[209]

Around 1539, Calvin wrote his *Petit traicté de la Cène* directly in French for the first time. After it was translated into Latin, Calvin sent it to Veit Dietrich with the following revealing comments: "I am accustomed to writing more carefully for those who understand Latin. However I made sure not only to express faithfully what I thought and write a brief account of the matter, but also to explain it clearly and straightforwardly." He continued by saying that in the *Institutes,* "I present and confirm the same doctrine more firmly by expressing myself in another way, and to my mind, more clearly."[210] Calvin openly acknowledged that switching to French meant adapting the message and losing some clarity in the process.

The Readership for Latin Books

The use of Latin in Calvin's edition of *De clementia* was natural because the author's work was directed at a scholarly audience. Indeed, Calvin rejected the critiques of the uninitiated, stating that he was only looking for the favor of "those who have penetrated the secrets of law."[211]

In contrast, when he began to defend the Gospel, Calvin sought a wider audience, at least according to his own statements. In 1534, speaking of the *Psychopanny-chia,* Calvin said, "I hope that my work will be very useful to the simplest and least-

---

[207]F. M. Higman, "Calvin and the Art of Translation" in *Western Canadian Studies in Modern Languages and Literature* 2 (1970): 7, 26. See Millet, *Calvin et la dynamique,* 763–870.
[208]CO, 12:627, 636.
[209]Herminjard, *Correspondance,* 7:183; and CO, 11:253.
[210]CO, 12:316.
[211]CO, 9:785–86.

educated people, and may also be of some use to those who are moderately learned."[212] At this point, however, he wrote his work in Latin. It was not translated into French until 1558, in spite of several requests by Farel. How were the "simplest people" to gain access to this refutation? Calvin seems to have had little interest in the matter.

The same question should hold true for the *Institutes,* since the primary goal of the work was to teach "some basics" to his compatriots who "hungered and thirsted for Jesus Christ." It is true that using Latin allowed Calvin to have his defense of French evangelicals read in the Holy Roman Empire. In these early years, despite his statements to the contrary, Calvin restricted his audience to the learned, though this approach may have been less the result of conscious choice than of the weight of his humanist training. Erasmus himself used only Latin in his statements about the need to translate the scriptures into the vernacular.[213]

From 1535 onwards, Calvin made increasing use of French in his printed works. Already in 1536, he worked on a French version of the *Institutes.* Over time, he reworked the text both in French and in Latin. However, Latin remained his preferred language, especially for corrections and additions to the *Institutes,* for exegetical commentaries, and for polemical works aimed primarily at German theologians.

A rather surprising statement from Calvin confirms his preference for Latin. In his introduction to the Psalms commentary, he described a project "which I have long considered, namely, to write something on the subject in French, so that people of our nation would not be completely deprived of help." But force of habit was stronger and once he had decided to start the work, he used Latin. "When I started to work on it, suddenly, contrary to my earlier intention, I somehow began to think of writing out in Latin, in draft form, the exegesis of a Psalm."[214] In short, though he planned to write in French, when he sat in front of a blank sheet of paper Latin "somehow" came to the fore.

Calvin's interest in bringing his works to the notice of international public opinion meant that the Reformer himself translated or had someone else translate his French writings into Latin. His concern over possible adverse reactions led Calvin to delay publishing the translation of his *Petit traicté de la Cène* until he had consulted with Farel on the appropriateness of the move, as it was important to consider the impact of the Latin publication of a text known in French for the past four years.[215] As Nicolas des Gallars noted, the *Traicté de la Cène,* which had been intended for the ignorant and unlearned, had proven useful even for scholarly audiences. Thus the Latin translation was intended both for educated readers and for those who knew no French.[216] Des Gallars highlighted the same themes in his translations of works

[212]CO, 5:169–70; and *Recueil,* 2.
[213]See below 282.
[214]CO, 31:14, 16.
[215]CO, 11:804.
[216]CO, 5:LI–LII.

against the Anabaptists and the *Traité des reliques.*[217] François Hotman too spoke of bringing the *Advertissement contre l'astrologie judiciaire* to the attention of "all those for whom our language is foreign."[218] Calvin's works against the Nicodemites also provide evidence of the need to translate works into Latin to have them understood by audiences in the German lands. Following pressing requests from a number of French readers to obtain the reactions of Luther, Melanchthon, and Bucer to the works, Calvin translated his two tracts into Latin and sent them to his three colleagues.[219] Claude Baduel followed the same approach after translating Calvin's *Quatre Sermons* at the Reformer's explicit request.[220]

In a letter dated 3 September 1546, Farel indicated his interest in seeing Calvin's written work reach a large audience, thanks to translations in Latin and in French. Farel congratulated his Genevan colleague on the Latin publication of his tracts against the Anabaptists and the Libertines, adding: "The same should be done for the book censorship done by those useless Paris theologians, and for other things that you have published in French."[221] Latin became vital when Calvin wanted to make the rest of Europe understand the doctrine that he had been teaching French speakers.

The Language of the "Ignorant and Uneducated"

From 1535 onwards, Calvin increasingly wrote in French. His first work published in the vernacular had a largely symbolic value. The text in question was a short preface that he wrote for the New Testament in the Olivétan Bible. However, Calvin retained some of his humanist training, as he also contributed a fictitious privilege for the work calling for the right to publish the Bible in the vernacular, but written in Latin![222]

In 1536, Calvin worked on translating his *Institutes* "during every free moment." Because he was so close to completing the work, he delayed sending a letter to François Daniel on several occasions.[223] He admitted as much to Daniel in a letter written in October 1536, when he was becoming aware of the urgency of his pastoral tasks in Geneva. Contact with these concrete issues convinced Calvin of the need to write in French. He began by offering to a popular audience a simple text: the 1537 Catechism, a summary of the *Institutes.* Here too Calvin wrote in Latin first before translating the work into French.[224]

---

[217]*B.C.1,* nos. 46/1, 48/4.

[218]*B.C.1,* no. 49/1.

[219]CO, 11:776–777, 826–30; and 12:7–12, 22, 26–27.

[220]*B.C.1,* no. 53/4; CO, 8:XXVI.

[221]CO, 12:379. See *B.C.1,* nos. 46/1, 44/3; and *B.C.2,* no. 58/7.

[222]B. Roussel, "Un privilège pour la Bible d'Olivétan (1535)? Jean Calvin et la polémique entre Alexander Alesius et Johannes Cochlaeus" in *Le livre et la Réforme,* ed. R. Peter and B. Roussel (Bordeaux: Société des bibliophiles de Guyenne, 1987), 233–61.

[223]Herminjard, *Correspondance,* 4:87–88; and CO, 10/b:62–64.

[224]*B.C.1,* no. 37/2.

In this middle period, Calvin considered starting a project that was never completed: translating Saint John Chrysostom's sermons into French. Calvin did leave a draft of a preface for this project. Olivier Millet suggests that this work was carried out during Calvin's second stay in Basel (April to August 1538), a likely hypothesis. This translation was intended to fill the role played later by the second version of the *Institutes* of 1539 and 1541: "to give access to Holy Scripture to the ignorant and untaught."[225] Calvin's draft preface contained an eloquent plea for the use of vernacular languages. Divine mysteries were to be revealed to all, and not just reserved for priests and monks. Thus while Calvin wished to expand his audience by using French, he also had a liking for Latin, so much so that he wrote his preface in that language.

Calvin's *Petit traicté de la Cène* was his first work written directly in French. While it was only published in 1541, it was undoubtedly written earlier, probably during his stay in Strasbourg or perhaps even prior to that.[226] The *Petit traicté de la Cène* exemplifies Calvin's use of French and Latin. Calvin had already dealt with the topic of the Lord's Supper in his *Institutes,* but he wanted to present his middle way to a wider audience. In a letter to Veit Dietrich dated 1546, he stated "my original intent was made clear in the simple and popular teaching method, adapted for use by the unlearned." Nicolas des Gallars's preface to the Latin version of the work confirms this: the French version was intended for the *illiterati* and was adapted for use by the most uncouth, whereas the Latin version was intended for scholars, the *literati homines.*[227]

In Strasbourg, Calvin made increasing use of French. In 1540, Melanchthon reacted to Charles V's proposal to hold private colloquies by writing a response on behalf of the members of the Schmalkaldic League. A request was made for a French translation of the work, primarily for the emperor, who according to Calvin himself had little knowledge of either Latin or German. Calvin carried out the translation, which was published in 1541.[228] Soon afterwards, still in collaboration with Bucer, Calvin sought to make the work of the Diet of Regensburg better known. While Bucer wrote a report in Latin on the meeting, Calvin provided a French version for his compatriots.[229]

Upon his return to Geneva, Calvin only used French for works that had a large target audience, above all the *Forme des prieres ecclesiastiques,* which served as a liturgical manual, and the *Catechisme.* Calvin also wrote a number of his polemical works

---

[225]CO, 9:831–38, esp. 831–33; and Millet, *Calvin et la dynamique,* 170–76.

[226]*B.C.1,* no. 41/4.

[227]CO, 12:316; and *B.C.1,* no. 45/7.

[228]Herminjard, *Correspondance,* 6:218–19; CO, 11:38–39; and R. Peter, "Calvin traducteur de Melanchthon" in *Horizons européens de la Réforme en Alsace,* ed. M. de Kroon and M. Lienhard (Strasbourg: Istra, 1980), 119–33.

[229]*B.C.1,* no. 41/1.

in French, including his tracts teaching against the Anabaptists, for the "poor faithful who are untaught and illiterate." "We must serve everyone," Calvin reiterated.[230]

The 1542 *Exposition sur l'Epistre de sainct Judas* and the 1543 *Exposition sur l'Epistre aux Romains* may well have been the result of strategies that Calvin subsequently abandoned.[231] When he returned to Geneva, he may have thought that the French-speaking population needed more basic spiritual food than was available in the unabridged Latin commentaries. The *Exposition sur l'Epistre de sainct Judas*—or Jude—was in all likelihood a reworked version of some of the topics Calvin had dealt with from the pulpit. As for the *Exposition sur l'Epistre aux Romains,* it was adapted from the Latin commentary. Rather than translate the whole, Calvin published a simplified version in French. After a few years, Calvin laid aside his policy of providing a scholarly version in Latin and a simplified text in French. From 1547 onward, Calvin published unabridged French translations of his biblical commentaries.

Calvin's preface to Melanchthon's *Loci communes* provides the clearest explanation of his views on the different audiences for Latin and French texts. Calvin declared that there would be no need to introduce the author if the work were written in Latin, for Melanchthon was "renowned among scholars." However "he is not as well-known by those of our nation who have never had much schooling."[232] Clearly, different educational levels separated the two audiences.

Calvin's concern for the "simple and unlearned" is displayed in one of the earliest French translations of his commentaries, on First Corinthians. The anonymous translator justified the work by referring to Calvin's concern for this uneducated audience.[233] The translator of the *Traité des benefices,* the second of the *Epistolae Duae* originally published in Latin in 1537, made the same observation in 1554. "This work was written in Latin in the form of an epistle, by a faithful servant of God and Jesus Christ, a pastor in His church. And because it is very important that even those who know no Latin can grasp the contents of this work, to be clear on what they can and should do regarding benefices, it seemed right to put it in the vernacular."[234]

Farel not only asked Calvin to translate his French works into Latin but also vice versa, especially for the *Psychopannychia* which Farel described in a rather convoluted manner as follows: "We need a French translation of your forceful assault, or even better your full siege of slumbering good people and wide-awake evil people."[235] Farel raised the issue of this French translation again in March 1551.[236] Clearly, the Neuchâtel Reformer was gravely concerned about the danger of Anabaptism.

[230]CO, 7:50.
[231]*B.C.1,* nos. 42/3, 43/4.
[232]CO, 9:847.
[233]See *B.C.1,* no. 47/5.
[234]See *B.C.1,* no. 54/11.
[235]CO, 12:379; *B.C.1,* no. 44/3; and *B.C.2,* no. 58/7.
[236]CO, 11:682, 199; and 14:82.

Other correspondents, such as Claude Baduel around 1547, requested that Calvin write French works dealing with pastoral issues, containing "precepts and advice to guide people in the path of duty and the search for piety."[237]

Toward the end of his life, when he translated his commentaries on the Pentateuch, Calvin explained the purpose of his work in a similar fashion: "so that our people can easily read this book."[238]

As Francis Higman noted, one can be more specific about the target audiences for Calvin's polemical writings in French, for he seems to have directed his tracts at two main audiences. His warnings about heresies (Anabaptists, Libertines, etc.) and about the Catholic church were intended primarily for a popular audience, the "most unlearned and untaught," "the somewhat-educated," the "people with a certain education," the "poor faithful who are untaught and uneducated."[239] In contrast, Calvin's works against the Nicodemites were directed at upper-class Christians. Indeed, this group included those who were attracted to the Reformation but did not dare to take the final step. Calvin's portrayal of these Nicodemites is unmistakable.[240]

Calvin's Works in Translation

According to available sources, Calvin himself only rarely translated his works from French into Latin.[241] He did so for his second *Catechisme* in 1545 and for his two tracts against the Nicodemites, ones he wished to transmit to German Reformers.[242] He clearly at times looked over translations done by members of his entourage. Such was the case for the letter to Sadoleto, a work that was available in two rival translations.[243] The same held true for the *Excuse de Jaques de Bourgogne,* translated by François Bauduin. Writing to de Bourgogne, Calvin noted, "Therefore, I am sending you his translation, which we reviewed together, not to improve it drastically, but only to see that the meaning of the text is truly expressed."[244] Calvin oversaw François Hotman's translation of his *Advertissement contre l'astrologie judiciaire,* since the Latin version includes documents that did not appear in the original French text.[245] Because most of these Latin translations were signed, we know that the main translator was Nicolas des Gallars. François Bauduin, François Hotman, and Claude Baduel also collaborated on the projects.

---

[237]CO, 20:385.

[238]CO, 20:199.

[239]Quotations from the *Psychopannychia* (CO, 5:169–70), from the *Advertissement contre l'astrologie* (CO, 7:516), and from the *Contre les anabaptistes* tract (CO, 7:50).

[240]Higman, *Style,* 165–69.

[241]See the list of translations and known translators in Appendix V.

[242]CO, 12:25; and *B.C.1,* no. 45/9.

[243]*B.C.1,* no. 40/7.

[244]CO, 12:575.

[245]J. Calvin, *Advertissement contre l'astrologie judiciaire,* critical edition carried out by O. Millet (Geneva: Droz, 1985), 32.

Translation from Latin to French was a different situation, since a range of different approaches were taken. At times, Calvin carried out the translation himself, as he did for his various editions of the *Institutes*. The defining characteristic of these translations is the author's free rendering of the original Latin text. Olivier Millet provided a good example of this by presenting parallel versions of a translated chapter of the *Institutes,* one done by Calvin and the other by Pierre de La Place. La Place, who carried out his work around 1540, endeavored to be faithful to the original, but achieved this only by being "verbose" while Calvin naturally felt free to select phrases from the Latin and reorder them to arrive at a more flowing French text.[246] As Calvin grew in experience in writing French, his French style increasingly differed from his Latin style. Those who have translated the 1559/60 *Institutes* have had to face the issue of these differences between the two works.[247] In fact, this contrast in styles enables us to establish which of his polemical pamphlets were also translated by Calvin himself.

The only exegetical commentary that Calvin translated into French was the one on the Pentateuch. Toward the end of his life, he not only wrote his Latin commentary on the last four books of the Pentateuch but also translated it. At the same time, he took the opportunity to revise the 1554 translation of his commentary on Genesis.[248] Indeed, he admitted enjoying the work: "I have begun to translate my commentaries on Moses into French, not only to make these works accessible to the faithful, but also because I needed to correct the numerous errors spread throughout the text. In fact, I have no regrets about doing the work."[249] Calvin also found time to enjoy reworking the French version of some of his shorter polemical pamphlets. It is not inconceivable that Calvin and his secretaries worked on these texts together.[250] One should also take into account the time lag between the publication of the original text and its translation. It seems to me unlikely that Calvin was the translator in the case of works that appeared in French many years after the original Latin text was published.

Conclusion

Calvin was torn between his humanist training and his pastoral vocation. Beginning in at least 1540, the Reformer and his entourage regularly referred to two audiences, one educated and international, the other French-speaking and more "untaught." Calvin and his colleagues justified the choice of one language or the publication of a translated work on the basis of this split audience. Over time, Calvin became more proficient in the use of French in a context in which French was increasingly common, at least in the theological domain.

[246]Millet, *Calvin et la dynamique,* 829–40.
[247]See Gilmont, "Les premières traductions," 175–88.
[248]*B.C.2,* no. 63/16, 64/5.
[249]CO, 20:199.
[250]Millet, *Calvin et la dynamique,* 885–87.

A few examples presented by Francis Higman provide concrete evidence for the evolution of Calvin's use of French from his first translation of the *Institutes* published in 1541, to the final version published in 1560. His choice of words increasingly diverged from the Latin original to more everyday words that were more reflective of the spirit of the French language. I will only note five of the examples Higman analyzes.[251] Indeed, one can find many more examples by consulting the critical apparatus in Jean-Daniel Benoît's edition of the *Institutes*.

1541	1560
sapience	sagesse
procedantes	issues
mutation	variété
denoter	enseigner
il appert	c'est chose notoire

Yet the choice of Latin in 1534 and 1535 to reach the "more untaught" in the *Psychopannychia* and teach "a few basics" in the *Institutes* indicates how profoundly Calvin's classical training affected him in his early years as a Reformer. At that time, he only had a theoretical sense of a popular audience. It was his experience in Geneva that led him to discover the realities of pastoral work.

3. BREVITY AND EASE OF WRITING

While avoiding repeating the studies of Calvin's style carried out by Francis Higman and Olivier Millet, it is worth gathering together some of the reactions of Calvin and his colleagues on the subject.

In his introduction to his lectures on Hosea, Calvin noted that his writings came at a high price in terms of the work involved: "after many long nights and much work, I have with difficulty done enough so that the church of God will receive some benefit from my writings...."[252] Calvin's sense of the burden of writing is clear, yet in most cases he worked very rapidly. Further on, he highlighted his care in writing and his concern for brevity: "in my works...when I have sufficient time to think about it, and apart from my efforts to work diligently, I try to write with the requisite brevity...."[253]

To present all the compliments Calvin's writings generated from his colleagues would take too long, so we will focus on three examples. In 1543, Melanchthon

---

[251] F. M. Higman, "Jean Calvin" in *Histoire de la littérature en Suisse romande*, vol. 1: *Du moyen âge à 1815*, ed. R. Francillon (Lausanne: Payot, 1996), 89.

[252] *B.C.2*, no. 57/3.

[253] *B.C.2*, no. 57/3.

thanked Calvin for dedicating his tract against Pighius to him. Melanchthon unhesitatingly suggested to Calvin that he should consider dealing with more important issues than free will, listing a few possible topics before adding, "I would like you to use your eloquence to present the doctrine on these key issues. Such work could strengthen our faithful, frighten our opponents, and help those who can yet be healed. Currently, which of us has a more brilliant and sharp debating style?" This quotation not only reveals Melanchthon's admiration for Calvin's style,[254] but also offers a low-key critique: Melanchthon would have preferred Calvin to use his talents in less controversial matters that would also be of more use to the church.

In 1550, after having read Calvin's commentaries on Genesis and Isaiah, Farel praised him extravagantly. "If God had not led you to deal with your subject concisely, plainly, and with such clarity, what would you bring up out of this sea of difficulties? Each century has had its own [exegetes] but no century can be compared to our own."[255] A few years later, Hotman gave a short summary of the qualities of Calvin's style: learning, discernment, and skill in debates.[256]

The "Requisite Brevity"

Calvin's focus on conciseness distinguishes him from his contemporaries, as he had a different understanding of style than did his friends Viret and Farel. Indeed, he rejected their more verbose approach. In 1549, Calvin elegantly expressed his dislike for their style. Farel had been asking for some time for Calvin's opinion on his most recent tract, the *Glaive de la parolle veritable,* while Calvin had been doing everything in his power to avoid having to express his viewpoint on the work. Left with no choice, he managed to extricate himself gracefully. "You know how much I admire [Saint] Augustine, but I cannot conceal the fact that I dislike his verbosity. It is true that my own conciseness may lead to a very dry style, but I have no intention of debating the merits of one method over another.... My only fear is that the somewhat heavy style [of your book] and wordiness of the presentation may detract from the brilliant sections that I did notice in it."[257] A few years earlier, Calvin rejected the idea of turning to Viret to write the *Apologie* of Jacques de Bourgogne for the same reason: Viret was too verbose.[258]

In his earliest work as a biblical commentator, in his dedication to his commentary on Romans, Calvin described the leading characteristic of an exegetical writer as "the love of brevity," knowing however that while Grynaeus shared his view, others saw things differently.[259]

---

[254]Herminjard, *Correspondance,* 8:342; and CO, 11:541.

[255]CO, 13:617.

[256]CO, 16:301–2.

[257]CO, 13:374.

[258]CO, 12:321; and *B.C.1,* no. 47/1. Higman has carried out a comparison of Calvin's style with that of Farel and Viret in "Calvin polémiste," *Études théologiques et religieuses* 69 (1994): 349–65.

[259]Herminjard, *Correspondance,* 6:74–75; and CO, 10/b:403.

Calvin's concern for a simple approach also linked him to Melanchthon. Calvin dedicated his tract against Pighius to Melanchthon for a number of reasons, the third of which was their common love for clarity of expression. "My polemical approach is simple and avoids affectation and pretense. For...you approve and prefer a simple and straightforward presentation that allows one to propose a topic clearly and put it before readers without concealing it in any sort of disguise."[260] Calvin repeated this compliment in his preface to the translation of the *Loci communes*.[261]

When Calvin was asked to look over a letter by Enzinas, he eliminated a number of passages. "I hope that you will realize what led me to trace [that is, cut out] many things, not that I disagreed with them, but they seemed superfluous to me, or at least they carried little weight with the recipient."[262] At the end of his life, Calvin continued to echo this viewpoint when he introduced his commentary on Joshua: "My brothers encouraged me to write a commentary on the book of Joshua. Until now, I have only reached chapter three, even though I am trying to be as concise as possible."[263]

A study of the length of Calvin's exegetical commentaries shows that over time they became longer and longer. The harmony of the Gospels reached 305,000 words, the commentary on the Psalms contained 465,000 words, while the harmony on the Pentateuch ran to 410,000 words. But if one compares the length of the commentaries to that of the corresponding biblical books, it appears that the length of Calvin's commentaries remained essentially constant. The only exception was his final commentary, on Joshua, which was significantly shorter.

Not everyone looked with favor on Calvin's concise style of writing. Many sixteenth-century authors felt that brevity led to lack of clarity. In his *Le grant et vray art de pleine rhetorique,* published in Rouen in 1521, Pierre Fabri stated explicitly that "if the matter is abbreviated and obscure, one should expand it and make it clear"[264] when dealing with texts to be translated. Similarly, in describing Calvin's revision work carried out in 1559, the translator of the *Commentaires sur le prophete Isaie* noted that among other changes, Calvin worked "to clarify what might have been unclear because of his brevity."[265]

Along the same lines, Bullinger felt that Calvin's work against Servetus was obscure because he was unduly concise.[266] Indeed, Calvin had warned Bullinger about this problem when he sent the book to Zurich: "This is a short book, written in haste,"[267] adding "in my short book, I have always been concerned that my brevity

---

[260]CO, 6:229; and *Recueil,* 257–58.
[261]CO, 9:848; and Millet, *Calvin et la dynamique,* 123–25.
[262]CO, 12:575.
[263]CO, 20:199; and *B.C.2,* no. 64/9.
[264]Quoted by Higman, "Calvin and the Art of translation," 13.
[265]See above 59.
[266]CO, 15:90; and *B.C.1,* no. 54/6.
[267]CO, 15:40.

may make matters somewhat unclear. However, I could not avoid this, and in fact I have deliberately kept the work concise for other reasons.... And I am aware that although I am concise in all my writings, this one is even more so than usual."[268] For his part, after reading Bullinger's remarks, Viret noted that the brevity that was criticized by some was enjoyed by others.[269]

In 1563, the link between brevity and obscurity resurfaced in the context of Calvin's writings against the Polish anti-Trinitarians. When considering whether he should write against them once more, Calvin stated, "the conciseness that I feel is necessary does not seem unclear to me."[270] In conclusion, let us recall that Calvin's chief complaint against having his sermons published was that they were excessively long-winded.

Ease of Writing

Calvin's response to Sadoleto provides an example of his fluid written style. The sixty-five-page in-octavo text of 11,500 words was written in six days, or an average of 2,000 words a day (corresponding to five or six pages of this book).[271] In passing, let us note Calvin's small joke: he was told by Antoine du Pinet that the latter was going to translate his letter. Shortly thereafter, Calvin remarked to Farel, "I did not even take a third as much time as has elapsed since he [Antoine du Pinet] wrote that he had started [the translation]."[272] In the first chapter of this book, I referred to another pamphlet written in the course of a few days in spite of a number of delays: Calvin's refutation of Caroli. The same held true for Calvin's first answer to Joachim Westphal. In this case, Calvin confidently declared, "As soon as I have a bit of time, I will start the work which will soon be finished."[273]

The need for a rapid response sometimes led him to shorten his work, as in the case of his answer to Pighius on free will. On 15 December 1542, Calvin stated that he wanted to complete the work in time for the next Frankfurt fair, leaving him less than three months to write a work of around 66,000 words.[274] Therefore, he restricted himself to refuting the statements made on free will and left predestination aside.[275]

As a skilled writer, Calvin could write on behalf of others, such as the Count of Furstenberg and Jacques de Bourgogne.[276] In the first instance, he had direct contacts with Furstenberg, but in the second case, Calvin communicated with de Bourgogne

---

[268]CO, 15:124.
[269]CO, 15:139–40.
[270]CO, 20:38–39; and *B.C.2,* no. 63/4.
[271]Herminjard, *Correspondance,* 5:372–73; and CO, 10/b:361.
[272]Herminjard, *Correspondance,* 6:116; and CO, 10/b:426.
[273]CO, 15:208.
[274]Herminjard, *Correspondance,* 8:220–21; and CO, 11:474.
[275]*B.C.1,* no. 43/3.
[276]*B.C.1,* nos. 39/3, 40/4, 47/1.

by correspondence, leaving fairly specific sources for later scholars. It is true that Calvin destroyed all the letters he had received from de Bourgogne after their quarrel, but for his part, de Bourgogne carefully preserved the ones from Calvin. Already in 1546, Calvin complained about the geographical distance between them: "The apology would be much easier to write if we were close by, rather than far away.... And for my part, I would have to fret over more than a hundred sections if we were unable to confer together to decide jointly what should be added or omitted."[277] Various factors delayed printing and the required revisions of the text: "Since the apology has not yet appeared, it would be useful to have any news that Maistre Valeran [Poullain] can provide.... [All this] means that the style should change and that we should add more connected sections."[278]

In his biography of Calvin, Colladon describes a further characteristic of the Reformer's mind, namely, the help Calvin received from his phenomenal memory. He was able to keep past events, whether personal or general, fresh in his mind. When interrupted during a dictation session, Calvin was able to pick it up again exactly where he had left off, without even having to ask where he had stopped, even after a delay of a number of hours. When confronting wrongdoers in the Consistory, he could recall earlier misdeeds that took place up to ten years earlier. When he taught or preached he did so without notes, apart from the text of scripture. As already noted, he never even wrote down where he had stopped at the end of a lecture or a sermon.[279]

The Commentator

Leaving aside the *Institutes,* which is once again an exceptional case, the vast majority of Calvin's works were commentaries, either bringing a text to light, especially the scriptures, or critiquing a text, as was the case for his polemical encounters with his adversaries. Calvin's approach was nothing new, since the exegetical method was rooted in classical culture, taken up by Christians, propagated in the Middle Ages by Muslim thinkers and Christian scholastics, and finally put to use by the humanists in their analyses of classical texts.

Calvin's first published work clearly belonged to this category: his edition of *De Clementia* brought together both Seneca's text and his own commentary.

Calvin's exegetical works that form the majority of his pastoral writings were also textual analyses. The author methodically followed the sacred text, line by line. Furthermore, Calvin analyzed scripture not only in his written commentaries, but also in his sermons and his exegetical lectures. Indeed, the key characteristic of Protestant scholarship lay first of all in its emphasis on scriptural exegesis in theological teaching, in contrast to glosses on the leading dogmatic summae. Moreover, Protestant

---

[277]CO, 12:321.
[278]CO, 12:420.
[279]CO, 20:108–9.

biblical interpretation focused on the literal meaning of the text, rather than on the four-fold interpretation favored by medieval scholars.

In his responses to writings by opponents, Calvin had no hesitation in providing a copy of the text that he was critiquing, thus allowing him to construct a point-by-point rebuttal. Having made use of this polemical technique for the first time in his response to Sadoleto, Calvin continued in this same vein throughout his career, and indeed, the technique was not a new one.[280] Many other sixteenth-century polemicists provided the full text written by their adversary, such as Luther and Silvester Prierias in their written debates in 1518 and 1520. In fact, Prierias was one of the very first to have the ninety-five theses printed.[281] Similarly, in 1533, when arguing against Cochlaeus for the right to read the New Testament in the vernacular, Alesius included his opponent's text alongside his own.[282] Likewise in 1544, during his controversy with Bartholomaeus Latomus, Bucer published both the Louvain theologian's attack and his own response in one book, the *Scripta duo adversaria*.[283] However, this practice was not commonplace. At times, the polemicist did follow the outline of his opponent's text step-by-step, but only provided the starts of phrases, as did Hieronymus Emser in his *Missae christianorum contra lutheranam missandi formulam assertio* in 1524.[284] Even on the Catholic side, people came to realize that providing too lengthy quotations by Protestant adversaries had the undesired effect of leading certain readers to retain only the Protestant passages, while leaving the refutations aside.[285]

However, providing an opponent's text in full did have the advantage of allowing readers to verify that the criticism of an adversary's positions was warranted, something that was not always possible when the polemicist merely cited phrases taken out of context from the opponent's work.

In practice, Calvin made use of several printing strategies. In most cases he provided his opponent's text at the start of the work, but he also tried two other approaches. The least common strategy was the one he used for his *Articuli facultatis parisiensis cum antidote:* on the left-hand page Calvin provided the articles of the Paris faculty together with a fake scholastic gloss, while on the right-hand page he

---

[280]*Epistola Sadoleti* (*B.C.1*, no. 39/5), *Consilium Pauli III* (*B.C.1*, no. 41/6), *Articuli Facultatis Parisiensis* (*B.C.1*, no. 44/6), *Admonitio paterna* (*B.C.1*, no. 45/13), *Acta synodi tridentinae* (*B.C.1*, no. 47/3), *Interim* (*B.C.1*, no. 49/6), *Calumniae nebulonis* (*B.C.2*, no. 58/1), *Impietas V. Gentilis* (*B.C.2*, no. 61/14). The *Defensio sanae doctrinae de sacramentis* (*B.C.2*, no. 61/14) is an exception, because Calvin's gloss on the text was intended to confirm rather than refute it.

[281]See P. Fabisch, "Silvester Prierias" in *Katholische Theologen der Reformationszeit*, ed. E. Iserloh (Münster: Aschendorff, 1984), 1:26–36.

[282]See above 116, note 222.

[283]See vol. 8 of the *Corpus catholicorum* (Münster: Aschendorff, 1924).

[284]See vol. 28 of the *Corpus catholicorum* (Münster: Aschendorff, 1959).

[285]U. Rozzo, *Linee per una storia dell'editoria religiosa in Italia, 1465–1600* (Udine: Arti Grafiche, 1993), 61.

presented his refutation.[286] At other times, he followed the standard pattern of an exegetical commentary, as in the case of the *Consilium paternum Pauli III* of 1541.[287]

Even when he did not provide the full text written by his opponent, Calvin's refutations did follow his adversary's arguments step-by-step, as was customary at the time. At the start of his pamphlet against Pighius, Calvin explained, "I will follow the order and method that he himself followed in his book. The only difference will be that instead of his attempts to display his abilities through stylish phrases, for my part I will be as careful as possible to be as brief and straightforward as I can."[288] Calvin's approach also provided a rationale for him to write quickly.

Yet his strategy was not without its problems. When he received Calvin's work written in response to the Bolsec affair, Viret said to Calvin, "Because you are responding to the attacks of an adversary, the structure of your work in terms of its order and method should be different from one that you would write of your own free will."[289] Beza, who was then in the same city as Viret, clarified their critique: "While I clearly notice that in this work you have preferred to follow the structure of your adversary['s work] rather than your own judgment, and that there is certainly justification for this project, especially as you have dealt with the same topic *ex professo* elsewhere, I would however have preferred that you start at the beginning."[290] In other words, committing oneself to following an opponent's line of argument made it impossible to include a number of one's own analyses of a topic.

Conclusion

In contrast to the attitude of many of his contemporaries, Calvin did not see clarity and brevity as contradictory. Instead, he made use of both qualities and was fortunate in being equally skilled in Latin and in French, and in having a clear and well-organized mind. As Francis Higman has shown, Calvin's style was different from that of other sixteenth-century writers, whether friends or adversaries. Calvin was skilled at presenting his topics in a precise and concise fashion and developed them straightforwardly by providing points of reference for his readers. His strategy involved using rhetorical devices to orient readers. Overall, Calvin simultaneously combined conciseness, clarity, and in-depth analysis.[291]

4. Calvin's Work Environment

By gleaning through disparate sources, one can peek through the doors of the house where Calvin lived in the rue des Chanoines from 1543 until his death. Three rooms

[286]*B.C.1,* no. 44/6.
[287]*B.C.1,* no. 41/6.
[288]CO, 6:237; and *Recueil,* 263.
[289]CO, 14:237.
[290]Beza, *Correspondance,* 1:81.
[291]Higman, *Calvin polémiste,* 365.

in the house are particularly important for our discussion: the *estude* or study; the *poêle* or main living area that served both as a dining room and living room; and finally, more surprisingly but quite importantly, the bedroom.[292]

Writing by Hand

Calvin dealt with his correspondence and the composition of his treatises by alternating between taking pen in hand himself and dictating. In 1557, when his first lectures were published, Calvin discussed his writing practices. He clearly stated that at times he made use of a secretary: "in my works, which I write at home or I dictate (when I have sufficient time to think about it)...."[293] At times, Calvin took up his pen, in spite of the fatigue that the work entailed. One should not forget that the work of a manuscript copyist changed very little between the medieval and early modern period; the pen, the ink, and the paper remained the same. Throughout this period, writing remained a laborious process, as evidenced by the complaints written by copyists in the colophons of their newly finished works.[294]

No copy of any of Calvin's printed works in its manuscript form has survived. Thus we have no direct evidence of how he prepared his manuscripts before sending them to the printers. However, a number of letters in Calvin's handwriting or taken down by secretaries have been preserved. Thus one can study the Reformer's handwriting and its evolution from 1533 onwards.

Calvin's handwriting was small, regular, and very flowing. His speed of writing is evidenced by the way in which he simplified characters and used abbreviations. He made use of this system from very early on, since these characteristics already appear in his first surviving letter.[295] Calvin's handwriting is not easy to read for those who have had little practice in it. An amusing comment from 1535 shows what Calvin's colleagues were up against: having just finished reading the first manuscript version of the *Psychopannychia,* Capito admitted to Calvin, "I have enjoyed the tone of your book very much, but I have not been able to study it in greater depth, because I find your handwriting is too small and unreadable."[296] One should not conclude, however, that Calvin scribbled his works. In fact, after a bit of practice Calvin's handwriting is quite readable, thanks to the regularity of his characters, except for some notes written in haste.

As we have seen, Calvin preferred to send letters written in his own hand out of respect for his correspondents. He only dictated his letters when sickness made it

---

[292]For information on Calvin's house, see Doumergue, *Jean Calvin,* 3:496–500.

[293]See *B.C.2,* no. 57/5.

[294]A. Kelders, "Les colophons des manuscrits datés de la Bibliothèque Royale comme source historique" in *Formules de copiste: Les colophons des manuscrits datés,* catalogue prepared by Th. Glorieux-De Gand (Brussels: Bibliothèque royale Albert Ier, 1991), 38–39.

[295]A. Matthey-Jeantet, *L'écriture de Calvin* (Le Locle: Courvoisier, 1909).

[296]Herminjard, *Correspondance,* 3:243; and CO, 10/b:45. Doumergue has assembled various examples of Calvin's handwriting in *Jean Calvin,* 1:559–66.

impossible for him to take up his pen.[297]

Where did Calvin work when he wrote in his own hand? One must assume that the *estude,* the room intended for this purpose, was where Calvin generally read and wrote. If my understanding of a note at the end of a letter to Farel in 1549 is correct, it seems that Calvin sometimes wrote in the *poêle.* After transmitting greetings from all his friends, "especially Normandie, Cop, and des Gallars," Calvin added "I am in fact writing to you in the *poêle.*"[298] The phrase *scribo enim a coena* does indeed explain the reason for the greetings and suggests that some of these friends may even have been in the room at the time.

Dictation

There is clear evidence on a number of occasions for writing via dictation— "when I have sufficient time to think about it"—for many of Calvin's works. In 1545, the Council provided Calvin with a secretary: "M. Calvin is somewhat ill, and would like to have someone to write at his dictation. It is decided that M. Trolliet or another, whichever one he prefers, be sent to him to take down the sermons."[299] The decision of the Council is somewhat amusing, since the nomination of Trolliet occurred during the very months when Calvin was struggling with the Council to have Trolliet dismissed from the ministry.[300] On another point, the secretary of the Council seems to have erred when he noted that Calvin was looking for someone to take down his sermons, given that Calvin did not prepare written texts before he preached.

More clear evidence of dictation practices surfaces in the 1549 *Advertissement contre l'astrologie.* In his dedication for the Latin translation, François Hotman explained, "Calvin wrote this work (I should instead say that 'he produced it' since I can truthfully affirm that he never took a pen in hand to write it, but that he dictated it to me as and when his schedule allowed)."[301]

Beza's description in his first biographical sketch undoubtedly relates primarily to the final years of the Reformer's life. "Being in such poor health, he slept very little, and most of the time was forced to keep warm in his bed, from where he also dictated most of his books, being continually productive and intellectually active."[302] In the second version of Calvin's biography, Colladon provided more details. He began by depicting the weeks in which Calvin did not have to preach: "On the days when he did not have to preach, he remained in bed, and had someone bring him some books by five or six o'clock, so that he could begin composing, having someone on hand to take dictation." Thus Calvin began his workday early, even though he stayed in bed.

---

[297]See above 36.
[298]CO, 13:451.
[299]RC 40, fol. 227v; and CO, 20:361.
[300]See below 265–66.
[301]CO, 7:XXXVIII. See *B.C.1,* nos. 49/1, 49/2.
[302]CO, 21:35.

One week out of two, he had to preach early in the morning, at 6 AM during the warmer months of the year, and at 7 AM in winter. "If it was his week [to preach] he was always punctual in starting his sermon and afterwards, having returned home, he went back to bed or simply lay on it fully clothed and, having a book to hand, turned back to his work." This description provides a mass of details: sometimes he got changed for bed, while at other times, he stretched out on his bed fully clothed. Colladon concluded, "this is how he dictated most of his books in the mornings, being continually and productively intellectually active."[303]

Des Gallars's remarks regarding the commentary on the Psalms flesh out this portrait. In 1555, at one point when Calvin was not in his bed, des Gallars happened to notice materials on a chair by the bed.[304] In the course of gathering material for the study of Calvin's correspondence, quotations from these sources show that Calvin intermittently dictated materials from his bed beginning in at least 1541.[305]

As des Gallars indicated, Calvin used notes to help him in the redaction process. Colladon confirmed this by specifying that Calvin requested books to be brought to him so he could make use of them in his writing. Indeed, the Reformer's writings contain so many quotations from ancient and contemporary authors that he must have used written sources. Although information on his reading practices is rare, Calvin seems to have been a careful reader who annotated his bedside reading material, a particularly apt expression in Calvin's case.[306]

Calvin's early awakening meant that he went to bed relatively early. When Castellio informed him that he would be leaving for Neuchâtel at first light the next day, he did so too late in the day to allow Calvin to write a letter to Farel yet that night. "I could not write that same day without putting my health at risk," he explained.[307] Thus Calvin did not work late in the evenings. Furthermore, he added, "I do not get up early enough to catch up with him [Castellio] the next morning." However, as noted above, he did begin work early. But on that day, he had another task to do first thing: "Add to this that I still had to prepare my sermon." Thus Calvin had a great deal to do in the morning, as he still had to prepare his sermon before preaching it.

Rereading and Revising

While Calvin produced his works rather quickly and in a flowing style, he did reread more or less attentively the works he dictated or wrote himself, although we do not have evidence of this practice for all of his writings. For instance, his polemical pamphlets, having been written and published in haste, were not reread, nor was his 1541 catechism, nor his 1557 commentary on the Psalms that was printed page-

---

[303]CO, 21:109–10.
[304]CO, 15:657.
[305]See above 35–36.
[306]See below 156–77.
[307]Herminjard, *Correspondance,* 8:78; and CO, 11:417.

by-page as he wrote it. Hotman's statement quoted above refers instead to an entirely dictated text.

Most of the evidence for Calvin's revision work comes from his writings based on oral teaching, such as the commentaries on Isaiah put together by des Gallars or the exegetical lectures prepared as a clean copy by Jonviller.[308] The more specific indications regarding the *Institutes* and the commentaries prove that these works were the result of a lengthy accumulation of notes and revisions done on the basis of numerous rereadings.

The revision process for the definitive 1559 and 1560 editions of the *Institutes* is relatively well known. As Jean-Daniel Benoît vividly described it, "One could say that Calvin worked with glue, a brush, and scissors, cutting up a printed text into fragments to add new sections, but only rarely eliminating a phrase or even a word of the text that had previously been printed."[309] All this work was accomplished with the help of secretaries. A letter by Nicolas Colladon, printed at the start of the 1576 *Institutes,* provides the richest source for the description of this process. "When Calvin revised this work for the last time and made it into an almost new work thanks to a better structure and a number of additions, our collaboration also increased. Indeed, when he was preparing the French version of the *Institutes* based on the upcoming revised [Latin] edition, he dictated a number of things, which were taken down sometimes by his only brother Antoine, and at other times by a private secretary. In many spots, he inserted pages taken from a previously printed French edition. Thus he often had to hand them over to be glued."[310]

A note from the printer at the start of the errata confirms this portrayal: "Because the copy of the present *Institutes* was difficult and hard to follow due to the additions written either in the margins of the book or on separate pieces of paper, it was impossible, in spite of our best efforts, to prevent all mistakes and omissions, which we ask you to forgive and correct as follows." Of the three changes indicated below, two were additions of seven and sixteen lines respectively.[311]

An analysis of the evolution of the *Institutes* between 1536 and 1560, both in French and in Latin, provides numerous traces of texts being established on the basis of one or more previously printed books. Thus the Latin 1539 edition contains some of the same typographical errors of the Latin catechism, indicating that the copy of the *Institutes* sent to the printer contained a number of pages printed in 1538.[312] The Latin 1559 edition was based on the 1553 Estienne edition, and left aside the Rovery reprint of 1554. Other writings were also inserted into the 1559 edition, such as the replies to Sozzini and Biandrata and the condemnation of Menno

---

[308]See above 52, 55.

[309]Benoît in Calvin, *Institution,* ed. Benoît, 1:11; and J.-D. Benoît, "D'une édition à l'autre de l'Institution: Comment Calvin travaillait" in *La Revue réformée* 11 (1960): 46–51.

[310]CO, 1:XLI.

[311]See *B.C.2,* no. 60/8, PP8r–v.

[312]O.S., 3:XV.

Simons.[313] The typesetters had more difficulty with the manuscript sections if one believes the remark of the *Opera Selecta* editors, who noted that there are fewer mistakes in the 1543 edition as compared with the 1539 edition, except in the chapters that were typeset on the basis of manuscript notes.[314]

Calvin used this technique from the early years of his career onward. When he revised his first version of the *Psychopannychia* in 1535, he explained to Christophe Fabri how he did it: "You should know that I have almost completely reorganized the book, without, however, adding or deleting much, but rather by structuring the work completely differently. I removed very little, but added other things and I have also changed a number of passages. Indeed, this study that I gave to Olivétan to read [the first version] contained my rather disjointed thoughts in notes, rather than organized in a clear and straightforward fashion, even if the work did contain a semblance of structure from the beginning."[315]

The revised Latin and French editions of the commentary on the Pauline Epistles published in 1556 provide a further example of this practice of expanding the text. Both editions explain the presence of an addition at the end of the work in the same way: "Because the author wrote this addition on a separate small sheet, the reader will forgive us if in printing the book we did not notice this sheet, and yet will appreciate (we hope) that having become aware of our mistake, we did not want to keep this addition from the reader. Thus it should be inserted on page 146 at line 6, after the word *Absurdité*."[316]

After the 1556 revision of the commentary on the Pauline epistles, Calvin continued to make small corrections in his copy of the work. Crespin had access to Calvin's copy in 1563, when the printer was authorized to complete a printing begun in 1557. The sheets printed in 1563 integrated Calvin's corrections directly into the text, but in the case of the material that had already been printed, Crespin provided a list of modifications in the errata. This list shows immediately that the revisions were not very major, as there were only eighteen changes for 360 in-folio pages.[317]

Preparing a Manuscript for Publication

The texts submitted to the printers contained a number of difficulties. For one thing, we have described the disorder of additions to be inserted into the text, but for another, when Calvin noted changes in his own handwriting, his small script was hard for the printers to decipher.

Early on, Calvin turned to friends or secretaries to help him prepare final drafts for printing. In 1535, the *Psychopannychia* was written out by a friend: Calvin wrote

---

[313]O.S., 3:XLI.
[314]O.S., 3:XIX; and *B.C.1,* no. 43/5.
[315]Herminjard, *Correspondance,* 3:349–50; and CO, 10/b:51–52.
[316]*B.C.2,* no. 56/1 on p. 886, no. 56/3 on p. 775.
[317]See *B.C.2,* no. 57/5; and below 189.

to Fabri, "Ever since it has been transcribed by Gaspard [Carmel], I have not looked it over."[318]

Antoine du Pinet carried out a similar task for Calvin for the second edition of the *Institutes*. On 1 October 1538, Calvin shared his concerns with Du Pinet: "I am very concerned about the publication of our catechism, especially as time is short. The copied-out material sent to me recently is dreadful."[319] A later passage from the same letter shows the importance of the work carried out by this volunteer scribe: "At this point I have to implore you to be faithful in your total commitment to this work, not only for my sake but for all good men. I wrote all this in such haste that I have not had enough time to reread what I wrote. But I will trust you, as you are used to my scratchings and even to my mistakes. In my last letter, I said how much I appreciated and enjoyed your work, to encourage you to continue." On 5 January 1539, Calvin returned to the topic: "I continue to implore you to work with care in correcting my work."[320]

The letter dated October 1538 shows how much confidence Calvin placed in Du Pinet, as he gave his scribe notes full of crossed-out passages and even mistakes. Du Pinet's responsibility was to put everything back in order, something the poor man did not manage to do at first since Calvin described Du Pinet's early attempts as dreadful.

The geographic distance between Calvin, at that time in exile in Strasbourg, and his secretary, who was a pastor at Ville-la-Grand, gave rise to this revealing exchange of letters. Subsequent traces of transcription work are much less frequent. For instance, in 1547, Calvin sent to Jacques de Bourgogne the translation of his *Excuse* "together with the French copy written out by [Jean de] Sainct-André."[321]

In a letter dated 1576, Nicolas Colladon said that he had reworked the French copy of the 1560 *Institutes*. "It was however necessary that someone check over the entire work at the end. For major changes had been carried out in a number of passages, so that due to the crossed-out sections and additions, most passages were rather muddled, difficult to read, and even wrong quite often, especially as secretaries do not always understand the words dictated by an author. At the request of his brother Antoine, . . . I have worked to reread, correct, and compare all the Latin and French sheets, just as they were in the author's drafts, so that the whole thing would be more reliable, clearer, easier, and in any event less muddled before being printed."[322] Colladon's work was not perfect, since the printer still complained about the state of the final draft, as we have noted above.

---

[318]Herminjard, *Correspondance*, 3:350; and CO, 10/b:52.
[319]Herminjard, *Correspondance*, 5:134; and CO, 10/b:261.
[320]Herminjard, *Correspondance*, 5:211; and CO, 10/b:307.
[321]CO, 12:575.
[322]CO, 1:XLI.

Conclusion

Calvin's technique of using both dictation and revision with pen in hand is not surprising. The next chapter on Calvin's reading practices will help to fill out a picture that is in no way startling in the context of the sixteenth century. One characteristic that defines Calvin more specifically is the combination of an orderly mind and a disorderly environment, especially in his study and in his manuscripts. I have already referred to Calvin's misplacing of the notes on Caroli.[323] One should also bear in mind that Calvin's home was a largely open setting in which friends came and went freely. Some malicious people even managed to steal from Calvin, as in the case of Pierre Dagnet, who also committed adultery with Antoine Calvin's first wife.[324]

The fact that Calvin accomplished much of this work while bedridden is, however, unique, and is tied to his health problems. There is no need at this point to revisit the analysis of Calvin's illnesses done by Emile Doumergue in conjunction with the medical historian Léon Gautier. Calvin gradually fell victim to a number of illnesses: migraines, pulmonary weaknesses that developed into tuberculosis, hemorrhoids, quartan fever, and finally gout. [325]There is strong evidence for all this in Calvin's letters, for like many men of his day, Calvin liked to tell his friends about his health problems. One can even imagine that at times the Reformer cleverly made use of his health issues to avoid having to intervene in certain matters.

All this, however, confirms the startling disparity between the energy of a man who was constantly sick and burdened with a thousand tasks and the abundance of printed works that he authored.

[323]See above 1–3.
[324]CO, 14:379, 406.
[325]Doumergue, *Jean Calvin*, 3:508–26.

CHAPTER FOUR

Reading Practices

In order to write books, Calvin read widely. We should therefore investigate what books were on his shelves, what his approach was to "the Book"—the Bible—and finally what his perspective was on other authors, such as the church fathers, the Greek and Latin classical writers, and medieval and early modern theologians.

1. CALVIN'S LIBRARY

Calvin's early years were spent surrounded by books, even though his 1538 exile led to a hiatus in his acquisition of materials for his own library. At his death in 1564 in the rue des Chanoines, Calvin left very little to his heirs in terms of material possessions, chief among which were his books. Alexander Ganoczy has brought to light what is known about the institution that received many of Calvin's books, the library of the Genevan Academy.[1]

Calvin's First Library

When John Calvin came to Geneva with his brother Antoine at the end of July 1536, he was en route from Noyon, where he had "put his affairs in order," and was planning to settle in Basel and Strasbourg.[2] At this point in time, Calvin seems to have been traveling light, but during his first stay in Geneva, managed to acquire enough books to constitute a fairly significant collection, as subsequent events will show.

The exile decree of 23 April 1538 led to the departure of John Calvin and Farel, but Antoine Calvin remained in Geneva. A few months later, in July 1538, Antoine sent a trunk to his brother in Basel, containing "things used on a daily basis."[3] At the

---

[1]A. Ganoczy, *La bibliothèque de l'Académie de Calvin* (Geneva: Droz, 1969).
[2]CO, 21:58.
[3]Herminjard, *Correspondance,* 5:56; and CO, 10/b:225.

time, John Calvin had only minimal financial resources, but in all likelihood Oporinus lent him enough to cover daily expenses. In a letter dated July 1538, while
thanking Louis du Tillet for a gift of money, Calvin explained that he did not want
to receive charity from his hosts, and that he would be able to live for a time on the
money Du Tillet had sent and "on some of my books."[4] Further passages indicate
that Calvin intended to sell his books that had remained behind in Geneva.

Indeed, once he had decided to accept Bucer's call to Strasbourg, Calvin discussed his financial situation with Farel. "If I do not want to be a burden to my
brothers there, I will have to live off my resources."[5] Shortly thereafter, he returned
to the topic when he turned down an offer of assistance from Du Tillet. "For now,
my food is free. The money from books will cover other costs apart from food, for I
hope that our Lord will give others' [books] to me as needed."[6]

Antoine Calvin left Geneva at the end of December 1538, and arrived in Strasbourg in early January 1539, finding lodging in his brother's house.[7] Antoine seems to
not have brought any books from Calvin's Genevan collection with him to Strasbourg.

Meanwhile, other events altered the situation. In January 1539, Calvin learned
of the death of Olivétan in Italy during 1538.[8] In his will, Olivétan named John and
Antoine as the heirs to half his estate. The executors were Christophe Fabri, pastor at
Thonon, and two other pastors of the Chablais.[9] The task of the executors was not
an easy one. Beginning in April, Fabri sent regular reports to Calvin, noting that he
had to gather up Olivétan's possessions that were scattered in different locations, do
a valuation of his books, and distribute them among Olivétan's heirs. Fabri's letters
are crucial because they allow us to discover that the seventy books the Calvin brothers received as a legacy constituted an exceptional collection of biblical and theological scholarship.[10]

Calvin had no plans to have the books brought to Strasbourg. In September
1539, he asked Fabri to sell all the books apart from a Hebrew Bible that he wanted
to keep for his own use. Calvin thanked Fabri for all his efforts, encouraged him to
reclaim all the books that Olivétan had loaned out, and trusted him implicitly to
carry out the sale of the books.[11] Fabri explained in February and August 1540 just
how difficult these tasks were.[12]

---

[4]Herminjard, *Correspondance,* 5:44; and CO, 10/b:221.

[5]Herminjard, *Correspondance,* 5:147; CO, 10/b:280; Herminjard, *Correspondance,* 5:278; and CO,
10/b:333.

[6]Herminjard, *Correspondance,* 5:165; and CO, 10/b:272.

[7]Herminjard, *Correspondance,* 5:204–5, 214; and CO, 10/b:303, 309.

[8]Herminjard, *Correspondance,* 5:228; and CO, 10/b:315.

[9]Herminjard, *Correspondance,* 5:306–7; and CO, 10/b:343.

[10]Herminjard, *Correspondance,* 6:13-27; CO, 10/b:364–69; and J.-Cl. Dony, "La bibliothèque
d'Olivétan" in *Olivétan traducteur de la Bible,* ed. G. Casalis and B. Roussel (Paris: Cerf, 1987), 93–102.

[11]Herminjard, *Correspondance,* 5:307 and 6:30–31; and CO, 10/b:343, 371–72.

[12]Herminjard, *Correspondance,* 6:184–86, 274; and CO, 11:21–22, 76–77.

Apart from the books that Fabri was accumulating in Thonon, Calvin still owned a number of books in Geneva, as evidenced in a letter of April 1539. Calvin told Farel that "in my books that are still in Geneva, there is enough to satisfy my landlord until next winter." In other words, Calvin expected to be able to cover the cost of his rent until the end of the year.[13] At that point in time, he knew that the city of Strasbourg would pay him a small salary beginning on May 1. On 31 December 1539, Calvin declared to Farel that "Michel du Bois has told me that he has sent you what is left of my books, together with my brother's clothes." Calvin asked Farel to sell what he could in Neuchâtel and to send the remainder to Basel at the first opportunity.[14] It is possible that this sale and transfer of possessions was not the only one Calvin organized.

In this context, we should note one of Calvin's later remarks. In 1542, Albert Pighius published his *De libero hominis arbitrio et divina gratia libri decem,* a general condemnation of the Reformation, including his critique of Calvin's 1539 *Institutes.* In the work, Pighius criticized Calvin for not having cited material by John Chrysostom or Jerome on free will in the section in which Calvin affirmed that no church father had written anything relevant on the subject. Calvin responded strongly to this attack: "Why therefore did Pighius not provide me with books? At the time I did not have any of those works, apart from a volume by Saint Augustine that had been lent to me. I believe I deserve to be forgiven because of my lack of books if I named two authors that I recalled had held an opinion, and left out the others that I had forgotten about at the time."[15]

It is almost certain that Calvin wrote the bulk of the second edition of the *Institutes* in Geneva prior to his exile in April 1538. One cannot rule out revisions done during his sojourn in Basel, since it was from Basel that he wrote to Du Pinet urging him to transcribe the text as well as possible.[16] Calvin told Pighius that he only had access to one book, and even that one had been lent to him. This account confirms what is known about Calvin's precarious situation in Basel. But one should probably note that Calvin's response to Pighius also served as a defense mechanism that could only be challenged with difficulty by his opponent. Calvin could situate the writing of the passage in question during his stay in Basel without fear of contradiction, and could quietly omit the fact that he probably had access to Oporinus's well-stocked library during his stay in the Basel printer's home. If he had no access to any editions by Chrysostom, how could Calvin have planned to translate the works of the Greek church father, as discussed below?[17]

Because of his lack of funds, Calvin did not acquire many books during his stay in Strasbourg. All of his possessions and those of his brother Antoine fit into a single

---

[13]Herminjard, *Correspondance,* 5:291; and CO, 10/b:340.
[14]Herminjard, *Correspondance,* 6:156; and CO, 10/b:441.
[15]CO, 6:336; and *Recueil,* 367.
[16]See above 40.
[17]See below 161–62.

cart. On 16 September 1541, the Genevan Council decided to pay the moving costs for Calvin and his family from Strasbourg to Geneva. The cart driver left for Strasbourg the next day, and returned on 8 October to Geneva, bringing "the wife and household of Master John Calvin" accompanied by Antoine.[18]

Calvin's Book Collecting in Geneva

To analyze the contents of Calvin's private library is a delicate task, in spite of the existence of the Genevan Academy library catalogue done in 1572, eight years after Calvin's death. There are two obstacles that make definitive conclusions difficult. First, Calvin was not in the habit of putting his name in his books. Second, a number of Calvin's books that were integrated into the Academy's collection after his death were sold in 1569.

Calvin gathered together a considerable number of books in his Genevan home. In his correspondence, there are many indications of books being sent to him, and examples of this practice are available throughout his second stay in Geneva. In 1545, François Bauduin, then in Paris, promised to send Calvin a number of works printed by Robert Estienne, including the Latin Bible, Eusebius's *Historia ecclesiastica* in Greek, and Tertullian's *Opera*.[19] Five years later, in 1550, Vergerio announced to Calvin that he was publishing a number of small booklets for the Italian market, and that he was sending a few copies to Calvin. Vergerio added that he had sent some other copies a few days earlier via a messenger that Vergerio did not entirely trust.[20] The following year, Haller in Bern sent Calvin a range of publications against the Council of Trent, written by the same Vergerio.[21] Shortly thereafter, Bullinger sent the same works in Italian. "I am sending to you what I received from M. Vergerio. I am giving these to you, as I would to a dear friend and close brother. I do not know Italian. However, I have kept the second copy, since he sent me two of them. I wonder whether you have received my fifth decade."[22] The final sentence refers to Bullinger's collection of his printed sermons.

Matthias Schenck sent Calvin the most recent work by Brenz on ubiquity. As a resident of Augsburg, Schenck could easily obtain the *De personali unione duarum naturarum* printed in Tübingen.[23] This last case is only one among many examples of works sent to Calvin for his rebuttal.

Calvin's will provides few details about his books. In it, Calvin named his heirs and asked his brother Antoine and Laurent de Normandie to "sell my belongings" without further specifications.[24] The Genevan Council asked Beza to obtain for the

---

[18]Herminjard, *Correspondance,* 7:289 n. 1.

[19]CO, 12:231.

[20]CO, 13:513.

[21]CO, 14:182, see 14:15; and F. Hubert, *Vergerios publizistische Thätigkeit nebst ein bibliographischen Übersicht* (Göttingen: Vandenhoeck & Ruprecht, 1893), 278–82.

[22]CO, 14:115.

[23]CO, 18:409.

[24]CO, 20:301; and Ganoczy, *Bibliothèque,* 16–18.

Academy library all the books that "he will find to be good and useful." The number of these books is unknown, but the magistrates paid 489 florins—leaving aside the sous and deniers—or around 233 livres tournois.[25] Two points of comparison enable us to determine the value of this amount. In 1539, Olivétan's seventy books were valued at 106 florins, or a little over 52 livres tournois. The 1569 after-death inventory of Laurent de Normandie's stock listed 278 bound volumes, and the whole was valued at a little less than 190 livres tournois.[26] Thus Alexander Ganozcy's estimation that Calvin had around 180 to 250 books is certainly not exaggerated. The two points of comparison suggest that in fact the number should be raised to between 300 and 350 volumes.

Not all of these books went into the collection of the Academy library because two years later, Beza purchased Peter Martyr Vermigli's library for the Academy. Given that the packing and transportation costs alone from Zurich to Geneva had come to 210 florins, the Council decided to sell the "useless" books.[27] The 1569 sale brought in 202 florins, or a little under 95 livres tournois, corresponding to around 140 volumes. We do not know whether these books were culled from Calvin's or Vermigli's own books.

The Contents of the Academy Library

A numerical analysis of the 1572 catalogue is difficult because one has to deal with disparate entities: catalogue entries, works, tomes, and volumes. There are 474 "items" that correspond to catalogue entries, for a total of 723 works. But these works were published in 844 different tomes, which were then bound into 554 volumes. If one considers the collection solely from the standpoint of different titles, there are 631 that still form part of the present-day collection of the Bibliothèque publique et universitaire. These 631 titles represent 85 percent of the works entered in 1572, a considerable percentage of the whole.

These books that have survived come from three main sources: the copyright collection, Calvin's books, and Vermigli's books. The copyright collection includes a part of the works printed in Geneva, principally between 1552 and 1564. Of the 109 Genevan titles, Alexander Ganoczy estimates that seventy-one come from this collection. A significant number of Vermigli's works can be identified thanks to ownership

[25]Herminjard, *Correspondance*, 6:24; and CO, 10/b:367. The prices have been converted from Savoyard florins "petits poids" to gold écus "au soleil" following the conversion table published by J.-Fr. Bergier in *Genève et l'économie européenne de la Renaissance* 1 (Paris: S. E. V. P. E. N., 1963): 439–40. The prices were then converted into *livres tournois* according to the tables produced by N. de Wailly, "Mémoire sur les variations de la livre tournois depuis le règne de saint Louis jusqu'à l'établissement de la monnaie décimale" in *Mémoires de l'Institut imperial de France: Académie des inscriptions et des belles lettres* 21/1 (1857): 254.

[26]See H. L. Schlaepfer, "Laurent de Normandie" in *Aspects de la propagande religieuse* (Geneva: Droz, 1957), 176–230; and Gilmont, "L'imprimerie réformée," 262–78.

[27]Ganoczy, *Bibliothèque*, 19–20.

marks or manuscript notes. However, a number of works remain in the doubtful category, for at times the marks are too infrequent to be identified with complete certainty. Furthermore, some binding work carried out between 1566 and 1572 may have regrouped works that in fact originally had distinct provenances. The identification of 195 works from Vermigli's collection is certainly optimistic.[28] One can also identify six works owned by François Bonivard. Finally, the collection also includes a number of works from various sources.

Is it possible to determine which books belonged to Calvin by working out which ones he did not own? This task is complicated because while one can prove that 45 percent of the books did not belong to Calvin, another 50 percent of the books have no indication of provenance enabling one to state how these works came to be part of the Academy library collection. Apart from seven books that contain a dedication addressed to Calvin, two others include manuscript notes that have been reliably identified as written by Calvin. Manuscript notes in another and the mark "J. C." on a fourth only provide ambiguous evidence. Anything further is in the realm of supposition, and one must remember that some of Calvin's books may have been sold as duplicates of ones owned by Vermigli.

Alexander Ganoczy's careful analyses combine two approaches. On the one hand, he examined the 1572 library catalogue, and on the other, he looked for information on Calvin's books in his correspondence. Yet even with these sources, conclusions remain tentative.

As regards the Bible, the library catalogue contains a number of Hebrew editions. Calvin made use of the Old Testament in its original language at the start of his lectures and sermons. The next section will consider what edition Calvin used. The Academy library contained fewer Bibles and New Testaments in Greek than Latin and French Bibles. Alongside the Bible itself, there were also reference works: concordances, dictionaries, and grammar books. Calvin's correspondence indicates that he acquired the 1545 Estienne Bible together with Vatable's annotations in five installments as each installment became available.[29] As for the French Bible, the Academy library did not include any of the editions that Calvin worked on: neither Olivétan's version nor either of Calvin's revised versions of 1545 and 1551. Of the four French Bibles in the 1572 catalogue, only the 1560 Estienne Bible was a significant marker in the history of Genevan Bible versions.[30]

The 1572 library presented an impressive collection of patristic works, containing the writings of no fewer than twenty-nine church fathers, but a list of these works does not match what Calvin read. For example, the 1572 catalogue only includes one work by Augustine, probably the 1543 *Opera omnia,* but this work was part of

---

[28]These numbers have been recalculated based on A. Ganoczy's remarks, by including the books of Jacques Bedrott (*Bibliothèque,* 20–22, 27–28).

[29]CO, 12:231; and Ganoczy, *Bibliothèque,* no. 50.

[30]See below 148–53.

Vermigli's library. Yet Augustine was a key figure for Calvin in terms of what he read.

Calvin's own library certainly contained a number of works sent to him by his friends. Among the works dedicated to Calvin were ones by Martin Bucer, Heinrich Bullinger, and John a Lasco. The Academy owned the complete works of authors such as Luther, Melanchthon, Zwingli, and Oecolampadius. While Calvin did quote from their works in the *Institutes* and elsewhere, there is no evidence that the works listed in the Academy catalogue were in fact owned by him. The Reformer clearly owned works by his colleagues Viret, Farel, and Beza. There is little evidence that these three authors sent their writings to Calvin, but a remark from Farel to Viret suggests that the three friends regularly exchanged works with each other. In 1557, Farel thanked Viret for sending him some new works, and he apologized for not doing the same for Viret. Farel then exclaimed, "you have given me so many [works] on so many occasions!"[31]

As a polemicist, Calvin also needed to be aware of the writings of his opponents. The 1572 library held a number of works by Joachim Westphal. A few of these contained provenance marks from Vermigli, but information from Calvin's letters suggests that he too owned a number of Westphal's works. The Genevan Academy collection also included Castellio's Latin Bible and his *De haereticis, an sint persequendi*. However, considerable numbers of the works Calvin critiqued did not appear on the shelves of the Academy library.

The writings of three Catholic theologians occupied considerable space in the Academy library, including Cajetan and Catharinus's exegetical, scholastic, and polemical works. These works may have come from Calvin's own library, as they contain no evidence of foreign provenance. One could therefore suggest that Calvin had an interest in these texts beyond the needs of polemic. Alexander Ganoczy has even wondered whether the presence of a significant number of scholastic writings by Cajetan, the father of neo-Thomism, is not indicative of Calvin's particular interest in a revived scholasticism. Cajetan and Catharinus were not the only contemporary theologians in the catalogue. John a Lasco had sent to Calvin the *Explicationes* of Ruard Tapper on the articles of the theology faculty of Louvain. The presence of works by Albert Pighius is no surprise since Calvin refuted his ideas in 1543 and 1552.

Calvin certainly had at his disposal various of the texts that he critiqued, even though these works did not find their way into the Academy library collection. It is true that he never quoted from contemporary Catholic theologians with much accuracy, but instead presented a general outline of their viewpoint without attributing positions to specific writers. At most, he mentioned a few names: Sadoleto, Eck, Pighius, and Cochlaeus in *De Scandalis* and Clichtove in *Verae christianae pacificationis ratio*.[32]

---

[31]CO, 16:386.
[32]CO, 8:38; and 7:641–42.

As for the works of medieval scholasticism that formed part of the Academy library's collection in 1572, they raise a question that I will mention only briefly at this point. Due to the lack of sources, scholars have wondered about the training Calvin received at the Collège de Montaigu. Although he was preparing for his diploma in the Faculty of Arts, various writers have suggested that Calvin came under the influence of the Occamist school during this period. The Academy library, however, displays a clear preference for the realist school, the *via antiqua,* including numerous theological and exegetical works by Thomas Aquinas. The *via moderna,* the nominalist approach of Duns Scotus and William of Occam, is notable by its absence. Did the selection of books in this area reflect Calvin's choice? Did it reflect his rejection of earlier intellectual influences? This matter is best left to specialists in the field.[33]

The extensive writings of sixteenth-century humanists met at the intersection of exegesis, linguistic studies, and philology. The 1572 collection contains Vermigli's copy of Erasmus's *Opera omnia.* Even if Calvin himself did not own this work, which seems unlikely, the writings of the Dutch humanist were certainly featured in Calvin's own collection. As indicated below, Calvin made frequent use of Erasmus's editions of the New Testament and his patristic texts. The other authors of note were Bibliander, Vatable, Lefèvre d'Etaples, Vivès, Guillaume Budé, Sadoleto, and Alciatus. These were philological, exegetical, or even philosophical works.

The Academy library owned a strong collection of works from classical antiquity both in Greek and in Latin, including significant numbers of works by poets, historians, and philosophers. One work that contains notes in Calvin's own handwriting brings together both Lucanus's *De bello civili apud Pharsaliam* and Seneca's *Tragoediae septem.* One should come back to this work to analyze the reasons for Calvin's admiration for Seneca, a sentiment that persisted well after the publication of *De clementia.* Calvin mentioned Seneca's works on numerous occasions, as well as those of Plato, Aristotle, and Cicero.

Classical works on both civil and church law also formed a part of the Academy library. It is possible that a number of these works were owned by Calvin. Among the volumes is the *Corpus juris civilis* along with several commentaries. Many of the authors in this section were people Calvin knew personally: Andreas Alciatus, François de Connan, François Bauduin, Charles du Moulin, and François Hotman. Gratian's *Decretum,* which Calvin made use of especially in his early career, also appears in the 1572 catalogue.

Finally, one should note that Olivétan owned a few French books in his library, including a copy of *Gargantua.*[34] This work was not passed on to Calvin, who had

[33]A. E. McGrath, "John Calvin and Late Mediaeval Thought: A Study in Late Mediaeval Influences upon Calvin's Theological Development," *ARG* 77 (1986): 58–78; A. Lane, "Calvin's Use of the Fathers and the Medievals," *Calvin Theological Journal* 16, no. 2 (1981): 149–205; and Ganoczy, *Le jeune Calvin,* 191–92.

[34]Herminjard, *Correspondance,* 6:23 n. 79; and CO, 10/b:367.

no liking for Rabelais, as shown by his fiery tirade on the subject from the pulpit.[35]

Conclusion

Although direct evidence about Calvin's book collection is lacking, one can build up a picture of it by gathering data from a range of sources. On the one hand, the cost of the books purchased by the Academy is high enough to prove that Calvin owned over 300 books. The Academy library catalogue offers a distorted picture of this collection, however, as only a part of Calvin's books was incorporated into the library, while the other part was sold off in 1569. Calvin's correspondence only supplies occasional information on purchases or gifts of books. Finally, the Reformer's writings provide evidence for his prolific reading. The following sections will examine these conclusions in greater depth.

2. THE BIBLICAL TEXT

Even those who have not studied Calvin extensively are often intrigued by his apparently contradictory attitude toward the scriptures. On the one hand, he placed a significant emphasis on the quality of vernacular translations, and on the other hand, in his own quotations from the biblical text, he displayed a somewhat cavalier attitude toward existing versions.

This section will not deal with the history of biblical translations or with the debates surrounding the legitimacy of these vernacular versions.[36] Nor am I qualified to assess Calvin's aptitude as a translator. My intention is to highlight Calvin's comments on his own work and that of his colleagues in this area and then to determine how he approached scripture.

Calvin's Choice of Bible

Which versions of the Bible did Calvin personally use, both in the original languages and in the vernacular? Several scholars have already examined this question, including the editors of the current edition of Calvin's sermons: first Jean-Daniel Benoît and Rodolphe Peter, then Thomas Parker with the help of Francis Higman, and finally Max Engammare. One should also mention the analyses carried out by Benoît Girardin.[37]

[35]CO, 27:261; and Chaix, *Recherches*, 82.

[36]P.-M. Bogaert and J.-Fr. Gilmont, "De Lefèvre d'Étaples à la fin du XVIe siècle," in *Les Bibles en français: Histoire illustrée du moyen âge à nos jours,* ed. P.-M. Bogaert (Turnhout: Brepols, 1991), 47–106, with a detailed bibliography 269–71; Engammare, "Cinquante ans de révision de la traduction biblique d'Olivétan: Les bibles réformées genevoises en français au XVI siècle," *Bibliothèque d'humanisme et renaissance* 53 (1991): 347–77; and B. T. Chambers has published a detailed bibliography of French Bibles: *Bibliography of French Bibles: Fifteenth and Sixteenth Century French-Language Editions of the Scriptures* (Geneva: Droz, 1983). For a general overview, see G. Bedouelle and R. Roussel, *Le temps des Réformes et la Bible* (Paris: Beauchesne, 1989).

[37]Benoît, *Supplementa calviniana* 5 (1964): XIII–XV; Peter, *Supplementa calviniana* 6 (1971): XL;

The Early Indexes of Biblical Quotations in the Institutes

Intrigued by this question already during Calvin's lifetime, his contemporaries drew up lists of the scripture quotations used in the *Institutes*. Valérand Poullain carried out the first attempt in 1549, using the Latin edition.[38] The preface to his work (published in 1550) reveals his doubts about the process.

> When I decided to establish these two indexes to assist your studies, Christian reader, I was hesitant from the very start. Since Calvin ... translated Biblical passages from Hebrew to Latin with great accuracy and care, I was worried that if I quoted these passages in his translation, the readers who are used to the current and common translation would be able to use the index only with great difficulty, because they have little knowledge of Hebrew. So basing myself on the advice of friends, it seemed best to not stray from the common and current translation.[39]

Augustin Marlorat encountered the same problem for the French version when he compiled a new index of biblical citations in the 1560 *Institutes*. In his preface dated 1 May 1562, he specified:

> As for the version that I followed, I hope that readers will not find it strange that I confined myself to the text itself as it appears in the Bible, rather than to what Master John Calvin put in his *Institutes*. For because he is an excellent and widely read man, and all his writings show how familiar he is with Holy Scripture, he does not always have the books open in front of him when he writes (since he does not need to) to put down word for word what he brings in from the Old and New Testaments. It is sufficient that the meaning is so well preserved and the sense of the words is so carefully observed.... Therefore, since I am sure that the author of the book would not object, nor would the readers find it strange, if we took the verses as they appear in the most recent version of the Bible...I decided to put in the passages of Holy Scripture differently in terms of the words as compared with how they appear in the *Institutes*.[40]

Marlorat's strategy was thus approved by the "author." One should highlight the fact that because Calvin carried out the French translation of this edition of the

---

Peter, "Calvin et la traduction des Psaumes de Louis Budé" in *Revue d'histoire et de philosophie religieuses* 42 (1962): 182–84; Parker, *New Testament,* 119–51; B. Girardin, *Rhétorique et théologique: Calvin, le commentaire de l'Épître aux Romains* (Paris: Editions Beauchesne, 1979), 164–67, 365–68; Parker, *Preaching,* 172–78; Engammare, "Paradis," 333–34, 343–44; Engammare, "Calvin connaissait-il la Bible?" 163–84; Parker, *Supplementa calviniana 3* (1995): XX–XXV.

[38]CO, 13:192.

[39]*B.C.1,* no. 50/16, fol. Aa1r.

[40]*B.C.2,* no. 62/8, fol. a1v.

Institutes, the biblical quotations that appear in the book were his own work.

Thus both Poullain and Marlorat observed the same phenomenon, but provided different explanations for it. For Augustin Marlorat, the differences were due to Calvin's citing the text freely from memory. For Valérand Pollain, the differences between the quotations and the commonly used translation were due to Calvin's unmediated use of the Greek or Hebrew original. This second explanation is probably closer to the truth.

The Old Testament

Calvin's practice in his exegetical lectures confirms this interpretation. In his 1561 edition of the lectures on Daniel, Jean de Laon provided the Hebrew text to be commented on at the start of each lecture. He gave several reasons for his innovation, the last of which is most interesting to us at this point. "Furthermore, as a highly skilled interpreter, Calvin commonly read each verse first in Hebrew, and then translated it into Latin."[41] This explanation portrays Calvin teaching with a Hebrew Bible in hand.

Was he using a monolingual Hebrew text, perhaps with rabbinical commentaries (Venice: Daniel Bomberg, 1517–18 or 1524–27) or a bilingual Hebrew-Latin version like the one produced by Sebastian Münster (Basel: Johann Bebel, 1534–35)? In 1539, when Calvin inherited a significant part of Olivétan's library, he had it all sold with the exception of a Bomberg Hebrew Bible.[42]

A number of these Hebrew Bibles appeared in the library of the Genevan Academy: Bomberg's two editions with notes in Vermigli's handwriting, and the Münster version without any marginalia.[43] The Hebrew Bible that had been owned by Olivétan did not appear in the catalogue. Was it sold as a duplicate? Did Beza perhaps keep it for himself? Once again we encounter the problem of lack of evidence regarding Calvin's personal book collection.

An analysis of the 1551 revision of the French Bible suggests that Calvin was using the second edition of the Münster Bible (Basel, 1546) at the time. The Genesis sermons confirm this thanks to a minor detail: the absence of a few words in the text Calvin commented on is explained by the fact that the Basel edition of 1546 accidentally skipped a line at that point.[44]

For the sermons, which Calvin prepared and delivered in French, we need to distinguish between the text transcribed at the start of each sermon and the quotations that appear in the body of the sermon itself. In the first case, the practice of the stenographers changed over the years. During the early years, Raguenier omitted

[41]CO, 40:523–524; and *B.C.2,* no. 61/20.

[42]Herminjard, *Correspondance,* 6:30–31; and CO, 10/b:371–72.

[43]Ganoczy, *Bibliothèque,* 159–160, no. 13.

[44]Engammare, "Cinquante ans," 357; Parker, *Supplementa calviniana,* 3:XX–XXV; and Engammare, "Paradis," 332–33.

Calvin's improvised version from the pulpit and used his personal copy of the Bible when preparing a clean copy of the sermon. That practice explains in part the differences between the text in the heading and in the body of the sermon.[45] But over time, Raguenier managed to take down everything, including Calvin's version of the biblical text, as in the Isaiah sermons preached between 1556 and 1559 and the subsequent Genesis sermons from 1559 to 1561. Because Calvin did not prepare notes for his sermons and freely improvised, his sermon often did not deal with all the verses that he had translated when he came into the pulpit. In his next sermon, he would go back to the passages he had left out, translating them once again before commenting on them. These repeat translations never matched each other and do not correspond to any known French Bibles of the time.[46]

Specific analyses of biblical quotations in Calvin's sermons generate two conclusions. First, his quotations are somewhat similar to the text of the Genevan Bibles of the time, yet they are not exactly identical. Second, the differences are largely due to Calvin's use of the Hebrew text. This observation holds true for the sermons on Micah, Isaiah, and Genesis, as well as for the commentary on the Psalms.[47] A number of Calvin's quotations can only be identified by consulting the Hebrew text.

Max Engammare's detailed analysis of twenty-four sermons on Genesis allows us to understand more clearly how Calvin used scripture when quoting from it. One quarter of his quotations of scripture deviate from any known text. Since these are quotations that he provided during the sermon, one can explain the small divergences between the biblical text and his quotations as a result of faulty recall. In fact, a comparison of the manuscript version of the sermons on the song of Ezekiel with the 1561 printed version shows that the editor had no hesitation in correcting erroneous biblical quotations.[48] Other differences were the result of rhetorical flourishes. But some of the divergences were more surprising: at times Calvin inserted images or personal ideas into the quotations. Furthermore, he created new verses, not only by mixing several passages of scripture together, but also by simply creating out of whole cloth "verses" that are not in the Bible.

Calvin's creation of these new "biblical verses" was the result of a gradual process. In order to make a stronger impression on his audience, the preacher emphasized a particular term, adding his own commentary to it. Subsequently, quoting from memory he would return to that gloss, but then did not link it to the biblical verse, instead linking it to his own commentary. Max Engammare, who carefully analyzed this procedure, adds that Calvin was not taking undue advantage of the scriptures, since he did not invent any new dogma based on a biblical quotation. In

[45]Peter, *Supplementa calviniana*, 6:XXXIX; Peter, "Calvin et la traduction," 183 n. 41; Parker, *Preaching*, 174–78.

[46]Parker, *Supplementa calviniana*, 3:XXIV–XXV.

[47]Benoît, *Supplementa calviniana*, 5:XIV; Parker, *Preaching*, 172–73; Engammare, "Paradis," 332–34; Peter, "Calvin et la traduction," 183–84.

[48]Higman, *Supplementa calviniana*, 3:XVII–XIX.

contrast, Calvin's practice of quoting scripture was different and much more controlled in his written commentaries.[49]

However, one should not envision Calvin working in solitude with only the Hebrew text of the Old Testament, since he also used other versions of the Bible. He certainly owned a first edition of Estienne's 1545 edition of the Bible, which provided side-by-side texts of the Vulgate and the new translation based on the Hebrew done by Leo Jud, accompanied by François Vatable's notes. François Bauduin sent this work to Calvin in sections, as it became available in print. The copy held by the Academy library may have been Calvin's.[50] As in the case of the New Testament, the Vulgate did have a significant influence on Calvin's interpretation of the Old Testament.

Finally, let us add to our study a detail that surfaced during the analysis of Calvin's 1563 revisions to the translation of his commentary on Genesis. As a reminder, the original 1554 Latin edition had been translated immediately by an anonymous secretary. In 1563, when he wrote his commentary on the rest of the Pentateuch and revised the commentary on Genesis, Calvin translated one of his commentaries for the first time. He took the opportunity to revise the 1554 translation. In doing so, he reread his version of the biblical text, and replaced "the Lord" with "the Eternal One" wherever the Latin original used "Jehovah." These alterations in the biblical text do not imply that he went back to the original Hebrew.[51]

The New Testament

For the New Testament, Calvin used the Greek text directly for his sermons and especially for his lectures. In the case of his sermons, the same evolution occurred as described above. During the early years, the stenographers did not write down Calvin's improvised translations. Thus the headings of the 1554 sermons on First Timothy use text taken from Jean Michel's 1544 Bible.[52]

Based on Calvin's philological discussions, it seems that he used a version done by Erasmus, one of Robert Estienne's editions with the notes of Vatable, and the Vulgate. Indeed, the Reformer had no hesitation in criticizing Erasmus's translation.[53]

Thomas Parker took the opportunity of the critical reedition of Calvin's commentary on Romans to try to identify Calvin's biblical sources more specifically. According to Parker, in his early commentaries, Calvin made most use of Simon de Colines's 1534 edition. From 1548 onwards, Calvin abandoned that version in favor of the Erasmus and Robert Estienne editions. Finally, the Genevan *textus receptus* became Erasmus's 1522 and 1535 versions as used by Estienne and then by Beza. Whenever Calvin deviated from Erasmus's translation—Calvin criticized him

---

[49]Engammare, "Calvin connaissait-il la Bible?" 167–79, 182.

[50]CO, 12:231, 84; and Ganoczy, *Bibliothèque*, no. 50.

[51]*B.C.2*, no. 64/5.

[52]Parker, *Preaching*, 174–78.

[53]See H. Feld's new critical edition of the *Commentarii in Pauli Epistolas ad Galatas, ad Ephesios, ad Philippenses, ad Colossenses* (Geneva: Droz, 1992), XXI–XXII, and the *Commentarii in Secundam Pauli Epistolam ad Corinthios* (Geneva: Droz, 1994), XXVII–XXVIII.

frequently—he readily returned to the Vulgate.[54] However, Benoît Girardin, who has closely studied Calvin's commentary on Romans, was not convinced by Thomas Parker's conclusions. Girardin believed that Calvin worked bilingually, putting both Greek and Latin on the same level. Parker's analysis only holds true if one focuses solely on the Greek version, leaving aside the remarks about the use of Latin. Girardin considers that Calvin was strongly influenced by the Vulgate.[55]

An analysis of the quotations in the *Psychopannychia* and the first edition of the *Institutes* shows that the young Reformer used several versions of the Latin Bible. He had a clear preference for the Vulgate, though he did not leave aside the versions prepared by Erasmus and Lefèvre.[56]

Even though there is no clear answer, one can conclude that Calvin knew of Erasmus's edition, that he used it, and that he critiqued it. He clearly followed with interest the work of Robert Estienne. Finally, modern scholars agree that Calvin made positive use of the Vulgate: both Thomas Parker and Benoît Girardin concur on this, together with those who have studied Calvin's use of the Old Testament. Yet are these references to the Vulgate the result of what he learned as a youth, or did he make a conscious philological choice to use the Vulgate? I lack the expertise to settle the question. Max Engammare favors the idea of youthful memories,[57] while Thomas Parker and Benoît Girardin believe it was a conscious choice on Calvin's part.

The French Versions of the Bible

From the Olivétan Bible to that of 1551

The first French Bible that was "Reformed" appeared in Neuchâtel in 1535.[58] Farel was the driving force for this work, in which Calvin played a modest role. He publicly supported the edition in one of the preliminary texts, a fictitious privilege that called for the right to publish vernacular Bibles.[59] In it, Calvin congratulated the translator, while defusing possible criticism. Indeed, he knew that "such a lengthy work sometimes leads to exhaustion." Olivétan himself made the same observation in his *Apologie du translateur.*

Calvin also wrote the preface for the New Testament. Because the New Testament was the weakest link in the translation, discussions began already in September 1535 to have it revised. Calvin stated that he was willing to put aside an hour a day for the translation, though Olivétan delayed the publication.[60] The outcome of Calvin's work on this project is unknown.

---

[54]Parker, *New Testament,* 119–51.
[55]Girardin, *Rhétorique et théologique,* 164–67, 365–68.
[56]Ganoczy, *Le jeune Calvin,* 193–94.
[57]Engammare, "Calvin connaissait-il la Bible?" 167.
[58]Chambers, *Bibliography,* no. 66; see esp. *Olivétan, traducteur de la Bible,* ed. G. Casalis and B. Roussel (Paris: Cerf, 1987).
[59]See B. Roussel's article above 116, note 222.
[60]Herminjard, *Correspondance,* 3:348–349; and CO, 10/b:51.

Soon after his return to Geneva in 1541, Calvin worked to revise Olivétan's version. Already in December 1542, he was "busy correcting the New Testament."[61] And in the following year, Jean Girard published a New Testament that explicitly states, "revised by M. Jehan Calvin."[62] Afterwards Calvin admitted that he had not overseen this edition with care and complained about the "significant and clumsy mistakes," though he did feel it was an improvement on the earlier translation.[63]

In 1546, Calvin did more than revise the New Testament alone. Instead, he turned to the entire Bible, though this time his name did not appear on the title page. In a signed preface, Calvin spoke of the man responsible for the revision in the third person: "A man was found who...." To carry out this work, Calvin turned to the 1535 Bible, which he praised, albeit with serious reservations. He noted "many mistakes" in two main categories. "The language [of Olivétan's translation] was crude and too far from the common and received practice." Hence Calvin focused on polishing and adapting the text "so that everyone can understand it better." Calvin deliberately omitted the reason for the second set of corrections. He simply stated that he had also corrected errors of interpretation: "He diligently worked to fully restore that which had been misunderstood, or corrupted, or translated too obscurely." But the Reformer did not directly criticize Olivétan's work.

Calvin was still not satisfied with his own revision, even though he felt it was an improvement on the earlier ones. He called for an expert in ancient languages, and wanted to see some skilled person "with enough free time" to devote a half dozen years to translating the Bible and then submit the work to a panel of experts.[64] This suggestion, which resurfaces in later editions, shows that the procedure that was finally used in the 1588 revision was already envisioned by Calvin in 1546.

The Genevans began a new revision in 1550, and once again, Calvin carried out the bulk of the work. He dealt with the New Testament, and when the publishers (in this instance Jean Crespin) proved to be uninterested, he looked after the Old Testament revisions as well. Calvin arranged to have Louis Budé check the translation of David, Solomon, and Job, while Beza checked the Apocrypha.[65] Calvin modified the 1546 preface in this new edition to highlight the work of Beza and of Louis Budé, who had since died.[66]

Searching for Competent Colleagues

Calvin did not give up on his hope to see a better translation of the Bible after 1551, encouraging Robert Estienne, for instance, to publish a new French version of the New Testament. Estienne settled in Geneva at the end of 1550, and soon began

---

[61]Herminjard, *Correspondance*, 8:220; and CO, 11:474.
[62]Chambers, *Bibliography*, no. 105.
[63]See below 216.
[64]CO, 9:826.
[65]CO, 13:655–56.
[66]Text quoted in Peter, "Calvin et la traduction," 190–92.

to produce Bibles once again, publishing editions of the scriptures in French for the first time. In 1552, Estienne asked Theodore Beza to carry out work on the scriptures,[67] while Estienne himself published a New Testament in Latin and French.[68] In his preface, Estienne admitted that he had revised his notes extensively because the ones in earlier editions "were too short, and contained a number of inaccuracies." Further on, he explained that the imperfections were due "in part to lack of time, in part also to the fact that I was not yet so advanced as to be a good and reliable guide, so that I satisfied neither myself nor others." The notes in his new edition were written with the help of experts. Estienne commented that the notes from the earlier editions had been "diligently examined by people well versed in the Holy Scriptures and in the pure proclamation of the word of our Savior Jesus" and were rewritten "with the counsel and advice of these friends." The transition from "people well-versed in the Holy Scriptures" to "friends" is significant. In any case in the context of Geneva in 1552, it is difficult to leave Calvin out of the leaders among the group of people well-versed in the scriptures. In 1553, Estienne published a complete version of the Bible in French, with fewer detailed explanations than he provided in 1552, although the aim of the publication remained the same.[69]

The concern for reliable editions of the Bible can also be seen in the search for faulty editions. Even though his name was not mentioned in the edict dated 26 November 1556, Calvin's concern and that of the magistrates was one and the same. "At this point we decided to bring order to the printing business, namely, to find knowledgeable and diligent proofreaders: and that no one be allowed to print the Holy Scriptures, translations, or commentaries without a license from the magistrates...."[70] A discussion that occurred in 1562 provides the grounds for these concerns. A pastor from the Poitou, Pierre Desprez, had officiated at the marriage of a brother-in-law and sister-in-law. His colleagues protested against this marriage and the synod of Poitiers condemned it in March 1561.[71] While agreeing to abide by this decision, Desprez attemped to justify his actions to Calvin by invoking, among other things, Leviticus 18, in particular "the notes that appeared in the Genevan Bibles printed by Antoine Rebul."[72] The verses in question were verses 16 and 18, which forbade a man to have sexual intercourse with his brother's wife and with the sister of his own wife. Each time, the notes specified that this ban was lifted after the death of the relative in question. At verse 16, the notes stated, "That is during his lifetime. For if the brother died without children, his brother

---

[67]CO, 14:401.

[68]Chambers, *Bibliography*, no. 167.

[69]Chambers, *Bibliography*, no. 172; E. Armstrong, *Robert Estienne, Royal Printer: An Historical Study of the Elder Stephanus* (Cambridge: Cambridge University Press, 1954), 228, 301; and Engammare, "Cinquante ans," 359–60.

[70]RC 52, fol. 118r. See also Chaix, *Recherches*, 17.

[71]J. Aymon, *Tous les synodes nationaux des Églises réformées de France* 1 (The Hague: Charles Delo, 1710), 30.

[72]CO, 19:309.

should marry the widow to give his brother descendents. Deut. 25." Similarly, alongside verse 18, the notes added, "If your wife is alive. For after her death, you may marry her sister." The Reformer responded sharply to this argument. "We were stunned at the notes included in Leviticus 18. The greed of the printers leads to much confusion, and because they search around like starving people to fill their margins to make more money, they also end up with temporary workers who are highly skilled at ruining the paper, among which we include this boastful man who claimed to have done marvels for Rebul's edition."[73] The edition (or rather editions) in question were very recent, for the first complete Bibles printed by Reboul appeared in quarto and folio editions in 1560. They contained abundant notes produced in the competitive environment that Calvin had condemned. The author of the notes is unknown.[74]

In 1557, after having completed a revision of the Latin Bible, Estienne planned to turn to the French version once more. He wished to have Antoine Chevalier revise the Old Testament translation,[75] but this did not happen. Instead, Estienne himself carried out that work, while Calvin and Beza revised the New Testament translation. In all likelihood, Beza carried out the bulk of the work, as was the case for the Latin New Testament printed in 1557.[76] Estienne died on 7 September 1559 before the work was done, so that in the end it was his son Henri who brought it to fruition. On 10 October 1559, the Company of Pastors signed a joint preface for this new edition, mentioning Calvin's work on earlier editions of the entire Bible. The Genevan pastors claimed to have asked "two of the members of our company, those who we felt were the most suitable, namely, M. Jean Calvin and M. Theodore de Beze" to revise the New Testament "while waiting to be able to deal with the translation of the Old Testament."[77] This Bible came off the presses in March 1560.[78]

The Genevan ministers' offhand approach to Robert Estienne's revision work is surprising. In the same volume in which his corrected version of the Old Testament appears, the pastors called for yet another in-depth revision. Furthermore, the Company of Pastors asserted that Calvin and Beza's revision work was carried out as a result of the company's initiative, while in fact Robert Estienne was the driving force behind the 1560 Bible.

One would have to analyze carefully the post-1560 editions of Calvin's commentaries in French to see whether he made use of the 1560 Bible. In the 1561 edition of the commentaries on the New Testament epistles, Badius updated the French text of

---

[73]CO, 19:369.

[74]Chambers, *Bibliography*, nos. 263–64, 253. I examined the folio Bible held by the Bibliothèque Sainte-Geneviève in Paris.

[75]Beza, *Correspondance*, 2:72–73.

[76]See below 153–54.

[77]CO, 9:830.

[78]Chambers, *Bibliography*, no. 261; Armstrong, *Robert Estienne*, 301–2; and Engammare, "Cinquante ans," 361, who feels that Estienne's revisions were only minor.

the scriptures. Yet his work remains ambiguous, since he fails to indicate the extent of the changes that were made. Badius wrote,

> The printer to the readers, Greetings. Fearing, dear readers, that the change in the translation of the text would leave you perplexed, I wanted to let you know that you have not lost anything in this change. For M. Calvin, the author of these commentaries, and M. de Besze, both being faithful teachers and pastors in this church, have used the gift of languages and other talents that they have received from the Lord, including interpretation and a healthy understanding of the clear meaning of the Holy Scriptures. They have recently worked to render the translation of the New Testament into our French language as truly, clearly, and easily as possible based on the Greek and the true meaning of the text. Their work and diligence has brought such light to our understanding of the true meaning, that no follower of the word of God can be anything but grateful to God for such a great and excellent gift given in our day to his poor church. Indeed, God called these two good men to carry out such a holy and necessary work. Therefore, you who will benefit from it, praise God forever, and be grateful to the instruments he used to give you such a great gift. Farewell.[79]

Calvin's interest in improving the translation of the Bible continued, given that he subsequently encouraged the efforts of another bookseller, Antoine Vincent, who sought to underwrite the costs of revising the translation of the Old Testament. On 1 October 1561, Calvin wrote to Beza, who was in Paris at the Colloquy of Poissy. Calvin mourned the death of two Hebrew scholars, Pierre Davantès and Antoine Chevalier, and requested Jean-Raymond Merlin's return to Geneva.[80] Calvin's concern went beyond the issue of Hebrew instruction in the Genevan Academy. Indeed, he noted to Beza: "It would be completely unfair to abandon [Antoine] Vincent, after he has committed so much money to this." This reference to Vincent's investment refers to the plans for the revision of the Bible. On 27 October, Calvin stated this explicitly to the Genevan Council.[81] Having managed to organize Merlin's return, Beza then sought to locate another linguist to be his colleague. After unsuccessfully trying to attract Jean de l'Espine,[82] Beza believed he had found an exceptional candidate in Antoine de Sainct-Ravy and one indication suggests that there was a link between Sainct-Ravy's prospective work and the bookseller Antoine Vincent. When he announced that he had recruited someone, Beza

---

[79]*B.C.2*, no. 61/8, fol. 6r.
[80]Beza, *Correspondance*, 3:174.
[81]CO, 21:764.
[82]Beza, *Correspondance*, 3:182.

laid out the candidate's financial requirements. To get Sainct-Ravy to agree, "I promised that any fair request would be put to our [Antoine] Vincent."[83] Thus Beza was hiring Sainct-Ravy for the bookseller. Unfortunately, Sainct-Ravy fell ill shortly after his arrival in Geneva and never recovered.[84] As a result, on 31 December 1561, Calvin once again asked Beza to locate a Hebrew scholar for him in France.[85] Nothing further is known about these attempts, but Antoine Vincent's project sank once the French wars of religion broke out.

The Extent of Calvin's Revision Work

Without going into the philological details of Calvin's task, it is worth outlining some of the main features of his work. Despite repeated assertions in his prefaces, Calvin's revisions were relatively superficial.[86]

A sentence from his 1546 preface reveals Calvin's main concern in the area of Bible translation work: not philological accuracy or the flow of the French text, but rather theological faithfulness. In his description of the revision work, speaking of himself in the third person, Calvin insisted on his exegetical expertise: "As for the meaning, based on the abilities God gave him and the judgment he gained through his lengthy and continual practice in the scriptures, he diligently worked to restore fully what had been misunderstood, or corrupted, or too obscurely translated."[87] His familiarity with scripture, rather than his expertise in ancient languages, was the foundation of his authority as a biblical translator.

The evolution in the critical apparatus in Genevan Bibles followed a similar path. While the notes included by Olivétan were primarily descriptive and literary, by 1536 the trend was to replace philological remarks with theological notes.[88] In all likelihood, Robert Estienne was the main person responsible for the move toward more extensive notes, since he added highly detailed summaries at the head of each chapter. As we have seen, Calvin followed the work closely, both for the 1552 New Testament and for the complete Bible printed in 1553.

Hence the Genevan revisions of the French Bible were not only rooted in their desire to ensure philological accuracy, but also in their pastoral and theological concerns. Calvin played a role in this transformation. In fact, very few scholarly editions of the Bible were produced in Geneva during Calvin's lifetime. These included original Latin versions done by Robert Estienne and Theodore Beza.

---

[83]Beza, *Correspondance,* 3:196; and L. Guiraud, *La Réforme à Montpellier* (Montpellier: Imprimerie générale du Midi, 1918), 1:77.

[84]Beza, *Correspondance,* 3:257 n. 10.

[85]Beza, *Correspondance,* 3:255.

[86]See O. Douen, "Coup d'oeil sur l'histoire du texte de la Bible d'Olivétan 1535–1560," *Revue de Philosophie et de Théologie de Lausanne* 22 (1889): 295; and Engammare, "Cinquante ans," 357.

[87]CO, 9:826.

[88]Engammare, "Cinquante ans," 350.

In contrast, no Hebrew editions appeared and those of the New Testament in Greek cannot really be considered as new, not even Estienne's 1551 Greek New Testament.[89]

A Latin New Testament revised by Theodore Beza appeared in 1557. In his preface, Beza referred to Calvin's encouragement and his willingness to read the manuscript over carefully.[90] A subsequent letter shows that Calvin did not have the time to follow that revision work closely, so he provided moral support above all.[91] In the 1565 reprint, Beza changed his preface, no longer referring to active collaboration on Calvin's part, but instead stating that he took up the translation work "impelled by Calvin's authority."[92]

Thus Calvin's declared intentions remained remarkably constant. From 1535 until 1561, he sought to improve the French translation of the Bible, paying particular attention to the New Testament. Already by 1546, he wanted to see specialists at work, overseen by a number of experts. Finally, when publishers like Robert Estienne and Antoine Vincent wanted to engage in such work, he gave them his active support.

Conclusion

As I indicated at the start, Calvin's attitude seems contradictory at first. On the one hand, he scrupulously watched over the quality of vernacular translations of the Bible, especially the French version, which he personally worked on. He dreamed of putting together a team of Hebrew scholars who would revise the translation of the Old Testament. Yet he also showed interest in all other editions of the Bible. He encouraged Robert Estienne and Theodore Beza to revise the Latin versions of the New Testament.

On the other hand, when he referred to scripture, whether in Latin or in French, his approach seemed cavalier. This attitude troubled his contemporaries and has caused concern to those preparing critical editions of his works. There are two possible explanations for his approach: for one thing, he often quoted from memory without transcribing the quotation "word for word"; for another, he preferred to make use of the text in its original language.

The key to this antinomian attitude lies undoubtedly in his focus on the importance of a true interpretation that went beyond word-for-word accuracy. Three pieces of evidence taken from different points of Calvin's career bear witness to this. In the eyes of the Reformer, the deep meaning of scripture is revealed less to the philologist than to the theologian.

Calvin's 1546 preface to the Bible shows his focus on giving readers a text that matched their capacities. Because these readers lacked "lengthy and continuous

[89]Armstrong, *Robert Estienne,* 300.

[90]The preface appears in Beza's *Correspondance,* 2:225–29, esp. 228.

[91]Beza, *Correspondance,* 3:73.

[92]Beza, *Correspondance,* 5:170.

practice" they did not have sufficient knowledge to find their way on their own. Thus, the use of reading guides was highly recommended. Because God had given these capacities to Calvin and because he had refined his judgment through many years of study, Calvin was not bound to existing translations. He and a few of his colleagues were able "to restore fully what had been misunderstood, or corrupted, or too obscurely translated."[93]

Calvin's view is also clearly expressed in a preface added in 1539 to the second edition of the *Institutes*. The work was presented as a guide enabling people to read the scriptures correctly. Although scripture did contain perfect doctrine, those "with little practice" could easily go astray. Therefore "the task of those who have received more knowledge than others from God is to help the unlearned in this matter." This was the raison d'être for Calvin's work: "it can be like a key and door to give access to all God's children to rightly and properly understand Holy Scripture."[94] As the following section will show, because he was aware of the gap that separated the bulk of Christians from the pastors who could read scripture correctly, Calvin first considered using the sermons of John Chrysostom to serve as an introduction to the reading of the Bible.[95]

In a sermon dated May 1555, we find the same rejection of the idea of "free interpretation" of the Bible. In commenting on the passage in Second Timothy where Paul asked "that Timothy divide the word of God aright," Calvin condemned those who felt they had no need to attend sermons since the Bible was sufficient for them. "Saint Paul shows us here that if we only have the Holy Scriptures, it is not sufficient if we each read it in private, but we have to have our ears filled with the doctrine taken from scripture, and that this doctrine be preached to us, so that we may be instructed."[96] Calvin compares the word of God to bread "with too tough a crust." We must "have the bread cut up for us, placed in our mouths, and have it prechewed for us." He continued in the same vein: "Many people may find the Holy Scriptures too obscure, but when they hear a faithful explanation of it, they will see clearly where previously all was darkness." According to Calvin, this was God's will: on one side were those who were called to teach, while on the other were the listeners.[97]

I believe this is the explanation for Calvin's attitude toward the dissemination of the Bible. On the one hand, he was careful to provide editions in which "the bread was cut up," intended for the bulk of the faithful; on the other hand, Calvin sought for himself the freedom given to those who were "well-versed" in the scriptures and who preferred to make use of the original languages.

[93]Chambers, *Bibliography*, no. 128; and CO, 9:826.
[94]Calvin, *Institution*, ed. Benoît, 1:25–26.
[95]See below 161–62.
[96]CO, 54:150. See R. Stauffer, "L'homilétique de Calvin," in *Interprètes de la Bible*, ed. R. Stauffer (Paris: Beauchesne, 1980), 178.
[97]CO, 54:150–52.

The primacy of theology over philology in Calvin's approach to the Bible marked a change from the humanist positions in the first years of the sixteenth century. We should remember that the scholastic theologians did not despise the scriptures, but they were convinced that the traditional interpretation formed the foundation of knowledge of the divine message and was much more important than a literal interpretation. In contrast, the humanists felt that the key was to return to the authentic text by patiently carrying out philological work.[98]

Although he did not reject textual analysis, Calvin reassessed the importance of the theological and even dogmatic dimension of biblical interpretation. Here one should reread his comments on other patristic and contemporary exegetical scholars to specify what criteria he used.[99] Let us only note at this point that Calvin's comment regarding John Chrysostom was that his interpretation of the Old Testament was weaker because he did not know Hebrew.[100] This statement shows that Calvin felt philological abilities were very important; yet as noted above, some of Calvin's doctrinal statements have no foundation in scripture.[101] Alongside literal exegesis, the Reformer read the Bible analogically and had no qualms about making use of this reading in polemical situations.[102]

3. Patristic and Classical Sources

Calvin's entry into humanist circles as a young man came via his edition of and commentary on a text by Seneca. The young pastor's entry into public life came during his statements at the disputation of Lausanne on Protestants' use of patristic sources. Calvin displayed his abilities early in both these domains.

Trying to draw up a list of all Calvin's readings is an impossible task. In 1950, François Wendel believed that identifying all the sources Calvin used would be an "enormous work…that no one has yet had the courage and patience to undertake."[103] Thereafter, many scholars have attempted to determine what texts had an influence on the Reformer, especially in terms of patristic sources. The most important studies for my approach are those that seek to understand concretely what and how Calvin read.[104] These works allow us to define the main characteristics of

[98]J. Verger, "L'exégèse de l'Université" in *Bible de tous les temps* (Paris: Beauchesne,1984), 4:199–232; J. Étienne, *Spiritualisme érasmien et théologiens louvanistes* (Louvain: Publications universitaires de Louvain, 1956), 172–74; and E. Rummel, *The Humanist-Scholastic Debate in the Renaissance and Reformation* (Cambridge, MA: Harvard University Press, 1995), esp. 96–125.

[99]See below 158, 172–73.

[100]CO, 9:834.

[101]See above 21–22.

[102]F. M. Higman, "L'analogie dans la pensée de Calvin" in *Analogie et connaissance* (Paris: Maloine, 1980), 1:118.

[103]Wendel, *Calvin,* 89.

[104]A detailed bibliography on patristics and medieval theology can be found in Lane, "Calvin's Use

Calvin's reading methods, including whether he quoted from primary or secondary sources, whether he expanded his range of readings during his career, and whether he quoted accurately from his sources.

The Lausanne Disputation in 1536 proves that Calvin was already well acquainted with patristic writings at this stage. He broke his silence when the Reformers were accused of holding the church fathers in contempt. Characteristically, he replied that if they truly despised the fathers, "we would not bother to read them and make use of their doctrine when the occasion arises." Going on the counteroffensive, Calvin attacked his opponents' ignorance, for they were not willing to "take the time to read their writings, something that we do gladly."[105] The quotations that Calvin then added to his discourse were clearly memorized and show how powerful his memory was. Calvin referred to a sermon by Augustine on the Gospel of John, "the eighth or ninth, though I am not sure of it." When citing the twenty-third letter by the same church father, Calvin specified that the section in question was "right near the end." He also debated attribution issues. Citing a commentary on Matthew, Calvin noted that it was "attributed to Saint John Chrysostom." In the case of the *De fide ad Petrum diaconum* attributed to Augustine, Calvin stated, "it is unclear whether he wrote it, or another ancient writer."[106] Modern scholars have decided that this text is apocryphal. As for the homily on John's Gospel, Calvin was also right to doubt his powers of recall: he was quoting from the thirtieth sermon.[107]

Before examining in greater detail Calvin's use of specific ancient writers, one should remember what role explicit quotations played in the writings of Calvin and his contemporaries. These quotations did not serve as references pointing back to the original text, but as appeals to authority. Thus, quotations from contemporary theologians or even from medieval scholastic writers were not attributed by name. Instead, the latter were generally referred to as a group, namely, the "sophists" or the "scholastics." Names of contemporary writers were also omitted, irrespective of their allegiance. Calvin rarely quoted from Erasmus, Luther, or Eck because their names did not carry weight in his argument.[108]

Calvin's use of patristic sources was first and foremost polemical, especially when he was targeting Catholics. He wanted to show that Protestants were seeking the primitive state of the church and that the Roman church had betrayed its origins. However, Calvin did not read the church fathers only to find material to use against the Catholics; instead, he searched the writings for an image of the early church that

---

of the Fathers," 191–200. For a general overview of Calvin's patristic and scholastic reading, see R. J. Mooi, *Het Kerk- en dogmahistorisch element in de werken van Johannes Cavlijn* (Wageningen: H. Veenman, 1965).

[105] Piaget, *Les actes*, 225.

[106] Piaget, *Les actes*, 226–27.

[107] L. Smits, *Saint Augustin dans l'oeuvre de Jean Calvin* (Assen: Van Gorcum, 1958): 1:120, 262.

[108] Lane, "Calvin's Use of the Fathers," 159–65. Lane also highlights Calvin's use of a few medieval scholars on 180 n. 216.

needed to be restored. These more positive quotations appear primarily in the biblical commentaries.

Patristic Sources

Early Contacts

From a very young age, Calvin had sufficient knowledge in patristics to be able to give an overview of the qualities of the leading church fathers. His unpublished preface to the project of translating Chrysostom's sermons explained why Calvin chose the writings of this church father. He noted that in the case of the Greek fathers, the works of Origen, Athanasius, Basil, and Gregory were available. Calvin rejected Origen, claiming he "unduly obscures the truth of scripture by his ceaseless allegories." The writings of the three others were too minimal in quantity to allow for any comparison with Chrysostom. For later periods, Cyril of Alexandria, "a truly eminent interpreter" could be ranked in second place among the Greek fathers. As for Theophylactes, "all of his qualities that are worthy of praise have been taken from Chrysostom." In terms of the Latin fathers, Calvin notes that the works of Tertullian and Cyprian call for a different sort of exegesis. Calvin criticized Hilary of Poitiers for lacking "the leading quality of exegesis, namely, discernment." For his part, Jerome only deserved lukewarm praise for his commentaries on the Old Testament, for he was "plunged in his allegories, with which he seriously distorts scripture." Jerome's commentaries on Matthew and Paul were more acceptable, though they reveal a man who was too unaware of ecclesiastical affairs. Ambrose was more successful: "there is no other apart from Chrysostom who has come closer to the true meaning of scripture." Calvin did however express some reservations: "If he had been blessed with as much doctrinal sense as intelligence, judgment, and ability, he would undoubtedly be ranked first among the expositors of scripture." Augustine was also a pious interpreter, but he provided too many details.[109]

This survey shows that Calvin was quite well-versed in Greek and Latin patristics already by 1538. The overview also displays a characteristic that reappeared in all of Calvin's writings, namely, his unwillingness to praise any author unreservedly and follow him blindly. Each of Calvin's positive assessments still contained reservations.

Augustine

We do not need to follow Luchesius Smits's argument as he retraces chronologically Calvin's direct or indirect quotations from Saint Augustine. Instead, our purpose is to shed light on a few leading trends. Calvin cited Augustine already in his commentary on Seneca, and gave Augustine a significant place in the first version of the *Institutes* in 1536. His knowledge of Augustine's thought continued to expand right up until the 1559 edition of the *Institutes*. In fact the key characteristic of

---

[109]CO, 9:834–35.

Calvin's body of work throughout his career is that it remained internally consistent, with each piece reinforcing the rest. Each time Calvin revised the *Institutes,* he made use of the fruit of his most recent writings, whether polemical or exegetical. Similarly, his other works benefited from the ideas that he worked out in the *Institutes.* We have already noted Calvin's strategy of recycling his own writings: this tactic is particularly clear when examining his reuse of quotations from Augustine.[110]

Calvin's awareness of Augustine's writings grew in tandem with the range of problems Calvin was called upon to deal with. In the first edition of the *Institutes,* he turned to Augustine primarily when providing explanations on the sacraments. The second version of the *Institutes* in 1539 was shaped by Calvin's study on the Epistle to the Romans in the same period and made significant use of Augustine when dealing with the issue of the depravity of human nature. At the same time, the work contained echoes of Calvin's earlier writings. The third edition of the *Institutes,* published in 1543, was shaped by Bucer's influence and that of the imperial diets, as well as by the research triggered by the foundation of a church in Strasbourg. This work contained more than twice as many quotations from Augustine and dealt not only with the church, pastors, and worship, but also with the freedom of the will and the sacraments. In the years following his return to Geneva, Calvin reread Augustine primarily for ammunition in his debate with Pighius. Furthermore, all of his tracts against Catholics made use of quotations from Augustine, in most cases ones that Calvin had not previously used. The 1550 *Institutes* echoed these passages, at least in part. Both Calvin's debates over the Lord's Supper with Westphal and Hesshusen and the controversy stirred up by Bolsec that led Calvin to clarify his doctrine of predestination resonated in the 1559 *Institutes.* After 1559, Calvin made very few new references to the North African church father.[111]

Calvin did not quote from Augustine constantly or in each of his writings. He quoted from Augustine on average once in every column of text in the *Institutes* as published in the *Opera omnia,* once in every two columns in the case of his polemical works, once in twenty-four columns for the biblical commentaries, and once in 400 columns for the sermons.[112]

Where did Calvin gain his knowledge of Augustine? In Calvin's day, there were two editions of Augustine's *Opera omnia,* one done by Amerbach and the other by Erasmus. Given the similar debates over attribution, titles of works, and certain textual variants, it seems that Calvin was using the edition prepared by Erasmus. In fact, one piece of evidence allows us to specify that Calvin was not using the 1543 reprint, but rather the original 1528–29 edition, though Vermigli's copy of the 1543 reprint has survived in the Academy library. Indeed, in 1543 Calvin asked Pighius to reread a passage of Augustine five lines above the passage that Calvin was quoting.

---

[110]Smits, *Saint Augustin,* 1:110–13.
[111]Smits, *Saint Augustin,* 1:25–117.
[112]Smits, *Saint Augustin,* 1:117.

However, this passage was only at that location in the 1528–29 full-page edition. The later editions were all printed in two columns.

In his early years, Calvin also made use of two very useful tools, namely, the *Decretum Gratiani* and Peter Lombard's *Libri IV sententiarum*. Both works were collections of quotations that nourished scholasticism in law and theology. Calvin openly made use of these sources, and gleefully used the Catholics' own favorite books against them. In fact, Calvin did not seek quotations only from Augustine for these works. Yet over time, Calvin left these works aside: from 1539 onwards, he stopped taking quotations from Peter Lombard and from 1543, he ceased to make use of the *Decretum*.

Calvin had to face his critics' objections: Pighius, Westphal, and Hesshusen also turned to Augustine's writings. Calvin's strategy was not only to reuse Augustine's texts, but also to set them in their context. Indeed, he invited his opponents to read more in depth. Not only did Calvin suggest to Pighius to read a passage located five lines above his quotation, but he also remarked, "Why does he not turn the page and find enough there to repress his wild screeching?"[113] Calvin made similar remarks to Westphal, but Luchesius Smits seized on the fact that Calvin failed to check his sources systematically: Calvin repeated some of Westphal's erroneous references.[114]

As for issues of authenticity, Calvin was largely dependent on Erasmus, who was the first to set aside a number of apocryphal texts supposedly written by Augustine. Calvin imitated Erasmus in being overly quick to reject certain treatises, but he still preserved a certain measure of independence by improving on certain critiques, rejecting certain sermons, or even sorting through apocryphal compilations to locate authentic fragments of Augustine's writings.[115]

Calvin's approach in specifying the source of his quotations also changed over time. At first he simply used vague references, but later became more and more specific, until 1543 when he carried out intensive work on Augustine. From that point on, he relaxed his standards once more. The vast majority of his 1,700 references are correct. Around a hundred errors were due in part to printers' mistakes. Only twenty-five errors were definitely due to Calvin, whether in the form of a mix-up between several of Augustine's works, careless use of sources, or at times even gaps in his memory. The majority of Calvin's quotations from Augustine were neither literal nor free, but rather, as in Luchesius Smit's phrase, "free-literal," and a number of these were undoubtedly written from memory.[116]

Luchesius Smits's study also allows us to determine that Calvin used the texts of the North African church councils from two sources: Gratian's *Decretum* and Pierre Crabbé's edition of the *Concilia omnia*. In the latter case, it seems that Calvin used

[113] CO, 6:296; and *Recueil,* 325.
[114] Smits, *Saint Augustin,* 1:201–12.
[115] Smits, *Saint Augustin,* 1:183–96.
[116] Smits, *Saint Augustin,* 1:237–48.

the 1538 Cologne edition rather than the 1551 reprint that survived in the Academy library.[117]

John Chrysostom

Calvin's admiration for the patriarch of Constantinople was manifest not only in his use of a relatively high number of quotations from this author. In fact, two particularly interesting pieces of evidence on this topic have survived. In the period between his exile from Geneva and the appearance of the 1541 French translation of his *Institutes,* Calvin planned to translate the saint's homilies into French. The most likely time frame during which he considered this project was the few months he spent in Basel between April and September 1538. The only surviving evidence of the project is Calvin's draft preface.[118] The aim of the document was similar to that of the second Latin edition of the *Institutes* in 1539, namely, to serve as a starting point for Bible reading. Calvin had admired John Chrysostom for many years, having cited him already in 1535.[119]

Calvin's preface reveals his enthusiasm for the Greek father's exegetical approach. Calvin was firm in his rejection of allegorical interpretation favored by Origen or Jerome. Instead, he praised Chrysostom's way of limiting himself to "the simple meaning of the words." Furthermore, Calvin felt that the literary genre of sermons was well suited for a wide audience. Yet we should note that Calvin's admiration was not blind. "I must admit that he too has points where he is inferior to others, points which deserve to be criticized." Calvin warned his readers against Chrysostom's doctrine of free will, which left too little room for grace, and explained that this failure was due to Chrysostom's excessive sensitivity to the reactions of the pagans.[120]

Alexander Ganoczy rediscovered an extremely rare edition of Chrysostom annotated by Calvin. The text in question is the 1536 Latin translation of John Chrysostom's works, published by Claude Chevallon in Paris. Most of Calvin's notes are in fact underlining; however, these marks enable us to establish which topics interested Calvin the most. This encounter with Chrysostom's works probably took place during Calvin's stay in Strasbourg. One can conclude that he read this Greek father's work in a Latin translation, and that he was struck above all by Chrysostom's rhetoric and his ability to illustrate pastoral subjects through the use of images appropriate for a broad audience.[121]

The parallel between the notes in this copy and Calvin's quotations of John Chrysostom in his subsequent works shows that the Reformer did not limit himself to reading Chrysostom on only one occasion or only one of his works. While only a

[117]Smits, *Saint Augustin,* 1:231–35; and Ganoczy, *Bibliothèque,* no. 74.
[118]CO, 9:831–38.
[119]Millet, *Calvin et la dynamique,* 170–76.
[120]CO, 9:835–36.
[121]A. Ganoczy and K. Müller, *Calvins handschriftliche Annotationen zu Chrysostomus: Ein Beitrag zur Hemeneutik Calvins* (Wiesbaden: Steiner, 1981); and Millet, *Calvin et la dynamique,* 176–81.

few passages quoted by Calvin in the 1539 and 1543 *Institutes* were in fact underlined in Chevallon's edition, Calvin's quotations of Chrysostom in his commentaries
are almost impossible to find in the underlined sections of the Chevallon edition. In
any case, Calvin would also have located a number of quotations from the Greek
father in Gratian's *Decretum* and Peter Lombard's *Livre des sentences*.

Cyprian

Anette Zillenbiller's study on Calvin's use of Cyprian confirms and refines the
analysis of Luchesius Smits on Calvin's use of Augustine.[122] Calvin's awareness of the
writings of the Carthaginian bishop certainly dates back to 1534–35. During these
first years of religious training, Calvin came into direct contact with Cyprian's writings; his stay in Strasbourg allowed him to deepen his knowledge of Cyprian. Calvin
mainly used Cyprian as an authority in questions about the church, and he proved
highly useful in controversies about the papacy that recurred during the religious
colloquies and in the years immediately afterwards. Calvin's increasing knowledge of
Cyprian also owed much to his contacts with leading German theologians, especially
Martin Bucer. After 1550, Calvin's use of new material from Cyprian was increasingly rare.

Calvin's main source of Cyprian was one of the editions of the *Opera omnia* prepared by Erasmus. The original edition appeared in Basel in 1520 and was reprinted
several times. The Academy library owned the 1540 edition that had belonged to
Vermigli.[123] As in the case of Augustine, a number of Calvin's quotations from Cyprian in his earliest works came from Gratian's *Decretum*. Calvin continued to make
use of the *Decretum* up to 1543, albeit less frequently.

Anette Zillenbiller's novel approach compared to that of Luchesius Smits was to
analyze the 1988 edition of Martin Bucer's *Florilegium patristicum*.[124] This work
consists of a collection of quotations sorted by theme, gathered together by the Strasbourg Reformer between 1530 and 1538. Thus, Bucer's influence on Calvin not
only made itself felt through conversations and suggestions regarding appropriate
reading, but also through sharing research materials.

Bernard of Clairvaux

Calvin's use of the last father of the Latin church indicates a clear evolution in
his perception of the Abbot of Clairvaux's thought.[125] Calvin's first references to

---

[122]A. Zillenbiller, *Die Einheit der katholischen Kirche: Calvins Cyprianrezeption in seinen ekklesiologischen Schriften* (Mainz: P. Zabern, 1993).

[123]Ganoczy, *Bibliothèque,* no. 62.

[124]M. Bucer and M. Parker, *Florilegium patristicum,* ed. P. Fraenkel, Martini Buceri Opera omnia,
ser. 2, Opera Latina 3 (Leiden: Brill, 1988)

[125]A. Lane, "Calvin's sources of St. Bernard," *ARG* 67 (1976): 254–83; and A. Lane, "Calvin's Use
of Bernard of Clairvaux" in *Bernhard von Clairvaux: Rezeption und Wirkung im Mittelalter und in der
Neuzeit,* ed. K. Elm (Wiesbaden: Harrassowitz, 1994), 303–32. I did not use A. Lane, *Calvin and Bernard*

Bernard were made in 1539, and were rather negative. Calvin even accused Bernard of semi-Pelagianism, a charge that does not hold water. At this point, Calvin only had vague and indirect notions of Bernard's thought, probably via Gabriel Biel. Indeed, it was Biel who accused Bernard of semi-Pelagianism. Calvin may have found this charge in Biel's *Commentarii in IIII sententiarum libros* or in Johann Altenstaig's *Vocabularius theologie,* first published in Haguenau in 1517.[126]

The 1543 *Institutes* marked a significant shift by including eight quotations from Bernard, several of which were quite lengthy. Calvin found in Bernard's writings comments on justification by faith and attacks on the corruption of the clergy. Calvin's controversy with Albert Pighius led him to cite new passages from Bernard on the issue of the human will. A number of his polemical treatises in the following years also quoted Bernard, while Calvin's biblical commentaries only rarely made use of a quotation from the French church father.

Anthony Lane considers that Calvin read Bernard in Strasbourg but did not take the book in question with him to Geneva. Beginning in 1542, Calvin made use of new quotations from Bernard, either quoting short passages from memory, as he did in 1543, or using other sources as intermediaries. This was the case, it seems, for Calvin's quotation of Bernard in his commentary on Genesis, a quotation that seems to have come from Aloisio Lippomani's *Caetena in Genesim ex authoribus ecclesiasticis,* published in Paris in 1546.[127]

Between 1552 and 1557, Calvin began to reread Bernard's *Opera omnia,* probably in the Basel edition of 1552, maybe even the copy that became part of the Academy library collection.[128] The results of this reading appeared in a quotation in the commentary on the Psalms and burst forth in the final edition of the *Insitutes* with fifteen new quotations from Bernard. These dealt with the doctrines of grace, justification by faith, and predestination.

Ecclesiastical History

Eusebius of Caesarea

Irena Backus has investigated Calvin's use of Eusebius as a source.[129] As in the case of the church fathers, Calvin consulted both the complete editions of Eusebius's writings and volumes of quotations. Among the works of Eusebius available in Calvin's day, the most likely were the Greek editions published by Robert Estienne:

---

of Clairvaux, Studies in Reformed Theology and History, n.s., no. 1 (Princeton: Princeton Theological Seminary, 1996), because the work only reached me after my monograph had gone to press.

[136]On Altenstaig, see V. Stegemann, "Altenstaig, Johannes," in *Neue Deutsche Biographie,* 1:215–16 (Berlin: Dunker & Humblot, 1953–).

[127]Lane, "Calvin's Sources," 273.

[128]Ganoczy, *Bibliothèque,* no. 86.

[129]I. Backus, "Calvin's Judgement of Eusebius of Caesarea: An Analysis," *Sixteenth Century Journal* 22 (1991): 419–37.

the *Historia ecclesiastica* printed in 1544, and the *Praeparatio evangelica* and the *Demonstratio evangelica* in 1545. Calvin definitely knew the first of these, since François Bauduin promised to send it to him from Paris in December 1545, while the second of these works found its way into the Academy library collection.[130] This Greek edition of the *Ecclesiastical History* was shortly followed by a Latin version, translated by Wolfgang Musculus, who added a number of ancient chronicles to it at the same time. This translation also appeared in the Academy library, but the volume in question previously belonged to Vermigli.[131] Alongside these works by Eusebius, Gratian's *Decretum* continued to be a possible source.

Irena Backus's analysis focuses less on when and why Calvin made use of the *Ecclesiastical History* than on his respect for his sources. In fact, the Reformer made few distinctions between the work of Eusebius and that of his successors. Our examination of a few examples suggests that Calvin's critical faculties operated in an intermediate zone: he was neither the father of historical criticism nor a dogmatician incapable of carrying out historical studies. In certain instances, he could analyze historical evidence, but he could equally well ignore the issue for doctrinal reasons. This conclusion is similar to the one we reached regarding Calvin's use of scripture: his work was philologically based but placed the primary focus on theology.

Humanism

Seneca Studies

Calvin's commentary on Seneca has given rise to a number of works on his approach to the classical philosopher. Calvin's scholarly knowledge displayed in his commentary on *De clementia* also surfaced once he began his religious work. In fact, one should examine along similar lines his interest in other classical writers such as Plato, Aristotle, and Cicero.

In his presentation of Seneca, done in the form of an advocate's speech, Calvin rated the philosopher as belonging to the second rank in terms of philosophy and Latin eloquence, only slightly behind Cicero. Clearly, these two writers, the two pillars of antiquity, played an important role throughout Calvin's career. The 1532 commentary also contained a large number of references to Quintilian. But Calvin the young humanist probably took most of his quotations from secondary sources, making use of contemporary authors instead. In a rather polemical fashion, Calvin also listed two pillars among his humanist peers, the first (for nationalist reasons) being Guillaume Budé rather than Erasmus, as one might have expected. Instead, Calvin ranked Erasmus in second place.[132] Ford Lewis Battles has established that a

---

[130]CO, 12:231; and Ganoczy, *Bibliothèque,* no. 39.

[131]Ganoczy, *Bibliothèque,* no. 71.

[132]J. Bohatec, *Budé und Calvin: Studien zur Gedankenwelt des französischen Frühhumanismus* (Graz: H. Böhlaus, 1950).

significant part of Calvin's classical knowledge came from a third contemporary, Filippo Beroaldo the elder.[133] These modern authors, together with Gratian's *Decretum,* enabled Calvin to gather together a significant proportion of the classical quotations that he scattered throughout his Seneca commentary.[134]

At that point, Calvin had only a limited knowledge of Greek. This situation continued to hold true for the next while, since Calvin's main reference on John Chrysostom was a Latin edition of his *Opera Omnia.*

Two pieces of evidence suggest that Calvin's interest in Seneca was revived around 1546. On the one hand, the Genevan archives have preserved a set of manuscript notes written by Calvin in preparation for a public statement on his part against luxury. Calvin had recently been asked by the Genevan Council to revise the ordinances insofar as they pertained to morals. On the other hand, Alexander Ganoczy has located a book containing Calvin's annotations in the Genevan Academy library. This work binds together seven of Seneca's tragedies with Lucian's *Pharsalus.*[135]

The annotations in this work are similar to those in the work by John Chrysostom, mainly underlined verses or sections highlighted in the margins by a vertical line. Sometimes we find brief remarks, around twenty in total. Half of the time these are textual corrections, instances where Calvin changed a letter or added a word. In the other cases Calvin explained why the underlined passage was significant: "voice of tyranny," "praise of life in the countryside," "words of a desperate man."[136]

The editors of these notes have focused on the themes that the Reformer highlighted, such as tyranny versus true power, stoic virtues, facing death, gods, and religion. In general, Calvin appeared to be establishing a reference file organized by theme. Thus, Calvin focuses both on the content and on the form of the work. Not only did he make corrections to the text from time to time, but he also underlined expressions that he found effective. This reading, which echoed many of the passages already used in Calvin's commentary on *De clementia,* shows how influential stoic philosophy was in Calvin's thought.

To these marginal notes one can add four manuscript pages entitled "De luxu" by the editors of the *Opera omnia.*[137] The four pages are an outline of a speech on the decline of Genevan morals and on the need to return to a more frugal and charitable way of life. Calvin may have used this outline as the basis for his speech before the Council of Two Hundred, mentioned in a letter to Viret written in May

---

[133]For more on this humanist, see M. Gilmore, "Filippo Beroaldo," in *Dizionario biografico degli Italiani,* ed. Alberto M. Ghisalberti (Rome: Instituto della Enciclopedia italiana, 1960), 9:382–84.

[134]F. L. Battles, "The Sources of Calvin's Seneca Commentary," *John Calvin,* ed. F. L. Battles et al. (Appleford: Sutton Courtenay Press, 1966), 38–66; and Millet, *Calvin et la dynamique,* 72–76.

[135]A. Ganoczy and S. Scheld, *Herrschaft, Tugend, hermeneutische Deutung und Veröffentlichung handschriftlicher Annotationen Calvins zu sieben Senecatragödien und der Pharsalia Lucans* (Wiesbaden: F. Steiner, 1982); and Millet, *Calvin et la dynamique,* 100–11.

[136]Ganoczy and Scheld, *Herrschaft,* 138.

[137]CO, 10/a:203–6; analysis and English translation in F. L. Battles, "Against Luxury and License in Geneva, a Forgotten Fragment," *Interpretation: Journal of Bible and Theology* 19 (1965): 182–202.

1547.[138] These pages contain a systematic set of quotations taken from classical authors (Seneca, Cicero, Juvenal, Perse, and Martial), from John Chrysostom, and from the Bible. Calvin followed his standard work practices: jotting a few references in the margins, writing down part of the quotation from memory, and paraphrases and reworkings of the original material.

Conclusion

Calvin was a widely read man according to the standards of his day. In the early years of his career as a Reformer, his readings were still few in number, and he used the two most traditional and accessible sources: Gratian's *Decretum* and Peter Lombard's *Livre des Sentences*. But over time, Calvin moved away from these to return *ad fontes*, following the humanist ideal. He went through the *Opera omnia* written by the various church fathers he quoted, such as Augustine, John Chrysostom, Cyprian, Tertullian, and Bernard. However, Calvin also still took advantage of any chance encounters with patristic sources, whether found in the writings of friends or opponents. His period in Strasbourg was a particularly fruitful one for his reading, thanks to the encouragement of Martin Bucer, who allowed Calvin to make use of his *florilegium patristicum*. Calvin's later readings in patristics and classics seemed to be shaped by the needs of the moment, as in the cases when debates forced him to strengthen his arguments. Depending on the topic under debate, Calvin read Augustine, Cyprian, or Bernard. In any case, once Calvin used a passage on one occasion, chances were high that he would reuse it in a later work.[139]

The church fathers mentioned in this chapter were not the only ones that Calvin quoted from regularly. Indeed, my list only reflects the current state of research. Based on the tabulation of direct quotations recently drawn up by Ramko Jan Mooi, there are many studies yet to be done on Calvin's readings in patristics, including on his use of Jerome, Gregory the Great, Ambrose, Tertullian, and Irenaeus, to list only those whose names recur most often.

Alexander Ganoczy made another important comment about Calvin's readings. He noted that he was struck by "the deep impression made on Calvin's works by the reading he had done shortly before taking up his pen. Clearly, Calvin was a different sort of reader. He assimilated very rapidly what he read, and was immediately impelled to write." The truth of Ganoczy's statement can be seen in Calvin's first works, the *De Clementia* and the *Psychopannychia*.[140] Another confirmation of Calvin's approach can be seen in the impact of Girolamo Muzio's *Vergeriane*. This work was published in Venice in 1550 and Calvin knew of its existence by January 1551. In the same month, Calvin attacked the pamphlet in a dedication to Edward VI.[141]

---

[138]CO, 12:531; and Ganoczy and Scheld, *Herrschaft,* 38 n. 249.
[139]Lane, "Calvin's Use of the Fathers," 189–90.
[140]Ganoczy, *Le jeune Calvin,* 61.
[141]See below 209.

4. Contemporary Authors

Establishing a systematic list of all traces of Calvin's readings would be too painstaking and lengthy, and would take up an undue proportion of this book. Thus I will not reexamine Calvin's encounters with the works of opponents against whom he wrote polemical treatises.[142] Rather than engage in a comprehensive overview, I intend to focus on a few trends.

"To Take Advantage of Others' Writings"

An Avid Reader

In 1543, Calvin added a quotation from Augustine to the end of his preface to the *Institutes*. He kept this quotation in subsequent editions and translated it as follows: "I count myself one of the number of those who write as they learn and learn as they write." In 1551, Calvin made a comment to Bullinger to the same effect. In March and August 1550, the Zurich Reformer had sent Calvin the third and fourth decades of his sermons.[143] Calvin wrote to thank him, sweeping Bullinger's protestations aside: "You claim that you did not send me your books so that I would learn something from you. For my part, just as I want my works to be of use to all pious men, so in return I gladly benefit from the writings of others. Truly, this is in fact fraternal communication."[144] These statements match Alexander Ganoczy's remark noted above.

Evidence from correspondence shows that Calvin was keen to read works by Reformers who were close to him: Bucer, Vermigli, Bullinger, and others. In 1546, when Calvin was worried that he had lost his commentary on Second Corinthians, he asked Viret to send the manuscript that Viret had been planning to submit to him as soon as possible. "Reading will provide a diversion and serve as a remedy against encroaching boredom."[145] Around 1555, when Calvin refused to publish a commentary on the Psalms, he stated (among other reasons) "that Martin Bucer, a very faithful doctor of the church, has worked on it with such knowledge, diligence, and faithfulness and has succeeded so well that at the very least it is not so crucial for me to get involved." Wolfgang Musculus had also written commentaries on the Psalms, published in Basel in 1551. Calvin recommended this writer, who "according to the judgment of well-advised people, has also received high praise in this area because of his diligence and hard work."[146] In 1554, Calvin told Vermigli how impatient he was to read the latter's commentary on Genesis, which had been due to appear for a num-

---

[142]See above 68–73.
[143]CO, 13:546–47, 636. The third decade became part of the Academy's library thanks to Bullinger's gift (Ganoczy, *Bibliothèque*, no. 184).
[144]CO, 14:74.
[145]CO, 12:367.
[146]CO, 31:14.

ber of years.[147] Toward the end of his career, when Calvin decided to intervene one final time in the debate on the Lord's Supper, he noted that the subject had already been dealt with by Oecolampadius, Bullinger, and Vermigli, and that it was only Hesshusen's stubbornness that impelled Calvin to return to this topic.[148]

A careful study of Calvin's writings shows that he did not restrict his reading to authors that he quoted from directly. In an earlier section, I indicated how quotations were used in his day: to refer to a particular work was not a means of noting a source, but rather a way to base oneself on an authority.

We should take note of one significant case of reading underpinning one of Calvin's works, namely, the pseudoprivilege he wrote for Olivétan's Bible. This pastiche, which may seem unconnected to events of the time, in fact clearly echoed a contemporary debate. Bernard Roussel has demonstrated that Calvin's statements were based on the controversy between Alexander Alesius and Johannes Cochlaeus on vernacular Bible translations. Calvin knew and made use of *An expediat laicis legere Novi Testamenti lingua vernacula,* which provided Alesius's text and refuted Cochlaeus. The work in question appeared in Dresden in 1533, shortly before Calvin wrote his pseudoprivilege.[149]

Reading the Leading Reformers

Martin Luther

We have already noted Calvin's deep and sincere admiration for Luther.[150] Our sources suggest that Luther had the greatest influence on Calvin in terms of his discovery of the Gospel. Because Calvin never learned German, he only read Luther's works in Latin and French translations.

Alexander Ganoczy's analysis of the 1536 *Institutes* allowed him to specify some of what Calvin read. The 1536 *Institutes,* described by Calvin and his friends as a catechism, owed a great deal to Luther's 1529 *Parvus Catechismus,* given that the outline of both works is identical. Calvin also made use of some of Luther's classic works: the 1520 *De captivitate babylonica* and *De libertate Christiana,* the 1519 *De sacramento Eucharistiae contio dignissima* translated into Latin in 1523, and the 1526 *Sermo elegantissimus super Sacramento Corporis et Sanguinis Christi* published in Latin in 1527.

Calvin ceaselessly proclaimed that he considered Luther "an excellent apostle of Christ, for his work and ministry above all others has restored the purity of the Gospel

---

[147]CO, 15:219–20.

[148]CO, 9:490; and *B.C.2,* no. 61/11.

[149]Roussel, "Un privilege," 233–60.

[150]See above 103–5. On the relationship between Luther and Calvin, see Doumergue, *Jean Calvin,* 2: 562–87; E. W. Zeeden, "Das Bild Martin Luthers in den Briefen Calvins," *ARG* 49 (1958): 177–95; Ganoczy, *Le jeune Calvin,* 139–50; and B. A. Gerrish, "The Pathfinder: Calvin's Image of Martin Luther" in *The Old Protestantism and the New: Essays on the Reformation Heritage,* ed. B. Gerrish (Chicago: University of Chicago Press, 1982), 27–48.

in our own time."[151] However, Calvin still felt entitled to express some reservations. Immediately after the Genevan *Confession de foy* had been approved by the Bernese ministers, Calvin wrote to Bucer: "If Luther could welcome us with our *Confession,* there would be nothing more I could wish for. However, he is not the only one deserving of consideration in God's Church." Calvin continued, blending praise ("I am absolutely convinced of his piety") and criticisms regarding Luther's obstinacy, focusing particularly on the doctrine of the Lord's Supper.[152] A few months later, still on the same subject, Calvin told Farel, "Luther is completely wrong, and I freely admit that I am dissatisfied with him."[153] But shortly thereafter, in October 1539, Calvin's admiration for Luther rose as a result of a minor incident. The German Reformer added a congratulatory note of approval for Calvin in a letter to Bucer. Calvin was very moved by this gesture and he rapidly told Farel all about it. In his 1556 *Secunda defensio,* Calvin in fact referred to Luther's approval.[154] On several occasions, Calvin insisted on Luther's human qualities, as in his *Ultima admonitio ad Westphalum:* "I would hope that whatever vices were mixed in with Luther's virtues would remain wholly forgotten."[155]

This preliminary analysis leads to a conclusion that holds true for other Reformation figures as well: Calvin read Luther with interest and benefited greatly from his readings, but he still preserved a critical mind-set and kept his distance at times. Shortly before the German Reformer's death, Calvin remarked to Melanchthon, "Even in the Church, we have to be careful how far we rely on men. Because disaster strikes when one man can do so much more than all the others."[156] To imitate such a model requires discernment. "O Luther," he exclaimed in his *Secunda defensio,* "you have left us very few men who have as many great gifts as you did; but you have left many who are like monkeys, attempting to mimic your holy way of glorifying yourself."[157]

Philip Melanchthon

Calvin's relations with Melanchthon had a completely different tone, even though they featured the same mix of respect and criticism.[158] In all likelihood, Calvin first encountered Melanchthon as the author of *De rhetorica* and *De dialectica.* These two treatises were regularly published in Paris beginning in 1522. Calvin

---

[151]*Defensio adversus calumnias Pigihii,* 1543 (CO, 6:250). See also *Supplex exhortatio ad Carolum Quintum,* 1543 (CO, 6:459, 473); *Secunda Defensio adversus Westphali,* 1556 (CO, 9:105); *Ultima admonitio ad Westphalum,* 1557 (CO, 9:238); and *Gratulatio ad Gabrielem de Saconay,* 1561 (CO, 9:448).

[152]Herminjard, *Correspondance,* 4:341–42; and CO, 10/b:138–39.

[153]Herminjard, *Correspondance,* 5:141; and CO, 10/b:277.

[154]Herminjard, *Correspondance,* 6:130–31, 165; and CO, 9:92.

[155]CO, 9:238; and *Recueil,* 1680.

[156]CO, 12:99.

[157]CO, 9:105; and *Recueil,* 1562.

[158]Doumergue, *Jean Calvin,* 2:538–61.

always displayed the greatest respect for Melanchthon's style, which served as a model for the Genevan Reformer.[159] When presenting Melanchthon to a French readership in the translation of the *Loci communes,* Calvin specified that there was no need to introduce Melanchthon to those who knew Latin, "because this author is better known than any other in the world in literary circles."[160]

Alexander Ganoczy has located in the *Institutes* traces of Calvin's in-depth reading of the *Loci communes.*[161] Melanchthon's systematic survey of Protestant theology clearly delighted the Frenchman, who not only used the work for his own benefit but also saw to the production of a French translation. We have already examined some of Calvin's reservations vis-à-vis certain of Melanchthon's viewpoints. Calvin's strategy of giving a positive interpretation to clashes caused by Melanchthon's refusal to go into great detail was typical of his approach when dealing with a theologian he valued. [162]

Calvin followed Melanchthon's written production closely. In 1539, he wrote to Farel, "If you have not yet read Philip's *De authoritate Ecclesiae,* I recommend that you do so. You will find that he is much less timid than he appears in his other writings."[163] Again, this work of Melanchthon was reprinted in French several times in Geneva between 1542 and 1550.

The two men became acquainted during various religious colloquies and found themselves in sympathy with each other. However, admiration and friendship still left room for a certain critical distance. Some have suggested that the preface to the French translation of the *Loci communes* voices some disagreements over free will and predestination. For his part, Melanchthon was glad to receive Calvin's treatise against Pighius, but expressed the wish that Calvin would focus on less abstruse theological topics. Melanchthon made this point in a stylish way and had no hesitation in subsequently returning to the topic.[164] Later relations between the two Reformers, while very revealing in terms of their temperament, have little to do with the issue of what Calvin read.

Ulrich Zwingli

The situation regarding Zwingli was very different. Once again, Calvin's first approach was shaped by his initial emotional response.[165] Calvin became acquainted with Zwingli and Oecolampadius's writings through Luther's critique of their memorialist outlook. In 1556, Calvin admitted, "having recently emerged a little from the darkness of the papacy, and having begun to develop a taste for healthy doctrine, I

[159]See the evidence gathered by Millet, *Calvin et la dynamique,* 122–25.
[160]CO, 9:847.
[161]Ganoczy, *Le jeune Calvin,* 150–56.
[162]See above 104–5.
[163]Herminjard, *Correspondance,* 6:131–32; and CO, 10/b:432.
[164]Herminjard, *Correspondance,* 8:342–43, 451–52; and CO, 11:541, 594–95.
[165]Doumergue, *Jean Calvin,* 2:567–69; F. Blanke, "Calvins Urteil über Zwingli," *Zwingliana* 11 (1959/1963): 66–92; and Ganoczy, *Le jeune Calvin,* 156–66.

read in Luther that Oecolampadius and Zwingli left nothing in the sacraments apart from austere figures and false representations, leading me to despise their books, so that for a long time, I did not read them."[166] However, Calvin did gain sufficient knowledge to shape his own opinion. In 1539, writing to Andreas Zebedee, a fervent follower of Zwingli, Calvin not only described Zwingli's perspective on the Lord's Supper as "false and dangerous," but also specified that "when I saw that this perspective was received with great applause by our own people, I did not hesitate to attack it while I was still in France."[167] In 1540, Calvin became annoyed when Zebedee continued to prefer Zwingli to Luther.[168]

As Alexander Ganoczy has shown, these reservations did not keep Calvin from gaining an in-depth knowledge of Zwingli's *Commentarius de vera et falsa religione,* published in 1525. The fact that Zwingli dedicated this work to Francis I may have led Calvin to do the same in 1536. Calvin made both positive and negative use of this source. At one point, he cited Zwingli's text without naming him, introducing the passage with the words, "some others say..." and then refuting the idea. More often, he borrowed ideas, sets of references, and expressions from Zwingli.

Calvin's suspicion of Zwingli persisted for many years. In 1542, in response to Viret, who probably told him that Zwingli's stance on the Lord's Supper was more nuanced, Calvin simply stated, "you can think what you want regarding Zwingli's writings. Indeed, I have not read everything. At the end of his life he may have retracted and corrected what he carelessly wrote earlier on."[169] Thus Calvin showed no interest in verifying Viret's statements for himself.

Was Calvin increasingly uninterested in Zwingli? One of his statements during Bolsec's trial may lead us to think so. In *De providentia Dei,* published in 1530, Bolsec had criticized Zwingli for having claimed that God is the author of sin. At first glance, Calvin's response seems contradictory: "As for Bolsec's statement regarding what Zwingli wrote in the book titled *De providentia Dei,* ... I have no doubt that it is an impudent slander, because even though I have not had time to read the book, I have found that Zwingli in fact says the exact opposite. In reality, in the eight or ten sheets that make up the book, Zwingli says more than twenty times that God is not the cause or author of sin."[170] The expression "read the book" should be taken to mean read in depth, since Calvin immediately afterwards stated that he had had access to the book—he even knew it had eight to ten gatherings[171]—and that he read it to locate at least twenty passages that contradicted Bolsec.

---

[166]*Secunda Defensio,* CO, 9:51; and *Recueil,* 1503.
[167]Herminjard, *Correspondance,* 5:318; and CO, 10/b:346.
[168]Herminjard, *Correspondance,* 6:191; and CO, 11:24.
[169]Herminjard, *Correspondance,* 8:123–24; and CO, 11:438.
[170]*RCP,* 1:106.
[171]Indeed, the work contained ten gatherings (Adams, *Catalogue,* 2:Z 218).

Martin Bucer

Prior to his departure from France, Calvin was suspicious of Martin Bucer, largely because of the sacramentarian controversy. However, Calvin read with care Bucer's *Ennarationes perpetuae in sacro quatuor evangelia,* which first appeared in 1527, and again in a revised version in 1530. Clear traces of this work can be found in the first edition of the *Institutes.*[172] Calvin continued to be interested in Bucer's writings. In May 1537, the Genevan Reformer asked Viret to bring from Lausanne a commentary by Bucer, possibly his commentary on the Psalms or the one on the four Gospels.[173] In January 1538, after having read various of Bucer's writings, Calvin did not hesitate to voice certain criticisms. In fact, Calvin's negative comments are surprising since he placed them in the middle of a long letter to Bucer encouraging him to calm tensions over the doctrine of the Lord's Supper. Claiming to speak on behalf of his colleagues, Calvin considered that Bucer went too far in his attempts not to upset anyone and that he ended up compromising with falsehood and harming the truth. Calvin's first comments were clear: "If you want everyone to accept Christ, you must not construct your own Gospel." Calvin then took a more nuanced approach, stating that he did not suspect Bucer of false doctrine, but that he felt Bucer's writings could trouble certain readers. Among the writings Calvin highlighted were the 1529 commentary on the Psalms, the refutation of Robert Ceneau, the *Defensio adversus Axioma Catholicum* of 1534, and "everything you have published since then."[174] Thus Calvin had no qualms about distancing himself from his close colleagues. Bucer did not hold a grudge against him, since he gave a glowing recommendation of Calvin to Myconius in 1538, when Myconius was a pastor in Basel. "Please help this outstanding man, who definitely has no equal, apart from Philip [Melanchthon] in terms of fervor, eloquence, and wisdom."[175] The following year, Bucer called Calvin to Strasbourg, leading to extensive personal contact between the two men and numerous exchanges of ideas.

Heinrich Bullinger

Calvin's relationship with Bullinger got off to a slow start. Calvin's reading of Bullinger's *Absoluta de Christi domini et catholicae eius ecclesiae sacramentis tractatio* marked a crucial juncture in their relationship. In 1547, the first phases of an agreement between Zurich and Geneva resulted from Calvin's in-depth examination of the work. Calvin scrutinized Bullinger's text very closely, combining general approval with detailed remarks, as we saw earlier. We also saw that Bullinger's response to Calvin on this matter was lukewarm. After a certain amount of sulking, Calvin's critical reading did not hinder the growth of a strong friendship.[176]

[172]Ganoczy, *Le jeune Calvin,* 166–78.
[173]Herminjard, *Correspondance,* 4:234; and CO, 10/b:96.
[174]Herminjard, *Correspondance,* 4:346–48; and CO, 10/b:142–44.
[175]Herminjard, *Correspondance,* 7:235; and CO, 11:272.
[176]See above 5–8.

Exegetical Writings by His Contemporaries

Based on Alexander Ganoczy's analysis of the first version of the *Institutes,* I have been able to indicate which leading works by his Protestant contemporaries Calvin read and made use of in this first Calvinist catechism. Calvin also focused on exegetical works written by his contemporaries. Two quotations will be sufficient to show that Calvin was a careful and critical reader. His 1539 dedication to Grynaeus shows that he began his commentary on Romans only after having read recent commentaries in depth, including those of Melanchthon, Bullinger, and Bucer. "Due to his doctrine, care, and skill in which he shines in every field, Philip Melanchthon has shed much light when compared with those who previously published their works. But because it seems that he intended to examine only that which was worth his attention, he spent much time over these sections, deliberately omitting many points that could trouble simple people. Bullinger followed suit. He too has been highly praised for his work. Indeed, he brings together a deft style and the doctrine for which he is highly thought of. Finally, Bucer's work acts as a colophon, thanks to all the commentaries he has published." Calvin's lengthy praise for Bucer focused on his wisdom, his extensive learning, and his precision in interpreting scripture. Calvin's only criticism was that Bucer was unduly verbose.[177]

Calvin's advice sent from Strasbourg in May 1540 provides another window on his reading at the time. Viret had asked for suggestions in preparing his lectures on Isaiah. In one short paragraph, Calvin drew up a concise bibliography. "In his lectures, Capito has a number of things that may help you considerably for your commentaries on Isaiah. But because he does not provide anything to his audience and has not progressed beyond chapter 14, his work will not be of much use to you at present. Although he does not lack subtlety, Zwingli often strays from the mind of the prophet, because he takes too many liberties. Although he is careless about the meaning of words and historical context, Luther is quite effective at presenting good doctrine. No one has done more on this book than Oecolampadius; however, he does not always hit the target. Overall, though human help may often be lacking, I hope however that God will not abandon you."[178] Calvin's overview was clear and concise.

Genevan Publications

In his debate with Gabriel de Saconay, Calvin encountered Saconay's criticisms regarding division among the Reformers. Saconay claimed that Luther's works were prohibited in Geneva. Writing about himself in the third person, Calvin replied, "For that matter, why would Calvin forbid the printing of Luther's books in Geneva, given that he has seen to it that even the worst books by his enemies have been printed? Even if this tone-deaf cantor was completely blinded by rage, he should still know very well that a few of Luther's works have been translated into French and

---

[177]Herminjard, *Correspondance,* 6:75–77; and CO, 10/b:403–4.
[178]Herminjard, *Correspondance,* 6:229; and CO, 11:36.

have been printed with both the name of Geneva and of the printer. As for his other works that have been printed elsewhere, they are on sale in the various shops."[179]

Saconay's comment does contain a grain of truth, however, as we shall see in the chapter on censorship.[180] In the early 1560s, Genevan censorship began to prohibit certain works because their authors were thought to be Lutheran or German. To understand Calvin's gradual shift on the subject, one must return to the case of Melanchthon's *Loci communes*. As we have seen, in 1546 Calvin encouraged the French reading public to read the book, reprinted by Crespin in 1551 with a preface by Calvin. Yet in 1559, plans for a new edition were set aside. In the intervening years, some of Calvin's opponents contrasted his views with those of Melanchthon on a number of occasions, even going so far as to refer to the French translation. In 1551, Jerôme Bolsec invoked Melanchthon, Bullinger, and Brenz against Calvin.[181] In 1552, Calvin had to reassure Laelio Sozzini that he and Melanchthon did not differ on the issue of predestination.[182] In a document sent to the Genevan Council in 1552, Jean Trolliet cited four pages from the translation of the *Loci* to support his own views on predestination. Calvin was then forced to admit "that Melanchthon's way of teaching is different from mine." He reiterated that Melanchthon had not wanted to enter into contentious matters because of his timidity and had been led by "unduly creaturely prudence." However, Calvin still ended with praise for his German colleague. "I honor Melanchthon both because of his excellent knowledge and because of his virtues, and above all because he has faithfully worked to sustain the Gospel."[183] This encounter predates the controversy with Westphal. Because matters deteriorated over time and discussions became more and more bitter, by 1559 it no longer seemed fitting to provide the *Loci communes* in French.

Calvin as a Critic

The Opinions of a Knowledgeable Reader

Calvin received many books for review, whether unpublished manuscripts or books that were already on the market. Calvin, Viret, and Farel were particularly active readers of each other's manuscripts. In the case of Viret's writings, Calvin seemed more willing to take the time to suggest revisions. In all likelihood, the work that Viret sent to Calvin in 1548 was *De la vertu et usage du ministere de la Parolle*. Shortly after receiving it, Calvin already made one comment. When he returned the manuscript, he had made only one change, namely, replacing one word with another that seemed more appropriate. "The rest without exception pleases me greatly."[184]

---

[179]CO, 9:448; and *Recueil,* 1843.
[180]See below 262–63.
[181]*RCP,* vol. 1, 91, 98.
[182]CO, 14:229–30; and Doumergue, *Jean Calvin,* 2:554, and n. 4.
[183]CO, 14:382.
[184]CO, 12:652, 654.

As for Farel's writings, Calvin was more reluctant to become involved. Farel wrote the *Forme d'oraison pour demander à Dieu la saincte predication de l'Evangile*, basing it on his 1543 *Oraison tres devote*. Farel sent the manuscript of his new work to Viret and Calvin. Christophe Fabri, Farel's assistant in Neuchâtel, explained to Farel that he would press Viret to read over the work and that if needed he would bring it to Calvin.[185] Viret read the manuscript with care, providing copious notes and highlighting the passages that were hard to decipher "which the printers should pay attention to." He guessed that Calvin would be too busy to read the manuscript. Indeed, Calvin indicated that he had received the manuscript but transmitted it directly to Jean Girard for printing.[186]

The account of Farel's last work, the *Glaive de la Parole*, provides a clearer picture of the process. Viret received the manuscript, but admitted, "The issue is Farel's style. It would be hard to change something unless a lot of things were changed."[187] Viret sent the manuscript on to Calvin with a series of specific comments. Calvin refused to deal with the text following Viret's careful reading of it and made a startling comment: "Given that I am unable to make my own works better, how equipped am I to deal with others' works?"[188] Farel was unhappy at Calvin's refusal to provide an opinion and insisted on a response. Left with few options, Calvin sought an explanation that would not hurt his old fellow Reformer. In a passage quoted earlier, he explained to Farel that his own concise style was very different from Farel and Viret's wordiness.[189] Thus Calvin preferred to have Viret provide feedback. Farel became very discouraged over these less than enthusiastic responses and spoke of abandoning the project. Viret, however, provided encouragement to Farel and the work was published in the end.[190]

Other writers also sought Calvin's advice. In 1542, Calvin's physician Benoît Textor sent from Mâcon a work by a local schoolmaster, Eloy du Verger. Textor provided detailed instructions: "While reading the work with care, write on a separate sheet the mistakes you find and send it to us afterwards. Furthermore, you will deal with the man in your usual way, that is, charitably, simply, gently, and mercifully, avoiding all insults."[191] Information is lacking on this minor author from Mâcon and none of Calvin's notes on this work have survived.

In March 1548, Miles Coverdale sent Calvin a Latin version of the *Book of Common Prayer* for possible publication.[192] The first English version of the prayer book appeared in March 1549. The creation of a new English liturgy, closer to a

---

[185]CO, 12:22–23.
[186]CO, 12:28–29, 32.
[187]CO, 13:335–36.
[188]CO, 13:347.
[189]CO, 13:374; and above 122–24.
[190]CO, 13:388, 393.
[191]CO, 11:477.
[192]CO, 12:671–72.

Reformed outlook, was the result of the accession of Edward VI in January 1547. As far as I am aware, Calvin did not respond to this dispatch.

In June 1548, François Hotman sent Calvin a preface for his comments. In all likelihood it was the dedication to a small legal treatise published in Lyon. Shortly afterward Hotman left Lyon for Geneva, where he worked as Calvin's secretary for a few months.[193]

When assessing the timeliness of a work, Calvin was able to make a distinction between his own personal opinion, which he shared with a few faithful correspondents, and reasons of simple expediency. When Jacques de Bourgogne suggested to Calvin that Bernardino Ochino's sermons be translated, Calvin explained his viewpoint in a few words: "I can tell you privately that [these sermons] are more useful in Italian than in other languages, mainly because of the man's name." Thus Calvin did not think highly of these texts, but he knew that Ochino's name had an impact. He added: "there is such a diversity of opinions that it is not a bad idea to attempt to bring some people in via this approach."[194]

When Calvin gave his opinion in 1548 on the *Traité très utile de Sainct Sacrement* by Valérand Poullain, his assessment was harsh: "these are limping texts." He explained that he had read the work the year before, not knowing its author. Calvin added to Viret, "If you want to lose both energy and time, you will immediately be able to see what there is to criticize."[195] Calvin's reservations about the work of a faithful disciple were also probably motivated by Poullain's lawsuit in Basel over a broken engagement. Calvin supported Jacques de Bourgogne against Poullain in this instance.[196]

Calvin's comment to Grataroli in 1559 undoubtedly referred to an unpublished work by Simon Grynaeus on the Lord's Supper. This text must have been put aside for a while, since Grynaeus died in 1541. Calvin's opinion of the work was mixed: "Even though Grynaeus's work does not displease me, I do not however think that it is effective in opposing the follies that disturb the church of today. This is why I have avoided such an ambiguous way of teaching."[197]

Conclusion

Calvin was a voracious and reflective reader who retained what he had read. His written corpus benefited from this slow accumulation of both ancient and more modern readings. A full assessment of Calvin as a reader will not be possible until the critical reedition of the *Opera omnia denuo recognita* is complete, assuming that

---

[193]CO, 12:717; and Baudrier, *Bibliographie lyonnaise: Recherches sur les imprimeurs, librairés, éditeurs, relieurs et fondeurs de lettres de Lyon au XVIe siecle* (Lyon: Librairie ancienne d'Auguste Brun, 1895–1921), 8:222–23.

[194]CO, 12:322.

[195]CO, 12:663.

[196]Denis, *Les Églises d'étrangers*, 245–50.

[197]CO, 17:431.

the editor of each volume will be able to discover which works Calvin in fact used.[198]

In terms of his choice of editions of classical authors' writings, Calvin displayed excellent critical judgment for his time. However, he did not blindly follow even renowned editors such as Erasmus, whether for the New Testament or the texts of the church fathers.

Calvin retained his critical judgment in all his readings. He gladly challenged his adversaries, but also noted doctrinal errors even in the works of authors he respected, whether they were church fathers like Chrysostom or Ambrose, or contemporaries such as Luther and Melanchthon. Calvin also criticized poor exegetical approaches, as in the case of Origen and Jerome, and undue verbosity, as in the case of Farel. Yet Calvin's stringent standards were not inflexible: he softened his assessments and even more so his public statements when the writer in question was a respected author, a friend, or a close colleague. One quotation will suffice. In 1539, Calvin explained to Zebedee that his respect for a man would never prevent him from exercising his critical faculties. "I do not hold such an immoderate and blind admiration for any man that would keep me from a steady judgment or from the value of the faith."[199]

5. AN ORDINARY CHRISTIAN'S BOOKS

The preceding sections laid out Calvin's own reading practices. But what did he think about what ordinary Christians should read? In contrast to Luther, he left no specific writings on the subject. Luther established a relatively clear distinction between Christians in general—*der gemeine Mann*—and the elite, whose role was to direct the church and the state. The elite were the only ones who could access all printed materials, while ordinary Christians had to make do with works in German, especially the catechism. Even the German Bible was intended primarily for pastors.

Luther's emphasis on the role of books in the education of future magistrates did not lead him to admire all printed texts unreservedly. Instead he was very critical of the great numbers of useless books that were published. Indeed, many of his contemporaries echoed the same theme. In short, Luther's position was nuanced and even hesitant in regards to the use of books, especially by the bulk of the population. He constantly reiterated the need to return to the Book of books: the Bible.[200]

Calvin did not explicitly deal with these issues. However, a study of his approach allows us to guess at some of his choices. The *Institutes* only explicitly

---

[198]This is an international project, the first volume of which was published by Droz in Geneva in 1992.

[199]Herminjard, *Correspondance*, 5:316; and CO, 10/b:345.

[200]Flachmann, *Martin Luther*, 119–225.

mentions reading once, and is referring to the Bible. Calvin stated that it was important that "each person make sure to read in private, but there should be masters and teachers to guide and help us."[201] In this passage, Calvin was returning to the fundamental need for assistance in interpreting scripture. A bibliographical analysis highlights a difference in this era between the Reformed and the Lutherans. The Reformed produced significantly more small-format editions of the Bible, indicating a more widespread practice of private reading of the sacred texts.

Did Calvin encourage the reading of other works? The history of Genevan printing provides evidence in response to this question. The chapter on censorship will show that the Genevan faithful were not allowed to read whatever they wanted. Calvin was fully aware that the Genevan printers sought to make a profit on any work, even a religious one. This negative facet of printing shows Calvin's concern to ensure that everyone had access to good books.

Based on what he prohibited, Calvin's recommended reading list was austere. Works of fiction or entertainment were forbidden. Even satire had limits: for instance, humorous works on God and truth were prohibited.[202] Attacks on corruption did not always meet with approval; for instance, the Genevan Council seized a pamphlet against the papacy because it led to "mockery and ridicule" rather than edification.[203] Calvin's austerity marked a change from the joyous effervescence of the first generation of Reformers, whose works were printed in Neuchâtel by Pierre de Vingle.

Calvin also dealt with the excessive number of bad books. Already in his first dedications, he attacked authors' ambitions to be published whatever the circumstances and he returned to this matter on several occasions. In the more restricted domain of biblical commentaries, Calvin noted that poor-quality works often outnumbered worthwhile editions.[204]

Overall, Calvin certainly favored individual reading by all the faithful. In this instance it seems that the Reformed did much to encourage everyone to read, without however authorizing free interpretation of the scriptures. Thus tension reigned between Christians' personal commitment and their submission to the control of the church.

[201]Calvin, *Institution,* ed. Benoît, 4.1.5.
[202]See above 106–7.
[203]See above 261–63.
[204]See above 45, 83, 84–85.

Chapter Five

Printing

Once books are written, they have to be printed. This task, which takes place after the creative process of writing is completed, will be the focus of this chapter. The two main questions that we will address are: how did Calvin select his printers? and how much knowledge did he have about the technical and economic constraints that printers faced? Before dealing with the second question, I will analyze Calvin's dedicatory epistles. The Reformer's use of this traditional practice is significant in terms of his relations with the publishing world.

1. Choosing a Printer

A study of the bibliography of Calvin's works shows that his approach varied widely, depending on whether the work to be printed was one he had written himself or one containing his oral teachings as recorded by third parties. Thus, this section is in two parts. The main one deals with the texts Calvin composed and wrote out himself, and the second shorter part provides a more rapid overview of his published sermons and lectures, the oversight of which was left to those who had supervised the note-taking process.

Works That Calvin Authored

A Small-Scale Start (Paris, 1531–32)

The Orléans student entrusted his first works to minor Parisian printers. When a group of Pierre de L'Estoile's followers decided to respond to Alciatus's critiques, their counteroffensive made use of the *Antapologia* written by Nicolas Duchemin in 1529. Calvin oversaw the printing in Paris, carried out by Gérard Morrhy,[1] and

---

[1] Ph. Renouard, *Répertoire des imprimeurs parisiens: Libraires, fondeurs de caractères et correcteurs*

added a dedication to the work.[2]

In the following year, Calvin had Louis Cyaneus, another small Parisian printer, produce his commentary on Seneca's *De Clementia*.[3] The author paid the printing costs and asked some of his friends to use the work in their university teaching in order to sell more copies. The edition was shared with an Orléans bookseller, Philippe Loré, who took charge of the part of the print run that bore his name on the title page. In 1533–34, Calvin himself taught on Seneca's treatise in the Collège de Fortet in Paris.[4] Overall, one gets the sense of a relatively unknown author struggling to break into the circle of the leading humanists. Yet Calvin had no lack of ambition, since his Seneca edition was intended to be a revision of the work by the great Erasmus, who was at the peak of his career at the time.

Johannes Oporinus and His Friends (Basel, 1536–38)

Following Nicolas Cop's sermon of 1 November 1533 and the Affair of the Placards of October 1534, Calvin left France and settled in Basel in January 1535 or slightly earlier. He found lodgings in the home of Conrad Resch and his wife Catherine Clein, a couple who had many ties to printing, not only in Basel but also in Paris and Lyon. Resch, one of the first booksellers to send Lutheran books into France, was also the godfather of one of Calvin's later printers, Conrad Badius.[5]

In Basel, Calvin built contacts with a group of printers to whom he remained loyal for a number of years. In 1536–37, this group consisted of Balthasar Lasius, Thomas Platter, Robert Winter, and Johannes Oporinus. Thomas Platter provided a highly colorful account of their work.[6] Calvin's encounter with these men was no coincidence, since both Platter and Oporinus were themselves scholars. The four men in the group formed an association around the same time as Calvin arrived in Basel. Oswald Myconius, a close friend of Platter's, sent a few letters in July 1535 to recommend the new printing firm to Calvin.[7] Although the manuscript of Calvin's *Institutes* was ready in August 1535, it only appeared in print in time for the March 1536 book fair. This group of printers was made up of novices, who only managed to bring out their first book at the end of 1535, but by March 1536, they had produced

---

d'imprimerie, depuis l'introduction de l'imprimerie à Paris, 1470, jusqu'à la fin du seizième siècle (Paris: M. J. Minard, 1945), 318.

[2]CO, 9:785–86.

[3]For the list of the printers of Calvin's works described in the *Bibliotheca Calviniana*, see *B.C.2*, 1089–106.

[4]*B.C.1*, no. 32/1.

[5]Droz, *Chemins*, 1:97–99. On Resch, see P. G. Bietenholz, *Basle and France in the Sixteenth Century* (Geneva: Droz, 1971), 33–35 and passim; Higman, *Diffusion de la Réforme*, 35, 49.

[6]Th. Platter, *Autobiographie,* trans. M. Helmer (Paris: Librairie Armand Colin, 1964), 105–11. Information on Calvin's stay in Basel can be found in Droz, *Chemins*, 1:89–126, though this section should be not be taken at face value. As for E. Le Roy Ladurie's work, *Le siècle des Platter* (Paris: Fayard, 1995), 189–91, it provides nothing except for a number of errors.

[7]CO, 10/b:47–50.

a number of important works, especially the correspondence between Zwingli and Oecolampadius.[8]

Even though the names of Platter and Lasius appeared on the title page as printers in the case of the *Institutes* and the *Epistolae duae,* Oporinus in fact did most of the work in bringing these two texts to print. He was the one who sent Calvin the first dozen copies of the *Epistolae duae* on 25 March 1537, promising to send more and offering him other works from his stock.[9] Both books were successful and their sales were strong. After arriving in Geneva, Calvin had a local printer bring out the *Confession de foy,*[10] but he remained faithful to his Basel friends when it came to his Latin works. He did, however, complain about the printing delays for the *Institutes*.

Later on, Calvin sent his *Catechismus* to Robert Winter, who had taken over from the Platter-Lasius firm and brought in Oporinus as his adviser.[11] Oporinus encouraged Calvin to rework the *Institutes* and Calvin began this task in Geneva. When he was forced out of that city, he found lodgings in the Latin school in Basel headed by Oporinus.[12] Thus Calvin had no shortage of opportunities to discuss his book projects at length with the humanist printer. Naturally, once he had settled in Strasbourg in September 1538, he sent the revised text of the *Institutes* to Robert Winter. However, the latter's lack of progress forced Calvin to turn elsewhere. Winter left the manuscript aside, missed the deadline of the 1539 spring book fair, and finally returned the manuscript to Strasbourg.[13]

However, Calvin made use of Robert Winter again in 1545, and sent him an anonymous pamphlet intended for circulation in Germany, the *Admonitio paterna Pauli III.* Calvin's choice proved to be a poor one. For one thing, the printed work was late in reaching Calvin; for another, the copy given to the Basel pastor Myconius contained an illegible first section, "due to some sort of dampness." Farel's assessment was harsh when he encountered the work during a visit to Basel. Writing to Calvin, he stated, "You should punish the printer who produced the Paul III so badly. Yet you had done such good work on this."[14]

Wendelin Rihel, the Faithful Supporter (Strasbourg, 1539–46)

When he settled in Strasbourg in September 1538, Calvin had no immediate plans to work with local printers, but was forced to do so due to Robert Winter's slow pace. Calvin then came into contact with the printer Wendelin Rihel, a scholar

[8]M. Steinmann, *Jahonnes Oporinus. Ein Basler Buchdrucker um die Mitte des 16. Jahrhunderts* (Basel, Stuttgart: Helbing & Lichenhahn, 1967), 11–12.

[9]*B.C.1,* nos. 36/1, 37/1; Herminjard, *Correspondance,* 4:208; and CO, 10/b:90–91.

[10]*B.C.1,* no. 37/2.

[11]*B.C.1,* no. 38/1.

[12]Herminjard, *Correspondance,* 5:20 n. 3, 146–47; and CO, 10/b:279–80.

[13]Herminjard, *Correspondance,* 5:214, 227; and CO, 10/b:310, 315.

[14]*B.C.1,* no. 45/13; and CO, 12:56, 38 [the letter should be dated 6 April 1545], 81.

who directed one of the largest printing houses in the city.[15] Calvin entrusted a number of works in succession to Rihel: his revised *Institutes,* the reply to Sadoleto, and his commentary on the Epistle to the Romans. Even after his return to Geneva, Calvin continued to send Rihel his exegetical works in Latin.[16] In a letter to Farel dated 1546, Calvin explained the reasons for his loyalty to Rihel. "As for my publications, I am not a free agent, at least in terms of the Pauline Epistles. You have already heard me say that during my stay in Strasbourg, Wendelin [Rihel] bound me to him because of his assistance, so much so that I would be condemned for ingratitude if I did not help him. Indeed, when I was in great financial need, he spent more than forty gold ecus on my affairs, and he was as prompt to look after my domestic situation as if I had hired him to do this. Thus it would now be unjust to refuse to send him the Epistles."[17] Beyond monetary issues, Calvin's statement shows how his status as an author had changed: he no longer had to seek out publishers. From then on publishers sought him out, and he helped them by entrusting a work to their press.

A number of events led Calvin to stop using Rihel's services. The temporary disappearance of Calvin's commentary on Second Corinthians in August 1546 showed him the dangers inherent in sending documents over long distances.[18] In the same time period, the printing of the *Brevis Instructio adversus errors anabaptistarum* led to a misunderstanding, probably due to distance factors. Without warning, Rihel omitted a dedication sent from Geneva for the work.[19]

The commentary that had gone astray in August 1546 was finally published in Geneva rather than in Strasbourg. The true reason for this was the Schmalkaldic War that began in July 1546 and that severely hampered the Strasbourg booksellers' freedom of movement. In April 1547, the situation worsened when Charles V's victory at Mühlberg left him in a position of strength. Hence Calvin took back his manuscript and had it printed in Geneva in 1548.[20]

Between 1542 and 1548, Valérand Poullain, who was briefly pastor of the French church of Strasbourg, worked as a liaison between Calvin and Rihel. Poullain probably oversaw the correction of proofs.[21] Finally, he also prepared the index for the 1550 *Institutes* in spite of his frosty relations with Calvin beginning in 1547.[22]

An Admiring Disciple: Michel du Bois (Geneva, 1540–41)

Already during his first stay in Geneva, Calvin had a local printer handle a work

[15]M. U. Chrisman, *Lay Culture, Learned Culture: Books and Social Change in Strasbourg, 1480–1599* (New Haven, London: Yale University Press, 1982), 4, 6, 14, 18.
[16]*B.C.1,* nos. 39/2, 39/4, 39/5, 40/3, 42/5, 43/5, 45/5, 45/11, 46/1, 46/2.
[17]CO, 12:391.
[18]See above 3–4.
[19]CO, 12:381; and *B.C.1,* no. 46/1.
[20]CO, 12:423; and *B.C.1,* no. 48/8.
[21]CO, 11:685, 12:216; and *B.C.1,* 130, 216.
[22]*B.C.1,* no. 50/16. On the Poullain affair, see above 176.

in French intended for a local audience. For this text, Calvin turned to Wigand Koeln, a printer who had been working in Geneva since 1519.[23] Yet some of Calvin's friends, especially Guillaume Farel, who always focused on propaganda via printed works, encouraged more modern and efficient printers than the aging Koeln to settle in Geneva. Jean Girard arrived in 1536, followed by Michel du Bois and Jean Michel in 1537–38. During Calvin's Strasbourg exile, Michel du Bois was among Calvin's most active supporters. In October 1540, he was one of the delegates sent by the Genevan Council to recall Calvin to the city.

With the support of Antoine du Pinet, who assisted Calvin in his task of writing from at least 1538 onward,[24] Michel du Bois attempted to become Calvin's printer of choice. On 4 October 1539, writing from Geneva to Calvin, Du Pinet stated,

> Congratulations on the successful publication of your catechism [a reference to the *Institutes*], but we still regret that we were not the ones chosen to bring this second edition out. Indeed, Michel du Bois came to me to complain: until now, he thought highly of your works and he had extended deadlines in order to have your works as the first fruits of his print shop, intending to dedicate his print shop to you. It is true that he owns varied and elegant typefaces that are certainly as good or better than those owned by German printers. Without wanting to speak ill of anyone, I have no doubt that books will be published in his print shop with more care and attention than in any other. For this man is the clear front-runner in terms of everything to do with the art of printing. Therefore, brother Calvin, I would urge you not to fail to entrust your nightly labors, as a Frenchman, to other Frenchmen.

Du Pinet's praise of Du Bois continued.[25] The appeal to Calvin's patriotism was certainly aimed at breaking the Reformer's bond with the Strasbourg printers, but also perhaps his links with the Piedmont native Jean Girard.

Whatever motives shaped Calvin's actions beginning in 1540, Du Bois obtained a part of Calvin's French works and even a Latin reprint.[26] In 1541, Calvin entrusted his *Psychopannychia* to Du Bois,[27] but the project collapsed, as did any future collaboration when the printer suddenly left Geneva at the end of 1541. Herminjard's hypothesis that Du Bois went bankrupt is generally accepted.[28]

---

[23]*B.C.1*, no. 37/2.

[24]See above 132–33.

[25]Herminjard, *Correspondance,* 6:37–38; and CO, 10/b:373–74.

[26]Herminjard, *Correspondance,* 5:211 and 6:37–38, 117; CO, 10/b:307, 373–374, 426; and *B.C.1*, nos. 40/6, 40/7, 41/2–4.

[27]See *B.C.1*, no. 42/5.

[28]See R. Peter, "Un imprimeur de Calvin: Michel du Bois," in *Bulletin de la Société d'histoire et d'archéologie de Genève* 16 (1978): 285–335. Further information can be found in L. Guillo, *Les éditions musicales de la Renaissance lyonnaise* (Paris: Klincksieck, 1991), 116–20.

An Inescapable Solution: Jean Girard (Geneva 1541–54)

Following Michel du Bois's departure, Calvin turned to Jean Girard, since he was then essentially the only good printer in the city.[29] His sole competitor, Jean Michel, who ran a print shop from 1538 to 1544, used an old and outdated Gothic typeface.[30] For a little less than a decade, Calvin first entrusted to Girard his French works, then his Latin polemic after 1543, and finally, after 1546, his exegetical works in Latin. In 1550, when new printing houses began to open in Geneva, Calvin progressively turned away from Girard.

The relations between the printer and Calvin were not as harmonious as one might imagine, given the lengthy catalogue of works described in the previous paragraph. Indeed, Girard got along better with Viret and Farel, and it was in fact Farel who called Girard to Geneva in 1536. Upon his arrival, Girard was perceived as a modern printer, using roman typeface for the first time in Geneva and following Olivétan in his quest for "modern spelling" with accents, cedillas, and other diacritical marks.[31]

In 1540, Girard brought out the Sword Bible. From a commercial perspective, this publication was a masterstroke. The newly fledged Reformation did not need a large folio Bible like the heavy Olivétan Bible, but rather a quarto volume, ideally suited for constantly traveling pastors. But the production of this Bible was a tactical error. Calvin never accepted this version because the revision work had been carried out without his agreement.[32] Nevertheless, Calvin remained in occasional contact with Girard during his Strasbourg exile.[33]

Girard was technologically adept and produced high-quality printed books. However, his financial skills were so minimal that he was always running short of funds. Given his decade-long monopoly, he should have become wealthy, but he ended up dying in penury. He relied on financial backers, who for the most part remain little known. One was Jean Chautemps and another, more peripherally involved, was Jean de la Maisonneuve. Both these men were Genevan citizens and leading merchants. Chautemps was a dominant force in the paper industry.[34] Another associate of Girard's was René de Bienassis, whose career is detailed below.

---

[29]S. R. Brandt, "Jean Girard, Genevan Publisher, 1536–1557" (thesis, University of California–Berkeley, 1992).

[30]G. Berthoud, "Les impressions genevoises de Jean Michel (1538-1544)," in *Cinq siècles d'imprimerie genevoise*, ed. J.-D. Candaux and B. Lescaze (Geneva: Droz, 1980), 1:55–88.

[31]S. Baddeley, *L'orthographe française au temps de la Réforme* (Geneva: Droz, 1993), 236–42.

[32]G. Berthoud, *Antoine Marcourt, Réformateur et pamphlétaire* (Geneva: Droz, 1973), 70–74; and Bogaert and Gilmont, "De Lefèvre d'Étaples," 70–71.

[33]Herminjard, *Correspondance*, 6:31, 186; and CO, 10/b:372, 11:22.

[34]A contract dated 1540 confirms Chautemps's role and reveals the participation of La Maisonneuve: J.-Fr. Bergier, "Le contrat d'édition de la Bible de l'épée, Geneva, 1540," *B.H.R.* 18 (1956): 110–13. On J. Chautemps, see Cartier, "Arrêts du Conseil de Genève sur le fait de l'imprimerie et de la librairie de 1541 à 1550," in *Mémoires et documents publiés par la société d'histoire et d'archeologie de Genève* (Geneva: Aubert-Schuchardt, 1888), 432–38, esp. 437–38.

From around 1545 to 1554, Girard also had links to the bookseller-turned-printer Simon du Bosc.[35] This link was somewhat suspect in 1554, given that Du Bosc worked closely with his uncle, Guillaume Guéroult. Guéroult, in turn, clashed with Beza over the translation of the Psalms and was an open sympathizer of Michael Servetus, whose *Christianismi restitutio* Guéroult printed in Vienne.[36]

A letter from Viret, dated July 1545, sheds light on Girard's situation. Writing from Lausanne, Viret intervened on Girard's behalf. "This good man is so severely hampered by a lack of funds that he may be forced to shut down his press unless help is found." Viret was hoping that a financial backer could be found to become Girard's associate. "I would recommend him [Girard] to you, but I know already that you consider him worthy of recommendation." Calvin's reservations vis-à-vis Girard undoubtedly explain why the printer turned to Viret for assistance rather than to Calvin, with whom he was in daily contact. Viret insisted on the matter, describing a situation that Calvin knew well. "Books these days do not sell well, while persecution flourishes. Many of those to whom he gave books to sell have perished."[37] In this last sentence, Viret was referring to the contracts binding book peddlers and the Genevan booksellers. Peddlers received the books as an advance and only paid for them once they made the sales. Thus peddlers who were arrested and executed represented a net financial loss for booksellers, as is well known in the case of Laurent de Normandie.[38]

From 1541 onwards, Calvin was thus forced to entrust his manuscripts to Jean Girard. During the first years, there is no evidence of tension between the two men in surviving sources. Indeed, in 1545, Calvin even displayed his confidence in Girard. The *Supplex exhortatio,* intended for Charles V, needed to have an appearance worthy of its imperial recipient. Bucer suggested having the work printed in Strasbourg, but Calvin gave it to Girard.[39] In reality, the only evidence of reservations on Calvin's part is that he made use of other printers prior to 1541. But Girard only owned one press[40] and the relative chaos that reigned there meant that he could not satisfy all the needs of the Reformers.

When he sent his *Brevis instructio* to Strasbourg in 1546, Calvin told Rihel that his translator, Nicolas des Gallars, "could not find anyone [in Geneva] who was willing to print the two texts he had translated into Latin."[41] This remark is probably

[35]A. Cartier, "Arrêts du Conseil de Genève," 520–21.

[36]E. Balmas, "Tra Umanesimo e Riforma: Guillaume Guéroult, "terzo uomo" del processo Serveto" in *Montaigne a Padova: E altri studi sulla letteratura francese del cinquecento* (Padua: Liviana, 1962), 109–218; and Balmas, "Guillaume Guérouelt e Théodore de Bèze: un curioso esempio di concorrenza letteraria nel XVI secolo," *Annali: Facoltà di Economia e Commercio Università di Padova* 1 (1969):1–40. See also below 270–71.

[37]CO, 12:105–6.

[38]Schlaepfer, "Laurent de Normandie," 180–82.

[39]Herminjard, *Correspondance,* 9:86–87; CO, 11:634–35; and *B.C.1,* no. 43/7.

[40]CO, 12:405.

[41]*B.C.1,* no. 46/1.

indicative of Girard's overwork rather than his inability to print Latin, since he had brought out des Gallars's Latin translation of the *Libellus de coena domini* in the previous year.[42]

A year later, when he sought to attract Jacques de Bourgogne to Geneva, Calvin even praised Girard. He noted that the *Excuse* written by his famous correspondent "would be better printed than elsewhere [Basel], namely, with a clearer typeface, better paper, and fewer mistakes."[43] A little later, Calvin explained to Jacques de Bourgogne that "the printing of the book has not yet started, because some of the characters in the typeface had to be recast. This is the typeface that was used to print the *Supplicatio:* it is very readable and visually appealing. The work will begin this week, God willing."[44] This quotation shows that Calvin cared about good-quality printing. Thus Girard made sure to have newly cast characters on hand to print the *Excuse,* which was addressed to the emperor.

Calvin's first complaints surfaced in 1547. Writing to Viret in August of that year, Calvin noted, "Girard has not yet delivered your preface, though I told him to bring it today."[45] The next year, one of Viret's works appeared without a preface. Calvin suspected that the printer was trying to cut corners for financial reasons, "And I believe there is another reason: they are worried they will run short of time to print my commentaries."[46]

Calvin's frustration with Girard boiled over in a letter to Farel in 1550: "Your work is not being printed and I do not know whether this is due to Girard's laziness, to the chaos that reigns in his print shop, or to his thoughtlessness in taking on too many works at once. I have already spoken to him about this more than once, and he has made solemn promises regarding this matter. For his part, Normandie has often asked him to speed up. The same holds true for the *Institutes,* which should have been finished before this month, and which is not yet ready. I wanted to let you know briefly what is happening, so that you might know that I have not been negligent. Girard does not react much to my pleas, and simply assures me that he will be working on it."[47]

Calvin's growing annoyance led to a gradual estrangement, especially as he found a new choice of printers once the print shops of Crespin and then of Robert Estienne opened their doors. In 1550, Girard still published all of Calvin's new works. In 1551, he continued to publish the commentaries that his press had been the first to print. The 1551 editions were either in French translation or in a collective Latin edition. In 1552, he printed a collection of Calvin's treatises with a preface

---

[42]*B.C.1,* no. 45/7.

[43]CO, 12:540; and *B.C.1,* no. 47/1.

[44]CO, 12:618. Calvin was referring to the bold roman font used in the 1543 *Supplex exhortatio* (*B.C.1,* no. 43/7).

[45]CO, 12:582.

[46]CO, 13:9–10.

[47]CO, 13:520.

by des Gallars. But Girard no longer had access to Calvin's new works. In 1553 and 1554, he only published the translations of two new commentaries.[48]

Girard did not take all this lying down. The final straw came when Calvin gave the task of printing the revised version of the commentaries on the New Testament Epistles to Robert Estienne. In Girard's eyes, he owned the rights to this work, since he had brought out its first edition. With Calvin's encouragement, Estienne let Girard know that the extent of the revisions meant that a transfer of the work to another printer was allowable. In August 1554, Girard, together with Simon du Bosc, asked the Genevan Council for a privilege for the works that the two men had published for the last twenty years. This move led to a reaction from Robert Estienne and Jean Chautemps, though the reasons for the latter's opposition to his former colleague are unknown. But in all likelihood, Girard's poverty from this point on was tied to the fact that his wealthy financial backers had cast him aside.[49] At first, Girard and Du Bosc's request received a favorable hearing in the Council, where opposition to Calvin remained strong. The councilors intended to establish the limits of Calvin's power. But on 10 September, the Reformer intervened directly, changing the state of play and annihilating any burgeoning opposition.

> "M. Calvin explained that he had heard that Messieurs have granted a privilege for his works and deeds, something he finds unreasonable, given that he is the author of the book. Previously there have been printers who printed poorly and made mistakes, and furthermore, if those who hold the privilege make some mistakes, he will have to bear the brunt of it. Therefore, he requested to be allowed to give his works to whomever he pleases, so that he can keep watch over his work and maintain his honor. Regarding Jean Girard, he will allow him to have the catechism, which will be more than enough for him to live on."[50]

Girard was finally cast aside. He never received any other new text written by Calvin, whose harsh phrase would be remembered: the catechism will be more than enough for him to live on. Girard did, however, manage to print the first major editions of Calvin's sermons.

The Proxies: René de Bienassis, Laurent de Normandie, and Others

Until his death, Calvin kept a close watch on the publishing world in Geneva. But over time, he gradually transferred oversight of the publications and their distribution to the leading booksellers, who also provided the necessary financing.

---

[48] *B.C.1,* nos. 51/2–4, 51/10, 51/11, 52/2, 53/2, 54/2.

[49] Geneva Archives de l'État, Registres du Conseil pour les affaires particulières, vol. 8, fols 117r, 118r, 124r, 125v, 126v, 131v (from 14 August to 4 September).

[50] RC 48:116ter (10/09/1554).

If my interpretation is valid, this phenomenon occurred already in 1546, with René de Bienassis.[51] Until now, this merchant, who had a vast income at his disposal, has been almost completely ignored. Printed and archival sources show that between 1546 and 1554 he oversaw and probably financed the publication of a large number of Calvin's works. He may in fact have already worked in the book trade in Lyon in 1543.[52] After 1550, Bienassis's support for Jacques de Bourgogne, Bolsec, and their friends led to increasingly cool relations between Bienassis and Calvin, and finally to an irreparable split.

Were there other financial backers like Jean Chautemps prior to 1546? There is no doubt that this merchant worked with Girard on other publications, such as the Sword Bible, but I have not found any evidence to suggest that he served as an intermediary between the author and the printer. Furthermore, during these years Calvin's main production took the form of short pamphlets, requiring only minimal financial outlay.

After 1550, Calvin's ability to do without Bienassis was strengthened by Laurent de Normandie who began to work in 1549. Until his death, Normandie assisted Calvin in the task of publication. The changeover from Bienassis to Normandie was a gradual one. When he arrived in Geneva in 1549, Normandie dealt with bookselling, but not book publication. However, he played a role already in 1550 for the Latin *Institutes* and in 1551 for the French version of the same work. Both of these texts were printed by Girard.[53] Bienassis continued to underwrite Calvin's works until 1551, apart from two further small investments in 1553 and 1554. In 1554, Normandie established a first booksellers' company and began to provide funds for publications.[54]

Although Normandie was never cast aside, other booksellers helped Calvin toward the end of his life. In 1559, Calvin's brother Antoine oversaw the publication of the definitive version of the *Institutes,* both in Latin and in French. He even helped his brother with the proofs and played a role in other later works by Calvin. As for the Lyon bookseller Antoine Vincent, he rapidly became one of Calvin's friends. Although Vincent probably never directly received any manuscript from Calvin, he was entrusted with an unsuccessful project of a French Bible and the edition of the Huguenot Psalter. As we shall see, he also played a role in the publication of Calvin's sermons.[55] Following this overview, let us return to a more detailed analysis.

---

[51]*B.C.1,* 244–46; and *B.C.2,* 1113.

[52]A translation of Erasmus's *Paraphrase sur toutes les epistres canoniques* (Lyon: Cl. La Ville, 1543) displays his motto, *Assez tost, si assez bien:* Baudrier, *Bibliographie lyonnaise,* 1:237. A copy of the work is held by the Universiteitsbibliotheek in Ghent, Acc. 9080).

[53]*B.C.1,* nos. 50/16, 51/11.

[54]Schlaepfer, "Laurent de Normandie," 179–230; and Gilmont, "L'imprimerie réformée," no. 2, 262–78.

[55]On Antoine Vincent's work in Geneva, see G. Morisse, "Le psautier de 1562," *Psaume* 5 (1991): 106–27. For more on the Bible translation project, see Beza, *Correspondance,* 3:175 n. 13 and passim.

The Turning Point of 1551

Settling in Geneva in 1548, Jean Crespin set up a press with the technical assistance of Conrad Badius and began by producing pamphlets containing extracts from the *Institutes*. Crespin soon obtained the printing rights for one of Calvin's new works, *De scandalis,* in Latin and in French.[56] In 1551, Crespin printed three of Calvin's major works: two commentaries and the revised French Bible.[57] In 1552, Calvin gave him the first part of the commentary on Acts to print and in 1554 he printed the second part.[58] From 1553 onwards, Crespin was displaced by other printers, as he never printed any further commentaries. However, he rapidly found a role as the preferred printer for Calvin's polemical works, a genre that was considerably less profitable.[59] Crespin may have been more adept at marketing these works for an international clientele, especially at Frankfurt. This hypothesis is more than likely, since the evidence suggests that he attended the book fairs more regularly than Henri Estienne, at least in later years.[60]

A dispute in 1556 shows that Crespin was barred from the most lucrative publications. In that year, he planned to bring out a midsized edition of the commentaries on the Pauline Epistles, to be bound with his own earlier edition of the canonical Epistles. According to Crespin, these texts were in the public domain. However, Robert Estienne, who had already taken this publication away from Girard, managed to put a stop to the print run that Crespin had already started. Crespin was forced to call a halt to his work, but did not destroy the sheets that had already been printed and instead kept them in stock. In 1563, when the work finally did enter the public domain, Crespin completed his edition and offered it for sale.[61]

Crespin's printed biblical commentaries were in Latin, since French translations of these works were entrusted to other printers. Jean Girard published the canonical Epistles,[62] while the brothers Antoine and Jean Rivery published the commentary on Isaiah,[63] and the Acts commentary was published by Philibert Hamelin.[64] René de Bienassis's influence can be seen in the works entrusted to Girard and Hamelin.

Laurent de Normandie and His Printers

Between 1549 and 1554, the management of Calvin's publications was reorganized for the long haul. Laurent de Normandie's first intervention in Calvin's published works took place in 1550. At the end of 1551, Robert Estienne established his printing house in Geneva. Finally, in 1554, Laurent de Normandie began to work as a book publisher.

---

[56]*B.C.1,* nos. 50/9, 50/12.
[57]*B.C.1,* nos. 51/5, 51/6; and Gilmont, *Bibliographie Crespin,* vol. 1, no. 51/3.
[58]*B.C.1,* nos. 52/3, 54/3.
[59]Gilmont, *Crespin,* 112–15.
[60]Gilmont, *Crespin,* 202.
[61]See *B.C.2,* no. 57/5.
[62]*B.C.1,* no. 51/10.
[63]*B.C.1,* no. 52/2.
[64]*B.C.1,* nos. 52/1, 54/1.

As a leading financier, Normandie did not run a printing house directly. Instead, he underwrote Conrad Badius's print shop and made use of other Genevan firms, especially that of Robert Estienne. From 1553 until his death in 1559, Estienne published the Latin version of all of Calvin's exegetical commentaries, as well as the definitive version of the *Institutes*.[65] He also published two of Calvin's polemical works in 1554 and 1555,[66] but, as noted above, this genre was soon left to Crespin. In 1553 and 1554, the French versions of the new commentaries were still produced by Girard.[67] From 1555 onwards, Conrad Badius, who was funded by Normandie, brought out the majority of the French translations of Calvin's works.[68]

After Robert Estienne's death in 1559, Badius printed an increasing number of Calvin's new works. It is true that at this point, Calvin was not writing many new commentaries.

When Badius left Geneva in 1562, Normandie turned to a number of smaller printers, in particular to Michel Blanchier and Jean Bonnefoy. Soon afterwards, François Perrin became Normandie's preferred printer. Thus Perrin was selected to print Calvin's commentaries on Joshua in Latin and French in 1564.[69]

All of these commentaries were overseen by Laurent de Normandie and his partner Philibert Grené, who defended their publishing rights against the horde of other printers. During the 1554 dispute over the monopoly of Calvin's works that had originally been printed by Girard, the counteroffensive was led by Robert Estienne and especially by Jean Chautemps, who were supported by Calvin. In the 1556 conflict between Robert Estienne and Jean Crespin over the commentaries on the Pauline Epistles, the two printers alone appeared before the Council. But in 1557, a joint request by Normandie and Grené focused on all of Calvin's New Testament commentaries, both in Latin and in French.[70]

Three years later, when the 1557 privilege was to expire, Normandie asked for and received an extension of the privilege. However, his victory was not complete, since the jointly printed edition done by Etienne Anastaise and Jean Bonnefoy was put on sale despite the extended privilege. Archival sources indicate that six months later, the printing quality of Anastaise and Bonnefoy's work was challenged, based on a report by Theodore Beza. I believe this challenge was a covert attack against competitors who had been allowed by the Council to publish works by Calvin in spite of Normandie's protests. The charges against Anastaise only bore fruit in January 1562. He was even sentenced to jail "for his major and serious faults of all kinds."[71]

---

[65] *B.C.1*, nos. 53/5, 54/8; and *B.C.2*, nos. 55/9, 56/3, 57/4, 59/4.
[66] *B.C.1*, no. 54/6; and *B.C.2*, no. 55/6.
[67] *B.C.1*, nos. 53/2, 54/2.
[68] *B.C.1*, no. 55/5; and *B.C.2*, nos. 56/1, 58/3.
[69] *B.C.2*, nos. 64/4, 64/9.
[70] See *B.C.2*, no. 56/1.
[71] See *B.C.2*, no. 60/1.

The Role of Antoine Calvin (1559–64)

During the final years of Calvin's life, Laurent de Normandie was no longer his sole advisor in publishing matters. The Reformer entrusted some editorial work to Antoine Vincent and above all asked his brother Antoine to oversee his works.

Antoine Calvin, who was inseparable from his brother from the moment he arrived in Geneva, first made an appearance in the world of printing with the final version of the *Institutes,* published in Latin by Robert Estienne in 1559 and in French by Jean Crespin in 1560. Firstly, Antoine Calvin's role was that of technical editor, helping his brother to proof the manuscript both directly and via Nicolas Colladon. Secondly, he acted as marketing director, funding the press and ensuring sales of the works.[72] In 1562, Antoine Calvin also oversaw the publication of Emmanuel Tremellius's *Enarrationes in Hoseam,* something that the Reformer pointed out to Tremellius.[73]

In the following years, Calvin finished his commentary on the Pentateuch, publishing it in Latin in 1563 and in French the following year. The Latin text was entrusted to Henri Estienne, the eldest son of Robert Estienne, who had brought out the 1559 *Institutes.* However, the son did not live up to the hopes of the Calvin brothers. Antoine turned to the Council to have them compel Henri Estienne to print the first sheet according to his directions. The Council even authorized Antoine Calvin to make use of another printer for the indexes, if necessary.[74] John Calvin complained about the excessive number of typographical errors in this edition.[75] As a result, when it came to the French version, Antoine Calvin turned to Henri's brother, François Estienne.[76]

The sources available do not provide enough information to know whether Antoine Calvin's arrival was a sign that his brother lacked confidence in Laurent de Normandie. Since the collaboration between the Reformer and the Noyon book merchant seemed to remain close, Antoine Calvin's presence should be seen as a new way of making use of people's talents rather than a sign of rivalry between two advisors.

Calvin's Oral Teaching

As we have noted, Calvin's circle relatively quickly sought to preserve a record of his sermons and lectures, and the Reformer agreed to the creation of a group of note takers to write down what he preached. After some debate, he also agreed to have his lectures recorded, so much so that in the end, Calvin systematically reviewed Jonviller's notes.[77]

---

[72]*B.C.2,* nos. 59/4, 60/8; and above 43–44; 130–31.

[73]CO, 19:565.

[74]Geneva, Archives d l'Etat, Registres du Conseil pour les affaires particulières, 13, fol. 57r; and *B.C.2,* no. 63/16.

[75] CO, 20:199.

[76]*B.C.2,* no. 64/5.

[77]See above 54–58; 73–80.

The Sermons

From 1549, the procedure for taking down Calvin's sermons functioned efficiently. The stenographers were paid by the Bourse française, which held all the rights to the works.[78] Whenever the sermons were put into print, the Bourse française asked for an equitable royalty.[79]

In 1554, some of the sermons taken down by Raguenier began to be published. Jean Girard started the process, publishing twenty-two sermons in 1554 and two in 1555.[80] At that time, Girard did not have the financial resources to bring out these works by himself, but there is no surviving evidence of the identity of the bookseller who obtained a manuscript from the Bourse. In any event, Girard's daring move is worth noting, especially since he had been forced away from publishing works by Calvin.

From 1557 onwards, Conrad Badius took over the work, publishing some of the most handsome collections of Calvin's sermons up until 1562. Laurent de Normandie's influence can be felt behind each of these editions. Already in 1558, Badius announced that these publications were part of a larger program.[81] After Badius's departure, Normandie continued to publish volumes of Calvin's sermons, entrusting one set to Pinereul in 1562 and another to Perrin in 1563. These two poverty-stricken printers relied on his commissions.[82]

Yet Normandie's monopoly was challenged in 1560, when independent printers brought out various collections of sermons. In spite of the fact that bibliographical studies provide a picture of anarchy in the Genevan printing world, these sermon collections were probably commissioned by one or two booksellers.

Although there is very little information about him, Pierre Juglier published two editions of sermons in 1560 and 1561.[83] Another volume of sermons was published in 1560 by Jean Dumont and Antoine Cercia.[84] In 1562, a consortium of six small printers prepared a collection of a few sermons with a preface by the pastor Jacques Roux.[85]

The leading bookseller Antoine Vincent certainly underwrote the volume of sermons on Job published in 1563, but he also bought extensive rights to the entire body of sermons beginning in 1561.[86] At that time, Vincent worked with the Genevan printer Jean de Laon.

[78]Gagnebin, "L'histoire des manuscripts," XIV–XXVIII.

[79]Droz, *Barthélemy Berton,* 46–52; and Gilmont, "L'apport de La Rochelle."

[80]*B.C.1,* no. 54/13; and *B.C.2,* no. 55/8.

[81]*B.C.2,* nos. 57/10, 58/5, 58/9, 58/10, 61/24, 62/22. Normandie's name is explicitly mentioned in the preface to the 1558 *Plusieurs sermons* (*B.C.2,* no. 58/5). Furthermore, Normandie had applied for permission to print Calvin's sermons (see *B.C.2,* nos. 58/5, 61/24).

[82]*B.C.2,* nos. 62/19, 63/21.

[83]*B.C.2,* nos. 60/4, 61/26.

[84]*B.C.2,* no. 60/12.

[85]*B.C.2,* no. 62/12.

[86]*B.C.2,* no. 63/22.

This list leaves aside reprints of works that entered the public domain. Our analysis shows clearly that the approach to sermon publication was different than it was for Calvin's other writings. Clearly the Bourse française had more leeway in this area. But it is likely that the Bourse waited for requests from booksellers instead of soliciting offers. This situation was due to the fact that Calvin had to be pushed to authorize each projected volume of sermons because he was always reluctant to see his sermons printed.

The Exegetical Lectures

We have already described the circumstances leading to the publication of Calvin's exegetical lectures. Following initial assistance from Nicolas des Gallars, the work was carried out by the brothers-in-law Jean Budé and Charles de Jonviller. Even though Jean Budé had more status (he signed the first prefaces), Charles de Jonviller oversaw the writing and printing process.

Because Jonviller was extremely particular about producing correct texts, he made the printers publish long lists of errata.[87] Constantly unhappy about the quality of their work, he went from one printer to another. The lectures on Hosea, the first of the twelve minor prophets, were brought out by Badius in Latin and in French in 1557. The Latin edition contained an errata sheet preceded by a lengthy self-defense from the printer.[88] Crespin carried out the bulk of the printing for the lectures on the minor prophets and came before the Genevan Council to request permission to publish the work. The French version was given to Nicolas Barbier and Thomas Courteau, booksellers with whom Crespin regularly worked. But the three men in fact worked for Jonviller, since he was the one who appealed to the Genevan Council when a conflict erupted over this edition.[89]

Jonviller selected a different printer for Calvin's lectures on Daniel. This time Budé and Jonviller requested permission to have the work entrusted to a protégé of Antoine Vincent, Jean de Laon. Archival sources confirm that Vincent played a role in this edition. However, Jonviller was unhappy with the end result. Once again, the outcome was a long list of errata in which the printer noted that typographical errors were unavoidable. Jean de Laon was still asked to bring out the French translation of the work. Antoine Vincent appeared in person before the Genevan Council to provide them with presentation copies of the work, both in Latin and in French.[90]

Jonviller returned to Crespin for the lectures on Jeremiah. Several sources provide details on the publication procedure. Jonviller covered all expenses, including the cost of the paper. On the day when he took delivery of 1,300 copies printed by Crespin, Jonviller sold them to three booksellers: Laurent de Normandie, Antoine

---

[87]See Gilmont, "La correction des épreuves."
[88]*B.C.2*, nos. 57/3, 57/8.
[89]*B.C.2*, nos. 59/5, 60/9.
[90]*B.C.2*, nos. 61/20, 62/14.

Vincent, and Nicolas Barbier. The excessive number of typographical errors again led to a long list of errata, in which Crespin in turn tried to explain the difficulties of the task.[91] The French translation of this work appeared in print after Calvin's death. This time, Jonviller turned to a Lyon printer, Claude Senneton. He too was forced to produce a long list of errata, but turned the situation to his advantage by attacking fellow printers who left out errata sheets and by depicting himself as a model to be imitated.

The Congrégations

Only a limited number of *congrégations* have survived, whether in manuscript or in print.[92] No details are available on how they were recorded; however, the fact that they were preserved in manuscripts that also contained sermons and that the first *congrégation* was printed alongside sermons suggests that the publication strategy for both *congrégations* and sermons was in fact similar.

Conclusion

Once Calvin became a successful author, he looked for high-caliber printers. His selection was based on quality issues and loyalty to his friends. Given that the Reformer had to deal increasingly with other responsibilities, from 1546 onwards he delegated authority to his advisors. However, he did not blindly hand over the reins, since he did not hesitate to weigh in on the side of his advisors in case of conflict.

Calvin's reservations about Girard, like his admiration for Robert Estienne, probably had several root causes. From a strictly typographical point of view, there was a clear difference between the two men. Girard was a former Waldensian Barbe, who had a long history of clandestine printing. His works were primarily smaller publications. There were only three folio volumes in his extensive catalogue. Girard preferred instead the octavo, or at most the quarto format. At a time when Reformed ideas had to penetrate a hostile world with great care, Girard preferred smaller, handheld formats. For his part, Robert Estienne never forgot that he had been a royal printer. To have an idea of what a luxury edition of this time would be like, one has to have held one of Estienne's Latin Bibles from his Parisian period and know how much paper cost at the time. When he came to Geneva, Estienne did not leave behind his appreciation for a quality product. Undoubtedly underwritten by Laurent de Normandie, the Latin commentaries published by Estienne were enormous folio volumes, printed in large characters with wide margins. In fact, one wonders how these works ever sold, both within Geneva and beyond its walls. But the fact remains that Calvin preferred this luxury printer.

Clearly, Calvin felt entitled to make certain demands since he knew that the

[91] *B.C.2*, no. 63/19.
[92] *B.C.2*, nos. 58/5, 62/6, 63/10; and above 80–81.

circulation of his writings was assured: he was truly in a dominant position in terms of his relations with the printing industry professionals.

2. THE ART OF DEDICATIONS

The use of dedications goes back hundreds of years. After the humanists brought them back into fashion, dedications continued to be used until the end of the ancien régime.[93] Dedicatory letters constitute a specific literary genre since they are personal letters read by a large audience. They need to combine all the charm of a private letter with the standards of a public document.

As Gérard Genette has shown, our analysis of dedicatory strategies should take into account the nature of the dedications: either private ones addressed to a friend or colleague, or public ones intended for political or religious figures.[94] This distinction is all the more important in that Beza followed the same division in 1564 in his biographical notes. Calvin "dedicated some of his works to private individuals as a show of thanks for a favor, or as a sign of friendship.... As for his other dedications intended for certain kings or princes or governments, his aim was to use these means to encourage some to persevere in the protection of the children of God, and to encourage the others to do the same."[95] Beza summed up the core intent in a few lines leaving us only with the task of explaining these remarks.

In this context, dedications will be considered in the narrow sense of the term, as a letter appearing at the start of a book and intended as a compliment to actual people. Therefore we will exclude any analysis of prefaces and marginal notes, including the preface of the Psalms Commentary written to *piis et ingenuis lectoribus*[96] and the

---

[93]For more on dedications as a literary genre, see G. Genette, *Seuils* (Paris: Editions du Seuil, 1987), 110–27. For an overview of dedicatory practices from the classical world to Luther's era, see H. Junghans, "Die Widmungsvorrede bei Martin Luther" in *Lutheriana: Zum 500: Geburtstag Martin Luthers,* ed. G. Hammer and K. Heinz zur Mühlen (Cologne, Vienna: Böhlau, 1984), 39–45. On medieval practice, see P. O. Kristeller, *Medieval Aspects of Renaissance Learning* (Durham: Duke University Press, 1974), 13–15. On the German lands and Erasmus, see K. Schottenloher, *Die Widmungsvorrede im Buch des 16. Jahrhunderts* (Münster: Westfalen, 1953). On England, see H. S. Bennett, *English Books and Readers, 1475–1557* (Cambridge: Cambridge University Press, 1952), 40–53; and his *English Books and Readers, 1558–1603* (Cambridge: Cambridge University Press, 1965), 30–55. See also B. Botfield, *Prefaces to the First Editions of the Greek and Roman Classics and of the Sacred Scriptures* (London: Henry George Bohn, 1861); as well as the work of Cl. Longeon in E. Dolet, *Préfaces françaises* (Geneva: Droz, 1979), 9-37; that of M. Lebel in J. Badius, *Préfaces de Josse Bade, 1462–1535: Humaniste, éditeur-imprimeur et préfacier,* ed. M. Lebel (Louvain: Peeters, 1988), 9–16; and that of R. Chartier, "Le prince, la bibliothèque et la dédicace," in *Le pouvoir des bibliothèques: La mémoire des livres en Occident,* ed. M. Baratin and Chr. Jacob (Paris: A. Michel, 1996), 204–23.

[94]Genette, *Seuils,* 122–23.

[95]CO, 21:36.

[96]CO, 31:13–36; and *B.C.2,* no. 57/4. For more on this commentary, see Gilmont, "La rédaction et la publication," 6–10.

dedication to the *De aeterna Dei praedestinatione* signed by all the Genevan pastors.[97] Based on these parameters, there are thirty-three items on the list of Calvin's dedications. (This list appears in chronological order in Appendix VI). Any interpreter of Calvin's dedications should note that his reputation grew considerably following his first Parisian publications. Already the first edition of the *Institutes* was a financial success. Beginning in the 1540s, Calvin knew that his works sold well. Hence Calvin's dedications were no longer those of a supplicant but were rather a prized compliment.

During his lifetime, Calvin published over a hundred different works.[98] Less than a third of these contained a dedicatory letter, including his major books: the *Institutes,* the biblical commentaries, and the exegetical lectures. Calvin's reluctance to see his oral lectures in print can be seen in the lack of a dedication in the first trial volume of these lectures, published in 1557.[99] The success of this first attempt pushed all his hesitations aside, and the successive volumes of the *Praelectiones* each contained a dedication. The majority of Calvin's dedications, twenty-six out of thirty-three, appeared in the three categories of his work described above. In contrast, his didactic and polemical works only rarely contained a dedication, whereas his sermons, only reluctantly published by the Reformer, never included a dedication.

Choosing a Dedicatee

The First Dedications

Calvin's oldest dedication appeared in another man's work, Nicolas Duchemin's *Antapologia.* This defense of Pierre de l'Estoile against Alciatus's attacks was prefaced by a poem by Duchemin addressed to the two sons of Adam Fumée and by a dedication to Claude de Hangest and Antoine de Lalaing, the son of the Count of Hoogstraeten.[100] Calvin added a dedication to his friend and fellow student at Orléans and Bourges, François de Connan.[101] Calvin used this letter as a means to lessen the conflict between the supporters of l'Estoile and Alciatus, or, as Olivier Millet termed it, Calvin's role was that of a *"moyenneur,"* or intermediary.[102]

This work shows how narrow Calvin's circle was at the time. Indeed, both Hangest and Connan reappeared in Calvin's next work: his 1532 edition of Seneca opened with a dedication to Claude de Hangest, commendatory of Saint-Éloi in Noyon.[103] This nobleman was a childhood friend and fellow student of Calvin's in

---

[97]CO, 8:253–56; and *B.C.1,* no. 52/4.

[98]See the systematic index of Calvin's published works in *B.C.2,* 1127–36.

[99]*B.C.2,* no. 57/3.

[100]This dedicatee, not identified by Fr. Wendel, was an illegitimate but later legally acknowledged son of Antoine de Lalaing, great chamberlain of Charles V. The young man became an apostolical protonotary and provost of Saint-Pierre de Cassel: A. Van Nieuwenhuysen, *Inventaire des archives de la famille de Lalaing* (Brussels: [Archives générales du Royaume], 1970), 47, 714.

[101]CO, 9:785–86.

[102]Millet, *Calvin et la dynamique,* 42.

Noyon, Paris, and perhaps also in Orléans.[104] In order to justify his audacity in publishing this work, Calvin also allowed himself to refer to the encouragement he had received from François de Connan.

The third recipient of one of Calvin's dedications was simply referred to as *amicus quidam*. Although the text of the dedication was written in 1534, it only appeared in print in 1542, as a preface to the *Psychopannychia*.[105] There are two possible hypotheses: either Calvin dedicated the work to an imaginary friend in order to bolster his daring in publishing the work, or the friend in question was a real person whose name could no longer appear in print in 1542.[106] To my mind, the second hypothesis seems to be closer to Calvin's usual behavior.

The next dedication, addressed to Francis I in 1535 and included in the *Institutes,*[107] is a famous but entirely atypical case. It is unlikely that Calvin consulted with the king on the appropriateness of his gesture or that he sent Francis I a copy of the work. Instead, this letter was intended more for the wider body of readers than for the king, as it did not contain any specific praise of the monarch or any justification on Calvin's part regarding his choice of dedicatee.[108] However, this dedication was a successful publicity strategy. At least two accounts from the period described the work by focusing on the dedication: "the catechism of a certain Frenchman addressed to the King of France," and "what Jean Calvin, a Frenchman, wrote to the French king."[109] The impact of this dedication is confirmed by the fact that it was also printed separately on its own.[110] Furthermore, Calvin seriously thought about writing another dedication for the definitive version of the *Institutes*. On 30 June 1559, he wrote to a councilor of the Elector Palatine:

> "given that they are currently printing my revised *Institutes,* which has been transformed into a new book and will appear in time for the next fair, a few of my friends have suggested that the prefatory letter to King Francis remain as a testimony to the father and the son, but that I should dedicate the book itself, which holds the first and most remarkable place among my commentaries, to the most illustrious Elector."[111]

In the end, this did not happen, but the suggestion itself confirms that although the letter to Francis I was important, it was not a true dedication.

---

[103]CO, 5:5–8.
[104]Herminjard, *Correspondance,* 2:410 n. 1; and Doumergue, *Jean Calvin,* 1:536.
[105]*B.C.1,* no. 42/5.
[106]For more on the purpose of this dedication, see Millet, *Calvin et la dynamique,* 442–44.
[107]*B.C.1,* no. 36/1.
[108]On Calvin's approach, see Millet, *Calvin et la dynamique,* 467–77.
[109]Herminjard, *Correspondance,* 4:23 n. 9.
[110]*B.C.1,* no. 41/2.
[111]CO, 17:578.

Private Dedications

Apart from the letter to Francis I, Calvin wrote dedications to monarchs between 1548 and 1563. In contrast, most of the personal dedications were penned between 1539 and 1550, if one leaves aside the 1556 work, in which the dedicatee changed. Thus as a Reformer, Calvin followed two different approaches. This evolution was linked to his increasing influence on the European religious scene.

Who were the ten individuals to whom Calvin dedicated his works? The first group of recipients includes those who could generally be categorized as Calvin's teachers: Simon Grynaeus, Melchior Wolmar, and Maturin Cordier.

When Calvin began to deepen his study of the scriptures in Basel in 1535, Grynaeus provided profoundly helpful guidance. Together, the two men developed an exegetical method. In dedicating his first biblical commentary to Grynaeus, Calvin also used him as a reliable authority.[112]

When Calvin dedicated one biblical commentary to Melchior Wolmar in 1546[113] and another to Maturin Cordier in 1550,[114] circumstances had changed. These tokens of thanks for his early teachers in Greek and Latin were flattering, for they came from a man who had become famous as a writer.

In between times, Calvin had turned his attention toward other figures. The 1543 dedication to Philip Melanchthon accompanied a polemical treatise attacking a Dutch theologian, Albert Pighius.[115] In his dedication, Calvin openly affirmed his close relations with the *praeceptor Germaniae*. In fact, these relations always remained cordial.

In 1546, Calvin dedicated a new biblical commentary to another highly renowned friend.[116] Jacques de Bourgogne, the second cousin of Charles V, was the highest-ranking noble to join the Reformation. Shortly thereafter, de Bourgogne's wife also requested a dedication. Calvin promised to offer her the first French tract that he would publish, though the project did not come to fruition.[117] The Bolsec affair produced such a rift in relations between Jacques de Bourgogne and Calvin that the Reformer removed the prestigious dedicatee's name from future editions of the commentary.

During 1549 and 1550, though he began to direct his attention toward kings and princes, Calvin still dedicated a few shorter commentaries on the Pauline Epistles to members of his circle. In 1549, Calvin dedicated a work to his two faithful companions in the Reformation, Guillaume Farel and Pierre Viret, publicly affirming the close bond between the three Reformers.[118] In 1550, Calvin sent a dedicatory letter

[112]*B.C.1*, no. 40/3.
[113]*B.C.1*, no. 48/8.
[114]*B.C.1*, no. 50/6.
[115]*B.C.1*, no. 43/3.
[116]*B.C.1*, no. 46/2.
[117]CO, 12:401, 425.
[118]*B.C.1*, no. 50/5.

to his physician, Benoît Textor, as a sign of gratitude for Textor's care of Calvin's wife.[119] But the commentaries dedicated in 1549 and 1550 to Farel and Viret, Cordier and Textor, were all rather short.

Laurent de Normandie's numerous bereavements when he arrived in Geneva in 1549 explain in part why Calvin dedicated a work to him. Prior to his exile in Geneva, Normandie carried out a number of duties for the king of France, the king of Navarre, the queen of Navarre, and for the dauphin. This eminent man provided great assistance to the Reformation cause, and Calvin's dedication to him appeared at the start of the *De Scandalis*.[120] Because this type of work normally did not have any introductory letter, it seems that on this occasion Calvin was looking for an appropriate place for his dedication, whereas many other times he looked for a dedicatee only once the work was complete.

This was his last private dedication for any of his new books. In 1556, when his commentaries on all the New Testament Epistles were republished in a collected edition, Calvin removed the name of Jacques de Bourgogne at the start of the commentary on First Corinthians. Instead, he dedicated his revised and corrected text to another foreign nobleman, the Italian Galeazzo Caracciolo, Marquis of Vico.[121]

Thus the list of Calvin's personal dedications is very short. From among his entourage, Calvin only selected his two longtime colleagues, Farel and Viret, and his physician, as well as a few famous friends: Jacques de Bourgogne, Laurent de Normandie, and Galeazzo Caracciolo. He left aside his faithful coworkers who labored under his direction, such as Jean Budé, Charles de Jonviller, and Nicolas des Gallars, as well as his favorite printers, including Robert Estienne and Conrad Badius. Among the leading Reformers, Melanchthon was an exception: Calvin did not dedicate any works to Bucer, Bullinger, or Vermigli.

The limited number of private dedications is due to two factors. On the one hand, Calvin only dedicated his minor works for exceptional reasons. Thus he did not have many opportunities to dedicate a book to a friend. On the other hand, beginning in 1548 his dedications for his major works, namely, the commentaries and the exegetical lectures, were reserved for public figures.

Public Dedications to Rulers

Calvin dedicated works to a vast array of kings and princes: the kings of France, Poland, England, Denmark, and Sweden, the Duke of Wurtemberg, the Lord Protector of England, the Elector Palatine, the future Henri IV, Prince Radziwill, and the sons of the Duke of Saxony. One should also add to this list the city councils of Geneva and Frankfurt.

---

[119] *B.C.1*, no. 50/7.

[120] *B.C.1*, no. 50/9.

[121] *B.C.2*, no. 56/3; and B. Croce, *Galéas Caracciolo, marquis de Vico*, trans. Jacqueline des Gouttes et al. (Geneva: Droz, 1965).

The dedication to Francis I was an exceptional case.[122] The other rulers to whom Calvin wrote dedications were the intended recipients of the dedications, since they were Protestant princes who were seen as benefactors and protectors of the Reformed church. In some cases, Calvin wanted to encourage this genuine attitude held by some of the dedicatees, while in other cases he hoped to generate such a sentiment. In any event, Calvin's approach was thorough: before writing the dedication, he made more or less in-depth inquiries on the monarch's attitude and ensured that the ruler received a copy of the work in question once it was printed.

Calvin's first dedication of this genre was directed to the Count of Montbéliard, who was also Duke of Wurtemberg.[123] Pierre Toussain sent Calvin regular reports on the religious situation in the count's lands. Toussain was the instigator of the dedication. He also gave the presentation copy to the prince and transmitted the ruler's thanks to Calvin.[124]

In the same year, Calvin also took note of the situation in England. The young Edward VI had ascended the throne a year earlier. Calvin first wrote a dedication to the Lord Protector, Edward Seymour.[125] Because this gesture was so well received, Calvin turned directly to Edward VI two years later, when the king was thirteen years old. The Reformer first dedicated his commentaries on Isaiah to the boy-king, but because that work had been transcribed by Nicolas des Gallars, Calvin added a dedication to Edward VI to his commentary on the canonical Epistles.[126] The revised version of the commentary originally transcribed by des Gallars appeared in 1559, just as Elizabeth I became queen. To celebrate the occasion, Calvin added a short dedication to the queen in his work.[127]

From 1548 onwards, Calvin wrote a series of dedications to princes. In 1549, Calvin presented his commentary on the Epistle to the Hebrews to Sigismund Augustus, king of Poland.[128] This gesture was the starting point for a cordial relationship with the Polish ruler. Other dedications did not have such happy outcomes: those addressed to Christian III, king of Denmark, and to his son Frederick did not generate any reaction.[129] As for Calvin's dedication to the sons of Duke Johann-Friedrich of Saxony, it elicited a polite, but chilly response.[130]

In 1559, Calvin turned to Gustav I, king of Sweden,[131] and in 1560 to Nicolas

---

[122]B. Roussel provides a general analysis of several other dedications by Reformers, intended for members of the French royal family in Peter and Roussel, eds., *Le livre et la Réforme,* 183–261.

[123]*B.C.1,* no. 48/7.

[124]*Lettres de la collection Sarrau,* 36 and n. 7.

[125]*B.C.1,* no. 48/9.

[126]*B.C.1,* nos. 51/5, 51/6.

[127]*B.C.2,* no. 59/1.

[128]*B.C.1,* no. 49/4.

[129]*B.C.1,* nos. 52/3, 54/3.

[130]*B.C.1,* no. 54/8.

[131]*B.C.2,* no. 59/5.

Radziwill, the most powerful prince of Poland and Lithuania.[132] This last dedication was a reworking of the ones that had been written for the king of Denmark and his son.

In 1563, Calvin also dedicated a work to the most faithful defender of Calvinism in the German lands, the Elector Palatine Frederick III.[133] Calvin's gesture fulfilled the aim that he had already had in mind for the definitive edition of the *Institutes*.[134] His final dedication was a reworking of the one presented to the sons of the Duke of Saxony. Calvin wrote it in 1563 for another young prince, Henri of Vendôme, the future Henri IV.[135]

Alongside ones intended for these rulers or future rulers, Calvin wrote two dedications to the magistrates of a city. The circumstances in each case were different, even though the dedications were written in successive years. In 1553, Calvin completed his commentary on the Gospel of John and offered it to the Council of his own city, Geneva.[136] This gesture coincided with the period of time in which the Perrinist party had continually been rejecting Calvin's authority. By asking the city authorities to continue welcoming refugees, Calvin was touching a sore spot in the conflict since one of the main complaints of his opponents was the massive numbers of French exiles arriving in Geneva. Two years later, when Calvin penned a dedication to the magistrates of Frankfurt, he was writing to friendly authorities.[137] When he asked the magistrates to continue keeping their doors open for refugees, Calvin's request was well received. As long as his wealthy aristocratic friends Johannes and Adolph von Glauburg remained influential, the Frankfurt council continued to support Calvin.

Dedications to Religious Authorities

On four occasions, Calvin dedicated treatises to a group of pastors. His intention was to impact the recipients in one way or another.

The church of Neuchâtel requested Calvin's tract against the Anabaptists, dated 1544. Naturally enough, Calvin dedicated the work to the pastors of the region.[138] In the same way, the translation of his catechism was dedicated to the pastors of East Friesland who had requested a Latin version of the work.[139]

Calvin's two other "ecclesiastical" dedications were linked to his debate with Joachim Westphal. In his first pamphlet that defended the 1549 *Consensus Tigurinus,* Calvin wanted to get all the Swiss churches involved. Calvin agreed with Bullinger

---

[132]*B.C.2*, no. 60/2.
[133]*B.C.2*, no. 63/19.
[134]CO, 17:578, 593.
[135]*B.C.2*, no. 63/16.
[136]*B.C.1*, no. 53/5.
[137]*B.C.2*, no. 55/9.
[138]*B.C.1*, no. 44/7.
[139]O.S., 2:72–74.

not to ask the churches for their official approval, but he did dedicate his text to them.[140] When he wrote the *Secunda defensio* two years later, Calvin dedicated the work to the pastors in Westphal's region, in Saxony and the southern German lands.[141] Calvin hoped, though probably not with great confidence, to isolate his adversary and gain the support of other German pastors.

A Collective Dedication

The 1561 dedication addressed to "all the faithful servants of God who want the reign of Christ to be properly established in France" is in a category of its own.[142] In it, Calvin provided a number of revealing statements about the role of his own writings, and about his links with France.

Written at the time of the Colloquy of Poissy, in this 1561 text Calvin explained everything that he had done for the restoration of the Gospel in France. He also reminds us of the preface that introduced his 1557 commentary on the Psalms, in which he laid out the bases of his vocation as a Reformer.[143] That preface, addressed to "pious and honest readers," cannot be considered a dedication in the strict sense. Yet it is interesting to note that Calvin's most significant statements on his vocation were concluded in letters written to a large audience.

How to Select a Dedicatee

Calvin's choice of specific recipients of his dedications was fundamentally shaped by his desire to promote the Reformation cause. Certain names were spontaneously selected by the Reformer, as was certainly the case for the dedication to Queen Elizabeth or the one to the Elector Palatine.

In other cases, Calvin's correspondents suggested a name to him. Thus the Duke of Somerset recommended dedicating a commentary to the archbishop of Canterbury or to the king of Poland.[144] In 1550, several of Calvin's friends, including Jan Utenhoven, insisted that he offer a commentary to the young Edward VI.[145] Denis Beurée suggested a dedication to the king of Sweden, Gustav I. Beurée was a Reformed Protestant living in the Swedish court who provided helpful information to Calvin on the religious situation in the country.[146] In 1557, Jan Utenhoven once again recommended a dedicatee, namely, the Duke of Lithuania, Nicolas Radziwill. This suggestion only bore fruit in 1560.[147]

---

[140] *B.C.1*, no. 55/6.
[141] *B.C.2*, no. 56/4.
[142] *B.C.2*, no. 61/20.
[143] See above 195 n. 96.
[144] CO, 13:270.
[145] CO, 13:626, 658. For suggestions from other correspondents, see ibid., col. 667.
[146] CO, 17:444; and *B.C.2*, no. 59/5.
[147] CO, 16:673.

On some occasions, Calvin sought a dedicatee who matched the message that he wanted to transmit. In 1554, Calvin wanted to condemn the Lutheran churches' lack of charity toward the Reformed from London who went into exile following the accession of Mary Tudor. Calvin wanted to turn to a German prince. Jean Sturm and Peter Martyr Vermigli recommended that he write a dedication to the sons of the recently deceased Duke Johann-Friedrich of Saxony. The Reformer followed their suggestion all the more readily as he had met the chancellor of Saxony in previous years.[148]

Normally, writers sought the agreement of the recipient before writing a dedication, or at least made inquiries among the recipient's entourage. Calvin knew this rule. Thus, in 1544, when Viret thought about dedicating one of his works to the Council of Bern, Calvin wrote that this plan only met with his approval "if you have first learned from the secretary that this gesture will not be unpleasant for them or dangerous for you."[149]

In terms of Calvin's private dedications, there are a few indications suggesting that he himself followed the practice outlined above. His dedication addressed to Simon Grynaeus and dated 18 October 1539 only appeared in print in March 1540. In between times, on 25 October, the dedicatee indicated his great satisfaction with the gesture.[150] Not only did Jacques de Bourgogne approve of the dedication Calvin wrote to him, but he even looked it over before it was published.[151] The same was true for the text of the dedication to the pastors of Neuchâtel. In fact, the pastors even made some requests for corrections.[152]

As for dedications to princes, several traces survive of inquiries regarding the appropriateness of the gesture, as in the case of the dedications to the Duke of Wurtemberg and to Edward VI. When Calvin considered writing a new dedication to the Elector Palatine for his definitive edition of the *Institutes,* the Reformer submitted his idea to one of the Elector's councilors, who deterred him from pursuing the idea. But in several instances no trace of Calvin's inquiries can be found in surviving correspondence. Thus we do not know why Calvin selected the kings of Denmark as dedicatees.[153] However, the dedication to Henri of Navarre begins with apologies for not having consulted the queen of Navarre before offering his dedication. Calvin explained that he had not realized that his work would be produced so swiftly and that his printer had suddenly told him the book would be ready for the September book fair. Therefore he hastily wrote his dedication.[154]

[148]CO, 15:148, 152–53, 188.
[149]Herminjard, *Correspondance,* 9:189; and CO, 11:687.
[150]Herminjard, *Correspondance,* 6:108–9; and CO, 10/b:427.
[151]CO, 12:260, 321.
[152]CO, 11:698–99.
[153]CO, 17:578, 593.
[154]CO, 20:116–17.

Yet Calvin did not always have access to reliable information. The request for a dedication to the king of Sweden, Gustav I, came from a Frenchman living in Sweden, a man whose name Calvin did not even know.[155] We know that the man in question was Denis Beurée and that he accurately explained that the heir apparent was favorably inclined toward the Reformed. Thus the dedication, together with the letters that accompanied the book, testify to accurate knowledge of the local situation. In the case of the Polish king, Calvin consulted the person who seemed to be the most reliable source at the time, namely, Floryan Rozwicz Susliga; Calvin mentioned this fact in his dedication. But Susliga was in fact a swindler who extorted money from various western princes and disappeared without a trace in April 1552.[156] When the treatise was republished, Calvin prudently removed all references to Susliga.

In the case of the 1563 dedication to the Elector Palatine, Calvin sought information but did not wait for the answer to his request. Various friends thought that his gesture was inappropriate, since he risked antagonizing the Lutherans.[157] Calvin received Bullinger's reaction too late to take it into account. He defended his approach by stating that he had asked for advice "in good time," but that he had not received any reply.[158] His persistence in dedicating a work to the Elector Palatine is all the more puzzling because a councilor to the Elector had explained to him four years earlier that his gesture was ill timed.

At times, surviving correspondence allows us to see what steps were taken to ensure that a copy of the work reached the dedicatees. Thus Pierre Toussain presented Calvin's work to the Duke of Wurtemberg.[159] The person presenting Calvin's commentary to the Duke of Somerset is unknown, but Richard Hill regretted that he had been unable to fulfill this role for the duke "who, as far as I have heard, was very appreciative."[160] Calvin's secretary, Nicolas de la Fontaine (who had previously served Jacques de Bourgogne), presented the books dedicated to Edward VI to the young monarch. De la Fontaine was sent to England specifically for this mission.[161] Regarding the work dedicated to the sons of the Duke of Saxony, the intermediary was a Genevan bookseller on his way to the Leipzig fair.[162] As for the commentary dedicated to the Council of Frankfurt, Jean de Saint-André, a colleague of Calvin's, brought it to the German city.[163] For the commentary dedicated to the queen of

---

[155]CO, 17:444.

[156]H. Barycz, "Voyageurs et étudiants polonais à Genève à l'époque de Calvin et de Théodore de Bèze (1550–1650)," in *Échanges entre la Pologne et la Suisse du XIVe au XIXe siècle* (Geneva: Droz, 1964), 73–76.

[157]CO, 20:72.

[158]CO, 20:134.

[159]CO, 12:668–69; and *Lettres de la collection Sarrau,* 34–37.

[160]CO, 13:136–37.

[161]See *Lettres de la collection Sarau,* 37 n. 2.

[162]CO, 15:260–61.

[163]CO, 15:765.

England, a new messenger was sent to London from Geneva.[164] Prince Radziwill was probably perceived as being less prestigious and farther away, so in this instance, Calvin sent the book to Frankfurt and asked Peter Dathenus to ensure that it reached Poland.[165] The most detailed information survives for the dedication to the king of Sweden, describing the route taken by the books from Geneva, through Emden, and into Sweden.[166]

The Purpose of Calvin's Dedications

The Goals of Dedications

Overall, sixteenth-century dedications had three main functions. The first of these was specifically dedicatory, namely, to build a link between the recipient and the author, and between the recipient and the topic of the book. Establishing a connection with a dedicatee had a double purpose. On the one hand, the author could hope for support and sponsorship in order to spread his work more effectively. On the other hand, dedications were often intended to solicit financial contributions. The publicity resulting from a dedication to a prince was generally highly favorable. For instance, as we have noted, the dedication to Francis I helped make the *Institutes* more widely known. Calvin's goal was never to obtain financial remuneration, even though some recipients did respond by providing a donation. A general survey of his dedications shows that Calvin's approach was never mercenary. In fact, he was even offended when Madame de Falais seemed to suggest that he had dedicated one of his commentaries to her husband in order to obtain something in return.[167] However, though he did not seek gifts he was capable of assessing the value of any that he did receive. Referring to his dedication to the Duke of Somerset, Calvin noted to Farel, "His wife has sent me a gift of an inexpensive ring. It is not worth more than four couronnes."[168]

The second purpose of a dedication was to serve as a preface, since the author could equally use the text to address a wider audience beyond the recipient and could also lay out the aims and content of the work.

Finally, according to humanist tradition, a dedication also served as a podium from which the author could speak out on current events. In extreme cases, the link between the topic of the book and the matters dealt with in the preface might be completely nonexistent.

Calvin's dedicatory letters fulfilled these three goals: they served as dedications in the narrow sense, prefaces, and even pamphlets on current events.

---

[164]CO, 17:490.
[165]CO, 18:171, 182, 188.
[166]CO, 17:454–56, 18:386–91.
[167]CO, 12:425.
[168]CO, 13:325.

Acknowledging Friends and Making Them Known

Apart from a few exceptions, Calvin's private dedications were short. Their main purpose was to express the author's appreciation. Calvin's aim in these dedications was to raise a monument to posterity in honor of the recipient[169] and to provide concrete proof of his friendship.[170] Thus he explained his personal ties to the recipient, justified his selection, and sincerely and specifically praised the dedicatee. We are not including the Parisian dedications of 1531 and 1532, since at that point in time the little-known young humanist was looking for sponsors to help bring his work to public attention.

Already in his dedication to Claude de Hangest, Calvin mentioned his personal contact with the recipient.[171] He followed the same practice on subsequent occasions by recalling discussions with Grynaeus,[172] acknowledging his intellectual debts to Wolmar and Cordier,[173] noting his and his wife's health issues in his dedication to his physician,[174] and highlighting his close friendship with Farel, Viret,[175] and Laurent de Normandie.[176] In his dedication to Melanchthon, Calvin unhesitatingly wrote, "Me amas autorem," or "You love me, the author."[177]

Dedications to Kings, Princes, and Magistrates

Public dedications had more complex purposes. By soliciting the patronage of a king or a prince, Calvin followed the practice of Erasmus, who had sought to build relations with high-ranking figures in order to foster academic studies and piety.[178] Calvin also claimed that he was not motivated by ambition, for he had learned "not to serve the theater of the world."[179]

Calvin's approach to these various rulers was low-key. He was aware that the Duke of Wurtemberg, the king of Poland, the sons of John-Frederick of Saxony, and the king of Sweden knew little or nothing about him.[180] On more than one occasion, he made use of the recommendation provided by someone from the recipient's own circle.[181] In his dedication to the Duke of Somerset, Calvin acknowledged "his low-born condition."[182] By contrast, the letter to Francis I that prefaces the *Institutes* made

---

[169]CO, 12:365.
[170]CO, 13:601.
[171]CO, 5:8.
[172]Herminjard, *Correspondance,* 6:74–75; and CO, 10/b:402–6.
[173]CO, 12:364–65, 13:525–26.
[174]CO, 13:598.
[175]CO, 13:477–78.
[176]CO, 13:601.
[177]CO, 6:229–30; and *Recueil,* 257.
[178]Erasmus, *Opus Epistolarum des Erasmi Roterdami,* ed. P. S. Allen (Oxford: Oxford University Press, 1992), letter no. 1593, 6:138.
[179]CO, 17:446.
[180]CO, 12:658, 13:281, 15:201, 17:446.
[181]CO, 12:658, 13:282, 15:201.
[182]CO, 13:17.

no mention of the author's status vis-à-vis that of the king. Calvin completely omitted any explanation as to why he was acting as advocate for his fellow believers.[183]

Calvin's compliments to the recipients overflowed with superlatives, thus creating portraits that presented an ideal rather than realistic picture of the dedicatees. However, he did do some research, in spite of his admission on one occasion that his sources were only rumors and published writings.[184]

Calvin's dedications to these princes were a gift (*munus*),[185] a public one, since they were brought before the whole world.[186] His aim was specifically to encourage his correspondents to pursue the work of the Reformation, or to make them open to the Calvinist cause. His intention was to be a spur (*stimulus*) in the defense of the true faith.[187] Yet this mission was more than Calvin could handle on his own: "as for you, I am calling you by name," he wrote to Edward VI, "or rather God himself through the mouth of his servant Isaiah is calling you to continue the restoration of the church."[188]

In some cases the aim was more specific. In 1553, Calvin asked the Genevan Council to continue to take in those who had been exiled on religious grounds.[189] Two years later, he turned to the magistrates of Frankfurt with the same message.[190] He asked Queen Elizabeth to welcome those who had been banished during the previous reign. On this occasion, however, he especially tried to erase the negative impact of the pamphlets published in Geneva against the rule of women. Hence he added a short sentence: "our Isaiah [the subject of the commentary] asks both kings and queens to be the sustainers of the church."[191]

The Reformer hoped that "the inclusion of a very famous name"[192] would provide a certain amount of publicity for his books, at least for some audiences, such as the Reformed in Neuchâtel or the king of Sweden's subjects.[193]

Many of the dedicatees, whether private or public figures, were intended to be models for others to follow: Jacques de Bourgogne as a model of religious faith,[194] the Duke of Wurtemberg as an example of moderation,[195] Laurent de Normandie,[196] Christian of Denmark as an example of a man who listened to God,[197]

[183]See Millet, *Calvin et la dynamique*, 464–77.
[184]CO, 20:116–22.
[185]CO, 13:17.
[186]CO, 13:281.
[187]CO, 12:659, 13:285.
[188]CO, 13:672.
[189]CO, 47:IV–VI.
[190]CO, 15:710–12.
[191]CO, 17:415.
[192]CO, 17:446.
[193]CO, 7:50–51, 17:446.
[194]CO, 12:258–60.
[195]CO, 12:659.
[196]CO, 13:599–602.
[197]CO, 14:293.

John-Frederick of Saxony,[198] and Gustav of Sweden as a model of equanimity in good times and in bad.[199]

The Link between a Book and Its Recipient

On more than one occasion, Calvin explained that he had selected the dedicatee on the basis of the theme of the work. At other times, he frankly admitted that he was offering his most recent publication.

In the case of Jacques de Bourgogne, the Reformer pointed to the parallel between the dedicatee and the subject of First Corinthians.[200] As for the Duke of Somerset, Calvin stated that he was not offering him an "improvised gift" but that "I have deliberately chosen what seemed to be most suitable for you."[201] Similar statements appear in other dedications.[202] The commentary on Isaiah dedicated to Edward VI led to a lengthy discourse on the similarities between Isaiah's message and the situation of the English king.[203] According to what Calvin wrote in the dedication to the sons of the Duke of Saxony, his original intention had been to dedicate the work to their father, John-Frederick, but Calvin had altered his plan after the duke's death.[204] However, evidence from his correspondence suggests that Calvin's explanation was not true and that in fact his choice of recipients had been made well after the duke's death.

At times, however, Calvin did explain in a straightforward fashion that his selection of works to be dedicated was random. In Wolmar's case, Calvin simply wanted to erect a monument to express his appreciation.[205] He offered the Duke of Wurtemberg "something he had available, ready to be published."[206] As for the king of Sweden, Calvin offered "a work of a reasonable length and worthwhile doctrine."[207] There was also no intrinsic connection between the lectures on Jeremiah and the dedication to the Elector Palatine.[208]

The Dedication as Preface

Calvin sometimes included in his dedications some information about the work that he was publishing, but he did not take undue advantage of this possibility. The dedications included in the pamphlets against Westphal were true prefaces. The first

---

[198]CO, 15:200.
[199]CO, 17:447.
[200]CO, 12:258.
[201]CO, 13:17.
[202]CO, 13:282, 601, 15:16.
[203]CO, 13:671–673.
[204]CO, 15:200, 148, 188; and above 202.
[205]CO, 12:365.
[206]CO, 12:658.
[207]CO, 17:446.
[208]CO, 20:72–79.

one set out the background to the controversy and summarized the content of the main text.[209] The second dedication offered a peace accord to the pastors of Saxony. Calvin proceeded to underline the shared viewpoints, after having laid out the matters over which there was disagreement.[210]

Similarly, Calvin's remarks about Moses and history that appear at the start of the dedication for the Genesis commentary were intended to whet the appetite of the readers for the work itself.[211]

As for the short treatise on exegesis that appeared at the start of Calvin's commentary on Romans, its location was ideal, especially as Calvin also used the dedication to situate his commentary in the context of his *Institutes*.[212]

We have already noted how frequently Calvin explained why he sought to publish his works. In the dedication to the 1531 *Antapologia,* he highlighted both his editorial work and the delays in bringing the book to press.[213] At times, he also used the dedications to justify his refutation of seemingly minor opponents or to provide a response motivated by his adversary's arrogance.[214] At the start of works that he had not written himself, Calvin specified the parameters of his authorial role each time, whether in the case of the Isaiah commentaries written out by Nicolas des Gallars[215] (but completely rewritten by Calvin for the second edition),[216] or for his lectures on the twelve minor prophets written out by Budé and Jonviller,[217] or for his lectures on Jeremiah.[218]

Pronouncements on Current Events

Many of the dedications contain attacks against the Roman Antichrist and his supporters. It is well known that the letter to Francis I defended the French evangelicals. In almost every dedication, attacks resurfaced against the Catholics, albeit adapted each time to suit differing circumstances.[219] In his commentary on Genesis, Calvin not only criticized Catholic exegesis, but also targeted the actions of some Protestants described as "professing the Gospel."[220] His dedication to the Christians of France was intended to link the content of the commentary to current events for a

---

[209]CO, 9:5–14.

[210]CO, 9:45–50.

[211]CO, 15:196–99.

[212]Herminjard, *Correspondance,* 6:74–78; and CO, 10/b:402–6. Good analysis by Girardin, *Rhétorique et théologique,* 277–86; see Ganoczy, *Le jeune Calvin,* 84; and J. V. Pollet, *Martin Bucer, études sur la correspondance* (Paris: Presses universitaires de France, 1962), 2:389–94.

[213]Herminjard, *Correspondance,* 2:315–17; and CO, 9:785–86.

[214]CO, 5:169–70; 6:229–30; 7:49; and 9:5–14, 45–47.

[215]CO, 13:669.

[216]CO, 17:413–15.

[217]*B.C.2,* no. 59/5.

[218]*B.C.2,* no. 63/19.

[219]CO, 6:229–32; 13:16–18, 283–85, 672–73; 143:292–96; and 47:IV–VI.

[220]CO, 15:199.

specific audience. Calvin showed how Daniel's situation and his prophecies were applicable to France in 1561.[221]

Calvin's dedication to Edward VI provides the template for an essay on current events. In it, Calvin attacked the reopening of the Council of Trent. Dated January 1551, the dedication was written shortly after the new convocation issued by Julius III.[222] In the same dedication, Calvin also targeted the *Vergeriane* by Girolamo Muzio, a work that had been published in Venice in 1550 and that came to Calvin's attention in January 1551.[223] As for the dedication to the Elector Palatine, it bore no relation to the prophecies of Jeremiah. Instead, Calvin used the dedication to summarize the controversy between Calvinists and Lutherans over the Lord's Supper.[224] The dedication to Prince Radziwill contained a violent attack against the actions of Stancaro and Biandrata.[225] In these instances, Calvin expounded his viewpoint at length, but at other times he had no qualms about adding occasional polemical comments to his dedications, though it would be too time-consuming to mention them all at this point.

How Effective Was Calvin's Approach?

One of his first public dedications, to the Duke of Somerset, was very well received. Given this favorable outcome, Viret encouraged Calvin to continue in the same vein: "Since we see that men of such high rank are affected, rejoice, and are motivated to sustain the faith more strongly, I think you should continue to do this, unless you have a more prestigious plan in mind."[226]

However, Calvin's previous dedication had only resulted in a few vaguely positive comments from the Duke of Wurtemberg and had no long-term consequences.[227]

The dedications to the kings of Poland and England should be ranked among the successes. In contrast, the dedication to Queen Elizabeth failed to diminish the queen's reservations.[228]

Some of Calvin's selections were clearly ill chosen, such as the one to the Elector Palatine. Furthermore, while Calvin could not have guessed that his dedicatee Nicolas Radziwill would later become the defender of the anti-Trinitarian churches, he might have been wiser to avoid criticizing the ideas of Giorgio Biandrata, whom Prince Radziwill trusted completely.

Meanwhile, the dedications to the king of Denmark and his son failed to soften the attitude of these two princes. And in contrast to what Jean Sturm and Peter Martyr

---

[221]CO, 18:614–24.
[222]CO, 15:30–37.
[223]CO, 14:15–16.
[224]CO, 20:72–79.
[225]CO, 18:155–61.
[226]CO, 13:270.
[227]*Lettres de la collection Sarrau*, 36; and CO, 15:196.
[228]CO, 17:490–92.

Vermigli had thought, those close to the sons of John-Frederick of Saxony responded politely to Calvin's dedication, yet still pointed out the areas where the Calvinists had split with Luther.

In the face of the most obvious failures, Calvin's preference was to change his dedications. On several occasions, he erased the name of one recipient and replaced it with another. Already in 1549, Calvin planned such a move for his project of a collective edition of the commentaries on the Pauline Epistles. Fearing that Duke Christopher of Wurtemberg would accept the terms of the Interim for the Montbéliard territory, Calvin wrote to Farel, "Definitely if Christopher becomes a defector, I will eliminate his name when the commentaries on all the Pauline Epistles appear."[229] Subsequently, in 1560, Radziwill's name replaced that of the Danish princes, and the future Henri IV replaced the sons of the Duke of Saxony in 1563.[230] In 1566, Calvin followed the same procedure by replacing Jacques de Bourgogne's name with that of Carraciolo.[231] He also removed the name of Susliga the swindler from the dedication to the Polish monarch.[232]

Each time, Calvin explained clearly the reasons for the change. He removed the name of the first recipients without trying to conceal the procedure. In fact, his text still made use of much of the material from the original dedication. Calvin's phrases in the new dedication to Carraciolo were typical:

> Would to God that when this commentary of mine first appeared I would not have known the one whose name I am now compelled to erase from this page where it previously appeared, or would I at least have known him well.... But it is with deep regret that I have to change my practice and remove someone's name from my writings and I am disappointed that this man, whom I had placed in a prominent place through my dedication, has fallen short and can no longer serve as a good example to others as I had hoped.[233]

Conclusion

This survey leads to a few observations. Calvin followed a two-step policy in terms of dedications. He began by dedicating works to private individuals. While he was not looking for material rewards, he did however hope that his chosen patrons would contribute to the reputation and spread of his work, especially in the case of his early publications. Later on, as his reputation grew, he set his dedicatees "in a prominent place," honoring them with a public letter.

---

[229] CO, 13:324.
[230] *B.C.2*, nos. 60/2, 63/16.
[231] In *B.C.2*, no. 56/3.
[232] *B.C.1*, no. 49/4.
[233] CO, 16:12.

From 1548 onwards, Calvin made more systematic use of dedications to princes and kings. His policy of public dedications is somewhat contradictory. On the one hand, Calvin's overall goal is clear: he wanted to use this type of text to gain the support of princes, either by encouraging rulers who already supported the Reformed cause or by trying to draw them into his orbit. But on the other hand, Calvin's choice of dedicatees seems rather haphazard. At times he made his selection on the basis of requests from people he knew little about, as in the case of the dedication to Gustav I of Sweden. At other times, he seemed uncertain over which prince to choose, as in 1554. "Given that my commentary on Genesis is now in press," he wrote to Farel, "I want to briefly raise the issue [of the London exiles] in the preface. But I have not yet found the best recipient for the dedication, in order to successfully tie in the problem to the right person. If you have any advice, please let me know."[234] Hence Calvin combined blind selection and carefully thought-out purposes.

Overall, sixteenth-century dedications are excessively flattering. Calvin's dedications did not follow that model, even though on several occasions he was less than sincere. When trying to gain the support of a prince who was not already favorably inclined, Calvin had no hesitation in piling on the compliments, while still preserving a certain balance. While it is fair to say that the portraits he painted were not realistic, at least they reflected the Reformer's hopes. For his part, Luther followed the same strategy.[235] As a skilled writer, Calvin wrote a wide variety of dedications. While he did follow the rules of the genre, he still pursued his desired goals.

3. Calvin's Knowledge of the Book World

Calvin was fully aware of publishing procedures and could follow the printing and dissemination of a book from start to finish. At most, over time he gradually freed himself from this task of oversight and left it to his entourage.

Prior to Printing

Layout Issues

Earlier chapters have shown how Calvin wrote out his text and had it prepared by secretaries. Did he do more than simply transfer the text to the printer?

Calvin left few explicit remarks on the outward appearance of books. Yet we can guess at his taste by noticing how he left aside the small and unadorned editions done by Jean Girard in favor of the deluxe editions prepared by Robert Estienne. To understand this, one has to have in one's hands a number of editions of the commentaries printed by Estienne: he used saint-augustine fonts that were a bit bigger

---

[234]CO, 15:148.
[235]Junghans, "Die Widmungsvorrede bei Martin Luther," 57.

than the usual cicero font, as well as very wide margins.[236] These terms, cicero and saint augustine, were part of the vocabulary of the day, which labeled the appearance of fonts by using evocative but vague names. Today, one would refer to using a twelve- or thirteen-point font, instead of eleven-point.

Calvin was also aware of the "calibration" constraints. In planning the size of a printed work, a printer would calibrate the manuscript, namely, determine the length of the text in order to plan for the correct number of pages. The result could be a textual constraint placed on the author, especially for the introductory and concluding sections, for which the printer might only set aside a limited number of pages. When Calvin dedicated his commentary on First Corinthians to Jacques de Bourgogne, he sent him the text with apologies. "Since writing my letters, I have changed my mind regarding the dedicatory letter for my commentary, for because it is very difficult to try to fill a certain number of pages and no more, I send it to you in final form, but on the condition that it will not be printed except with your permission."[237] In the *Bibliotheca Calviniana*, I suggested that this passage indicated that a printed proof rather than a manuscript had been sent. This situation would have been exceptional, especially as Calvin was living so far away from his printer. It may be simpler to believe that Calvin had first intended to discuss what topic the dedication should deal with but that he abandoned this project in favor of a text designed to fit the space provided by the printer. However, Calvin left this correspondent entirely free to prevent the publication of the dedication. Leaving aside these possible interpretations, the phrase "to try to fill out a certain number of pages and no more" definitely refers to calibrating a text, a common procedure in handling manuscript texts.

The setup of the *Excuse de Jaques de Bourgogne* gave rise to an abundant correspondence, highlighting Calvin's interest in all the aspects of printing. Because the work was addressed to Emperor Charles V, both the setup and the paper had to be of high standard. To achieve this, Calvin preferred to have the work printed in Geneva rather than Basel. "...It would be better-printed here than there, that is with better fonts, better paper, and fewer mistakes."[238] When printing of the work began in Geneva in November 1547, the printer's concern for quality led him to "have certain font characters recast. This font was used to print the supplication readably and attractively."[239] Calvin was referring to the large roman font, equivalent to our sixteen-point font, used in the *Supplex exhortatio*, proving that for this 1542 work intended for the emperor and the members of the diet, special care was taken over the outward aspect of the work.[240]

---

[236]*B.C.1*, no. 54/8; and *B.C.2*, nos. 55/9, 56/3, 57/4. See above 194.
[237]CO, 12:260.
[238]CO, 12:540.
[239]CO, 12:618.
[240]*B.C.1*, no. 43/7.

The author also focused on choosing a title. Until September 1547, the work is referred to in letters as the *Apologie.* Yet when he was almost ready to have it printed, Calvin selected the definitive title. "The best title seems to me to be: Excuse composée... de laquelle il faict confession. Indeed the word apology is rare in French."[241]

Jacques de Bourgogne wanted to have his motto and his family crest appear in the work. Calvin discussed where to place them in the text[242] and then had them molded in lead, probably by Jean Duvet, an engraver who had regularly spent time in Geneva since 1539 and who died there in 1556.[243]

Calvin also had definite opinions on the preparation of an alphabetical subject index. Nicolas Colladon pointed this out when the French *Institutes* was being prepared in 1551. At the request of Laurent de Normandie, Colladon agreed to enlarge the previous index.

> To compile it, I admit that I used to make use of Calvin's advice in numerous places.... I recall that one night, as he was having dinner at the home of Normandie, he took the index that was in the Latin version of his *Institutes,* and after requesting a pen, he went through the index, crossing out and cutting out numerous unnecessary entries, or even false and inaccurate ones (which explains why many people are disappointed by indexes in books), showing me a better path to follow.[244]

Advice and Directives to Printers

Because he wrote many books and occasionally collaborated with booksellers (as we shall see below), Calvin gained such ascendancy that he could partially direct the printer's production.

In the 1540s, Calvin and Farel exercised indirect oversight over the work of Jean Girard, as noted in testimony from 1544, 1545, and 1546.[245] However, it would be an exaggeration to believe, with Eustorg de Beaulieu, that only works examined by Calvin could be printed in Geneva.[246] Indeed, shortly thereafter, de Beaulieu's poem *Chrestienne resjouyssance* annoyed Farel: "I am surprised that [Girard] printed the sheets disfigured by Eustorg [de Beaulieu] to the detriment of readers, and, I imagine, not without expenses both for the press and the work accomplished. On this

---

[241]CO, 12:587.

[242]CO, 12:577.

[243]CO, 12:618; and M. Campagnolo, "Le créateur de la monnaie de Genève," in *Jean Duvet, le Maître à la licorne,* ed. Chr. Cherix (Geneva: Cabinet des estampes, 1996), 15.

[244]J. Calvin, *Institutio* (Lausanne: Excudebat F. le Preux, 1576), fol. **1v; and O.S., 3:XXXIV–XXXV.

[245]CO, 11:722; and 12:29–30, 372–73, 405.

[246]CO, 12:44; and Pidoux, *Psautier,* 2:27.

point, I would ask for more censorship on your part, so that vain frivolities of this type are not published."[247]

In 1553, when Bullinger learned that a Genevan printer wanted to republish some of Oecolampadius's biblical commentaries, the Zurich pastor contacted Calvin. He asked Calvin to ensure that the text was respected, because the Strasbourg reprints of his commentaries on Jeremiah and Ezekiel contained interpolations. In fact, based on the preface and the errata sheet in Crespin's edition, it seems that the setup of the text was quite difficult.[248]

In 1563, Bullinger worked to ensure that the rights of his Zurich printer, Christoph Froschauer, were maintained. Thus, when Bullinger sent two newly printed works, he asked that they not be shown around to avoid pirated editions.[249]

Other requests indicate activity in the area of book sales. In 1558, Jean Sturm wanted to support a small-scale Italian bookseller, Guido Bicillo, and sought to obtain a number of Genevan works for him at a reduced price. Sturm asked Calvin to provide Bicillo with the same financial arrangements as Crespin and his Genevan colleagues provided to Jean Garnier.[250]

One of Calvin's requests to the Genevan Council reveals matters that to my knowledge have never been studied until now. In November 1551, Calvin asked the Council to grant a privilege for someone "who has published Origen in Venice" and who had already received privileges from "the emperor, the king of France, the Venitians, and the magistrates of Basel." The work in question was the *In evangelium Joannis explanationum tomi XXXII,* edited by Ambrogio Ferrari, also known as Ambrogio da Milano, a Benedictine scholar who clashed with the Inquisition fifteen years later. The volume was published by the Spinelli brothers.[251] Since Calvin intervened on behalf of "someone who has published," he had probably been approached by the Spinelli brothers. He was in fact in contact with the world of Venetian printing, as seen through the request of John Cheke, discussed below.[252] As far as I am aware, the names of these Italians have not yet been mentioned in Calvin studies.

During Printing

Correcting Proofs

In the sixteenth century, correcting proofs was a particularly laborious task. Indeed, most printers used the continuous printing technique. In order to proceed

[247]CO, 12:405.

[248]CO, 14:534; and Gilmont, *Bibliographie Crespin,* no. 53/9.

[249]CO, 19:666.

[250]CO, 17:24–25; and Gilmont, *Crespin,* 199 and n. 50.

[251]RC 46, fol. 90v (12/11/1551). Copies of this edition can be found in London in the British Library, 3805.bb.16, and in Paris at the Bibliothèque Nationale, C.2130. For more on Ambrogio Ferrari, see M. E. Cosenza, *Biographical and Bibliographical Dictionary of the Italian Humanists* (Boston: G. K. Hall, 1962), 2:1382.

[252]See below 240–41.

as efficiently as possible, the forms were used for printing as soon as each form was set up. As soon as a form was printed, it was sent back to the typesetters, who then reorganized the characters in the form. A normal-sized print run in Geneva was around 1,350 copies, which meant that two forms were printed daily: the recto and verso of a single sheet. Thus the proofreader had to check the proofs twice a day. If the proofreader was not a professional hired by the master-printer, he had to live close to the printing house, in order to provide the constant supervision required throughout the book production period.[253]

Calvin's first role in the world of printing was in fact to correct the proofs of Nicolas Duchemin's *Antapologia* in 1531. In his dedication, Calvin explained that the author "especially wanted to ensure that his work did not reach readers in a corrupted and mutilated form. Therefore, when he heard that I was planning on leaving for Paris, he asked me, on the basis of our friendship, to ensure that printing errors were avoided. I was delighted to accept the task, with the proviso that I would not be blamed for any errors apart from ones due to negligence." As Aimé-Louis Herminjard pointed out, in spite of Calvin's diligence, a list of errata was still necessary: there were fourteen corrections in thirty printed sheets. The twelve errors in the gatherings B through F are printed on the last page of gathering G, whereas the two corrections in book G are printed at the end of the prefatory booklet A.[254] This example shows that Calvin paid more attention to rereading the whole work than to correcting the sheets as they came off the presses.

In 1536, Calvin left Basel "immediately after" the publication of his first version of the *Institutes*.[255] It seems clear that he oversaw the printing of this work. In contrast, proofreaders working for the printing house dealt with the *Epistolae duae*. Oporinus reminded Calvin of this fact and praised their high-quality work. Oporinus even referred to a few passages "which left us puzzled" and for which Grynaeus and "your Louis" (an unidentified figure) were consulted.[256]

Calvin's letter to Farel, sent from Strasbourg in 1539, contains a statement that is difficult to interpret. Right from the start, the writer complained about his numerous responsibilities. Then he specified, "because this messenger wanted to take the start of my book with him, I had to reread almost twenty sheets."[257] Calvin cannot have been referring to correcting proofs, since these sheets were not being sent to Rihel, but to Farel. Calvin may possibly have been rereading an already printed text. There is clear evidence for the practice of rereading following printing, since the work contains an eighteen-line errata list.

[253]J.-Fr. Gilmont, ed., *Le livre, du manuscit à l'ère électronique,* 2nd ed. (Liège: Editions du C. E. F. A. L., 1993), 57–61.

[254]Herminjard, *Correspondance,* 2:317 and n. 9.

[255]CO, 31:26.

[256]Herminjard, *Correspondance,* 4:208; and CO, 10/b:91.

[257]Herminjard, *Correspondance,* 5:286–87; CO, 10/b:337; and *B.C.1,* no. 39/4.

Calvin's Bible editions were at times carelessly done, as evidenced by the 1546 New Testament. In it, Calvin provided a notice denouncing "the serious and major errors" that were featured in the earlier New Testament, which "indicated on the title page that I had revised and corrected it."[258] Keen to distance himself, Calvin stated "it is true that I revised it, though I did it in haste, especially as I had another urgent work in hand at the time." Calvin was referring to the treatise against Pighius that he wanted to complete in time for the Frankfurt fair in spring 1543.[259] He insisted on the matter, stating that the edition would have been much better "if they had followed the manuscript I wrote, and if the mistakes had not crept in from elsewhere." However, he felt that his own work had been good. "In any event, the translation that was done was still better that previous ones." In this criticism of the 1543 reprint, Calvin acknowledged the importance of proofreading, though he admitted that he had not carried out that task.

Overall, Calvin was not a good proofreader, because he worked too fast. Successive editions of the *Institutes* show that the author reused previously printed pages without correcting all the typographical errors. Therefore, his 1554 criticism of the quality of Jean Girard's work is surprising, as Calvin seems to be less than honest in his declaration. We should recall that Calvin appeared before the Genevan Council to retain control over the copies of his works and to be able to entrust these to Robert Estienne and Conrad Badius. In his appearance on 10 September 1554, the Reformer reminded his hearers that he "was the author of the work," and complained of being victimized by printers "who worked carelessly and made mistakes." If the Council were to grant the requested privilege, Calvin declared that he would be at the mercy of these printers: if they made mistakes "he would always be blamed."[260]

Thus at this point, Calvin complained that he would have to take responsibility for printers' typographical errors. A year later, he took a very different approach. During the famous *congrégation* on 16 October 1551, Bolsec criticized the translation of a verse from Proverbs, used in the French *Institutes*.[261] Several of Calvin's enemies made use of this remark. In 1555, accused before the Bern council of having slandered Calvin, Jean Lange ended up admitting to having made a few statements "based on a passage in *Le livre de la predestination et providence de Dieu* written by the said master Jehan Calvin." The Bern Council noted that "the said Master Jehan Calvin has in fact admitted that the mistake and error was not his fault but that of the printer's." The tribunal concluded: "we have seen that the printer's error was a serious one with major repercussions, and that master Jehan Calvin, as the author of

[258]Chambers, *Bibliography*, no. 132. The text of Calvin's notice appears in Herminjard, *Correspondance*, 8:448–49 n. 15.

[259]*B.C.1*, no. 43/3; Herminjard, *Correspondance*, 8:220; and CO, 11:474.

[260]RC 48, fol. 116ter.

[261]R. M. Kingdon et al., *Registres de la Compagnie des Pasteurs* (Geneva: Droz, 1962–), 1:81.

the book, was responsible for correcting the said error prior to printing and publication, and thus eliminating the scandal this has caused. Thus it seems to us that the blame that he wished to lay on the printer should rightfully be placed on him, and his excuses in this matter are judged to be inadmissible."[262] The mistake in question was a typographical error in a verse from Proverbs. "Dieu a créé toutes choses à cause de soy-mesme, voire l'inique au jour de sa perdition." If "iniquité," was printed instead of "inique" God becomes the author of evil. This mistake that appeared in the French edition of the *Institutes* in 1541 reappeared in 1545.[263]

Calvin immediately sent a written protest to the Bern council, explaining: "as for the error that everyone can see came from the printer, the petitioner is hurt at the thought that the mistake is being attributed to him, as if he were a proofreader for a printing house. This is not his occupation. And even then, the mistake is not that serious, given that everyone, from unlearned idiots to little children, is able to reestablish the meaning of the sentence by looking at the surrounding text."[264] Calvin complained to Bullinger in the same vein: "to prevent me from being able to defend myself, I am being blamed falsely and for no reason for the damage caused by a certain error that even children can see was done by the editor. In fact, the council has decreed that each time printers make a mistake, the authors of the book should be blamed."[265] However, Calvin's opponents did not forget Bern's condemnation. When the first investigation of the Perrinists took place immediately after 16 May 1555, the Consistory gathered information on statements made by Philibert Berthelier. It seemed he had mentioned "Mr. Calvin's sermons and [writings on] predestination that had been condemned as heretical in Bern."[266] Though this information muddles various elements, the reference to the Bernese condemnation is clear.

At the time, Calvin was clearly under attack, and he had to make do with whatever justification he could. The fact that the typographical error of 1541 reappeared in 1545 confirms what has already been said about Calvin's writing and translation techniques.[267] This habit of blaming printers for mistakes indicates that he tried to keep his distance from the final publication stages of his writings.

Toward the end of his life, when he had more leisure for the task of writing, Calvin noted the typographical errors in the Latin edition of his commentary on the Pentateuch. He was alerted to this by the conflict between his brother Antoine and

---

[262]CO, 15:544.

[263]Prov. 16:4, quoted in the *Institutes*, 1.3.23.6. See Benoît's edition, 3:440, and O.S., 3:400. The various pieces of evidence brought together in *B.C.2*, 1114–15 have been clearly put into perspective by W. H. Neuser, review of *Bibliotheca Calviniana*, by Rodolphe Peter and Jean-François Gilmont, *Theologische Literaturzeitung* 119, no. 12 (1994):1086–87.

[264]CO, 15:550, 21:601.

[265]CO, 15:572, 610.

[266]R. Consist. 10, fol. 30v (28/05/1555).

[267]See above 130–32.

Henri Estienne over the publication rights to this work.[268] In translating the work into French, Calvin noticed "the numerous errors spread throughout the text."[269]

A Concern for Spelling

Calvin was clearly not as conscientious as Beza when it came to reviewing printed works. In 1552, Beza provided an interesting insight into his concern for accuracy in establishing a printed text. Having recently completed the translation of one of Bullinger's treatises, *The Perfection of Christians,* Beza decided against having it printed in Geneva because of the 1551 edict of Châteaubriand.[270] Yet he regretted having to take this step, because he would have then had a reason to travel from Lausanne to Geneva to oversee the correction of the proofs. While entrusting the manuscript to Bullinger to have it printed in Zurich, Beza gave extensive instructions: "Make sure that the person who oversees the proofreading pays attention not only to the French language but also to stylistic issues and that he be as careful as possible in the task of proofreading."[271] This concern is not surprising given that Beza was a humanist who had his own viewpoint on French spelling.[272]

In contrast, Calvin had little interest in these matters. His early education left him accustomed to old-fashioned spelling. According to Susan Baddeley, it was in part due to Calvin's influence that modern spelling, sought by Olivétan and used by Girard, and which peaked in 1540, gradually gave way to a return to more traditional spelling.[273] Francis Higman brought to my attention the fact that this interpretation leaves Beza's influence aside. In his 1550 *Abraham sacrifiant,* Beza called for a moderate spelling reform, in order to make texts more readable. Indeed, it was around 1550 that the return to a more traditional spelling took place in Geneva.

Is there anything to be learned from the punctuation of Calvin's works? Albert-Marie Schmidt thought so: "we have scrupulously observed the original punctuation, believing that we had no right to convert a *rhetorical punctuation* designed to highlight the different emphases of the discourse to a logical punctuation, used primarily for purposes of understanding."[274] Yet over twenty years ago, Francis Higman indicated that punctuation was primarily added by the printer "and the end result, rather than making the text clear, is often fickle, to the point of being positively perverse."[275] Although they have not settled the debate regarding responsibility for

---

[268]*B.C.2,* no. 63/16.

[269]CO, 20:199; see *B.C.2,* no. 64/5.

[270]See below 273.

[271]Beza, *Correspondance,* 1:76.

[272]Baddeley, *L'orthographe française,* 243–52.

[273]Baddeley, *L'orthographe française,* 236–42, 272–82, 424.

[274]J. Calvin, *Trois Traités,* annotated by A.-M. Schmidt (Paris: Editions, 1934), 27. H. Estienne et al., the editors of the *Discours merveilleux de la vie, actions et deportements de Catherine de Médicis, Royne-mère* followed the same practices (Geneva: Droz, 1995), 111.

[275]J. Calvin, *Three French Treatises,* ed. F. M. Higman (London: Athlone Press, 1970), 44.

punctuation, Olivier Fatio and Françoise Bonali-Fiquet have modernized the punctuation to make the texts more readily understandable.[276] Olivier Millet offers his own suggested punctuation that "tries to convey the oratorical rhythm of Calvin's sentences."[277] In any event, the matter remains an important one. Indeed, in his work on a later century, H. Gaston Hall has highlighted the importance of punctuation in reading Molière.[278]

Responsibility for spelling and punctuation is difficult to assign in early printed works, because the printed text that has come down to us was shaped by the author, the printer, and his proofreader, as well as by the typesetters. Depending on the personalities and interests of each party, the combination of influences could vary.[279] Referring to possible mistakes that could occur in printing, Jean Crespin noted punctuation issues: "at times, one can find sentences without clear commas, colons, or periods."[280] It would, however, be wrong to assume that no rules applied to the choice of punctuation. Etienne Dolet was the first to dedicate a few pages to French punctuation.[281]

In Calvin's specific case, I would suggest that he played no role in the punctuation of his works, because of his lack of interest in correcting proofs.

Following the Pattern of the Frankfurt Fairs

For booksellers seeking an international audience, participating in the Frankfurt fairs was essential. Twice a year, the leading publishers gathered in the Büchergasse. The spring fair, which began twenty-four days before Easter, lasted twenty days, whereas the autumn fair was held from 8 to 21 September. Printers were obsessed with meeting the deadlines of the fairs. Works had to be completed in good time to be launched at the fairs. Hence the extensive number of books completed in January–February and July–August.[282]

Calvin was fully aware of this phenomenon, as a brief glance at his correspondence will show. In 1538, his plans to provide a new edition of the *Institutes* took shape, but the Basel printer worked slowly. On 5 January, Calvin stated, "We will

[276]Calvin, *Des scandales,* 40; and J. Calvin, *Lettres à M. et Mme de Falais,* ed. Fr. Bonali-Fiquet (Geneva: Droz, 1991), 33.

[277]Calvin, *Advertissement,* 43.

[278]H. G. Hall, "Ponctuation et dramaturgie chez Molière," in *La bibliographie matérielle,* ed. R. Laufer (Paris: Editions du Centre national de la recherche scientifique, 1983), 115–41.

[279]See my review of S. Baddeley's book in *B.H.R.* 57 (1995): 244–51.

[280]See the note that appears before the errata in the *Praelectiones in Librum Prophetiarum Jeremiae* (Geneva: Jean Crespin, 1563), fol. FF5v.

[281]E. Dolet did so in *La manyere de bien traduire d'une langue en aultre* (Lyon: Chés Estienne Dolet, 1540). This text also appears in N. Catach, *L'orthographe française à l'époque de la Renaissance* (Geneva: Droz, 1968), 305–9; on contemporary punctuation, see also 71–82 and 295–304.

[282]For more on the Frankfurt book fair, see A. Ruppel, "Die Bücherwelt des 16. Jahrhunderts und die Frankfurter-Büchermessen," in *Gedenkboek der Plantin-dagen 1555–1955* (Antwerp: Vereeniging der Antwerpsche Bibliophielen, 1965), 239 and J. W. Thompson in his presentation of H. Estienne, *The Frankfurt Book Fair* (Amsterdam: G. Th. Van Heusden, 1969).

have to delay publication of my work until the next fair."[283] A few weeks later, he noted bitterly, "It is now put off until the next fair."[284]

In December 1542, regarding his reply to Albert Pighius, Calvin explained to Farel, "I want my response to appear in time for the next fair."[285] Because time was short, Calvin only refuted the six books dealing with free will. As for the four books on predestination, Calvin announced at the end of his work, "I will leave this topic aside until the next fair."[286]

The Zurich publication of the *Consensus tigurinus* in early March 1551 was too late. Calvin complained to Bullinger about this on 12 March. "Your letter should have arrived two weeks ago. Then the book would have appeared in time for the Frankfurt fair."[287]

On 31 December 1553, Calvin announced to Bullinger, "The booklet against Servetus will be published in time for the next Frankfurt fair."[288] In the last days of May 1554, Calvin explained to John a Lasco that "Genesis is taking up all my time until the fair."[289]

When considering a new dedication for the final edition of the *Institutes,* Calvin presented the matter in the following manner in June 1559: "My *Institutes,* now revised and transformed into a new work, is currently being printed so as to be ready for the next fair."[290]

On 19 July 1563, Charles de Jonviller informed Hans Wolf about the work that had recently been published in Geneva. "M. Calvin's commentaries on the harmony of the four books of Moses are being printed by Henry Estienne. The same Calvin's lectures on the prophecies and lamentations of Jeremiah are being published by Crespin. I hope that these works will be on sale at the next fair." Crespin had to rush to get the work done, for a note at the end of the errata explains that he had two presses working simultaneously to complete the print run.[291]

The deadline of the fairs even influenced the pace of writing. Referring to a short document that was dealt with earlier, Calvin explained that he had delayed writing the work: "Because it was such a short piece, I decided to wait to write it until the time of the fair."[292]

Calvin's comment around 20 July 1550 on the collective edition of the Pauline commentaries proves that he knew how to estimate how long a print run would take: "Now the printers are rushing with Paul. But I fear that they have begun later

[283]Herminjard, *Correspondance,* 5:214; CO, 10/b:310; and *B.C.1,* no. 39/4.
[284]Herminjard, *Correspondance,* 5:227; and CO, 10/b:315.
[285]Herminjard, *Correspondance,* 8:220–27; CO, 11:474; and *B.C.1,* no. 43/3.
[286]CO, 6:404; and *Recueil,* 438.
[287]CO, 14:74.
[288]CO, 14:723; and *B.C.1,* no. 54/6.
[289]CO, 15:143; and *B.C.1,* no. 54/8.
[290]CO, 17:578, and *B.C.2,* no. 59/4.
[291]CO, 20:66; and *B.C.2,* nos. 63/16, 63/19.
[292]CO, 13:488; and above 90–91.

than they should have. If the work does not appear in time for the next fair, it will have other companions."[293] The end of the sentence indicates that, if the book was not ready in time for the next fair, it would be completed in time for the subsequent one. As the work in question was extensive, containing 189 sheets, the printing task would require several months. In July 1550, Calvin must have considered that the printing work was well underway, since he thought it unlikely, but not impossible, that it could be completed in the space of two months.

Dating Dedications

Do the dates of the dedications provide any information on the actual pace of writing? Based on verifiable cases, three hypotheses are possible: the date provided is the actual date when the dedication was written, or it was added by the printer when the work came off the press, or, more rarely, the date is symbolic. Since the dedication date is often close to the date in the colophon, it is not surprising that out of thirty-one dated dedications, eight are dated in January, two in February, six in July, and five in August. Two thirds of the dated dedications, therefore, correspond to periods shortly before the Frankfurt fairs.

We cannot carry out these analyses without noting that the printed dates are often approximations. The best example of this comes from the work published in 1557, where the colophon states that the work was completed on 20 August, whereas Beza was already sending Bullinger the final printed sheets of the work from Lausanne on 18 August.[294]

Several dedications provide the actual date when they were written; in fact, this was the most common occurrence. Thus, the letter to Francis I was dated 25 August 1535, suggesting that the work was intended for the autumn fair, but it was finally only completed in March 1536 for the spring fair.[295] Calvin's dedication to Grynaeus, dated 18 October 1539, was immediately sent to the dedicatee, who responded on 25 October, but publication was only completed in March 1540.[296] The *Psychopannychia*, published in 1542, begins with a dedication dated 1534 and a preface dated 1536. There is no clearer evidence that this work had been written well before it was published.[297] The dedication to Wolmar, dated 1 August 1546, retained this date, even though the original manuscript of the commentary it accompanied went missing in August 1546, so that the whole work was only finally published in 1548.[298] The dedication to Farel and Viret is dated 29 November 1549, even though the printing of the commentary only got underway a month later.[299]

---

[293]CO, 13:606; and *B.C.1*, no. 51/10.
[294]See *B.C.2*, no. 57/11.
[295]See *B.C.1*, no. 36/3.
[296]*B.C.1*, no. 40/3.
[297]*B.C.1*, no. 42/5.
[298]*B.C.1*, no. 48/8.
[299]*B.C.1*, no. 50/5; and CO, 13:499.

The practice of leaving it to the printer to insert a date surfaces first in Nicolas Duchemin's *Antapologia*. Because he was in Paris overseeing the printing, Calvin could write and sign his own dedication on 6 March. However, this was not the case for Nicolas Duchemin. Thus either Calvin or the printer dated the author's dedication 1 March. The case of the dedication to the pastors of Neuchâtel is clearer, since the text was written and submitted to the recipients in March, and was returned to Calvin in April, yet the dedication was dated 1 June, a date that was close to the completion date of the printing, expected imminently on 31 May.[300]

The short interval between the dedication date and the completion of the print run indicates that Calvin, who lived not far from the print shop, waited until the final days before writing his preface. Works printed by Robert Estienne, who was more prone than most printers to indicate the date of completion, show that there usually was a time gap because the dedication date was later than the date in the colophon. Calvin's commentary on John did not quite conform to this rule, because the dedication, dated 1 January 1553, was very close to the colophons, which indicated either 31 December or 1 January.[301] The Genesis commentary came off the presses on 20 July 1554, and the dedication was dated 31 July. But only on 7 August did Calvin announce "My preface on Genesis is currently being printed...."[302] In the following year, his commentary on the synoptic Gospels was completed by the printer on 17 July, but the dedication date is 1 August. In 1557,[303] the commentary on the Psalms came off the presses on 15 July, while the dedication date was 23 July.[304] When Calvin apologized for not having consulted Jeanne d'Albret before choosing to dedicate a work to the future Henri IV, Calvin clearly stated that he wrote the dedication when he heard that the work was nearly entirely printed.[305]

The only issue remaining is that of symbolically significant dates. Calvin dated his dedication to his compatriot Laurent de Normandie on 10 July, specifying that it was the "day of my birth," while announcing ten days later, "I hope that this winter they will publish the *De scandalis* book." In mid-August, he referred to the process of writing the book and obtained printing permission for it on 1 September. Thus this text was written and printed significantly after the date given in the dedication.[306] When Calvin signed his dedication to the Genevan Council on 1 January 1553 and provided a copy of the book to the dedicatees on 5 January, his actions were not in any way extraordinary.[307] Yet a year earlier, the Genevan pastors as a group signed a joint dedication to the city Council also on 1 January. The pastors

---

[300]CO, 11:689, 698–99, 722; and *B.C.1*, no. 44/7.
[301]*B.C.1*, no. 53/5.
[302]*B.C.1*, no. 54/8; and CO, 15:209.
[303]*B.C.2*, no. 55/9.
[304]*B.C.2*, no. 57/4.
[305]See above 203.
[306]*B.C.1*, no. 50/5; and CO, 13:606, 623.
[307]*B.C.1*, no. 53/5.

offered the Council a treatise on predestination linked to the Bolsec affair. Bolsec, an opponent of Calvin's, was expelled from Geneva on 23 December 1551. In early January 1552, Calvin began to write something on the subject. On 21 January, the work was complete along with the preface, since it was submitted to the Council on that date. On 25 and 28 January, the Council asked Calvin to soften his stance in the preface.[308] This date therefore seems to be symbolic, even though one should not completely discount the hypothesis that Calvin began the writing process by working on the dedication. In this case, the various dates make sense, since Calvin had begun writing in early January.

Overall, the most common practice suggests that Calvin indicated the actual date on which he finished writing his dedications. Because he usually wrote these once the print run was completed, this date was close to the first day of sale for the book. This should be our working hypothesis, given that other indications are lacking.

Financing

On the topic of Calvin and money, while much has been written on Calvinism and capitalism and on attempts to legitimize money lending, Calvin's concrete attitude toward money and businessmen has not yet received the attention it deserves. While Calvin was clearly not motivated by money, he did not share Saint Francis of Assisi's disdain and refusal to take material circumstances into account, for example. Calvin knew that money was necessary. He even wanted to make it fruitful without becoming its slave. Via his brother and his associates, Calvin was in regular contact with financiers and high-flying merchants. Although malicious enemies denounced Calvin's fondness for riches even during his own lifetime, these accusations were a result of his contacts with the world of business. Not everyone understands that one can be in contact with the business community yet remain untainted by it.[309]

Calvin's earliest interactions with the world of printing made him aware of the economic underpinnings of the business. In 1532, he had his Seneca commentary, *De Clementia,* printed at his own expense, "which has used up more money than you can imagine," he told a friend.[310]

Before becoming well known and settling permanently in Geneva, Calvin went through serious financial struggles. As noted earlier, he received substantial assistance from Wendelin Rihel, his Strasbourg printer. During Calvin's stay in Strasbourg,

---

[308]*B.C.1,* no. 52/4.

[309]H. Meylan, "Un financier protestant à Lyon, ami de Calvin et de Bèze, Georges Obrecht" in *D'Érasme à Théodore de Bèze,* ed. H. Meylan (Geneva: Droz, 1976), [117–124]; and H. Meylan, "Calvin et les hommes d'affaires," in *Regards contemporains sur Jean Calvin* (Paris: Presses universitaires de France, 1965), 161–70. A. Biéler, *La pensée économique et sociale de Calvin* (Geneva: Droz, 1959), does not study the Reformer's personal outlook, but instead analyzes his pronouncements on wealth and poverty (see especially 306–45).

[310]Herminjard, *Correspondance,* 2:417–19; and CO, 10/b:20–22, bearing in mind the corrections noted in *B.C.1,* no. 32/1.

Rihel spent more than forty gold écus to help him,[311] and gave him "enough to cover the extra costs" of reprinting the *Institutes* in 1539.[312]

Since few traces of Calvin's financial concerns vis-à-vis the printing world survive, we will focus on one of the rare instances when money issues did surface, namely, in connection with the *Excuse à MM. Les nicodémites*. Calvin's violent polemics against Protestants who participated in Catholic ceremonies for the sake of a quiet life led to numerous reactions among his target audience. Antoine Fumée, a councilor in the Paris Parliament, asked Calvin to have his opinion verified by Luther, Melanchthon, and Bucer. Fumée added that he would reimburse any of the costs incurred in this mission.[313] Indeed, in early 1545, Claude de Senarclens was sent to Wittenberg and Strasbourg to garner responses that were added in subsequent editions of the text.[314]

The printing of the *Excuse de Jaques de Bourgogne* was paid for by the author. Calvin sent very detailed financial reports to the sponsor. After describing the engraving of the prince's coat of arms, Calvin added, "I trust that you will not be upset that one écu was spent in order to have the matter dealt with in a timely fashion."[315] In January 1548, his report on the edition provided details: "a hundred copies will cost you approximately one écu." This estimate included the costs of drawing up the coat of arms, that is, the salary of the engraver, his meals, and the printing costs of the eight hundred copies printed. Calvin allowed the printer to keep a hundred for himself. "The seven hundred, all costs included, come to seven écus."[316] The unit cost seems entirely reasonable. Seven écus for seven hundred copies of a work that was printed on five sheets, works out at a cost of slightly more than one denier tournois per sheet (1.08 exactly). Focusing on a period twenty years later, H.-J. Bremme established that the average production cost varied between 1.4 and 1.7 deniers per sheet.[317]

In October 1552, Francisco de Enzinas wanted to publish a Spanish translation of the Bible and was looking for a publisher. Enzinas turned to Calvin for advice.[318] He was hoping for a large-scale work containing some six hundred illustrations. Calvin wrote back to him in January, by which point Enzinas had already succumbed to the plague. "Regarding the matter that you entrusted to me, I have discussed it with eight or more of my friends." Because Calvin was eager to see the Bible made available in every language, he wanted Enzinas's project to succeed.

[311]CO, 12:391.

[312]Herminjard, *Correspondance*, 5:291; and CO, 10/b:340.

[313]Herminjard, *Correspondance*, 9:444–48; CO, 11:826–30; and Boehmer, *Spanish*, 1:204–5.

[314]CO, 12:6–12, 25–26, 27, 61–62, 72; and *B.C.1*, no. 45/9.

[315]CO, 12:618.

[316]CO, 12:655.

[317]H.-J. Bremme, *Buchdrucker und Buchhändler zur Zeit der Glaubenskämpfe: Studien zur Genfer Druckgeschichte, 1565–1580* (Geneva: Droz, 1969), 31.

[318]F. de Enzinas, *Epistolario*, ed. I. J. García Pinilla (Geneva: Droz, 1995), 634–35; and CO, 14:402.

Therefore he began to solicit opinions from as many people as possible, but only one publisher, Etienne Trembley, indicated any interest. Calvin listed the others' objections. Firstly, the project needed a cash investment: "few of the men have access to cash (indeed, they have invested their fortunes elsewhere)." Secondly, a Spanish Bible was not expected to sell well: "the sale of the books will be slow and painstaking." Furthermore, "even if the book sales proceed more rapidly than they had thought, they will still not bring in enough to match the total expenses which will have to be made." Calvin listed the expenses: preparing the text, a trip to Geneva for Enzinas, and correcting proofs "especially if you decide to bring an assistant from Paris." Calvin reiterated the concerns about the lack of readers and the danger of a high price for the end product.[319] Calvin's analysis was a professional one, which left him torn, since he had no way of countering the booksellers' objections in spite of the usefulness of the project. In any event, Enzinas's death put a sudden stop to the idea.

The German translation of the *Response à l'interrogatoire nagueres faict à Jehan de Poltrot touchant la mort du Duc de Guise* shows how competent and effective the Genevan and Zurich Reformers could be in the realm of book production. On 17 July 1563, Calvin sent the pamphlet to Bullinger, suggesting that it be published in German. "The work is very sellable, so that booksellers should not worry about making a loss."[320] The following day, Beza brought up the matter again, adding two other pamphlets regarding the religious conflict in France.[321] These letters reached Zurich in early August. Georg Keller, known as Cellarius, carried out the German translation of the work. The printer, Christoph Froschauer, declared that he was ready to have the work completed in time for the September fair, so long as the translation was brought to him in time. "I am speeding up the process, for as you know, there are not many days left for printers to work before the fair."[322] On 22 August, Bullinger announced to Calvin that the young Froschauer had promised to print the work in spite of the delays caused by the translator.[323] The project was successful in the end: "This French pamphlet published for the Admiral against Poltrot was printed in German by Froschauer, and more than a thousand copies were sold in Frankfurt."[324]

Calvin played a direct role in this propaganda project. But from around 1546 onward, he usually delegated the oversight of his publications to his entourage, because although he had the requisite ability, his time was taken up by other priorities.

---

[319]Enzinas, *Epistolario*, 644–45; and CO, 14:432–33. One of Etienne Trembley's sons married a daughter of Antoine I Vincent (E. Droz, "Antoine Vincent, La propagande protestante par le psautier," in *Aspects de la propagande religieuse* [Geneva: Droz, 1957], 291).

[320]CO, 20:65.

[321]Beza, *Correspondance*, 4:169–70; and CO, 20:110.

[322]Beza, *Correspondance*, 4:180; and CO, 20:130.

[323]CO, 20:136.

[324]CO, 20:161.

The Circulation of Books

Transmitting Books in Sheet Form

Sixteenth-century printing techniques involved producing a complete print run of a given form on a daily basis. Thus the final sheets slowly grew in number. Even though the author might not have followed the proofreading process closely, he could gradually gain a sense of the work in its printed form. This practice, which led to the creation of errata sheets, also left numerous traces in contemporary correspondence. It was quite common for authors to send friends the first part of a work being printed, or for a correspondent to ask for the remaining sheets, so as to have a complete copy.

The first case in Calvin's correspondence is that of Olivétan's Bible. Calvin complained that he had received an incomplete copy, which he could neither bind nor use until the missing sheets were sent to him.[325] On 9 March 1544, Valérand Poullain sent from Strasbourg an incomplete work by Bucer, promising to send the remainder once it was ready.[326] The case of the 1545 *Admonitio paterna Pauli III* is more unusual, because the work was printed in Basel. On 27 March, Calvin still had only the first booklet. He sent this material on to Myconius, informing him that the work should be on sale in Basel, where Myconius lived.[327] In 1551, when Bullinger and Calvin decided to publish the *Consensio mutua* of 1549, the Zurich printers took the lead. The work was very brief, amounting to only two printed sheets. On 27 February, probably because a messenger was available, Bullinger sent Calvin a copy of the first sheet, printed on only one side. The complete work left Zurich for Geneva on 7 March.[328] The availability of a messenger, this time Francesco Lismanini, allowed Calvin to send Bullinger the first part of the 1555 *Defensio sacrae doctrinae de sacramentis*.[329] In 1557, Calvin sent the Zurich Reformer the incomplete *Praelectiones in Oseam*,[330] and did the same for the *Ultima admonitio ad Westphalum* on 7 August 1557. Calvin's explanation for his actions highlights his polemical passion: "I preferred to send you the incomplete work, rather than keep you in suspense." On 18 August 1557, Beza sent the last sheets of the work from Lausanne.[331]

As indicated below, Ambrosius Blaurer was one of Calvin's keenest correspondents when it came to collecting everything published by the Reformer. In December 1556, he obtained the printed sheets of the *In librum psalmorum commentarius*. Even though the work came off the presses in July 1557, it was only in December that Blaurer asked for the sheets that he still needed to complete his copy. "I would

---

[325]Herminjard, *Correspondance*, 3:349; and CO, 10/b:51–52.

[326]CO, 11:685.

[327]CO, 12:56; and *B.C.1*, no. 45/13.

[328]CO, 14:55, 69.

[329]CO, 15:358–359; and *B.C.2*, no. 55/6.

[330]CO, 16:412; and *B.C.2*, no. 57/3.

[331]CO, 16:565; Beza, *Correspondance*, 2:85; and *B.C.2*, no. 57/11.

like to have everything that precedes the a1 booklet, and everything after the q1 booklet, that is, everything that comes before page 1 and after page 256."[332] Blaurer's request was very specific: he knew that the preliminary pages—"before page 1"—were printed last.

Advertising

It does not seem that Calvin played any direct role in the advertising techniques used in some of his works. Instead, the responsibility for this approach lay with the booksellers.

The end of the title of the 1536 *Institutes* would fit in well with the blurbs used by modern-day publishers: "A work worth being read by all who care about piety. Newly published."[333] Such a phrase was undoubtedly the work of the Basel printers Platter, Lasius, or even Oporinus.

Wendelin Rihel shared his colleagues' eagerness to praise the worth of their products. In 1539, the new edition of the *Institutes,* "finally matches its title." Rihel repeated the expression in 1543 and 1545, going much further in these two later editions, including on the title page an encomium of Calvin by Jean Sturm. In the 1545 French edition, Girard printed Sturm's text more discreetly, on the verso of the title page. "John Calvin is a man of penetrating judgment and admirable doctrine, gifted with a prodigious memory. It is marvelous to see how he expressed himself on all topics in his writings, both abundantly and purely. His *Institutes of the Christian Religion* provide clear evidence of this. After having it published for the first time, he expanded it, and has now completely perfected it. Indeed, I know of no one who has written more perfectly, to demonstrate true religion, correct morals, and eliminate abuses. And whoever grasps even the main points of the matters he teaches about in this book, is quick to believe that he is perfectly well-versed in these matters."[334] Calvin's reaction to this promotional praise is unknown. Given that the work was printed in Strasbourg while he was in Geneva, Calvin would not have been able to exert direct control over this matter. Although Sturm's quotation did reappear in subsequent Latin and French editions, it no longer appeared on the title page, perhaps at Calvin's request.

Calvin's remark, made a few months earlier in July 1542, probably regarding the publication of the *Psychopannychia,* highlights his sensitivities in this domain. Writing about an unidentified admirer, he said, "It is surprising, unless our praise-giver believes that I should be more upset that readers will not get to see on the first page these extensive and rather fulsome compliments he directs at me." Calvin's comments are unclear. Was a publisher suggesting including laudatory remarks on a title page? Perhaps. In any event, Calvin poked fun at the "encomiast" and, later in the

---

[332]CO, 16:335, 350, 723; and *B.C.2,* no. 57/4.
[333]*B.C.1,* no. 36/1.
[334]*B.C.1,* nos. 39/4, 43/5, 45/5, 45/6.

same letter, he refused to submit to the greed of this man, which suggests that there were business interests at stake in this affair.[335]

Wendelin Rihel stretched the truth once again when the *Psychopannychia* was reprinted. Although the title was changed, the work itself remained the same, thus obviating the claim on the title page: "A work written seven years ago, now in print for the first time."[336] When he published the Latin translation of the pamphlets against the Anabaptists, Rihel noted: "Now translated for the first time from French into Latin."[337]

Jean Girard, who took over from Rihel as Calvin's printer, emphasized the original character of the reprints, but in a more reserved fashion. The 1550 Latin *Institutes* was presented as follows: "based on the author's very latest revisions, now expanded in a few places and corrected in innumerable spots." Girard also noted the existence of the indexes.[338] For the 1551 French *Institutes,* Girard also underlined Calvin's role: "Composed in Latin by John Calvin and translated into French by his own hand and then newly revised and expanded." This same sentence appears in all the new editions up to 1557, even when the text itself remained unchanged.[339] The collective edition of the commentaries on the Pauline Epistles did, however, provide a revised text. Girard noted this fact, stating, "based on the author's most recent revisions."[340] A more unusual phrase appeared on the title page of the *Opuscula omnia,* a collected edition of Calvin's tracts. Girard noted that the work included a tract "published here for the first time." The pamphlet in question was *De aeterna Dei praedestinatione,* which appeared on its own in the same month, brought out by a different publisher.[341]

When he began publishing Calvin's works in 1550, Jean Crespin emphasized that these were new works: "newly written treatise" appeared on the title pages of *Des scandales* and *De la predestination eternelle.*[342] In most cases, his statements were true. The 1554 reprint of the commentaries on the canonical Epistles simply indicated, "second edition."[343] The reprint of the Isaiah commentary was indeed "revised by the author himself, expanded and perfected thanks to substantive work." In some ways, Crespin was echoing the author's own statements in his dedicatory epistle to the queen, where Calvin began by saying. "I have spent so much energy and care in improving this commentary that it can rightly be considered as a new work."[344]

---

[335]Herminjard, *Correspondance,* 8:80; and CO, 11:418.
[336]*B.C.1,* no. 45/11.
[337]*B.C.1,* no. 46/1.
[338]*B.C.1,* no. 50/16.
[339]*B.C.1,* nos. 51/11, 53/7, 54/10, 57/6.
[340]*B.C.1,* no. 52/8.
[341]*B.C.1,* no. 52/4.
[342]*B.C.1,* nos. 50/12, 51/8, 52/5, 52/6.
[343]*B.C.1,* no. 54/4.
[344]*B.C.1,* no. 59/1; and CO, 17:414.

The reprint edition of the commentary on the Acts of the Apostles in 1560 led to a major clash between Crespin and Calvin. The original work had appeared in two successive volumes, the first published in 1552 and the second in 1554. In 1560, Calvin revised the text of his commentary. Crespin still had a stock of unsold copies of volume two, in the 1554 version. The publisher told Calvin in early August 1560 that he had completed the printing, although in fact he had only printed the revised first volume. Adding a title announcing that the edition was "revised by the author himself and strengthened by numerous additions," Crespin in fact brought to the Frankfurt fair a composite work, containing parts from 1560 and from 1554. In October 1560 his strategy was uncovered and Crespin was thrown into prison "for having changed some titles of the commentaries on Acts against the intention of M. Calvin." The charge was clarified on the following day. The printer was accused "of having stated in the title that the book had been revised, which was false and of having lied to the said M. Calvin, saying that the revised version had come off the presses, which was untrue." Crespin was made to recall the copies sent to Frankfurt and was barred from selling any more of them until he had completed the second part of the work. The colophon of that second volume is in fact dated 1561.[345]

Crespin also specialized in another form of advertising, namely, indicating the name of the dedicatee on the title page of a work. Seven of Calvin's works followed this pattern. Apart from Laurent de Normandie, all the dedicatees were monarchs. Leaving aside the 1536 *Institutes,* only Crespin provided the dedicatee's name on the title page. Girard and Estienne, who each published a substantial number of dedications, never followed Crespin's approach, perhaps because they did not believe this practice contributed to book sales.

Robert Estienne's approach contrasted with that of his Genevan colleagues in a number of ways. His preference was for simple, short titles, and he avoided advertising slogans as much as possible. His reprint of the Latin *Institutio* in 1553 had a very short title, merely highlighting the inclusion of indexes.[346] In the final edition of 1559, Estienne provided a more lengthy description of the new elements of the work: "expanded so significantly that it could almost be considered to be a new work." But this phrase may in fact be the work of his son Henri, who oversaw the printing process during his father's final illness. While the phrase was fully accurate in 1559, it was reused without qualms in subsequent reprints.[347] The 1560 French edition offered a similar formulation: "Newly produced in four volumes, divided into chapters, in an organized and methodical fashion. The work is expanded so significantly that it can almost be considered a new work." Crespin's phrase reappeared

---

[345]Archival documents cited in *B.C.2,* no. 60/2.
[346]*B.C.1,* no. 53/6.
[347]*B.C.2,* nos. 59/4, 61/15, 61/16.

in every following edition. Only Jacques Bourgeois removed the word "newly" and the final sentence, "The work is expanded... new work."[348]

The only time that Robert Estienne produced the text of a revised commentary, he indicated the fact to his readers in a clearly modest fashion: "the reader will notice that this is the latest revised version of these commentaries when he reads them and compares them to previous editions." Crespin preserved this phrase in the edition he began in 1557 and completed in 1563 following his conflict with Estienne.[349]

Conrad Badius, whose task was primarily to handle French editions, liked to note that the work was "newly translated." This phrase appeared on the title page of the *Chant de victoire,* the *Psychopannychie,* and the *Response de Jehan Calvin et Theodore de Besze* against Castellio.[350]

In the case of the exegetical commentaries, Badius used a phrase similar to the one used by Estienne. In the 1556 commentary on the Pauline Epistles, Badius noted, "When reading and comparing this edition to the others, you will clearly see that the author revised and expanded everything."[351] In 1561, when he correlated the biblical text with the new edition of the Bible, Badius added to his sentence: "and that the translation of the text is done as perfectly as possible."[352] All the later editions, whether in 1556 or 1561, literally copied Badius's title.[353] Indeed, Badius used a very similar phrase on the title page of the commentaries on the Catholic Epistles, and his approach was copied by those who reprinted his work.[354] As for the commentaries on the Gospels and the Acts of the Apostles that he printed in 1561, Badius presented them as substantially reworked texts: "The whole work has been diligently revised and almost newly translated, both the text and the commentary, as can be seen if one compares the earlier editions with this one."[355] A Lyon edition of 1562 echoed Badius,[356] but the honest-minded Jacques Bourgeois did not follow suit in 1561. Bourgeois's approach was followed in subsequent editions, even those published in Lyon.[357] Finally, Badius produced a commentary on the Psalms, claiming that "this translation is so revised and so carefully compared to the Latin, that one can consider it to be a new edition."[358]

In Lyon Sebastien Honorat, who published a number of Calvin's exegetical commentaries in 1562 and 1563, copied Badius's phrases and added them to the

---

[348]*B.C.2,* nos. 60/8, 61/17, 61/18, 62/7, 62/9, 62/10, 62/11, 62/12, 63/14, 64/11. Bourgeois's reprint is no. 62/8.

[349]*B.C.2,* nos. 56/3, 57/3.

[350]*B.C.2,* nos. 55/4, 58/7, 58/8, 59/8.

[351]*B.C.2,* no. 56/1.

[352]*B.C.2,* no. 61/8; and above 152.

[353]*B.C.2,* nos. 60/1.1, 62/4, 62/5, 63/8, 64/3.

[354]*B.C.2,* nos. 56/1, 60/1.2, 62/4.2.

[355]*B.C.2,* no. 61/7.

[356]*B.C.2,* no. 62/3.

[357]*B.C.2,* nos. 62/1, 62/2, 63/6, 63/7, 64/1.

[358]*B.C.2,* no. 61/9, no. 63/9.

title page of the commentary on the Acts of the Apostles when he published the work separately.[359]

Complimentary Copies and Advertising

Finally, Calvin worked hard to let his friends know about upcoming publications. The works in question were primarily his own, although throughout his career, his correspondence contained innumerable bibliographical references concerning countless works. Evidence for this can be found in a 1543 letter from Pellikan in Zurich, asking Calvin about Robert Estienne's exegetical publications.[360] During periods of confessional conflict, correspondents were at least as curious about opponents' writings as about those written by friends.

Already in April 1532, when attempting to advertise and sell copies of his edition of Seneca's *De clementia,* the young author organized the distribution of copies to his friends. He sent one to Philippe Loré, and asked him to send five copies to Bourges for various recipients.[361]

As regards the rest of Calvin's career, in some instances a dedication in a surviving copy indicates that the recipient received a complimentary copy. Yet these instances are rare. In most cases, any information available comes from Calvin's correspondence, thus explaining the rather fragmentary nature of the data.

Surprisingly, Viret and Farel rarely thanked Calvin for sending complimentary copies of books and instead restricted themselves to giving their opinion on the content of the works. It may be that they considered this exchange of books perfectly normal, except in cases when buying the book locally would be quicker than waiting for the arrival of a messenger. At least this seems to have been the procedure as evidenced by the few indications located in Calvin's correspondence. As a rule, the route taken by book bearers was the same as that taken by letter carriers, namely, from Geneva to Lausanne and from Lausanne to Neuchâtel. Thus in 1554, Viret noted that he had received the pamphlet on the Trinity against Servetus. "I received yesterday the books that you sent. Thank you very much. I will see to it that Farel gets sent one as soon as possible."[362] It was when the distribution failed that Calvin's correspondents' complaints show how the system usually operated. In 1557, Farel was unable to locate a copy of the *Ultima admonitio* against Wesphal and reported that he had searched for it unsuccessfully at Neuchâtel and Lausanne.[363] Calvin was puzzled: "Given that my reply to the Saxons is for sale in Lausanne, Beza should have a copy. Why did he not give it to you? You would certainly have received it sooner if it had not been for the fact that I assumed you had read it before a reliable

[359]*B.C.2,* nos. 62/3.2, 63/7.2.

[360]CO, 11:517–18, 527.

[361]Herminjard, *Correspondance,* 2:418–19; and CO, 10/b:21. For information on the recipient's identity, see *B.C.1,* no. 32/1.

[362]CO, 15:23.

[363]CO, 16:606.

messenger was available."[364] Hence Calvin had not sent anything from Geneva, because he thought it would be more efficient for Beza to do so from Lausanne. On another occasion, Viret had a stock of a few copies of the pamphlet *Contre la secte phantastique des libertins* in Geneva, allowing him to send a copy to Gwalter.[365]

Another close colleague who made no mention of Calvin sending him complimentary copies was in fact Beza himself. Yet when he lived in Lausanne from 1549 to 1559 he was in regular touch with Calvin. The only trace of a book being sent was that of the *Responsio ad versipellem mediatorem* of 1561, a work printed in Geneva after consulting Beza, who was then in Poissy and Paris.[366]

Before listing a number of Calvin's correspondents who received copies of his works, we must mention the largest publicity effort detailed in the sources. The work in question was the *Excuse de Jaques de Bourgogne,* one hundred copies of which were retained in Geneva by Calvin. He explained to Jacques de Bourgogne: "The aim has been to have the work spread in France by these means. I have sent out around fifty copies here and there, including to Madame de Ferrare, although this should not prevent you from sending her a copy with a letter."[367] Clearly, this was a rather unusual book intended for a large audience. We should note that the copies distributed by Calvin were part of the batch for which Jacques de Bourgogne did not have to pay.

Martin Bucer, who had encouraged Calvin's written work since at least 1538, probably received complimentary copies from Calvin on a regular basis. The only evidence of this is in the case of the 1549 *Interim adultero-germanum.*[368]

Calvin's Greek teacher, Melchior Wolmar, received several complimentary copies. His copy of the first *Institutes* is currently in Freiburg-am-Breisgau.[369] The 1550 reprint of the work was sent to Wolmar by Beza. Wolmar also received a copy of the commentary on John, which is now held in London.[370] Wolmar only obtained the 1554 commentary on the Acts of the Apostles in 1556, at Beza's suggestion.[371] When sending the work, Calvin apologized for not having sent his commentaries on Acts sooner. "I have had so much work here [in Geneva] that I did not even think of sending the commentaries on Acts."[372]

In contrast, there is much evidence that Calvin sent numerous books to Heinrich Bullinger. The two men met each other for the first time in Basel in 1536. Shortly thereafter, Calvin sent the Zurich pastor a copy of his *Institutes.*[373] He then

[364]CO, 16:623.

[365]CO, 12:77; and *B.C.1,* no. 45/4.

[366]*B.C.2,* no. 61/22; and Beza, *Correspondance,* 3:187, 195.

[367]CO, 12:655.

[368]CO, 13:148.

[369]Freiburg-am-Breisgau, Universitätsbibliothek, Rara N 239 de; and *B.C.1,* no. 39/4.

[370]London, British Library, C.28.m.9; and *B.C.1,* no. 53/5.

[371] Beza, *Correspondance,* 2:51.

[372]CO, 16:284; and *B.C.1,* no. 54/3.

[373]Herminjard, *Correspondance,* 6:196 n. 3.

sent Bullinger the 1543 *Supplex exhortatio ad Carolum Quintum.* Bullinger responded, saying he had received the copy, which is now in Paris.[374] In July 1548, a French student brought him the *Acta synodi tridentinae,* which came off the presses in December 1547. The delay was probably due to the problems in finding a carrier to transport the book.[375] In July 1548, Bullinger requested that Calvin send him everything that was being printed in Geneva, especially the *Commentari in quatuor Pauli epistolas* and the *Commentarii in secundam epistolam ad Corinthios.* Bullinger added, "Please send me these books. I am not asking for them as a gift; I am not so bold as to request another present right after just having received one. I will be happy to pay the cost." When Calvin fulfilled this request in January 1549, he explained, "I would have sent you my commentaries on the five Pauline Epistles sooner, except that I thought they would be available where you are. Given that messengers go from here to Zurich only infrequently, I was in fact worried that you would pay more in transport costs than in the purchase cost. I am now sending you the work on Second Corinthians and the four next ones."[376] Meanwhile, in December 1548, Bullinger thanked Calvin for the commentary on the Epistles to Timothy.[377] The copy of the *De vitandis persecutionibus* of 1549, together with the additional booklet of 1550 sent by Calvin to Bullinger, is currently in Paris.[378] However the copy of the 1549 *Interim adultero-germanum* with the 1550 *Appendix,* is held in Geneva. This work had been sent to Bullinger by Calvin in January 1549.[379] Evidence from correspondence then indicates that Bullinger received numerous polemical works whose contents were often a matter for debate between the Zurich pastor and his Genevan colleague, including the 1554 *Defensio orthodoxae fidei de Trinitate,*[380] the *Defensio sanae doctrinae de sacramentis* of 1555,[381] the *Secunda defensio contra Westphali calumnias* of 1556,[382] the *Ultima admonitio ad Westphalum* of 1557,[383] and the *Dilucida explicatio* against Tilemann Hesshusen.[384] This list gives rise to at least two observations. Given that we know, thanks to autographed copies, that certain books were sent, though there is no trace of this in the two men's correspondence, this means that the letters do not allow us to build a comprehensive list of all the books sent. Furthermore, on the basis of their correspondence it appears

---

[374]Bibliothèque de la Société de l'histoire du protestantisme français, 8o 11709 (1) Rés; CO, 11:708; and *B.C.1,* no. 43/7.

[375]CO, 13:6; and *B.C.1,* no. 47/3.

[376]CO, 13:6, 165; and *B.C.1,* nos. 48/7, 48/8.

[377]CO, 13:116; and *B.C.1,* no. 48/9.

[378]Bibliothèque de la Société de l'histoire du protestantisme français, 80 11709 (3) Rés; and *B.C.1,* no. 49/5 and no. 50/11.

[379]Musée historique de la Réformation, A50(49); CO, 13:166; and *B.C.1,* nos. 49/6, 50/1.

[380]CO, 15:38, 40, 90; and *B.C.1,* no. 54/6.

[381]CO, 15:375–376; and *B.C.2,* no. 55/6.

[382]CO, 16:11; and *B.C.2,* no. 56/4.

[383]CO, 16:595; and *B.C.2,* no. 57/11.

[384]CO, 18:350, 357; and *B.C.2,* no. 61/11.

that Bullinger only received copies of Calvin's commentaries in 1548 and 1549, and then only at his request. However, it is hard to believe that Calvin did not send him any sample of his exegetical work. Calvin's comments in 1549 regarding transport costs being higher than the cost of the books themselves indicate that economic considerations could slow the book trade. The frequent time lag between a book's completion and a copy being sent shows that one had to wait for a reliable courier who was willing to take on the extra burden.

In spite of incomplete data, we can identify other recipients of these complimentary copies. Simon Sulzer, who was a pastor in Bern between 1541 and 1553, was one of Calvin's regular correspondents. Sulzer received the 1543 *Defensio sanae doctrinae adversus calumnias Pighii*. His copy is held in Strasbourg.[385] Shortly thereafter, he received the *Supplex exhortatio ad Carolum Quintum*.[386] In 1544, the physician Benoit Textor, then living in Mâcon, thanked Calvin for sending the *Articuli parisiensis cum antidoto*.[387]

Oswald Myconius, Oecolampius's successor, informed Calvin that his 1543 *Supplex exhortatio ad Carolum Quintum* was not available for sale in Basel. Calvin then sent him a copy: "Since you are so keen to obtain my work, I am sending you a copy."[388] Calvin sent a copy of his 1550 *Appendix libelli adversus Interim* to Laelio Sozzini, with whom Calvin had recently become acquainted. Sozzini had not yet at this stage displayed his Anabaptist tendencies. Calvin sent copies of the same work also to Celio Secondo Curione, who taught in Basel, and to Claude Baduel, who was still living in Nîmes.[389]

Calvin's first attack against Westphal, the *Defensio sanae doctrinae de sacramentis*, was dedicated to the Swiss pastors. Calvin therefore sent copies to all the dedicatees, and also to Charles du Moulin, who was in Tübingen at the time, and to the Montbéliard pastor Pierre Toussain. Calvin explained to Toussain that he had prudently omitted his name from the list of dedicatees.[390]

The 1556 *Secunda Defensio contra Westphali calumnias* was equally extensively distributed. The only surviving traces of this distribution, however, are the copies sent to Peter Martyr Vermigli, who was then in Strasbourg,[391] and, more surprisingly, to Gaspard Nydbruck, an imperial councilor who was quietly Protestant. Nydbruck, who had attended Calvin's exegetical lectures in Strasbourg, wrote to him to ask his advice about the writing of the Magdeburg *Centuries*. Nydbruck's letter explains why Calvin sent him his anti-Lutheran work together with the following

---

[385]Bibliothèque nationale et universitaire, R 100439; Herminjard, *Correspondance,* 8:256; CO, 11:501; and *B.C.1,* no. 43/3.

[386]Herminjard, *Correspondance,* 9:155; CO, 11:672; and *B.C.1,* no. 43/7.

[387]CO, 11:824; and *B.C.1,* no. 44/6.

[388]CO, 11:726, 733; and *B.C.1,* no. 43/7.

[389]CO, 13:554, 573, 587–88.

[390]CO, 15:382, 384.

[391]CO, 16:34–35; and *B.C.2,* no. 56/4.

disclaimer: "If possible, I would rather spend my time writing other things. But thanks to your keen understanding, you will see why my position requires me to engage in this combat."[392] This gift is one of the rare cases in which a book was sent to someone whom Calvin knew only in passing.

Finally, in his later years, Calvin sent several complimentary copies of his works to an Augsburg schoolteacher, Matthias Schenck. In 1561, Schenck thanked him for sending three short works, in March for the *Dilucida explicatio* against Hesshusen and in October for two other works, probably the *Gratulatio ad G. Sacconnay* and the *Impietas Valentini Gentilis detecta*.[393]

In short, Calvin aimed to make his written works known in a wide range of settings. It seems that he sent out more complimentary copies of his shorter polemical works than of his large exegetical commentaries.

Sales

Calvin's correspondents regularly asked him to send them a wide range of books, not only his own. He even played a role in more large-scale bookselling endeavors or in purchases that were only indirectly linked to publishing. He also acted as Ambrosius Blaurer's go-between in 1561, in order to have Genevan paper sent to Winterthur and Constance.[394]

Working Together with Booksellers

Already in 1532, Calvin was striving to recoup his investment in *De clementia*. He asked professors in Paris, Bourges, and Orléans to lecture on his work so that a number of students would buy it. Calvin also made arrangements with an Orléans bookseller, Philippe Loré, to have a number of copies printed listing Loré's name on the title page.[395]

In 1539, during his Strasbourg exile, Calvin established a strong bond with Michel du Bois, who settled in Geneva as a bookseller in 1537 and then became a printer in 1540. Calvin tried to have Du Bois sell his new *Institutes* in Geneva and later his commentary on the Epistle to the Romans by providing him with a stock of copies. However, Du Bois turned out to be a mediocre businessman. In April 1539, Calvin had to remind Du Bois of his debts. In December 1539, Du Bois replied, complaining that the *Institutes* were hard to sell and that he was overstocked. Calvin suggested to Du Bois that he send a hundred copies to Neuchâtel in order to avoid returning the unsold copies to Rihel. However, as Calvin noted to Farel, if the books

---

[392]CO, 20:446, 20:445–47, 448–50.

[393]CO, 18:408–9, 19:55; and *B.C.2,* nos. 61/11, 61/13. On Schenck, see J. Bolte in *A.D.B.,* 31:56.ß

[394]*Briefwechsel der Brüder Ambrosius und Thomas Blaurer, 1509–1548,* ed. Tr. Schiess (Freiburg am Breisgau: F. E. Fehsenfeld, 1912), 3:649–50.

[395]Herminjard, *Correspondance,* 2:417–19; and CO, 10/b:20/22, bearing in mind the corrections noted in *B.C.1,* no. 32/1.

were sent on from Geneva, "we will have to find someone else willing to take them on." A status report of July 1540 notes that Du Bois had sent many books to Neuchâtel. As well as sixty-seven copies of the *Institutes* and 182 copies of the commentaries on Romans, Du Bois also transferred between ten and twenty copies each of five other commentaries by Capito, Bucer, and Oecolampadius. In spite of this lack of success, Calvin still wanted to help Wendelin Rihel and therefore asked Farel to try to sell the stock. Calvin established price parameters for his own books: ten batz, or at least nine. If the order was a large one, Farel was authorized to go as low as eight batz. If the batz or plappart, Bernese coinage, was truly worth thirty to thirty-two deniers,[396] Calvin therefore was asking for between one livre and one livre five sous per work. Even when taking transportation costs into account, this seems to be a very steep price. In September, Farel received the parcel and opened it in Maturin Cordier's presence. Farel was able to place a few copies of the *Institutes* in a Lausanne bookshop but was unsure what to do with the remaining books. In October 1540, Calvin arranged to have sixteen copies sent back to Strasbourg. In July 1541, he asked Viret, who was then in Geneva, to collect forty-eight florins owed to Rihel. In all likelihood the debtor was once again Michel du Bois, who left Geneva at the end of 1541, probably as a result of bankruptcy.[397]

Calvin's comment to Christophe Fabri, who was in Thonon at the time, is connected to the Genevan stock of Rihel editions. In September 1539, Fabri asked Calvin for a copy of his *Institutes* and of his commentary on Romans, if they had been published. Fabri even laid out the best route: Strasbourg–Basel–Neuchâtel–Thonon, and specified that he would foot the bill.[398] But Calvin did not comply, for, as he explained, he had been unable to find any adequate courier, "because the transport costs will be almost as much as the value of the book itself. And since it could not be sent to you quickly for this reason, I thought it would be better if you bought it from Michel [du Bois]."[399]

On his return to Geneva, Calvin continued to remain abreast of bookselling issues. When Viret arrived in Geneva at a time when Calvin was away, he found various quantities of Calvin's works in the latter's home. "I took the liberty of taking a few booklets from your house, namely, the catechism and the *Psychopannychia,* because I saw that you had numerous copies."[400]

In 1549, Calvin acted as a go-between in two bookselling deals. On 19 January, a Berthoud schoolteacher, Conrad Curio, transmitted an order from a Zurich bookseller requesting two hundred copies of Calvin's work against the Augsburg Interim.

---

[396]M. Körner, "Plappart," in *Dictionnaire Historique et biographique de la Suisse,* 5:307.

[397]Herminjard, *Correspondance,* 5:291; 6:156, 256, 295–96, 339; and 7:186, 252; CO, 10/b:340, 441, and 11:63–64, 80–81, 100, 254, 282; and *B.C.1,* nos. 39/4, 40/3.

[398]Herminjard, *Correspondance,* 6:26; and CO, 10/b:368.

[399]Herminjard, *Correspondance,* 6:32; and CO, 10/b:372.

[400]CO, 12:84.

The Zurich bookseller also asked for a few copies for himself and his friends, and solemnly promised to pay the bill as soon as possible.[401]

The other transaction was more complicated, because it involved filling an order from Italy. Baldassare Altieri, one of the main proponents of the Reformation in Venice in the first half of the sixteenth century, took the opportunity of a trip to the Swiss lands in 1549 to order several hundred copies of Calvin's works. In June 1549, Altieri worked out with Bullinger the minute details of his order. Haller in Bern would order the books from Calvin. The books would be sent to Zurich care of Froschauer, and Laelio Sozzini would deal with getting them to Venice. Because the original order has since been lost, only partial lists of the requested books are available. There were at least seven different works, with twenty to fifty copies of each requested. The transaction only took place after several reminders. On 12 September, Haller could finally confirm that he had received the books ordered from Girard and he sent them on immediately to Zurich. The later stages of the transfer of the books to Venice are not known.[402]

Occasional Smaller Transactions

Sometimes it is difficult to find a particular book in one's local bookshop. Sixteenth-century readers were already aware of this problem. A few correspondents handled the matter by turning directly to the author.

"The work is unavailable for purchase" in Basel. In this instance, the book in question was the *Supplex exhortation ad Carolum Quintum*.[403] In Zurich in 1548, Bullinger could not find Calvin's exegetical commentaries that had been published in the first months of that year.[404] Already in March 1549, his *Interim germano-adulterum* had sold out.[405] And in 1557, Farel complained that he was unable to find the *Ultima admonitio adversus Westphalum* either in Neuchâtel or in Lausanne.[406] In the same period, the Schaffhausen pastor Jacob Rueger made a fruitless search for a number of pamphlets by Calvin and Beza.[407] Bartholomeus Hagen's criticisms about "the carelessness of our booksellers" refer to the booksellers of Augsburg and Swabia.[408]

The complaints coming from Wroclaw in 1551 were more commonplace. After telling Calvin that "all of Poland is eagerly reading your works, so much so that no other works are as successful," Ambrosius Moiban added, "I would like to see the

---

[401]CO, 13:161; and *B.C.1*, no. 49/6.

[402]Bullinger, *Korrespondenz mit den Graubündern*, 1:472–75; and CO, 13:317–18, 327–28, 367, 386–87. More detailed information appears in *B.C.1*, no. 49/5.

[403]CO, 11:726; and *B.C.1*, no. 43/7.

[404]CO, 13:6.

[405]CO, 13:213.

[406]CO, 16:606.

[407]CO, 18:417–18.

[408]CO, 19:332. On Hagen, see J. Hartman in *A.D.B.* 10:332.

catalogue of your commentaries because such works are too seldom imported here."[409] In the following year, Moiban reiterated his comments about the great popularity of Calvin's works in Poland and Hungary and repeated his earlier phrase almost word for word: "I would like to see the catalogue of your works. For too few such works are imported in our area."[410]

The Biel pastor Ambrosius Blaurer was Calvin's most faithful correspondent when it came to Calvin's written works and acquired copies of these texts from the author himself. Beginning in 1553, Blaurer wrote constantly to Calvin on this matter. For example, Blaurer told Calvin that he was waiting for a good opportunity to buy and bring back to Biel a copy of Calvin's commentary on John. Blaurer added: "Please make sure that I receive a catalogue of all the works that you have published over the years." Calvin gave a complimentary copy of the commentary on John to Blaurer but also sent him at the same time four copies of the *De aeterna Dei praedestinatione*, asking only for the bookseller's price.[411] On 11 February 1554, Calvin sent Blaurer a number of books, including three copies of his *Defensio orthodoxae fidei de trinitate* and his *Quatre sermons*. He added to the parcel Beza's *Epistola Magistri Passavantii*.[412] In February 1554, Calvin sent Blaurer his commentaries on the Acts of the Apostles, "following the conditions that you set, namely, that I receive the price for it here from that trustworthy man." Calvin also explained that because his 1552 *Opuscula* were being published in one volume, he did not feel he needed to give Blaurer a list of all his writings.[413] But the books that were sent did not always reach their destination. Blaurer's silence regarding the *Secunda defensio contra Westphalum* could only be due to such a problem. "Therefore," Calvin wrote, "I suspected that the copy I had sent to you had not reached you so I promptly sent you a copy at your expense." Wanting to avoid too many expenses for his correspondent, Calvin explained to Blaurer that he had not sent Crespin's *Acta martyrum* to Biel. "I was worried about burdening you with this cost."[414]

We have already mentioned that Calvin sent out the first sheets of his commentary on the Psalms in December 1556. After receiving these sheets, Blaurer promised, "when I receive the remainder, I will pay the printer in full."[415] In December 1557, Blaurer asked for the rest of the Psalms commentary and Calvin's lectures on Hosea. Blaurer added, "This is a pressing yet friendly request to have you tell me about everything important printed this year by your printers and that you consider worthwhile for us to read."[416] In February 1558, Blaurer thanked his correspondent, asking him to send him any new works

---

[409]CO, 13:638.

[410]CO, 14:307. On Moiban, 1494–1554, see *A.D.B.* 22:81–82 and 36:790.

[411]CO, 14:459, 474; and *B.C.1,* nos. 52/4, 53/5.

[412]CO, 15:25; and *B.C.1,* nos. 52/9, 54/6.

[413]CO, 15:24–25; and *B.C.1,* no. 52/8.

[414]CO, 16:145; and *B.C.2,* no. 56/4.

[415]CO, 16:350; and *B.C.2,* no. 57/4.

[416]CO, 16:723–724; and *B.C.2,* no. 57/3.

with the commentaries on Isaiah and another copy on Hosea. Make
sure that you first receive payment for these. I believe that the works you
recently sent me will sell reasonably well here. For the sake of our
friendship, I ask you not to go to any expense for me. You will have
done enough if you simply tell your household servant to see to it that
our representative receives from your printer the works that I would
like, and that the printer is paid by our representative.[417]

Blaurer's remarks regarding book sales in Biel show that he was not only buying
books for himself. Indeed, at times he purchased several copies of the same work. In
April 1561, Blaurer inquired once more about Calvin's new releases and asked for his
treatise against Hesshusen "once Liner has paid you for it."[418] Blaurer was referring
to Hans Liner, a merchant from Saint Gallen, who regularly traveled to Lyon and
acted as a messenger for many Swiss pastors. In July, Blaurer noted that he had
received the commentaries on Isaiah and on the Acts of the Apostles, but he had not
yet received Calvin's lectures on the minor prophets.[419] In October, Blaurer sent to
Calvin the Latin translation of a book by Brenz, but asked that Calvin send it back if
he already owned it. Thus Blaurer was not blindly generous.[420] The final mention of
books in Blaurer's correspondence dealt with the lectures on Daniel. In December
1561, Blaurer told Calvin that he was disappointed when he found out from Hans
Liner who was traveling through Biel that he had a copy intended for the St. Gallen
pastors. Blaurer felt that Calvin should have known that he too wanted that work.
Instead, he was forced to wait for another opportunity.[421]

    Other references to book orders in Calvin's letters are few and far between.
From Lyon, Claude Baduel ordered the 1551 commentary on Isaiah, adding, "I will
pay what I owe for the book itself and the transport costs."[422] Christophe Piperi-
nus's order of Calvin's commentary on the synoptic Gospels highlights the risks
inherent in sending books: "Please send via this messenger this unbound book, but
wrap it well so that it can travel safely to me through the storms."[423] Writing from
Basel, Simon Sulzer worried about the cost of two commentaries that he had probably already received, namely, the commentary on the Psalms and the lectures on the
minor prophets.[424] In April 1561, the Schaffhausen minister Jacob Rueger asked
Schaffhausen merchants who passed through Geneva to buy several pamphlets by
Calvin and Beza. It seems that Rueger was not confident about the merchants' good

---

[417]CO, 17:42; *B.C.1*, no. 51/6; and *B.C.2*, no. 57/3.
[418]CO, 18:420–22; and *B.C.2*, no. 61/11.
[419]CO, 18:538; and *B.C.2*, nos. 59/1, 59/5, 60/2.
[420]CO, 19:86–87.
[421]CO, 19:156; and *B.C.2*, no. 61/20.
[422]CO, 14:69; and *B.C.1*, no. 51/6.
[423]CO, 15:821. See also *B.C.2*, no. 55/9.
[424]Beza, *Correspondance*, 3:56; and *B.C.2*, nos. 57/4, 59/5.

sense, since he asked Calvin or Beza to oversee the purchases.[425] In the same period, the son of one of Calvin's fellow students from Orléans and Bourges, François Daniel, ordered two copies of the *Institutes* from Calvin. The young man knew that the work was sold by Antoine Calvin.[426]

In October 1554, John Cheke, who was in Padua at the time following his trip through Geneva, complained about being unable to find any good books.

> ...I would like to have a few to read this winter. If I knew how to pay for them or where to go in Venice to deposit funds to pay for them, I would be sure to ask you to send me the small Estienne Bible with notes and whatever else is available on the prophets. I study them with pleasure. But I definitely do not want you to do this unless you tell me where to go in Venice to deposit the money.[427]

I only located one instance where one of Calvin's correspondents thanked him by sending him a book in return. The humanist Johannes Sinapius made an extended stay in the court of Ferrara before returning to Franconia. It was from Ferrara that he wrote in January 1557 to thank Calvin for the two books printed in 1552, one by Calvin and the other by Robert Estienne. As a token of thanks, Sinapius sent Calvin "no gold in exchange for base metals, but rather base metals in exchange for gold," namely, a defense of the Society of Jesus, recently published in Vienna, probably The *De Societatis Jesu initiis, progressu, rebusque gestis nonnullis* of 1556.[428]

Services Rendered

The only remaining subject to mention is that the booksellers' travels allowed them to provide assistance to the Reformers in a variety of ways, chiefly by transmitting letters, books, and news. The Frankfurt fair was the ideal place to find out about recent publications, especially those of opponents. As Viret wrote to Farel in 1543, "Given that I have no definite information regarding the books he has asked for, I will wait until Guillaume [du Bosc] returns from the fair."[429] In 1549, he made a similar remark: "But we will probably have more accurate news about this matter when our booksellers return from Frankfurt."[430] In 1556, during the height of his conflict with Westphal, Calvin wrote to Farel: "I think that the Frankfurt fair will

---

[425]CO, 18:417–18.

[426]CO, 18:415; and *B.C.2,* no. 59/4.

[427]CO, 15:267.

[428]CO, 16:375–76. On Sinapius, see I. Guenther, "Johannes Sinapius," in *Contemporaries of Erasmus: A Biographical Register of the Renaissance and Reformation,* ed. P. G. Bietenholz (Toronto: University of Toronto Press, 1987), 3:254–55. For more on the book Sinapius sent, see C. Sommervogel, *Bibliothèque de la Compagnie de Jésus* (Toulouse: privately published, 1911–30), 11:4–5.

[429]CO, 11:521.

[430]CO, 13:398.

bring us many books by the Saxons. We will have to talk this over together when we meet next with Viret."[431]

In 1536, when Calvin took part in the disputation of Lausanne, he wrote to his friend from Orléans, François Daniel. He began by explaining his three-month silence. He had been preoccupied by many tasks, and then "the August [Lyon] fair was over in the meantime, a particularly convenient time to send letters." There would be little need to comment on this statement except for the fact that the Lyon fairs were at least as important for Geneva as the Frankfurt ones. The Lyon fairs took place four times a year for two weeks: beginning on the first Monday after 6 January, on the ninth day after Easter, on 4 August, and 3 November. Calvin's letter to Daniel on 13 October was written with the November fair in mind.[432]

In 1538, when Calvin retreated to Basel, his friend Du Tillet suggested to him that he provide Calvin with financial assistance. To organize the transfer of funds from Paris to Basel, Du Tillet naturally recommended using the services of Conrad Resch, with whom Calvin had stayed in 1535–36.[433]

During his time in Strasbourg, Calvin did not limit his contacts to Wendelin Rihel alone. He also made use of the services of another scholarly printer, Kraft Müller, better known by his Latin name, Crato Mylius. Mylius was a former student of Melanchthon. From 1539 to 1561, Mylius regularly served as a messenger between Strasbourg and Wittenberg, Worms and Ulm.[434]

In the first years after his return to Geneva, Calvin established links with the Lyon book world. In 1541, he was aware of Etienne Dolet's psalter project.[435] He was also in contact with Jean Frellon, who served as a go-between in 1543 for some fund transfers and who exchanged letters with Calvin in 1546.[436] Marcellin Beringen, who worked with his brother Godefroy as a printer, received and transferred letters intended for Calvin in 1546. Beringen was a humanist who had contacts with Basel's scholarly circles.[437]

The earliest Genevan printers and booksellers had little impact beyond the city's borders. The only exception was Guillaume du Bosc, who sometimes attended one of the fairs.[438] Thus it was the Zurich bookseller Christoph Froschauer who handled the sale of the *Acta synodi tridentinae* in 1547 in Frankfurt.[439] After 1550, Frankfurt became a crucial crossroads for international communication. Calvin pointed out

[431]CO, 16:76.

[432]Herminjard, *Correspondance,* 4:87–88; and CO, 10/b:63.

[433]Herminjard, *Correspondance,* 5:108; and CO, 10/b:245. On Resch, see above 180.

[434]Herminjard, *Correspondance,* 6:130, 400, 7:188; CO, 10/b:432, and 11:131, 255.

[435]Herminjard, *Correspondance,* 7:374; and CO, 11:357.

[436]CO, 11:648, and 12:281–82, 370. On Jean II Frellon, see Baudrier, *Bibliographic lyonnaise,* 5:154–271.

[437]CO, 12:457–58. On the Beringen brothers, see Guillo, *Les éditions musicales,* 114–16.

[438]CO, 11:521.

[439]J. Cochlaeus, *Joannis Calvini in Acta Synodi Tridentinae Censura, et Ejusdem Brevis Confutatio circa Duas Praecipue Calumnias* (Mainz: F. Behem, 1548), fol. D5r-v ; and *B.C.I,* no. 47/3.

this fact to the Polish noblemen who wrote to him. Because he was in Frankfurt in September 1556, the Polish nobleman's letter reached him late, and he decided to wait until the next fair to answer them, "because at this fair, he explained, there is always a greater opportunity to write letters."[440] When Calvin wanted to send a presentation copy of one of his works to Prince Radziwill in Poland, he transmitted it once again via Frankfurt, where Dathenus entrusted the package to Sebastian Pech.[441] Pech was John a Lasco's former secretary, who had become a bookseller in Poland and regularly traveled between Poland and Frankfurt.[442]

Another case is that of a Wurtemberg pastor who was searching for one of Calvin's works and suggested to the Reformer on 27 February 1554: "I would appreciate it if next quarter, when your merchants head to Frankfurt, you give it [the book in question] to your printers." From Frankfurt, the pastor's own contacts would bring the book back to him.[443]

However, Frankfurt was not the only possible meeting point. We have already mentioned Lyon. Surviving letters also show that the Genevan bookseller Jacques Derbilly traveled to Regensburg in 1557 and that he carried letters from the Regensburg pastor Martin Schalling.[444] When Nydbruck began writing to Calvin, he suggested using Oporinus as a courier between Geneva and Vienna.[445] Similarly, Valentin Paceus was encouraged to send to Strasbourg the letters he was writing from Leipzig and intended for Geneva.[446]

To conclude these shorter and more lengthy journeys, it is worth reminding ourselves of the danger of letters going astray. We have already recounted the story of the loss of Calvin's manuscript copy of his commentary on Second Corinthians.[447] In a letter to Calvin in late November 1557, François Hotman not only complained about the disappearance of an earlier letter, but also asked Calvin to make inquiries about the man who had carried the mail. The man in question was a printing worker who had been employed for many years by Rihel in Strasbourg and had recently been hired by Crespin in Geneva. Hotman noted that he had already questioned Rihel's proofreader, who had given a positive assessment of the worker's talents. Thus Hotman asked Calvin to pursue inquiries in Geneva.[448]

Conclusion

Calvin was clearly well acquainted with the world of printing and bookselling. He knew what work was carried out in a print shop, how typesetting and layout

[440]CO, 16:420.
[441]See above 204.
[442]CO, 176:379–80, 420, 600; 18:118, 182; and 20:277.
[443]CO, 15:52.
[444]CO, 16:408, 598, 651.
[445]CO, 16:88.
[446]CO, 13:593.
[447]See above 3–4.
[448]CO, 16:714.

were done, what proofreading entailed, and what the average workload was. Yet he was even more aware of the constraints facing those who selected works to be published. Publishers had to have sufficient funds to underwrite the production of the work, advertise it, and sell it. The fairs, and the Frankfurt fair in particular, were ideal places to launch new works.

Calvin matched his writing tempo to the needs of the booksellers. If he had a short tract to write, he waited until the next fair was coming up to start work. If he had to write a dedication, he waited until his printer told him the work was off the presses before composing it.

Although Calvin had first come into contact with a printing house at age twenty-two, and a year later personally paid for the printing of his first book, he did not always oversee the production of his written works as closely throughout his entire life. Already by the mid-1540s, he handed over part of the oversight of his publications to friends in the bookselling business. In particular, he no longer proofread his books. However, he did not turn his attention completely away from this industry, and he remained interested in what happened to his books.

Overall, it seems that right up to his last days, the Reformer continued to display a high level of interest in the distribution and sale of his works. His correspondents constantly asked him to send them his works, and he unhesitatingly responded by using the Genevan printers as go-betweens.

Chapter Six

Censorship

The issue of Calvin and censorship can be considered from two different perspectives: Calvin as a censor, and Calvin as a subject of censorship. Furthermore, this dual approach took place in various geographic settings, whether in Geneva or beyond its borders. In his own city-church, the Reformer sought to control the production of Geneva's printers, yet he too had to receive permission to print, leading at times to clashes. Outside Geneva, Calvin also attempted to censor certain works published in Protestant areas, while at the same time dealing with prohibitions issued by Catholic authorities. These are the themes that will be dealt with in this chapter.

1. The Censor in Geneva

The Legal Foundations of Genevan Censorship

Until 1550, the output of the Genevan printing industry was minimal, given that there was only a handful of printers, and in several years, only one. In the early years, no censorship laws were in place. The process began due to an incident that occurred during Calvin and Farel's exile. In 1539, Girard printed a book by Marie d'Ennetiè-res and Antoine Froment under a false name. Because the work in question criticized the pastors, it was immediately brought to the attention of the Council; the work was confiscated and those responsible for producing it faced charges.[1]

Nine days after the printer's arrest, the Council issued its first edict. No work could be printed without prior authorization from the magistrates. A few months later, on 19 September, the Council ordered the creation of a copyright library: the first copy of any printed book had to be deposited in the *maison de ville*. The authorities' rationale is worth noting: they had taken this measure in order to prevent the

---

[1]Cartier, "Arrêts du Conseil de Genève," 533–35; Chaix, *Recherches*, 15–17; and Berthoud, *Antoine Marcourt*, 65–70.

printing of books "in which the honor and glory of God are rejected." The conflict that had erupted in May was due to the work's critical attitude toward the pastors. Thus the religious aspect of censorship was put forward as a rationale from the very start. On 6 January 1540, even stricter controls were put in place. Once a book had received printing permission, a signed manuscript copy had to be deposited with the Council.[2]

The earliest rules were therefore quite straightforward: the Council was the only authority charged with censorship issues, and carried out its mandate through pre-printing authorizations. No publications could escape censorship, and printers had to furnish both a manuscript copy of the work prior to printing and a printed copy after the task was completed. Starting in 1539, the Council regularly called on the pastors to evaluate religious publications. In January 1559, this practice became formal law. At the request of two pastors, one of whom was Theodore Beza, the Council decided to systematically send to the pastors all the works that were brought to the civil authorities for printing authorization. Two or three of the pastors were to examine and sign the works. Hence from 1559 onwards, Genevan works were subject to a double censorship. The pastors' justification for this measure is worth noting: "works printed in this city carry great weight wherever the faithful are, but there are some risks, in that some people who correct works add in mistakes or bad things."[3] In July 1559, the Council members even asked the ministers to keep a record of printing permissions, parallel to the list held by the Council.[4] Because these records have not survived, their very existence is open to question.

Censorship in Practice

The day-to-day practice of censorship was much less clearly defined than the legislation. The main way to learn about the practice of censorship is to analyze the records of the Genevan Council. Indeed, these records contain a certain number of requests for permission to print as well as the Council's response on a regular basis. However, the gap between the number of requests recorded in the registers and the actual number of printed books is very large. Over two-thirds of works printed never appear in the registers. In fact, this proportion varied depending on the printers. Jean Crespin and Eustache Vignon appeared more infrequently in the registers than their colleagues. In Crespin's case, only thirty printing permissions for his works appeared in the registers, while his total production amounted to 250 editions.[5]

Before accusing Genevan publishers of systematic negligence, we should note that not all the permissions that were granted were recorded in the registers. For instance, one of the Psalter editions contains an extract of a privilege not recorded

[2]RC 33, fols. 115v, 122v, 292v (9–19 Sept. 1539); and RC 34, fol. 3v (6 Jan. 1540).
[3]RC 54, fol. 357v (16 Jan. 1559).
[4]RC 55, fol. 76r (31 July 1559).
[5]Bremme, *Buchdrucker,* 70 nn. 22–23; and Gilmont, *Crespin,* 81.

elsewhere.[6] In some cases, a conflict over publishing rights led a publisher to defend his monopoly granted because of a printing permission that does not appear in the registers. For example, Crespin requested a privilege for a work by Sleidanus that had been published a year earlier. The Council specified that it was "a work whose publication we authorized."[7] In all likelihood, some works received tacit permission to be printed, as was probably the case for reprints. Legislation to this effect came into force only in 1568, but in all likelihood it merely made common practice official.[8]

There is clear evidence that some works were printed without authorization. Indeed, some of the authors whose works were involved were quite famous. However, the printers were generally the ones who faced the penalties.

The 1550 case of Jean Girard was an extreme one, since he printed a book that had been explicitly banned by the Council. Because no copy of the work has survived, it is difficult to get a clear picture of the incident. The book was authored by Benoît Textor, Calvin's physician, and was entitled, *Le testament et la mort de la femme de Pierre Viret*. According to the recollections of a contemporary, the book detailed the celestial visions experienced by Viret's wife shortly before her death. She saw the skies opened and the chairs ready for Farel and her husband.[9] The Council prohibited the printing of the book on 20 January on the grounds that "most of the said work contains things that are not religiously relevant," and expressly prohibited the author from having the book published anywhere else. On 5 May, Girard was sent to the Council for having ignored the ban, and he was imprisoned on 11 May. The next day, Calvin intervened on his behalf and managed to have him released with "a severe reprimand." In theory, the entire print run was destroyed, but some copies survived and circulated surreptitiously, leading to satirical comments from the Reformers' enemies. Viret, who was probably one of the instigators of the work, felt it necessary to appear before the Council of Geneva to clear his name. This incident was one episode in the ongoing conflict between Calvin and his political opponents.[10]

In 1554, Theodore Beza and Guillaume Guéroult clashed over their translations of the Psalms. Guéroult took the opportunity to publish a small poem attacking Beza. Responding immediately, Beza slipped a poem into his new edition of the Psalter. The poem was entitled "To the jealous donkey." Although both works had received general printing permissions, the insulting poems had clearly not been submitted to the Council. Though both printers were threatened with jail time, they ended up simply being reprimanded.[11]

---

[6]This Psalter was printed by Rivery in 1565: see Pidoux, *Psautier,* 2:150.

[7]RC 53, fol. 209r–v (29 June 1557).

[8]Bremme, *Buchdrucker,* 70.

[9]Quoted by J. Barnaud in *Pierre Viret: Sa vie et son oeuvre, 1511–1571* (Saint-Amans: G. Carayol, 1911; repr., Nieuwkoop: De Graaf, 1973), 314 n. 3.

[10]Cartier, "Arrêts du Conseil de Genève," 486–92 together with the information provided in the preceding footnote.

[11]The entire account is given in Pidoux, *Psautier,* 2:68–72. See also Balmas, "Guéroult," 1–40.

In 1556, Antoine Cercia appeared with two printed works in hand and requested a printing permission for them. The Council seemingly accepted his request. A week later, Simon du Bosc brazenly requested a privilege for a work that was printed without authorization. The Council hardly reacted, simply ordering that the work be examined "in the usual fashion."[12] Du Bosc returned to the matter a few days later, asking for the privilege. He was turned down, but did receive printing permission without any other complaint.[13]

In 1559, Beza came before the Council bearing two books that had been printed without permission. His rationale was the urgency of the deadline due to the upcoming Frankfurt fair. The Council decided that they would "accept the excuse this time around."[14]

Lesser-known printers faced greater penalties from the Council. In 1558, Zacharie Durant was sentenced to three days in prison for having printed the *Anthitese des pseaumes contre le pape* without permission. His unsold stock was to be destroyed.[15] In July 1559, Jacques Bourgeois spent a day in prison for having printed "without permission" the placards written by a new arrival in Geneva, a man who intended to settle in Geneva as a physician.[16] In May 1563, Vincent Brès faced charges for having sold an ABC book containing theological errors. Called before the Consistory in August, he admitted that he had been lying when he claimed that the work was done by the Genevan pastors, but he blamed an absent pastor, Pierre d'Airebouze. Two weeks later, Brès admitted that his second explanation was also a lie. He also confessed "that he had not asked permission from Messieurs to have it printed." Because he was facing the Consistory, he was excommunicated and threatened with being sent before the Council.[17]

Few printers seem to have respected the rule of asking for permission before starting a print run. One obvious example is the first edition of Crespin's martyrology. By April 1554, the work was in press. By July, a Strasbourg correspondent had already received over half of the printed sheets. But Crespin only appeared before the Council on 14 August to request "that he be allowed to print" his volume. He received the authorization a week later, with one restriction, namely, that he remove the words "martyrs" and "saints" from his text. The requirement was somewhat problematic given that the work was already printed with the title *Livres des martyrs*. Crespin's solution was to print a new preliminary booklet using another title, but he continued to sell (in all likelihood far away from Geneva) a few *Livres des martyrs*, some of which have survived until now.[18] The city councilors seem to have been

---

[12]R. Part. 10, fol. 111r (31 July 1556).
[13]RC 51, fol. 247r (4 Aug. 1556); and R. Part. 10, fol. 145v (20 Oct. 1556).
[14]RC 55, fol. 8v (17 Feb. 1559).
[15]RC 54, fol. 170v (2 May 1558).
[16]R. Crim., 1559–1561, fol. 33v (4 July 1559).
[17]RC 58, fol. 531r (17 May 1563); and R. Consist. 20, fols. 96v, 121r (5 and 31 Aug. 1563).
[18]Gilmont, *Crespin*, 166–67.

unaware of Crespin's strategy. Badius's case in 1560 was very different. Just as he requested a printing permission for his *Satyres de la cuisine du pape,* the councilors learned that the book was already in print. In spite of Badius's explanation that his presses were idle and that Laurent de Normandie had suggested that he start the printing process, the Council members decided that Badius had shown "disregard and disobedience" and he was condemned to three days in jail.[19]

In 1557, Robert Estienne printed Calvin's *In librum psalmorum* commentaries without requesting printing permission. When the printer appeared before the Council with the printed volume in hand, he explained that he received the manuscript sheet by sheet as the printing process moved along. In spite of their generally positive relationship with Calvin—this incident took place after 1555—the Council was displeased. The councilors sent a delegation to Calvin and instructed Estienne to follow the regulations.[20]

The same disregard for procedures appeared when it came to the requirement to provide printed copies. In many cases, the printers provided copies of their works when they were trying to obtain something from the Council. Thus, a week after being reprimanded for having printed Calvin's Psalms commentary, Estienne presented to the Council "one copy of each work he had printed since his first days in Geneva."[21] In August 1562, Crespin provided a copy of the *Thesaurus linguae graecae* the day before he presented a request regarding a dispute over the sale of the *Thesaurus* itself.[22] When Badius brought to the Council copies of Beza's speech at the Colloquy of Poissy in 1561, he was reprimanded on two grounds: he had already offered the work for sale, and he had not provided any copies for the copyright library.[23]

In his study of the Academy library, Alexander Ganoczy accurately remarked that the copyright library rules operated "with a bit less disregard" from 1552 to 1565. He even noted a clear improvement in 1555 that should be tied to the crushing of the Perrinist faction. His analysis is perceptive, except when he praises the generosity of Robert Estienne. A study of the Council registers shows that Estienne's ostensibly generous actions were motivated by strong reasons of self-interest.[24]

On several occasions, the Council had to reiterate its edicts, especially regarding the need to obtain an authorization prior to printing. This occurred in 1556, again in 1560 when new printing regulations were issued, and once more in 1563 when the Council limited the number of presses.[25] But the rules were also reasserted at other times such as in 1557 when Estienne published Calvin's Psalms without permission,

[19]RC 55, fol. 170v (5 Jan. 1560).
[20]RC 53, fols. 252v, 255v (27 and 29 July 1557); and Gilmont, "La rédaction et la publication," 8.
[21]RC 53, fol. 262r (5 Aug. 1557).
[22]RC 57, fol. 95r (6 Aug. 1562); and R. Part. 13, fol. 38v (7 Aug. 1562).
[23]RC 56, fol. 246v (6 Oct. 1561).
[24]Ganoczy, *Bibliothèque,* 13–17.
[25]RC 52, fol. 118r (26/22/2556); and Chaix, *Recherches,* 20–25, 32.

and in 1563 when Jean-Baptiste Pinereul was allowed to restart the printing of the Psalter that the Council had recently stopped. On these occasions, the Council decided to remind all the printers of the regulations.[26] In November and December 1557, the councilors suddenly became concerned about the nonobservance of copyright library regulations. On 25 November, Robert Estienne was asked to bind the copy of the work he had deposited in the copyright collection. On 3 December, when the pastor Michel Cop offered a bound volume for the copyright library, the Council members reminded him that the printer was to give an unbound copy to each Council member. Finally on 7 December, the councilors decided to remind all the printers of their obligations in this domain.[27]

The Censors

In the best-case scenario, the records noted the printer's request for printing permission and a few days later noted that the authorization had been provided. But in many instances, the records only indicate one of the two steps: either the request or the decision taken. Usually, the terms used in the records are very general, as was the case for Beza's *Confession de foy*. On 16 September 1558, the councilors decided "to have it examined." Four days later, they authorized the printer to start on the work: "since the report indicates this is a good work, he may print it."[28] The decision was normally taken after a report on the work had been received. Sometimes, the records provide the name of the councilor who had to obtain a report on the work and, much more significantly, the name of the person or persons asked to examine the work.

There are only slightly more than one hundred such cases recorded during Calvin's lifetime. Even then, the information is at times rather vague. For instance, the records may indicate that the councilor had received feedback from "learned men" or "masters."[29] In three cases, the works in question were submitted to a large committee. A work by Chappuys on the plague was authorized in 1543 after a "meeting with the pastors, physicians, and barber-surgeons of the city."[30] In 1552, when the newly arrived Robert Estienne presented a list of works he intended to publish, the Council consulted "the pastors, the doctors, and learned men."[31] In 1556, when Zacharie Durant presented a work by Antoine Chanorrier, it was sent to "scholars."[32]

[26]On Estienne, see above 149–51, 189–90. On Pinereul, see RC 58, fol. 46r (29 Apr. 1563).

[27]R. Part. 11, fol. 144r (25 Nov. 1557); and RC 53, fols. 444r, 445r, 450r (3 and 7 Dec. 1557).

[28]RC 54, fols. 286r, 289r (16 and 20 Sept. 1558).

[29]RC 44, fol. 308v (23 Jan. 1550); R. Part. 5, fol. 34r (21 Dec. 1551); and RC 51, fol. 189v (19 June 1556).

[30]RC 37, fol. 150r (10 July 1543).

[31]R. Part. 6, fol. 105r (1 Dec. 1552).

[32]RC 51, fol. 189v (19 June 1556).

Otherwise, reviewers of the works tended to be divided into three categories, according to the records: the pastors as a group, Calvin himself, and the Consistory. Yet the Council also took its decisions after having consulted other people, as detailed below. To my mind, however, analyzing the data based on these references seems flawed because the references are so few and far between. Furthermore, comparisons over time are unreliable because of the preponderance of references in later decades. Prior to 1550, few indications of the procedure survive, whereas these became more numerous from 1550 to 1554, and doubled again in number in later years.

Throughout the period, the pastors in general or Calvin in particular were consulted on a regular basis, though more frequently after 1555. In 1559, a year when Calvin was often sick, the pastors as a group were asked their advice more often. The Council conferred with Calvin over printing issues much less frequently in 1559 and 1560. At times, Calvin was called upon jointly with others like Farel,[33] Abel Poupin,[34] Beza,[35] or together with the rest of the pastors.[36] Clearly, when the Council called on the ministers in general, they sometimes in fact meant Calvin, as was the case with a 1558 request when the magistrates requested the opinion of the pastors but the report was presented by Calvin.[37] However, when the Council called on the pastors, Calvin was not automatically consulted even though the names of other individual pastors or groups of them only appeared in the records after 1555. These ministers included Abel Poupin,[38] Nicolas des Gallars,[39] François Bourgoing,[40] Pierre Viret,[41] and Jacques des Bordes.[42] In 1563, Bourgoing even received a small honorarium for his work "following the earlier rulings" as the registers stated.[43] This mention of payment for the censors is the only one as far as I am aware.

The Consistory was first and foremost in charge of controlling public morals. Thus, it is understandable that the Consistory was concerned when a "scandalous" publication was available, whether printed locally or brought in from outside Geneva. In particular, the Consistory was the main actor in the struggle against Gabriel Vigean's almanacs, which will be described below. In contrast, the Consistory's activity in assessing manuscripts prior to printing is more surprising. Between 1560 and 1564, the Consistory registers detail three cases and in two instances the Council registers explicitly mention the Consistory's report.[44] However, in other

[33]RC 37, fol. 150r (10 July 1543).

[34]R. Part. 6, fol. 13r (1 July 1552).

[35]RC 56, fol. 210r (30 June 1561).

[36]RC 45, fol. 48r (15 July 1550).

[37]RC 54, fol. 234v, 240v (15 and 21 July 1558).

[38]RC 51, fol. 23v (24 Feb. 1556).

[39]RC 51, fol. 63r, 252v (23 Mar. 1556, 3 Aug. 1556); and RC 56, fol. 15r (1 Mar. 1560).

[40]RC 51, fol. 63r (23 Mar. 1556); and RC 58, fol. 47v (3 May 1563).

[41]RC 55, fol. 173r (11 Jan. 1560).

[42]RC 58, fol. 64r (14 June 1563).

[43]RC 58, fol. 47v (3 May 1563).

[44]R. Consist. 17, fol. 113r (11 July 1560) and RC 56, fols. 59r–v (11 and 12 July 1560); R. Consist.

cases the Council sent manuscripts to the Consistory without any assessment recorded in the Consistory registers. This situation may be due to the fact that the councilors were somewhat vague in distinguishing between the body of pastors and the Consistory.[45] Indeed, in two of the three cases noted in the Consistory registers, the minutes state explicitly that the decision was made after having heard the report of one or two pastors. Thus sending a work to the Consistory was equivalent to submitting the text to the pastors.

Superstitions in the Almanacs and ABC Books

Before analyzing the usual work of the censors, we must consider a phenomenon that clearly displays the limits of the Reformation's impact in the early years. At the beginning, those overseeing the printing industry were on the lookout for traces of "papist idolatry." In spite of the censors' efforts, two kinds of works were able to resist such pressures for a number of years. These were the almanacs and ABC books, traditional texts that some Genevan customers wanted to see remain unchanged. Already in 1543, the Council authorized the printing of a psalter with music and prayers if the Hail Mary was omitted from the text.[46] Over the years, almanacs containing "a number of superstitions" were printed and sold by two small-scale booksellers, Gabriel Vigean and Nicod du Chesne, in spite of the repeated complaints of the pastors and the Consistory. Gabriel Vigean had inherited an older typesetting font from his father Wigand Koeln. Beginning in 1553, Vigean worked together with Nicod du Chesne, a minor bookseller and bookbinder. The two struggled to survive using a range of strategies. Because they employed old Gothic fonts, they were likely rarely busy. Their production was limited to works that could easily be sold.[47]

Calvin intervened for the first time in December 1546.[48] From this point onward the Consistory was involved in searching out these almanacs. Calvin's first intervention led to Vigean's appearance before the Consistory. Among other superstitions the Consistory condemned was the fact that the almanacs indicated "the best day to enjoy the company of women." Vigean proved to be accommodating and offered to submit his almanacs to the Consistory.[49]

In September 1548, Calvin renewed his attack, this time before the Council, criticizing both the Gabriel Vigean almanac and his ABC books.[50] A year later,

---

20, fol. 10r (6 Jan. 1564) and RC 58, fol. 145r (10 Jan. 1564); R. Consist. 21, fol. 2r (16 Mar. 1564) and RC 59, fol. 21v (17 Mar. 1564).

[45]RC 55, fol. 24v (28 Mar. 1559); and RC 56, fols. 11r, 42v, 59v, 245r (19 Feb. 1560, 24 May 1560, 12 July 1560, 29 Sept. 1561).

[46]RC 37, fol. 121v (9 June 1543).

[47]Cartier, "Arrêts du Conseil de Genève," 439–52, 455–67.

[48]RC 41, fols. 262v, 285v (14 Dec. 1546, 17 Jan. 1547).

[49]R. Consist. 3, fols. 1, 10 (6 and 27 Jan. 1547).

[50]RC 43, fol. 186r (6 Sept. 1548).

Calvin reiterated his charges and this time the printer was sent to prison.[51]

It seems that the muted reaction of the civil powers was due to their lack of concern, since the conflict with Gabriel Vigean lasted beyond 1550, when Nicod du Chesne began to work with him. The Consistory intervened several times without any explicit mention in the surviving sources of any direct action by Calvin. In July 1551, Du Chesne was criticized for having bound Catholic missals. Appearing before the Consistory, he "angrily admitted that he did it to earn a living and that he offended neither God nor Messieurs [the magistrates]."[52] The Consistory denounced him to the Council, which merely collected additional information, including personal verbal attacks of Du Chesne against Calvin.[53] On 1 September, the Consistory decided to bar him from the Lord's Supper,[54] and on 3 September, the Council prohibited him from printing and selling breviaries. The next day the magistrates returned to the issue of Du Chesne's insults against Calvin.[55]

In September 1553, the Consistory complained of a disturbance caused by Nicod du Chesne, who burst into the chamber and threatened certain members of the group. The bookseller was very upset about the Consistory's oversight of the community members' morals.[56] Shortly thereafter, he was accused of having Gabriel Vigean print almanacs and ABC books full of superstitions in his own shop. On 28 September, Du Chesne vigorously denied this before the Consistory and put the blame for the deed on the brother and brother-in-law of Jean Girard. These two men admitted to having printed a few sheets without having been able to see the whole volume.[57] Vigean and Du Chesne were interviewed on 12 October. Vigean admitted everything and even added that Du Chesne wanted to have him print books of hours following Lausanne usage. For his part, Du Chesne continued to deny everything.[58] When sent before the Council, both booksellers were merely reprimanded.[59] Once again, Vigean was called before the Consistory regarding his almanacs on 21 December 1553 and was reprimanded by the Council on 8 January.[60] Yet Vigean imperturbably continued to produce the same almanacs. In September 1554, the Consistory threatened to remand him before the Council members, adding accusations about his marital life.[61]

The struggle against traditional Catholic almanacs, begun in earlier years, still was not won by the mid-1550s. These publications with a Catholic outlook still

[51]RC 44, fol. 290v (23 Dec. 1549).
[52]R. Consist. 6, fol. 49r (30 July 1551).
[53]RC 46, fol. 24v (3 Aug. 1551).
[54]R. Consist. 6, fol. 58r (1 Sept. 1551).
[55]R. Part. 4, fol. 284r (3 Sept. 1551); and RC 46, fol. 52r (4 Sept. 1551).
[56]R. Part. 7, fol. 134v (4 Sept. 1551).
[57]R. Consist. 8, fol. 56r (28 Sept. 1553).
[58]R. Consist. 8, fol. 58v (12 Oct. 1553).
[59]R. Part. 7, fol. 161r (16 Oct. 1553).
[60]R. Consist. 8, fol. 79r (21 Dec. 1553); and R. Part. 7, fol. 212r (8 Jan. 1555).
[61]R. Consist. 9, fol. 126v (6 Sept. 1554).

found faithful purchasers. In February 1556, the Consistory decided once again to draw the Council's attention to Vigean's publications.[62] A few days later, Calvin made a formal complaint about the printer's publications as well as about his dissolute lifestyle. Vigean was sent to prison and was again told not to print almanacs.[63] In 1557, Calvin again complained before the Council about Gabriel Vigean and his almanacs. This time the accused was put in prison and condemned.[64] There is no clear evidence about his lifestyle up to 1559. On 15 August 1557, Nicod du Chesne was executed for having collaborated with exiled Genevans living in Bernese territory who ceaselessly criticized their native city.[65]

In order to contain this continual wave of corrupt almanacs, in February 1554 Badius was authorized to distribute almanacs "from which superfluities have been removed."[66] In May 1558, he received a five-year privilege for a publication free of superstitions or witchcraft and also managed to have other almanacs burned. A few months later, Badius brought up the matter "because the population takes no notice of these works."[67] In 1560, a disgruntled Badius asked to be freed from his promise to print almanacs unless he could obtain a monopoly. He also asked not to have to print them in red and black so that he could sell them more cheaply.[68] In all likelihood, he obtained what he wanted since in November 1561 he raised the matter again and obtained a three-year privilege.[69] Following his departure to Orléans, the tradition of sanitized almanacs continued since Olivier Fordrin received permission to print them in October 1563 "so long as he uses some red ink."[70] However, some elements of Catholicism still remained in Genevan editions of the almanacs, since Calvin condemned them again in 1563.

Calvin's Direct Control

Between 1542 and 1550, Calvin held a certain amount of oversight of Genevan publications in spite of the resistance of the Council and part of the population. At the time Jean Girard was responsible for almost all the publications, though these were few in number. Thanks to Calvin's authority, the Reformer held at least indirect influence over Girard's work without having to turn to the Council, as detailed above.[71]

---

[62]R. Consist. 10, fol. 90 (6 Feb. 1556).

[63]RC 53, fols. 39r, 43v, 50v (8–15 Mar. 1556).

[64]R. Consist. 12, fols. 7r, 8v–9r (25 Feb. 1557, 4 Mar. 1557); and RC 53, fols. 39r, 43v (8 and 11 Mar. 1557).

[65]Cartier, "Arrêts du Conseil de Genève," 462–66.

[66]R. Part. 8, fol. 4v (16 Feb. 1554).

[67]RC 54, fols. 172r, 333r (5 May 1558, 21 Nov. 1558).

[68]RC 56, fol. 87r (14 Oct. 1560).

[69]RC 56, fol. 268v (25 Nov. 1561).

[70]RC 58, fols. 112v, 115r (22 and 29 Oct. 1563).

[71]See above 214–15.

Furthermore, during the same period, the Council consulted Calvin either personally or together with the rest of the pastors. There are few specific references during this period, yet it seems that the Council's usual practice was to consult the church authorities. The only exception was a work on the plague, which was accepted as long as it was "corrected by the physicians and surgeons of the city."[72]

Calvin clearly played a leadership role prior to the stabilization of the pastoral corps that occurred around 1546–1547. One instance of Calvin's role is the case of the New Testament printed by Jean Michel in 1543. This New Testament was Calvin's version, to which Michel added the summaries of a certain Claude Boysset. At the time Calvin was away from Geneva. Panicked at the thought of anyone daring to amend one of Calvin's works, two of his colleagues, Abel Poupin and Matthieu de Geneston, thought they could see "major errors and mistakes" in the summaries. In spite of repeated requests from the Council, the two men could not prove their accusation. Finally, on his return Calvin gave a Solomonic decision, probably in order to protect his two fellow pastors. The Reformer maintained that there were "several mistakes" in the text, but suggested that the publication still be authorized, so long as both the name of Geneva and Calvin were left out. A subsequent letter from Benoît Textor noted the attacks by friends of Jean Michel regarding this matter. These men believed that Calvin's decision was unworthy and baseless. Historians still wonder today about the theological reasons for the two pastors' concerns.[73]

From 1550 onwards, the Genevan printing industry began to grow and the Council's oversight expanded, although the general atmosphere was very fraught. Calvin's opponents, some of whom were on the Council, tried to limit his influence on censorship by calling on Beljaquet, Trolliet, and their allies, as explained below. For its part, the Consistory condemned Vigean's publications without getting much solid support from the Council. However, the Council continued to request the opinion of Calvin and the other ministers on numerous works. This apparently contradictory approach was due to the division of Calvin's opponents and supporters into two camps, often equally represented on the Council. It is not worth listing all the works that Calvin was asked to scrutinize; however, a few specific interventions should be noted. Acace d'Albiac's verse translation of the book of Job was authorized "so long as the three verses marked for removal are in fact removed."[74] Also, when Girard asked to be allowed to print Calvin's sermons, the Reformer was naturally consulted.[75]

After the crushing of the Perrinist faction, Calvin frequently provided advice about the appropriateness of publishing a given work. Most of the time, the authorization was granted without problems.[76] A few manuscripts were turned down because

---

[72]RC 36, fol. 144r (14 Oct. 1542).

[73]RC 37, fols. 138r–v, 140r, 143v, 146v, 148r, 150r, 209r (26 June 1543–31 Aug. 1543); R. Part. 1, fol. 73r (6 July 1543); CO, 11:821–823; and Berthoud, "Les impressions genevoises," 1:69–70.

[74]R. Part. 5, fols. 143r, 148r (26 and 31 May 1552).

[75]RC 47, fols. 172v, 174r (2 and 3 Sept. 1553); and R. Part. 7, fol. 226v (1 Feb. 1554).

[76]RC 51, fols. 70r, 203r, 206v (27 Mar.–3 July 1556); RC 53, fol. 165r (7 June 1557); RC 54, fols.

"it is not worth printing them."[77] According to the registers, as many manuscripts were sent to Calvin as to the pastors in general. As indicated earlier, by January 1559, two or three ministers were to examine each work, though this general rule may have been honored more in the breach than in the observance. Beginning in 1559, the Council at times turned to the Consistory, but there was a certain amount of overlap between transmitting a work to the pastors and to the Consistory.

The 1560 ordinances created three positions for overseers of the printing industry. On 4 March, Beza, François Chevalier, and Jean Budé were appointed to these posts.[78] Already on 21 April of the following year, Beza was excused due to his workload in the Academy. While Nicolas Colladon was the suggested replacement,[79] Louis Enoch in fact filled the vacancy. He was explicitly referred to as overseer in June 1561, but he was probably already in office in May.[80] The main task of the overseers was to police the printing industry, but from time to time they were also asked to look over some copies of works.

From then on Calvin and the pastors were also consulted about works with political connotations. Calvin was asked to look over the *Ample declaration faite par M. le Prince de Condé,* and he agreed with the Council's suggestion that the work be published without listing the printer or place of publication. The Reformer was so interested by the text that four days later he provided an expanded version of it.[81] Later in 1562, the pastors approved the tale of the persecutions in Angrogne, though because the work contained criticisms regarding the Duke of Savoy, the text could only be published on the condition that "the name of the city be omitted."[82] In January 1563, the Council turned to Calvin once again to decide whether it was worth publishing a political pamphlet by Jacques Spifame, a "declaration regarding the war in France."[83]

Calvin was also consulted regarding the publication of his own work taken down by secretaries, his sermons,[84] his exegetical lectures,[85] and even regarding the ecclesiastical ordinances that he "had revised while they were being written out."[86]

Economic and Technical Issues

Given the growing success of the Reformed movement, printing began to become

---

25v, 170v, 193v, 224v, 226r, 230r, 234v, 240v (28 Dec. 1557–21 July 1558); and RC 56, fols. 133r, 176v (17 Jan. 1561, 17 Apr. 1561).

[77]RC 54, fols. 145v, 148v (8 Apr. 1558, 11 Aug. 1558).

[78]RC 56, fol. 15v (1 Mar. 1560).

[79]RC 56, fol. 177v (21 Apr. 1561).

[80]RC 56, fols. 193r, 205v (20 May 1561, 9 June 1561).

[81]RC 57, fols. 39v, 40v, 43v (16–21 Apr. 1562).

[82]RC 57, fols. 54v, 57v (12 and 18 May 1562).

[83]RC 57, fol. 187r (17 Jan. 1563).

[84]RC 54, fols. 196r, 198v (27 and 30 May 1558); and RC 56, fols. 28r, 35r (11 Apr. 1560, 3 May 1560).

[85]RC 56, fol. 191v (19 May 1561); and RC 57, fol. 145r (3 Nov. 1562).

[86]RC 56, fols. 244r, 260r (29 Sept. 1561, 10 Nov. 1561).

a lucrative economic sector. Calvin was frequently consulted by the Council about conflicts over his writings or the Bible, works that excited the envy of publishers.

In 1557, Laurent de Normandie and Philibert Grené wanted to extend their privilege for Calvin's New Testament commentaries. In contrast to the situation in August 1554, this time the Council conferred with the author of the commentaries.[87]

Two years later, printers came into conflict over the new translation of the New Testament revised by Calvin and Beza. Beza, who had carried out most of the work, received financial support from Robert Estienne. The son and heir of Estienne planned to take advantage of the situation and defended his monopoly. Agreeing with Calvin's opinion, the councilors gave Henri Estienne a privilege for three years not only for the New Testament but also for the whole Bible.[88] When the other printers as a group complained about the monopoly in 1560, Calvin did not intervene directly. A trio made up of the syndic Claude Roset, Beza, and Budé decided to keep the three-year privilege for the entire Bible and to reduce the privilege for the New Testament by fourteen months.[89]

The Psalter was another Genevan best seller. Already in December 1555, Simon du Bosc, who proposed a new edition of the Psalms combining prose and verse translation, asked for a privilege to protect his edition. When Calvin was consulted on the issue, he requested that all the printers be asked for input. The Council granted the privilege without there being evidence of any extensive consultation process.[90] In the meantime, the cantor Pierre Vallette created a form of musical notation combining the notes in their score and the names of the notes spelled out. Here too, Calvin was consulted before the cantor obtained his privilege.[91]

The vast scale of the fully versified Psalter edition is well known. This enterprise served both as propaganda for the Reformed and as a commercial endeavor benefiting not only the printers but also the Bourse française.[92]

When the deacons responsible for the care of the foreign poor requested a special privilege for ten years—the usual duration being only three years—the Council turned to Calvin and Beza for advice. They agreed and the privilege was granted on the condition that a solution be found that was fair for all the printers.[93] A year later, when the task was underway, the deacons came to complain about booksellers who were not keeping their promises. Once again, the Council sought Calvin's opinion.[94]

[87]RC 53, fol. 335v (17 Sept. 1557); and above 186–87.

[88]RC 55, fols. 121r, 122v (5 and 6 Oct. 1559).

[89]RC 56, fols. 24r, 26v (28 Mar. 1560, 4 Apr. 1560); and R. Part. 12/2, fol. 53v (2 Apr. 1560).

[90]RC 50, fols. 64r, 69r, 79v (12–24 Dec. 1555).

[91]R. Part. 9, fol. 163v (10 Jan. 1556).

[92]E. Droz, "Antoine Vincent," 276-93; and G. Gorisse, "Le psautier de 1562," in *Psaume: Bulletin de la recherche sur le psautier huguenot* 5 (1991): 106–27.

[93]RC 56, fols. 210r, 213v (30 June 1561, 8 July 1561).

[94]RC 57, fol. 130r (2 Oct. 1562).

In the meantime, the pastors intervened because of other problems in the printing industry. In January 1559, when Calvin was housebound due to illness, Theodore Beza and Louis Enoch requested that printed works be subject to stricter
oversight and that the pastors check the printing authorizations.[95] In August, des
Gallars and Beza asked to have the printing industry sorted out because "there is disorder and divisions among the printers, even between master-printers and journeymen."[96] The pastors' request led to the printing ordinances of 13 February 1560.
On 12 February, Beza presented the regulations to the Council.[97] Once the overseers of the printing industry went into action, the struggle over the print quality of
published works intensified. Calvin became involved on several occasions, especially
given that poor-quality books included editions of the Bible as well as editions of his
own work.

In December 1560, the overseers accused three printers of negligence: Jean
Anastaise, Jean Bonnefoy, and Jean-Baptiste Pinereul. All three were suspended and
Anastaise's printing of one of Calvin's commentaries was stopped.[98] In the following
days, these penalties were slightly reduced.[99] Before the end of the month, the over-
seers accused another printer, Jacques Bourgeois, and repeated their criticisms of
Pinereul and Anastaise.[100]

In May 1561, Calvin seized the initiative once more, though his complaints
mainly dealt with issues of content. He stated that there were works for sale in
Geneva "in which passages of scripture are misused, and which can only lead to
scandal." He attacked the use of falsified places of publication. The Reformer also
probably had in mind foreign books sold by the city's booksellers.[101]

The overseers' complaints of December 1560 had Calvin's support, since he
came to the Council on 12 January 1562 to point out that it was too lax. He noted
that the suspensions suggested by the overseers were lifted too swiftly. The Council
listened to him and asked the overseers to examine all the printers in a systematic
fashion. In the course of this investigation, several printers had their license to run a
printing house suspended.[102]

The large-scale printing of the Psalter led to renewed competition between
printers. Those who prepared poor-quality work were brought to the attention of
the authorities.[103] A report submitted on 27 January did not limit itself to sorting
out the issues of investments and relative quotas among the printers. Instead, it also

[95]RC 54, fol. 357v (16 Jan. 1559).
[96]RC 55, fol. 87r (28 Aug. 1559).
[97]RC 56, fol. 6r (12 Feb. 1560).
[98]RC 56, fol. 114v (12 Dec. 1560).
[99]RC 56, fols. 116r–v, 219r (13–17 Dec. 1560).
[100]RC 56, fol. 123r (27 Dec. 1560).
[101]RC 56, fol. 184v (5 May 1561).
[102]RC 56, fol. 292r (12 Jan. 1562).
[103]RC 56, fol. 297v (22 Jan. 1562).

made specific technical complaints about mistakes in certain psalters, including errors in the music in François Jaquy's edition, worn-out typeface in the first part of Jean Durant's large-size psalters, and the uneven page setup in his 32° psalters. Complaints were also made about the poor-quality paper in Jean Rivery's psalters. Zacharie Durant got away with minor criticism about the tiny font he used in his Bibles "because of the difficulties this causes," but he was prohibited in the future from using these "nonpareilles" characters, corresponding to a five- or six-point font. The Council ended the process by ordering a new examination of all the printers and the restriction of the number of their presses.[104] The Council continued to be forgiving, since on 7 February, it called in seven printers and only gave them "a severe reprimand" before returning to them the fines they had been condemned to pay.[105]

In May 1563, Calvin and Beza once again criticized the "abuses and major errors in the printing industry of this city." They noted "several scandals" and even heresy in the ABC books printed by Vincent Brès and then by Michel Blanchier and François Estienne. The pastors asked that all the ABC books and abridged catechisms be confiscated. The works were indeed seized and the sorting process began a few days later.[106] This time, there is tangible proof that a certain number of publications were set aside. On 2 July, Jean Chautemps, one of the city's leading papermakers, bought the condemned *palettes* (the local name for ABC books) at a low price, to make cardboard.[107]

On 22 June, Pinereul again requested permission to reopen his printing business in spite of the overseers' opinion to the contrary. One of the overseers then announced that the new printing ordinance was ready.[108] The overseers asked Calvin to intervene personally, undoubtedly to give more weight to their endeavor. On 26 June, he appeared before the Council to ask that the printers be called to a general assembly and given a warning. He specified that the controversial ABC books were sometimes added as appendices to Bibles.[109] The next day, the Council issued an ordinance restricting the number of presses that each printer could run. Three days later, the Council requested that the papermakers be more disciplined.[110]

All of these moves show the importance that Calvin placed on the effective management of the printing industry. The overseers were certainly more strict in their requirements than was the Council. Calvin and Beza had to intervene regularly to support the overseers.

Given this situation, it is not surprising that Calvin's advice was even sought over the advisability of opening a printing shop. In 1560, in the case of Robert

[104]RC 56, fol. 300r–v (27 Jan. 1562); and RC 57, fol. 8r (16 Feb. 1562).
[105]RC 56, fol. 304v (5 Feb. 1562).
[106]RC 58, fol. 53r, 59v (17 and 26 May 1563).
[107]RC 58, fol. 72v (2 July 1563).
[108]RC 58, fol. 67r (22 June 1563).
[109]RC 58, fol. 68v (24 June 1563).
[110]RC 58, fol. 69r (25 June 1563).

Bréard, Calvin's advice was to have him assessed by experts.[111] As for Claude de Huchin, Budé and Calvin noted a point that counted against the candidate: he was one of the journeymen who had fought to have Wednesday as a day off.[112] Calvin's opinion was also sought in the case of François Perrin, who had been suspended from printing by the Council but who was supported by his patrons Laurent de Normandie and Philibert Grené.[113]

Having dealt with these economic and technical issues, I would like in closing to suggest one hypothesis. Beyond all the rationales presented so far for banning a book, we should perhaps also consider in certain cases the existence of a lobby that controlled Genevan printing. During his lifetime, Calvin was Geneva's most prolific published author and he entrusted the management of his publications to Laurent de Normandie, who later worked together with Calvin's own brother Antoine.[114] When the Vincent family set up their business in Geneva, Calvin also entrusted major bookselling endeavors to them.[115] And in 1560, when it came time to choose three men to oversee the printing industry, three close friends of Calvin were appointed: Theodore Beza, Jean Budé, and François Chevalier.[116]

Toward the end of his career, the impoverished Jean Girard sought to defend his printing privileges. Indeed, he had been the first to publish Calvin's own works. In 1554, just as he was about to receive the Council's support for his request, Calvin forcefully intervened and destroyed all Girard's hopes. "Regarding Jean Girard, it will be sufficient for him to have the catechism, which will be enough for him to make a living."[117] Similarly, when Theodore Beza and Guillaume Guéroult clashed over the versified translation of the Psalms, Calvin put all his weight on the side of his disciple and friend. Calvin was already hostile toward Guéroult due to his behavior. Hence the Reformer accused the printer before the Council, noting that Guéroult "is not well-versed in French and knows no Latin."[118]

This hypothesis also seems to have been shared by Claude de Huchin. Starting in June 1561, this printer had been trying vainly to open a printing house. A few months earlier, Huchin had clashed with Conrad Badius. Two of the overseers, Beza and Chevalier, were appointed to deal with the matter, but Huchin refused to involve Beza, telling him that he was "both judge and opponent." Poor Beza was all the more insulted when Huchin "repeated that his judges were his opponents and his opponents were his judges" after Badius had made his own statement about the dispute. Beza immediately brought the matter before the Council, which decided to

[111]RC 56, fols. 60r, 68r (15 July 1560, 12 Aug. 1560).
[112]RC 56, fol. 254r (28 Oct. 1561); and Chaix, *Recherches,* 27–29.
[113]RC 56, fol. 294r (13 Jan. 1562).
[114]See above 189–91.
[115]See the information gathered in *B.C.2,* 1105.
[116]See Chaix, *Recherches,* 67. François Chevalier, whose career began in 1556, was one of Calvin's supporters (Naphy, *Calvin,* 209, 211, 217–19).
[117]RC 48, fol. 116ter; and above 186–87.
[118]For more on this affair, see Balmas, "Guéroult," 13.

hear the accused man and possibly send him to prison. This affair left no further traces in the sources.[119] While Huchin might have been at least partially correct in his assessment, his timing was unfortunate, as seen in his ongoing difficulties in trying to open a printing house in Geneva.

Calvin's authoritative role combined with the status and wealth of the men of his circle explain why the Council granted the group's requests so willingly. In any of the conflicts over major publishing endeavors such as the Bible and the Psalter, Normandie and his friends always ended up on the side favored by the printing overseers. In the case of lucrative enterprises such as editions of Calvin's commentaries, members of this inner circle also obtained privileges that their competitors failed to get. Is this simply a coincidence? I must however add that I have found one case where Calvin and two city councilors were asked to adjudicate a dispute between Robert Estienne and Nicolas Barbier in July 1557. Their collective decision found Estienne in the wrong.[120]

Criticisms Directed against Rejected Works

The preceding sections have shown how conscious the Genevan authorities were of the need for quality printing in Geneva, thanks in part to the input provided by Calvin and the printing industry overseers. We have also noted comments regarding the style and literary worth of published works. Thus when François Bonivard wished to publish a volume of spiritual songs, the Council had the work examined and then asked to have it "put in better French rhyme."[121] The French translation of a medical treatise by Eucharius Rösslin on the origin of man had two flaws: it "was badly translated and contained several medical errors."[122] In terms of politics, the Genevan authorities were keen to avoid clashes with more powerful neighbors. Even in this area, one that more clearly fell under the Council's direct jurisdiction, Calvin's opinion was sought, at least after 1555.

Yet religious concerns came first. The Council members accepted one work "having heard that these books are not against God"[123] and rejected another "because it does not provide much edification,"[124] or in another instance, because "there is little point in printing it, and because it contains things that should not be published much."[125]

In many cases, specific explanations for the Council's decisions are lacking. Some authors whose previous works had been published in Geneva saw their proposed

---

[119]RC 56, fol. 174 (11 Apr. 1561). On Huchin, see Chaix, *Recherches*, 167–68; and Bremme, *Buchdrucker*, 176–77.

[120]RC 53, fols. 242r, 248r (19 and 23 July 1557).

[121]RC 50, fols. 48v, 64r (28 Nov. 1555, 12 Dec. 1555).

[122]RC 57, fols. 180r, 197r (4 and 29 Jan. 1563).

[123]RC 38, fol. 330r (18 Aug. 1544).

[124]RC 36, fol. 146r (17 Oct. 1542).

[125]RC 56, fol. 170v (3 Apr. 1561).

manuscripts turned down. The list of rejects includes the sermons of Jean Garnier,[126] the *Vraie épée de la foi* by Barthelemy Causse,[127] a translation of Vermigli's *De coelibatu sacerdotum et votes monasticis,*[128] and Bullinger's *Adversus anabaptistas.*[129]

As previously noted, Calvin increasingly distanced himself from the Lutherans in the late 1550s.[130] In 1558, a French translation of the Augsburg Confession was turned down.[131] In 1559, the authorities refused to allow a reprint of Melanchthon's *Loci communes.*[132] Similarly, a "certain book revised by Philip Melanchthon" was only authorized on the condition that "it be revised and corrected by a few of the pastors." The Council specified that the publisher would bear the costs of the revision.[133] The Council's rationale was clearer when it turned down Brenz's commentaries on Exodus and Leviticus "given that the said Brenz writes badly and is a sacramentarian."[134] In the same vein, the Council allowed the publication of the first Magdeburg *Centuries* "so long as only the old stories are printed from that book, leaving out the doctrine of the Lutherans and Germans who put the book together."[135]

Some polemical works did not meet with the approval of the Genevan pastors. For instance, they refused to authorize the publication of works of this type by Vermigli and Bullinger. When Thibaud Jourdain offered his *Pot aux roses de la prestraille papistique* together with a few French and Latin letters for children, he was asked to have the work printed elsewhere. In fact, Jourdain found a more welcoming printer in Lyon.[136] This is the third of the anti-Catholic works discussed in this chapter, all of which ran into trouble with the Council. The *Antithese des pseaumes contre le pape,* printed by Zacharie Durant in 1558, was prohibited because it "was more likely to lead to mockery and satire than to edification."[137] In 1560, Badius faced problems because of his *Satyres de la cuisine du pape,* although in this case the book explicitly received printing permission.[138]

Concerns over theological accuracy led to requests to Louis Enoch to make "a

[126]RC 53, fol. 196v (24 June 1557).

[127]RC 55, fol. 20r (17 Mar. 1559).

[128]RC 55, fol. 139v (6 Nov. 1559), and J. P. Donnelly, *A Bibliography of the Works of Peter Martyr Vermigli* (Kirksville, MO: Sixteenth Century Journal Publishers, 1990), 31.

[129]RC 56, fol. 170v (3 Apr. 1561); and J. Staedtke, *Heinrich Bullinger, Bibliographie* (Zurich: Theologischer, 1972), vol. 1, no. 396.

[130]See above 173–74.

[131]RC 54, fols. 163r, 166v (26 and 28 Apr. 1558).

[132]RC 55, fols. 18r (14 Mar. 1559).

[133]RC 55, fols. 84v, 88r (22 and 29 Aug. 1559).

[134]RC 55, fols. 120r, 128r (3 and 16 Oct. 1559).

[135]RC 55, fol. 29r (10 Apr. 1559).

[136]RC 55, fols. 84v, 85v (29 and 30 July 1563). Two copies of this work are held in the Bibliothèque Nationale in Paris (D2. 4235; Rés D2. 4236).

[137]RC 54, fol. 170r (2 May 1558).

[138]RC 55, fol. 170v (5 Jan. 1560).

few corrections" to his 1560 work, *La vraye histoire contenant l'inique jugement contre Anne du Bourg*.[139]

Some of the rejections were due to issues of church politics. I am intrigued by the difficulties faced by Jan Utenhoven's *Simplex narratio*. The book tells the tale of the problems faced by the members of the Flemish Church of London following their expulsion from England. The manuscript of the book was submitted to the Council and was rejected by the Consistory according to Calvin. He wrote to Utenhoven that the authorities' decision was motivated by their wish to avoid controversy with the Lutherans.[140] However, the Consistory registers are completely silent on this matter. Utenhoven, who had sought refuge in Poland, wanted to know what had happened to the manuscript. The Polish printer Sebastian Pech located it in Crespin's printing house and had it printed by Oporinus in Basel. Calvin's explanation is surprising. The Genevans' focus on appeasement is an unlikely rationale given that the various pamphlets against Westphal had just recently been issued in quick succession, without waiting for Beza's new onslaughts! Furthermore, although the Genevans refused to publish the manuscript they had no hesitation in making use of it. Beza did so in his *De Coena Domini*, which attacked Westphal and was published in February 1559, while Crespin also made use of it in his 1561 martyrology.[141]

Another response of the Genevan authorities shows how much importance was placed on promoting Calvin and Beza's writings. Jean Rivery requested authorization for a running commentary on the synoptic Gospels, containing extracts by numerous authors. The pastors felt the work was good. However, "it seemed to them that the one who composed the work should not have taken sentences from the commentaries of Monsieur Calvin and Monsieur de Beze." According to the pastors, the danger was that "readers will leave these longer works aside and take up this shorter one." Therefore, Rivery's request was denied.[142]

Genevan self-censorship explains why there were relatively few prohibitions issued against foreign books. In most cases, the books seized were individual copies, and seizures were infrequent.[143] In 1550, a certain Don Gueri appeared before the Consistory to be reminded of his promise to destroy his wife's Anabaptist books. Gueri was forced to deny the rumor that he had said his wife continued to read these books as well as the Koran.[144] In 1551, the Council barred the sale of "a book against Christians, printed in Normandy."[145] The work in question was by Artus

---

[139]RC 56, fol. 51r (18 June 1560).

[140]RC 54, fol. 318r (31 Oct. 1558); and CO, 17:379.

[141]J. H. Hessels, *Ecclesiae Londino-Batavae archivum* (Cambridge: Typis Academiae Svmptibvs Ecclesiae Londino-Batavae, 1889), 2:120; G. Moreau, "Contribution à l'histoire du Livre des maryrs," *BHSPF* 103 (1957): 185; and Gilmont, *Crespin,* 141–42.

[142]RC 57, fols. 154r, 159r (19 and 27 Nov. 1562).

[143]See Chaix, *Recherches,* 82–83.

[144]R. Consist. 5, fol. 64v (11 Sept. 1550).

[145]RC 45, fol. 275v (18 May 1551).

Désiré, and its preface directly targeted the Genevan pastors. Published in Rouen in 1550, the book had as a title *Les combats du fidelle papiste pelerin romain contre l'apostat priapiste tyrant à la synagogue de Geneve.*[146] In 1553, a recently dismissed schoolteacher named Jean Collinet was called before the Consistory because he had circulated a manuscript translation of the dedicatory letter intended for Castellio's Latin Bible.[147] In 1555, several journeymen printers were questioned over a Bible that had supposedly circulated in Geneva, containing notes by David Joris, a Dutch Anabaptist who was living in a semiconcealed fashion in Basel at the time.[148] In 1556, the Consistory condemned the *Golden Legend,* though one should also note that the book's owner was in trouble for not attending church.[149] In March 1559, the authorities seized three volumes of *Amadis de Gaule* from different owners. The Consistory requested that the Council order the books to be burnt, "given that they only serve to corrupt and deprave the youth and furthermore they are only lies and fantasies." Aware of even minor details, the Consistory noted that the works entered Geneva "en blanc," namely, in loose-leaf form, and that they were bound in the city.[150] In the following year, the Consistory examined a Lyon imprint, *La Fontaine de vie,* and judged it to be "full of idolatry and filth." The bookseller who brought the work to Geneva faced charges and all copies, whether sold or unsold, were gathered up for burning.[151] In 1562, the authorities were concerned about a political-religious work printed in Lyon, the *Catéchisme du cardinal de Lorraine.* This time, the end result was a simple reprimand and a recommendation "to read other books."[152] But the work that caused the Consistory the gravest concern was the *Conseil à la France désolée* by Castellio. Two copies of the work were seized as they were being bound. These copies had been sent from Basel to Castellio's cousin, Michel Châtillon.[153] Yet all in all, this list remains short, mainly including a few works of Catholic piety, a few novels, and works written by Castellio or his friends.

Conclusion

Overseeing the Genevan printing industry was straightforward in Calvin's day, due to the small size of the city and the Reformed commitment of most of the

---

[146]See F. S. Giese, *Artus Désiré, Priest and Pamphleteer of the Sixteenth Century* (Chapel Hill: UNC Dept. of Romance Languages, 1973), 86–92.

[147]R. Consist. 8, fol. 62v (26 Oct. 1563).

[148]R. Consist. 10, fol. 70v (28 Oct. 1555).

[149]R. Consist. 11, fol. 78v (12 Nov. 1556).

[150]R. Consist. 15, fols. 21v, 31v (2 and 9 Mar. 1559).

[151]R. Consist. 17, fol. 41r (28 Mar. 1560). More research should be done on this case, since the work in question could not have been the 1560 edition of *La Fontaine de vie* of which bibliographers are aware. That edition was dated September 1560 (Baudrier, Bibliographie lyonnaise, 4:327).

[152]R. Consist. 19, fol. 120r (12 Aug. 1562). I have not Been able to identify this *Catéchisme* printed in Lyon.

[153]R. Consist. 20, fols. 22r, 104v, 127v (25 Mar. 1563, 19 Aug. 1563, 9 Sept. 1564); and Buisson, *Castellion,* 2:225–26.

printers. In terms of theology, in most cases all that was needed was to adjust a few confessional nuances. However there were some focal points of resistance, often among those who felt nostalgic for the past and were determined to use old style almanacs or traditional Catholic ABC books. Some resistance also came from friends of dissidents such as Castellio.

As a last resort, the civil authorities were the ones who exercised censorship. Prior to 1555, when the Perrinist faction still had members on the Council, the end result was regular conflict. Once the faction was forcefully removed, Calvin intervened much more often. While he served as consultant, he also sought to attack the overly lax approach of the Council.

The oversight of bookselling was not restricted to religious issues. The civil authorities also worried about the political repercussions caused by certain works, and focused on the literary and typographical quality of books printed in Geneva.

While overall Genevan-printed books remained faithful to the Reformed approach, the authorities' control over the printers only functioned to a certain extent. The Council registers do not paint the portrait of a perfectly well-oiled system, but instead show signs of constant improvisation. In contrast, the Consistory was much more vigilant and strictly controlled what could be read in Geneva.

2. CENSORED BY THE GENEVAN COUNCIL

Period Before 1550

Even before Calvin's return to Geneva in 1541, the civil authorities' suspicion of him, as evidenced by his forced departure in 1538, remained strong. The Genevans' request to have him answer Sadoleto did not mean that a full reconciliation had taken place. For instance, when on 6 January 1540, two Genevan citizens together with the printer Michael du Bois asked to be allowed to reprint Calvin's letter to Sadoleto that had previously been published in Strasbourg, the Council ordered that the Genevan pastors be consulted. Furthermore, on 12 January, the minister Jean Morand was asked to write a new reply, as if Calvin's response had not been satisfactory. However on 30 January, the authorities allowed Calvin's letter to be published.[154] The hesitant attitude of the Council shows that its concerns were long-lived.

After Calvin's return, his works followed the same path toward publication as any other, namely, being submitted for scrutiny before being authorized.[155] The only clash over these procedures occurred in 1548, when the councilors became uneasy over the attack on Charles V's Interim. The magistrates' main fear was that the emperor would feel personally targeted. Calvin was aware of these potential

[154]RC 34, fols. 3v, 15r, 63r (6–30 Jan. 1540).
[155]RC 35, fols. 364r, 499v (18 Oct. 1541, 14 Feb. 1542).

problems, since two days before the request for printing permission was made, he told Farel, "If by chance our council permits the publication of what we have presented against the Imperial Interim, I will send you a copy via the next messenger. But given that [Jean] Trolliet is telling his colleagues that there is no need for so many books and sermons, I fear that his power is such that we will have to look for a printing press elsewhere."[156] Jean Trolliet was a Genevan citizen, a former monk who had many supporters in the city. He had been Calvin's persistent enemy ever since the latter had denied him a post as pastor in 1545.[157] Right away, he resurfaced as one of Calvin's censors.

On 29 November 1548, René de Bienassis brought the request to print the *Interim adultero-germarum* to the Council, who dealt with the matter on the following day. The Council decided that two of the magistrates "must meet with the said Calvin to know about the content of this response, so as to be sure that it contains no attacks against princes. If it only contains criticisms of Papal abuses, the request should be granted."[158] This discussion must have been lively based on Calvin's report to Farel on 12 December. "We have finally received permission to print the tract, after I chided many people. Furthermore, they brought me a copy, so that it will be printed with my guarantee, and based on my decision. And when I think of the insults our brothers have to bear, I almost feel like I am fighting against phantoms in the dark."[159]

A few months later, des Gallars submitted the *Pro J. Calvino ad ineptias J. Cochlaei responsio*. Because the work contained a number of overly personal attacks on two theologians who were members of the emperor's court, the Council members ordered that the work be toned down. "Be it resolved that if he wants to have this response printed, these insults have to be removed and replaced with some strong admonitions."[160]

Shortly thereafter, when Calvin presented his commentary on the Epistle to the Hebrews, the work was accepted without being examined, though the printing permission was issued twice, at a twelve-day interval.[161]

The Period of Major Conflict

During the years 1551 to 1554, immediately prior to the defeat of the Perrinist party, censorship operated in a particular way. While the city councilors still consulted Calvin and the pastors on a regular basis, the authorities also submitted theological works on a regular basis to physicians or lawyers. Two of these men were Calvin's opponents: the aforementioned Jean Trolliet and the physician Louis Beljaquet.

---

[156]CO, 13:110.
[157]Doumergue, *Jean Calvin*, 6:19–21, 162–69; Naphy, *Calvin*, 94–96, 152, 171–72, 174, 212–13.
[158]RC 43, fols. 253v, 255v (29 and 30 Nov. 1548).
[159]CO, 13:126; and *B.C.1*, no. 49/6.
[160]RC 44, fol. 25v (21 Feb. 1549).
[161]RC 44, fols. 53v, 62v (25 Mar. and 5 Apr. 1549).

Trolliet often displayed his dislike of Calvin, while Beljaquet's attitude can be inferred from the fact that he was forced out of the Council of Sixty after the riots in 1555.[162]

Yet the period began promisingly. When Calvin requested permission to have his *De scandalis* printed in September 1550, his request was granted without any requirement to have the book examined.[163]

But on 21 January 1552, when Calvin wanted to publish his justification against Jerôme Bolsec, he encountered a new breed of censors. He appeared in person to present his request, and explained the purpose of the book, which had been called for "in Italy as well as elsewhere." He added that the main body of the text was preceded by a joint preface that the pastors wanted to dedicate to the Council. Claiming that the manuscript was in Lausanne at the time and was being examined by Theodore Beza, Calvin only brought the dedication to the Council. The Council ordered that a complete copy be provided and planned to have it examined by Beljaquet and Trolliet.[164] On 25 January, the Council minutes record an early reaction to the preface. The entire Council supported the censors' criticisms, stating that "several slurs" in the pastors' dedication had to be corrected.[165]

By 28 January, the two delegates had scrutinized the entire book. While they praised it, they also condemned the excessive use of insults: they noted that the work was "praiseworthy and important and well-based, and deserves to be printed. Yet there are several verbal insults that could do with being omitted."[166] There is no direct evidence of Calvin's reaction to this critical review. But a few months later, in August 1552, when he presented another manuscript, the *Quatre sermons,* he took a more cautious approach. He had a supportive syndic, Jean-Ami Curtet, present the request on his behalf, and he specified two conditions. First, Calvin did not want his work to be examined by Trolliet, and second, if the work was turned down, he asked to be allowed to have the work printed elsewhere. The Council accepted these conditions.[167]

But in between times, the Council continued to entrust works to its lay censors. In March 1552, Luther's commentary on Galatians was submitted to a mixed committee that included the pastor Abel Poupin and two physicians: François Chappuys and Beljaquet.[168] Subsequently, one of Bucer's commentaries was sent to Beljaquet, Trolliet "and the others."[169] In 1553 and 1554, Beljaquet was consulted at least five times: twice along with Trolliet, once with Chappuys, and once alone.

---

[162]Naphy, *Calvin,* 212.
[163]RC 45, fol. 79v (1 Sept. 1550).
[164]RC 46, fol. 138v (21 Jan. 1552).
[165]RC 48, fol. 140r (25 Jan. 1552).
[166]RC 48, fol. 142r (28 Jan. 1552); see *B.C.1,* no. 52/4.
[167]*B.C.1,* no. 52/9, 465–66.
[168]R. Part. 5, fol. 88r (8 Mar. 1552).
[169]R. Part. 6, fol. 323v (29 Dec. 1552).

One of the manuscripts they considered was not described in the records.[170] The others were Pierre Viret's *Nécromancie papale,*[171] a collection of songs by Simon du Bosc,[172] and Beza's *De haereticis puniendis.*[173]

However, in the case of Calvin's own writings the magistrates' attitude varied depending on whether he was presenting polemical pamphlets or exegetical commentaries. In September 1552, Calvin cautiously brought in his commentary on John, even going so far as to say that "he did not dare have it printed without authorization because of the edicts." However, the magnanimous councilors indicated that they had every confidence in him: "he can be responsible for whatever he prints or gives to others to print."[174] In contrast, the civil authorities were much more suspicious of his polemical treatises. Although Calvin gave his word of honor that he had only included material "that was faithful to God and to the honor of this city" in his justification of Servetus's execution, the Council still sent a four-man delegation to him to talk over the matter.[175]

In December 1554, Calvin's exasperation over the issue of his work defending the *Consensus Tigurinus* reached its peak. The registers of the Council were rather low-key regarding this text: the request, examination, and permission process was completed in twenty-four hours.[176] But in a letter to Farel, Calvin exploded. He could not stand the fact that the Council had chosen to submit his work to the censors in spite of the fact that it had already been approved by the Zurich pastors. He admitted that he almost consigned the text to the flames. "I was so angry that I declared to the four syndics that even if I lived for another thousand years, I would never publish another single line in this city." He added that he was unsure what to do with his commentary on the synoptic Gospels.[177] Was his threat effective? It seems instead that his exegetical works were more readily authorized. In January 1555, his commentary on the concordance of the Gospels was allowed on the simple condition that Calvin take responsibility for its content.[178]

Some of the other decisions taken by the Council barely conceal the aim to teach Calvin's party a lesson in the area of orthodoxy itself. In August 1554, Council member Pierre Tissot, one of Calvin's opponents, criticized Crespin for having used the word "martyr" in his martyrology. At the time, Crespin complied, but a few months later, after the fall of the Perrinists, Calvin harshly condemned from the pulpit those who considered themselves as "great upholders of the Gospel" but who could not

[170]RC 47, fol. 84v (30 May 1553).

[171]RC 47, fol. 101r (26 June 1553).

[172]R. Part. 7, fols. 151v, 157r (29 Sept. and 9 Oct. 1553).

[173]RC 48, fol. 92r (19 July 1554).

[174]RC 46, fol. 274r (19 Sept. 1552).

[175]RC 47, fols. 191v–192r, 200v (11 and 26 Dec. 1553).

[176]RC 48, fols. 168r–v (24 and 25 Dec. 1554).

[177]CO, 15:356.

[178]RC 48, fol. 184r (28 Jan. 1555).

stand the word martyr.[179] A careful scrutiny of the Council records may reveal similar confrontations.

Earlier on, in December 1551, the Council and the pastors clashed over the issue of singing Psalms. Having received the agreement of the Council, and certainly basing himself on the pastors' advice, the cantor Louis Bourgeois had corrected printing errors in the music of the psalms. His revised edition led to confusion among worshippers, who had become used to the faulty melody. The Council forgot about its earlier authorization and decided to put Bourgeois in prison. Calvin then intervened in a full Council meeting to "remonstrate" with the councilors, noting that the changes had been made with their agreement to correct the mistakes made by the Lyon printers. The Council members refused to give ground and kept Bourgeois in prison, releasing him only the next day. A week later, the pastors returned to the fray. The Council members still held that Bourgeois had overstepped the bounds. It seems likely that Calvin had spoken about the matter from the pulpit, for on 15 December, the Council minutes referred to "yesterday's exhortation done by Mr. Calvin," who was then called in to receive "gracious remonstrances."[180] This incident shows the limits of the pastors' power when it came to a matter that seems to have been in their realm of expertise, namely, psalm singing.

Between August and September 1554, the Council had no qualms about supporting the request for a privilege presented by Jean Girard and his associate Simon du Bosc, in spite of Calvin's opposition. The Reformer had to intervene forcefully before the civil authorities gave way.[181]

After the Perrinists' Defeat

The sea change that resulted from the victory of Calvin's supporters in 1555 is clear. Increasingly, his requests for printing permission were granted without any required scrutiny of the text. Some of his works still went through a review process, as in the case of his lectures on the twelve minor prophets in 1558. The text was approved the day after printing permission was requested, even though the manuscript itself was not yet complete.[182] In contrast, Calvin received permission to print the following works without any form of review: his final edition of the *Institutes,* his *Dilucida explicatio* against Hesshusen, Pierre Richer's writings against Villegagnon, Calvin's commentaries on the Pentateuch, and his condemnation of Valentino Gentile.[183]

---

[179]Gilmont, *Crespin,* 169–70.

[180]RC 46, fols. 106r–v, 109r, 115v, 116v–117r (3–15 Dec. 1551); P. Pidoux, "Les origines de l'impression de musique à Genève" in *Cinq siècles d'imprimerie genevoise,* ed. by J.-D. Candaux and B. Lescaze (Geneva: Société d'histoire et d'archéologie, 1980), 1:96–108.

[181]See above 186–87.

[182]RC 54, fols. 266v, 268r (25 and 26 Aug. 1558); and *B.C.2,* no. 59/5.

[183]RC 55, fol. 39r (2 May 1559); RC 56, fols. 114v, 200r, 213v (12 Dec. 1560 [see *B.C.2,* no. 61/11] 6 June 1561, 8 July 1561); and RC 57, fol. 184r (12 Jan. 1563).

Calvin and his printer Robert Estienne may have become too used to this favorable climate. Their procedures regarding Calvin's commentary on the Psalter were certainly cavalier. The book's colophon is dated 15 July, and Calvin's preface is dated 23 July. Yet Estienne only requested permission to print the work on 27 July. In fact, he presented to the Council a printed copy of the work in question. The Council reacted awkwardly, unwilling to let this impertinent approach slide, yet reluctant to confront Calvin directly. In the end, the Council sent a delegation to Calvin to remind him that all printers were to observe the edicts. Two days later, Estienne obtained his printing permission, together with a low-key reprimand.[184] This episode provides the only note of conflict between Calvin and the Council regarding publications issued between 1555 and 1564.

Conclusion

In short, the high points and low points of Calvin's relations with the Genevan Council illustrate effectively the kind of balance of power he sought between civil and religious authorities. Geneva was not a theocracy, one in which the Council was directed by the church. Even when Calvin managed to force out his political opponents, the Council did not simply become blindly devoted to his cause. However, his strong personality did enable him to gain an important role, as shown by the fact that he was consulted over the political repercussions of certain works, a task that otherwise clearly fell under the remit of the civil authorities.

3. Censorship Outside Geneva

Calvin as a Censor

Although Calvin was reasonably successful at controlling the Genevan printers, how did he deal with books published in other more or less friendly Protestant areas? What were his options when works were printed in other Protestant cities like Frankfurt, Basel, or Bern?

In general, Calvin's letters contain many complaints on this issue, as he found that effective actions were difficult, if not impossible. In 1547, Andreas Rappenstein received permission from the Council of Bern to publish a critique of Calvinist church discipline. In response, the Reformer complained, "What will become of us if everything can be printed thanks to the support of the magistrates, the elimination of legal penalties, and the silence of the judges?"[185]

Calvin was more likely to meet with success when he attacked Servetus's *Christianismi restitutio*. As a reminder, the Spanish anti-Trinitarian had persuaded Balthasar

---

[184]RC 53, fols. 252v, 255v (27 and 29 July 1557).
[185]CO, 12:570.

Arnoullet to print his work discreetly in an out-of-the-way printing house. In fact, the Lyon printer had opened a second printing house in 1551 in Vienne, in the Dauphiné and entrusted its operation to his brother-in-law Guillaume Guéroult. Arnoullet received an honorarium from Servetus and thus looked the other way and let Guéroult do his work. In order to minimize leaks, Guéroult had the work printed in a temporary workshop in an isolated house. Once the print run was finished, Servetus gave five containers of the books to Pierre Meyrieu, a font maker from Lyon, and also asked Jean Frellon to send a barrelful of copies to Frankfurt, in the care of Jacques Berthet. A third consignment of books was probably sent to Geneva itself. In any event, Frellon, who was unaware of the ferocity of Servetus's attacks against Calvin, sent two copies of the work to the Reformer himself.

This courtesy launched a manhunt for Servetus and his printers. Via Guillaume de Trie, Calvin gave Servetus's name to a Catholic friend who immediately sent the dossier to the inquisitor Matthieu Ory. A few sheets from the *Christianismi restitutio* were included in the packet. Because these first attempts failed due to insufficient evidence, the Genevans sent more documents, which reached Matthieu Ory in the same roundabout ways. This time, the inquisitor managed to get confessions from some of the accused. Ory also successfully seized and destroyed the containers held by Pierre Meyrieu. At the same time, Arnoullet was arrested while Guéroult fled to Geneva. Sent before the Catholic judges, Arnoullet claimed to be an innocent man tricked by his brother-in-law. Probably in order to display his honesty, he asked Jacques Berthet to destroy the barrel of books sent to Frankfurt.

Arnoullet's letter to Berthet came across Calvin's desk. Immediately, Calvin made every effort to have the barrel of books disappear. Thomas Courteau, a printer who worked for Estienne, went to Frankfurt in September 1553 to see that this destruction did take place. His task was supported by a letter from Calvin to the Frankfurt pastors. The Reformer was even able to provide specific information as to the location of the barrel and indicated that he hoped the works would be burnt, for they risked spreading pestiferous poison. As for the copies Calvin received from Frellon, these were probably burnt along with Servetus, since his death sentence included the clause that his work be destroyed by fire. During his execution, two or three works were chained to his neck. However, not everything was destroyed by fire, since three copies of the work have survived.[186]

A few years later, during his violent controversy with Joachim Westphal, Calvin's friends in Frankfurt managed to prevent Westphal from making use of the city's presses.[187] Meanwhile, a proofreader in Strasbourg sent Calvin's friends a copy of a German work by Westphal on baptism. The proofreader took with him two sheets containing attacks against Calvin. Calvin's friends believed that the work had

[186]CO, 14:599–600; CO, 8:75–757; Baudrier, *Bibliographie lyonnaise,* 10:93–102; Doumergue, *Jean Calvin,* 6:265–75, 352–64; and Droz, *Chemins,* 4:1–9.

[187]See *B.C.2,* no. 56/4, 610–12.

been commissioned in Frankfurt. However, it seems that this text never made it into print.[188] Later on, in 1561, Calvin's friend from Strasbourg, Jean Sturm, managed to have a work by Hesshusen seized, especially because of its criticisms of the Elector Palatine.[189]

Supported by the French Reformed churches, Calvin limited the spread of Jean Morély's *Traicté de la discipline et police ecclesiastique,* published in Lyon in April 1562, prior to the national synod held in Orléans. The synod president Antoine de la Roche Chandieu, who was one of Calvin's staunchest supporters, ably managed the situation so as to have the work condemned. However, Morély did not give up so easily. Instead, he attempted to have the decision reversed, even going to Geneva on several occasions. Finally, in early September he prudently sought refuge in flight while the Council, noting that Morély had gone into exile of his own accord, ordered that a copy of the work be publicly burnt on 16 September 1563. A week earlier, one of Morély's closest friends, the apothecary Pierre Touillet, was called before the Consistory because he owned a copy of the *Traicté* and had lent it to his brother-in-law. Touillet did not let himself become flustered by these criticisms, but after leaving the Consistory session he prudently fled the city.[190]

As for the issue of any kind of control over the output of the Basel presses, there was nothing the Genevans could do. A vast number of works written by Protestants who criticized Calvin appeared in Basel. In 1553 and 1554, Beza condemned a series of unwelcome publications often printed by Oporinus's printing house. These works included Bibliander's *Protoevangelium,* the *Historia apostolica* attributed to Abdias, as well as the *Historia* by Nicephorus. If one includes Castellio's *De haereticis an sint persequendi,* the Genevans' sense of frustration is palpable. Beza stated, "I wish the people of Basel would be given a serious warning to clear up this filth promptly." Shortly thereafter, he also condemned Johannes Funck's *Chronologia.*[191] In 1557, Farel complained to Bullinger about Oporinus's publication of a Latin translation of the *Theologia germanica.* Farel suspected that either David Joris or Jean Bauhin was responsible for the text and vehemently criticized Oporinus: "Oporinus seems to be ready to produce anything without any selection process, allowing everyone to go wherever they want and however they want."[192] A few months later, Beza heard about an Antwerp edition of the same text. However, this was probably only a projected publication, since the *Theologia germanica* was only republished by Plantin in 1558.[193]

This account indicates that two very different situations held sway in Protestant printing. In Geneva itself, Calvin was able to exercise stringent oversight of the world

---

[188]CO, 16:196–97.

[189]*B.C.2,* no. 61/11, 810–11.

[190]R. Consist. 20, fols. 129r–v (9 Sept. 1563); and Ph. Denis and J. Rott, *Jean Morély (ca 1524–ca 1594) et l'utopie d'une démocratie dans l'Église* (Geneva: Droz, 1993), 57–60.

[191]Beza, *Correspondance,* 1:135; and 104, 114, 123, 130, 133–34.

[192]CO, 16:549–50.

[193]Beza, *Correspondance,* 2:82–84.

of printing, first and foremost over works printed in the city but also over foreign imports. In contrast, his influence over the rest of the Protestant world was weaker and he had to work very hard to limit the spread of a book that he did not like.

Resistance to Catholic Censorship

The reality of Catholic censorship and its increasingly hard-line approach were a constant source of concern for the French-speaking Reformers, even though Calvin did not say a great deal about the subject in his correspondence.

Beginning around 1542, "heretical" publications printed in Geneva began to circulate in France. Though their numbers were small until 1550, in the next decade editions proliferated, reaching their peak around 1562. The outbreak of the wars of religion and the establishment of Protestant presses in France itself contributed to the major drop in production of these works after 1565.[194]

In various letters, the Reformers showed that they understood their printers' tactics, which can be gauged by examining Genevan works of the period. These tactics included the page setup, the selection of printers' names and places of publication, as well as the spread of the books undertaken by daring peddlers.

In 1550, Viret sent to Bullinger the French translation of *La source d'erreur* that had recently been published by Jean Girard. Viret apologized, "I am sorry that it is not printed in a better font. But this has been done in order to lessen the weight of the book, so that it can be transported more easily. This is how the printer is trying to adapt to French needs, because they receive harsh penalties if they are ever caught with such books."[195]

In 1552, writing again to Bullinger, Beza explained the situation of the Genevan book industry. "As for the French books you were telling me about, the situation in this day and age is such that works of this kind can hardly be bought for hard cash in these areas. But our printers have become adept at trusting a few men, who are commissioned to secretly spread these booklets among the French churches. This task often puts the printers in danger, because once these men, who are not dishonest, are caught with their works, they lose their lives for the name of Christ." It is hardly worth underlining the unconscious cynicism of the last sentence, which seems more concerned over the losses sustained by the printers than over the deaths of the peddlers. It is worth noting that this explanation was intended for the Zurich printers who produced the *Perfection des chrestiens*. Beza sought to explain under what conditions their work could circulate in France.[196]

Among the chief difficulties caused by the Édict of Châteaubriand promulgated on 26 June 1551 was the clause that banned the importing of any book "from

---

[194]Higman, *La Diffusion de la Réforme*, 207–13; and Higman, "Le domaine francais, 1520–1562," in *La Réforme et le livre*, ed. J.-Fr. Gilmont (Paris: Cerf, 1990), 111–17.

[195]CO, 13:511.

[196]Beza, *Correspondance*, 1:88–89.

Geneva and other lands and places notoriously separated from the church of the Holy apostolic See." This measure reiterated an earlier edict dated 11 December 1547. At the same time, the edict prohibited any publication that omitted the name of the author and publishing information.[197]

For a while at least, the Genevans were deeply concerned about these threats. Bullinger wanted to have the French translation of the *Perfectio christianorum,* dedicated to Henri II, published in Geneva. While Beza did translate the manuscript, he then found himself facing a dilemma. If the work indicated that it was printed in Geneva, the book would surely provoke the anger of the king. Yet concealing the name of the city and of the printer would arouse the suspicions of the police. "It is against the law to use the name of another city." Thus the work was finally printed in Zurich.[198]

Even before that, the Genevan printers had become used to printing without stating the name of the city in all or part of their printed output. The same hide-and-seek game occurred regarding the names of the author and printer. Writing to Calvin, Farel commented on the technique, referring to the *Supplex exhortatio ad Carolum Quintum.* Some copies appeared without the author's name: "you ensured that part of the works were printed with your name, and part without. This deliberate choice on your part means that the book will circulate and be read more easily. If your name can smooth the path of this book in the eyes of the princes and leaders of the Empire, then the copies with your name in them will have served their purpose. If this situation leads to envy, others will avoid the book, but they will have to be discerning."[199]

The starting point for Genevan legislation on printing came in 1539. The cause of the conflict was an *Epistre* by Marie d'Ennetières, printed with a falsified place of publication: "At Antwerp, by Martin Lempereur." In the same year, Girard published Marguerite de Navarre's *Le miroir de l'ame pecheresse* with two printers' addresses, one true and the other false: "printed in Avignon, by Honorat d'Arles." A work published by Jean Michel between 1538 and 1542 made use of another kind of false address that could be immediately detected through its use of irony: "printed in Rome, in the Castle of the Holy Angel." The text in question was Luther's pamphlet that compared the Pope to Jesus Christ.

After the Genevan Council officially banned false places of publication, the practice largely disappeared. In contrast, printers regularly omitted the place of publication and author's name in a number of copies or in the entire print run.

As far as I know, Crespin was the only one who took the risk of producing works under a seemingly plausible fake name, and did so without being detected by the Council. In 1552, he published a Bible that stated "printed in Avignon, by Jehan

---

[197]Higman, *La diffusion de la Réforme,* 190–92.
[198]Beza, *Correspondance,* 1:76.
[199]Herminjard, *Correspondance,* 9:131–32; CO, 11:565; and *B.C.1,* no. 43/7.

Daniel," as well as a prayer book supposedly printed in Lyon. In 1556 and 1557, he produced five works in Spanish indicating they were published in Venice, either by Juan Philadelpho or by Pedro Daniel. François Hotman's work, *De statu primitivae Ecclesiae,* gave a hybrid printer's address: "Hierapoli, apud Jo. Crispinum." More surprising is the fictitious—and rather imaginative—address placed in a work that was directly overseen by Calvin, namely, the *Libri duo apologetici* against Villegagnon, printed by Badius in 1561 with the following address: "Excusum Hyerapoli, per Thrasibulum Phoenicum."

A few years earlier, Calvin had maneuvered around this very restrictive law. In 1547, when talking with Jacques de Bourgogne about the printing process for his *Excuse,* Calvin suggested that the work be printed in Geneva. He added, however, that the Council would probably refuse, because they would worry about the city's name appearing on the title page of such a highly political work.[200] Even though it was printed in Geneva, the first print run of the text bore the name of Wendelin Rihel of Strasbourg. However, the Strasbourg city authorities were very upset about this tactic, even though Jacques de Bourgogne had consulted Bucer on the matter. According to its proponents, the work could hardly harm Strasbourg "since it appears to have been published almost two years ago, when there was no tension" with the emperor. From this remark, we gather that the work had also been antedated. In order to placate the Strasbourg magistrates, Jacques de Bourgogne had to modify the initial and final booklets.[201] Unfortunately there are no surviving copies of that first print run, from which Calvin sent fifty copies into Catholic areas. The sole surviving copy of this work comes from the second, revised print run.

The Genevan authorities consistently condemned the use of false addresses. In 1553, when the Consistory wanted to send Vigean and du Chesne before the Council because of their almanacs, the Consistory noted an additional misdemeanor: they had printed the works with a false address, purporting to have been published in Lyon.[202] In 1555, Jacques Poullain was reprimanded for having produced part of his print run under the false address of Lyon, and furthermore, he had done so without authorization. He was compelled to correct the faulty copies.[203] It may be the case that false addresses were more common than first thought, since Calvin included a criticism on the subject in his declaration to the Genevan printers in May 1561: "these works contain several false items, including stating that they were printed in certain places, when this is untrue."[204]

When Guillaume Guéroult's relations with the Council soured, he was blamed for having indicated that one of his works was printed "with privilege," though this

[200]CO, 12:495, 540.
[201]CO, 12:657–58; and *B.C.1,* no. 47/1.
[202]R. Consist. 8, fol. 58v (12 Oct. 1553).
[203]RC 49, fol. 55v (22 Apr. 1555).
[204]RC 56, fol. 184v (5 May 1561).

was not the case. His nephew, Simon du Bosc, was called in and warned not to include Guéroult's name on his future publications.[205]

Yet the Council had no objection to having the city's name omitted altogether. In fact, this strategy was a requirement when publications seemed to be politically dangerous. We have mentioned several cases of this kind already, such as the New Testament printed by Jean Michel, in which Calvin did not want his own name or the name of the city to appear.

Conclusion

Once outside Genevan territory, Calvin's influence on book production was very limited. He had little success in imposing his standards of orthodoxy on other Protestants. Beyond the open conflicts that divided various Protestant confessional groups, there remained a significant number of differences even among those who were close to Calvin and remained in dialogue with him. In Geneva there were few focal points of resistance, especially after 1555, but Calvin's opponents found refuge in nearby areas including the pays de Vaud, or in Basel, slightly further afield. Indeed, Basel's extremely liberal attitude was particularly aggravating for Calvin and his friends.

The task of bringing Genevan publications into Catholic lands in spite of censorship was primarily undertaken by printers, booksellers, and peddlers. The Genevan booksellers established a whole network to distribute these books. Calvin himself was not directly involved in this work, but he was fully aware of the difficulties involved. Indeed, how could it be otherwise, given his close friendship with Laurent de Normandie, one of the leading figures in the Protestant book trade in France?

[205]RC 49, fol. 136v (19 July 1555).

Chapter Seven

Conclusion

Calvin's work as an author was one task among many for a very busy man. His regular schedule in Geneva included two sermons on Sundays, morning sermons on weekdays every second week, and exegetical lectures on the first three days of alternate weeks. Sermons and lectures each lasted an hour. Beyond that, he attended the Consistory meetings on Thursdays and the *congrégations* on Fridays. At the same time, Calvin also dealt with a thousand and one issues regarding the church. For instance, on the day in 1548 when he blocked the maneuver of Antoine du Pinet before the Council, he was forced to abandon his plans to deal with correspondence in the hours between the morning sermon and lunch. Instead, he had to rush to the city chambers and spend the entire morning there in meetings.[1] The published Consistory registers show how many small matters Calvin handled. Many of his close friends provide a portrait of Calvin being constantly interrupted as he worked. In 1549, for example, des Gallars could not read to Calvin more than the commentary on two to three verses at a time.[2] Beza also depicted Calvin's multitasking in a rather lively way in his second Apologia against Claude de Sainctes, published in 1568 or 1569.[3] It was in this rather hectic context that Calvin wrote both his letters and numerous tracts and commentaries.

From Working at His Desk to Working from His Bed

How did Calvin handle the writing process? At times, he took up the pen himself. When composing a letter, he felt it was polite to write it in his own hand. Yet his poor health led him to work from his bed on a regular basis, and hence he was

---

[1]CO, 12:667; and above 29.

[2]CO, 36:11–12.

[3]This edition is lost, though its text survived thanks to Theodore Beza, *Tractationes theologicae* (Geneva: Eustache Vignon, 1573), 1:334–406. For a translation of the relevant section, see Doumergue, *Jean Calvin,* 3:502.

forced to make use of his secretaries. Toward the end of his life, he was more willing to dictate his correspondence. As for his treatises, he tended not to take up the pen himself unless he was proofreading. In his final years, when he was less likely to be disturbed, he tried to set aside the first hours of the day for writing. On the mornings when he had to preach, he went back to bed when he returned from church. Then he would gather together some notes and some books, and would call on a secretary to take dictation.

But his door was always open, and therefore he had to cope with numerous interruptions to his work. Yet his exceptional memory allowed him to take up his work again exactly where he had left off in his dictation. Colladon's biography emphasizes Calvin's excellent memory, which served him well both in the religious oversight of the city and in his own scholarly work.[4] In part, his powers of recall compensated for the disorder among his papers and in his study.

Because he was always under the pressure of deadlines, Calvin worked fast. He was able to compose a polemical response in a few days. At the same time, he also dealt with long-term projects by returning to previous publications on a regular basis. He followed this pattern for his *Institutes* but also for his commentaries, which he reread and revised often. The final edition of the *Institutes* was the result of an extensive gathering together of notes and revisions. Calvin's approach was to take earlier versions, preferably in printed form, and to add new reflections to them, mirroring his recent theological experiences and his current reading.

The more research I carried out on this topic, the more a specific characteristic of Calvin's activity came to the fore. The Reformer almost always wrote in a hurry. He waited until the last minute before writing short pamphlets, for instance until the looming deadline of the Frankfurt fair. He waited until his treatises were almost completely printed before writing the dedicatory epistle. He waited until he knew a messenger was available before writing a letter. He waited until it was nearly time for his exegetical lecture before preparing for it. In short, he seemed to be an overworked person who managed his schedule by only responding to the most pressing requests.

This day-to-day pressure can also be seen in his choices in terms of public dedications in his books. Calvin's global outlook probably took clear shape between 1548 and 1550. From then on, he wanted to use these works as springboards for the Reformation. But the concrete task of choosing dedicatees, like that of choosing a specific topic, was in fact dealt with on a case-by-case basis, depending on the issues of the day.

Reading and Writing

Reading and writing are two complementary activities. Calvin was an active reader, of both classical and contemporary authors. In the early years, he used traditional sources of medieval scholasticism, such as Gratian's *Decretum* and Peter

---

[4]CO, 21:108–9.

Lombard's *Sentences*. But he eventually left these aside in favor of *Opera omnia* collections. He also took advantage of any information from contemporary writings to which he gained access. If needed for a debate, he went back to his books to strengthen his arguments.

Calvin also read his contemporaries' writings. Throughout his life, he remained affected by his encounter with Luther's work. He also read the works of leading Reformers including Bucer, Vermigli, Bullinger, and even Zwingli and Oecolampadius. He took a keen interest in his friends' writings, such as those of Viret, Beza, and Farel. He remained abreast of the work penned by his Catholic or Protestant opponents. Finally, he also focused on medieval and early modern scholasticism. Calvin was a thorough reader, long retaining what he had read, and his own writings benefited from this continuous accumulation of readings.

Calvin was an excellent writer who combined clarity and conciseness in his texts. He also benefited from having an extremely clear and well-organized mind, and from being equally fluent in Latin and French. He certainly was talented enough to write in a wide range of literary genres, though he did not allow himself to engage in satire.[5] He largely left poetry aside, apart from his *Epinicion Christo cantantum* of 1540 and his few attempts (rapidly forgotten) to translate some of the Psalms into French.

In contrast to many of his contemporaries, whose writings were characterized by a meandering style that took many detours, Calvin made his points clearly and concisely. He developed his argument by providing readers with reference points, using rhetorical techniques effectively to guide them to the intended goal.

Calvin's reluctance to have his sermons published adds an essential element to this portrait. Not only did Calvin try to distance himself from the muddled style of improvised speaking in his writings, but he was also aware of the great distinction between oral and written discourse. One of Calvin's main reasons for resisting the idea of having his sermons published was their excessive wordiness. When he published his writings, he wanted to produce short, unhurried, well-polished, and well-structured commentaries.

His opposition to the plan was overcome. And yet, one should recall that in the case of the works that he presented as "unhurried," the reality was that they were often the result of rushed writing, pressured by printers' deadlines or upcoming book fairs. In fact, Calvin made a startling statement: "Given that I do not have the ability to improve my own writings, how able am I to look after the writings of others?" However, one must bear in mind that he wrote this in order to avoid having to give Farel feedback on one of the latter's works.[6]

[5]See above 106–7.
[6]See above 174–75.

Latin or French?

For Calvin, selecting what language to write in was difficult, since he was torn between his humanist education and his vocation as a pastor. At first, he turned to Latin, even when addressing "the most unlearned." I sense that in 1534 and 1535 he was not even aware of this issue. At that point, he saw Latin as his only option.

From at least 1540 onwards, Calvin and his colleagues commonly affirmed that there were two main bodies of readers, one of which was highly educated and international, while the other was "more untaught" and French-speaking. From then on, Calvin used both languages and even improved his command of the French language. When he returned to Geneva, he intervened in various polemical debates in both French and Latin. He was also very willing to translate his own writings, the *Institutes* in particular. However, he entrusted to others the translation of longer works such as his commentaries and lectures. At one point in 1555, he contemplated writing a commentary on the Psalms in French, but he quickly dropped the idea. In 1563, he took great pleasure in undertaking a translation of the commentary on the Pentateuch. It is at this point that one realizes that Calvin's life span coincided with a sea change in the use of languages. Between 1535 and 1564, the use of French in biblical and theological writings became commonplace. In fact, Calvin's writings in French played a role in this transition.

Calvin and the Book World

Beginning in his student days, Calvin focused on publishing, more specifically on overseeing print runs and obtaining funding. Already when he was in Paris he went into printing shops on a regular basis. He knew about the pace of production and the difficulties involved in typesetting a text created from scattered characters into an octavo sheet. Yet his own style of editing, involving successive textual additions, made printers' lives more difficult. Because Calvin did not have the necessary patience to provide clear corrections, he only scanned superficially the printed texts that he then gave to the printers. Calvin trusted his secretaries, even to the point of allowing them to proof his manuscripts. Hence typographical errors could be transmitted from edition to edition without him realizing it. He also did not check his marginal references. It was only when alphabetical indexes were prepared that it became clear that mistakes had been perpetuated from one edition to the next. In spite of efforts to provide clear copies of his manuscripts, the printers were unable to supply the perfect version of his work that Calvin was looking for.

Calvin had little interest in preparing indexes for his works. In the case of the final version of the *Institutes,* the printers probably had his agreement to declare that no new index would be provided, on the grounds that the work was so well-structured that any reader could immediately find an answer to any question. However, customers disagreed and an index had to be prepared in 1559. When Colladon revised the index to the French edition of 1551, Calvin merely made some quick suggestions, providing an example of a few model entries. He left it to his secretary to complete the work.

In short, while Calvin understood the operating procedure of printing presses, he had no great interest in closely following the process. He only paid close attention to the printing of a book when the work of an important friend was being produced, as in the case of the *Excuse de Jaques de Bourgogne*. Under ordinary circumstances, René de Bienassis, Laurent de Normandie, Antoine Calvin, and others dealt with this task, and only called upon him when there were problems.

Calvin rapidly became a popular author, enabling him to then seek out high-quality printers. Calvin made his choice of printers based on quality issues and ties of friendship. His preference for Robert Estienne and Conrad Badius was due to the high level of intellectual and printing skills displayed by these two famous representatives of Parisian humanist printing. While Calvin appeared to be less impressed by the efficiency of the small format editions intended for clandestine networks in Catholic countries, he was very attracted to Estienne's beautiful folio editions. Clearly, Calvin was a bibliophile. However, he knew that to spread his ideas on a wider scale, he needed to rely on smaller-sized volumes, especially for works intended for Catholic lands. Though I have not located specific sources for the following assessment, it seems to me that the Reformer viewed this popular propaganda more as an unavoidable necessity than as a way to highlight his message.

Calvin always remained in close contact with booksellers. They were part of his social milieu ever since his student days and his brother Antoine was an active participant. Clearly, Calvin was more attuned to book circulation and distribution problems than to printing issues. Indeed, he was aware that the key to a book's success was to make it accessible to readers.

I noted earlier that one should avoid an exaggerated sense of Calvin's importance, one that would look for Calvin's explicit agreement in any event that occurred in Geneva during his lifetime. While I wish to maintain this statement, I also note that his relations with printers and his role in censorship indicate that he was quite active, even in terms of more minor decisions. His opinion was sought on numerous books. He intervened directly in actions taken against many works that contained errors or superstitions. Furthermore, he also played a role in encouraging printers, helping both to make their works known and even to sell them. In all likelihood, he did delegate some responsibilities in the oversight of printing and bookselling, but his presence remained tangible. As soon as a powerful voice was required, Calvin came to the fore.

Calvin and His Peers

Compared to other leading figures of his day, Calvin's knowledge of the printing industry was not out of the ordinary. Well-known authors such as Erasmus and Luther were well-acquainted with printers and took action in the realm of printing technology in order to ensure that their works would reach a wide audience.

In contrast, the approach of Ignatius of Loyola remained medieval, even though he was more than twenty years younger than Erasmus and about eight years younger than Luther. The message spread by Loyola and his companions was based on preaching, private conversations, and correspondence. Although his conversion undoubtedly came through reading books, Ignatius himself never wrote any. Only one Latin edition of his *Exercitia spiritualia* appeared in 1548. Later, when the Jesuits began to focus on educating youth, Ignatius sought inexpensive texts for the Jesuit schools. It was with this aim in mind that he intended to set up a printing press in the Roman College in 1556.[7] Clearly, printed books were not one of Loyola's major concerns. This observation leads to questions regarding when and how the Jesuits began to focus on printing, for they definitely began to do so before the end of the sixteenth century.

For their part, Erasmus,[8] Luther,[9] and Calvin were each highly aware of the technical and financial constraints of the printing world. All three men favored this form of communication. They each selected their printers carefully, choosing humanists who could understand both printing techniques and the content of their works.

Yet some differences between the three remained. Erasmus was not a pastor; though he did have numerous disciples, he did not establish a church. While he strongly supported the concept of vernacular Bible translations, as in his 1519 *Paraclesis,*[10] he only used Latin in his own works. He did not go beyond the circle of established printing centers, since he used high-quality printers in Venice, Basel, Antwerp, and Louvain.

The conflict between Erasmus and Edward Lee displays the skill with which Erasmus and his friends made use of printing. The humanist even succeeded in keeping his adversary out of the main printing houses in the Seventeen Provinces. In his debates with the Louvain theologians, Erasmus did not use the same weapons as his opponents. He had printed books on his side, whereas his opponents controlled the churches and the university lecture halls. In this confrontation, printed texts and public oral discourse met face to face.[11]

---

[7]G. Castellani, "La tipografia del Collegio romano," *Archivum historicum Societatis Jesu* 2 (1933): 11–16; and H. Becher, "Ignatius und das Buch," *Stimmen der Zeit* 159 (1956/1957): 321–31.

[8]See L. Jardine, *Erasmus, Man of Letters: The Construction of Charisma in Print* (Princeton: Princeton University Press, 1993).

[9] Apart from H. Flachmann's monograph listed below, see J. L. Flood, "Le livre dans le monde germanique à l'époque de la Réforme," in *La Réforme et le livre, l'Europe de l'imprimé (1517–v. 1570),* ed. J.-Fr. Gilmont (Paris: Cerf, 1990), 43–48, 59–62; H. Volz, "Die Arbeitsteilung der Wittenberger Drucker zu Luthers Lebzeiten," *Gutenberg Jahrbuch* (1957): 146–54; H. Wolf, *Martin Luther, Eine Einführung in Germanistische Luther-Studien* (Stuttgart: Metzier, 1980); H. Wendland, "Martin Luther, seine Buchdrukker und Verleger," in *Beiträge zur Geschichte des Buchwesens im konfessionellen Zeitalter,* ed. H. G. Göpfert, P. Vodosek, et al. (Wiesbaden: O. Harrassowitz, 1985), 11–35; and M. U. Edwards, *Printing, Propaganda and Martin Luther* (Berkeley: University of California Press, 1994).

[10]P. Mesnard, "La Paraclesis d'Érasme," *Bibliothèque d'humanisme et renaissance* 13 (1951): 26–34.

[11]A. Vanautgaerden, "Le grammairien, l'imprimeur et le sycophante ou comment éditer une querelle théologique en 1520 [Érasme et Lee]," in *Les Invectives,* ed. A. Vanautgaerden (Bruxelles: La

Like Calvin, Luther established a church. Both men shared a pastoral outlook, leading them to make prolific use of their respective vernacular language. High-caliber printers were attracted both to Wittenberg and to Geneva thanks in part to the impact of the Reformers. Yet political circumstances meant that Wittenberg was not the only center of Lutheran book production. The fragmented nature of the German lands meant that numerous printers transmitted the Reformer's ideas. Yet Luther was not always happy about this, not because of copyright issues, but because poorly prepared copies tended to distort his message. Hence Luther found it more difficult than Calvin to control the spread of his works.

Luther was also more prone than Calvin to make a strong link between oral communication and writing. A significant proportion of Luther's works were sermons and academic lectures. Even more so than Calvin, Luther tended to write in response to specific events.[12]

Unlike Calvin, Luther often spoke about the social role of books. As we have seen, Luther gave books a place in the creation of the kingdom. However, he did differentiate between the scholarly purpose of books, for men who were called to leadership roles in church and state, and the popular purpose, for ordinary people who were to limit themselves to the catechism and some German works.

Many current scholars tend to repeat Luther's table talk statement that printing is "God's final and greatest gift." However, this positive statement is counterbalanced by his many complaints about the large number of bad books.[13] Calvin also complained at times about the overabundance of bad books.[14]

Leaving these nuances aside, the crucial issue is to note how familiar the world of printing was to Erasmus, Luther, and Calvin. I believe that their contacts with the printing industry were greatly helped by their collaboration with highly educated master printers, whom the Reformers and humanists saw as genuine collaborators.

The Pace of Writing

When considering Calvin's total printed output, one should make a distinction between exegetical texts and polemical tracts. *The Institutes of the Christian Religion* belongs with the biblical commentaries, while we will leave the very infrequent ecclesiastical writings aside in this analysis, given that they were so few in number.

The exegetical commentaries were the result of a large-scale project begun as early as 1538, one that Calvin worked on systematically whenever he found time to do so. In contrast, his polemical works sprang up in response to specific events. Calvin's opponents were not all equally important in his eyes: he seems to have been

---

Lettre Volée à la Maison d'Erasme, 1997), 11–32, esp. 28.

[12]Flachmann, *Martin Luther;* and M. Lienhard, *Martin Luther, un temps, une vie, un message* (Paris: Le Centurion; Geneva: Labor et fides, 1983), 303–23.

[13]Flachmann, *Martin Luther,* 119–74.

[14]See above 178.

more concerned about some than about others. Here too, Calvin's state of mind played a role: at times he approached his writing task with enthusiasm, whereas at other times he was disgusted at the idea of writing because of his opponent's despicable nature. His early rule about not harming Protestant unity was broken when he saw the gnesio-Lutherans attacking the poor Flemish exiles from London. Until 1553, Calvin happily targeted Catholics and attacked radical factions within Protestantism. After 1553, he also trained his sights on the Lutheran theologians from Saxony, whom he refused to acknowledge as brothers.

Calvin's biblical commentaries were directly linked to his oral instruction, specifically to lectures in the Academy and to the Friday *congrégations*. Furthermore, beginning in 1556, his exegetical lectures were systematically taken down and published. The likelihood of his commentaries being based on a sermon cycle was much lower. In any case, Calvin was constantly immersed in the study of the Bible. For instance, he read over the French translation of the scriptures and preached sermons on two or three books of the Bible at a time, working his way through chapter by chapter in each instance. He also engaged in scriptural exegesis in his lectures in the Academy and, together with his colleagues, he studied yet another book of the Bible in the *congrégations*. As the number of his printed works grew, he reversed his procedure and took advantage of his written work when preparing his oral instruction.

The *Institutes* remained his core work. Calvin focused on it during his entire career as a Reformer, from 1534/35 to 1559/60. This work contained the key outcomes of his pastoral and theological activity, his participation in religious colloquies, and his numerous polemical encounters. Over time, the *Institutes* contained the heart of his message and he only rarely deleted a paragraph.

The overall picture of his writing output, in terms of published work, is a relatively simple curve shaped by certain key events. The first part of the curve shows steady growth, as Calvin managed to produce almost 100,000 words in 1538. His Strasbourg exile reduced his pace of writing, since he went back down to 40,000 words in 1541. His return to Geneva and restructuring of the Genevan church did not leave Calvin much free time, though his output began to reach over 100,000 words in 1544. The curve then remained steady until 1550, when Calvin entered into the most productive phase of his writing career. He even produced more than 250,000 words per year in this period. The political power struggles in Geneva did not affect this pace of writing. In fact, the high point of Calvin's activity as a writer occurred in 1555, as if the political struggle had motivated Calvin to write more and more. Indeed, the defeat of his opponents led to a gradual reduction in his activity as a writer. From 1558 on, the decrease was steeper, though the numbers did go up again during the last four years of his life. The main cause for this decrease was undoubtedly Calvin's worsening health. His partial withdrawal from public life during his last few years helps to explain the resurgence in his writing activity during that period.

This general curve for his polemical works mostly follows the pace of Calvin's exegetical and pastoral writings. Only between 1541 and 1549 does the path of the polemical writings diverge. During the first years after his return to Geneva, Calvin focused most of his writing energy on producing polemical works. Following a peak of 80,000 words in 1544, the proportion of Calvin's output devoted to polemic dropped to reach a plateau of between 30,000 and 40,000 words, decreasing even to below 20,000 words after 1558.

This data appears in Appendix I. Though the data is subject to interpretation, it does, to my mind, help clarify the information that a simple list of titles would provide. We should not put a brief pamphlet of a few pages and a lengthy commentary requiring many years of work on the same footing. Yet the rapid succession of many polemical texts also indicates a significant area of Calvin's output after his return to Geneva in 1541. These data also highlight the significant amount of material produced by Calvin between 1550 and 1557.

The Vocation of a Reformer

Everything Calvin did was underpinned by his sense of calling. Whether he was preaching, producing commentaries on scripture, or engaging in political matters, Calvin saw himself as a servant of the truth. When he preached from the pulpit, he believed that he was the conduit of God's word. In one of his sermons on Genesis, Calvin stated that God "sent people who faithfully expound the Holy Scriptures, who strengthen us in faith, and help us grow in the fear of God.... And we should not consider sermons as coming from mortal men, but instead we should raise our eyes higher, so that we receive with reverence that which we know has come from on high, namely, from God."[15] God's hand gave to Calvin the responsibility for the church of Geneva. In a short space of time his perspective extended beyond the walls of the city. Calvin's growing authority is evidenced in his increasingly frequent interventions. At times Calvin acted on his own initiative, but he also often responded to external requests. His international reputation allowed him to begin dedicating his works to Protestant princes and kings beginning in 1548.

Calvin's sense of calling led to two outcomes. The first is less obvious: Calvin was very humble in that as a Reformer his authority did not come from within himself, but from another. Yet it was precisely this assurance that he drew from his submission that was at the root of his unbearable intolerance. In the context of our current topic, his rigidity was particularly apparent in his polemical writings. Yet even if Calvin did often react on the spur of the moment, in a fit of fury, as he himself admitted, he still did control his pen to a certain extent. If needed, he would quietly pass over certain truths, in order not to overly upset some of his audience.

[15]Engammare, "Paradis," 332.

His entire expository work on the Bible, one of his main occupations, was also based on an aristocratic understanding of his mission. Because the Christian masses were unable to understand scripture on their own, someone needed to explain it to them. Hence Calvin placed great importance on sermons and Bible translations. Those with training in scripture could knowledgeably reread the Hebrew and Greek originals and interpret them accurately. Hence Calvin was tireless in his activity in the teaching office. This function was a gift of God, a gift that Calvin increased through constant research and study.

This approach to Holy Scripture provides the picture of an exegetical scholar who made use of the lessons inherent in the humanists' philological method, while at the same time not leaving scholastic tradition completely aside. Calvin's interpretation of scripture was based on reading original texts, but his theological talent as an interpreter guided his understanding of scripture. In fact, unlike Erasmus or Theodore Beza, Calvin did not publish any philological study of scripture. Instead, he drew doctrines and ethical principles from the Bible. His approach signaled the rebirth of scholasticism in the Reformed world. This Reformed outlook still had to face political influences. We have already discussed Calvin's debate with Bolsec over predestination. Clearly, Calvin hardened his position in order to crush his opponent and thus prove the truth of his cause. If he had admitted that he was in the wrong, Calvin would have put his position as a Reformer in jeopardy.[16] Political ramifications—in a broad sense—also surfaced in his relations with Bullinger and the other Strasbourg Reformers.[17]

Calvin did not yield unreservedly to truth when engaged in polemics; he admitted that he would sometimes omit to mention matters that would harm his cause.[18] In spite of the fact that he avoided excessive exaggeration, his compliments in his dedications did part company with objective assessments.[19] When Bullinger and his colleagues asked him to make changes in his first answer to Westphal, he managed to satisfy them at least partially, without causing undue friction.[20] His 1543 intervention in the New Testament affair clumsily combined an analysis of the complaints about the work with the aim to salvage his colleagues' reputations.[21] His willingness to take responsibility for proofreading varied depending on the context.[22] His answer to Pighius regarding his patristic readings must not be taken literally, given that Calvin only highlighted aspects that were in his favor.[23]

---

[16]See above 22–24.
[17]Bouvier, *Henri Bullinger*, 43–163.
[18]See above 95–96.
[19]See above 211–12.
[20]See above 97–99.
[21]See above 254–55.
[22]See above 216–18.
[23]See above 137.

Like a good lawyer, Calvin took advantage of every possible argument on his side and had no qualms about quietly passing over the awkward ones. As a master politician, he was also capable of taking over a situation that bothered him in order to avoid being swamped by it. This was the case, for instance, when he alerted other Reformers about Nicodemism.[24] Subsequently, Calvin opposed the idea that the French churches should develop a confession of faith. But once he realized that he had no power to prevent it from happening, he took the lead and proposed his own version.[25]

On several occasions, he criticized himself for his laziness and inertia. However, the charges seem barely credible when one considers all that he accomplished. His criticisms are indicators of his impatience and the excessive nature of his extremely sensitive temperament. Many of his circumstances, in particular his poor health, did not allow him to make all his dreams into reality. He often tended to express his disappointment in extravagant terms. When he encountered an obstacle, his reaction was stark: he would burn his manuscript, never write again, never publish anything again. His decision to write was motivated by external factors: a request by his circle of friends and colleagues, or as the result of his emotional reaction to an event or a work that he read. Even though he tried to master his sensitive nature, Calvin sometimes experienced violent physical reactions.

Indeed, his extreme sensitivity meant that he needed to have the emotional support of close friends. As a Reformer and specifically as an author, Calvin never worked in isolation even though he was the dominant figure in his setting. While he was confident of the quality of his writings, Calvin still had no hesitation in submitting them to his colleagues before publication. His primary colleagues for feedback purposes were his closest friends, men like Farel, Viret, and Beza. Calvin's attempt to work with Bullinger on the first response to Westphal was not a success because the comments from Zurich were too numerous and too detailed. Hence Calvin stopped sending his manuscripts to Bullinger prior to printing, although he maintained cordial relations with the Zurich Reformer.

To end this section, I cannot resist commenting on a rather perceptive remark by Ernst Walter Zeeden. In his analysis of the image of Luther as seen in Calvin's correspondence, Zeeden noted that Calvin had a high regard for the German Reformer, but that he did not consider Luther to be infallible. Calvin criticized Luther for being too stubborn and too willing to believe the flattery of his circle. Instead, Calvin saw his German counterpart as a starting point, one to be surpassed. Ernst Walter Zeeden believed that these same critiques could be applied to Calvin himself. Just like Luther, Calvin saw himself as an infallible exegete and his own circle's admiration for him, evident in the first biographies penned by Beza, echoed the adulation Luther received.[26]

---

[24]See above 108.
[25]See above 67–68.
[26]Zeeden, "Das Bild Martin Luthers," 177–95.

Books in Their Rightful Place

Calvin was a book lover. He read extensively, he wrote fluently and extensively, he owned a fine collection of books, and he was well acquainted with the publishing world. However, in spite of its importance, Calvin's activity as a writer was neither his only occupation nor his most time-consuming one. Yet his initial dream had definitely been to focus calmly on writing. In 1536, when he discovered the urgent nature of the pastoral work in Geneva and Lausanne, he had to leave his quiet study once and for all. Even his exile from Geneva did not allow him to make his dream a reality, since Bucer persuaded him to establish a French church in Strasbourg.

From that point on, his schedule included oral instruction, the oversight of the Company of Pastors as its moderator, Thursday Consistory meetings, the *congrégations* on Fridays, letter writing, private and public interventions in Genevan affairs and in those of Reformed churches across Europe, and so forth. Thus writing works for publication only made up one facet of his activities.

The combination of two factors led to a decline in the place of the book in the range of communication methods used by Calvin. On the one hand, Calvin's spoken words were so effective that the Reformer tended to prefer this direct contact. On the other hand, his sense of vocation led him to prioritize the work of organizing the Genevan church. As he stated in 1542, his chief goal was to serve his own era and his "current vocation."[27] At that time, writing biblical commentaries was put on the back burner. His reference to his "current vocation" was based on a distinction between pastoral work directed toward his contemporaries and writings intended not only for readers of his day but also for future generations.[28]

Indeed, his written works became one of the best means of transmitting his influence to later generations. Thanks to his books, especially the *Institutes* and the biblical commentaries, Calvin influenced not only scholars who knew Latin but also less well-educated readers. Prior to the end of the sixteenth century this readership could acquaint itself with Calvin's texts not only in French, but also in Dutch, English, and German, not to mention other languages where translations were more sporadic, such as Italian, Czech, and even Spanish. Furthermore, we should not forget the highly valuable impact of education and religious instruction provided by two small works dating from the last months of 1541: the *Catechisme* and the *Forme des prieres*.

Theology and Typography

Did the development of printing shape the work of theologians, especially that of Calvin? Because I do not have enough in-depth knowledge about Calvin's theology to give a definitive answer, I will limit myself to a few comments.

[27]CO, 11:418.
[28]See above 17.

My sense is that Calvin's theology was mainly rooted in the Middle Ages. Scholasticism, which is in fact a theology and a philosophy of the book, is based on teaching derived from textual commentaries. In most of his writings Calvin either commented on scripture to emphasize its importance or commented on the writings of an opponent in order to attack him. Furthermore, scholasticism invented a new way of reading, namely, rapid scanning in search of authoritative citations. In the same way, Calvin enriched his theological reflections through readings, whether from primary sources or from collections of citations.

Yet Calvin distinguished himself from the scholastics by following the scriptural approach advocated by the humanists. His aim was to recover the literal meaning of scripture by finding out the meaning intended by the author. Here too, the approach was tied to a certain kind of book developed during the manuscript era in Florence, one that featured a simple and uncluttered page.

The invention of printing did not dramatically alter the habits of western intellectuals nor the ordering of society. Elizabeth Eisenstein has suggested that printing was one of the main factors that led the western world into the modern era.[29] Her opinion is not shared by all.[30] From my point of view, the new invention led to a quick revolution, whose social impact was especially felt beginning in the eighteenth century when private reading became a factor in the French Revolution.

However, from the time of the Reformation onward, printing led to a clear acceleration in the rate of communication. For Calvin, the increase in the number of critical editions of works by the church fathers provided him with tools that were unavailable to earlier generations. At the same time, the constant clash with ideas in printed polemical works forced writers to sharpen their prose. The increased knowledge of languages meant that it was no longer possible to have the biblical text say whatever the commentator wanted. But the sixteenth century saw only the early stages of development of a critical mind-set that began to flourish in later centuries.[31]

Therefore, my answer to the question is to place Calvin in a transitional phase, one in which printing was beginning to shape intellectual life without altering it in a fundamental fashion. In any event, Calvin's grave concerns about images goes against one of printing's chief points of pride, namely, producing multiple copies of specific illustrations.[32]

---

[29] E. L. Eisenstein, *The Printing Press as an Agent of Change,* 2 vols. (Cambridge: Cambridge University Press, 1979).

[30] See, for example, R. Chartier, "De l'histoire du livre à l'histoire de la lecture: Les trajectoires françaises," *Archives et Bibliothèques de Belgique* 60 (1989): 161–89.

[31] Laplanche, "Controverses et dialogues," 2:318–21; textual criticism began in the seventeenth and eighteenth centuries: L. D. Reynolds and N. G. Wilson, *D'Homère à Érasme: La transmission des classiques grecs et latins* (Paris: Editions du Centre national de la recherche scientifique, 1984), 142–65.

[32] W. M. Ivins Jr., *Prints and Visual Communication* (Cambridge: Routledge & Kegan Paul, 1953).

And to Conclude this Conclusion

My careful study of Calvin's works and correspondence and of the Council and Consistory registers has reconfirmed some of my ideas about the Genevan Reformer. These include his lively intellect, his speedy pace of work, his intolerance, his influence over his colleagues, and his knowledge of printing and publishing. Yet on several occasions I was surprised by what I found in the sources. Here are some of the surprises.

The information I gathered together about his temperament indicated that Calvin was emotionally fragile, subject to major physical reactions to stress. His indigestion, caused indirectly by the Damoiselle du Verger in 1540, seems to provide a portrait of Calvin that is at odds with the usual depictions.

Calvin's overall activity was marked by both haste and impatience. In spite of what he occasionally said, Calvin never took the time to do something in a "leisurely" fashion. He described his own publications as "embryos barely formed in the womb." It is all the more remarkable that the quality of his works and their impact were so great.

It is equally surprising to learn that all this work was undertaken by a "lazy" man, and that the floods of polemical attacks came from a man who avoided "skewering" his opponents. Calvin had no qualms about contradictions, especially when he reacted in anger.

Furthermore, I must admit that a word count of his published works shows that he was surprisingly productive from 1550 to 1557. In spite of his endless struggles against the criticisms of the Perrinists, Calvin managed to produce an extensive exegetical corpus during these years. The peak of this work took place in 1555. In fact, the victory over the Perrinists led to a gradual decrease in Calvin's output.

Finally, those who have edited Calvin's sermons are used to the picture of Calvin going from sermons to lectures, from lectures to the *congrégations,* and from the *congrégations* to work on his commentaries. Yet I feel that the Reformers' biographers do not highlight sufficiently Calvin's continuous exegetical work, carried out concurrently on several books of the Bible. The Genevan instructional system compelled him to constantly read and teach on the Bible. He was not lying when he said that he based his teaching on scripture. To my mind, few theologians of the period could boast of such extensive exegetical work.

Hence Calvin was a man of the modern era in several respects. He did not merely make use of printing, but rather used its opportunities to the utmost. Living during a transitional phase in linguistic terms, and in spite of his clear preference for Latin, he also wrote in French and was one of the leading participants in the development of written French in theological works. As a writer, Calvin became aware of the gap between written style and oral rhetoric and of the difference between treatises intended for publication and sermons. Hence he perceived that written works had their own identity, thus proving that reading in the sixteenth century was no longer only done aloud but also silently to oneself.

Yet Calvin remained a man of his time, a time of profound change. He used printing, this new invention that had begun to take root. As a good humanist he used Cicero's language, but turned to French in his work as a pastor. He wrote and published works intended for his contemporaries, both those near at hand and far away, not to mention future generations. Yet his primary vocation remained the oversight of the Genevan church, a mission he fulfilled by giving pride of place to the word.

APPENDIX 1

Calvin's Productivity

This listing only deals with texts written by Calvin and published in his lifetime. It leaves aside his sermons, his lectures, and his correspondence.

The word count is based on the number of words in a column of the *Opera Calvini*. When it came to revised works, especially the *Institutes*, I did a rough estimate of the increase in the length of the text resulting from each revision. I did not include Calvin's translations nor his revisions of the translations of the Bible. As much as possible, I have used the earliest editions of Calvin's writings.

The numbers in parentheses refer readers back to the numbering system used in the *Bibliotheca Calviniana*.

		Number of Words
1531	Preface to the *Antapologia* by N. du Chemin	600
1532	Commentary on *De clementia* by Seneca (32/1)	58,000
1534	*Psychopannychia* (42/5)	22,000
1535	1st Latin *Institutio* (36/1)	85,000
1535	Privilege for the Olivétan Bible	1,500
1535	Preface to the Olivétan New Testament	5,000
1536	*Epistolae duae* (37/1)	26,000
1537	*Instruction et confession de foy* (37/2)	16,000
1538	2nd Latin *Institutio* (39/4); based on a total of 200,000 words	115,000
1538	Preface to *Catechismus* (38/1)	2,500
1539	*Petit traicté de la Cene* (41/4)	11,000
1539	*Commentarii ad Romanos* (40/3)	107,000
1539 [Mar]	Reply to Sadolet (39/5)	11,500
1539 [Sept]	*Declaration du conte de Furstenberg* (39/3)	7,000
1540 [Feb]	*Seconde Declaration du conte de Furstenberg* (40/4)	12,500
1541	*Actes de la journée imperiale de Regensburg* (41/1), translation of Latin documents: 37,000 words	—
1541	1st French *Institution* (41/3)	—
1541	*Epinicion Christo cantatum* (44/8)	1,200

1541 [Oct]	*Forme des prieres*	16,000
1541 [Nov ?]	*Catechisme de l'Eglise de Geneve*	23,000
1542	3rd Latin *Institutio* (43/5); based on a total of 250,000 words	50,000
1542	*Exposition sur l'Epistre de Judas* (42/3)	3,700
1543	*Advertissement*… treatise on relics (43/2)	16,000
1543	*Petit traicté monstrant que doit faire un fidele entre les papistes* (43/6), revised translation of one of the *Epistolae duae* together with a letter dated 1540	16,000
1543 [Feb]	*Defensio sanae doctrinae adversus calumnias Pighii* (43/3)	66,000
1543 [Dec]	*Supplex exhortatio ad Carolum Quintum* (43/7)	29,000
1544	*Advertissement sur la censure de Sorbonne* (44/3)	4,000
1544	*Articuli Facultatis Parisensis cum antidoto* (44/6)	15,000
1544	4th Latin *Institutio* (45/5), simple revision	—
1544	2nd French *Institution* (45/6)	—
1544 [Mar]	*Brieve instruction contre les anabaptistes* (44/7)	33,500
1544 [Nov]	*Excuse à MM. les nicodémites* (44/9)	8,000
1545 [Feb]	*Contre la secte des libertins spirituelz* (45/4)	36,000
1545 [Mar]	*Admonitio paterna Pauli III, cum scholiis* (45/13)	8,000
1545 [Aug]	*Pro G. Farello adversus P. Caroli calumnias* (45/10)	17,000
1545 [before Nov]	*Commentarii in 1^{am} ad Corinthios* (46/2)	101,000
1546	*Histoire d'un meurtre de Jehan Dias* (46/5)	2,000
1546 [Aug]	*Commentarii in 2^{am} ad Corinthios* (48/8)	56,000
1547	*Excuse de Jaques de Bourgogne* (47/1)	9,500
1547 [Nov]	*Acta synodi tridentinae, cum antidoto* (47/3); based on a total of 50,000 words	35,000
1547 [Aug]	…*avec une epistre contre un cordelier de Roan* (47/7)	6,500
1548 [Feb]	*Commentarii in 4 Pauli epistolas* (48/7)	119,000
1548 [July]	*Commentarii in epistolas ad Timotheum* (48/9)	52,500
1548 [Dec]	*Interim adultero-germanum* (49/6)	31,000
1549	*Advertissement contre l'astrologie judiciaire* (49/2)	10,000
1549 [May]	*Consensio mutua*	2,900
1549 [May]	*Commentarii in epistolam ad Hebraeos* (49/4)	71,000
1549 [Nov]	*Commentarii in epistolam ad Titum* (50/5)	13,000
1550 [Jan]	5th Latin *Institutio* (50/16); based on a total of 275,000 words	25,000
1550 [Feb]	*Commentarii in 1^{am} ad Thessalonicenses* (50/6)	15,500
1550 [Mar]	*Appendix libelli adversus Interim* (50/1)	4,000
1550 [July]	*Commentarii in 2^{am} ad Thessalonicenses* (50/7)	11,500
1550 [July]	*In omnes Pauli epistolas* (51/10), completely revised and expanded, thanks to the addition of the commentary on the Epistle to Philemon	3,000
1550 [Sept]	*De scandalis* (50/9)	34,000
1550 [Dec]	*Commentarii in Isaiam,* written out by des Gallars (51/6) 340,000 words	—
1551	3rd French *Institution* (51/11)	—
1551 [Jan]	*Commentarii in epistolas canonicas* (51/5)	100,000
1552 [Jan]	*De aeterna Dei praedestinatione* (52/4)	41,000

1552 [Mar]	*Commentarii in Acta Apostolorum,* I (52/3) Written beginning in 1550	118,000
1552 [Sept]	*Quatre sermons* (52/9)	26,000
1553 [Jan]	*In Evangelium sec. Johannem commentarius* (53/5)	170,000
1553 [Feb]	6th Latin *Institutio* (53/6)	—
1554 [Jan]	*Commentarii in Acta Apostolorum,* II (54/3)	95,000
1554 [Feb]	*Defensio orthodoxae fidei de Trinitate* (54/6); based on a total of 70,000 words	61,000
1554 [July]	*In 1ᵘᵐ Mosis librum commentarius* (54/8); written beginning in 1550	230,000
1554 [Nov]	*Defensio sanae doctrinae de sacramentis* (55/6)	11,000
1555 [June]	*Harmonia ex tribus Evangelistis composita* (55/9); written beginning in 1554	305,000
155F [Jan]	Revision of commentaries on the New Testament Epistles (56/3)	—
1556 [Jan]	*Secunda defensio contre Westphali calumnias* (56/4)	24,000
1557	*Brevis responsio de praedestinatione* (57/2)	3,500
1557	*Responses a certaines calomnies et blasphemes* (57/9)	2,500
1557 [July]	*In librum psalmorum commentarius* (57/4); written starting at least in 1555	465,000
1557 [Aug]	*Ultima admonitio ad J. Westphalum* (57/11)	41,000
1558 [Jan]	*Calumniae nebulonis de providentia cum responsione* (58/1)	12,000
1559 [Jan]	*Commentarii in Isaiam* (59/1), revision bringing the work to 410,000 words, of which the new sections totaled	135,000
1559 [Aug]	Last revision of the *Institutio* (59/4); based on a total of 450,000 words	175,000
1559 [Aug]	Revision of *Commentarii in Acta Apostolorum* (60/2)	—
1560	Last French revision of the *Institution* (60/8)	—
1560 [June/Dec]	*Dilucida explicatio de vera participatione carnis et sanguinis Christi* (61/11)	29,000
1561	*Gratulatio ad Gabrielem de Saconay* (61/13)	11,500
1561 [July]	*Impietas Valentini Gentilis detecta* (61/14)	3,000
1561 [Oct]	*Responsio ad versipellem mediatorem* (61/22)	11,500
1561 [Dec]	*Responsio ad Balduini convicia* (62/27)	5,500
1562	*Response à un certain Holandois* (62/16)	3,500
1562 [Nov]	*Confession de foy pour presenter à l'Empereur* (64/7)	7,000
1563 [Jan]	*Brevis admonitio ad fratres Polonos* (63/4)	2,000
1563 [May]	*Epistola qua fidem admonitionis apud Polonas confirmat* (63/12)	1,500
1563 [July]	*Mosis libri quinque cum commentariis* (63/16). Revision of the Genesis commentary on the other four books of the Pentateuch. Calvin began the work in 1561 or even perhaps in 1559.	412,000
1564	*In librum Josue commentarius* (64/9)	54,000

Exegetical Commentaries and Oral Teaching

The commentaries are listed by the date when Calvin finished writing them. Below each entry, if available, is an indication of the oral teaching that served as the basis for the commentary. The numbers in parentheses refer to the numbering system in the *Bibliotheca calviniana*.

Chronological List of Commentaries	Number of Words
1539 [Oct] *Commentarii ad Romanos* (40/3)	107,000
=> lectures given in Geneva in 1537 (?)	
1545 [Nov] *Commentarii in 1^{am} ad Corinthios* (46/2)	101,000
=> lectures given in Strasbourg in 1539–1541 (?)	
1546 [Aug] *Commentarii 2^{am} ad Corinthios* (48/8)	56,000
=> lectures given in Strasbourg in 1539–1541 (?)	
1546–48 *Commentarii in 4 Pauli epistolas* (48/7)	119,000
1548 [July] *Commentarii in epistolas ad Timotheum* (48/9)	52,500
1549 [May] *Commentarii in epistolam ad Hebraeos* (49/4)	71,000
=> focus of the *congrégations* until 1549	
1549 [Nov] *Commentarii in epistolam ad Titum* (50/5)	13,000
1550 [Feb] *Commentarii in 1^{am} ad Thessalonicenses* (50/6)	15,500
1550 [July] *Commentarii in 2^{am} ad Thessalonicenses* (50/7)	11,500
1550 [July] *In omnes Pauli epistolas* (51/10). Complete revision and addition of the commentary on the Epistle to Philemon	3,000
1550 [Dec] *Commentarii in Isaiam,* written by des Gallars (51/6) 340,000 words	—
=> sermons from 1546 and lectures from 1549–1550	
1551 [Jan] *Commentarii in epistolas canonicas* (51/5)	100,000
=> *congrégations* from 1549–1550	
1552 [Mar] *Commentarii in Acta Apostolorum, I* (52/3)	118,000
=> sermons from 1549 to 1553 (first part)	
1553 [Jan] *In Evangelium sec. Johannem commentarius* (53/5)	170,000
=> *congrégations* from 1550 to 1553	

1554 [Jan]	*Commentarii in Acta Apostolorum II* (54/3)	95,000
	=> sermons from 1549 to 1553 (second part)	
1554 [July]	*In 1um Mosis librum commentarius* (54/8)	230,000
	=> lessons from 1550 to 1552	
1555 [July]	*Harmonia ex tribus Evangelistis composita* (55/9)	305,000
	=> congrégations from 1553 to 1555	
1556 [Jan]	*Révision des commentaires des Épîtres du N. T.* (56/3)	—
1555–57 [July]	*In librum psalmorum commentarius* (57/4)	465,000
	=> lectures from 1552 to 1555	
1559 [Jan]	*Commentarii in Isaiam* (59/1): the revised text came to 41,000 words, of which the new section made up	135,000
	=> sermons from 1556 to 1558	
1559 [Aug]	Revision of the *Commentarii in Acta Apostolorum* (60/2)	—
1563 [July]	*Mosis libri quinque cum commentariis* (63/16). Revised commentary on Genesis and writing of a new commentary on the other books of the Pentateuch.	412,000
	=> congrégations from 1559 to 1562	
1564	*In librum Josue commentarius* (64/9)	54,000
	=> congrégations from 1563 to 1564	

Chronological List of the *Congrégations*, with the Corresponding Commentaries

From an unknown starting date until 1549: Hebrews
=> 1549 [May]   *Commentarii in epistolam ad Hebraeos* (49/4)
From 1549 to 1550: Canonical Epistles
=> 1551 [Jan]   *Commentarii in epistolas canonicas* (51/5)
From 1550 to 1553: Gospel of John
=> 1553 [Jan]   *In Evangelium sec. Johannem commentarius* (53/5)
From 1553 to 1555: Synoptic Gospels
=> 1555 [July]   *Harmonia ex tribus Evangelistis composita* (55/9)
From 1555 to Aug. 1559: Psalms
=> may have played a role in Calvin's commentary published in 1557 (?)
From Sept. 1559 to Nov. 1562: Harmony of the 4 books of the Pentateuch
=> 1563 [July]   *Mosis libri quinque cum commentariis* (63/16)
From Nov. 1562 to May 1563: Galatians
From June 1563 to Jan. 1564: Joshua
=> 1564   *In librum Josue commentarias* (64/9)
Beginning in Jan. 1564: Isaiah

Chronological List of Topics of Calvin's Exegetical Lectures

In 1537: Romans (?)
=> 1539 [Oct]   *Commentarii ad Romanos* (40/3)
In 1539–1540: 1st Corinthians and 2nd Corinthians (?)
=> 1545 [Nov]   *Commentarii in 1^{am} ad Corinthios* (46/2)
=> 1546 [Aug]   *Commentarii in 2^{am} ad Corinthios* (48/8)
From 1541 to 1549: unknown topics

From 1549 to 1550: Isaiah

    => 1550 [Dec]   *Commentarii in Isaiam*, written out by des Gallars (51/6) based on sermons and lectures from 1546

From 1550 to 1552: Genesis

    => 1554 [July]   *In 1um Mosis librum commentarius* (54/8)

From 1552 to 1555: Psalms

    => 1557 [July]   *In librum psalmorum commentarius* (57/4) From this point on, the text of the lectures was brought to print by J. Budé and Ch. de Jonviller

From 1556 to 1558: *Osée et les autres Petits Prophètes*

    => 1557 [Feb]   *In Hoseam Prophetam praelectiones* (57/3)

    => 1559 [Jan]   *Praelectiones in duodecim Prophetas minores* (59/5)

From June 1559 to Apr. 1560: Daniel

    => 1561 [Aug]   *Praelectiones in librum prophetiarum Danielis* (61/20)

From Apr. 1560 to Jan. 1563: *Prophéties et Lamentations de Jérémie*

    => 1563 [July]   *Praelectiones in librum prophetiarum Jeremiae et Lamentationes* (63/19)

From Jan. 1562 to Feb. 1564: Ezekiel (cycle interrupted by illness)

    => 1565 [Jan]   *In viginti prima Ezechielis capita praelectiones* (65/6)

List of Sermon Cycles that Served as the Basis for Written Commentaries

In 1546: Isaiah

    => 1550 [Dec]   *Commentarii in Isaiam*, written out by des Gallars (51/6) based on sermons and the lectures from 1549–1550

From Aug. 1549 to Sept. 1553 (Sunday mornings): Acts of the Apostles

    => 1552 [Mar]   *Commentarii in Acta Apostolorum*, I (52/3)

    => 1554 [Jan]   *Commentarii in Acta Apostolorum*, II (54/3)

From July 1556 to Sept. 1558 (on weekdays): Isaiah

    => 1559 [Jan]   *Commentarii in Isaiam*, revision of the text written up by des Gallars (59/1)

APPENDIX 3

Polemical Treatises in Chronological Order

Starred titles are ones where Calvin did not explicitly state that he was the author. The numbers at the end of each title refer back to the numbering system in the *Bibliotheca calviniana*.

Psychopannychia with a dedication (1534) and a preface (1536): 42/5
Epistolae duae (1537): 37/1
Bildtnüs eins neuwen Propheten (1539): 39/2
* *Declaration faicte par Guillaume conte de Furstenberg* (1539): 39/3
Sadoleti epistola and Calvin's response (1539): 39/5
* *Seconde declaration faicte par le Conte de Furstemberg* (1540): 40/4
Petit traicté de la saincte Cene (1541): 41/4
* *Les actes de la journée imperiale tenue en la cite de Reguespourg* (1541): 41/1
* *Consilium Pauli III et Eusebii Pamphili explicatio* (1541): 41/6
Advertissement du profit qui reviendroit... reliques (1543): 43/2
Defensio doctrinae adversus calumnias Pighij (1543): 43/3
Petit traicté monstrant que doit faire un fidele entre les papistes (1543): 43/6
Supplex exhortatio ad Carolum Quintum (1543): 43/7
* *Advertissement sur la censure de Sorbonne* (1544): 44/3
* *Articuli Facultatis Parisiensis cum antidoto* (1544): 44/6
Brieve instruction pour armer contre les erreurs des anabaptistes (1544): 44/7
Excuse à Messieurs les nicodémites (1544): 44/9
Contre la secte phantastique des libertins (1545): 45/4
* *Pro G. Farello adversus Petri Caroli calumnias, defensio* (1545): 45/10
* *Admonitio paterna Pauli III, cum scholiis* (1545): 45/13
* *Excuse de Jaques de Bourgoigne* (1547-1548): 47/1
Acta synodi tridentinae cum antidoto (1547): 47/3
Epistre contre un cordelier de Rouen (1547): 47/7, p. 195–229
Advertissement contre l'astrologie judiciaire (1549): 49/2
Interim adultero-germanum (1549): 49/6, et l'*Appendix* (1550): 50/1
De scandalis (1550): 50/9
Consensio mutua in re sacramentaria (1551)
De aeterna Dei praedestinatione (1552): 52/4
Quatre sermons fort utiles pour nostre temps (1552): 52/9
Defensio orthodoxae fidei de trinitate (1554): 54/6

Defensio sanae et orthodoxae doctrinae de sacramentis (1555): 55/6

Secunda defensio contra Westphali calumnias (1556): 56/4

Brevis responsio ad diluendas nebulonis calumnias (1557): 57/2

Responses à certaines calomnies et blasphemes (1557): 57/9

Ultima admonitio ad Westphalum (1557): 57/11

Calumniae nebulonis de occulta Dei providentia, cum responsione (1558): 58/1

Dilucida explicatio de vera participatione carnis et sanguinis Christi. Responsum ad fratres Polonos (1561): 61/11

Gratulatio ad Gabrielem de Saconay (1561): 61/13

Impietas Valentini Gentilis detecta (1561): 61/14

Responsio ad versipellem mediatorem (1561): 61/22

Response à un certain Hollandois (1562): 62/16

Responsio ad Balduini convitia (1562): 62/27

Brevis admonitio ad fratres Polonos (1563): 63/4

Epistola qua fidem admonitionis ab eo editae apud Polonos confirmat (1563): 63/12

Ad quaestiones Georgij Blandratae, responsum (1560) published in 1567

Reformation contre Antoine Cathelan, published in 1566

Systematic Plan of *Tractatus omnes* (1576)

The *Tractatus* provided the Latin version of Calvin's treatises. The list below therefore gives the Latin title where available, but the date in parentheses after the title is the date of the first edition, whether in Latin or French.

The numbers at the end of each title refer back to the numbering system in the *Bibliotheca calviniana*.

Part one: Instruction, contains:

De Coena Domini (1541): 45/7
Epinicion, Christo cantatum (1544): 44/8
Catechismus ecclesiae Genevensis (1542)
Precum ecclesiasticarum formula (1542)
Supplex exhortatio ad Carolum Quintum (1543): 43/7
De scandalis (1550): 50/9
Formula confessionis fidei scholae Genevensis (1559)
Confessio fidei ut coram Sua Caesare Majestate ederetur (1564): 64/7

Part two: Refutations, divided in seven sections, contains:

Section one: Against Papists
Sadoleti epistola and Calvin's response (1539): 39/5
Defensio doctrinae adversus calumnias Pighij (1543): 43/3
Admonitio paterna Pauli III, cum scholiis (1545): 45/13
Articuli Facultatis Parisiensis cum antidoto (1544): 44/6
Admonitio de reliquiis (1543): 48/4
Acta synodi tridentinae cum antidoto (1547): 47/3
Interim adultero-germanum (1549): 49/6, and the *Appendix* (1550): 50/1
Responsio ad versipellem mediatorem (1561): 61/22
Preface to the *Ad Fr. Balduini convicia responsio* of Theodore Beza (1563), followed by the
    Responsio ad Balduini convitia (1562): 62/27
Gratulatio ad Gabrielem de Saconay (1561): 61/13
Censura, seu brevis refutatio calumniarum Anthonii Cathalani mendicabuli (1566)

Section two: Against Anabaptists and Libertines
Psychopannychia (1542): 42/5
Brevis instructio adversus errores anabaptistarum (1544): 46/1
Adversus sectam libertinorum (1545): 46/1
Epistre contre un cordelier de Rouen (1547): 47/7

Section three: Against Pseudo-Nicodemites
De fugiendis impiorum illicitis sacris (1537): 37/1, p 3–44
De christiani hominis officio (1537): 37/1, p 45–78
De vitandis superstitionibus (1543) with the *Excusatio ad Nicodemitas* (1544) and supplementary texts: 49/5, 50/11
Homiliae sive conciones IV (1552): 53/4
Confutatio cuiusdam Hollandi (1562): 62/16

Section four
Admonitio adversus astrologiam iudiciariam (1549): 49/1

Section five: Against Anti-Trinitarians
Fidelis expositio errorum Michaelis Serveti, et brevis eorundem refutatio (1554): 54/6
Valentini Gentilis impietatum brevis explicatio (1561): 61/14
Ad quaestiones Georgij Blandratae responsum (1567)
Responsum ad fratres Polonos ad refutandum Stancari errorem (1561): 61/11
Brevis admonitio ad fratres Polonos (1563): 63/4
Epistola qua fidem admonitionis ab eo editae apud Polonos confirmat (1563): 63/12

Section six: In Support of Predestination
De aeterna Dei praedestinatione (1552): 52/4
Brevis responsio ad diluendas nebulonis calumnias (1557): 57/2
Calumniae nebulonis adversus doctrinam de providentia et Calvini responsio (1558): 58/1

Section seven: On the True Understanding of the Lord's Supper
Consensio mutua in re sacramentaria (1551)
Defensio sanae et orthodoxae doctrinae de sacramentis (1555): 55/6
Secunda defensio contra Westphali calumnias (1556): 56/4
Ultima admonitio ad Westphalum (1557): 57/11
Dilucida explicatio de vera participatione carnis et sanguinis Christi (1561): 61/11, p. 3–92
Optima ineundae concordiae ratio, si extra contentionem quaeratur veritas (1561): 61/11, p. 93–100

APPENDIX 5

French and Latin Translations

This list only deals with works written by Calvin himself. Therefore, it leaves aside both his lectures and sermons.

The numbers in parentheses refer back to the numbering system in the *Bibliotheca calviniana*.

Latin Works

Psychopannychia
>   Written in 1534, revised in 1536: 1542 (42/5)
>   Anonymous French version: 1558 (58/7)

Institutio
>   Written and revised: 1536, 1539, 1543, 1550, 1559 (36/1, 39/4, 43/5, 50/16,59/4)
>   French version by John CALVIN: 1541, 1545, 1551, 1560 (41/3, 45/6, 51/11,60/8)
>   Latin summary *Catechismus:* 1538 (38/1)
>   French version by John CALVIN: 1537 (37/2)

Epistolae duae
>   Written in 1537 (37/1)
>   Extensively revised version of the first letter translated by John CALVIN into French: *Petit traicté monstrant que doit faire un fidele entre les papistes:* 1543 (43/6); this treatise was retranslated into Latin by John CALVIN in 1545: 1549 (49/5)
>   Anonymous French version of the second letter: *Traité des benefices:* 1554 (54/11)

Responsio ad epistolam Sadoleti
>   Written in 1539 (39/5)
>   Anonymous French translation revised by John CALVIN: 1540 (40/7)

Commentarii in Epistolam ad Romanos
>   Written by 1540 (40/3)
>   Anonymous French version: 1550 (50/4); partial version: 1543 (43/4)

Epinicion Christo cantatum
>   Written in 1541, published in 1544 (44/8)
>   French version by Conrad BADIUS: 1555 (55/4)

Defensio sanae doctrinae adversus Pighium
>   Written in 1543 (43/3)
>   Anonymous French edition: 1560 (60/10)

Supplex exhortatio ad Carolum Quintum
> Written in 1543 (43/7)
> French version, perhaps by John CALVIN (according to O. Millet): 1544 (44/12)

Articuli Facultatis Parisiensi cum antidoto
> Written in 1544 (44/6)
> French translation by John CALVIN: 1544 (44/4)

Admonitio paterna Pauli III
> Written in 1545 (45/13)
> Anonymous French translation: 1556 (56/5)

Commentarii in priorem epistolam ad Corinthios
> Written in 1546 (46/2)
> Anonymous French translation: 1547 (47/5)

Commentarii in secundam epistolam ad Corinthios
> Written in 1546, published in 1548 (48/8)
> Anonymous French translation: 1547 (47/6)

Acta synodi tridentinae cum antidoto
> Written in 1547 (47/3)
> French translation by John CALVIN: 1548 (48/3)

Commentarii in quatuor Pauli epistolas
> Written in 1548 (48/7)
> Anonymous French translation: 1548 (48/6)

Commentarii in utranque epistolam ad Timothaeum
> Written in 1548 (48/9)
> Anonymous French translation: 1548 (48/5)

Commentarii in epistolam ad Hebreos
> Written in 1549 (49/4)
> Anonymous French translation: 1549 (49/3)

Consensio mutua
> Written jointly by Calvin and Bullinger in 1549, published in 1551
> Anonymous French translation: 1551 (Genève)

Interim adultero-germanum
> Written in 1549 (49/6)
> Anonymous French translation: 1549 (49/9)

Commentarii in epistolas ad Thessalonicenses
> Written in 1550 (50/6, 50/7)
> Anonymous French translation: 1551 (51/4)

Commentarii in epistolam ad Titum
> Written in 1550 (50/5)
> Anonymous French translation: 1550 (50/3)

De scandalis
> Written in 1550 (50/9)
> French translation by John CALVIN: 1550 (50/12)

Commentarii in epistolam ad Philemonem
> Text published in the collected edition of 1551 (51/10)
> Anonymous French translation: 1551 (51/3)

Commentarii in epistolas canonicas
> Written in 1551 (51/5)
> Anonymous French translation: 1551 (51/2)

Commentarii in Isaiam
> Written by Nicolas des Gallars: 1551 (51/6); major revision by Calvin: 1559 (59/1)
> Anonymous French translation: 1552 (52/2)

Commentarii in Acta Apostolorum
> Written in 1552 and 1554 *(5213, 54/3)*
> Anonymous French translation: 1552 et 1554 (52/1, 54/1)

De aeterna Dei praedestinatione
> Written in 1552 (52/4)
> Probably translated into French by John CALVIN or revised by him: 1552 (52/5)

Commentarii in Joannis evangelium
> Written in 1553 (53/5)
> Anonymous French translation: 1553 (53/2), later revised by Nicolas COLLADON (letter
> from Collodon to Morcuard published in the 1576 Lousanne edition of the *Institu-
> tion*: 1576, fol. **2r)

Commentarii in Genesim
> Written in 1554 (54/8)
> Anonymous French translation, revised by John CALVIN in 1564 (54/2)

Defensio orthodoxae fidei de Trinitate
> Written in 1554 (54/6)
> French version by John CALVIN: 1554 (54/5)

Harmonia ex tribus evangelistis composita
> Written in 1555 (55/9)
> French version by Nicolas COLLADON (letter from Colladon to Marcuard published in
> the 1576 Lousanne edition of the *Institution,* fol. **2r): 1555 (55/5)

Defensio doctrinae de sacrementis
> Written in 1555 (55/6)
> Anonymous French translation: 1555 (55/2)

Commentarii in Psalmos
> Written in 1557 (57/4)
> Anonymous French translation: 1558 (58/3)

Brevis responsio ad diluendas calomnias de praedestinatione
> Written in 1557 (57/2)
> Anonymous French translation revised by Theodore BEZA: 1559 (59/8)

Gratulatio ad Gabrielem de Saconnay
> Written in 1561 (61/13)
> French version by John CALVIN: 1561 (61/10)

Responsio ad versipellem mediatorem
> Written in 1561 (61/22)
> Anonymous French translation: 1561 (61/21)

Mosis libri quinque cum commentariis
> Written in 1563 (63/16)
> French version by John CALVIN: 1564 (64/5)

Commentarii in librum Josue
> Written in 1564 (64/9)
> Anonymous French translation: 1564 (64/4)

French Texts

Petit traicté de la S. Cene
    Written between 1537 and 1540, published in 1541 (41/4)
    Latin version by Nicolas DES GALLARS: 1545 (45/7)
Forme des prieres ecclesiastique
    Written in 1540 and 1542, published in 1540 (Strasbourg) and 1542 (Geneva)
    Anonymous Latin translation: 1552 (Geneva)
Catechisme
    Written in 1541
    Latin version by John CALVIN: 1545 (Strasbourg)
Traité des reliques
    Written in 1543 (43/2)
    Latin version by Nicolas DES GALLARS: 1548 (48/4)
Brève instruction contre les anabaptistes
    Written in 1544 (44/7)
    Latin version by Nicolas DES GALLARS: 1546 (46/1)
Excuse à Messieurs les nicodémites
    Written in 1544 (44/9)
    Latin version by John CALVIN in 1545, published in 1549 (49/5)
Contre la secte des libertins
    Written in 1545 (45/4)
    Latin version by Nicolas DES GALLARS: 1546 (46/1)
Epistre contre un cordelier de Rouen
    Written in 1547 (47/7)
    Latin version probably by Nicolas DES GALLARS: 1552 (52/8)
Excuse de Jacques de Bourgogne
    Written in 1547 (4711)
    Latin version by François Bauduin revised by John CALVIN: 1548 *(4811)*
Advertissement contre l'astrologie judiciaire
    Written in 1549 (49/2)
    Latin version by François Hotman revised by John CALVIN: 1549 (49/1)
Quatre sermons
    Written in 1552 (52/9)
    Latin version by Claude BADUEL: 1553 (53/4)

APPENDIX 6

Calvin's Dedications

The numbers in parentheses refer back to the numbering system in the *Bibliotheca calviniana*.

[1] Dedication to François de Connan, 6 Mar. 1531 (O.C. 9:785–86). Nicolas Duchemin, *Antapologia*. Paris: Gérard Morrhius, 1531. In–4°.

[2] Dedication to Claude de Hangest, abbot of Saint-Éloi in Noyon, 4 Apr. 1532 (32/1). Seneca, *Libri duo de clementia*, commentary by John Calvin. Paris: Louis Cyaneus; Orléans: Philippe Loré, 1532. In–4°.

[3] Dedication to an anonymous friend, 1534 (42/5). *Vivere apud Christum non dormire animis sanctos, qui in fide Christi decedunt, assertio.* Strasbourg: Wendelin Rihel, 1542. In–8°.

[4] Dedication to Francis I, 25 Aug. 1535 (36/1). *Christianae religionis institutio.* Basel: Thomas Platter & Balthasar Lasius, 1536. In–8°.

[5] Dedication to Simon Grynaeus, 18 Oct. 1539 (40/3). *Commentarii in epistolam Pauli ad Romanos.* Strasbourg: Wendelin Rihel, 1540. In–8°.

[6] Undated dedication to Philip Melanchthon, [Feb. 1543] (43/3). *Defensio sanae et orthodoxae doctrinae adversus calumnias A. Pighii.* Geneva: Jean Girard, 1543. In–4°.

[7] Dedication to the pastors of Neuchâtel, 1 June 1544 (44/7). *Brieve instruction pour armer contre les erreurs des anabaptistes.* Geneva: Jean Girard, 1544. In–8°.

[8] Dedication to the pastors of East Friesland, 28 Oct. 1545. *Catechismus Ecclesiae genevensis.* Geneva: Jean Girard, 1545. In–8°.

[9] Dedication to Jacques de Bourgogne, 24 Jan. 1546 (46/2). *Commentarii in priorem epistolam Pauli ad Corinthios.* Strasbourg: Wendelin Rihel, 1546. In–8°.

[10] Dedication to Melchior Volmar, 1 Aug. 1546 (48/8). *Commentarii in secundam epistolam ad Corinthios.* Geneva: Jean Girard, 1548. In–4°.

[11] Dedication to the Duke of Wurtemberg, 1 Feb. 1548 (48/7). *Commentarii in quatuor Pauli epistolas: ad Galatas, ad Ephesios, ad Philippenses, ad Colossenses.* Geneva: Jean Girard, 1548. In–4°.

[12] Dedication to the Duke of Somerset, 25 July 1548 (48/9). *Commentarii in utranque Pauli epistolam ad Timotheum.* Geneva: Jean Girard, 1548. In–4°.

[13] Dedication to King Sigismund-Augustus of Poland, 23 May 1549 (49/4). *Commentarii in epistolam ad Hebraeos.* Geneva: Jean Girard, 1549. In–4°.

[14] Dedication to Guillaume Farel and Pierre Viret, 29 Oct. 1549 (50/5). *Commentarii in epistolam ad Titum.* Geneva: Jean Girard, 1550. In–4°.

[15] Dedication to Maturin Cordier, 17 Feb. 1550 (50/6). *Commentarii in priorem epistolam Pauli ad Thessalonicenses.* Geneva: Jean Girard, 1550. In–8°.

[16] Dedication to Benoît Textor, 1 July 1550 (50/7). *Commentarii in posteriorem epistolam Pauli ad Thessalonicenses.* Geneva: Jean Girard, 1550. In–8°.

[17] Dedication to Laurent de Normandie, 10 July 1550 (50/9). *De scandalis.* Geneva: Jean Crespin, 1550. In–4°.

[18] Dedication to Edward VI, 25 Dec. 1550 (51/6). *Commentarii in Isaiam prophetam,* written out by Nicolas des Gallars. Geneva: Jean Crespin, 1551. In–2°.

[19] Dedication to Edward VI of England, 24 Jan. 1551 (51/5). *Commentarii in epistolas canonicas.* Geneva: Jean Crespin, 1551. In–2°.

[20] Dedication to Christian III of Danemark, 29 Mar. 1552 (52/3). *Commentariorum in Acta Apostolorum, liber I.* Geneva: Jean Crespin, 1552. In–2°.

[21] Dedication to the Genevan Small Council, 1 Jan. 1553 (53/5). *In Evangelium secundum Johannem commentarius.* [Geneva]: Robert Estienne, 1553. In–2°.

[22] Dedication to Prince Frederich of Denmark, son of King Christian III, 25 Jan. 1554 (54/3). *Commentariorum in Acta Apostolorum liber posterior.* Geneva: Jean Crespin, 1554. In–2°.

[23] Dedication to the sons of Duke Johann-Friedrich of Saxony, 31 July 1554 (54/8). *In primum Mosis librum commentarius.* [Geneva]: Robert Estienne, 1554. 1n–2°.

[24] Dedication to the pastors of the Swiss churches, 28 Nov. 1554 (55/6). *Defensio sanae et orthodoxae doctrinae de sacramentis.* [Geneva]: Robert Estienne, 1555. In–8°.

[25] Dedication to Frankfurt's magistrates, 1 Aug. 1555 (55/9). *Harmonia ex tribus Evangelistis composita, adiuncto seorsum Johanne.* [Geneva]: Robert Estienne, 1555. In–2°.

[26] Dedication to the pastors of Saxony and lower Germany, 5 Nov. 556 (56/4). *Secunda defensio de sacramentis fidei contra Westphali calumnias.* [Geneva]: Jean Crespin, 1556. In–8°.

[27] Dedication of the commentary on First Corinthians to Galeazzo Caracciolo, 24 Jan. 1556 (56/3). *In omnes Pauli Epistolas atque in Epistolam ad Hebraeos, item in canonicas Commentarii.* [Geneva]: Robert Estienne, 1556. In–2°.

[28] Dedication to Elizabeth, Queen of England, 15 Jan. 1559 (59/1). *Commentarii in Isaiam prophetam.* Revised edition. Geneva: Jean Crespin, 1559. In–2°.

[29] Dedication to Gustov I of Sweden, 26 Jan. 1559 (59/5). *Praelectiones in duodecim Prophetas quos vocant minores.* Geneva: Jean Crespin, 1559. In–2°.

[30] Dedication by Calvin to Nicolas Radziwill, 1 Aug. 1560 (60/2). *Commentarii integri in Acta Apostolorum.* [Geneva]: Jean Crespin, 1560 (1561). In–2°.

[31] Dedication to the Christians of France, 19 Aug. 1561 (61/20). *Praelectiones in librum prophetiarum Danielis.* Geneva: Jean de Laon, 1561. In–2°.

[32] Dedication to Frederich III, Elector Palatine, 23 July 1563 (63/19). *Praelectiones in librum prophetiarum Jeremiae et Lamentationes.* Geneva: Jean Crespin, 1563. In–2°.

[33] Dedication to Henri de Vendôme, future King Henri IV, 31 July 1563 (63/16). *Mosis libri quinque cum commentariis. Genesis seorsum, reliqui quatuor in formam harmoniae digesti.* Geneva: Henri Estienne, 1563. In–2°.

Bibliography

MANUSCRIPT SOURCES

Freiburg-am-Breisgau, Universitätsbibliothek, Rara N 239 de
Geneva, Archives de l'État, Registres du Conseil
Geneva, Archives de l'État, Registres des Sentences criminelles
Geneva, Archives de l'État, Registres du Conseil pour les affaires particulières
Geneva, Archives de l'État, Registres du Consistoire
Geneva, Musée historique de la Réformation, A50(49)
Geneva, Bibliothèque Publique et Universitaire, Ms. Fr. 3817 and 3871–3873
Ghent, Universiteitsbibliotheek, Acc.9080
London, British Library 3805.bb16
London, British Library C.28.m.9
Paris, Bibliothèque de la Société de l'histoire du protestantisme français, A 465
Paris, Bibliothèque de la Société de l'histoire du protestantisme français, 8o 11709 Rés.
Paris, Bibliothèque Nationale, C.2130
Strasbourg, Bibliothèque nationale et universitaire, R 100439

PRINTED PRIMARY SOURCES

Adams, Herbert M. *Catalogue of Books Printed on the Continent of Europe, 1501–1600 in Cambridge Libraries.* 2 vols. London: Cambridge University Press, 1967.

Aymon, Jean. *Tous les synodes nationaux des Églises réformées de France.* The Hague: Charles Delo, 1710.

Badius, Josse. *Préfaces de Josse Bade, 1462– 1535: Humaniste, éditeur-imprimeur et préfacier.* Edited by Maurice Lebel. Louvain: Peeters, 1988.

Beza, Theodore. *Correspondance de Théodore de Bèze.* Edited by Hippolyte Aubert et al. Travaux d'humanisme et renaissance. Geneva: Droz, 1960–.

———. *Histoire ecclésiastique des Englises réformées au royaume de France,* edited by G. Baum and E. Cunitz. Nieuwkoop: B. de Graff, 1974.

———. *Theodori Bezae Vezelii, volumen Tractationum Theologicarum.* 1:334–406. Geneva: Jean Crespin, 1570.

Bible. Translation by Olivétan. Neuchâtel: Pierre de Wingle, 1535.

Bucer, Martin, and Matthew Parker. *Florilegium patristicum.* Edited by Pierre Fraenkel. Martin Buceri Opera Omnia, series 2. Opera Latina 3. Leiden: Brill, 1988.

Bullinger, Heinrich. *Korrespondenz mit den Graubündern.* Edited by Traugott Schiess. Vol. 3. Nieuwkoop: B. de Graaf, 1904–6.

Calvin, John. *Advertissement contre l'astrologie judiciaire.* Critical edition by Olivier Millet. Geneva: Droz, 1985.

———. *Calvin's Commentary on Seneca's De clementia.* Introduction, translation, and notes by Ford Lewis Battles and Andre Malan Hugo. Leiden: E. J. Brill, 1969.

———. *Commentaires sur le prophete Isaie.* Geneva: Fr. Perrin, 1572.

———. *Commentarii in Secundam Pauli Epistola ad Corinthios.* Edited by Helmut Feld. Geneva: Droz, 1994.

———. *Commentarii in Pauli Epistolas ad Galatas, ad Ephesios, ad Philippenses, ad Colossenses.* Edited by Helmut Feld. Geneva: Droz, 1992.

———.*Commentary on the Book of Psalms.* Edited by James Anderson. Grand Rapids: Eerdmans, 1949.

———. *Défense de Guillaume Farel et de ses collègues contre les calomnies du théologastre Pierre Caroli par Nicolas des Gallars.* Translated by Jean-François Gounelle. Paris: Presses universitaires de France, 1994.

———. *Des scandales.* Edited by Olivier Fatio. Geneva: Droz, 1984.

———. *Deux congrégations et exposition du catéchisme.* Edited by Rodolphe Peter. Paris: Presses universitaires de France, 1964.

———. *Institutes of the Christian Religion.* Edited by John T. Mc Neill. Translated by Ford Lewis Battles et al. Philadelphia: Westminster Press, 1960.

———. *Institutio.* Lausanne: F. le Preux, 1576.

———. *Institution.* Edited by Jean-Daniel Benoît. Paris: J. Vrin, 1957–1963.

———. *Joannis Calvini in Acta Synodi Tridentinae censura, et ejusdem brevis confutatio circa duas praecipue calumnies.* Mainz: F. Behem, 1548.

———. *Lettres à M. et Mme de Falais.* Edited by Fr. Bonali-Fiquet. Geneva: Droz, 1991.

———. *Opera quae supersunt omnia.* 59 volumes. Edited by Eduardus Cunitz et al. Berlin: C. A. Schwetschke 1863–1900.

———. *Opera selecta.* Edited by Peter Barth and Wilhelm Niesel. 5 vols. Munich: C. Kaiser, 1926–59.

———. *Plaidoyers pour le comte Guillaume de Furstenberg.* Edited by Rodolphe Peter. Paris: Presses universitaires de France, 1994.

———. *Praelectiones in librum Prophetiarum Jeremiae.* Geneva: Jean Crespin, 1563.

———. *Psychopannychia; or, the Soul's Imaginary Sleep between Death and Judgement.* Vol. 3 of *Selected Works of John Calvin: Tracts and Letters,* edited by Henry Beveridge and Jules Bonnet. Grand Rapids: Baker Books, 1983.

———. *Recueil des opuscules.* Edited by Theodore Beza. Geneva: J.-B. Pinereul, 1566.

———. *Supplementa Calviniana.* Vol. 2, *Sermons sur le livre d' Esaïe chapitres 13–29,* edited by G. A. Barrois. Neukirchen-Vluyn: Verlag der Buchhandlung des Erziehungsvereins, 1961.

———. *Supplementa Calviniana.* Vol. 3, *Sermons sur le livre d' Esaïe chapitres 30–41,* edited by Francis M. Higman, Thomas H. L. Parker, and Lewis Thorpe. Neukirchen-Vluyn: Verlag der Buchhandlung des Erziehungsvereins, 1995.

————. *Supplementa Calviniana.* Vol. 5, *Sermons sur le livre de Michée,* edited by Jean Daniel Benoît. Neukirchen-Vluyn: Verlag der Buchhandlung des Erziehungsvereins, 1964.

————. *Supplementa Calviniana.* Vol. 6, *Sermons sur les livres de Jérémie et des Lamentations,* edited by Rudolphe Peter. Neukirchen-Vluyn: Verlag der Buchhandlung des Erziehungsvereins, 1971.

————. *Three French Treatises.* Edited by Francis M. Higman. London: Athlone Press, 1970.

————. *Trois traités.* Annotated by Albert-Marie Schmidt. Paris: Editions, 1934.

Chambers, Bettye Thomas. *Bibliography of French Bibles: Fifteenth and Sixteenth Century French-Language Editions of the Scriptures.* Geneva: Droz, 1983.

Cochlaeus, Johannes. *De interim brevis responsio.* Mainz: Behem, 1549.

————. *Joannis Calvini in Acta Synodi Tridentinae Censura, et ejusdem brevis confutation circa duas praecipue calumnias.* Mainz: F. Behem, 1548.

De Enzinas, Francisco. *Epistolario.* Edited by I. J. García Pinilla. Geneva: Droz, 1995.

Dolet, Etienne. *La manyere de bien traduire d'une langue en aultre.* Lyon: Etienne Dolet, 1540.

————. *Préfaces françaises.* Geneva: Droz, 1979.

Erasmus, Desiderius. *Opus epistolarum des Erasmi Roterdami.* Vol. 6. Edited by Percy S. Allen. Oxford: Oxford University Press, 1992.

————. *Paraphrase sur toutes les epistres canoniques.* Lyon: Claude La Ville, 1543.

Estienne, Henri, et al. *Discours merveilleux de la vie, actions et deportements de Catherine de Médicis, Royne-mère.* Geneva: Droz, 1995.

Fatio, Olivie et al., eds. *Registres de la compagnie des pasteurs de Genève.* 13 vols. Geneva: Droz, 1962–.

Herminjard, Aimé Louis. *Correspondance des Réformateurs dans les pays de langue française, 1512–1544.* Geneva: H. Georg, 1866–97.

Hessels, J. H. *Ecclesiae Londino-Batavae archivum.* Vol. 2. Cambridge: Typis Academiae Svmptibvs Ecclesiae Londino-Batavae, 1889.

Lambert, Tom, and I. S. Watt, eds. *Registres du Consistoire de Genève au temps de Calvin.* Vol. 1. Geneva: Droz, 1996.

Nouveau Testament (Geneva: J. Gerard, 1551).

Peter, Rodolphe, and Jean François Gilmont. *Bibliotheca Calviniana: Les oeuvres de Jean Calvin publiée au XVIe siècle.* Vol. 1, *Écrits théologiques, littéraires et juridiques, 1532–1554.* Travaux d'humanisme et Renaissance 255. Geneva: Droz, 1991.

————. *Bibliotheca Calviniana: Les oeuvres de Jean Calvin publiées au XVIe siècle.* Vol. 2, *Écrits théologiques, littéraires et juridiques, 1555–1564.* Travaux d'humanisme et Renaissance 281. Geneva: Droz, 1994.

————. *Bibliotheca Calviniana: Les oeuvres de Jean Calvin publiée au XVIe siècle.* Vol. 3, *Écrits théologiques, littéraires et juridiques, 1565–1600.* Travaux d'humanisme et Renaissance 339. Geneva: Droz, 2000.

Platter, Theodore. *Autobiographie.* Translated by M. Helmer. Paris: Librairie Armand Colin, 1964.

Schiess, Traugott, ed. *Briefwechsel der Brüder Ambrosius und Thomas Blaurer, 1509–1548.* Freiburg am Breisgau: F. E. Fehsenfeld, 1912.

Stelling-Michaud, Sven, ed. *Le Livre du Recteur de l'Académie de Genève (1559–1878)*. 6 vols. Geneva: Droz, 1959–1980.

Sturm, J. *Quarti antipappi tres partes riores*. Neustadt: M. Harnish, 1580.

Zwingli, H. *Sämtliche Werke*. Vol. 14. Zurich: Theologischer, 1959.

SECONDARY SOURCES

Armstrong, Brian G. "The Bolsec Controversy on Predestination." *Sixteenth Century Journal* 25 (1994): 747–50.

Armstrong, Elizabeth. *Robert Estienne, Royal Printer: An Historical Study of the Elder Stephanus*. Cambridge: Cambridge University Press, 1954.

Arnold, Matthieu. *La correspondance de Luther: Étude historique, littéraire et théologique*. Mainz: Philipp von Zabern, 1996.

Backus, Irena. "Calvin's Judgement of Eusebius of Caesarea: An Analysis." *Sixteenth Century Journal* 22 (1991): 419–37.

Baddeley, Susan. *L'orthographe française au temps de la Réforme*. Geneva: Droz, 1993.

Baker, J. Wayne. "Jérome Bolsec." In *Oxford Encyclopedia of the Reformation*, edited by Hans J. Hillerbrand, 1:188–89. New York: Oxford University Press, 1996.

Balmas, Enea. "Guillaume Guéroulet e Théodore de Bèze: Un curioso esempio di concorrenza letteraria nel XVI secolo." *Annali: Facoltà di Economia e Commercio. Università di Padova* 1 (1969): 1–40.

———. "Tra umanesimo e Riforma: Guillaume Guéroult, 'terzo uomo' del processo Serveto." In *Montaigne a Padova: E altri studi sulla letteratura francese del cinquecento*, 109–218. Padua: Liviana, 1962.

Barnaud, Jean. Pierre Viret. *Sa vie et son oeuvre, 1511–1571*. Saint-Amans: G. Carayol. 1911. Reprint, Nieuwkoop: De Graaf, 1973.

Barth, Fritz. *Calvin und Servet*. Bern: A. Francke, 1909.

Barycz, Henryk. "Voyageurs et étudiants polonais à Genève à l'époque de Calvin et de Théodore de Bèze (1550–1650)." In *Échanges entre la Pologne et la Suisse du XIVe au XIXe siècle*, 73–76. Geneva: Droz, 1964.

Battles, Ford L. "Against Luxury and License in Geneva, a Forgotten Fragment." *Interpretation: Journal of Bible and Theology* 19 (1965): 182–202.

———. "The Sources of Calvin's Seneca Commentary." In *John Calvin*, edited by Ford L. Battles et al., 38–66. Appleford: Sutton Courtenay Press, 1966.

Baudrier, Henri-Louis. *Bibliographie lyonnaise. Recherches sur les imprimeurs, libraires, éditeurs, relieurs et fondeurs de lettres de Lyon au XVIe siècle*. 12 vols. Lyon: Librairie ancienne d'Auguste Brun, 1895–1921.

Bäumer, Remigius. "Albert Pigge." In *Katholische Theologen der Reformationszeit*, 1:98–106. Münster: Aschendorff, 1984.

Becher, H. "Ignatius und das Buch." *Stimmen der Zeit* 159 (1956/57): 321–31.

Bédouelle, Guy, and Bernard Roussel. *Le temps des Réformes et la Bible*. Paris: Beauchesne, 1989.

Belle, E. *La Réforme à Dijon des origines à la fin de la lieutenance générale de Gaspard de Sauls-Tavanes, 1530–1570*. Dijon, Paris: Damidot frères, 1911.

Bennett, Henry S. *English Books and Readers, 1475–1557.* Cambridge: Cambridge University Press, 1952.

———. *English Books and Readers, 1558–1603.* Cambridge: Cambridge University Press, 1965.

Benoît, Jean-Daniel. "D'une édition à l'autre de l'Institution: Comment Calvin travaillait." *La Revue réformée* 11 (1960): 39–51.

———. "L'année 1559 dans les annales calviniennes." *Revue d'histoire et de philosophie religieuses* 39 (1959): 103–16.

Benzing, Josef. *Lutherbibliographie: Verzeichnis der gedruckten Schriften Martin Luthers bis zu dessen Tod.* Baden-Baden: Heitz, 1966.

Bergier, Jean François. *Genève et l'économie européenne de la Renaissance.* Paris: S. E. V. P. E. N., 1963.

———. "Le contrat d'édition de la Bible de l'épée, Geneva, 1540." *Bibliothèque d'humanisme et renaissance* 18 (1956): 110–13.

Berthoud, Gabrielle. *Antoine Marcourt, Réformateur et pamphlétaire.* Geneva: Droz, 1973.

Berthoud, Gabrielle, et al. *Aspects de la propagande religieuse.* Geneva: Droz, 1957.

———. "Les impressions genevoises de Jean Michel (1538–1544)." In *Cinq siècles d'imprimerie genevoise,* edited by Jean-Daniel Candaux and Bernard Lescaze, 1:55–88. Geneva: Droz, 1980.

Bertrand, D. *La politique de S. Ignace de Loyola. L'analyse sociale.* Paris: Cerf, 1985.

Biéler, André. *La pensée économique et sociale de Calvin.* Geneva: Droz, 1959.

Bietenholz, Peter G. *Basle and France in the Sixteenth Century.* Geneva: Droz, 1971.

Blanke, Fritz. "Calvins Urteil über Zwingli." *Zwingliana* 11 (1959–63): 66–92.

Boehmer, Edward. *Spanish Reformers of Two Centuries from 1520. Their Lives and Writings.* Vol. 3. Strasbourg, 1874. Reprint, New York: B. Franklin, [1962].

Bogaert, Pierre, and Jean-François Gilmont. "De Lefèvre d'Étaples à la fin du XVIe siècle." In *Les Bibles en français,* edited by Pierre Bogaert, 47–106. Paris: Brepols, 1991.

Bohatec, Josef. Budé und Calvin. *Studien zur Gedankenwelt des französischen Frühhumanismus.* Graz: H. Böhlaus Nachfolger, 1950.

Borgeaud, Charles. *Histoire de l'Université de Genève,* Geneva: Georg & Co., 1900.

Bornert, René. "L'Église française de Strasbourg." In *La Réforme protestante du culte à Strasbourg au XVIe siècle (1523–1598). Approche sociologique et interprétation théologique,* edited by René Bornert, 193–200. Leiden: Brill, 1981.

Botfield, Beriah. *Prefaces to the First Editions of the Greek and Roman Classics and of the Sacred Scriptures.* London: Henry George Bohn, 1861.

Bouvier, André. *Henri Bullinger le successeur de Zwingli d'après sa correspondance avec les réformés et les humanistes de langue française.* Neuchâtel and Paris: Delachaux et Nestlé, 1940.

Braekman, Emile Michel. "Les interventions de Calvin." In *La dispute de Lausanne, 1536: La théologie réformée après Zwingli et avant Calvin,* edited by Eric Junod, 170–77. Lausanne: Bibliothèque historique vaudoise, 1988.

Brandt, Steven Russell. "Jean Girard, Genevan Publisher, 1536–1557." Ph.D. diss., University of Calilfornia–Berkeley, 1992.

Bremme, Hans Joachim. *Buchdrucker und Buchhändler zur Zeit der Glaubenskämpfe: Studien zur Genfer Druckgeschichte, 1565–1580.* Geneva: Droz, 1969.

Buisson, Ferdinand. *Sébastien Castellion, sa vie et son oeuvre, 1515–1563.* Etude sur les origines du protestantisme libéral français. Paris: Hachette, 1892.

Büsser, Fritz. H. Bullinger, Briefwechsel. Zurich: Theologischer, 1973.

Cadier, J. "La confession de foi de La Rochelle: Son histoire, son importance." *La Revue réformée* 86 (1971): 47.

Campagnolo, Matteo. "Le créateur de la monnaie de Genève." In *Jean Duvet, le maître à la licorne.* Geneva: Cabinet des estampes, 1996.

Candaux, Jean Daniel, and Bernard Lescaze, eds. *Cinq siècles d'imprimerie genevoise.* Geneva: Société d'histoire et d'archéologie, 1980.

Cantimori, Delio. "Spigolature per la storia del Nicodemismo Italiano." In *Ginevra e l'Italia,* 179–90. Florence: G. C. Sansoni, 1959.

Cartier, Alfred. "Arrêts du Conseil de Genève sur le fait de l'imprimerie et de la librairie de 1541 à 1550." In *Mémoires et documents publiés par la Société d'histoire et d'archéologie de Genève* 23, 361–529. Geneva: Aubert-Schuchardt, 1888.

Casalis, Georges, and Bernard Roussel, eds. *Olivétan traducteur de la Bible.* Paris: Cerf, 1987.

Castellani, G. "La tipografia del Collegio romano." *Archivum historicum Societatis Jesu* 2 (1933): 11–16.

Catach, N. *L'orthographe française à l'époque de la Renaissance.* Geneva: Droz, 1968.

Cavallo, G., and Roger Chartier, eds. *Histoire de la lecture dans le monde occidental.* Paris: Seuil, 1997.

———. *Storia della lettura nel mondo occidentale.* Rome, Bari: Laterza, 1995.

Chaix, Paul. *Recherches sur l'imprimerie à Genève de 1550 à 1564: Étude bibliographique, économique et littéraire.* Geneva: Droz, 1954.

Chaix, Paul, Alain Dufour, and Gustave Moeckli. *Les livres imprimés à Genève de 1550 à 1600.* Geneva: Droz, 1966.

Chartier, Roger. "De l'histoire du livre à l'histoire de la lecture: Les trajectoires françaises." *Archives et Bibliothèques de Belgique* 60 (1989): 161–89.

———. "Le prince, la bibliothèque et la dédicace." In *Le pouvoir des bibliothèques. La mémoire des livres en Occident,* edited by M. Baratin and Chr. Jacob, 204–23. Paris: A. Michel, 1996.

Chrisman, Miriam. *Lay Culture, Learned Culture. Books and Social Change in Strasbourg, 1480–1599.* New Haven: Yale University Press, 1982.

Cosenza, Mario Emilio. *Biographical and Bibliographical Dictionary of the Italian Humanists.* Vol. 2. Boston: G. K. Hall, 1962.

Cottret, Bernard. *Calvin. Biographie.* Paris: J. C. Lattès, 1995.

Covelle, A.L. *Le livre des bourgeois de l'ancienne république de Genève.* Geneva: J. Jullien, 1897.

Croce, Benedetto. *Galéas Caracciolo, marquis de Vico.* Translated by Jacqueline des Gouttes et al. Geneva: Droz, 1965.

De Greef, Wulfert. *Johannes Calvijn, Zijn werk en geschriften.* Kampen: De Groot Goudriaan, 1989.

———. *The Writings of John Calvin: An Introductory Guide.* Grand Rapids: Baker Books, 1993.

De Wailly, N. "Mémoire sur les variations de la livre tournois depuis le règne de saint Louis jusqu'à l'établissement de la monnaie décimale." In *Mémoires de l'Institut impérial de France. Académie des inscriptions et des belles lettres* 21/ 1 (1857): 254.

Delumeau, J. *Rome au XVIe siècle.* Paris: Hachette, 1975.

Denis, Philippe. "La Bible et l'action pastorale." In *Le temps des Réformes et la Bible,* edited by Guy Bedouelle and Bernard Roussel, 515–44. Paris: Beauchesne, 1989.

————. *Les églises d'étrangers en pays rhénans (1538–1564).* Paris: Belles Lettres, 1984.

————. "Jacques de Bourgogne, seigneur de Falais." In *Bibliotheca dissidentium. Répertoire des non-conformistes religieux des seizième et dix-septième siècles,* edited by A. Séguenny, 10–11. Baden-Baden: V. Koerner, 1984.

————. "Jean Laski et le retour au papisme." In *Les Églises et leurs institutions au XVIe siècle. Actes du Ve colloque du Centre d'Histoire de la Réforme et du Protestantisme,* 3–17. Montpellier: Université Paul Valéry, 1978.

————. "La prophétie dans les Églises de la Réforme au XVIe siècle." *Revue d'histoire ecclésiastique* 72 (1977): 289–316.

Denis, Philippe, and Jean Rott. *Jean Morély (ca. 1524–ca. 1594) et l'utopie d'une démocratie dans l'Église.* Geneva: Droz, 1993.

Donnelly, John Patrick. *A Bibliography of the Works of Peter Martyr Vermigli.* Kirksville, MO: Sixteenth Century Journal Publishers, 1990.

Dony, Jean Claude. "La bibliothèque d'Olivétan." In *Olivétan traducteur de la Bible,* edited by Georges Casalis and Bernard Roussel, 93–106. Paris: Cerf, 1987.

Douen, Orentin. "Coup d'oeil sur l'histoire du texte de la Bible d'Olivétan 1535–1560." *Revue de Philosophie et de Théologie de Lausanne* 22 (1889): 295.

Doumergue, Émile. *Jean Calvin, les hommes et les choses de son temps.* 7 vols. Lausanne: G. Bridel, 1899–1927.

Droz, Eugenie. "Antoine Vincent: La propagande protestante par le psautier." In *Aspects de la propagande religieuse,* 276–93. Geneva: Droz, 1957.

————. *Barthélemy Berton, 1563–1573.* Geneva: Droz, 1960.

————. *Chemins de l'hérésie: Textes et documents.* 4 vols. Geneva: Droz, 1970–76.

Dupèbe, J. "Un document sur les persécutions de l'hiver 1533–1534 à Paris." *Bibliothèque d'humanisme et renaissance* 48 (1986): 405–17.

Edwards, Mark U. *Printing, Propaganda and Martin Luther.* Berkeley: University of California Press, 1994.

Eisenstein, Elizabeth L. *The Printing Press as an Agent of Change.* Cambridge: Cambridge University Press, 1979.

Encyclopédie de Genève. Vol. 4, *Les Institutions.* Geneva: Association de l'Encyclopédie de Genève, 1985.

Engammare, Max. "Calvin connaissait-il la Bible? Les citations de l'écriture dans ses sermons sur la Genèse." *Bulletin de la société de l'histoire du protestantisme français* 141 (1995): 163–84.

————. "Cinquante ans de révision de la traduction biblique d'Olivétan: Les bibles réformées genevoises en français au XVI siècle." *Bibliothèque d'humanisme et renaissance* 50 (1991): 347–77.

————. "Le Paradis à Genève: Comment Calvin prêchait-il la chute aux Genevois?" *Etudes théologiques & religieuses* 69 (1994): 329–47.

————. "Pierre Caroli, véritable disciple de Lefèvre d'Etaples." In *Jacques Lefèvre d'Etaples (1450?–1536): Actes du colloque d'Etaples les 7 et 8 novembre 1992,* edited by Jean François Pernot, 55–79. Paris: Champion, 1995.

————. "Des sermons de Calvin sur Esaie découverts à Londres." In *Calvin et ses contemporains*, edited by O. Millet, 69–81. Geneva: Droz, 1988.

Étienne, Jacques. *Spiritualisme érasmien et théologiens louvanistes*. Louvain: Publications universitaires de Louvain, 1956.

Fabisch, Peter. "Silvester Prierias." In *Katholische Theologen der Reformationszeit* 1, edited by E. Iserloh, 26–36. Münster: Aschendorff, 1984.

Ficker, Johannes. *Die Anfänge der akademischen Studien in Straßburg*. Strasbourg: J. H. Ed. Heitz, 1912.

Fischer, Daniele. "Nouvelles réflexions sur la conversion de Calvin." *Etudes théologiques et religieuses* 58 (1983): 203–20.

Flachmann, H. *Martin Luther und das Buch*. Tübingen: J. C. B. Mohr, 1996.

Flood, John L. "Le livre dans le monde germanique à l'époque de la Réforme." In *La Réforme et le livre, l'Europe de l'imprimé (1517–v. 1570)*, edited by Jean-François Gilmont, 29–104. Paris: Cerf, 1990.

Fraenkel, Pierre. "Trois passages de l'Institution de 1543 et leurs rapports avec les colloques interconfessionnels de 1540–41." In *Calvinus ecclesiae genevensis custos*, 149–57. Frankfurt am Main: P. Lang, 1984.

Gagnebin, Bernard. "L'histoire des manuscrits des sermons de Calvin." In *Supplementa Calviniana*, Vol. 2, *Sermons sur le livre d'Esaïe*, edited by G. A. Barrois, XIV–XXVIII. Neukirchen-Vluyn: Verlag der Buchhandlung des Erziehungsvereins, 1961.

Ganoczy, Alexandre. *La bibliothèque de l'Académie de Calvin*. Geneva: Droz, 1969.

————. *Le jeune Calvin: Genèse et évolution de sa vocation réformatrice*. Wiesbaden: F. Steiner, 1966.

Ganoczy, Alexandre, and Klaus Müller. *Calvins handschriftliche Annotationen zu Chrysostomus: Ein Beitrag zur Hemeneutik Calvins*. Wiesbaden: Steiner, 1981.

Ganoczy, Alexandre, and Stefan Scheld. *Herrschaft, Tugend, hermeneutische Deutung und Veröffentlichung handschriftlicher Annotationen Calvins zu sieben Senecatragödien und der Pharsalia Lucans*. Wiesbaden: F. Steiner, 1982.

Gardy, Frédéric. *Bibliographie des oeuvres théologiques, littéraires, historiques et juridiques de Théodore de Bèze*. Geneva: Droz, 1960.

Geisendorf, Paul F. *Théodore de Bèze*. Geneva: Labor et fides, 1949.

Genette, Gérard. *Seuils*. Paris: Editions du Seuil, 1987.

Gerrish, Brian Albert. "The Pathfinder: Calvin's Image of Martin Luther." In *The Old Protestantism and the New: Essays on the Reformation Heritage*, 27–48. Chicago: University of Chicago Press, 1982.

Giese, Frank S. *Artus Désiré, Priest and Pamphleteer of the Sixteenth Century*. Chapel Hill: UNC Dept. of Romance Languages, 1973.

Gilmont, Jean-François. *Bibliographie des éditions de Jean Crespin, 1550–1572*. Vol. 2. Verviers: Librairie P. M. Gason, 1981.

————. "Calvin et la diffusion de la Bible." In *La Bible imprimée dans l'Europe moderne*, 230–42. Paris: Bibliothèque nationale de France, 1999.

————. "Comment Calvin choisissait-il ses imprimeurs?" *Australian Journal of French Studies* 31 (1994): 292–308.

————. "L'apport de La Rochelle et du royaume de France à la diffusion des écrits de Calvin (1560–1600)." In the forthcoming proceedings of the colloquium "Le livre entre Loire et Garonne." Niort, Paris: Association des amis d'Agrippa d'Aubigné, Librairie Honoré Champion, 1998.

———. "La censure dans la Genève de Calvin." *La censura libraria nell'Europa del secolo XVI.* Edited by U. Rozzo, 15–30. Udine: Forum, 1997.

———. "La correction des épreuves à Genève autour de 1560." To be published in the Mélanges Elly Cockx-Indesteege.

———. "Les épîtres dédicatoires de Jean Calvin." In *Prologues et préfaces de la Bible, xve–xvie siècles,* edited by Bernard Roussel and Jean-Daniel Dubois. Paris: Cerf, 1998.

———. "L'imprimerie réformée à Genève au temps de Laurent de Normandie (1570)." *Bulletin du bibliophile* 2 (1995): 262–78.

———. *Jean Crespin, un éditeur réformé du XVIe siècle.* Geneva: Droz, 1981.

———. *Le livre, du manuscrit à l'ère électronique.* 2nd ed. Liège: Editions du C. E. F. A. L., 1993.

———. "L'oeuvre imprimé de Guillaume Farel." In *Actes du Colloque Farel Neuchâtel,* 29 septembre–1er octobre 1980. *Revue de théologie et de philosophie* 2 (1983): 122–23.

———. "Les premières traductions de l'Institution de la religion chrétienne." In *Festschrift for Peter De Klerk,* edited by Wilhelm H. Neuser, Herman Selderhuis, and Willem van't Spijker, 175–88. Heerenveen: J. J. Groen, 1997.

———. "La rédaction et la publication du commentaire des Psaumes de Jean Calvin." *Psaume. Bulletin de la recherche sur le psautier huguenot* 10/11 (1995): 6–10.

———. *La Réforme et le livre: L'Europe de l'imprimé (1517–v. 1570).* Paris: Cerf, 1990.

———. "Les sermons de Calvin: De l'oral à l'imprimé." *Bulletin de la société de l'histoire du protestantisme français* 141 (1995): 142–62.

Gilmore, M. "Filippo Beroaldo." In *Dizionario biografico degli Italiani,* edited by Alberto M. Ghisalberti, 9:382–84. Rome: Instituto della enciclopedia italiana, 1960–.

Ginzburg, Carlo. *Il nicodemismo: Simulazione e dissimulazione religiosa nell'Europa del '500.* Turin: G. Einaudi, 1970.

Girardin, Benoit. *Rhétorique et théologique: Calvin, le commentaire de l'Épître aux Romains.* Paris: Editions Beauchesne, 1979.

Godin, Andre. *Spiritualité franciscaine au XVIe siècle: L'homéliaire de Jean Vitrier.* Geneva: Droz, 1971.

Gorisse, G. "Le psautier de 1562." In *Psaume. Bulletin de la recherche sur le psautier huguenot* 5 (1991): 106–27.

Guenther, Ilse. "Johannes Sinapius." In *Contemporaries of Erasmus: A Biographical Register of the Renaissance and Reformation,* edited by Peter Bietenholz, 3:254–55. Toronto: University of Toronto Press, 1987.

Guillo, L. *Les éditions musicales de la Renaissance lyonnaise.* Paris: Klincksieck, 1991.

Guiraud, Louise. *La Réforme à Montpellier.* Montpellier: Imprimerie générale du Midi, 1918.

Haag, Eugène, and Emile Haag. *La France protestante.* Edited by Henri Bordier. Paris: Librairie Sandoz et Fischbacher, 1877–88.

Hagen, Kenneth. "What Did the Term Commentarius Mean to Sixteenth-Century Theologians?" In *Théorie et pratique de l'exégèse,* edited by Irena Backus and Francis Higman, 13–38. Geneva: Droz, 1990.

Halkin, Léon. *Erasmus ex Erasmo. Érasme éditeur de sa correspondance.* Aubel: P. M. Gason, 1983.

Hall, H. G. "Ponctuation et dramaturgie chez Molière." In *La bibliographie matérielle,* edited by R. Laufer, 115–41. Paris: Editions du Centre national de la recherche scientifique, 1983.

Heyer, H. *L'Église de Genève: Esquisse historique de son organisation.* Geneva: A. Jullien, 1909.

Higman, Francis M. "L'analogie dans la pensée de Calvin." *Analogie et connaissance* 1 (1980): 113–23.

———. "Calvin and the Art of Translation." In *Western Canadian Studies in Modern Languages and Literature* 2 (1970): 5–27.

———. "Calvin polémiste." *Études théologiques et religieuses* 69 (1994): 349–65.

———. *La diffusion de la Réforme en France, 1520–1565.* Geneva: Labor et Fides, 1992.

———. "Le domaine français, 1520–1562." In *La Réforme et le livre,* edited by Jean François Gilmont, 105–54. Paris: Cerf, 1990.

———. "Jean Calvin." In *Histoire de la littérature en Suisse romande.* Vol. 1, *Du moyen âge à 1815,* edited by Roger Francillon, 81–93. Lausanne: Payot, 1996.

———. "La place de la polémique dans l'oeuvre écrite de Calvin." In *Le contrôle des idées à la Renaissance,* edited by J. M. De Bujanda, 113–39. Geneva: Droz, 1996.

———. *The Style of John Calvin in His French Polemical Treatises.* Oxford: Oxford University Press, 1967.

Hillerbrand, H. J., ed. *The Oxford Encyclopedia of the Reformation.* New York and Oxford: Oxford University Press, 1996.

Holtrop, Philip C. *The Bolsec Controversy on Predestination, from 1551 to 1555.* Lewiston, NY: Mellen, 1993.

Hubert, Friedrich. *Vergerios publizistische Thätigkeit nebst ein bibliographischen Übersicht.* Göttingen: Vandenhoeck & Ruprecht, 1893.

Ivins, William Mills. *Prints and Visual Communication.* Cambridge: Routledge & Kegan Paul, 1953.

Jardine, Lisa. *Erasmus, Man of Letters: The Construction of Charisma in Print.* Princeton: Princeton University Press, 1993.

Junghans, Helmar. "Die Widmungsvorrede bei Martin Luther." In *Lutheriana. Zum 500. Geburtstag Martin Luthers,* edited by Gerhard Hammer and Karl-Heinz zur Mühlen, 39–65. Cologne, Vienna: Böhlau, 1984.

Junod, Eric, ed. *La dispute de Lausanne, 1536: La théologie réformée après Zwingli et avant Calvin.* Lausanne: Bibliothèque historique vaudoise, 1988.

Kalma, J. J. "Poppius, Menso." *Biografisch lexicon voor de geschiedenis van het Nederlandse protestantisme,* 2:370–71. Kampen: Kok, 1978.

Kelders, A. "Les colophons des manuscrits datés de la Bibliothèque Royale comme source historique." In *Formules de copiste: Les colophons des manuscrits datés,* 38–39. Brussels: Bibliothèque royale Albert Ier, 1991.

Kingdon, Robert M. "Calvin and the Establishment of Consistory Discipline in Geneva: The Institution and the Men who Directed it." *Nederlands archief voor kerkgeschiedenis* 70 (1990): 158–72.

———. "Compagnie des pasteurs." In *The Oxford Encyclopedia of the Reformation,* edited by Hans J. Hillerbrand, 1:392–94. New York: Oxford University Press, 1996.

———. "Consistory." In *The Oxford Encyclopedia of the Reformation,* edited by Hans J. Hillerbrand, 1:416–17. New York: Oxford University Press, 1996.

Kline, Michael B. *Rabelais and the Age of Printing.* Geneva: Droz, 1963.

Körner, M. "Plappart." In *Dictionnaire historique et biographique de la Suisse,* 5:307. Neuchâtel: Adminnistration du dictionnaire historique et biographique de l Suisse, 1921–33.

Kristeller, Paul Oskar. *Medieval Aspects of Renaissance Learning.* Durham: Duke University Press, 1974.

Labarthe, Olivier. "La relation entre le premier catéchisme de Calvin et la première confession de foi de Genève." Unpublished thesis, Geneva, 1967.

Lane, Anthony. *Calvin and Bernard of Clairvaux.* Princeton: Princeton Theological Seminary, 1996.

———. "Calvin's Sources of St. Bernard." *Archiv für Reformationsgeschichte* 67 (1976): 253–81.

———. "Calvin's Use of Bernard of Clairvaux." In *Bernhard von Clairvaux: Rezeption und Wirkung im Mittelalter und in der Neuzeit,* edited by Kaspar Elm, 303–32. Wiesbaden: Harrassowitz, 1994.

———. "Calvin's Use of the Fathers and the Medievals." *Calvin Theological Journal* 16, no. 2 (1981): 149–205.

Laplanche, François. "Controverses et dialogues entre catholiques et protestants." In *Histoire du christianisme des origines à nos jours.* Vol. 8, *Le temps des confessions,* 299–321. Paris: Fayard, 1992.

———. "L'enseignement universitaire." In *Histoire du christianisme des origines à nos jours.* Vol. 8, *Le temps des confessions, 1530–1620/30,* 1066–77. Paris: Desclée, Fayard, 1992.

Le Coultre, Jean Jules. *Maturin Cordier et les origines de la pédagogie protestante dans les pays de langue française (1530–1564).* Neuchâtel: Secrétariat de l'Université, 1926.

Le Roy Ladurie, Emmanuel. *Le siècle des Platter.* Paris: Fayard, 1995.

Lienhard, M. "Controverses et dialogues entre Luthériens et Réformés." In *Histoire du christianisme des origines à nos jours.* Vol. 8, *Le temps des confessions, 1530–1620/30,* 281–99. Paris: Desclée, Fayard, 1992.

———. *Martin Luther, un temps, une vie, un message.* Paris: Le Centurion; Geneva: Labor et fides, 1983.

Longeon, Claude. *Premiers combats pour la langue française.* Paris: Librairie générale française, 1989.

Massaut, Jean-Pierre. *Josse Clichtove, l'humanisme et la réforme du clergé.* Liège, Paris: Les Belles Lettres, 1968.

Matthey-Jeantet, A. *L'écriture de Calvin.* Le Locle: Courvoisier, 1909.

McGrath, Alister E. "John Calvin and Late Mediaeval Thought: A Study in Late Mediaeval Influences upon Calvin's Theological Development." *Archiv für Reformationsgeschichte* 77 (1986): 58–78.

Ménager, Daniel. "Théodore de Bèze, biographe de Calvin." *Bibliothèque d'humanisme et renaissance* 45 (1983): 231–55.

Mesnard, P. "La Paraclesis d'Érasme." *Bibliothèque d'humanisme et renaissance* 13 (1951): 26–34.

Meylan, Henri. "Calvin et les hommes d'affaires." In *Regards contemporains sur Jean Calvin,* 161–70. Paris: Presses universitaires de France, 1965.

———. "Un financier protestant à Lyon, ami de Calvin et de Bèze, Georges Obrecht." In *D'Érasme à Théodore de Bèze,* edited by Henri Meylan, 213–20. Geneva: Droz, 1976.

Millet, Olivier. *Calvin et la dynamique de la parole.* Paris: H. Champion, 1992.

———. "Calvin pamphlétaire." In *Le pamphlet en France au XVIe siècle,* 9–22. Paris: Centre V. L. Saulnier. Université de Paris–Sorbonne, 1983.

Monter, E. William. "The Consistory of Geneva, 1559–1569." *Bibliothèque d'humanisme et renaissance* 38 (1976): 467–84.

Mooi, Remko Jan. *Het Kerk-en dogmahistorisch element in de werken van Johannes Calvijn.* Wageningen: H. Veenman, 1965.

Moreau, Gerard. "Contribution à l'histoire du livre des martyrs." *Bulletin de la société de l'histoire du protestantisme français* 103 (1957): 185.

———. *Histoire du protestantisme à Tournai jusqu'à la veille de la révolution des Pays-Bas.* Paris: Les Belles Lettres, 1962.

Morisse, Gerard. "Le psautier de 1562." *Psaume* 5 (1991): 106–27.

Mülhaupt, Erwin. *Die Predigt Calvins, ihre Geschichte, ihre Form und ihre religiösen Grundgedanken.* Berlin: W. de Gruyter, 1931.

Muller, Richard A. "The Bolsec Controversy on Predestination from 1551 to 1555." *Calvin Theological Journal* 29 (1994): 581–89.

Naphy, William G. *Calvin and the Consolidation of the Genevan Reformation.* Manchester: Manchester University Press, 1994.

Nauta, Doede, et al. *Biografisch lexicon voor de geschiedenis van het Nederlandse protestantisme.* Kampen: Kok, [1978–].

Neuser, Wilhelm H. Review of *Bibliotheca Calviniana,* by Rodolphe Peter and Jean-François Gilmont. *Theologische Literaturzeitung* 119, no. 12 (1994): 1086–87.

Nicole, P. D., and Christophe Rapin. "De l'exégèse à l'homilétique: Evolution entre le commentaire de 1551, les sermons de 1558, et le commentaire de 1559 sur le prophète Esaïe." In *Calvinus ecclesiae Genevensis custos,* edited by W. H. Neuser, 159–62. Frankfurt am Main: P. Lang, 1984.

Olson, Jeannine E. *Calvin and Social Welfare: Deacons and the Bourse française.* Selinsgrove, London, Toronto: Susquehanna University Press, 1989.

Pannier, Jacques. *Les origines de la confession de foi.* Paris: F. Alcan, 1936.

Parker, T. H. L. *Calvin's New Testament Commentaries.* London: SCM Press, 1971.

———. *Calvin's Old Testament Commentaries.* Edinburgh: T & T Clark, 1986. Reprinted with minor corrections, 1993.

———. *Calvin's Preaching.* Edinburgh: T & T Clark, 1992.

Peter, Rodolphe. "Calvin et la traduction des Psaumes de Louis Budé." In *Revue d'histoire et de philosophie religieuses* 42 (1962): 175–92.

———. "Calvin traducteur de Mélanchthon." In *Horizons européens de la Réforme en Alsace,* edited by Marijn de Kroon and Marc Lienhard, 119–33. Strasbourg: Istra, 1980.

———. "La première édition de l'Institution de la religion chrétienne de Calvin." In *Le livre et la Réforme,* edited by Rodolphe Peter and Bernard Roussel, 17–34, 115–17. Bordeaux: Société des bibliophiles de Guyenne, 1987.

———. "Les premiers ouvrages français imprimés à Strasbourg." In *Annuaire de la société des amis du Vieux-Strasbourg* 4 (1974): 73–108; 8 (1978): 11–75; 10 (1980): 35–46; 14 (1984): 17–28; 17 (1987): 23–37.

———. "Un imprimeur de Calvin: Michel du Bois." In *Bulletin de la société d'histoire et d'archéologie de Genève* 16 (1978): 285–335.

Peter, Rodolphe, and Jean Rott. *Les lettres à Jean Calvin de la collection Sarrau.* Paris: Presses universitaires de France, 1972.

Peter, Rodolphe, and Bernard Roussel, eds. *Le livre et la Réforme.* Bordeaux: Société des bibliophiles de Guyenne, 1987.

Piaget, Arthur. *Les actes de la dispute de Lausanne, 1536.* Neuchâtel: Secrétariat de l'Université, 1928.

Pidoux, Pierre. "Les origines de l'impression de musique à Genève." In *Cinq siècles d'imprimerie genevoise*, edited by J. D. Candaux and B. Lescaze, 1:96–108. Geneva: Société d'histoire et d'archéologie, 1980.

———. *Le psautier huguenot du XVIe siècle: Mélodie et documents.* Vol. 2. Basel: Edition Baerenreiter, 1962.

Pollet, Jacques V. *Martin Bucer, études sur la correspondance,* Vol. 2. Paris: Presses universitaires de France, 1962.

Renouard, Philippe. *Répertoire des imprimeurs parisiens: Libraires, fondeurs de caractères et correcteurs d'imprimerie, depuis l'introduction de l'imprimerie à Paris, 1470, jusqu'à la fin du seizième siècle.* Paris: M. J. Minard, 1945.

Reusch, Franz H. *Die Indices Librorum Prohibitorum des sechzehnten Jahrhunderts.* Tübingen: Litterarischer Verein, 1886.

Reynolds, Leighton D., and Nigel G. Wilson. *D'Homère à Érasme: La transmission des classiques grecs et latins.* Paris: Editions du centre national de la recherche scientifique, 1984.

Rott, Jean. *Correspondance de Martin Bucer: Liste alphabétique des correspondants.* Strasbourg: Palais Université, 1977.

———. "Documents strasbourgeois concernant Calvin." In *Regards contemporains sur Jean Calvin: Actes du colloque Calvin, Strasbourg 1964,* 28–49. Paris: Presses universitaires de France, 1965.

Roussel, Bernard. "François Lambert, Pierre Caroli, Guillaume Farel et Jean Calvin (1530–1536)." In *Calvinus servus Christi: Die Referate des congrès international des recherches calviniennes,* edited by Wilhelm H. Neuser, 35–52. Budapest: Presseabteilung des Ráday-Kollegiums, 1988.

———. "Un privilège pour la Bible d'Olivétan (1535)? Jean Calvin et la polémique entre Alexander Alesius et Johannes Cochlaeus." In *Le livre et la Réforme,* edited by Rodolphe Peter and Bernard Roussel, 233–43. Bordeaux: Société des bibliophiles de Guyenne, 1987.

Rozzo, U. *Linee per una storia dell'editoria religiosa in Italia, 1465–1600.* Udine: Arti Grafiche, 1993.

Rummel, Erika. *The Humanist-Scholastic Debate in the Renaissance and Reformation.* Cambridge, MA: Harvard University Press, 1995.

Ruppel, A. "Die Bücherwelt des 16. Jahrhunderts und die Frankfurter-Büchermessen." In *Gedenkboek der Plantin-dagen 1555–1955,* 239. Antwerp: Vereeniging der Antwerpsche Bibliophielen, 1965.

Schlaepfer, Heidi Lucie. "Laurent de Normandie." In *Aspects de la propagande religieuse,* 176–230. Geneva: Droz, 1957.

Schmitt, Charles B. "The Correspondence of Jacques Daléchamps (1513–1588)." *Viator* 8 (1977): 399–434.

Schottenloher, Karl. *Die Widmungsvorrede im Buch des 16. Jahrhunderts.* Münster: Westfalen, 1953.

Scribner, Robert W. *Popular Culture and Popular Movements in Reformation Germany.* London: Hambledon Press, 1987.

Smits, Luchesius. *Saint Augustin dans l'oeuvre de Jean Calvin.* Assen: Van Gorcum, 1958.

Sommervogel, C. *Bibliothèque de la Compagnie de Jésus.* Toulouse: privately published, 1911–30.

Speelman, Herman A. *Calvin en de zelfstandigheid van de Kerk.* Kampen: Kok, 1994.

Staedtke, Joachim. *Heinrich Bullinger, Bibliographie.* Vol. 1. Zurich: Theologischer, 1972.

Stauffer, Richard. "Brève histoire de la Confession de La Rochelle." *Bulletin de la société de l'histoire du protestantisme français* 117 (1971): 355–66.

———. "L'homilétique de Calvin." In *Interprètes de la Bible,* edited by Richard Stauffer, 167–81. Paris: Beauchesne, 1980.

———. "Les Sermons inédits de Calvin sur le livre de la Genèse." *Revue de Théologie et de Philosophie* 98 (1945): 26–36.

Stegemann, V. "Altenstaig, Johannes." In *Neue deutsche Biographie,*1:215–16. Berlin: Duncker & Humblot, 1953–.

Steinmann, M. *Johannes Oporinus: Ein Basler Buchdrucker um die Mitte des 16. Jahrhunderts.* Basel, Stuttgart: Helbing & Lichenhahn, 1967.

Taylor, Larissa. *Soldiers of Christ: Preaching in Late Medieval and Reformation France.* New York: Oxford University Press, 1992.

Thompson, James W. *The Frankfurt Book Fair.* Amsterdam: G. Th. Van Heusden, 1969.

Turchetti, Mario. *Concordia o toleranza? François Bauduin (1520–1673) e i "moyenneurs."* Geneva: Droz, 1984.

Vanautgaerden, A. "Le grammairien, l'imprimeur et le sycophante ou comment éditer une querelle théologique en 1520 [Érasme et Lee]." In *Les Invectives,* edited by A. Vanautgaerden, 11–32. Bruxelles: La Lettre Volée à la Maison d'Erasme, 1997.

Van Nieuwenhuysen, A. *Inventaire des archives de la famille de Lalaing.* Brussels: [Archives générales du Royaume], 1970.

Verger, J. "L'exégèse de l'Université." In *Le moyen âge et la Bible,* edited by Pierre Riché and Guy Lobrichon, 199–232. Paris: Beauchesne, 1984.

Volz, H. "Die arbeitsteilung der Wittenberger Drucker zu Luthers Lebzeiten." *Gutenberg Jahrbuch* (1957): 146–54.

Vuilleumier, Henri. *Histoire de l'Église réformée du Pays de Vaud sous le régime bernois.* Lausanne: La Concorde, 1927–33.

Wagenmann, J. A. "Karg, Johannes" In *Allgemeine deutsche Biographie,* 15:120–21. Berlin: Duncker & Humblot, 2003.

Wendel, François. *Calvin, sources et évolution de sa pensée religieuse.* Paris: Presses Universitaires de France, 1950.

Wendland, H. "Martin Luther, seine Buchdrucker und Verleger." In *Beiträge zur Geschichte des Buchwesens im konfessionellen Zeitalter,* edited by Herbert G. Göpfert, P. Vodosek, et al., 11–35. Wiesbaden: O. Harrassowitz, 1985.

Wilcox, Peter. "The Lectures of John Calvin and the Nature of His Audience, 1555–1564." *Archiv für Reformationsgeschichte* 87 (1996): 136–48.

Wolf, Herbert. *Martin Luther, eine Einführung in Germanistische Luther-Studien.* Stuttgart: Metzier, 1980.

Zeeden, Ernst Walter. "Das Bild Martin Luthers in den Briefen Calvin." *Archiv für Reformationsgeschichte* 49 (1958): 177–95.

Zillenbiller, Anette. *Die Einheit der Katholischen Kirche: Calvins Cyprianrezeption in seinen ekklesiologischen Schriften.* Mainz: P. Zabern, 1993.

Index

325